What Others Are Saying about *The Bones of Makaidos*. . . .

It is fitting for the last book in the Oracles of Fire series to be the best. *The Bones of Makaidos* captured me from the very beginning. Bryan Davis's ability to vividly depict scenes is at its best in the final installment of his best selling fantasy series. You will not be able to put the book down!

—**Grant Miller** (Age 15)

Beloved characters, both new and old, grace the pages of this tale and beckon you to enter their world one last time as they fight against the growing darkness around them. The tapestry masterfully woven is finally complete. But is it really the end?

—**Anne K. Riley** (Age 19)

After reading the rest of the Oracles of Fire and Dragons in our Midst books, I find *The Bones of Makaidos* to be a smashing ending. It's so nice to find not one, but two book series that are so enthralling, adventure-packed, inspiring, and God honoring.

—**Rebecca Vath** (Age 16)

I laughed; I cried; I shared with each character's joy and suffering. I could not put this book down, even to go to bed. *The Bones of Makaidos* pulled me in from cover to cover. Bryan Davis has saved the best for last! This book is definitely one you don't want to miss.

—**Sarah Pratt** (Age 15)

This book is absolutely amazing. It's thrilling to join in with all of these characters' adventures once again! I can't keep my hands away from the book. It's sad to know that this will be the last one, but it's great anyway! A must-read for sure!

—**Danielle Diez** (Age 14)

Bryan Davis has done it again! I knew Mr. Davis was an excellent author, but I was amazed to find myself double-taking and rereading pages as my jaw dropped. You will be up late into the night reading *The Bones of Makaidos* telling yourself, "just one more chapter" over and over again. Possibly Mr. Davis's best yet!

—**Jacob Eggert** (Age 13)

The Bones of Makaidos is, in my opinion, the best book that Mr. Davis has written yet! The events in this book left me bewildered, and they completely change your outlook on this entire series. It's a work of art!

—**Anna Bjela** (Age 13)

The Bones of Makaidos is a tale of love, courage, sacrifice, and redemption; a wonderful end to an awesome series. All I can say is: What a ride!

—**T. McCarville** (Age 18)

In *The Bones of Makaidos,* action will spike your adrenaline; suspense will urge you to read on; sacrifice and salvation will bring you to tears, and the characters will encourage you to trust in God more than ever before.

—**Regan Hickman** (Age 15)

I've cried more in this book than the other seven put together—some were tears of sadness, but most have been tears of joy. Each time you read it, it'll be just as powerful as the first time, if not more. All loose ends will be tied, and when you read the last page, you'll be left with a sense of peace that's hard to describe.

—Connie Wolters (Age 27)

If you don't think the Oracles of Fire series can get any better, then think again. This book outdoes the rest! Prophecies are fulfilled, and any questions from the last seven books are answered. *The Bones of Makaidos* is my favorite of Mr. Davis's books, and I know it will be yours too.

—Taylor Ward (Age 15)

The Bones of Makaidos is a fitting end to the best series of books I have ever read! In the ultimate battle of good versus evil, I felt joy at surprise reunions and sadness over the loss of loved ones. In the end I was left with a happiness that can only come from experiencing God at work in this world of ours.

—Rachel Tettleton (Age 16)

"I want you to win my heart. I want you to fight for me, sweat for me, bleed for me. . . ." *The Bones of Makaidos* captures the hearts of readers, brings them into the lives of all the characters, and shows that God is always there, and if you have faith, he will reward you.

—Kendra Williamson (Age 13)

In *The Lord of the Rings: The Two Towers,* King Theoden said "If this is to be our end, then I would have them make such an end, as to be worthy of remembrance." Mr. Davis has accomplished this and then some.

—Hayley Cox (Age 17)

The Bones of Makaidos is an epic adventure that brings the wonderful elements of the series together into an ultimate climax. Well done, Mr. Davis!

—Kenny Donovan (Age 17)

The Bones of Makaidos is my favorite book. There's adventure, excitement, and romance all mingled together. At times I feel like all of the characters are real, like I'm going right along with them in their adventures. Most of all, these books have strengthened my faith. Thank you, Mr. Davis!

—Jenn Morgan (Age 12)

Throughout the first seven books, Billy, Bonnie, Walter, Ashley, Sapphira, and Elam have grown closer to each other and stronger in their faith in Elohim. Now, together with the rest of the Oracles of Fire, they face their final battle, the fiercest challenge, preceding the ultimate reward.

—Bryce McLemore (Age 15)

In this rousing conclusion, Bryan Davis has penned a tale of betrayal and endurance, of faith, hope, and love. Of humor. Of other worlds and of a majestic people in whom the lights of chivalry and honor have not gone out. Indeed, *The Bones of Makaidos* is a masterpiece of Christian literature.

—Holli Herdeg (Age 16)

The Bones of Makaidos

Bryan Davis

Living Ink Books
An Imprint of AMG Publishers
Chattanooga, Tennessee

The Bones of Makaidos
Volume 4 in the Oracles of Fire® series
Copyright © 2009 by Bryan Davis
Published by Living Ink Books, an imprint of AMG Publishers
6815 Shallowford Rd.
Chattanooga, Tennessee 37421

ISBN 13: 978-088957-874-3
ISBN 10: 0-89957-874-8
First printing—March 2009

ORACLES OF FIRE and DRAGONS IN OUR MIDST are registered trademarks of AMG Publishers

Cover designed by Bright Boy Design, Inc., Chattanooga, Tennessee
Interior design and typesetting by Reider Publishing Services,
    West Hollywood, California
Edited and proofread by Dan Penwell, Rick Steele, and Sharon Neal
Map illustrated by Jim Brown, Clayton, North Carolina
"Family Tree" image ilustrated by Jared Sloger, Papillion, Nebraska

Printed in Canada
15 14 13 12 11 10 09 –T– 8 7 6 5 4 3 2 1

Library of Congress Cataloging-in-Publication Data
Davis, Bryan, 1958-
  The bones of Makaidos / Bryan Davis.
     p. cm. -- (Oracles of Fire ; v. 4)
  Summary: As the fiery wall of Abraham dies away, the people of Second Eden wait for the coming war, unaware that a spy has come among them.
  ISBN-13: 978-0-89957-874-3 (pbk. : alk. paper)
  ISBN-10: 0-89957-874-8 (pbk. : alk. paper)
  [1. Dragons--Fiction. 2. Demonology--Fiction. 3. Christian life--Fiction.
4. Fantasy.] I. Title.
  PZ7.D28555Bon 2009
  [Fic]--dc22
                                        2009006633

For every Oracle of Fire who reads this,
I pray that your heart's flame blazes once again
as these words reignite a passion that can
never be extinguished.

ACKNOWLEDGMENTS

After eight books and over a million words, this story has come to an end. It would be impossible to thank every person who offered a helpful hand in the creation and polishing of these works, so please forgive any omissions.

Thank you to my wife and children. You helped me in more ways than I can count, from conception, to gestation, to birth. This story would have remained a crazy dream without you.

Thank you to the folks at AMG, especially Dan Penwell. You took a chance on a strange new idea as well as an unproven author. I can't thank you enough.

This new book, the longest in both series, required the editing prowess of many willing helpers, including some of my faithful readers, so I send my thanks to Peter Blaskiewicz, Connie Wolters, and Holli Herdeg for poring over the two hundred thousand words and offering their suggestions.

And most of all, thank you to my Lord and Savior, Jesus Christ. You implanted the flame within me that helped me understand what an Oracle of Fire is. Without You, I would be nothing.

AUTHOR'S NOTE

The Bones of Makaidos is the fourth book in the **Oracles of Fire** series and is related to the **Dragons in our Midst** series. The numbers in the diagram below show the best reading order for the two series. Although the books are stacked vertically to indicate the chronological order of the story line, they should be read in the numbered sequence.

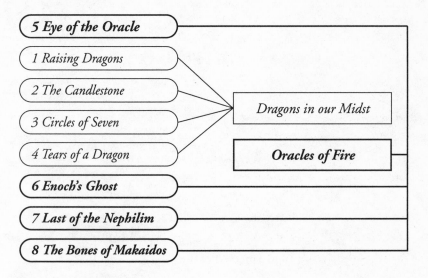

For readers unfamiliar with the previous books, I recommend reading the first seven before this one. As a minimum, read *Enoch's Ghost*, including the recap at the end of that book, as well as *Last of the Nephilim*. This story concludes all earlier adventures that readers explored in a multidimensional land, a journey guided by the *Oracles of Fire*.

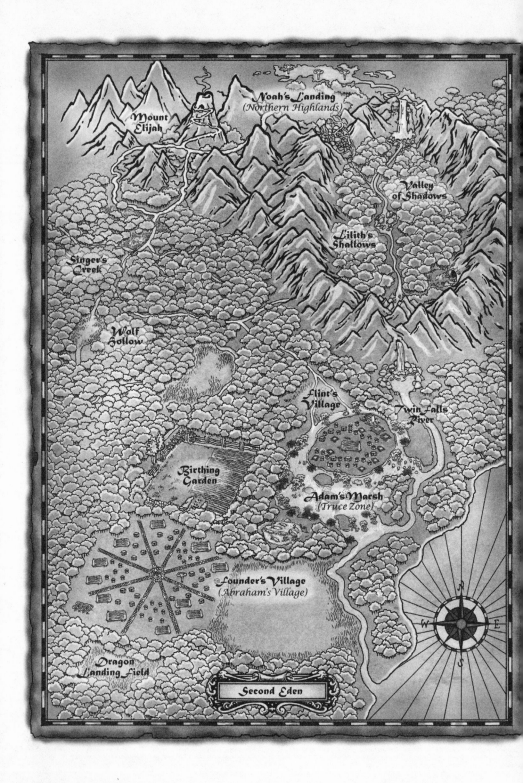

Mount
Elijah

Noah's Landing
(Northern Highlands)

Valley
of Shadows

Lilith's
Shallows

Singer's
Creek

Wolf
Hollow

Flint's
Village

Twin Falls
River

Birthing
Garden

Adam's Marsh
(Truce Zone)

Founder's Village
(Abraham's Village)

Dragon
Landing Field

Second Eden

CONTENTS

CONTENTS

BOOK 2
FROM THE ASHES

x

An Oracle's Call

A tender heart that burns with fire,
A contradicting blend;
With words of heat, I scald the soul,
And with my words I mend.

An Oracle of Fire born
To sacrifice and bleed,
For hungry souls, I spend my life
To meet their every need.

Yet, Oracles of Fire burn;
They pierce, they scald, they sear
Corrupted souls in dark abodes
Who cower there in fear.

The light has come! Begone, you shades,
Who hide in blackest mire!
I free the captives, loose their chains,
And give them holy fire.

While some will carry vibrant light,
The fearful drop the torch;
Courageous souls absorb the fire,
While others fear the scorch.

Yet, flames from God must pierce your breast
To purge the dross of sin
And make your silver wholly pure
And light the flame within.

A bridge awaits, a risky path,
The cross of Christ displayed
A broken body, blood, and tears;
A tomb for us inlaid.

I call you now to cross the bridge,
To take the scarlet key.
To gain the burning, tender heart,
And walk the path with me.

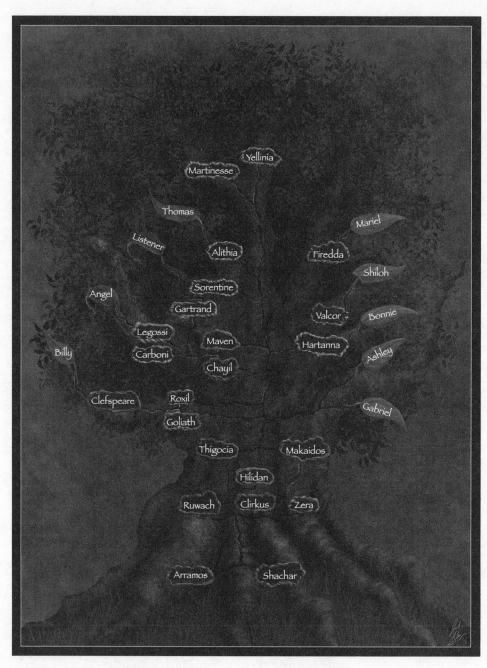

THE DRAGON FAMILY TREE

PROLOGUE

Mardon stood at the edge of the precipice and peered into the chasm. The sheer rock faces on each side plunged until they seemed to meet in the apparently infinite depths. Stepping back, he turned to a lady draped in a red cloak, Semiramis, her hood lifted over her auburn locks. "Mother, how do you propose that we descend?"

Lowering her hood, Semiramis gazed into the bright sky. "Arramos said he would show us the way during Second Eden's eclipse cycle. Since that eve is upon us, he will fly here soon. He is quite anxious to send us into that world."

A crystalline egg orbited Mardon's head, flashing crimson light from within. As it stopped in front of his eyes, its familiar voice, Sir Devin's voice, penetrated his mind. "Will you trust the instructions of a dragon?" Its eyes, no more than two reddish ovals, blinked. "Arramos is the most devious of the accursed race."

Mardon stared at the light, concentrating his thoughts on its center. *If you want to gain a new body, I suggest that you withhold your misgivings. I put our plan into motion to roust the girl and her*

dragon friends, so my promise to give you a chance to kill her will soon be fulfilled.

"And my desire to capture her is the reason I put up with you. Although I have bigger draconic prizes in mind, I will mount that demon witch's head on a pedestal so I can see it from anywhere in my leisure room."

Mardon cringed but said nothing. It was no use talking sensibly to the mad dragon slayer. Their crusades lay at opposite ends. Devin wanted nothing more than to kill all who possessed dragon blood, whether they were full-blooded or merely human offspring of former dragons. He had no spiritual ideals, only a lust for killing.

Shaking his head, Mardon let his gaze follow a narrow footbridge to the other side of the chasm. He sought after so much more than slaying reptiles. Doing away with dragons and their kin was merely a stepping-stone toward the ultimate in spiritual ascensions, the unification of humanity with the heavenly host. Such a feat would demonstrate to all realms that the son of King Nimrod had finally taken his place at the side of the Majesty on High.

As he scanned the skies alongside his mother, Mardon avoided further eye contact with Devin. The cruel slayer might be able to read unguarded thoughts, and if he caught any hint that their purposes differed so greatly, he might cause problems.

Soon, a dragon flew into sight, reddish against the blue sky and carrying something in one of his clawed feet. Seconds later, in a flurry of wings and wind, Arramos set down a bucket and landed several paces from the chasm's precipice. After drawing in his wings, he stared at Mardon with pulsing red eyes. "It is time for your transformation," he growled.

Mardon tried to steel himself, but tremors weakened his legs. "Transformation?"

Laying a hand on the back of his head, Semiramis crooned. "A disguise, my dear. Some of the Second Eden inhabitants know you too well." She turned toward Arramos and nodded at the bucket. "What is this, my lord?"

"Water from the river of the Prism Oracle," Arramos said. "It will help us complete the transformation."

"I see." Semiramis eyed the water. "That oracle has powers beyond what I knew."

Arramos's voice lowered to a rumble. "There is much you do not know."

"Well, if it's just a disguise …" Mardon squared his shoulders. "I'm ready."

Arramos snorted twin jets of fire, coating Mardon from his head to his chest.

"Ahhhrg!" Mardon dropped to his knees. Pain ripped across his face. He reached for his mother and tried to scream, but his desperate gasp brought a stream of blazing heat into his mouth and throat, scorching the tender skin inside.

Semiramis grabbed the bucket and poured half of the water over his head. Then, adding gentle splashes with the remainder, she took care to soak every inch of melting flesh. When the bucket ran dry, she slung it to the side and glared at Arramos, her lips pressed tight.

3

Mardon fanned his face, barely missing Devin's egg as it floated near his cheek, apparently unhurt. "It still burns!" His voice sounded gravelly, like that of a dying old man. "It feels like my skin is melting!"

"Ah, yes," Arramos said with a chuckle. "Fire tends to do that. It will likely torture you for days or weeks to come."

Semiramis shook her fist, her voice spiced with rage. "So this is his disguise? What do you have in mind for me? Mummification?"

"Don't tempt me." His eyes flaming, the dragon's head swayed as he studied her from head to toe. "It is crucial that your beauty remains intact."

Her fingers loosened, but she maintained her violent glare. "My beauty, as you judge it, will be my undoing. The genius dragon girl and the Foley boy will surely recognize me."

"Indeed. Exactly what I hope for. You will appeal to their sense of mercy, and your loving care for this wretched burn victim will be proof of your repentance."

"So my disguise is …"

"Righteousness." Arramos tipped his head back and laughed. "The same disguise so many humans use to fool their fellows in every walk of life."

Semiramis lowered herself to her knees. With quick, angry motions, she helped Mardon strip away his smoldering shirt. "Loving my son will not be an act. My goal all along has been to put him on a throne of glory."

"All in good time. Surely ascension to such a throne will include healing. That should be another incentive to ply your trade well."

Clenching her teeth, she wedged her words between short, shallow breaths. "Incentive? After torturing my son, you speak of incentives? Why should I do anything you say?"

"I hold the ultimate dagger over your head, your life and your son's life. I can see to it that you survive in Second Eden in spite of your current state of deadness, but my power will not avail you if you try to enter Heaven. Surely you have wondered how your dead souls would survive. And have you not also wondered how you will be able to defeat the host of Heaven with an army of mortals from the Earth? Compared to them, your army would be a swarm of gnats."

Semiramis turned to Mardon. Her expression gave her away. She had wondered. In fact, those questions had haunted both of them for centuries.

Looking at Arramos again, she murmured, "Go on."

"The Oracles are the key. They have eaten fruit from the Tree of Life, so their makeup has been altered. Unable to die a natural

4

death, they are now like the angels. Since Mardon knows an Oracle's genetic code and her weaknesses, he should be able to learn the secret and pass along her power to the two of you and your armies, thus enabling all of you to become like the sons and daughters of God."

"I see." Semiramis eyed Mardon again. "Can you do this thing? It could be our only chance. If need be, I can temporarily incapacitate an Oracle with a sleeping powder."

Mardon pondered the idea. Since the Oracles originated as plant creatures, they possessed photosynthetic code. Through their eyes, they always had the ability to capture light that could be used for manufacturing energy. He could use tainted light on one of them and confuse her photosynthetic cells, causing them to expend energy rather than produce it, thereby deteriorating her body. In theory, her life-sustaining system would have to respond by battling the photosynthetic cells. She would literally be at war with her own body. Then, by getting samples of cells before degeneration began and after her body battled back, he could figure out how the life-sustaining code worked, reverse engineer it, and replicate it for others.

His throat still on fire, he pushed through the pain. "I have an idea. It would weaken an Oracle at first, but we could use her cellular structure later for our benefit. To begin the process, I must have close contact, at least for a short time."

"One of the Oracles resides in Second Eden," Arramos said to Semiramis. "You will have to gain her trust. Your skill as a deceiver will be put to the test."

Semiramis crossed her arms, her tone softening. "How will I deal with the dragons from Earth? I cannot fool their danger-sensing abilities."

"You are no danger to them. Only Makaidos, king of the dragons, has power great enough to sense danger toward others. Still, you must continue to guard your thoughts well, for the mind reader will try to see past your façade."

5

"Ashley?" Semiramis shook her head. "She will not be a problem. I have learned how to block her mental penetration. Her inability to see past my defenses will make her suspicious, but there will be no proof she can use against me."

"Very good." Arramos spread out his wings. "Let us fly now to Second Eden."

"Fly?" Semiramis asked. "How so?"

"The portal the Nephilim used remains open, though it is only a one-way passage to those who lack my power. It has been very useful for transporting new allies and one very old … shall we say … *crystalline* weapon for our eventual confrontation. I have been given permission to move parts of two circles of Hades to Second Eden, the great abyss that once imprisoned the Watchers as well as the village of the sixth circle where Morgan held Shiloh prisoner. That village now resides in Second Eden as a buffer between here and there. I can take you as far as Morgan's prison, and, from that point, you are on your own." Arramos lowered his head to the ground, creating a staircase. "The eclipse is upon us. Let us make haste."

"Very well." Semiramis took Mardon's hand and helped him climb the spiny steps.

As soon as they settled between two tall spines, Devin's crystal flashed in front of Mardon's eyes. "I warned you about dragons," the slayer said. "And this one has betrayed you. Will you trust me now?"

Still racked with pain, Mardon nodded at the egg and spoke to it with his mind. *Let us make our plans in secret. Perhaps we both can achieve our goals and thwart those of the dragon. Trust me. My mother is not pleased with this plan, and she has already told me how she will bring you back to life in a way that will surprise everyone, perhaps even Arramos.*

BOOK 1
REFINING FIRES

1

CHAPTER

HIDDEN GEMS

Bonnie looked down at the magma far below. As the slow-moving river boiled, heat rose from the depths and warmed her skin, a refreshing change from the chilly air that normally filled the tunnels and chambers in the nether regions of Hades. If she stayed here much longer, she would have to take her sweatshirt off. Her long-sleeved T-shirt and jeans would be enough to keep her warm.

While small whirlpools spun in slow rotations, huge gas bubbles erupted on the surface and popped, spewing ash and steam upward in swirling clouds of sulfur-permeated air. The entire stream churned from right to left, at half the speed of a normal walking pace.

Standing between Sapphira and Shiloh on the rocky ledge, Bonnie unfurled her wings and rested a tip on each girl's shoulder, ready to pull them back should they lose their balance. Shiloh, Bonnie's nearly identical cousin, matched her height, but Bonnie had to reach down a few inches to cover Sapphira, the petite Oracle of Fire. Both companions wore matching outfits, sweatshirts and jeans, perfectly suitable for exploring the sometimes narrow caves. Shiloh also wore a ring with a red rubellite, making her ready to pretend to be Bonnie, just in case.

"I don't understand how it could ever have been harmless," Bonnie said as she fanned her face with her hand. "It's scalding even way up here."

"Oh, it's deadly now." Sapphira picked up a fist-sized stone and tossed it into the chasm. The moment it struck the current, a plume of steam shot from the contact point, sending reddish black fragments high into the air. "When most of the portals closed a long time ago, it turned into normal molten rock."

"Normal?" Taking a step back, Shiloh blew a strand of dampened hair from her face, her British accent as pronounced as ever. "As if anything's normal in this place."

"You're sweating," Bonnie said. "What are you wearing underneath?"

Shiloh lifted her sweatshirt, revealing a T-shirt with a lion on the front. "It's the Narnia shirt you gave me in the sixth circle. It's too warm for two layers and too cold for just one."

Bonnie shielded her eyes from the river's glow and scanned the other side of the chasm. Rising heat warped her view, making the rocks on the opposite wall hard to define. As undulating light from the restless source below created strange shadows all across the sheer rock face, one shadow seemed constant, a protruding lip of stone. "What's over there?" she asked, pointing. "I think I see another ledge."

Sapphira pulled back her stark white hair and tied it with a rubber band. "There *is* a ledge. When there was a portal nearby, my eyesight was sharper, and I spotted a tunnel opening on the other side. Even now I sense something, as if a weak or distant portal is around, but I don't know where it could be. Anyway, I never figured out how to get across the chasm to check it out."

10

Flipping Sapphira's ponytail with the tip of her wing, Bonnie grinned. "Now we have a way to get there."

"I wouldn't try it," Shiloh said. "The updrafts from that crazy pot of stone soup could toss you around like a feather in a storm."

Bonnie let her wings droop. "I guess it'll have to stay a mystery." She looked again at the opposite ledge. Shadows continued to stalk its surface, so real they seemed alive. But, of course, they were the result of the odd light, nothing to worry about. With Yereq guarding the only entrance to the mines, no one could intrude on them.

"Speaking of mysteries ..." Sapphira turned toward an opening in the wall behind them. "The only place left to show you is the kiln level, where Elam used to make magnetite bricks with Raphah. I've never even been there myself."

"Why not?" Shiloh asked. "If you were here for centuries, you had plenty of time."

"It was a forbidden zone for years and years, and after everyone left, Chazaq wasn't around to lower the platform in our elevator shaft. It's a long drop, much farther than what we climbed to get to this level, so if I went down there, I thought I might never get back up. And now the rope's not even long enough to go that far. When Bonnie's fully healed, maybe we can give it a try. She might be able to boost us with her wings."

Bonnie nodded. It had been about a month since her mother left with Acacia through a portal to Second Eden. They had used a section of the elevator rope Sapphira had cut to climb through the cross-dimensional hole. Bonnie and Shiloh had also tried to climb, but the portal collapsed, and rocks fell through, sealing the hole and injuring Bonnie's shoulder. Fortunately, as an anthrozil, the photoreceptors in her blood helped her heal quickly, though not as quickly as she would have healed in the sunlight.

Sapphira lifted her hand and whispered, "Give me light." A blaze erupted in her palm, a small fireball, bluish white and

11

sparkling. "Ready for the climb back up? I think it's only about a half hour until Gabriel's supposed to come."

"About twenty-five minutes," Shiloh said, looking at her watch. "We can make it, if Bonnie's up for the climb."

Bonnie rubbed her shoulder. "It feels good, but I could use another dip in the hot springs after Gabriel leaves."

Sapphira touched a pouch that had been sewn to her jeans waistband, perfectly sized to hold Enoch's ovulum, a crystalline egg at least five times the size of a hen's egg. "Let's go. I left the ovulum in our hovel. I'm kind of nervous about being without it."

As Sapphira led the way toward the tunnel, Bonnie followed, looking back as she walked. The fireball cast an azure glow across the chasm, though not enough to see the other side clearly. As the light shrank away from the expanse, a strange shadow took shape, growing larger by the second.

Bonnie turned and spread her wings. "Sapphira! Shiloh! Run!"

As the two looked back, Bonnie grabbed each of them around the waist and lifted off the ground. Beating her wings, she scooted through the exit passageway and into the tunnel. The moment she lowered them to the floor, Sapphira jerked free. She stepped back toward the passage, spread out her arms, and shouted, "Ignite!"

Her body burst into flames from head to toe, her hands ablaze in white hot tongues that shot three feet in front of her. "Who's there?" she called, her voice deeper than usual.

In the light of Sapphira's flames, the shadow vanished. A human male walked through the exit, his hands raised to block the heat. "Hey, Sapphira! Cool your jets!"

Bonnie laughed. "It's Gabriel!"

"In the flesh." Dressed in a long-sleeved flannel shirt and khaki cargo pants, he nudged Bonnie's side. "Your wings look awesome. Did you never lose them, or did you get them back?"

"I'm not supposed to tell. I'm not even sure you're supposed to know I have them."

"Oh, well," Gabriel said, shrugging. "Cat's out of the bag ... or the backpack, I guess."

Sapphira lowered her hands and let the flames dwindle to a fireball in one palm. "How did you get here without us seeing you?"

Gabriel pointed toward the chasm. "I flew across that crazy lava river. Quite a ride, that's for sure."

"I lived here for multiple millennia," Sapphira said, "and I never found a passage to that side."

"Leave it to me to get lost looking for you." Grinning, he gave her a wink. "Actually, there's a way to get there from the lowest level. It's kind of a steep climb, though."

Shiloh elbowed his ribs. "Okay, mystery boy, spill the story. How did you get to the lowest level?"

He walked back toward the ledge. "Come on. I'll fly you over there one at a time, and we'll talk. Yereq's there, too, and a few other surprises you'll have to see to believe."

"Yereq's there?" Sapphira said as she and the others followed. "Who's guarding the entrance?"

"Walter's dad." Stopping close to the edge, Gabriel looked into the depths. "You should see him. He looks pretty cool with an assault rifle, and Walter's mom is there, too. She had a pump-action shotgun. Anyway, since we couldn't find you in the hovel or the springs, Yereq hung a new rope in the elevator shaft and lowered us to the bottom. He's stronger than a gorilla and climbs like one, too. I told the others to wait while I checked out the tunnel that led up here."

Bonnie reached over with a wing and tapped his shoulder. "How about if I carry Sapphira and you carry Shiloh?"

"Sure." Gabriel shrugged. "If they're not queasy about a rough ride."

Shiloh raised her arms. "Lock and load, Batman. I'm ready for anything."

13

As Gabriel wrapped his arms around Shiloh, Sapphira copied her pose. "Bonnie, are you sure you can carry me?"

"That's why I picked you." Bonnie slid her hands around Sapphira's slim waist and pressed her chest against her back. "You're the lightest one here. I once carried Billy from our schoolyard all the way to the top of a mountain. He probably weighs almost twice as much."

Gabriel pointed a wing at Bonnie. "I learned this the hard way. The heat will push you higher, so keep your webbing at an angle, almost like you're descending, and you can glide most of the way across. Maybe three wing beats will do it."

"Got it."

Gripping Shiloh tightly, he flapped his wings and lifted toward the chasm. Almost instantly, a rush of air thrust him higher, but he quickly corrected and glided away.

"Last one there has to kiss Morgan," Shiloh sang out.

Bonnie followed, keeping her wings tilted forward. At first, she dropped, raising a gasp from Sapphira, but when she adjusted to catch more of the rising air, she ascended toward the opposite ledge, flapping slowly to compensate for the inconsistent surges from below. The heat dried her eyes and cheeks, delivering a painful sting, and her wings felt weak, having had so little exercise in the caverns of Hades.

Boosted by a final thrust of rising air, Bonnie flew over the wall's protruding lip and released Sapphira, who jogged to a graceful stop. Bonnie flapped again to keep her balance and managed not to stumble.

Gabriel extended an arm toward a low-clearance hole in the wall. "Follow me, ladies." He ducked under the arch and disappeared, Shiloh staying one step behind him.

"They'll need light." Sapphira created another fireball and hurried through the opening.

As soon as the glow faded, Bonnie took another draw from the sulfur-rich air. If only Billy could see this place. He'd be amazed. But he was probably seeing even more amazing things himself, going on adventures in Second Eden she could only dream about. Of course, being with him would be awesome beyond words, but staying here for now would have to do. After all, that's what God wanted. Nothing else mattered.

"Aren't you coming?" Gabriel called, his head sticking out through the hole.

"Sorry. I got lost in thought." Collapsing her wings and ducking low, she hustled under the arch and followed Gabriel as he walked, hunched-over, toward a light in the distance.

"Don't stand straight yet," he said. "The ceiling's pretty low for a while."

Keeping her eyes on Gabriel's wings, Bonnie scrambled along the pebbly floor until they reached Sapphira. The petite Oracle stood without bending, while Shiloh and Gabriel remained stooped. "Now you see why Yereq didn't follow me." He pointed into the darkness. "Sapphira, if you please. There aren't any hazards between here and there."

Sapphira marched ahead, her fireball now brighter than ever. Shiloh kept two steps behind, while Gabriel took Bonnie's elbow, slowing her pace as they followed. "Are you doing okay?" he whispered.

"My shoulder's healed, if that's what you mean."

"That, too, but I was wondering about staying down here. Sapphira's used to it, and Shiloh stayed alone for forty years, so she can handle it."

Bonnie smiled. Images of Gabriel's past appearances ran through her mind. When she was only six years old, he appeared to her in the form of radiant energy, and she thought he was an angel. "My guardian angel is a wonderful, caring young man."

"Young? Do you know how old I really am?"

"Sixty, maybe?"

Gabriel laughed under his breath. "Older, but nice try."

"And how old is Shiloh?" Bonnie asked. "Fifty-five?"

"Something like that."

"Hmmm …" Bonnie pressed her lips together, trying to hide a grin. "Close enough, I think."

"Close enough?" Gabriel squinted at her. "What are you suggesting?"

"Suggesting?" Bonnie tried to read his eyes, but shadows blocked her view. "What were *you* thinking?"

"Never mind."

This time, Bonnie let her smile break through. Everyone knew of Gabriel's attachment to Shiloh, but he was too embarrassed to admit it.

Finally, the ceiling angled up, allowing her to stand upright. The tunnel widened into a well-lit chamber, a square room about thirty feet across. Freestanding ovens lined each of three walls. Their chimneys rose toward holes in the ten-foot ceiling, though they came short by various distances. Their crumbling tops, likely penetrating the ceiling holes at one time, revealed their age and lack of recent use.

Flickering lanterns sat on the floor. A person crouched or stood near each one, most of them women, except for Yereq and an old man wearing sandals and a forest-green medieval tunic that overlapped dark knee-length breeches.

Bonnie eyed the elderly gentleman. With a bright white aura surrounding him, he seemed ghostly, even semitransparent. For a moment, he would be solid, then a shimmer would pass across his body, allowing a split-second view of the rock wall behind him. With scattered white hair covering his ears and bright sparkling eyes, he seemed familiar. In a way, he resembled Professor Hamilton, her former teacher who passed away after a battle with Devin the dragon slayer. Yet, since she missed him so much, every lively old gentleman brought back thoughts of her beloved professor, though they didn't really look alike.

Bonnie followed a trail of light from his aura to one of the women. She carried the ovulum in her cupped hands. Like a movie projector, it seemed to create the aura and the man within.

Gabriel gestured toward each person in turn. "Bonnie, Shiloh, and Sapphira, I would like to introduce you to Rebekah, formerly Legossi; Dallas, the woman holding the ovulum, was once Firedda; Elise, also known as Carboni; Dorian, who once flew the skies as Yellinia; Kaylee, who, when dressed in scales, answered to the name of Alithia; Jordan, known to the dragon clan as Martinesse; and Tamara, affectionately dubbed Sorentine by her fire-breathing family members."

He took a deep breath and exhaled heavily. "Whew! I practiced that for hours."

"Excellent!" The elderly man clapped his hands. "And I am Enoch, prophet of the Most High. And of course," he said, motioning to a giant man sitting near a corner, "you already know Yereq."

17

Gabriel let his wings sag. "Sorry. I was going to introduce you next."

"It's quite all right. Sapphira and Shiloh already know me." Enoch reached for Bonnie's hand, but his fingers passed right through hers. "And Bonnie saw me from the window of her motel room."

"I *thought* I recognized you," she said. "It was dark that night, so I didn't get a good look."

"Nor I at you. And although we can now see that you have wings, you and everyone here must guard that secret. A day may come when we can use the ignorance of others to our advantage. And plans for the future are why I arranged this meeting. I am in my viewing room at Heaven's Altar where I can see almost anything

I request, and I can project my image if the Lord so allows. The ovulum is very useful as my hologram-generating device."

Sapphira laid a hand on her empty pouch. "How did the ovulum get here? I left it in my hovel."

Gabriel pointed at himself. "I found it there. When I picked it up, it started talking. Scared me half to death."

"I apologize for the scare." Enoch began pacing in a small circle near the center of the room, glancing at each person as he made the circuit. "The people in the land of Second Eden are preparing for a great battle, and they are woefully unprepared. They have only recently had to take up arms to ward off infrequent attacks from small bands of shadow people, who are relatively weak compared to the forces that will someday come against them. The enemy will eventually include the entire race of shadow people as well as another tribe of humanlike creatures that has no name, as far as I know. A cadre of Nephilim will join them, and one of the mightiest of all dragons, Goliath, will surely enhance their power and strategic maneuvers."

Tamara, a slender brunette who now sat cross-legged near a kiln, hissed, then quickly covered her mouth. "I … I am sorry. Old … um … habit."

Bonnie smiled at her. Obviously some of the former dragons didn't speak English very well. Wearing a long dress and smock, and her hair tied in pigtails, Tamara looked like an overgrown child, complete with a cute smile and dimples.

Enoch waved his hand. "Some habits die hard, and some we must retrieve and again make our own. Each one of you dragons, for one reason or another, has chosen to take part in the human race. Yet now I am asking you to return to your draconic states and join the battle in Second Eden, at least as many of you as possible."

A low rumble sounded from somewhere above, making the ground tremble. Enoch looked up, his bushy white eyebrows scrunching down. "Yereq, will you please investigate?"

18

When Yereq climbed to his feet, his head rose to within inches of the ceiling. He bowed to the prophet. "Shall I take a messenger who will send word in case I become involved in a battle?"

Just as Gabriel raised his hand, Rebekah shot to her feet, her waist-length blond tresses swaying as she rose. "Send me. The winged boy will be of greater use here if escape is necessary."

Enoch nodded at her. "Then make haste. We will fill you in on the details later."

Rebekah stripped off a zippered jacket, revealing a long-sleeved baseball-style jersey tucked into loose-fitting camo pants. She jerked up a lantern and swung toward Yereq, fire in her eyes. "Let's make tracks!"

As soon as the giant and former dragon disappeared into another tunnel, Enoch continued, his pace of delivery much faster now. "You cannot transform into dragons until you arrive in Second Eden, and the available portals are dangerous, so we must get you there by way of a new kind of transport. Marilyn Bannister, the human wife of Clefspeare, is building a device called Apollo that will, in combination with Sapphira's power, create an entirely new portal opening."

Sapphira raised her hand. "Father Enoch?"

"Yes, my child." His tone seemed patient, but his eyes kept glancing at the ceiling. Even though he wasn't actually in the chamber, somehow he could perceive direction of sound.

"What about the portal in the museum room? I sense that it's still there, but when I try to reopen it, I see that the passage is blocked by rocks."

"The portal is still there. Apparently, someone has again plugged the hole at the top of Mount Elijah, so the inhabitants of Second Eden must break through in order for us to use it again. I have no way of knowing why they have not done so, because my viewing portal to that world was limited to the ovulum. Even I cannot travel there at this time."

19

Forming her hands into a cradle, Sapphira took the ovulum from Dallas. Enoch's projection drifted with the egg's movements. "Maybe we should try to get this to Second Eden. It would be more useful in their hands than in mine."

Another rumble sounded, louder this time, followed by a stronger tremor. Bonnie and Gabriel flapped their wings to steady themselves, while Enoch stood upright, unaffected.

When everything settled, Enoch scanned the chamber's inhabitants. "I heard the quake, and by your reactions, I assume the tremor was powerful."

"Yes, Prophet," Gabriel said. "A real shaker."

Enoch sat down. As his body hovered just above the stone floor, he stroked his chin. "This is quite unexpected. I have no idea what is causing the seismic disturbances."

Sapphira stood next to him, her head only inches higher than his. "Shall I try to go to the surface?"

"Alone?" Gabriel asked. "Without a weapon?"

Enoch chuckled. "Sapphira Adi, the Oracle of Fire, *is* a weapon."

Sapphira blushed. "Then shall I go?"

"No, child. We will await word from Rebekah. Let us rest and have faith."

She sat down and crossed her legs. "I have several questions, if you don't mind."

"Then ask." Enoch glanced again at the ceiling, listening. "My meeting agenda is on hold until we learn what is afoot."

Sapphira began counting on her fingers. "When will the Apollo device be finished? Does this mean Bonnie and Shiloh and I don't have to stay here? And ..." Her cheeks flushed a deep cherry red. "Will I get to see Elam soon?"

Enoch patted her hand, though, again, he made no real contact. "I am a prophet, dear one, but I do not have all the answers. Regarding Apollo, without Ashley there to help, Marilyn has only

Larry to guide her, so I cannot guess when it will be finished. I arranged for helpers to come to her aid, but it remains to be seen how much benefit they will be. So, while I evaluate the dangers on the surface, you will stay here, at least until we test Apollo. The purpose of this meeting was to gather all the former dragons in a safe place and inform you of our plans."

"That makes sense." Sapphira bit her lip before continuing. "And what about Elam?"

"Ah, yes, my old friend, Elam." Enoch gazed at her, pausing for a moment as a faraway look passed across his eyes. "It is difficult to know how God will bring people together, or if he will at all, so I cannot answer. I hope the two of you will be united at last, but I think divinely arranged marriages are relatively rare."

"Like Billy and Bonnie?" Gabriel asked.

Enoch smiled at Bonnie before shifting to Gabriel. "Merlin's prophecy seems to indicate an eventual union between two people of similar characteristics, but they are not named. And the poem also does not reveal when, where, or how it will take place."

21

"But isn't Bonnie closely related to Billy?" Gabriel asked, scratching his head. "Something like second cousins or first cousins once removed? I can never figure that out."

Enoch laughed gently. "They are related through their dragon lineage, and God's laws allow for unions between closer dragon relations than they do for human ones. Billy and Bonnie, however, are quite safely within the limits for both species." He pointed at Gabriel. "On the other hand, take for example you and Shiloh. Although she is your niece, which would disqualify a union between the two of you in the code for humans, since that relationship is of draconic origin, you could be married."

Gabriel's cheeks turned even redder than Sapphira's had. "Yeah," he said, running his shoe along the floor. "I get it."

Bonnie sneaked a glance at Shiloh. Her face, too, had flushed, and a barely perceptible smile bent her lips.

Dallas stood up. "I hear footsteps."

Rapid clops sounded from the tunnel. Seconds later, Rebekah burst into the chamber, her lantern swinging. Breathless, she bent over and laid a hand on her chest. "Explosions. ... Men with jack-hammers ... Two with guns."

With a beat of his wings, Gabriel glided to her side. "How about Mr. Foley? Is he okay?"

After taking a deep breath, Rebekah straightened and shook her head. "He's wounded, as is his wife. Yereq put them in a safe place before he began fighting the invaders."

"Did Yereq collapse the entrance tunnel?" Sapphira asked. "That was our plan in case of attack."

"He said he was going to, but I left before he could do it."

"We gotta get up there," Gabriel said. "With my wings helping, I can climb that rope in a heartbeat."

Sapphira leaped to her feet. "I'll go. I'm the lightest. Gabriel can use the rope to pull me from the upper level, and I can help with hauling up the others."

"Count me in," Bonnie said, raising her hand.

As Shiloh and the former dragons chimed in with their calls offering to help, Enoch waved his arms. "Come together! Hurry!" When they gathered around, so close they penetrated his aura, he spoke with a solemn tone. "Do not act in haste. You are the reason the invaders have come. If you pop out of your hole, they will pick you off. Go in stealth, and proceed with caution."

"Understood." Gabriel picked up a lantern. "Follow me!" He exited through the tunnel, the glow of his lantern bobbing with his quick march.

Sapphira gave the ovulum to Bonnie. "You stay at the back of the line and use this for light." Carrying a ball of fire in her hand, Sapphira hurried to follow Gabriel. Shiloh went next, then Rebekah and the other former dragons, some carrying lanterns. When the last one filed out, Bonnie looked at Enoch. With only

two weak lanterns on the floor, the glow from the prophet's hologram seemed brighter than ever.

"I have to catch up," she said, "but something's been bothering me." She touched the side of her waist, as if gripping a belt.
"It feels like something's tied to me, but when I try to grab it, I
can't feel anything. Even when I take off my clothes to bathe in
the springs, I think it's still there."

Enoch leaned close. "I cannot try to feel it for you. Have you
asked Sapphira?"

"She can't feel it or see it. Neither can Shiloh."

"Hmmm…" His eyes brightened, as if energized by his drilling
stare. "I have an idea about what this might be, and it could be of
grave concern, but while I ponder it, you should hurry and join
the others." The hologram faded along with the aura. "I hope to
see you again soon."

Bonnie picked up one of the lanterns, blew out the other, and
rushed into the tunnel. Ahead, light appeared. As it grew brighter
and closer, a voice sounded in the distance. "Bonnie, is that you?"

23

"Yes, Shiloh." Flapping her wings to give herself a push, Bonnie scooted toward her. "Thank you for waiting."

"No problem." Shiloh's eyes sparkled as she winked. "I figured
we'd better make like twins before we showed our faces."

Bonnie nodded. It was time to get their backpacks on, just in
case.

CHAPTER

HELPERS

Sliding his sword from its scabbard, Edmund edged close to the door. "Stay hidden, Madam. I will investigate."

Marilyn smiled at the noble knight. Dressed in a pair of Jared's jeans and one of Billy's West Virginia sweatshirts, he seemed out of place with his sword and shield. "Don't worry, Edmund. The Caitiff wouldn't ring the doorbell."

"Ah! You are right." Keeping the sword behind his back, he opened the door. "Yes? May I help you?"

A low "ahem" sounded, then a hesitating voice. "Uh … don't the Bannisters live here?"

Marilyn peeked around Edmund. The teenager standing on the porch seemed very familiar. Could it be? Adam Lark?

"Yes, they live here. I am Edmund, knight of the—"

"Adam!" Marilyn called, pulling the door fully open. "Come on in!" She patted Edmund on the shoulder. "It's okay. He's … a friend."

Adam wiped his feet on the welcome mat and stepped inside. Flashing a grin, he nodded at Edmund. "What's with the sword?"

"Young man," Edmund said, bowing, "I am protecting this house while the other men are away."

Adam pulled up his T-shirt, revealing a handgun in a waist holster. "My Glock is better than a sword, at least for me. I had to shoot one of those monsters just yesterday."

Edmund cradled his sword in his palms. "Yes, my good fellow, but a blade is more effective with these creatures, because—"

"It's okay, Edmund," Marilyn said. "I'm sure you can talk later."

"That would be a pleasure." Edmund bowed and backed out of the way.

Giving Adam a warm smile, Marilyn closed the door. "What brings you here?"

Adam pulled an envelope from his back pocket. "This note." He handed it to her. "Check it out."

Marilyn withdrew a folded letter and read the beautiful script out loud.

26

Dear Adam,

As you are well aware, not all is right with our world. While the number of Caitiff has certainly decreased, more and more souls long thought dead are appearing at their former homes, frightening the current residents. Not only that, people claiming to be infamous scoundrels—Hitler and Stalin, to name only two—have surfaced, and DNA tests have proven their claims.

The situation is dire, Adam, and it is time for you to step up and be the hero God has recently called you to be. Because you are acquainted with the Bannisters and are aware of Billy's, shall we say, special gift, I am asking you to go to his house and offer your services. Tell Mrs. Bannister that you have considerable skills in electronics and can help her with the Apollo project. Please arrive at five in the afternoon on the date you receive this letter.

Sincerely,
Enoch, Prophet of the Most High

Marilyn refolded the note and slid it back into the envelope. "Well, that's quite a surprise."

"Yeah." Adam nodded at the letter. "Is it some kind of joke?"

"It's not a joke." Marilyn guided Adam farther inside and lowered her voice. "So you know about Billy's ... uh ... gift?"

Adam shrugged. "I figured it out. When Dr. Whittier kidnapped my father and started preaching about slaying dragons, I kind of put two and two together. I never told anyone and kind of laid low until all the dust settled. But when I got that letter, I decided to go ahead and check it out."

"And you have skills in electronics?"

He nodded. "Ever since my father came home, he's been teaching me. Dr. Whittier's a creep, but I think he sobered my dad up. Things've been a lot better lately."

She laid a hand on his back. "Well, let me show you what we're doing. We—"

The doorbell rang.

"I will get it," Edmund called.

This time he opened the door without hesitation. A teenaged girl stood on the porch. Wearing glasses, an old "Pittsburgh" sweatshirt, and a long flowing skirt, she peered inside. "Is this ... the Bannister residence?"

Edmund gave her a half bow. "It is, indeed. Won't you come in?"

Shivering in the draft, she extended an envelope to Edmund. "I got this letter, and—"

Edmund nodded toward Marilyn. "If you please, Miss, give it to the lady of the house, Mrs. Bannister."

As Edmund swung the door closed, the girl again extended the envelope, her arm still shaking. "Mrs. Bannister, I think this will explain why I'm here."

"A message from Enoch?" Marilyn asked as she took the letter.

The girl's eyes grew wide. "How did you know?"

Marilyn winked at Adam. "It's happened before." She opened the enclosed note and again read out loud.

Dear Carly,

I write to you with an urgent request. Your dear friend Bonnie Silver is in grave danger, and you might be able to make a difference in the outcome of her trials. At this very moment, she is hiding in a secret place, but forces of great evil stalk her constantly.

From the moment the two of you met on a bus in first grade, she has entrusted you with many secrets, including her greatest secret, and her recent letters to you have described some of her circumstances, using, of course, the code the two of you developed for such messages.

I ask you now, Carly, to go to the Bannister home at 1545 Cordelle Road in Castlewood, West Virginia. I am well aware of the dangers of solitary travel for a young lady such as yourself, but the situation is grave, and I am sure you will want to help your dear friend.

Please tell Mrs. Bannister that you are skilled with computers and can help her with the Apollo project. Be sure to arrive at five in the afternoon on the date after you receive this letter.

Sincerely,

Enoch, Prophet of the Most High

"So, you're Carly," Marilyn said.

"Yes." Carly offered her hand. "I'm glad to meet you."

"Any friend of Bonnie's is a friend of mine." Marilyn shook Carly's hand gently. "How did you get here?"

"I took the bus from Pittsburgh and transferred in Morgantown. Then I walked from the Castlewood bus station. That's why I'm a little late. I didn't know how far it was."

"It's five miles to the bus station!"

"Yes ... I know that now."

Marilyn shook her head. "You poor thing. No wonder you're shivering so."

Carly touched her sweatshirt. "I have layers underneath. I thought I'd be warm enough."

"Your parents must be worried sick. Would you like to call them?"

Carly dipped her head low. "Uh … Neither of my parents wanted me, so I live in a group foster home. I often go for long walks, so they might not miss me until dinnertime."

"Oh, Carly! And you came by yourself, even with all the Caitiff lurking!" Marilyn took her into her arms and hugged her close. "We'll have to get in touch with someone at your home, but you're welcome to stay here as long as you want."

"Thank you." Sniffing, Carly drew back. "I appreciate it."

Marilyn set a hand on her hip. "Well, I wonder how many more helpers will be coming."

After glancing at a clock on the wall, Edmund peered out a window next to the door. "It is ten past five, and I see no one else."

Adam extended his hand toward Carly. "Adam Lark, friend of Billy Bannister. If you know Bonnie, I'm sure you've heard of him."

29

"Nice to meet you," she said, shaking his hand. "And, yes, Bonnie goes on and on about Billy in her letters."

"Figures. Everyone knew she and Dragon Breath were crazy about each other."

Carly tilted her head. "Dragon Breath?"

"Never mind. I'd better get used to calling him Billy."

Marilyn glanced toward the rear of the house. "Shall I introduce you to Apollo and my project team?"

"Sure," Adam said.

Carly nodded. "Yes, thank you."

"And I will patrol the perimeter," Edmund said, sliding his sword into its scabbard. "If there is trouble, I will sound the usual alarm."

Marilyn winced. Edmund meant the trumpet he had found at the Foleys' home some months back. She gave him an uneasy smile. "A shout will be fine, thank you."

Opening the door, Edmund nodded, disappointment clear in his expression. "As you wish, Madam."

Marilyn led the new helpers through a hallway and stopped at a closed door near the back of the house. "Just to let you know in advance, you're about to meet Shelly and Larry. Shelly is our neighbor, and Larry is ... well, you'll see."

She swung the door open, releasing a low-pitched hum from the room. Inside, the drone of cooling fans pushed against them like a sonic wall, and the breeze from an air conditioner made Carly push her hands into her sweatshirt's front pouch.

Shelly, dressed in dark gray sweats, sat in a swivel desk chair just outside a glass-enclosed chamber, typing at a keyboard while watching a display mounted on the chamber's exterior. The transparent walls took up most of the rear half of the computer room. The walls made up the housing for a ceiling-high box of metal and plastic—Larry the supercomputer. Covered with notched dials, flashing diodes, and plasma monitors, to Adam and Carly he probably looked like something straight from the Starship Enterprise.

As the trio walked in, Shelly spun in her chair and stood up. Flashing a nervous smile, she pulled Marilyn's sleeve, drawing her close as she whispered, "So ... why are you letting Adam Lark in on our secret? And who's the girl?"

"Take a breath, Shelly. It's okay." Spreading out an arm, Marilyn turned in a slow circle. "Adam and Carly, this is Larry's abode."

Carly's eyes grew wide as she and Adam surveyed the room. Marilyn followed their gazes. From flowcharts on the walls to the monitors on Larry's panels to flashing lights, animated graphs, and beeping speakers on his control screen, the work area was definitely impressive.

Marilyn stepped between Adam and Carly and set a hand on each of their shoulders. "Larry, I would like for you to meet Adam Lark and Carly ... uh ..."

"Masters," Carly said.

A voice, a blend of computerized and normal human speech, sounded from the mounted screen. "Greetings. I have recorded Carly's voice and will store it for future security use. My database already contains an entry for Adam Lark. Hmmm … Billy's notes are not exactly flattering."

"Yeah." Adam shifted his weight from foot to foot. "We kind of didn't … I mean—"

"Erase that entry," Marilyn said, "and create a new one. We're starting with a clean slate."

"Old entry deleted. New record stored, complete with voiceprint."

"Now …" Marilyn led them to a ten-foot-long wooden table abutting the wall opposite Larry. "This is our workspace for assembling Apollo."

Carly used a pair of tweezers to lift a silicon chip about the size of a thumbnail, one of the many computer parts scattered across the table. "What exactly is Apollo?"

Marilyn picked up Apollo by one of its foot-long dowels. Except for the rectangular shape of its inner glass enclosure, Apollo, a virtual twin of its predecessor, looked more like an old-fashioned hourglass than a cross-dimensional portal device.

As she tilted it, a glass door swung open on tiny hinges, and a cat's-eye marble rolled out onto her palm. "It's supposed to be a portal opener. The original one created a flash of light made up of exactly the right wavelengths to create a window to another world." She showed them the marble. "This is exactly the size and weight of something we want to transport to another realm, so we keep it in there for our tests. So far, it hasn't worked."

Adam's eyes bugged out, but he stayed quiet. Obviously the talk about another realm had given him a shock.

"So," Marilyn continued, "we want to send a gem called a rubellite. It's needed to increase the power of Excalibur, the legendary sword. We're hoping to get it to Billy and Walter so they can install it in the sword's hilt."

31

Carly touched one of the four dowels. "Bonnie wrote to me about this. Sometimes I wondered if her stories could possibly be true, but seeing this makes them come alive."

"Did she include her adventures in Hades?" Marilyn asked.

"If you mean the Circles of Seven," Carly said. "Yes, she did."

Marilyn closed Apollo's glass door. "Well, that's related to what's going on here. Hades has combined with Earth, and the appearance of strange creatures and the resurrection of dead people are the result of the merging. Billy and Walter are in another realm called Second Eden. For some reason, that place is the key for getting everything back to normal."

Adam pointed at the floor. "So all the chaos in the world can be traced to what's been going on in this house?" He let out a whistle. "This is getting cooler all the time."

"Cool, yes, but dead serious, too. We're going to help them by any means we can, and if sending the rubellite works, we'll try to open a portal big enough to send people."

"So what do we do?" Carly asked.

Marilyn set Apollo down. "Building this much was easy. The hard part has been getting the electronics to work. They're housed in a cap that snaps on to Apollo's top ..."

For the next few hours, Marilyn explained the device and how her tests had failed to this point. She even replicated the failures three times to give her two new helpers hands-on experience. With her adoptive daughters, Stacey, Rebecca, and Monique, away at a church function, she had plenty of time to recount many of their adventures. Finally, after eating a late dinner, they returned to the worktable.

"So," Marilyn said. "Any ideas? Adam? Carly?"

Adam ran his fingers through his scraggly shock of dark hair and leaned over the table. As his Castlewood Valley High School T-shirt rubbed against the edge, he peered into Apollo's glass enclosure. "The flash wasn't very bright, nothing like the wattage you're supposed to be getting."

"If that's the case ..." Carly smoothed out a schematic, a collection of printed pages taped together, and pointed at a microprocessor symbol near the bottom of one of the pages. "I think this one's the culprit."

"Could be." A few inches taller than Carly, Adam looked down at her, gesturing with his hands as he spoke. "Since Apollo flashed, it must've gotten the signal from Larry, but the flash was too weak. Something must have told the generator the wrong electromotive force."

Carly pointed at the microprocessor symbol again. "Since that chip has the math coprocessor, and since the coding calls for higher precision, we might have a rounding problem somewhere in the calculations. Rounding might not matter sometimes, but precision is crucial in this case. If one of the earlier numbers is wrong, the error gets worse and worse with every line of math code."

"So, the processor calculated the wattage wrong?" Marilyn asked.

"Well, voltage," Adam said. "That drives the wattage. But, yeah."

33

Carly tapped a finger on Apollo's top. "If we can swap out that chip, we can test Adam's theory right away."

Crossing her arms, Marilyn gave Adam and Carly an admiring gaze. Adam had changed so much since his bullying days at Castlewood Middle School. And Carly's computer skills had already been a godsend. "Okay!" Marilyn said. "Let's give it a shot."

Carly's eyes darted from one side of the table to the other, searching across scattered chips, diodes, and resistors. "Do we have another one here?"

Marilyn looked back at Shelly. She was sitting once again at Larry's control panel. "Do we have any more of Ashley's zeta chips?" Marilyn asked.

"Probably." Shelly stared at a flat monitor mounted on a wall panel as she pecked on a keyboard. "I'll check inventory."

"You may use verbal inquiries, Shelly. My parsing engine has fully integrated your voiceprint as well as your biography—Shelly Foley, twenty-one-year-old daughter of Carl and Catherine, sister of Walter, and one-time hostiam for—"

"Stifle it!" Shelly pointed a rigid finger at the monitor. "Just tell me if we have—"

"Any of Ashley's zeta chips?"

Shelly rolled her eyes. "Give me a break, Larry. If you already knew what we wanted, why'd you give me such a hard time?"

"To allow time for background processing. I wanted to check our usual suppliers for the raw materials. Our inventory shows zero zeta chips, but an epsilon chip would likely suffice. It is an older generation but quite functional for this application, though it lacks Ashley's newer communications protocol."

"Will that be a problem?" Marilyn asked.

"Only in that it will make transmissions a few milliseconds slower."

Shelly jumped up from her seat and headed for the hallway door. "I'll get the chip." She stopped, twirling her shoulder-length brown hair as she looked back. "Need anything? Drinks? Cookies?"

"I don't." Marilyn touched Adam's shoulder. "How about you?"

"The pizza made me thirsty. Anything non-diet."

"Water would be great," Carly said.

Marilyn nodded at Shelly. "Water for everyone, thank you."

Adam picked up Apollo's top, a black disc about the size of a hockey puck. "You think Ashley might hire someone like me? I mean, after I graduate, of course."

"Maybe she could take on an intern before you graduate. You certainly have the skills." Marilyn let out a silent sigh. With Adam and Carly around, they would probably eventually get Apollo working. But what would that mean? So many events had to fall into place. Who might find the rubellite once they transported it

34

to Second Eden? How would that person know to give it to Billy? Leaving so much to faith felt like jumping into a dark pit, but what choice did she have? Somehow she had to provide a path for her men to march home ... her men ... Jared and Billy.

Marilyn clenched her fist. They had to come back. They just had to.

While Carly and Adam pored over the schematic, whispering to each other, Marilyn sat in the control desk chair. "Larry, I hope you don't mind if I ask again, but—"

"I am a computer, Marilyn. I do not get weary of questions. I constantly monitor the communication ports, both conventional and cross-dimensional, especially Ashley's tooth-transmitter protocol, and there are no messages."

Marilyn rested her chin in her hand. No word from Jared or Billy in a month. Were they all right? If so, what could they be doing in Second Eden that would prevent them from returning? Did they have a way to return at all?

Shelly popped back into the computer room, a small plastic bag pinched in her fingers. At the bottom of the bag lay a tiny black chip. "Found it!"

"Perfect!" Carly said, reaching for the bag.

Adam slid Apollo closer to her. "Let's fire it up again."

"I'll get the water now." Shelly hustled out of the room.

As Marilyn rose from the chair, a phone on the desk chimed. She jerked it up. "Hello?"

"Mrs. Bannister?" The voice was deep, almost like a lion's growl, yet drowned in static.

"Yes. Who is this?"

"I am Yereq."

She glanced at the caller ID number—Carl Foley's cell phone. "Yes, Yereq. Is something wrong?"

Again the voice seemed weak, as if submerged in water. It broke up at times, creating gaps between words. "Mr. Foley is hurt,

35

and I cannot ... I am unable to get help. I pressed a button on this ... and your name appeared ..."

Marilyn swallowed and tried to keep her voice calm. "Yereq, where is Mrs. Foley?"

"She ... also hurt ... breathing ... not talking."

"She's unconscious but alive?"

"Yes."

"Listen carefully. After we're finished, press the end button. Then push nine, then one, then one again and the send button. It's probably green. Do you see those?"

After a few seconds, he said, "Yes. I understand."

"Good. That's the number for emergency calls. Tell the operator where you are and that you need an air ambulance. Do it now." Marilyn hung up the phone and exhaled loudly, feeling a sudden loss of energy. Just staying calm for Yereq had drained her reserves.

Shelly walked back in, carrying four bottles of water. "I heard the phone."

"It was Yereq. He says your parents are hurt."

Shelly dropped two of the bottles. "Did he say how bad?"

Marilyn jumped up and collected the bottles. "Only that he couldn't get help. With all the static it was hard to hear him."

Shelly's voice squeaked. "Can you call him back?"

Marilyn shook her head. "Yereq had a bad signal, and he's probably trying to call nine-one-one right now, so I don't want to confuse him with a call-waiting beep. We can hunt down the hospitals in the area and contact them."

"I am printing out a list of hospitals within a hundred miles of that location," Larry said. "The closest major health center is in Kalispell, Montana."

Shelly jerked the sheet from Larry's output bin and grabbed the phone. "I'll start calling. Maybe someone can tell me if an ambulance was dispatched."

While Shelly punched in the first number, Marilyn joined Adam and Carly at the table. "Will you two be able to do this by yourself?"

"Sure," Adam replied. "It'll be a breeze."

"Good." She rolled the marble into his hand. "How long do you think?"

"I have to take out a circuit board." Holding Apollo by one of its dowels, he set the marble inside the glass enclosure. "Probably about ten minutes."

"That might give us enough time to get news on Walter's parents." Crossing her arms over her chest, Marilyn walked toward Shelly as she waited with the phone against her ear, apparently on hold.

Marilyn sighed. On hold. With her husband and son off in another world, her life had been "on hold" for so long! Were they safe? Were they even alive? And what could she do once she arrived in Montana? Of course, she would have to find someone to look after Stacey, Rebecca, and Monique before she took off, but that wouldn't be a problem. They had stayed at friends' houses before.

She watched Adam as he feverishly worked on Apollo, Carly looking on. That strange device was their only hope for piercing the curtain of questions, and the answers couldn't come soon enough.

37

CHAPTER

The Vacants

Billy stopped on Mount Elijah's steep incline and wrapped his cloak tighter around his body. The frigid wind tore through the woolen material, chilling his skin. Elam had warned him that the higher elevations were much colder than the valleys, but with the potential for battle looming, he had declined to wear more layers. A swift march up the slope would have to be enough to keep him warm.

Looking back at Walter, he raised a battle shield to block the wind and pressed a finger against his lips. "Let's keep it down."

Puffing white streams over his own shield, Walter joined him, whispering. "How much farther?"

Billy pointed. "You can see the top. The path will switch back twice more before we get there."

Walter angled his head to see the pinnacle. "Is that a fire?"

"Looks like they're trying to stay warm." Billy reached under his cloak and withdrew Excalibur from a belt scabbard. "Get ready."

Walter opened his cloak, revealing the hilt of a sword. "I've got your back."

"But who has our front?" Billy scanned the cloudy twilight skies. From the stories Valiant told, Second Eden had never experienced such overcast conditions, but ever since Angel's lie a month ago, rain and snow had come to the land in regular cycles. With no need for the watering mists and with the next eclipse due, would the fountains erupt and flood the Valley of Shadows as before? If so, what effect would the rising water have on Abraham's wall of fire, the protective shield that kept Flint, Goliath, and their armies from attacking the villages?

Billy grabbed Walter's sleeve and pulled him close. "When we get to the north face again, we'll hold there until Pegasus rises. It looks like the sky's clearing in that direction, so maybe we'll see the eclipse, and we can listen for the fountains. But whether we hear them or not, when it gets totally dark, that's when we run the rest of the way to the top and attack. Excalibur's light should scare them half to death. And if it doesn't, the dragons will."

"If they show up on time." Walter looked up at the darkening sky. "No sign of them yet."

"Dad will wait until the last minute. No use letting themselves be seen too soon. He and Hartanna know what they're doing."

"Yeah, but Valiant's description of these goons makes me wonder if your father has ever faced anything like them before. And what if they really have candlestones?"

Billy nodded. Walter was right. Valiant had called them "Vacants," empty of soul, emotions, or capacity for pain, humanoid creatures Abraham had once mentioned as if from a fairy tale. The villagers had spoken of altered tribes, but most of them had seen only the shadow people. Now, as if resurrected from ancient history, this tribe had returned to Second Eden. Why? No one knew. But since they stalked about the woods and mountains north of Founders Village but hadn't attacked the village itself, they seemed content to keep Abraham's people close to home, forcing Elam, Valiant, Sir Barlow, and others to maintain as many guards as possible.

Still, they had accosted the village's patrol, making the path to Mount Elijah dangerous, so the band of Vacants guarding the top of the volcano would have to go, and with only a narrow access trail available, it seemed best to Elam to send two warriors for a surprise attack. With Acacia now fully rested, she could try again to open the portal in the volcano's throat, if it still existed at all. Clefspeare had tried to clear the Vacants out once before but grew weak as he approached. Could that mean these creeps had a candlestone? Who could have given it to them? And how could they know that it weakened dragons?

Pointing with Excalibur, Billy whispered, "Let's move. Remember, we'll stop at the next switchback. That'll be the north face."

Soft-stepping on the gravelly path, they eased around the mountain and out of its shadow. Pegasus came into view, barely visible over the horizon. Although partially veiled by thin clouds, it shone a swath of yellowish moonlight across an array of peaks and valleys, creating a stunning portrait of a river-fed landscape, the western side of each mountain shrouded in shadows.

As a sliver of darkness passed over the edge of the huge moon, wind pummeled their bodies and flapped their cloaks. Billy pulled up his hood and pressed his back against the mountain. The rocky wall didn't shield him from the wind, but at least it held his cloak in place.

Walter joined him at his side and pointed toward a valley. "The fountains are supposed to be somewhere over there."

"I see bubbles in the river," Billy said. "I'll bet that's where they spring up."

"Yep. They're about to blow, all right."

"Perfect. The noise should help."

Leaning his head against the mountain, Walter looked at Billy. "You ever think back to how all this started? I mean, how we teamed up?"

Billy nodded. "When did you first know I was different?"

"When you breathed on your Pop-tart on the bus, and it toasted on the spot."

"That soon? I didn't know you noticed."

"I didn't know your breath would turn into fire, but I noticed." Walter pulled out his sword. "And I'm glad I did. Life's been awesome ever since."

The shadow crossed the moon's halfway point, further darkening their surroundings. "Are you ready for another battle?" Billy asked.

"Fire up that sword, and I'll follow the glow."

"Just a couple more minutes, I think." Listening for a rush of water, Billy kept his gaze locked on the skies. Just a hint that his father lurked nearby would be a big help. These Vacants sounded as bad as the Nephilim, maybe worse. And with Excalibur acting in an unpredictable manner, who could tell how effective it would be? Still, it had always provided at least a bit of light, and the blade was as sharp as ever. If necessary, he could also use his fire breathing, but that would have to wait until they engaged the Vacants in close conflict. He didn't want to accidently scorch Walter.

When the last slice of Pegasus drained away, Billy summoned a bare glow from Excalibur, just enough to see the path in front of him, a path wide enough for the two of them to march side by side. He stepped away from the mountain and whispered, "Ready?"

Walter sidled up close. "Let's do it."

Craning his neck, Billy listened for the fountains. Although the wind whistled past his ears, a sudden rush burst through. Water raged somewhere in the distance.

Billy threw off his cloak and charged ahead, Excalibur leading the way. With Walter in the darkness behind him, he concentrated on the path, resisting the urge to summon a brighter light. The closer they could get without alerting the Vacants, the better.

As he rounded the final switchback, a shout reached his ears, then another. Excalibur's glow covered the mountaintop, revealing several scurrying shadows on its flat surface. Two shadows charged down the path, both with blades reflecting the glow, but before they could reach Billy, a blast of fire ripped across the sky and doused the pair with flames, fanned by beating wings that rushed by in the darkness above.

Billy and Walter hopped over the writhing, burning bodies and ran on. Another stream of orange splashed onto the very top of the mountain, energizing the Vacants' campfire. With flames now illuminating the scene, Billy made a quick count. About five of the goons remained. Not a problem.

All five charged, swords bared and spears raised. Billy waded into them, slashing with all his might, shooting fire from his mouth, and blocking their blows with his shield. After dismembering one and setting another ablaze, he burst through to the other side and swung around. Walter battled two Vacants, swiveling back and forth to meet their swords with his, while a third approached from his rear.

As Billy set his feet to attack again, dizziness flooded his mind. Nausea boiled in his stomach. Was a candlestone around? No matter. He had to fight.

"Walter! Behind you!" Walter spun, but too late. The Vacant stabbed him in the side with a spear. As Walter slumped to his knees, Billy charged, again slashing with Excalibur, but this time only smoke spewed from his mouth.

After crashing into one of the Vacants and knocking him down the slope, Billy lopped the head off the one who stabbed

Walter and kicked its body off the side of the mountain. In the distance, a shadow fled away, probably an escaping Vacant.

His shoulders now sagging, Billy faced the final opponent, a tall brute of a man. With a spear uplifted and ready to throw, the Vacant held something in his other hand, something that emitted a dim beam of light.

Billy gulped. His arms wilted, unable to lift his sword and shield. He couldn't fight. He couldn't even run. His legs refused to budge.

Just as the Vacant slung his spear, a voice bellowed from above. "Son! Drop to your belly!"

Billy threw himself to the ground. The spear swished over his head. A thud sounded, then a ripping noise. Soon, only the rush of water and the whistling wind reached his ears. With strength returning to his muscles, he pushed up to his hands and knees and turned toward Walter. "You all right, buddy?"

Now on his stomach, Walter clawed the path, groaning. "Nope. Guess again."

"I'm coming." As Billy crawled toward him, a sudden wind beat his hair into a frenzy. A dragon landed on the volcano's flat top, its wings outstretched.

"Son!" Clefspeare called. "Are you wounded?"

"I'm okay, but Walter's pretty bad."

Clefspeare raised his head and trumpeted. When his call died away, he shuffled his body toward Billy. "I signaled Hartanna. She carried the candlestone bearer to his doom, but she is now weak. I will take Walter to our healers, and she will carry you back to the village as soon as she is able."

"I'll check out the hole," Billy said. "That's what we came for."

"It is dark. Be careful. We will return with Acacia in the daylight." With a beat of his wings, Clefspeare rose into the air, passed over Billy, and picked up Walter in his claws. Rising and falling in the whipping wind, the great dragon disappeared in the darkness.

Billy climbed to his feet and, clutching Excalibur, staggered toward the portal hole on the mountain's flat top. He summoned the brightest glow the sword would give and passed the light across the volcano's throat. A pile of boulders plugged the hole. The Vacants must have torn down the remnants of the wall that once arched over this circular floor and rolled them in.

He leaned against the pile. There was way too much debris to dig through by himself, and Acacia would be needed to open the portal. No use wearing himself out before she arrived.

As he searched the dark skies, a sliver of Pegasus appeared from behind its eclipsing shadow. Light seeped out and spread across the starry canopy, turning it purple and magenta. The rush of water eased, a sure sign that the eclipse had reached its waning minutes.

He looked at the river's source. Fountains still pushed water well above the surface, breaking off chunks of ice as the flow surged past the edges of a glacier. With light continuing to clarify every detail, he walked to one of the dead Vacants and used the flat of his blade to turn the creature's head face up. Although his facial features somewhat resembled that of humans—two eyes, one nose, one mouth—their sizes and positions differed. The mouth sat lower, near the chin, much smaller than normal, more like a guppy's mouth. Its eyes, still open, were also lower, one on each side of a central nose, if you could call it a nose. It looked more like a doorknob with breathing holes. And the eyeballs? As big as ping pong balls yet as dark as coal, they reflected the moon, seemingly without a defined iris or pupil.

As the glow from Pegasus continued to brighten, he moved the sword to the Vacant's arm, the site of his fatal wound. Covered with a metal-reinforced sleeve, an elbow-length stub oozed dark blood. Was the blood black, or just dark red?

Billy looked away. Just two years ago this sight would have made him gag, but now it brought a sense of heaviness—so much fighting, so much bloodshed, so much evil in every realm. And now he was a warrior, called to battle on every front. Sure, he had become strong, and he had courage. And, yes, he could handle a sword with the best of them. But what good was all of that when his primary reason for wielding his sword was far away in another world? Would he ever see Bonnie again?

As he walked back to the volcano's throat, he looked again at the massive moon, as bright as two Earth moons now that its time of darkness had slipped away. This place was so different—shadow people, Vacants, odd swamp folks, and a peaceful group of humans training for battle while a protective wall of fire slowly ebbed.

Yes, it was different … and dangerous, even to the point of death, especially now for Walter. Would he even survive his wound?

Billy picked up one of the stones plugging the hole and heaved it down the slope. At least he could move some of this stuff out of the way while he waited. It would take his mind off Bonnie and Walter.

After a minute or so of hauling rocks, he sat down on one of the larger ones. He was wrong. Images of his friends stayed locked in his mind. He looked up at the sky. Hartanna couldn't show up soon enough.

After stopping at their hovel to put on their backpacks, Bonnie and Shiloh ran side by side through the main corridor, Bonnie carrying a flickering lantern. Because of the delay, they had to hurry to catch up with the others.

Bonnie stopped at the mouth of the escape tunnel to her right, a narrower passage that ascended at a sharp angle. "Lights out?"

"Probably a good idea," Shiloh said. "Sapphira can always relight it with her patented, 'Ignite.'"

Lifting the glass, Bonnie blew out the flame. Now in darkness, she whispered, "A little slower now."

The two scurried up the incline, feeling the walls on each side as they climbed. Soon, shouts and a clamor of metal on rocks echoed through the passage.

"The girl's on fire! What is she, a demon?"

Craning her neck to listen, Bonnie slowed her pace further. That was a male voice, strained and unfamiliar.

"Sapphira!" someone else called. "Get back! He's got a gun!"

Bonnie grabbed Shiloh's arm. "That was Gabriel!"

As they dashed ahead, a bright glow came into view and guided their way. When they neared the source, they crept close to the wall, staying in the shadows. Sapphira stood at the center of the tunnel, completely ablaze in white flames that spread from one wall to the other. Behind her, Gabriel shielded the former dragons with his wings.

Three men stood on Sapphira's far side, one with a rifle poised at his shoulder. A pile of rubble blocked the way beyond them, dust swirling from an apparent collapse. The rushing air proved that a vent somewhere still allowed passage to the outside.

47

"Vlad," the tallest man shouted. "Shoot her! Just shoot her!"

"I can't!" Vlad's rifle trembled. "She's just a girl, Nolan! I can't shoot a girl."

Her white hair streaming in the flames, Sapphira formed a fireball in her hands. "Do you want to see me throw like a girl?"

A short, bearded man climbed up the pile of rubble. "She's a demon, I tell you. I'm outta here." He disappeared through a hole in the rocks.

Sapphira threw the ball against the pile. White-hot flames splashed all around. "That was a warning," she said as she fashioned a new ball. "The next one will roast your flesh."

Nolan snatched the rifle. "If you won't do it, I will!"

Gabriel burst through the wall of flames and leaped for the gunman. The moment he reached for the barrel, the rifle went off with a loud pop.

Sapphira's body snapped back and dropped to the ground. Her flames dwindled as the gunshot's echo reverberated in the tunnel.

"Sapphira!" Bonnie scrambled toward her.

Nolan kicked Gabriel in the groin, then smacked the side of his head with the barrel, sending him crashing against the wall. Gabriel slumped and slid to the floor, out cold, or worse.

Now with only lantern flames lighting the tunnel, Nolan turned the rifle toward Bonnie, Shiloh, and the others as they huddled around Sapphira. "Vlad, find the one they call Bonnie and get her out of here."

Bonnie angled her face toward the shadows. She had to protect her secret and get to Second Eden. If she couldn't hide or escape from these intruders, all would be lost.

"I'm Bonnie," Rebekah said, rising to her full height. "Take me, and leave the others alone."

Nolan jerked a photo from his shirt pocket. Holding it close to his eyes, he glanced between it and Rebekah. "Liar!" He handed the photo to Vlad. "Use this to find her. I'll cover you."

Bonnie kept her head low, listening to Sapphira's rapid breaths. Blood spilled from a shoulder wound, and her eyelids fluttered. "I'm okay," Sapphira whispered. "Let him get close, and I'll—"

"I'm Bonnie." Shiloh stood and stepped into the lanterns' glow, faking an American accent. "Now put down that gun, and I'll go without a fight."

Vlad set the photo close to Shiloh's face. "She's the one, all right."

"Get her in the chopper and tie her up," Nolan said, waving the rifle toward the exit hole.

Vlad pulled a dagger from his belt and pressed the tip against Shiloh's chin. "Get moving."

As Shiloh climbed the rubble, Nolan lowered the barrel. "Now that we have what we came for, the rest of you stay here for ten minutes. Then you're free to go."

48

After looking back at Gabriel, Shiloh disappeared through the hole, followed seconds later by Vlad.

"Where are you taking her?" Rebekah demanded.

Nolan smirked. "To someone who pays very well, but I'm sure he would be rather angry with me if I revealed his identity or his whereabouts." He backed toward the rubble, a hint of unsteadiness in his step. "Now, if you'll excuse me."

Sapphira reached for Bonnie's hand. "Help me up," she whispered. "I hear pain in his voice. It's happening."

"What's happening?" Still angling her face away from the gunman, Bonnie locked wrists with Sapphira and hoisted her to her feet. "What are you talking about?"

"You'll see." Sapphira faced Nolan as he climbed the pile, the rifle still pointed her way. "Feeling bad, Nolan?" she asked.

He paused at the edge of the hole and squinted at her. His head lolled like that of a drunken man. "I ... I feel fine."

Sapphira reached to her shoulder, smeared blood onto her palm, and showed it to Nolan. "He who spills the blood of an Oracle of Fire will surely die."

Heaving shallow, choking breaths, Nolan clutched his shirt as he gasped his words. "You *are* a demon ... or some ... some kind of witch."

Sapphira's hand ignited from the heel to the tips of her fingers. The blood sizzled and burned away. "Tell us where your partner is taking Bonnie."

With sweat streaming down his three-day beard, Nolan gagged, barely able to speak. "Will you ... let me ... live?"

"Tell us!" Sapphira shouted. "You are in God's hands now."

Nolan stared at his hands with wide eyes. The fingers touching his rifle smoldered, as if on fire. Then, sparks erupted from the tips, like holiday sparklers—white and orange. He threw down the gun and shook his hand, but the flames ate away his fingers, faster and faster.

49

The fingers on his other hand ignited, then his feet and lower legs. He collapsed, rolled down the pile of rubble, and writhed on the ground, every extremity ablaze, including his scalp. His arms now just flailing nubs, he screamed. "Curse you! Curse you all, dragons and demons alike!"

Bonnie turned her head. It was awful, just too awful. Flickers of light from his engulfed body painted the wall, and his fading screams and the odor of burning flesh assaulted her senses. Soon, all was quiet.

Turning back, Bonnie looked for him but found only a heap of bones, charred and smoldering.

Rebekah picked up the rifle and pointed it at the escape hole. "I'll need three to come with me. The rest of you stay here to help our wounded. Alithia, check on Gabriel."

One of the former dragons, a short, stocky lady, ran to Gabriel's side and pressed her fingers against his throat. "He's alive."

After Rebekah climbed through the hole, Dallas and two others followed. Then, when all three had disappeared, Rebekah poked her head back through. "Hide the bones. I'll send someone back with a report as soon as I can."

Bonnie stooped beside Gabriel and touched his caretaker's arm. "Does he need a doctor?"

"I am a doctor ... Kaylee Saunders, M.D." She pulled Gabriel's eyelids up and peered in. "He's unconscious. Let's get some water."

Rotating her wounded shoulder, Sapphira looked at Bonnie. "Can you lead them to the spring?"

"Of course." Bonnie peeked at Sapphira's back but saw no blood, no obvious exit wound. "And you'll need to soak, too. Maybe Dr. Saunders can get that bullet out."

"I'd like to wait for word on Shiloh," Sapphira said, "and the Foleys and Yereq."

Bonnie picked up a lantern and held it close to Sapphira's shoulder. Blood dampened a splotch the size of two hands. "No way. We have to clean that wound and stop the bleeding. Besides, those guys might come back for their partner."

"So we have to make sure they can't." Wincing, Sapphira glared at the hole in the rubble. "I'm still well enough to stop them."

Dr. Saunders looked up at one of the other former dragons. "Dorian, hide the bones and stand guard. If someone comes through besides one of our own, come and warn us."

"How will I find you?" Dorian asked. "I know not the path to the spring."

Bonnie pointed into the darkness. "Go to the end of this tunnel. Turn left, then right again when you hear the sound of water."

"Very well." Dorian bowed her head. "If they pursue me, I will lead them away from your refuge and then return and warn you."

While the other former dragons carried Gabriel, Sapphira and Bonnie led the way, Sapphira with a weak ball of fire in her hand and Bonnie with a lantern in hers. Whenever they jostled him, Gabriel mumbled a few indecipherable words.

Bonnie kept a close eye on Sapphira. At times, her gait wobbled as she negotiated the descent, but she always managed to straighten again. With her white eyebrows bent low and her red lips pursed, she seemed to be battling intense pain. That bullet had likely damaged more tissue than she had let on.

When they reached the passage to the spring, the sound of falling water and a rush of wet air filled the tunnel. After traversing a short path, they entered an enormous chamber. Their lights flashed into the upper reaches, revealing a cathedral-like ceiling.

Steamy springs cascaded from three holes near the top of a flowstone wall, dropping down a stair-step array of flat rocks before joining into one stream. At each level, water collected in pools behind and around the rocks, some neck-deep and some barely deep enough to scoop up a handful. Overhead, stalactites dripped cool limestone water, making the chamber feel like a storm had just passed as the sodden branches of imaginary trees trickled their excess on passersby.

Bonnie set her lantern by one of the deeper pools, her favorite place to sit and soak. The rocks within the stream formed a bench, perfect for relaxing. When she sat in this pool, the surface reached up to her neck, and a waterfall poured a hot shower just beyond her feet, sending a warm current her way.

The former dragons laid Gabriel gently on the stone floor. Tamara sat next to him and propped his head on her thigh. "His breathing is good," she said. "He's still mumbling, but his eyes are closed."

"Then Sapphira is our priority." Dr. Saunders eyed her shoulder. "If I cut the bullet out, am I subject to the Oracle's curse? You will certainly bleed more."

"No worries," Sapphira said. "Paili once removed a splinter from my foot. I bled, but she was fine. Apparently, if the bloodletting is for healing rather than for harm, you're safe."

"That's good enough for me." Dr. Saunders reached for Sapphira's shirt. "Let's get this off and have a look."

Sapphira glanced at Gabriel. "Okay, but—"

The doctor followed her line of sight. "Don't worry. He's unconscious. I think he'll see only stars for quite a while."

As she pulled up the bottom hem, Gabriel called out, "Wait!"

Dr. Saunders lowered Sapphira's shirt. "Ah! You're awake!"

Gabriel sat up, holding a hand against his forehead. "I might be seeing stars, but I don't want to risk seeing any other heavenly bodies."

"Ladies," Bonnie said with a smile, "we have a true gentleman among us."

Sapphira pointed at a plastic basin near a lower pool. "There's a sponge in that basin. Someone can take that and help Gabriel back to the tunnel."

Bonnie stepped down the stony staircase, filled the basin with cooler water from an estuary pool, and she and Tamara supported Gabriel as they walked to the outer passage. After helping him sit with his wings spread comfortably behind him, Bonnie mopped the back of his head with the sponge. "There's some blood here."

"Yeah, I felt it. I don't think it's too bad." Opening his eyes fully, he looked at Bonnie. "So ... what happened to Shiloh?"

As she wrung out the sponge, Bonnie tightened her jaw. "They took her," was all she could manage.

Gabriel's wings fell limp. "I see."

Bonnie swallowed down a painful lump. For some reason, Shiloh's sacrifice brought feelings of shame. Why didn't the real Bonnie stand and say, "I'm Bonnie"? But what choice did she have? Enoch had told her to stay hidden, to keep her wings secret. And now this very event might have been the one Enoch had planned for, to use Shiloh as a decoy to keep the real Bonnie safe.

But that didn't help much. Poor Shiloh now sat in the clutches of a stranger who promised to take her to some unnamed person who obviously didn't have her best interests in mind. What would he do if he discovered she wasn't the real Bonnie? How long could Shiloh keep up the charade?

Again dabbing his head wound, Bonnie told Gabriel what happened during the moments he lay unconscious. Although the events themselves seemed to transpire in slow motion, unfolding in the span of several minutes when they occurred, retelling them took far less time.

"So," she said, wringing out the sponge again, "we're waiting on word from Rebekah, and those guys might come back to find out what happened to Nolan."

"I don't think they're worried about retrieving a hack like him, but if they figure out Shiloh's not who she says she is ..."

"That's what I was thinking."

53

"Then we need to set a trap," Gabriel said, "something that'll keep them from ever returning."

"Like what?"

"We'll ask Sapphira." Gabriel leaned on one hand and reached for Bonnie with the other. "In the meantime, help me up. I want to go outside and see if I can help Rebekah."

Bonnie shook her head. "No way. You might have a concussion. I'm sure Rebekah can handle it. She seems like a ball of fire."

"Did someone mention my name?"

Bonnie turned toward the voice. As lantern light grew closer, the silhouettes of two females took shape, and their faces clarified. "Keep going, Bonnie," Rebekah said, smiling. "I was enjoying your conversation."

"It's nothing I wouldn't say to your face. You're a real go-getter." Bonnie raised her eyebrows. "So what did you find out?"

Rebekah gestured toward the escape tunnel. "I saw two helicopters taking off. One looked empty except for the pilot, and Vlad sat in the front passenger seat of the other one. I thought I saw Shiloh in the back, but I wasn't sure. There were two dead guys on the ground, pretty much mangled, like a wild beast had torn into them. I guess Yereq did that before he left. I saw a lot of blood, but no sign of anyone else."

"So Yereq must have taken the Foleys somewhere to get help," Bonnie said. "And he tried to block the tunnel before he left."

"And we finished the job." Dallas pointed at herself with her thumb. "Dorian and Elise are still back there sweeping up bones."

"So we're trapped?" Bonnie asked.

Gabriel managed a pain-streaked smile. "If Rebekah is as smart as I think she is, she made sure we have a way out."

Rebekah grinned at Dallas. "What did I tell you?"

Dallas rolled her eyes. "You were right, as usual."

"So you did?" Bonnie said. "How?"

"Oh, you'll see soon enough." Rebekah stooped next to Bonnie. "So how's the hero?"

Gabriel ran a hand through his hair. "Singed a few follicles and put a new dent in my head, but with all these brilliant ladies taking care of me, I'll be as good as new in no time."

"And Sapphira?" Dallas asked.

"I think the doctor wanted to do surgery, but I'm not sure how she can. We have a razor blade, and I'm sure Sapphira can sterilize it, but without anesthesia …"

A shrill cry sounded from the springs, followed by a muffled moan. A pain-filled lament filled the tunnel, its echo repeating several times before it faded away.

Tears flooded Bonnie's eyes. With Shiloh in trouble, Gabriel hurt, Yereq missing, and Sapphira suffering through surgery, everything seemed to be going wrong all at once.

She looked around at her three companions, each face darkened by worry and the dimness of the tunnel. In many ways, this place felt like the candlestone, a dark prison that forced its captives to wait for outside help while trusting in friends in higher places.

55

She took Gabriel's hand, barely able to speak. "Will you sing a prayer with me?"

"You bet." Gabriel slid back against a wall and rested his head. "What song?"

"The one you taught me when I was six years old, remember?"

"How could I forget?" Gabriel let out a long sigh. "I've sung it a hundred times since then, especially while you were in the candlestone."

"I was just thinking about that place. How did you know I was in there?"

Gabriel caressed her hand. "I saw you. I was with you."

"You were? If you were light energy, why didn't I see you? I could see everyone else in there."

"You didn't see me? I surrounded you when you first got there, when Devin tried to grab you."

"You were the cage of light?"

He nodded. "Apparently, God allowed me to become visible when you needed me most."

"Like in the bedroom when I was six." Bonnie again imagined that day long ago when Gabriel first appeared to her. She had been devastated by her father's cruel remarks about her wings, and Gabriel comforted her with a song.

"Right," Gabriel said. "And when Palin was ready to cut you open on your thirteenth birthday. My energy field somehow lit up a poster of a guardian angel, and the glow let Palin see you. I think when he figured out that you were a girl, he couldn't kill you. So he just left. I guess he never told Devin."

"That's amazing! I didn't even know that happened!"

Gabriel smiled. "I wish I could tell you all the ways God protected you. Maybe now that we'll be together for a while, I can. But I think when you were six, that was the most special time."

"Me, too. The prayer has stayed in my mind ever since." Now on her knees, Bonnie gave him a hug and kissed his cheek. "I don't think I could've made it without you, but …"

"But what?"

"I feel so ashamed. When you never became visible again, I kind of forgot about you. I started wondering if you were just in my imagination, you know, the hopeful dream of a six-year-old. Then, when I turned thirteen, I saw Sapphira. She told me you were there, so that's when I started hoping again, hoping I really had a guardian angel, but I never told anyone, not even Billy. I wasn't sure anyone would believe me."

A tear dripped down Gabriel's cheek. He looked at her for a moment, his chin trembling. "I think—"

Another shriek sounded from the springs chamber, long and sharp, then a series of halting wails.

Bonnie covered her mouth and breathed her words through her fingers. "Poor Sapphira!"

Gabriel straightened. "We'd better start singing." He looked up at Rebekah and Dallas. "Care to join us?"

Both ladies sat on the floor, cross-legged. "If we don't know the words," Rebekah said, "we'll hum along."

Bonnie settled beside Gabriel and clutched his hand tightly. Everything seemed so dark, so hopeless. When she was in the candlestone, her song always made her own body brighter and created a shield that protected her from Devin. Now it felt like she needed a shield more than ever, and a cascading waterfall of light to chase away the shadows.

Taking a deep breath, she began singing, and Gabriel joined in on the second word.

> Whither shall I go from thy spirit? Or whither shall I flee
> from thy presence?
> If I ascend up into heaven, thou art there: If I make my
> bed in hell, behold, thou art there.
> If I take the wings of the morning, and dwell in the utter-
> most parts of the sea;
> Even there shall thy hand lead me, and thy right hand shall
> hold me.
> If I say, Surely the darkness shall cover me; even the night
> shall be light about me.
> Yea, the darkness hideth not from thee; but the night
> shineth as the day:
> The darkness and the light are both alike to thee.

57

Exhaling heavily, Bonnie looked at each of her fellow singers in turn. All eyes glistened. In each face, sadness blended with hope. Despair had fled away.

Still holding Gabriel's hand, Bonnie loosened her grip. They had done all they could do here. It was time to add action to their prayers.

She stood and helped Gabriel to his feet. "Let's set that trap we talked about," she said. "I'm ready to catch a few kidnappers."

4

CHAPTER

THE HEALER

Billy slid down Hartanna's flank and landed flat-footed on the grass. "Thanks for the ride!" he said as he adjusted his scabbard belt.

With Pegasus now high overhead, Hartanna's features were clear in the bright moonlight. "Please bring back a report as soon as possible. Walter is very dear to all of us."

"Don't worry. I will." Billy sprinted toward the village as fast as his mail, cloak, and scabbard would allow. Since they had landed in the field near the birthing garden instead of the dragon landing area, he would enter the village from the north, nearer Abraham's former home. Since Elam didn't want to assume too much, he had declined the villagers' offer to have him live there, choosing a less prestigious hut instead. It lay vacant because of the deaths of the couple who once lived there, both victims of the rampage by Goliath and the Nephilim when they entered Second Eden a month ago.

The villagers later converted Abraham's house into a triage station for wounded soldiers. With the firewall keeping their main

59

enemies at bay, only a few troops had need of it, those who had suffered minor injuries from skirmishes with the Vacants who had ventured too close to the villages.

When Billy arrived at the triage hut, he paused next to one of two dragons painted on either side of the door. Now warm from his run, he shed his cloak, tucked it under his arm, and pushed the door open.

Inside, Walter lay on a raised cot near the back, well away from the cold draft breezing in from the street. Ashley and Steadfast stood on either side, Ashley with her back to the door and both leaning over Walter's body. Neither one looked up to see who had come in.

After easing the door closed, Billy walked closer. "How is he?"

"If you have an extra hand," Ashley shouted, "get it over here now!"

He dropped his cloak and ran across the floor, dodging a row of cots as he loosened his scabbard belt and let it fall. With a hop over the last cot, he joined Ashley. She and Steadfast had both hands inside a gash in Walter's chest.

Ashley spat out her words. "Alcohol on the table! Douse your hands and come back!"

On a table near the wall, Billy found a glass bottle, poured a splash into his palm, and washed. "Okay!" he called, leaping back. "What now?"

Keeping her fingers in place, Ashley pulled aside Walter's skin with the heel of her hand. Blood flowed freely and dripped down Walter's ribcage. "See what I'm holding?"

Billy peered inside. "A vein?"

"An artery. Grab it."

Praying for a strong stomach, Billy reached in and pinched the wet artery. "Like this?"

"Perfect." Ashley let go and dashed to the table. Blood spewed from her other hand's release point, spraying Billy's shirt. Two seconds

60

later, she jumped back with a needle attached to a long strand of thin black thread. "Okay, just keep holding it until I say so."

Billy bit his lip hard. So much blood! And the wound looked awful. But it didn't matter. Duty called.

Ashley poked the needle into Walter's artery and began stitching around it. Apparently the Vacant's spear had sliced through it, and now she had to splice the loose ends together. As she worked, the delicate artery seemed to line up and seal itself effortlessly, as if the combination of her stitching and her healing touch cauterized the vessel.

Ashley looked up at Steadfast. "Doing okay over there?"

"Yes." A bead of sweat trickled from Steadfast's forehead down to his clean-shaven cheek. "These veins are not leaking badly. I am able to hold them until you are finished there."

"Good. I'll just be another minute." Ashley blew hair out of her eyes. "I hope it works. I helped stitch up Valiant, but it was nothing like this. And every stitch seems to wear me out."

After another minute or so, she tied the thread and cut it with a small knife. "Okay, Billy. Take a breather and wash up." She gestured toward the door. "You'll find a pitcher pump out back."

Billy pulled his hands from Walter's warm body. Out in the fresh air and free from the viselike hold, his fingers, now dripping blood, felt cold and cramped. He paused, staring at Walter's nearly motionless body. Nausea churned. A blanket of heaviness weighed down his shoulders. What would happen? After all the dangers they had faced, would a stupid monster from another world bring Walter's life to an end?

"Billy!"

Ashley's sharp voice shook him out of his daydream.

"What?"

"Get washed up," she said, her tone now calm. "I'll need your clean hands again in just a minute."

Billy ran to the door, pushed the latch button with his wrist, and forced the door open with his foot. With the great moon still

61

bright, and lanterns lining the street, finding the pump in the back proved to be no problem. After scrubbing his hands and then his face, he hurried back, finding Ashley tying off another stitching job.

He showed her his hands. "What now?"

Ashley nodded toward the table again. "See the little bottle, the brown one?"

"Uh-huh."

"Put one drop of that stuff on your finger and smear it under Walter's tongue."

Billy stepped over to the table and pulled a cork from the tiny bottle, no bigger than an eye dropper bottle. "What is it?"

Steadfast, two fingers still in Walter's wound, looked his way. "An elixir Angel created. It discourages blood loss."

"Probably some kind of clotting enhancer," Ashley said. "We have to do something more to stop the bleeding than this patch-work job I'm doing."

Billy let a drop leak onto the tip of his index finger. Pressing Walter's cheeks together with one hand, he pushed the medicated finger into the opening and rubbed the tip under Walter's tongue.

Walter jerked his head and bit down lightly on Billy's finger before settling down. Billy withdrew his finger and shook out the pain. "Done."

"Thank you." Ashley snipped a thread and reached for a bloodstained rag. "Steadfast will close the incision. I have to check his pressure."

She picked up a makeshift blood pressure cuff from the supply table. As she wrapped Walter's arm with the sleeve—a bladder, of sorts, constructed from rabbit gut—she looked at Billy. "When your father brought Walter here, we weren't sure how badly he was hurt. He was conscious, but when his blood pressure kept dropping, we knew he must have had internal bleeding. Then he conked out, and we knew we had to go in."

She pumped up the sleeve with a bulb, also made from some kind of animal gut. "He stayed kind of delirious. He kept trying to get up and charge back into battle, so Steadfast knocked him out with another one of Angel's home brews."

Releasing the air, Ashley watched a needle move across a bleached leaf painted with hand-numbered pressure readings. "I didn't have time to look for my stethoscope, but with my sensory gifts, I can feel the pulse changes." She closed her eyes for a moment, then unwrapped the sleeve. "Eighty-five over fifty. We might need some blood."

Billy rolled up his sleeve. "I'm O positive."

"Same here, but I don't know what Walter is. Steadfast says Angel had a way of knowing who was compatible with whom, but it's based on matching their companions somehow. Since that won't work with Walter, we'll stick with what we know. O is a universal donor, but if Walter's a negative, our RH factor could be a big problem."

Billy looked again at Steadfast, now stitching Walter's skin closed. After Angel went up in flames with Abraham, the poor guy was called into service as a surgeon after being little more than a medical orderly. Still, he knew enough to help, and between him and his Eve, Pearl, they worked nonstop.

"So, we'll chance the RH factor if we have to," Billy said. "I mean, giving him our blood beats bleeding to death."

"Right." Her hands red, Ashley brushed her tangled hair back with her forearm. Dressed in blood-dappled white T-shirt and a pair of jeans that were obviously slept-in, she looked exhausted from head to toe. "Steadfast is really good at stitching. I think the process drains my healing power, so it's best to let him take over on the less-critical ones."

Billy looked past Ashley. Steadfast, a thirtysomething male, just like all the other patriarchs in the village, meticulously worked the needle and thread. A nearly transparent egg floated close to his ear, its barely visible eyes looking on and wobbling, as if nodding

63

approval at Steadfast's work. At the other end of the thread, Walter's skin lifted, still bloodstained, as two flaps joined tightly together. His chest raised and lowered in time with his breaths, shallow and gurgling.

Even with his shirt off, Walter looked warm enough. Glistening with sweat, his body, more muscular and hardened than Billy had ever seen it, glowed in the light of the lantern's dancing flame. "So, how bad was the damage?"

Ashley looked back at Walter, concern sagging her brow. "The spear sliced a gash in his lung."

"Sliced a lung?" Billy laid a hand on his chest. "Ouch!"

She nodded. "Thank God it missed his heart, but it cut enough blood vessels to kill him. We patched him up the best we could, so we'll just have to monitor him for more bleeding."

He looked back at the door and lowered his voice. "Are you up for a full-blown healing?"

She matched his tone. "When Walter was passing out, I didn't have time to get Acacia to try it. But now he might be out of danger, and you know what Elam said."

Nodding, Billy replayed the recent event in his mind, their first discovery of the Vacants. Valiant had been patrolling alone in the woods to the north and came upon at least a dozen of them. They attacked, and Valiant fought ... well ... valiantly. After killing three of their party, he managed to escape, but he suffered multiple spear wounds.

He staggered back to Founder's Village, where Ashley attempted a healing with Acacia providing the fire. It worked, at least for Valiant, but Ashley nearly cooked. Her temperature spiked to 106 and stayed above 104 for three days. Now, a full week after she was finally able to get out of bed, she still tired easily. And Acacia seemed drained as well. She didn't feel fully recharged until yesterday. Elam gave both a stern command not to try any further healings unless someone would surely die without the attempt.

"We could ask your mother to try again," Billy said. "Just because her healing power hasn't worked on humans here, it doesn't mean it'll never work."

Ashley touched his arm. "Billy, it's all right. Trust me. If I thought Walter was about to die, I'd do it in a heartbeat."

"Should we fly him up to the hospital, then?"

"That won't do any good. We brought the heart and lung machines down yesterday. Cliffside's going to land the entire hospital soon. No sense in keeping it flying around up there when the worst of the bad guys are trapped behind the wall of fire."

Billy looked again at Ashley's hands, slender and strong. A ring decorated one of her fingers, a red gem shining from its mount. "How'd you learn so much about surgery?"

"Doc taught me. Bonnie's father, I mean. Since we kept quite a few animals, we sometimes had to do some minor surgery. Instead of taking them to the vet, Doc showed me how. He went to medical school, but after he got his MD, he didn't like seeing all the suffering and death, so he turned to pharmacy."

Billy offered a sympathetic nod. Ever since Dr. Conner died heroically after their battle against Devin in the underground laboratory, he had often wondered about how great an asset Dr. Conner would have been. Now his talents seemed wasted. "I guess we could really use him."

"You bet." Ashley crossed her arms over her chest and huffed a sigh. She glanced at Walter before shifting back to Billy. Her brow drooped again, along with her sad eyes. "How are you doing?"

Billy picked up his sword belt and fastened it around his waist. "Okay, I guess. No wounds."

"No, I mean—" She laid a hand on his chest. "I mean here. It's been a month with no contact."

"Yeah. I knew what you meant." He clutched Excalibur's hilt and massaged its smooth surface. "And I think you already know the answer."

65

Pressing her lips together, she nodded. "When I'm tired, I can't control this mind-reading thing very well. Sorry for butting in on your emotions."

"No big deal." He glanced at her hand, still pressed gently against his chest. She was obviously tired and mentally drained. "Emotions are all I have left," he said, "and I'm kind of wearing them on my sleeve."

"I know. Me, too." Pulling her hand back, she looked at Walter again. Steadfast had covered his torso with a sheet and was now checking his pressure. Since he lacked Ashley's sensory powers, he was using her makeshift stethoscope to listen for the heartbeat. "I see you found it," she said.

Steadfast nodded, his eyes trained on the meter. "It was next to the laundry bin."

"Sorry. I remember now. I put it there this morning." Looking more exhausted than ever, she turned back to Billy and lowered her voice to a whisper. "You know, I like the people here, and I know how important our work is, but sometimes I just want to go home. Do you know what I mean?"

"Sure. I think about that a lot."

"How badly do you miss home? I mean, I know you must really miss Bonnie, right?"

Heat flowed into Billy's cheeks and ears. "When you butt in, you really butt in."

She clenched her fist and scolded herself. "Get with it, Ashley! Don't be such a relational clutz!"

"Don't worry about it. I shouldn't have said it that way. I mean, I do miss Bonnie ... a lot ... and I miss my mother, too. But we've been so busy here, the only time I think about it is when I go to bed. But that doesn't last long. I'm so exhausted, I conk out right away."

"I know. You and Walter have been training constantly. Either that or out on patrol."

He pointed at her. "Look who's talking—Miss Never Sleeps. You're either a doctor, a mechanic, or an inventor. If you don't rest more, you're going to have a breakdown."

Looking at the floor, she nodded. "I know, I know. But who else is going to do those things?"

"I can't argue with that." Billy glanced at Walter again. Steadfast had finished taking his pressure. He probably would have reported anything unusual. "Speaking of inventions, any news on your radio project?"

As a weak smile appeared, Ashley's voice perked up. "My tooth transmitter still works. It's not nearly strong enough to call home, but it's perfect for communicating locally. And I altered Merlin's radio frequency without a problem."

"Any luck with that?"

She shook her head. "I can't get anywhere with the magnets. The field they create isn't strong enough to make a crack in the dimensional wall. Without at least a tiny opening, Larry wouldn't be able to hear me even if I sent a megawatt signal."

Billy painted a picture in his mind—his mother operating Larry's console. Without communications, their only hope was to find a portal. Acacia would have to try again at Mount Elijah, the sooner the better. "If Walter seems out of the woods in the morning," he said, "I'll take Acacia and Listener up to the volcano and see what we can see."

"Okay, check back here first thing. I'll let you know how he's doing."

"You're staying here? Doesn't Steadfast have this shift?"

"He does." She dragged a cot close to Walter's and sat down. "I just want to be here in case he needs me."

Billy sat next to her, adjusting his sword to make room. "I don't need to be a mind reader to know that something's up between you two."

Her cheeks flushing, Ashley suppressed a smile. "That noticeable, huh?"

"Your sleeve is covered with it."

She brushed her sleeve and let her smile break through. "Walter and I are like this, Billy." She slid closer, hip to hip. "We're friends, partners, fellow warriors, but not lovers. Ever since we worked together to help you and Bonnie navigate the Circles of Seven, we've fought together and bled together. But you know what? We trust each other so much, it's like we're building a foundation for something else later on."

"You mean when Walter's old enough."

She nudged his side. "Who says you're not a mind reader?"

"When would that be? Three years? Five years?"

"It's hard to tell. This place has changed us so much, it's like we're maturing at double the normal speed. He already looks more like a man than a boy."

"Yeah. I noticed. Maybe it's something in the air here." Billy rose to his feet. "I'd better get to bed. Gotta climb a volcano tomorrow."

Ashley showed him her bloody hands. "I'll get cleaned up and then sack out."

"Want me to bring you a change of clothes?"

"No. I don't want you to wake Emerald. She's an early riser. I'll be fine."

Billy walked to the head of Walter's cot and gazed at his friend's ashen face. Still gurgling as he breathed through his open mouth, Walter's eyes darted under his lids. Whatever Ashley had used to put him under didn't slow down his mind. He was likely fighting even now, probably skewering a few more of those Vacants.

Gripping Walter's shoulder, Billy whispered, "Get well soon, buddy. I need you at my side."

As he turned to leave, Ashley caught his pant leg. "Will you pray for Walter?"

"Sure. When I get back to the hut, I'll pray until I fall asleep."

"No. I mean now." Her brow arched up. "Please?"

"Uh, yeah, sure." Taking her by both hands, he lifted her to her feet. As they faced each other, she closed her eyes and tilted her head upward. Billy traced a tear stain from the point it exited her eye, through her cheek's contours, and down to her chin. This would be hard. Although he found praying easy and liberating, doing so out loud in a way that would comfort someone else seemed out of reach. But he had to give it a try, just pretend Ashley wasn't there and say what was on his mind.

Compressing her hands lightly, he spoke in a low tone. "Father, you know how much we both love Walter. He's such a good friend—brave, loyal, and always trying to make people smile. If he dies, we know he would go to a better place, but ..." He paused. With his throat narrowing and his voice breaking up, this was getting even more difficult than he imagined.

Ashley's fingers tightened around his, and she broke in, her voice just as tremulous. "But we really need him here ... so if you don't mind ... please let him stay for a while, at least until ..."

Her hands began to pull away, but Billy held them fast. It seemed that their physical connection helped her thoughts and feelings flow. Now the mind reader had become a mind writer. He knew exactly what she wanted to say.

"So please let him stay," Billy continued, "at least until we can tell him how much we love him."

As he opened his eyes, he let her hands slide away. After dabbing new tears with her shirt sleeve, she kissed him on the cheek and whispered, "Thank you."

On the way to the door, he picked up his cloak and slung it over his shoulder. Then, pulling the door open, he looked back.

Ashley sat once again on the cot, her eyes wide and wet. He gave her a nod, hoping she could read the brotherly love pouring from his heart. "Good night, Ashley."

She replied in a weak voice. "Good night, Billy. I'm glad I can count on you."

Adding a wave as he kept an eye on Ashley, Billy called out, "Good night, Steadfast. Take good care of both of them."

Steadfast wiped his bloody hands on a rag and waved back. "I will. You can count on that."

After once more glancing at Ashley, Billy walked out and closed the door. Something was wrong. Ashley seemed to want something, but what? Could her ability to sense emotions also transmit messages somehow, or were they both so tired that every little twitch and change in body posture seemed to communicate more than it was meant to?

70

Now out in the cool breeze again, Billy pushed his arms through the cloak sleeves, fastened the collar clasp, and pulled up his hood. He looked toward the birthing garden. Now that it was likely well past midnight, his father would have relieved Thigocia and settled down for his turn as the birthing garden's watch dragon.

Billy strolled that way. Wearing a black cloak and hood, he probably looked like a ghostly shadow wandering through the midnight wind. It was a good thing the village folk slept deeply at these hours, even Cliffside, who normally guarded this field. With dragons taking over that duty, Elam put him on daytime woods patrol, a responsibility he relished. Actually marching out to possible battles definitely beat standing on the garden periphery night after night with nothing to do but whistle all-clear signals to his fellow guards.

While marching across the grassy meadow between the village and the garden, Billy caught sight of a pair of glowing dots, scarlet and pulsing—Clefspeare's eyes shining red. Even with the beams turned off, the fiery pupils were easy to see. "Dad," Billy called. "It's me."

"Yes, son," came a deep, rumbling voice. "I know, though your scent is not quite the same."

Billy brushed his hands together. "Probably Walter's blood. I was deep in it for a while."

"And how is our valiant soldier faring?"

With his snout now close, the dragon's breath caressed Billy's face with warmth. "Not great, but Ashley's taking good care of him. He—"

"Mercy!" The plaintive female voice came from the field's western border, close to the twin fir trees, Hilidan and Zera. "O virtuous dragon, I beg for mercy!"

Clefspeare's eyebeams flashed and locked on a feminine form staggering toward them with another figure, probably male, at her side. "Who goes there?" Clefspeare growled.

Now within three or four paces, the woman dropped to her knees, her hands clasped. "O mighty dragon, I beg you not to breathe on us with your punishing flames. Another dragon, Arramos by name, has hurled his fiery wrath at my son, and he would not survive another blow."

The man, still standing at her side, covered his face with his hands.

"Step out of the woman's shadow," Clefspeare ordered, "and show yourself."

Trembling, the man took a step and stopped again. With Pegasus as bright as ever, his details sharpened. Shorter than average and dressed in a typical villager's garb—cotton long-sleeved tunic and woolen trousers—he slowly lowered his hands from his face, revealing the telltale marks of recent burns.

Billy grimaced. With swollen cheeks, charred eyebrows and scalp, and practically no lips, this guy was a pitiful mess.

"Where did you see Arramos?" Clefspeare asked.

71

Rising to her full height, the woman stepped into the moon's glow. A lovely angular face and smooth complexion made her seem too young to have an adult son. Yet, with a hood covering her hair, any possible grayness stayed hidden. She pointed toward the western border. "We saw him out there, beyond that wall."

A growl rose from Clefspeare's gullet. "I sensed no danger."

"Great dragon, I know so little about your kind, so I do not know how your danger sense operates. How far does it extend? We were at least a thousand paces away, well into the prairie."

"I see." Clefspeare extended his neck, bringing his head close to the woman. She cringed but stayed still while he sniffed her face, then her hands. "I sense no danger from her, and her words carry the ring of truth. If Arramos has come to Second Eden and yet lurks nearby, our danger has increased a hundredfold."

The woman clasped her hands again. "Good dragon, do you have a doctor in this village? My son requires care."

"We have no doctor, but perhaps we can help." Clefspeare turned to Billy. "Has either Ashley or Steadfast cared for burn victims?"

"Not that I know of, but I'm sure they can do something. They have some pain relievers and an ointment that'll take down swelling."

The woman grasped Billy's hand and kissed it. "Thank you. Please lead us to these medicines. I have no money, but I will work for you."

"From what village do you hail?" Clefspeare asked. "And what is your name?"

"We come from a faraway land not yet known to these people." She swept back her hood, revealing shining hair that fell to her shoulders. "And my name is Semiramis."

72

5

CHAPTER

ELAM'S JOURNAL

Her right arm in a sling, Sapphira knelt and touched the floor of the tunnel with her free hand. She rubbed her finger along the cracked stone, squinting at the surface in the light of three lanterns carried by Bonnie, Rebekah, and Dallas.

Bonnie edged close and looked over Sapphira's shoulder, careful not to cast a shadow. What could she be looking for? While Gabriel and the others had gone on a journey outside to search for Yereq and the Foleys, Sapphira had said she would stay and set a trap for any future invaders. For some reason, she had chosen this spot, a point where the escape tunnel intersected at right angles with one of the main tunnels.

In one direction, this passage led to the living quarters, and in the other, it split into two wide corridors. Following the left passage would lead someone to the growth chamber section and another trio of tunnels, and wandering through the one on the right would surely get a person lost. It led into a honeycomb of narrow shafts that funneled into more rooms that Bonnie had not had time to explore.

On her one journey into that section, it had taken her three hours to find her way back. Probably only Sapphira could walk through that maze without losing her way. After so much time alone in these caves, she likely had the entire network mapped out in her mind.

Finally, Sapphira pointed at the floor. "There should be a cavity below us, and the rock layer here is no more than a foot thick all along this tunnel. That's why Morgan put the girls' living quarters that way." She pointed in the direction of the hovels. "The giants had no reason to go there, so there was no risk collapsing the floor."

"But hasn't Yereq been walking through here when he brings you supplies?" Dallas asked.

"He has. That's why this intersection might work for setting a trap." Sapphira again passed her hands along the floor surface. Her fingers rippled with tiny flames. "The cracks are bigger than before. It's almost exactly the same as the layer that covered the abyss Paili and I found thousands of years ago. It's fragile and close to breaking."

Bonnie joined Sapphira on her knees. The cracks, indeed, had widened since the first time she had noticed them, now a few millimeters across in some places. The light from Sapphira's hands plunged deeply into the fissures, like sunshine in a narrow canyon.

"So our plan," Sapphira continued, "is to break through the floor and cover the hole. I should be able to heat the rocks enough to loosen them, but we'll need something heavy to punch through. One of us could look for a shovel or a pick on the mining level, but they might be too brittle to use by now."

"Let's get the rope from the elevator shaft," Rebekah said, "and tie it to an anchor. Once you get it heated up, one of us could jump on the spot while hanging on to the rope."

Sapphira raised a finger. "One item I forgot to mention. The cavity leads straight to the magma river. If you can't hang on to the rope, you're done for."

74

"Then can you just heat it up slowly?" Bonnie asked. "To test how weak it gets?"

"I suppose so. If it starts collapsing, I can probably get away in time."

Bonnie stripped off her backpack, releasing her wings. "I'll hold on to you just in case."

Pressing a palm on the floor, Sapphira took in a deep breath. "Stand clear."

As Rebekah and Dallas backed away, Bonnie stayed close and clutched Sapphira's shirt. The Oracle's hand suddenly blazed. As fire shot out from under her palm, redness crawled along the floor, as if blood were seeping from wounds in Sapphira's hand.

Soon, the heated area spread out in a three-foot-wide circle, orange at the perimeter and red changing to white closer to her hands. When the widening arc reached Sapphira's denim-covered knees, she scooted back to avoid the superheated stone.

A cracking noise blended in with a chorus of hisses and sizzles, sounding like a bonfire fueled by green wood. Sapphira lifted her hand and slid back farther. "I think it's pretty weak now."

Rebekah pushed a flat rock with her foot and slid it past the perimeter of heated stone. "Try hitting it with this."

Still holding Sapphira, Bonnie pushed the rock over the hottest spot, then, unfurling her wings, she stepped on it, careful to keep most of her weight on her other foot. More cracks sounded, but the floor didn't give way. How much pressure could she add? Of course she could jump back in time, even fly if she had to, but should she risk it? Probably not. It wasn't worth it to—

Suddenly, the entire tunnel shook. Unable to brace herself, Sapphira toppled forward and smacked her head against the floor. The weakened stone collapsed, swallowing Bonnie and Sapphira.

As they slid into the hole, Bonnie lurched forward and wrapped her arms around Sapphira's waist. Now falling freely in a cavernous chamber, she unfurled her wings and flapped, slowing their plunge.

75

Shouts sounded from above. "Are you all right? Can you fly back up here?"

Bonnie couldn't answer. Not yet. Her wings billowing with warm, rising air, she had to orient herself and figure out which way was up. Flying in a slowly ascending circle, she found the hole above. Rebekah and Dallas crouched at the edge, looking down.

"I'm all right," Bonnie grunted.

Gasping for breath, Sapphira managed, "I'm all right, too."

Rebekah reached down. "Can you get her up here? Dallas and I can catch her."

"I can't hover," Bonnie said. "But I'll see what I can do. Get ready."

While Rebekah and Dallas looked down from the hole in the flat ceiling, Bonnie flew in a wider circle, dipped for a moment, and then zoomed up, flapping madly as she boosted Sapphira toward four outstretched hands.

Rebekah latched on to the wrist of Sapphira's good arm. Bonnie's momentum drove her into the ceiling, smacking her head. Dazed, she fell again, but managed to twist her body back into flying position. Again riding the drafts, she looked up at the hole. While Rebekah pulled Sapphira's arm, Dallas grabbed the back of Sapphira's jeans and hoisted her the rest of the way.

Rebekah reached down again. "You're next."

Rubbing her head, Bonnie eased higher. Her wings brushed against the ceiling, and she passed just out of reach of Rebekah's hands. As she circled again, Sapphira shouted from the hole. "You could land on the chasm floor next to the magma river and then hike to the overlook back where we met Gabriel. From there, flying up with the rising air shouldn't be too hard."

"I'll give it a try," Bonnie said.

Sapphira pointed. "When you get to the bottom, make sure you walk in that direction. It'll be hot, but there should be room on the chasm floor to stay clear of the river."

"Got it."

Letting herself fall into a circling dive, she surveyed the chamber. At least twice as big as the springs room, the gap between the bare rock walls narrowed at the lower levels and converged into a fissure about six feet across.

Bonnie aimed for the crack and pulled in her wings. She plunged through, tears streaming as hot dry air whipped across her face. Once she came out into the open, the gap widened again, revealing the chasm and channel she had seen from the precipice, though at a different point on the river.

After orienting herself again, she flapped her wings and headed in the direction Sapphira had told her, flying well above the churning magma. She grimaced at the blistering heat. Why not just fly all the way to the ledge? It would be better than walking. No use getting too close to the river.

The channel, now about fifty feet from one wall to the other, veered to the right, then back to the left, narrowing as it continued. Soon, Bonnie approached a place where the walls jutted out, creating a pinching point, too narrow to fly through, though near the ground it widened, providing plenty of space for walking.

This had to be the reason Sapphira suggested going on foot. Maybe with her enhanced vision she had seen this tight passage from her vantage point on the ledge. If so, maybe the destination would soon be in sight.

As she descended, Bonnie winced at the scalding heat. There was no way she could land without getting cooked.

She angled back up and made a slow circle. When Sapphira walked down there, back when the river acted as a portal to another world, the floor level wasn't as hot. In her hurry, she likely hadn't thought about that.

Bonnie looked up. The tight fissure she had dropped through loomed above, much too narrow for a return flight. Somehow she would have to build a lot of speed, shoot the channel's gap with her wings folded, and catch an updraft before crashing into the river.

After flying up to the narrow gap in the ceiling, she angled her body toward a spot in the fissure about halfway between the ceiling and the river. Then, half falling and half gliding, she zoomed toward it.

Again searing heat stung her eyes and instantly dried the sweat dripping from her pores. The gap between the protruding walls drew closer and closer, apparently deeper from the fissure's front entry to its rear exit than she had thought. When she pulled in her wings, would her momentum get her through before she dropped too far? Maybe, maybe not. But there seemed to be no other choice. She had to go for it or be stuck there flying in circles forever.

Just before slicing through, she jerked in her wings, leaving them out enough to catch a little bit of updraft. Now plunging at a sharp angle, the tips of her wings scraped the side walls. The air grew hotter. The magma drew closer, singeing, scorching, blistering.

As her lips cracked, Bonnie screamed, "Help me!"

With one mighty flap, she shot through the fissure's exit, then expanded her canopy. Beating her wings furiously, she fought the dive. Pain roared through her mainstays. Heat seared the membranes. She felt like she was on fire.

After swooping within five feet of the river, she leveled out and began a slow climb, too slow to keep the heat from baking her skin. The magma boiled and popped below. A droplet splashed on her sleeve, instantly setting it on fire.

Crying out, she flailed her arms and beat out the flame. Her wings now scraped and weary, and her body dehydrated and half-cooked, it was all she could do to ascend even a few feet. Soon, however, she rose above the danger point, out of reach of the bubbling soup. Now it was time to look for the ledges leading to the tunnels. Either side would do.

Still flapping with all her might, Bonnie looked up. There, maybe a hundred feet ahead, both ledges jutted out into the chasm. She aimed for the one on her right, the ledge leading to the brick kiln room. It looked slightly lower and closer.

She summoned a burst of energy, flapped her wings, and shot upward. The rising air buoyed her effort, but a swirling air current swept her to the side and slammed her against the wall.

Fluttering her wings to stay in place, she clawed at the wall until she caught hold of a rocky lip. She pushed the toes of her shoes against the slick face, but they slipped, unable to find solid footing. Something hurt down there, something hot.

Twisting her neck, she looked down. Her pant leg smoldered at the cuff, stinging her ankle. Would a blaze spring up? Hanging on with all her might, she slowed her wings, not wanting to fan the flame.

She rubbed her sweaty face against her upper sleeve. Now what? Push off and try to fly again? That might work, but another slap against the wall could knock her out. Then she'd be nothing more than a quick flash of fire and a puff of smoke.

She looked up. Fifty feet to climb with no other protrusions to grab. It was impossible.

Licking her dry lips with a dry tongue, she set her feet against the wall and—

"Bonnie! Catch this!"

A rope fell across her shoulder. Grabbing it, she looked up again. Rebekah stood at the ledge holding the other end.

"I've got you," Rebekah shouted. "Use your wings to help."

Pressing her feet against the stone, Bonnie spread out her wings, flapped slowly against the rising air, and scrambled up the wall. When she crested the ledge, she fell forward to her knees and slapped her palms on the ground, panting.

Rebekah patted her on the back. "You look like you had a rough ride."

"I did." Bonnie flopped backwards to her seat and batted at her pant leg to snuff the sparks. "Let's not try that again."

"We don't have to. The hole you made is perfect. Sapphira's working on covering it up." She waved across the expanse and called, "I've got her, Dallas. We'll meet up top."

Bonnie looked that way. Barely visible as she stood on the opposite ledge, Dallas waved in return and disappeared in the shadows.

"So," Rebekah said as she wound the rope into a coil, "it looks like you should visit Dr. Saunders."

"Probably." Bonnie smacked her dry lips. "I need some water before we do anything."

Rebekah hoisted the rope coil over her shoulder, rings of perspiration dampening her shirt at the underarms and chest. "We'll have to wait for Dallas to drop us a line. We brought the only ropes, so she and Sapphira will have to figure out how to fish it up to the top level first."

Heaving a sigh, Bonnie climbed to her feet. Her mouth and throat were so parched, she had to drink something soon. Her sweat had dried, and no more emerged in spite of the heat.

When they entered the low tunnel, Rebekah picked up a dim lantern and led the way. Feeling dizzy now, Bonnie spoke, hoping to shake away the daze and forget about her terrible thirst. "Did you find out what made the tunnel shake?"

Rebekah slowed to let her catch up. "No. We didn't have anyone available to go up top to find out."

"So is Sapphira alone?"

"Until Dallas gets back, yes. But I don't think we have to worry about her. She should be registered as a lethal weapon."

Bonnie stayed quiet. Even with Rebekah's reassurances, thinking about Sapphira up there alone felt awful. Getting shot made her seem so much more fragile, and her loss of blood had weakened her quite a bit.

When they arrived at the kiln room, Rebekah headed straight for the other exit tunnel and stopped at its opening. "You look like you're ready to drop."

Bonnie blew out a tired breath. "I can make it."

"Rest here for a while." Rebekah pointed at a raised part of the floor. "Have a seat, and I'll check on the elevator shaft and come back for you when Dallas drops the rope."

"Great. Thanks."

Rebekah picked up a dark lantern next to the door, lit its wick using hers, and left it at Bonnie's side.

Lowering herself while stretching her pain-filled wings, Bonnie sat on the foot-high step and tried to swallow, but with her throat so dry, the motion felt like shoving down desert sand. Her head swam, as if an ocean's surf ebbed and flowed from one side of her head to the other. If she didn't get something to drink soon, she'd pass out for sure.

She leaned over and rested her head on the step, bracing herself with her hand, her fingers overlapping the edge. As she gripped it, something moved underneath her fingertips. She peered under the ledge and looked at the face of the step. A loose section of stone had shifted, revealing a hollow space behind it.

What could it be? With her vision blurred and swirling, everything seemed like part of a dream—hazy, out of reach, incomprehensible. It was probably broken by centuries of natural crumbling, but, even in her foggy vision, the dividing line between the movable stone and the surrounding fascia seemed distinct, not a random crack.

Pushing in one side of the section, she opened it further. Something lay inside. A book? She reached in and withdrew a small volume, about the size of a diary, but another object lay in there as well. Reaching farther, she grasped a glass vial, small enough to enclose in her hand. A handwritten label wrapped around its middle, bearing an odd script.

81

ὃς δ' ἂν πίῃ ἐκ τοῦ ὕδατος οὗ ἐγὼ δώσω αὐτῷ, οὐ μὴ διψήσει εἰς τὸν αἰῶνα.

She peered into the bottle. Sealed with a corklike stopper, it seemed about a third full of liquid of some kind, transparent and more viscous than water.

She tried to swallow once more. Just looking at liquid made her throat ache more than ever. Feeling dizzy again, she turned her attention to the book, hoping to distract herself. She opened the cover, feeling its supple leather and the rough twine that tied the pages together at its spine. It had to have been put there recently, certainly not millennia ago when Elam lived here. It would have rotted by now. Still, maybe Hades made things age differently. Who but Elam could have stored a book in a room that had been abandoned for so long?

She studied the first page. It held more strange letters, yet they differed from those on the bottle. She thumbed through the pages and stopped at the last one. What was this? English words?

Drawing the book closer, she read the text.

I believe my time here is short, so short that I wonder if I will have opportunity to finish this entry and bind it with the others. And I wonder if it matters at all. If I make a hurried escape or am dragged to a death sentence, who will ever read this missive, this journal of tortured body and tortured thoughts? Only God knows.

Because of my refusal to betray Mara, Morgan is losing her patience with me. I think she is likely to kill me, but she is a hard one to predict. Yet, no matter what tortures she brings to bear, no matter how much flesh she rips from my back, I will never, never betray my beloved Mara. She who brought food to my starving body, carried in the most precious of vessels, I could never betray, nor even entertain an unkind thought. Once a lump of coal, she is now a gem. The pressures of her slavish strife have fashioned a polished diamond—pure, strong, and of infinite value.

Friend, I hope you are able to read my hastily scrawled letters. It is a strange occurrence that as I rub the juice of the fruit of the Tree of

Life on its pages, hoping its properties will preserve it for whoever
finds it as an antiquity, the words transform into odd characters that
I cannot fathom. Is it a miracle? Perhaps. I can only hope that God
will use it for good and carry my thoughts of love to a generation that
needs them, for although my story is one of heartbreak and pain, a
glimmer of light persists. My faith in God has never died. No matter
what happens to me, I know that one day I will stand unashamed in
his presence, and I hope that my beloved will stand with me.

 Until that day, the fetters I bear are but a passing annoyance,
for I know that the coming Messiah will deliver me from the chains
of this realm and take me to a higher plane. Yet, I look forward to
giving my body and soul to Mara in the bonds of marriage, the
shackles of unconditional love, and in breathing this prayer, I am
content to let God's will be done.

Bonnie rubbed her eyes, but in her dehydrated state, no tears
flowed. These words of Elam's were so beautiful, so full of faith!
What a treasure of a man he must be—another diamond forged
by the trials and tribulations of never-ending hardships.

She closed the journal and hugged it to her chest. Obviously
Elam meant for this to be read by anyone, so she could show it to
Sapphira. She would be able to read any of the languages.

Looking at the vial of liquid again, Bonnie imagined Elam
pouring out drops and rubbing them over the pages. At first it
seemed so strange, but was it really? The same fruit that kept him
and Sapphira alive and young for centuries might also maintain
parchment, but how could it translate written words into a more
modern language? A miracle? Why not? Wasn't it already a miracle that fruit from the Tree of Life could keep the book intact? And
weren't words associated with eternal life? Didn't Jesus say, "The
words that I speak unto you, they are spirit, and they are life"?

With her throat again aching, Bonnie eyed the liquid. Was she
allowed to drink it? Why not? There was nothing saying she
shouldn't. She picked at the label, a thin strip of parchment. Might
this text be a warning of some kind?

She pulled out the stopper, poured a drop on her fingertip, and smeared it across the label, making sure to cover the entire text. Within seconds, the words transformed into:

But whosoever drinketh of the water that I shall give him shall never thirst.

Bonnie tried to swallow, but the grit in her throat wouldn't let the muscles finish the motion. The liquid in her grasp would soothe her aching throat and end her torture. But was she allowed to take it? Did finding this vial mean that God would allow her eternal life on earth?

As she continued staring at the liquid, so clear, so desirable, an image appeared in her mind, the first circle of Hades where she argued with the dragon. He had tempted her to look into a pond to see the scales she had felt on her face. The temptation to acquiesce was so strong! While she fought the urge, it felt like snakes were biting her. Yet, that time, she had received a solemn warning not to look into any mirrors, so giving in wasn't a real option. As a child of God, she had to obey her one and only master.

But what about this time? There had been no command not to drink the liquid. This water of life would not only soothe the pain that was every bit as bad as the striking serpents, it would also likely give her long life and maybe even …

Healing? She looked at a burn on her hand where a splash of magma had taken a bite out of her flesh. Raw and swelling, it hurt like crazy, but still nothing like the desperate thirst that ravaged her entire body.

Again applying a single drop to her finger, she swabbed her burn. It stung at first, but within seconds, the welt shrank and disappeared. The patch of skin, now smooth and pink, looked healthier and younger than the surrounding area.

Bonnie held the vial in her open palm and stared at this priceless treasure. There was no longer any doubt. She knew what to do. Standing up, she put the stopper back in the bottle and slid it into her pocket. She would give it to Sapphira and heal her shoulder.

6

CHAPTER

VISITORS

S emiramis," Clefspeare said. "The name is familiar to me, but I
cannot place it."

She lowered herself to her knees again. "I have nothing to hide,
great dragon, and I will tell you my story, but I beg you to let us
be on our way to any medical aid you can supply. My son is in
great need."

Billy looked at his father, waiting for a signal. With all those
burn wounds, this poor guy needed help, and fast, but he wasn't
about to offer help before the two newcomers passed his father's
scrutiny.

Clefspeare nodded. "Son, take them to triage. When both have
had sufficient rest, I want to talk to them further."

"Yes, sir." Billy grasped the man's arm. "Do you need support?"

"I would be glad of it, young man."

His voice seemed raspy, like shoes dragging across sandpaper.
Billy pushed his shoulder under the man's arm and helped him
walk. "I'm Billy Bannister. What's your name?"

"Hunter. My companion believes I am a hunter, but I have yet to prove it."

Out of the corner of his eye, Billy caught a glimpse of Hunter's companion floating near his neck. It was slightly bigger than most, and a bluish light shone from within, making its egg shape clear.

Semiramis helped from the other side. "Let us hurry, Master Billy. I fear that infection might soon set in."

When they arrived at Abraham's hut, Billy pushed the door open and peered inside. Ashley lay sleeping on her cot next to Walter's, which had been lowered to a normal level. Steadfast sat on a short bench with the blood pressure sleeve hanging over one of his slumped shoulders.

"We have a new patient," Billy said, keeping his voice low.

Steadfast jumped up and hurried toward them. "A burn victim?"

"A wicked dragon spewed his hellish fire," Semiramis said. "When my son is well, he will hunt that beast and fulfill his destiny."

Steadfast helped Hunter lie down on a cot and knelt at his side. "Billy," Steadfast said, pointing at the equipment table, "please fetch that lantern. It is my brightest one. And the jar of salve. It should be labeled, 'Healing Ointment.'"

"Will do." Billy grabbed the lantern and jar and brought them back. "Can you help him?"

"Help? Yes." Steadfast pried a rubber lid from the jar. "Heal? I have my doubts."

While Semiramis eyed him carefully, Steadfast dipped his finger into the jar and smeared yellow ointment on Hunter's cheek.

Hunter cringed but didn't cry out. Still, his entire body trembled.

Steadfast dipped into the jar again. "He reacts with pain. Shall I continue?"

"My son is brave," Semiramis said. "Do not spare the healing ointment."

Steadfast applied the salve and rubbed it in from Hunter's scalp to just below his charred lips. With every push on his skin, Hunter jerked but stayed silent.

As he put the lid back on, Steadfast looked at Semiramis. "I can give him something to help him sleep."

"Yes," she said, nodding. "I think that would be best."

Steadfast pointed. "Billy, there is a clear crystal vial near the back of the table."

"Got it." Billy retrieved a tiny oval bottle with a flat bottom. Inside, the medicine was so clear, it seemed invisible.

Steadfast pulled out a stopper and poured a drop into Hunter's mouth. Within seconds, his trembling stopped, and his breathing grew heavy and easy. "Now," Steadfast said as he handed the bottle back to Billy, "we can talk about his condition."

"Good doctor," Semiramis said, laying a hand on his arm, "do me the kindness of a blunt word. It is not a service to tell me less than all you know."

87

"First, my good lady, I am not a doctor, so blunt or not, my word may well be little more than the chittering of a monkey. Yet, I will give you my opinion. His burns are not life-threatening, but they are irreversible. He will wear his scars for the rest of his days."

"I see." She drew her hand back. "With all these fine potions and ointments, surely there is someone in this village who possesses more medical knowledge."

"We had a doctor with considerable skill, but she is no longer here." He nodded at Ashley, still sound asleep on her cot. "I have, however, extraordinary counterparts, this young lady as well as my Eve. We also have a man named Patrick and his wife, Ruth. Patrick has no formal medical training, but he is quite adept at first aid, while Ruth was once a nurse."

Semiramis looked at Ashley, her eyes widening. "Oh!" She quickly covered her mouth.

"Do you know Ashley?" Billy asked.

Lowering her hand, she nodded. "In the land where I live, I was the guardian of Zeno's Chasm. I saw her there."

Billy searched for her companion but found none. "The land where you live? You mean, you're not from Second Eden?"

"No, but my son is."

"Then how did you—"

"Oh, Master Billy, that is a long story, and I will gladly tell you when I am summoned again to the good dragon outside, but since I fear what Ashley will tell you when she wakes, I will give you a summary. You see, I was in service to the dragon who burned my son's face. The wretched lizard betrayed us, curse his name, and banished me to this world. But while in his service, I tried to prevent Ashley and her company from crossing a most dangerous bridge. Not only did I fear for their lives, I knew the dragon Arramos would surely destroy them for making the attempt. He sent giants to shake them from the bridge, and I was powerless to stop them. My fear is that Ashley will think I was in league with those giants and claim that I am your enemy."

"Maybe not," Billy said. "It's tough to fool her."

"Yes, I knew right away that she has a gifted mind, but as I watched those giants deal so treacherously with her and her friends, I sensed an intense anger ... a righteous anger, mind you, but truly intense."

"Well, don't worry too much. I'll talk with her. She can't deny the evidence. I mean, it's obvious Hunter's no friend of Arramos."

"Very true, Master Billy." Semiramis stifled a yawn. "I apologize. Ours has been a very long journey."

Billy looked at Steadfast. "Any vacancies in the village?"

"Since Ashley is here, her bed at Emerald's home is likely empty. We can find a more permanent option when daylight comes."

"I'll escort her." Billy took off his cloak and offered it to Semiramis. "Ready?"

"Ah!" Semiramis said, taking the cloak. "This village is populated by gentlemen."

As Billy guided her along the dark street, Semiramis said nothing. She just sighed now and then as she glanced at the moon. After waking Emerald and her father and making the bedding arrangements, Billy turned to go.

Semiramis caught his sleeve. "Wait."

He spun back. "Yes?"

"Your cloak." She let it slide off her sleeves and then slowly down her body. "The night is long and cold."

"Thanks," he said, reaching for the cloak. "You're right."

As she released it, she let her fingers glide along his forearm. "And I take it that you have no Eve to keep you warm?"

His cheeks heating up, Billy drew back and shook his head. "It'll be a while before I'm ready for that."

"I see." Semiramis bowed her head. "Good night, Master Billy." With that, she closed the door.

A shiver ran up and down his spine. Was it really that cold? Or was Semiramis's manner just a bit too friendly? The females of Second Eden had been more affectionate than those at home, apparently innocently oblivious to how a lingering touch might affect most males of the species, at least those from Earth. And Semiramis's touch seemed more powerful than most—electric, sensual, something that aroused his sense of wariness.

He pushed his arms through the cloak sleeves, raised the hood over his windblown hair, and hurried toward Elam's home. With only a few hours till daylight, there wasn't much time to sleep. Not only did he have to get up early to take Acacia to Mount Elijah, Elam would want to know all the details about the newcomers, Semiramis and Hunter.

Now exhausted, Billy shuffled to the door and eased it open. Inside the one-room hut, Elam lay sleeping on a straw-stuffed mattress near the left wall. After slipping off his shoes and cloak, Billy tiptoed to a mattress on the opposite wall, watching for any sign of Elam awakening. With darkness covering Billy's movements, Elam would likely sleep on. The warrior chief had worked on training the troops with Sir Barlow all day, and the exercises he had put himself and the others through were often brutal.

Billy and Walter had joined the regimen during the past four weeks and collected blisters and calluses on hands and feet. But it wasn't all bad. The expanding pectorals and bulging biceps, as well as their newfound quickness and agility, made it all worth it.

As Billy lay down, he let out a quiet sigh. Every muscle seemed to sigh with him, as if deflating after another grueling day. Even his brain seemed to leak, too tired to spark anything more than the simplest thoughts. There was so little time now for reflection and prayer. If only—

"Billy?"

He turned toward Elam. With the door closed, darkness shrouded the gap between them. "Yes. I'm here."

"You're back so late. Is everything all right?"

Billy imagined Elam's form, perhaps propped on an elbow. "Well … no. But it's all under control."

"What happened on Mount Elijah? Did you find Vacants?"

"A few. Walter and the dragons and I cleared them out. I'll tell you about it in the morning."

"Sounds good. Thanks."

Billy settled again and stared into the darkness, listening to the marsh peepers raising a racket from a nearby pond. *Sounds good*, Elam had said. But was it good? Not really. With Walter hurt so badly and a pair of strangers in town, everything felt as dark as the room, heavy somehow, stifling. Something was definitely wrong, but what? The feeling wasn't exactly like danger sensing, more like an uneasiness in the pit of his stomach. Could it be from the hideous burns on Hunter's face? Semiramis's electric touch? The sight of Walter's blood spewing from his sliced-open body?

As Elam turned, crackling the straw in his bed, Billy looked his way. The warrior chief seemed restless. No wonder. With so many pressures on his shoulders, anybody would lose sleep. But this guy, the grandson of Noah himself, surely had more wisdom than anyone else around, so he probably felt the uneasiness in the air.

Billy closed his eyes and let the weariness take control. The dawning of a new day would likely bring answers to his questions, for good or for evil.

With Rebekah supporting one side and Dallas the other, Bonnie staggered into the springs chamber. Water splashed and licked at the stones as it rushed downward, but the sound was pure torture. Relief lay close by, but not close enough. Her feet dragged, as if slogging through sticky clay.

Finally, the two women lowered her to her knees near one of the cooler pools. Bonnie set down Elam's journal, dipped her hands into the shallow rock basin, and splashed her face. Then, taking another double scoop, slurped the water as fast as her swollen tongue would allow.

Ah! It was so good! How could sulfur-tinged water carry such a rich and delicious flavor? It was heavenly!

As she continued to drink deeply and wash her parched skin, a whispered conversation drifted past her ears.

"Oh, thank God Bonnie's okay."

That was Sapphira's voice. She seemed shaky, upset about something. Bonnie slowed her drinking and glanced their way.

"Did you learn the reason for the tremor?" Rebekah asked.

Sapphira, now dirty from head to toe, braced herself on Rebekah's elbow. "Our exit tunnel caved in even more, so I think the collapse caused the shake. Nobody was around, so I don't know if the others got buried or if they're safe on the other side. I tried digging through, but the rocks are way too heavy."

91

"Especially with one shoulder out of commission," Dallas said.

Tucking the journal under her arm, Bonnie rose to her feet and pulled the vial from her pocket. "Put this on your wound."

Sapphira took the vial and lifted it close to her eyes. As a rippling fire spread across her fingers, the liquid inside seemed to carry a phosphorescent glow. "What is it?"

"Juice from the fruit of the Tree of Life. It has healing properties. I put a little on one of my burns, and it disappeared."

Sapphira pulled the stopper from the top. "Where did you find it?"

"Hidden in the brick kiln room." Bonnie showed her the journal. "It was next to this. I couldn't read much of it, only the last page, but I'm sure it's Elam's."

"Elam's?" Her hands now jittery, Sapphira gave Rebekah the vial. "Would you apply it, please?"

Rebekah slid Sapphira's shirt down her shoulder and began stripping off the blood-soaked bandage. "This will probably hurt."

"It's worth it." Wincing, Sapphira took the journal and opened it to the first page. "It's written in Hebrew."

As her eyes moved back and forth across the text, her lips quivered, and her voice trembled. "It's Elam's journal. He ... he's writing about how he feels after meeting me through the hole in the wall. Before that, he never had a reason to write, because every day was the same, just one day after another of baking bricks, getting whipped by Nabal, and searching for food until he fell asleep on the floor. But now that he met me ..." Sapphira choked on her words. "He has a reason to live ... and he wants to leave a lasting record of his love for me ... and the secrets he learned that he wasn't allowed to reveal until someone discovered this journal."

"Secrets?" Bonnie asked.

Sapphira nodded. "I suppose I'll have to read it one page at a time to find out what he—"

Rebekah made a shushing sound. "Now hold still for a second. I'm going to pour this directly over the stitches."

"Shouldn't you take them out first?" Bonnie asked.

"And open the wound?" Rebekah's brow furrowed. "I should say not. Her bleeding would be profuse."

Bonnie touched a hanging strand from one of the stitches. "Wouldn't it be easier to pull them now than later when her skin is healed?"

"Hmmm. . . ." Rebekah said. "I see your point."

"Our first-aid kit is still on that rock." Sapphira pointed at a large, flat stone near one of the bathing pools.

Dallas hurried to the rock. "I'll get it."

Soon, Rebekah began cutting and pulling out the stitches, applying a little of the juice after each one. "This is working splendidly. Blood pours out. I sprinkle a few drops. The cut seals."

"Thank you." Sapphira read the journal, cringing at every cut and pull.

Bonnie looked over her other shoulder and scanned the ancient text. Some of the words had been set in stanzas as if arrayed in poetic lines.

"This makes sense," Sapphira said, running a finger from right to left on a line. "Elam says he's going to rearrange the pages. Hebrew works start at the back and go to the front, but he received a prophecy that told him to start at the front for future readers."

"Elam received prophecies?" Bonnie asked.

Sapphira nodded. "Enoch once told Elam that he was a prophetic heir, sort of like the way Elisha took Elijah's mantle and became a powerful prophet."

"Are any of the prophecies written in the journal?"

Sapphira pointed at the page again. "This might be one. It's a poem, so if I translate it, it will lose its rhyme and meter."

"I still remember Hebrew," Rebekah said, "but no use wasting time reading it in both languages."

93

Sapphira pressed her finger on the page and moved it along each line, pausing between them as she translated. "Elam says there's a dark world ... a realm below all others ... reserved for neither good nor evil ... a valley of dead souls who cannot ascend to Paradise ... or descend into the Lake of Fire ... because they yet have a purpose in the land of the living ... to escape this valley, they must be called by name ... into the world in which their purpose is to be fulfilled. ... A day will come when a king will plunge into that valley ... and wait for his resurrection call ... but it can come only when precious blood is freely given ... by one who is as white as snow. ... Two virgins will offer their blood ... one to make a warrior invincible ... and one to resurrect a king."

Sapphira lifted her finger from the page and looked at the others. "And there is a way to enter that realm from the magma river view."

"Well, my dear," Rebekah said. "Your skin is as soft as a baby's backside."

Sapphira rotated her shoulder. "It feels perfect."

Rebekah slid Sapphira's shirt back in place. "I saved a few drops for Bonnie's burns and scrapes, and then we should see if the four of us can clear a path to the outside."

"And then ..." Sapphira closed the book and rubbed the cover lovingly. "Maybe we can see if there's a king in that valley of souls."

Marilyn jogged across the grass. The edge of a deep pit was now in sight. After flying with Shelly on a commercial airline to Kalispell, she borrowed a small private plane from a friend of Jared's and flew it to the hilltop where Ashley's home once stood. With the bad weather and such a small ground strip, the landing had been rather harrowing, so feeling solid earth beneath her feet boosted her energy.

She stopped at the edge of the pit and looked down. High winds whipped her hair, and the depth made her head swim.

Thousands of feet below, people moved, looking more like animated toys than real humans. She checked the pistol in her shoulder holster. It was firmly in place.

She pulled a phone from her pocket and read the signal meter. Nothing. Not a surprise, though. The static-filled call from Yereq had let her know that mobile phone service was lousy in this area and probably even worse at the bottom of the pit.

"So," she murmured, "we'll execute plan B."

She withdrew a makeup compact from her jacket, opened it, and searched for sunlight. With clouds racing overhead, the sun peeked out intermittently, providing a bright ray for only a second or two at a time. She angled the mirror and caught the sun in the reflection. A shaky circle of light danced on the grass. As she turned the mirror, the circle dove into the pit and instantly reappeared on the floor.

Another cloud blocked the sun. The circle vanished. Marilyn tapped her foot, keeping the mirror at the same angle as she waited. Soon, the sun flashed another beam. She guided the light toward the people and waved it across them, but it lasted for only a moment. Again the sun hid behind a cloud, this one larger and denser. There would be no more rays for a while.

95

A flicker of light caught her eye. She looked at the people below, all now standing still. The light flashed again. They had seen her.

Waving both arms, she shouted, "It's Marilyn! I need transport!"

She lowered her arms. Of course, her voice might not have carried that far, but the signal proved that they likely knew who she was. Gabriel would probably fly up, but with thousands of feet to ascend, it might take a while.

Hugging her jacket close, she looked toward Kalispell and replayed Shelly's recent phone call. Shelly had rushed to the hospital in a taxi, and Marilyn was getting the smaller plane ready for takeoff when Shelly's call came in.

. . . .

"Dad's in critical condition. He took bullets in his chest and back, and he lost quite a bit of blood."

"Is he going to be all right?" Marilyn asked.

"The doctor thinks so. I donated blood, and so did Mom. We're all the same type."

"Then your mother must have recovered."

"She woke up when Yereq carried her out of the pit. Then he went back and hauled Dad out. That's when Dad lost a lot of blood. It's not an easy climb."

"I can imagine."

"Then he carried Dad to the highway, and Mom waved down a guy driving a flatbed truck. When he saw a ten-foot-tall man carrying a bloodied body, he wasn't exactly keen on giving them a lift, but Mom talked him into letting them all ride in the back."

"It's a good thing she was there."

"You bet. And Yereq, too. If not for him, Dad would be dead for sure. He's not out of the woods, and he's still unconscious, but his vitals are pretty strong. By the way, Yereq's probably already back at the pit. He was pretty anxious to return and protect Sapphira."

Marilyn touched her cell phone, now in her jeans pocket. If only she could call for an update. Shelly had sounded fairly confident, but a hint of worry darkened her voice.

Soon, Gabriel came into sight, his wings beating against the fierce wind. After a few more minutes, he rose above the rim, and with a final surge, he landed next to Marilyn.

"Whew!" He laid a hand on the back of his head. "That knock on the noggin I took is still throbbing."

Marilyn touched his hand. "Are you sure you can carry me down?"

"Yeah." He brushed dirt from his jeans and long-sleeved T-shirt. "You're a pilot, so you won't puke if it gets bumpy, right?"

Lifting her arms, she laughed. "Let's go, flyboy. Don't spare the speed."

"You asked for it." Standing behind her, Gabriel slid his arms around her waist and leaped into the hole. As they dropped, Marilyn's stomach pushed into her throat, taking her breath away. The wall of rock zoomed upward, and the floor rushed toward her so fast, the objects below blurred.

Soon, Gabriel unfurled his wings, slowing the plunge. His hands pushed into Marilyn's abdomen and squeezed out her last gulp of air. As he glided to the ground, the pressure eased, allowing her to take in a breath as well as the sight below. Several women stood with hands on hips peering into a hole in the wall, some dressed in jeans and others in long skirts, all covered with dirt.

Gabriel landed in a trot, releasing Marilyn as he slowed. "Is Yereq ready?" he asked.

"Almost," one of the women said. "It's the last of the dynamite, so he's making sure it's placed perfectly."

As the woman pushed back her tangled hair, Marilyn recognized her smudged face—Dorian, once called Yellinia. These former dragons had all gathered in Castlewood before traveling to Montana and had spent enough time in Marilyn's home for everyone to become acquainted.

Marilyn quickly scanned the others—Elise, Kaylee, Jordan, and Tamara. "I take it Rebekah and Dallas are still inside with Bonnie and Sapphira," she said.

Gabriel nodded. "It looks like the collapse was pretty massive, so we might not be able to blast through it, but Yereq says he'll dig it out eventually. We're just trying to give him a head start."

"What is that?" Dorian asked, pointing toward the sky.

Marilyn looked up. A gleam reflected one of the sun's passing rays, blinding her for a moment, but when another cloud blocked the light, the object became clear—a helicopter.

"Chopper," Gabriel said. "And it's heading this way."

97

"Shall I find Yereq?" Tamara asked as she leaned toward the tunnel entrance.

Dorian touched Tamara's hand. "Call his name as you feel your way along the wall and watch for his lantern."

Tamara nodded, ducked under the low arch, and disappeared.

As the helicopter, a large transport unit, descended, Gabriel waved toward the tunnel. "Take cover in the dark. Out in the open, we're fish in a barrel."

The other four dragon women skulked into the cave while Marilyn stayed at Gabriel's side. "I'm packing a Glock inside my jacket," she said.

Gabriel stared at the chopper. "How many rounds?"

"If that helicopter's full of bad guys, not enough."

"Got a plan of action?"

Marilyn touched one of Gabriel's wings. "I think you'd better stay out of sight and be ready to fly out of here with one of the women."

"But I should stay and—"

"What are you going to do, slap them with your wings?" She gripped his taut bicep. "Save the heroism for the escape flight."

Folding his wings tightly, Gabriel backed toward the tunnel. "I'll watch. If you get in trouble, I'm flying you outta here first. Yereq can protect the others."

As he faded in the tunnel's darkness, the helicopter settled to the ground, raising a cloud of sand. A muscular man stepped out from the pilot's seat, and a tall sinewy woman emerged from the back passenger door, both dressed in army camouflage, complete with high boots and caps that shadowed their eyes. Each carried an automatic rifle tucked under an arm.

Marilyn patted the outside of her jacket and felt the shape of her weapon. With that kind of firepower approaching, her pistol seemed no more than a toy.

The man stopped within ten paces of Marilyn, set his feet, and spoke in a commanding tone. "If you surrender peacefully, no one will get hurt. Tell your company to come out of the cave and file quietly to the helicopter."

Shouting over the din of the beating chopper blades, the woman waved at someone inside the passenger compartment. "Get out before I use you for target practice!"

A hairy little man hopped out and looked all around, confused and scared. Another followed, then a third. Soon, at least ten of the creatures had gathered, the whipping wind tossing the hair on their bodies about. One of them dragged an old backpack on the ground. Dressed only in ragged gray loincloths, they looked more like diapered chimps than men.

Marilyn tensed her jaw. The Caitiff. Why had the soldiers brought those foul beasts here?

The man waved his gun toward the helicopter. "Get on board. If no one comes out from that hole, I will count to five and start shooting into it."

Marilyn walked as slowly as she dared. Would Gabriel swoop out and jerk her off the ground? Or was he thinking they'd both get shot out of the sky?

The female soldier marched toward her, gesturing for the Caitiff to follow. She patted down Marilyn's jacket and pulled the Glock from the inner holster. "You got any other surprises in there, honey?" she asked as she slid the gun behind her belt.

Marilyn shook her head. "Where are you taking me?"

"You'll find out soon enough." She looked at the male soldier. "Jackson, let's clear them out."

Jackson raised the rifle to his shoulder and fired a round into the cave. A muffled shriek erupted from near the entry, then silence ensued.

"Wait!" Gabriel called. "Hold your fire." He emerged, cradling a woman. As blood trickled down her dangling arm, he scowled at Jackson. "What kind of idiot would shoot into a dark cave?"

Jackson pointed the rifle at Gabriel. "A soldier who wouldn't mind putting a hole through your head, freak."

99

Gabriel didn't flinch. "If I wasn't carrying an innocent woman you just shot, I'd salute you for your courage."

"Cut the bravado." He aimed toward the cave again. "How many more dragon-kind are in there?"

"Just one." Gabriel turned that way. "Might as well give it up, Dorian."

As he set the wounded woman on the ground, Marilyn peeked at her. It was Tamara. Her eyes closed, she breathed through her mouth, her chest rising and falling in rapid, shallow bursts. Keeping her eyes on Jackson, Marilyn began edging closer to Tamara, hoping to offer some help, but how could she do anything with armed thugs around?

Dorian emerged from the tunnel, her head low and her hands in the pockets of her denim jumper.

"Any others?" Jackson asked.

Keeping her stare low, Dorian shook her head.

"We'll see about that." Jackson fired at least a dozen more rounds into the tunnel, spraying them from side to side. Then, pulling a flashlight from a belt clip, he nodded at the female soldier. "I'm going in, Olsen."

As he waved the beam, Jackson kept the rifle at his hip, a finger on the trigger. When he disappeared inside, Olsen barked at the Caitiff. "Take another sniff to remind yourselves of the dragon scent."

The one carrying the backpack lifted it to his nose and sniffed. Then, like a pack of anxious dogs, the others gathered around and did the same, each one fidgeting and scratching himself after his turn. With every second, their agitation grew. As they jumped in place, they looked more like monkeys than ever.

"When I give you the signal," Olsen said, "go in there and find the dragons."

"Dragons," they echoed, jumping even higher now. "Dragons!"

Olsen called into the tunnel. "Jackson! Is it clear?"

A shrill whistle sounded from within. Olsen furrowed her brow and stalked toward the entrance. "What's going on?"

Dorian withdrew a clenched fist from her pocket and pressed something with her thumb. An explosion boomed from the cave, sending out a shock wave that knocked Olsen to her seat.

In a flash of wings, Gabriel zoomed to her, snatched the rifle, and kicked her in the face, knocking her flat. One of the Caitiff grabbed his wing and jerked him to the ground, and two jumped on his back. The others rushed into the cave, whooping, the lead one carrying a flashlight.

Marilyn tackled one of the brutes and beat his hairy body with her fists. Dorian wrestled the one clutching Gabriel's wing and slung him away. As Gabriel fought off the third, a loud voice boomed from the cave. "Gabriel! Marilyn! Dorian! Let them go and stay down!"

Marilyn flattened her body. Shots rang out, and the three Caitiff flopped to the ground. As soon as the gunshot echoes died away, she jumped up and looked at the tunnel. Yereq stood at the entrance, Jackson's rifle at his shoulder, ready to fire. The Caitiff writhed in pools of dark blood, and Olsen lay on her back, apparently unconscious.

Tamara rose to her knees and pushed her hair back, smiling. "My acting good?"

"You certainly fooled me," Marilyn said. "The blood looked real."

"Blood real." Tamara pointed at her arm. "Cut on stone."

"The tunnel is open," Yereq said, "and some of the Caitiff went through. I was unable to stop them."

Gabriel brushed sand from his clothes. "Let's go. If Sapphira set the trap, maybe we can help the Caitiff fall in." He handed Olsen's rifle to Dorian. "Keep an eye on her."

Marilyn retrieved her own gun from Olsen and pointed it at one of the wounded Caitiff, but she didn't have the heart to shoot the struggling beast again. "Bullets only slow them down," she said to Dorian, "so be careful."

"We should go now." Yereq picked up a lantern at the entrance and led the way through a haze of swirling dust. Soon, he stopped at a deep cleft in the wall. "While we hid in this alcove, the gunman walked into our trap, and he is now no more."

Kaylee and Elise stepped out from the recess, followed by Jordan. "Was anyone hurt?" Kaylee asked.

"Yes." Marilyn pointed toward the exit. "Take Jordan and Elise, and see what you can do out there."

"The Caitiff," Gabriel said. "Did you see them?"

Kaylee nodded toward the tunnel's down slope. "They passed us by. One paused for a second and sniffed around, but he took off again."

Marilyn pushed her gun back to her holster. What could that mean? If Bonnie and Shiloh exchanged clothes and backpacks, maybe those beasts had Bonnie's scent in their nostrils and had picked up her trail.

She patted Yereq on the arm. "Let's get back to the mines. There's no telling what damage those little devils might do before we can get there."

THE RIVER PORTAL

"Well, so much for that." Rebekah tossed a splintered pick handle to the ground. "Save your hands, ladies. We'll have to come up with another plan."

Bonnie sat on a boulder and looked at her palms. Dirty and blistered, they weren't tough enough, nor was any of her party strong enough to dig through the tons of stone in the collapsed tunnel. Although she could have healed her hands with the two or three drops she saved in Elam's vial, it wasn't worth it. Better to keep it for an emergency. "Gabriel knows we're here," she said. "He and Yereq will figure out a way to get in."

"And what if they try to blast through?" Dallas asked. "Another collapse?"

Rebekah kicked a rock across the floor. "My guess is they won't risk it for a while. They know we have food and water, and now we're safe from outside interference. But they might try to communicate, maybe with tapping noises."

"I agree." Sapphira picked up a lantern. "May I suggest that you and Dallas stay here while Bonnie and I look for the portal Elam wrote about?"

Rebekah took the lantern and extinguished the flame. "After a water break, sure. We can come back here and listen."

"And we'll relieve you when we come back." Sapphira snatched up the pick handle, set it ablaze, and led the way as the four walked to the end of the escape passageway. She stopped at the mouth of the larger tunnel and used her bare foot to sweep dirt over an exposed corner of the blanket that concealed the hole in the floor.

Dimming her flame, she turned to the others. "It looks pretty natural, don't you think?"

Bonnie stooped and touched the covering with a finger. "Only if it stays this dark. Someone with a bright lantern might notice and—"

An ear-splitting bang shot through the tunnel, and the ground shook violently.

Bonnie jumped away from the trap. "What was that?"

As grit rained down from the ceiling, coating their heads and shoulders, Rebekah held up her lantern. "Sapphira, give me some light."

Sapphira pointed at the wick. "Ignite!"

As a lively flame erupted, Rebekah extended her arm into the escape passage, creating an orange halo in the dusty air. "Maybe someone is blasting their way in."

"That's fine if it's Gabriel," Dallas said. "But how can we safely find out?"

Rebekah lifted a finger to her lips. "Shhh. Let's listen for a minute."

Folding her wings in tightly, Bonnie eased into the tunnel. Echoes of tapping sounds reached her ears, small rocks falling to the floor, then the clinking of metal—picks or shovels striking stone.

Rebekah pointed at Bonnie. "Your wings are exposed, so you and Sapphira stay here. Dallas and I will check it out."

"You don't have a weapon," Bonnie called as they marched up the dim tunnel's incline.

"If it's Gabriel, we don't need one. If it's someone else, we'll be back in a hurry." Soon, the light faded away.

Sapphira handed Bonnie the pick handle, now burning with a small flame. "This will give us a chance to look at Elam's journal." She pulled it from behind her jeans waistband and opened it to a page she had marked with an old lantern wick. The ovulum, now back in its pouch, bobbed with her movements.

Bonnie held the flame closer to the page. The handwritten letters were thick and bold in one entry but weak and barely readable in another, probably reflecting Elam's exhaustion when he wrote it. Still, bold or not, none of the odd characters made sense.

"This Hebrew poem," Sapphira said, running her finger along the text, "is cryptic. We'll have to figure out the symbolism. It talks about liquid fire, which is probably the magma river, and water stirred by an invisible oar, which might be the whirlpool Elam and I went through to get to Dragons' Rest."

105

Bonnie nodded. "That makes sense, but it's obviously too hot down there now."

"Right, so we have to figure out the rest. It says to obey the command Moses neglected, and Nebuchadnezzar's dream will awaken. Yet, fear not, for he who ..."—she squinted at the words—"made alive, I think would be the best way to say it. He who made alive Balaam's lowly servant can do the same for a face of granite."

"Balaam's lowly servant," Bonnie repeated in a whisper.

Sapphira looked at her. "I've read the story of Balaam, but I don't remember a servant."

"Balaam had a donkey that spoke to him. Maybe that's what it means by making his servant alive."

"I suppose a donkey could be a servant. What about the other parts?"

Bonnie blinked at the text, still a mess of indecipherable marks. "Well, the command Moses disobeyed was to speak to a rock that gave them water in the wilderness. And Nebuchadnezzar had a dream about a statue made out of gold and silver and clay. Then a stone crushed the statue and became a mountain."

"I remember that." Sapphira kept her finger on the page. "So it sounds like we have to speak to a face of granite."

"Have you seen any granite that looks like a face?"

"The cliff that overlooks the magma river is granite. When I was down at the side of the river where Elam and I waded in, I tried to find a place to climb up, but I don't remember anything that looked like facial features."

"Was that when Paili fell from the cliff?" Bonnie asked.

"Right. I guess I didn't notice anything but her."

The sound of running footsteps clopped toward them. Bonnie turned and looked up the incline. A light bounced in the distance, getting closer in a hurry.

Rebekah's voice broke the silence. "That blast punched a hole through the rubble." When she arrived, she stopped and gasped for breath.

Dallas joined her a half second later. Puffing, she pointed back into the tunnel. "A bunch of strange creatures are gathering on this side of the debris."

"Strange creatures?" Sapphira asked. "What did they look like?"

"Covered with hair, more like monkeys than men, but they wore loin cloths and spoke to each other, so they couldn't be monkeys."

"Did they see you?" Bonnie asked.

"I'm not sure. They didn't seem to. They just sniffed and snorted and jumped up and down."

"They had a bright flashlight," Rebekah said, "so I kept the lantern behind me. I would guess there were at least six of them, but they were still coming through the hole. They'll probably head this way as soon as they're all through."

Bonnie pointed at the hidden trap. "Maybe the first few would fall in, but it couldn't possibly catch them all. They'd have to be pretty stupid."

"If you saw them," Dallas said, "you might be more confident. They make monkeys look like Einstein."

"We can't fight that many." Rebekah nodded toward the springs chamber. "Should we hide at the waterfall?"

Sapphira sidestepped the trap. "You and Dallas hide there. Near the ceiling where the springs come out, you can climb behind the falls. When you swim under the rock, you'll come out in an air pocket with enough room for both of you. There's a vent, so you should have plenty of air."

Rebekah forked her fingers at Bonnie and Sapphira. "What about you two?"

107

"We'll head down the shaft and then the river overlook," Sapphira said. "If they show up there, I should be able to send a few over the edge."

"What if there are more than just a few?" Dallas asked.

"Then we'll have to deal with that." Sapphira tucked the journal behind her waistband. "You and Rebekah go. It might take you a little while to get hidden. I'll stay here until the last second."

Rebekah gave her an inquisitive look. "Why?"

"If they're just creeping along, they'll see the hole. So I'm going to make sure they're in a hurry."

"Bait the trap?" Rebekah gave Sapphira a thumbs-up. "Good idea."

As soon as the two former dragons left for the springs, Sapphira took the pick handle from Bonnie and crept a few feet into the escape tunnel. As she crouched, she appeared to be listening, her white hair shining in the glow of her flame.

Bonnie tiptoed in and crouched next to her, careful not to make a sound.

"If they figured out that Shiloh's an impostor," Sapphira whispered, "they're probably coming for you."

Bonnie nodded, holding her breath as she listened. The fire on Sapphira's stick dwindled, now barely the size of a match flame. In the dim light, the sides of the passage seemed to get narrower, funneling the slightest sounds from the depths—a scratching noise, a click, a tap. Were they even real? Or were they figments, tricks her anxious mind played to get her to run?

Soon, a whisper pierced the silence, then another, though the words seemed foreign, more like guttural chatter than human speech. A circle of yellow light came into view, distant, yet growing by the second.

Sapphira clutched Bonnie's wrist and whispered, "Get ready."

Bonnie tightened her leg muscles. She mentally traced a path to the elevator and imagined the climb down, already difficult enough without strange monkey men chasing her. But there wasn't another option.

As Sapphira rose slowly to her feet, Bonnie did the same. Sapphira pressed the stick into Bonnie's hand and whispered, "When I say run, you go first. Don't worry about me."

Bonnie nodded. "Don't take too many chances."

Suddenly, the stick blazed. "Bonnie!" Sapphira shouted. "Someone's out there! We have to hide! Run!"

Bonnie turned and, dodging the hidden hole, sprinted toward the elevator shaft. With her wings giving her a boost, she zipped along, but as she neared the shaft, the breeze blew out her flame. Now in darkness, she groped for the opening in the wall, looking back for any sign of a white-haired girl with a ball of fire riding on her palm.

Finally, her hand passed across a gap. She reached in, grabbed the rope, and looked back again. More shrieks erupted in the darkness. Had some of the creatures fallen into their trap? Was Sapphira trying to increase the number of victims somehow?

A hand touched her shoulder. "Let's get going!"

"Sapphira? How did you—"

"I know my way around in the dark. Climb down! Hurry! I'll be right behind you."

Bonnie swung out into the shaft and let the rope slide through her hands, braking with her shoes only when the burning sensation in her fingers grew too painful. Within seconds, she felt the breeze from the next level's opening and swung to the floor, then quickly backed away to make room.

The sound of bare feet slapping the stone followed. A fireball appeared. As it grew to the size of a baseball, it illuminated Sapphira's palm and face. She whispered, "Come on," and ran through the tunnel.

Bonnie dashed after her, again propelling herself with her wings. "How many of the ape men were there?"

"I think four fell in the trap," Sapphira called back, "but there were at least six more. I'm not sure if they saw which way I ran."

As they jogged along the stony path, they passed by a tiny spring pouring from a one-inch-wide hole in the wall. A bucket collected the water, but it had long since overflowed. The excess spilled to the floor and ran down a network of shallow cracks.

When they reached the entry arch to the magma river overlook, Sapphira stopped and set a hand on her chest. "Whew! That's the farthest I've run in centuries."

Bonnie looked back. "I think I hear something, that chatter those creatures make."

"Let's get out of sight." Sapphira snuffed out her fire and guided Bonnie through the entrance. When they neared the ledge, the river provided all the light they needed.

Stretching out her wings, Bonnie looked over the side. "You came here to try to find the face, didn't you?"

"We couldn't all fit in the other hiding place anyway, and this was the first alternative that came to mind."

"So if the face is on the cliff underneath us, do we speak to it from up here or from down there?"

"We might as well try from up here first," Sapphira said, "but what do we say to it?"

Bonnie looked back at the tunnel. The sound of monkey chatter drew closer. "Moses was supposed to get water from his rock, so maybe we should ask this one for water."

"It's worth a try." With Bonnie holding to her shirt, Sapphira leaned over the edge and shouted at the wall below. "Would you please give us some water?"

No reply came, only the low rumble of partially molten rock grinding against the walls on either side of the river.

As Bonnie pulled Sapphira back, a light appeared on the tunnel wall just outside the entryway. Bonnie spread out her wings. "They're coming!"

"Fly me to river level," Sapphira said. "We could ask the wall from down there."

"It's too hot to land." Bonnie looked out over the chasm again. "Maybe we could fly in front of the cliff and find a face. If it has ears, we can talk into one. If all else fails, we'll head to the other ledge."

"It's worth a try. But it will be faster and safer if you search without me. Remember the updrafts."

Two hairy men crept toward them, one bearing a thick club and the other a flaming torch.

Bonnie pointed. "You can't stay here with them."

"I'll fend off the monkey men." Sapphira stepped back from Bonnie and spread out her arms. Her entire body erupted in flames, sending their attackers scurrying. "Now hurry. I can't do this for very long."

Flapping her wings, Bonnie leaped out over the chasm. A surge of hot air pushed her higher, but she quickly adjusted and angled down toward the cliff wall. Flying in a tight oval, she scanned the granite surface. Two deeply set clefts near the top could easily be eyes, and a rugged protrusion just below them made for a crooked but passable nose.

She flew lower. After flapping once, she let the upwelling breezes keep her in a glide. A deep hole, round and craggy, made the face seem like it was trying to blow out a flame. Yet, with the wall staying flat as far as she could see, there seemed to be no place for ears anywhere.

As she swept closer to Sapphira, she shouted. "No ears. I'm going to ask as I pass by the mouth."

Sapphira, still in flames, kept her arms spread wide, while shadows jumped up and down nearby. "Okay, but I'm running out of energy."

Bonnie flew back to the face. Just before reaching the circular mouth, she shouted, "Please give us water!"

Nothing happened. Bonnie passed by the mouth, made a tight one-eighty turn, and flew toward it again. Suddenly, water gushed out in a geyserlike surge. It blasted against her side and thrust her across the chasm and into the far wall. Her wing bent painfully against the rock, but its strong mainstay cushioned the impact, allowing her to push off with her feet and fly toward the precipice.

Now dripping wet from her waist down, Bonnie had to beat her wings hard to stay aloft. The hot updrafts had vanished, and her right wing faltered, likely bruised by the impact.

Her flames dwindling, Sapphira grunted as she flung fireballs at the approaching monkey men, now several in number. "You can do it!" she called. "You're almost here!"

With a final thrust, Bonnie lunged back to the ledge and stopped just short of Sapphira's flames. The attackers ran away, the last one with a flashlight in his grip. As they retreated in the inner tunnel, the glow dwindled for a few seconds before steadying. Quiet chatter echoed from wherever the hairy beasts had stopped.

"I guess they're regrouping." Sapphira shut off her inferno. "Good thing. You can't fly me anywhere until I get cooler." She touched Bonnie's shoulder. "Are you all right?"

Bonnie shook her wings, throwing off streams of water. "Just a bruise, I think." She hustled back to the edge and looked down. A three-foot-wide column of water shot from the face's mouth and plunged into the river. Huge plumes of steam rocketed upward, filling the chamber with a misty cloud.

"Whew!" Bonnie waved a hand at the vapor. "I got back just in time. That steam would have cooked me."

Sapphira fixed her gaze on the river. "And now we might have another problem."

Bonnie joined her. Below, at the point where the water struck the magma, the river solidified. As the hardening magma piled up behind it, the flow of molten rock rose with the growing wall.

"How high can it go?" Bonnie asked.

Sapphira pointed at the far wall. "I think it will eventually seep around the sides of its own barricade, but with the water flowing faster than the magma, it's hard to tell."

Bonnie stared through the rising vapor. "It looks like the waterfall's making a pool, and it's swirling."

"I noticed," Sapphira whispered. "That must be our portal."

Bonnie glanced back at the entry. The flashlight's glow stayed steady. The monkey men still lurked, but they seemed to be coming no closer. "So do we go through it?" she asked, matching Sapphira's low tone. "Or do we fly to the other ledge and warn Rebekah and Dallas about the rising magma?"

"I can't see it rising all the way up here. Once it gets higher than the water source, there's nothing to dam it up."

"Will our new portal stay open if the magma creeps around the sides? I mean, if hardening magma caps it off, we might not get back."

"It's hard to say, but considering the prophecy, I think we have to see what's there." Sapphira touched the wounded wing. "Are you able to carry me down?"

Bonnie pulled her wing to the front and massaged a bruise on the outer part of the mainstay. "I think so. Going down should be easier than crossing the chasm."

A shriek sounded from the tunnel. In the shadows, a line of hunched men drew near, snarling. One of them carried the bucket Bonnie had seen in the tunnel.

"The monkey-man fire department is here." Sapphira pulled Bonnie toward the edge. "Let's fly!"

A wave of water flew over them. Her hair dripping, Bonnie wrapped her arms around Sapphira's waist. Just as one of the creatures leaped, she vaulted into the air. The beast's momentum carried him over the side, and he plummeted, his hairy limbs flailing.

"When we get down there," Sapphira shouted, "I'll let you know if I sense a portal."

A loud bang sounded in Bonnie's ears, then another. "Did you hear that?"

"Gunshots? Did those freaks get reinforcements?"

"Maybe. Let's hurry." Staying close to the near wall, Bonnie flew around the column of steam and drifted downward from the cooler side. As they closed in on the whirlpool, the swirling water grew clear. It spun downward at least ten feet, guarded by a wall of steam and mounting rock that separated the pool from the oncoming magma.

"I can feel it!" Sapphira yelled. "The portal!"

"Do we just dive right in?"

"What's the worst that could happen? We'd get wet."

Bonnie grimaced. The words *we could drown* came to mind, but she decided it would be better to stay quiet. Elam's prophecy had come true so far, so this portal had to lead somewhere. But to a dark world beneath all others? Would that be worse than drowning? Yet, with her injured wing aching, there seemed to be no other option.

113

As she neared the mouth of the whirlpool, she folded in her wings, held her breath, and plunged in feetfirst. The water, hot enough to sting her skin, sucked them down. Then, like a slide at a theme park, it zipped them along a twisting path. With her eyes closed, she could only feel the sensations—bubbles brushing past her face, a sense of coolness as the water tempered, Sapphira's warm body in her arms, and a continued downward pull into a seemingly endless coil.

Her lungs now begging for air, and the rush of water slowing, she opened her eyes. Darkness blinded her. Thousands of bubbles continued to blow past, but not enough to allow her to catch a gulp of oxygen. Within seconds she would have to try, or else faint.

Just as she opened her mouth to gather bubbles, she burst out of the water. Her shoes struck soft turf, and she tumbled into a somersault, flying over Sapphira and sliding to a stop on her back.

Blinking, she sat up and looked behind her. Sapphira had already risen to her knees. In the dimness, she appeared as a dripping gray shadow against a darker background.

Bonnie climbed to her feet and helped Sapphira get up. "Can you call for some fire?" Bonnie asked.

Sapphira shook her hands, slinging droplets. Then, raising a palm, she whispered, "Give me light."

Nothing happened.

She added a hint of sternness to her voice. "Give me light."

Again, nothing happened.

"Are you too wet?" Bonnie asked.

"I don't think I'm any wetter than I was at Morgan's swamp." She blew on her hands. "Maybe I flamed out scaring those monkey men. I'll try again in a minute."

A low voice rumbled from somewhere nearby. "You have no power here, dread Oracle. At least, not yet."

8

CHAPTER

A New Dragon

Churning her arms and legs as fast as she could, Marilyn puffed. If Yereq didn't slow down soon, she would have to fall back and follow his lantern light instead of his sprinting body. Sure, it was easy enough for Gabriel to keep up. He had wings to give him a boost, while she had nothing but weary legs. Following these two was like trying to compete with Superman and the Flash.

Finally, Gabriel and the giant slowed to a stop. Marilyn caught up and braced her hands on her knees as she tried to catch her breath. The two were looking down into a hole at the intersection between the escape and main tunnels.

"What happened?" she asked.

"It's the trap," Gabriel said. "I see the light from the magma river way down below. I hope some of the beasts fell into it."

Marilyn peered over the edge. "Where do we look for Bonnie and Sapphira?"

Gabriel set a finger on Yereq's stomach. "You know the mines better than we do. What do you think?"

"I will search this level," Yereq replied. "It has the most rooms and mazes, and I know them well. I suggest that you and Marilyn go down the elevator shaft and check the next level. You need only search the magnetite channels and the magma river overlook. If you do not find them, you can go to the brick kiln level where we met them earlier."

After picking up another lantern near the wall and lighting it, Yereq left it on the floor, sidestepped the hole, and headed toward the springs chamber in a quick march.

Gabriel handed the new lantern to Marilyn. "Hang on to this. We'll take a shortcut straight down. If they're at the overlook, this has to be the fastest way."

"Let's split up," she said. "Since you'll have light from the river, I'll go down the shaft with the lantern. That way we'll cover more ground."

"Do you know how to get there? Won't you need protection?"

"Don't worry. Just give me directions." She patted her holster. "I have a protector right here."

"Right." He pointed into the darkness. "Follow the tunnel until you see an open doorway cut into the rock wall to your right. There's a rope that'll lead you to the next level down." He touched the lantern. "Can you climb while holding that?"

She looked at the narrow handle on the top of the lantern. "I'll hold it in my teeth if I have to."

"Good. After we search that level, I'll fly you back up. See you at the overlook." Folding in his wings, Gabriel leaped into the hole.

Marilyn didn't bother to watch his progress. She had to hurry.

Jogging in the direction he had pointed, she waved the lantern from side to side to illuminate every cleft in the dark walls. Staring past the flickering light and trying to pick up a nondescript black hole seemed impossible, but soon it came into sight.

She set the lantern handle between her teeth, grabbed the rope, and, braking with her shoes, climbed down hand over hand. It was hotter in the shaft, and the work raised a quick sweat. Within a few seconds, a draft cooled her skin. Had she reached the next level? With the lantern's glow blinding her eyes, she couldn't see an exit hole.

She pushed a foot against the far wall, hoping not to crash into anything. As she swung, her hair brushed against something, probably the top of the lower doorway. She dropped to solid ground, released the rope, and pulled the lantern from her mouth.

"Whew!" She mopped her forehead with her sleeve. "Now to find the overlook."

Again holding the lantern out in front, she passed by a dark chamber. She stopped and lifted the lantern close to a sign on the wall next to the gaping entrance. The strange lettering probably revealed exactly what was inside, at least to someone who could read the language.

Extending her light, she stepped in. Her shoe pushed something heavy, making a scraping noise. She set the lantern on the floor and touched a wooden handle with curved metal on the opposite end. It looked like a rusted pick. As she lifted it, the handle crumbled in her grasp.

"The mines," she whispered.

Trying to quiet her pounding heart, she turned the lantern's brightness up and tiptoed in. When Yereq mentioned searching the magnetite channels, she had imagined a network of trenches with sweating girls driving their picks into hard rock while a brute of a man ripped their backs with a barbed whip. Of course, the girls were gone, but as she stepped down into a trench, it seemed that the pain of every lash pierced her mind, and the anguished cries of little slave girls drifted through the stale air.

She stooped and picked up a flat glass disk. On the inside, black particles covered the bottom. They looked like iron filings, the kind she had used for magnet experiments in school. A scrap of an old dress lay nearby, torn and bloodied. She snatched it up

117

and clutched it tightly in her fist. Those poor girls! The torture they endured must have been the worst of nightmares!

As she let the scrap fall, she straightened and looked into the darkness. This place had to be massive, far too big to search thoroughly. Maybe if they were close, they would respond to a call. If not, she could come back after checking the overlook.

"Bonnie!" she shouted.

The name echoed in the chamber, fading with each reverberation.

"Sapphira!"

Again, the name echoed. The sound seemed to travel along multiple corridors, as if conducting a search in the deep recesses of the mines.

Marilyn listened. Besides the sound of her own breathing and a slight trickle of water somewhere in the distance, nothing reached her ears.

After calling each name twice more, she climbed out of the trench and returned to the tunnel. As she hurried on, strange sounds emanated from the darkness in front of her, a combination of running water and …

She squinted. "Monkey chatter?"

Creeping slowly now, she passed a fountain springing from the wall, explaining one of the sounds. As she continued, the shrieking clamor heightened. A light appeared to the right, revealing another arched passage. The light danced, seemingly in time with the chanting beasts.

Marilyn set the lantern down and pulled out her gun. Even if bullets just slowed the Caitiff down, a few well-placed shots might be enough to send a monkey into the magma river.

With her back against the wall, she slid closer, listening. A girl somewhere within the adjacent chamber called out, "Let's fly!"

Extending the gun with both hands, Marilyn leaped in front of the opening. Behind a wall of jumping Caitiff, two with flaming torches, Bonnie vaulted from a ledge with Sapphira in her arms, both dripping wet. One of the Caitiff fell in their wake and disappeared.

"Back off!" Marilyn shouted as she stalked toward the other Caitiff. "Get out of my way!"

The hairy men, now about seven in number, turned as one. Snarling, one leaped toward her, but with a quick aim she shot it through the chest. As it dropped to the ground, she turned the gun back on the others. "Who's next?"

One of the Caitiff threw a bucket. She ducked, but it glanced off the side of her head, making her stagger. Squealing, the Caitiff lunged. She fired shot after shot. One fell, then another. But three made it through her hail of bullets. A hairy hand grabbed her gun. Two others latched on to her wrists and bowled her over. A torch fell beside her ear, something metal struck her head and flashed a light in her eyes, and an arm covered her mouth.

She yelled into its smelly skin, her voice muffled. "Get off me, you disgusting ape!"

Just as one of the beasts turned her gun toward her, it flew backwards into the darkness. A second disappeared, releasing her wrists. Finally, the one covering her mouth jumped off and backed away slowly.

Marilyn grabbed the torch and leaped to her feet. Extending the flame, she illuminated the area. Gabriel, his wings spread wide, pointed another torch at the Caitiff. "If you don't want to follow your buddies into the chasm, then get out now!"

The lone Caitiff turned and sped out through the passageway.

Marilyn ran to the edge of the precipice. "Did you see where Bonnie went?"

"Bonnie? You saw her?"

"She jumped off with Sapphira in her arms."

She looked down into the depths. Water poured from a hole somewhere in the wall, but with the magma river's glow dying

119

from the cooling effect, and steam rising in a billowing column, she couldn't see anyone.

Marilyn cupped her hands around her mouth and called out as loudly as she could, "Bonnie!"

Gabriel threw down his torch and beat his wings. "I'm going in."

"Be careful!"

He leaped straight out, then dropped. As he fanned his wings, he slowed his descent and disappeared into the plumes of white.

Marilyn continued her calls, shouting for Bonnie and Sapphira again and again until her voice grew hoarse. With the roar of water and the loud hiss of venting steam, her cries seemed to hit a barrier and die away.

After a few minutes, Gabriel flew back to the ledge, soaking wet and puffing. With a shake of each wing, he cast off hundreds of droplets. Some splashed on Marilyn's cheek, hot and stinging.

"Sorry about that."

She rubbed her cheek. "It's okay. I've had worse burns."

"I know what you mean. Flying here through the channel nearly fried me."

"Any sign of them?"

"Not a trace." He turned back toward the chasm and looked down. "The water's rising like crazy, and I didn't have a light."

She pushed the torch into his hand. "Then try again. We have to find them."

"Not with this," he said, pushing it back. "That steam will put it out in a heartbeat."

"Then maybe ..." Waving the torch near the ground, she scanned the area. "I felt something hit me, something metal that flickered in my eyes."

The firelight raised a sparkle a few feet away. Gabriel leaped toward it and snatched up a flashlight. "This should do it."

"Any sign of my gun?"

"Nope. I think it went into the soup with the first one I yanked off you."

"Okay." She rubbed her head where the flashlight had hit her. "Better get going."

"I'm on my way." With a leap, he dove into the chasm again.

Marilyn shuffled back to the tunnel, her head aching. She searched for her lantern, but it was nowhere to be found. With a huff, she murmured, "The Caitiff must have taken it."

Now with only a dwindling torch, she hurried back to the edge and waited. The beast that escaped might return soon, and who could tell if there were any others in the matrix of tunnels?

After several minutes, Marilyn sat down in a shadow near the wall. No use yelling for Gabriel. He probably couldn't hear her anyway, and she didn't want to alert anyone else to her presence.

The flames at the end of her torch wilted, then died away. Probably all for the best. Now to anyone walking by, she would be undetectable.

Soon, lantern light appeared in the tunnel again. Marilyn froze. She glanced back and forth between the chasm and the passageway. How many of those monsters were coming? Where was Gabriel now?

A massive figure lumbered onto the ledge, his lantern illuminating his bearded face.

Marilyn jumped up. "Oh, Yereq! I'm so glad to see you!"

He offered a smile, but his expression quickly turned serious. "Where is Gabriel?"

She nodded toward the chasm. "I'm pretty sure I saw Bonnie fly Sapphira down there, so he's trying to find them."

"Since I was unable to locate anyone on the upper level," Yereq said, "I tried to climb down to the kiln chamber, but it was flooded, so I decided to find you."

Marilyn kept her gaze fixed on the white clouds rising from the boiling water below. They jetted upward only a few feet in

121

front of her, vanished into the darkness above, and reappeared in swirling streams that rocketed down, then back up again after bouncing off the swelling river. "This place will be like pea soup in a few minutes," she said. "Gabriel had better hurry."

The magma's glow continued to weaken, and with thick vapor filling every cubic inch of air, the chamber grew darker and darker. Pops and sizzles diminished until only the sound of falling water reached their ears.

Soon, another sound drew near, flapping wings and heavy grunts.

"It's Gabriel!" Marilyn stepped as close to the edge as she dared and searched the sea of white fog. "I can't see him anywhere."

Yereq knelt, reached over the precipice, and hoisted Gabriel up to the ledge, a handful of shirt in his huge hand. After setting him upright, Yereq raised the lantern near Gabriel's face. "Did you see them?" Yereq asked.

Water streamed from Gabriel's soaked hair and down his reddened cheeks. "No sign of them," he said, puffing quick breaths. "I thought I saw a swirl in a pool, so I dove in. It didn't lead anywhere, and the water was scalding, so I climbed out." He took a deeper breath and let it out slowly. "Magma was spilling in, and while I was flying around, it hardened over the first pool and now the sideways geyser is making a lake over the new layer."

"So will it keep making layers of rock and water until it fills the chasm?" Marilyn asked.

He nodded, slinging water up and down. "Looks that way, at least for a while. The cooling magma built a wall a little ways upstream, so it overflows, cools down, and keeps building the wall."

"So where could Bonnie and Sapphira have gone?"

"Nowhere down there, unless there was a portal. When I was in an energy state, I could sense a portal, but not now." He nodded toward the other side of the chasm. "I'm going across to check the brick kiln room."

She grabbed his drenched sleeve. "Yereq already went there. It's flooded."

"Then I'll search the tunnel. Maybe they're hiding out in between." He took the lantern from Yereq, then, with a quick flap, he leaped into the vapor and disappeared, leaving Marilyn and Yereq in the darkness.

"If he doesn't find them," Marilyn said, "we'll have to leave and come back as soon as possible with search lamps and maybe even scuba gear."

Yereq kept his gaze locked on the fog. "I have heard of such equipment. Are you trained in its use?"

"I'm certified, but not for cave diving. If this chamber fills up, it'll be very dangerous. I'll have to find an expert."

For a few minutes, silence ensued, save for the constant splashing from below. Then the familiar beating of Gabriel's wings drew near, and lantern light pierced the fog. He landed in a graceful walk, stepping between Marilyn and Yereq as he folded in his wings.

123

"I struck out." Water streaming down his worried face, Gabriel nodded toward the chasm. "It's filling up pretty fast. We'd better go topside."

Marilyn touched his arm. "We'll get search equipment and come back."

He paused, looking forlornly at the rising steam. "If there's anything to come back to."

After climbing to the first level and hurrying through the escape tunnel, they rushed out into the daylight. Blinking, Marilyn looked around. Dorian sat cross-legged on the ground next to two dead soldiers, the rifle in her lap. Kaylee, Tamara, Elise, and Jordan were all at the helicopter, Kaylee studying the controls and the others standing just outside the pilot's door.

"I had to shoot the woman," Dorian said. "She is no longer among the living. The man is dead, as well."

Kaylee called from the pilot's seat. "Marilyn, this is not my field of expertise. Have you ever flown a helicopter?"

"Not one this big, but I should be able to handle it." Marilyn marched toward them. "We'll need it if we're going to get search equipment down here."

After everyone except Yereq boarded the helicopter, Marilyn started the blades rotating. Yereq stooped at her side, the shining lantern again in his grip. "If you see them," she shouted as she passed her cell phone to him. "Push number three and hold it down for two seconds. It will dial the phone Gabriel has."

Gabriel reached into his pants pocket. "If it's not too wet."

"And if that doesn't work," she continued, "dial nine-one-one like you did before. You might have to climb to the top to get cell service."

"I understand. I will continue searching until you return. At the very least, I should try to find the last Caitiff. If he is still prowling, Bonnie and Sapphira are not safe."

She touched her holster. "Do you need a weapon?"

"I have my sword, and the dead soldiers left their rifles. I know how to use them."

"Great. We'll be back as soon as we can." She lifted the helicopter into the air and guided it slowly upward. The surrounding walls seemed closer than before. Of course, it was an illusion, but with the swirling wind, it wouldn't take much of a gust to sweep them close enough to brush the tail against the rocks. The higher they rose, the more susceptible they would be to the winds at the surface.

Soon, however, they had flown safely above the crater's lip and were rising still higher. The mountain's bald top came into view, the borrowed airplane still parked near the forest's edge.

Marilyn wrapped her fingers around the cyclic stick. Flying the plane would be a lot easier, but the helicopter had more passenger room, and transporting people and equipment from one vehicle to the other would be too time consuming. Experienced or not, she would have to make do.

124

"Okay," she said as she turned the helicopter toward town, "let's get everyone up to date and plot our strategy."

Bonnie swung toward the voice. Dread Oracle? Who could have said that?

She whispered to Sapphira. "Did you hear a voice?"

"I heard, but I didn't like the tone."

Bonnie cleared her throat. "Who's there?"

The voice returned, this time with a low echo following each word. "The guardian of the expectant ones, the warden who watches the fruit of unopened wombs, the caretaker of the forsaken but not forgotten. So you see, I am all three."

She narrowed her eyes. Something moved out there, something large and dark. But how far away was it? Everything was warped. The man's reply, if it was a man at all, seemed to beg her to ask what his strange words meant. Should she play along? Or should she go straight for the heart of the matter?

"Who are you?" she asked.

"A guardian."

Sapphira clutched Bonnie's arm and whispered, "Wait. Let me."

"I was hoping you would."

"Guardian," Sapphira said, "you speak in riddles. Are you able to tell us plainly who you are and where we are?"

"Some now, some later." The voice carried no hint of friendliness or malice. "The learning ladder is better climbed a rung at a time rather than in leaps and bounds."

Darkness faded. Like dawn on a cloudy day, muted light illuminated their surroundings. Behind them, a head-high waterfall fed a swiftly flowing brook, shallow by all appearances. To each side, a wall of black mountains sealed them in, perhaps a mile or so away, though their height likely skewed the distance. In front, a verdant field lay before them with human-shaped statues dotting the landscape, one within reach.

125

A column of white mist swirled around the statue, dressing the polished black stone with a semitransparent veil. With every orbit around the stony face, the vapor seemed to animate the features, giving life to the eyes, nose, and mouth. Wrapped in fog, an arm stretched slowly toward Bonnie and Sapphira. Starting at the tips of its fingers, stone morphed into flames, making a crackling sound as the transformation inched along. Muscles rippled on the forearm, and a fiery sleeve took shape over the bulging bicep.

Bonnie latched on to Sapphira's elbow and backed away. "I don't think it wants a hug."

"Not likely." Sapphira raised her free hand. "Give me a fire-ball!" She looked at her uplifted palm. Nothing appeared.

Now engulfed in flames from its waist up, the figure took a step. As if breaking the façade away with its crunching weight, the stony boot crumbled, revealing more flames.

"It's too slow to catch us," Bonnie said, her retreat keeping pace with the statue's advance. "I wonder what it is."

"Once it's finished transforming, it might be a lot faster, so we'd—"

"You are solid rock!" The voice seemed to thunder across the land. The flaming man stopped in mid-step and hardened to stone again.

Bonnie looked up at the ash gray sky, searching for an airborne creature, something large enough to bellow such a resounding command, but nothing appeared.

A low voice droned. "It is wise to my eyes to avoid the citizens of this valley. You are likely not prepared to face them or displace them."

Bonnie again looked for the speaker of the rhyming words. A large red dragon stood near the brook, maybe a dozen feet away, the end of its tail flicking the water.

Pushing back her wet hair, she narrowed her eyes again, trying to get a good look at the dragon. This scene was so much like the first circle in the Circles of Seven, even the heaviness, a dragging weight that was worse than the effect of her saturated clothes.

"Do you fear me?" the dragon asked, his voice low but not unpleasant.

"Well ..." Bonnie peeled her sweatshirt over her head and began wringing it out. Maybe it would be best to show confidence in spite of their circumstances. "*Should* I fear you?"

The dragon's eyes flashed dark blue, and his voice lowered to a growl. "Only my enemies need fear me. My friends revere me."

"Hmmm. . ." Bonnie squinted at him. He didn't answer the question, very much like the deceitful dragon in the circles. During that encounter, the dragon had tried to get her to look into a pool, in violation of a command to avoid reflections. If this one was trying to play games with her mind, she would have to be on the alert.

Sapphira stepped ahead of Bonnie. "What's your name? And how did you know to address us in English?"

Extending his neck, the dragon brought his head closer and spoke in what sounded like an old and lovely language.

Sapphira set her hands on her hips. "No, I don't prefer ancient Hebrew. I'm just trying to figure out who you are and where we are."

"You two are inquisitive for a pair of intruders." The dragon shuffled toward them and stopped within a wing's reach. "Tell me, if two alien beings barged into your home and demanded answers to their inane questions, would you be pleased or pestered?"

While Sapphira aimed a suspicious stare at him, Bonnie pondered his words. With only the dragon and statues in this land, a human could be considered alien, yet the statues seemed human enough. Apparently hewn out of some kind of black rock, they were roughly shaped and indistinct, though the faces carried more detail. "I would be pestered," she finally said.

"Why did you hesitate?" the dragon asked. "Is truth so precious in your land that you must speak it sparingly? Do you consider the cost of truth before you spend it? Or do you merely lend it at your leisure?"

Bonnie looked at Sapphira. With her hands still on her hips and her brow bent low, Sapphira seemed unwilling to play this dragon's game. Bonnie copied her pose, hoping to show her distrust, but for some reason, her arms and legs felt heavy and stiff. She had to raise and lower her feet as if marching in place to keep her blood circulating. And she had to answer. This dragon represented their only source of knowledge.

"It's fair to say that truth is precious in my world," Bonnie said. "There are many liars, as well as those who would use our words against us, making us hesitant to reveal all we know. Yet, among friends, we are glad to speak truth without reservation."

The dragon let out a long "Hmmm," then added, "Is that so?"

Sapphira dipped her knee as if offering a curtsy and flavored her tone with a lovely formality. "Please pardon our intrusion and our many questions, but since we all find truth to be valuable, is it not reasonable for us to seek it and for you to dispense it?"

The dragon gave them a slow nod. "Reasonable to ask? Yes. Reasonable to expect answers? Not necessarily. For the one bearing answers is sometimes obligated to hold his tongue. For some, truth is an incisive sword, a light in low luminance, a path to protection, yet, as the other lass has already indicated, in other hands, truth is a divider, a stone hurled to inflict injury, a club to beat down those who lack opportunity to light lamps of their own."

Bonnie let his words soak in. They seemed profound, more straightforward than those of the dragon in the Circles of Seven. And this dragon alternated between lovely prose and abrupt, in-your-face declarations, sometimes alliterating and sometimes speaking with rhymes. He was definitely not the evil dragon from the first circle.

"It is wise," the dragon continued, "to learn in what manner someone will wield a sword before equipping her with one. Quite often this discernment requires a test to prove both worth and wisdom, and those of integrity never fear the light that such a test would bring, for light is the key to every locked door."

"Very well." Sapphira bowed her head. "Since we have no opportunity to prove our worth, may we have leave to explore this land ... to light our own lamps, as you say?"

"Have you grown weary of conversing with me?" Twin lines of smoke rose from his nostrils. "Do you think that I am unable to light your lamps? Ask me a question. I will give you a truthful answer."

Bonnie looked down at her legs. Her jeans were caked with dried mud. She stamped her foot lightly, making it break away and relieving a buzzing tingle.

"A truthful answer?" Sapphira spread out her arms. "What is this place, and who are you?"

"I invited a singular question," the dragon replied, "and you have offered a pair of puzzlers. Is requiring only one a reasonable request?"

"It's reasonable. I just wanted to save a little time."

"Ah, yes. Time. A tantalizing topic." The dragon set his head near Sapphira's and drilled his shining stare at her eyes. "Tell me, do you believe that God exists within a time framework, or is he outside of time, able to see every past and future event as if they were present?"

"Why does that matter?" Sapphira asked. "I'm just trying to figure out where we are."

Bonnie glanced once more at her heavy legs. As before, mud covered her pants from knees to ankles. She stomped both feet, loosening the dirt again.

"Explaining where you are," the dragon said, "is dependent on your understanding of time."

As the dragon droned on, Bonnie looked at Sapphira's legs. They, too, were coated with drying mud, and her feet seemed locked in place. Bonnie took Sapphira's hand and pulled her to the side, forcing her to move her feet. The mud cracked and flaked away.

129

"Why did you do that?" Sapphira asked.

"Just trust me." Bonnie shifted back to the dragon. "It's been nice talking to you, but we really need to go and learn about this place ourselves."

"Has it *really* been nice talking to me?" he asked. "Or is this an idiomatic pleasantry by which you are hiding the truth of the matter?"

Keeping hold of Sapphira's hand, Bonnie walked back the way they came. "We're going."

"You may go," the dragon said as daylight waned. "But you must begin without a flame or a flicker. As you discover the truths of my realm, your vision will be restored."

Bonnie wheeled back toward the dragon. Darkness blanketed everything in sight until only a pair of pulsing blue eyes floated in the midst. "I will provide you with a few of truth's precious gems," he continued. "First, you who claim to cherish the true treasures have neglected to secure a most precious valuable. Since the waterfall was your source of entry, I suggest you search the river. Second, you have no reason to assume that the creatures you meet in this place will tell you the truth. And third ..." The eyes drew so close, Bonnie could feel the dragon's hot breath on her cheeks. "There is only one way to escape. That truth you must also learn on your own, but it might be a terrible truth that you will be unable to bear."

The eyes vanished, leaving Bonnie and Sapphira in complete darkness. A shiver ran along Bonnie's soaked skin. She checked for her necklace. It was gone, likely stripped over her head by the rushing water, but would the dragon be aware of that? "Do you know what valuable he was talking about?" she asked.

"Maybe ..."

Bonnie waited, listening to the swish of Sapphira's wet clothes. A low groan followed.

"The ovulum and Elam's journal are gone!"

9

CHAPTER

A REUNION

Where did you last remember having them?" Bonnie asked.

"The ovulum was still in my pouch when we were on the ledge, and the journal was tucked behind my waistband, so they must have dropped out in the whirlpool. Since I was so wet, I guess I didn't notice the change."

"Come on." Bonnie groped for Sapphira's hand. "He said to search in the river."

As soon as she felt Sapphira's grip, Bonnie led her toward the sound of running water. "I don't think it's deep, and won't the ovulum glow? It should be easy to find."

"It doesn't always glow, and when it does, it's usually when I'm holding it. And the journal's probably waterlogged somewhere."

"True," Bonnie said. "We'd better concentrate on the ovulum." She thought about mentioning the journal's protective coating, but would that also protect it from water? She decided not to bring that up and raise potentially false hopes.

As their feet sloshed into the edge of the river, Sapphira drew back her hand. "I don't trust that dragon. Everything he said about truth being precious to him might have been a lie."

"I know what you mean," Bonnie said. "I've dealt with a lying dragon before, but he might be telling the truth about where the ovulum is. It's worth a try." She waded into thigh-deep water. At least she wouldn't have to worry about mud collecting on her clothes in here.

When it began getting shallower again, she moved back to the deepest section, stooped, and searched the sandy bottom with her fingers. "Do you know if it floats?"

Sapphira splashed next to her. "I don't remember it ever being in water."

"If it sinks, then it's likely to be in the middle instead of the sides, but if it floats, then the current might take it past us."

"And it might have already floated beyond this point."

132

Bonnie grimaced. Sapphira was right. This search might be a fool's game, but what else could they do? Consulting Enoch about this place and how to escape might be their only hope.

As she shuffled forward, listening to the sound of the nearby waterfall, the cold current chilled her skin, making her shiver again.

"It's getting colder," Sapphira said.

"I noticed." Bonnie had to clench her teeth to keep them from chattering. "I wonder why. I thought we might get used to it after a while."

A gentle laugh arose, far away and drifting on the wind. It sounded wonderfully alive and carefree.

"Did you hear that?" Bonnie asked.

"A woman laughing?"

"I think so."

"Just a second ago," Sapphira said, "I thought I heard a man talking. It's almost like he told a joke, and the woman laughed."

Bonnie shuddered, yet not from the chill of being wet. The feeling that someone was watching never seemed so real before. It felt like cold, curious fingers petted her bare forearm, raising a thousand new goose bumps.

As they pressed on, the sound of falling water grew louder. The riverbed descended, signaling the deeper pool dredged out by the plunging force. Strangely enough, a sense of warmth flowed across Bonnie's skin.

"Feel that?"

"I do." Sapphira ran a slippery finger across Bonnie's arm. "And the water feels oily, like it has some kind of petroleum in it. If there's a spring at the bottom, then this pool might be really deep. And if the ovulum sank, then—"

"It is quite deep, ladies."

Bonnie stopped. A male voice? Where did it come from?

"Who's there?" she asked.

"Bonnie, don't you recognize my voice?"

The sound came from the riverbank to her right. She turned that way and replayed the words in her mind. The voice was familiar, but hearing it in total darkness made it seem heavy, frightening. "I'm sorry," she said. "I don't—"

Sapphira grabbed Bonnie's arm and whispered, "Remember what the dragon said? Don't give away truth so fast."

"Right." Bonnie pressed her lips together. The voice still buzzed in her brain. It was so tantalizing, like a cry from her past, a call she couldn't possibly ignore.

Sapphira cleared her throat. "May I ask who is addressing us?"

"I am Dr. Matthew Conner, Bonnie's father."

A new chill ran up Bonnie's spine. "My father? But he died. I saw him die."

"So did you, Bonnie, and now you breathe the breath of life."

Bonnie stood upright, now in waist-deep water. The voice did sound like her father's, though younger, more like the father she

133

knew when she was about six years old. "How did you come back to life?"

"I did not say that I came back to life. I only mentioned your resurrection, not mine."

Sapphira clutched Bonnie's wrist. "He's being evasive, Bonnie. I don't think—"

"The other water wader speaks again." He chuckled in a friendly manner. "May I suggest that the one standing on solid ground might be the one making more sense right now?"

"We might as well get out," Bonnie said. "If the ovulum sank, we won't find it until we have some light."

As the two trudged over to the bank, Bonnie felt a strong grip on her hand and a helpful pull. She didn't bother to resist.

The man released her and continued. "Do you know where you are, Bonnie?"

"We've been trying to figure that out, but the dragon—"

"The dragon wouldn't tell you, right?"

Bonnie let a laugh flavor her reply. "He's not exactly free with information."

"It took me a while to learn that lesson." The man's voice grew warm and caring. "Think about it, Bonnie. You saw me die at the hands of Devin, but when you visited Heaven, did you see me there?"

Bonnie's heart sank. Remembering the city of ivory and the streets of shimmering gold should have sparked joy and anticipation, but now, like every time she thought of that holy place, her emotions seemed torn. No, she hadn't seen him there, and ever since that visit, she forced herself to sweep away every thought that her daddy had instead been condemned.

"Your hesitation speaks volumes," he said. Fingers combed back her wet hair, and his voice trembled, filled with sorrow. "Sweet daughter, did you think I had gone to Hell?"

Bonnie swallowed hard. Sweet daughter? It was like an echo, a long lost dream. The words bathed her ears with fresh joy, the

134

joy her images of Heaven should have kindled with every thought. How old was she when her father last uttered that phrase? Four? Five? When her wings started growing, the terms of endearment ended, replaced by ... "Freak of nature," she whispered out loud.

The fingers pulled back. "What did you say?"

Bonnie pressed her lips together again. With tears welling, her voice cracked as her words poured out. "Daddy, you called me a freak of nature. I heard you. I was only about six, but I remember. I was playing with my dolls, and ... " She felt smaller, vulnerable and weak. "You ... you said it to Mama. It hurt. It really hurt a lot. And you never called me your sweet daughter again."

Her tears burst forth. Strong arms wrapped her up. A hand stroked her head and another rubbed her shoulder. "Oh, Bonnie! I'm sorry. I'm so, so sorry!"

She laid her head on his chest and wept. Her hands curled into fists, begging to pound his chest, yet her arms ached to hug him in return. She tried to speak, but her words came out in spasms. "Daddy ... I ... I love you. But ... but you hurt me so bad. When I didn't see you in Heaven ... I wasn't sad ... not really. I just ..." She threw her arms around him and pressed closer. "Oh, Daddy, I love you so much!"

135

The hands continued stroking her head, and his familiar voice, that tender voice from long ago, whispered in her ear. "I love you, too, sweet daughter. Never again will you fear the hateful words that imprisoned you. They are gone forever."

She blinked. Although tears blurred her vision, his shirt came into view. The darkness had faded, not much, but enough to see the man in her arms. She looked up at his face. Yes, it was Daddy. His face was the youthful one she remembered from her younger days. Although tears streamed down his cheeks as he gazed back at her, his eyes sparkled with delight.

"Bonnie," he said, his voice now weak and forlorn, "will you please forgive me?"

She tightened her grip and again pressed her head against his chest. "With all my heart."

As she pulled back, a brisk warm breeze freshened the air. She felt lighter, as though gravity had decreased by half. Even her clothes had given up their dragging effect. Had the breeze dried them that quickly?

With her hand still clutching her father's, Bonnie turned to Sapphira. "Look! It's my daddy!"

Sapphira stood at the edge of the waterfall's pool, her hair and clothes still dripping. "Bonnie, I can't look. It's still dark."

"Dark?" Glancing at her father, she walked to her and waved a hand in front of her eyes. She neither flinched nor blinked, and her pupils stayed dilated. "Very strange."

"That's one of the odd characteristics of this place," her father said. "The residents here have differing perspectives based on what they've learned, or allowed themselves to learn, and their perspectives become reality."

Bonnie looked downstream. The dragon was nowhere in sight. The statue that had nearly come to life stood motionless near the river's edge, and other stony figures marked the landscape both near and far. "Like those statues?"

"So it seems. Most were here before I arrived, but one man showed up later. He soon turned to stone."

"Why didn't you become a statue?"

"I did become one. I met the dragon, and we had a long discussion about truth and how the space-time continuum works. By the time we finished, I couldn't move. Then, when the other man arrived, I was able to listen to the conversation between him and the dragon. It wasn't long before he, too, became a statue, but it seemed as if his arrival somehow allowed me to break free. The dragon shouted for me, but I escaped before I could solidify. My feet began to catch on fire, so I ran through the edge of the river. Ever since, I've just stayed out of the dragon's sight."

"I don't blame you." Bonnie took Sapphira's hand. "Now if we could figure out how to get Sapphira to see, we might be able to search the pool for the ovulum."

Sapphira rubbed one of her arms. "The water is oily, Dr. Conner. Do you know why?"

"I hadn't noticed." He touched her skin and raised his finger to his nose. "It's a strong odor. Could it be camphor?"

After Sapphira smelled the back of her hand, her voice sharpened. "I think you're right!"

"Why the alarm?" Bonnie asked.

"It's the odor of Morgan's witchcraft. I smelled her brews so many times, I couldn't possibly forget. And it's the same thing I smelled when Goliath called to Roxil, back when Gabriel and I were trying to rescue her from Dragons' Rest."

Bonnie's father crossed his arms over his chest. "It seems that I have much to learn about this girl, don't I?"

Setting a hand over her mouth, Bonnie grinned. "I'm sorry. You were never introduced."

After Bonnie explained who Sapphira was, including a rapid-fire sketch of her life as an underborn and her most important adventures, she finished with a loud exhale. "And now we're looking for the ovulum to see if Enoch can tell us what's going on."

"Very interesting." Bonnie's father sniffed his finger again. "Sapphira, you might not be aware of this, but I am trained in pharmacy. It's no wonder Morgan used camphor in her spells. It has many analgesic properties, and, as she and other witches likely believed, it supposedly has spiritual properties. It was used to exorcize an evil spirit and to reduce certain bestial urges."

Blinking again, Sapphira reached for Bonnie. "I can see better now. It's still pretty dark, but I can tell it's you standing there."

"Revelations of truth are opening your eyes." Bonnie's father stroked his chin. "I'm learning as much by your visit as you are."

Sapphira stepped into the pool. "This feels like a portal. My eyesight is getting really sharp." As she lifted a hand, a ribbon of fire sprouted from her palm and spun into a fireball. "Look. My flames are back."

"But you can't light a transporting fire in the water," Bonnie said.

"No, but the camphor oil has a source in this world." Sapphira waded farther out. "With my portal eyesight, maybe I won't have to go very deep to figure out where it's coming from. And maybe the ovulum's down there, too."

"You're diving in?" Bonnie asked.

"Sure. I was hoping you'd come with me." Sapphira blew out the fireball in her palm. "Do your wings keep you from swimming?"

"Actually, they help me, but—"

"Then we should go together, just in case."

"Just in case what?" Bonnie asked as she stepped into the pool.

"I have no idea, but trouble is better faced in twos."

"Or threes." Bonnie's father waded in with the girls. "I have seen strange shadows in this pool. Maybe it was my imagination. Then again, maybe not."

With a jump, Sapphira dove in. Bonnie followed. She opened her eyes and found the Oracle gliding effortlessly downward, her body undulating as if she were a white-haired mermaid.

Bonnie angled her wings and pushed against the water. Like two massive flippers, they shot her forward. Holding her nose, she equalized the pressure and looked back. Her father gave her an "Okay" sign. He couldn't move as quickly, but he could see well enough to follow.

Now about fifteen feet down, she caught up with Sapphira. With bubbles rising from her nose as she hovered, the Oracle pointed into the darker depths. A faint glow pulsed, red in a sea of black.

Bonnie thrust with her wings and shot toward the glow, continuing to equalize pressure as she dove. With her eyes burning and the slimy sensation increasing, the water felt like cooking oil. When she reached bottom, she found the ovulum lodged between two rocky knobs. Tiny bubbles percolated from dozens of pores in the pumicelike floor, popping as they rose toward the surface.

Grabbing the ovulum, Bonnie pulled, but the knobs held it fast. With her lungs aching, she couldn't afford a delay. She pulled again. Still no movement.

Her father lunged past her and grasped the egg. Flexing his muscles, he jerked it free. Bubbles poured out, thousands, big and small. Sapphira joined them, frantically waving her arms and pointing toward the surface.

A shadow loomed over them. As it drew closer, light from above faded. Red pinpoints appeared in the shadow, bright and angry.

Sapphira waved an arm, shouting a warped cry. Her own bubbles blended with the chaotic mix. As her palm swept through the effervescence, sparks erupted. Then, like lightning arcing across the sky, the sparks leaped from bubble to bubble, igniting the gas within.

139

With rising bubbles feeding the storm, a web of electrical pulses surrounded the swimmers. Every popping bubble that struck Bonnie's skin felt like a hornet's sting. All three batted at the swarm. Above, the shadow continued to hover, as if waiting to pounce should the victims swim out of the hive.

Sapphira waved both arms around her body and swept the water in a circle. Bonnie did the same, touching her father with her foot to get him to join in. Soon they created a vortex. As the web of sparks swirled around them, Bonnie's chest felt like it was about to explode. Her body demanded oxygen. She had to breathe … now!

The orbiting web of sparks blurred into long, fuzzy streaks. Soon, everything went black. The oily wetness streamed down her arms and legs, like slippery worms sliding across her skin. She sucked in air. Finally! Although saturated with camphor and garlic, it was the sweetest breath she had ever taken.

Blinking, she searched for her father and Sapphira. She dared not whisper. Who could tell what evil lurked in this dark place? A dripping sound reached her ear, multiple streams hitting a solid floor. She craned her neck. Wet clothes? These weren't her own wet clothes. The drips came from about five feet away.

Taking a step, she reached out and touched someone, a shorter person, soaked, yet warm. Grabbing a handful of wet material, she pulled the person close and whispered, "Sapphira?"

"Shhh," came the reply. "Enoch is speaking to me." As Sapphira turned, the ovulum's glow appeared.

"I'll be quiet," Bonnie said, "as soon as I find my father."

"I don't think he came with us."

"Then he had to face that dark creature we saw?"

"I think so." Sapphira shushed Bonnie again and lifted the ovulum close, still whispering. "Bonnie's here, Father Enoch. Please repeat what you told me."

The prophet's low voice emanated from the crystalline egg, stirring the red mist within, but static blended with the voice, as if the signal came from a distant radio station. "Sapphira asked why the ovulum glowed," Enoch said. "I have been calling you from my viewing room at Heaven's Altar, and my call brought light to the ovulum's inner mist."

The radiance darkened, then sparked with life again, the shifts in power coinciding with the surges of static. "Sapphira told me," Enoch continued, "that your father is present in your current realm."

"Yes," Bonnie said. "There's no doubt about it." Now that her eyes had adjusted to the ovulum's light, she looked around the room. A square of stone walls surrounded them, the closest one maybe four feet away, while the others stood at least five times farther. The near wall displayed rows of ornate columns with indistinct murals in between. The red glow dispersed above, revealing no cap on this stony box of a room, but the lack of moving air gave evidence that some kind of roof sealed them in.

"Very interesting," Enoch said, his voice still distant and scratchy. "Since your father and I never crossed paths at Heaven's Altar, I wondered what became of him, so a few months ago I consulted the Prism Oracle. Dr. Matthew Conner stood in the Oracle's spray without hood, crown, or walking stick, indicating that he had, indeed, passed from life on Earth. But it also means that he was neither in Heaven nor in Hades. I searched the Bridgelands and as much of Second Eden as I could, but I found no trace of him."

"Is there any way you can find out if he's okay?" Bonnie asked. "I mean, did Sapphira tell you about the creature in the pool?"

"She told me. Since your father is already dead, yours was the greater danger. Only those in Hades need fear the second death. My guess is that he escaped unharmed."

141

"Then where are we?" Bonnie asked. "Another afterlife realm of some kind?"

"As one who lives in Heaven's Altar rather than Heaven itself, I have very little access to those who know more than I do. Occasionally I have the opportunity to speak to a passing angel, but they are usually in a great hurry, and my inquiry about Dr. Conner pales in importance to whatever task the angel has been called to accomplish. Still, a Seraph paused for a moment to tell me about a place your father might be, a realm called the Valley of Souls."

"The Valley of Souls," Bonnie repeated in a whisper.

The ovulum's light faded to a bare hint of a glow, diminishing Enoch's voice further. "I had never heard of it. I consulted my books but found no such entry, and I had no further opportunity to consult an angel."

Sapphira breathed another shush. "I hear something." She pushed the ovulum back into her pouch, covering its light.

A dragging sound filtered in, each slide followed by a thump. The noise grew louder by the second, and a throaty grunt punctuated the thumps.

A tiny flame sprouted from Sapphira's finger. "We'd better hide," she said, pulling Bonnie toward the wall. They crouched behind one of the Ionic columns, not quite wide enough to hide them both. Sapphira blew out her flame and whispered "Shhhh." They crouched and peered around the marble pillar, straining to listen.

Slide. Clump. Oomph. Slide. Clump. Oomph.

In a distant hallway, a flicker of orange light appeared. As it expanded, a shadow expanded with it. Draconic in shape, the shadow stretched upward and arched along the curve of a domed ceiling. Below, the creature casting the shadow took shape, a dragon, the same dragon they had seen by the river, carrying a lantern with one clawed hand and a chain with the other.

142

After each step, it jerked the chain, and a trailing object thumped against the floor. As he drew closer, his lantern illuminated a large stone table at the center of the room. About four feet in height and at least ten feet long, it looked like a place for a large family to gather.

The dragon set the lantern on the table. The light danced across an array of three-legged wooden mounts. They looked like stands that might hold a display, maybe a book or a framed photo, but they were empty. A taller mount sat in the middle of the table, also empty. Stubby candles surrounded the central mount, their colors indiscernible.

Giving the chain a final jerk, the dragon brought the trailing object into view—a statue, human in shape and size, apparently one of the figures they had seen near the waterfall's river. The dragon set it upright, carefully balancing it next to the table. With his hands raised, the petrified man seemed to be singing, as if lifting up a psalm of praise.

After looking it over, the dragon breathed a stream of fire and covered the statue in flaming tongues from top to bottom. Like mud streaming from a filthy child, the statue's black coat washed away, leaving behind a flaming man, still frozen in his worship position.

As if thawing from a deep freeze, the man began to slump, his limbs as fiery as Sapphira's when she kept the monkey men at bay. The dragon caught him with a foreleg and picked up a small bottle from the table. After taking out a stopper with his teeth, he poured a single drop on top of the man's head. Dense fog crawled along the man's scalp and filtered down over his face and shoulders. Soon, the fog enveloped his entire body, veiling him and the dragon's limbs completely.

For a moment, all was silent. Then, a huff sounded, and the fog blew away. An egg-shaped crystal about the same size as the ovulum sat in the dragon's cupped hand. He placed it gently on the center mount, picked up a hefty stylus, and scratched something down in a huge open book.

143

After putting the bottle on the table and picking up the lantern, he turned. He sniffed the air. Blue beams, much wider than the narrow lasers other dragons used, swept slowly across the wall adjacent to where Bonnie and Sapphira hid. They crouched low and squeezed behind the column.

The beams passed the corner and began tracing their wall, pausing as they met each column. When the beams reached the girls' hiding place, they paused again, then moved past.

The blue lasers flicked off. Frowning, the dragon turned again and shuffled into the hallway. Soon, with the sound of the dragon's sliding steps dying away, the lantern's aura shrank.

With the dying light still enough to guide them, Sapphira tiptoed out and crept toward the table. Bonnie followed, peering down the hallway. No sign of the dragon.

Sapphira relit her fingertip and touched it to the wick of one of the candles. As its flame sparked, she snuffed her own flame and slid the candle close to the book.

"What about the ovulum?" Bonnie whispered. "Is Enoch still with us?"

Sapphira opened her pouch and peeked at the egg. It was completely dark. "I think we lost the signal."

"Then we're on our own." Bonnie studied the book. Thousands of oddly shaped symbols covered the parchment, more like tiny cartoon characters than letters or numbers. With no apparent rows or columns, the symbols seemed random, a mosaic of scattered shapes.

"I can't read this," Sapphira whispered. "It's a language I've never seen before."

Bonnie touched one of the characters, a birdlike creature. "Maybe it's like hieroglyphics. The pictures represent—"

A string of whispered words rose from the page, strange and guttural. Bonnie jerked her hand away and stepped back. "What was that?"

"It's an old language." Sapphira narrowed her eyes. "Roughly translated, it said, 'Dragon essence recognized. Language recognized. Translation in progress.'"

"Dragon essence?" Bonnie pointed at herself. "It detected that in me?"

"That's my guess. Maybe it's like a password. Only a dragon is allowed to see what all this stuff means."

Bonnie squinted at the page. The symbols darkened and lifted from the parchment, growing and morphing as they elevated. The bird transformed into a dragon with purple scales. Two humans rode on its back, a man and a girl strapped into seats, the girl apparently the pilot as she slapped the dragon's neck and whistled.

Backing away with Sapphira, Bonnie looked at the corridor again. Would the dragon hear the commotion and return? She froze in place, unable to hide. The sight was too mesmerizing, almost hypnotic.

The dragon, about the size of a human hand, flew several inches above the book, which had become a valley scene, a forest with a river running through it. As soon as it landed, the man slid down and helped the girl dismount. After speaking quietly for a moment, they looked up at the sky. Another dragon approached, a white one, also carrying two riders.

The man scooped up the girl, ran into the forest, and stopped at a cave. Trembling, he shouted into the cave's opening. "Oracle! I have come with the sacrifice. Are you there?"

A brilliant light poured from the cave, and someone answered, but the rush of the river and the beating wings of the approaching white dragon drowned out the voice.

The man leaped away from the blazing light. Caressing the girl's cheek, he spoke to her, but again, the surrounding noise made the words impossible to hear.

145

Sapphira tugged Bonnie's sleeve. "I know that man," she whispered. "He's Makaidos, king of the dragons. That's his human form. I met him in Dragons' Rest."

"Enoch told my mother that Makaidos sacrificed himself to save Roxil and Ashley, and now his bones have the power to regenerate." Bonnie edged closer to the scene. "With all the fire and fog, I couldn't tell for sure, but that man looks like the statue the dragon brought in here. If he's Makaidos, his human name is Timothy."

Sapphira joined her. "I thought he looked familiar, too. They're probably one and the same."

"If so," Bonnie said, "it would make sense for the dragon to have the book open to his page."

"But he looked younger when he came out of the statue, maybe early twenties."

"Shhh!" Bonnie pointed at the scene. "Look!"

Timothy held a dagger against the girl's throat. A woman shuffled toward him on her knees, her hands clasped, while another man looked on. Suddenly, Timothy pushed the girl toward the woman and dashed into the cave. The light transformed into a rush of flames. As cries of "Timothy! No!" rang out, the scene crumbled and fell to the page.

Bonnie tiptoed back to the table and touched the book. "Could this hold the stories behind all the people here?"

"That's what I was thinking."

Bonnie studied the page again. Near the bottom, an English entry, penned in lovely script, read:

Makaidos, also known as Timothy. Scheduled to be recalled from the Valley of Souls to Second Eden. Implanted in ovulum. Mounted in transport position. First attempt failed when residents did not call upon him by name. Goliath, also known as Dragon, transported in his place from an alternate ovulum mount. Because of the freedoms granted to Goliath, if he resurrects as a dragon, he will likely retain his memory of his time here and remember that his son also dwells in the valley. Makaidos will also remember this place, but only if those in Second Eden are wise enough to learn of the necessary sacrifice. Otherwise, he will not survive.

She looked at the array of wooden mounts on the table, one holding the egg the dragon had made. Were the others the "alternate" mounts? Could this place be a resurrection portal of some kind? She nudged Sapphira and whispered, "Is your eyesight sharper here?"

"I think so. And I feel a heaviness. It's a portal, for sure."

A flicker of light caught Bonnie's attention. She looked down the hallway. Nothing but darkness.

She lowered her voice even further. "Should we see where that corridor goes?"

Sapphira matched her tone. "I'm thinking the book might tell us. It's safer that way."

"I wonder if it has an index of some kind." Bonnie marked the page with one finger, pressed another finger behind the last page, and flipped to the back of the book. As before, dozens of odd symbols covered the parchment, but these seemed more organized, as if lined up in two columns. She touched a symbol at the top that appeared to be one of the column headings, larger and darker than the entries beneath it.

The book's voice returned. "Destination Earth."

She touched the other heading. Again, the voice rose. "Destination Second Eden."

"Look." Bonnie pointed at the first column. "This list is a lot shorter than the other one."

"I think I'm getting the picture." Sapphira set her finger on a symbol in the Earth column. "Try this one."

As soon as Bonnie touched the entry, the voice responded in monotone. "Lazarus of Bethany. Called back to Earth by the Son of God."

147

She moved her finger to another line.

"Dorcas, otherwise known as Tabitha. Called back to Earth by Peter, the apostle."

Bonnie stared at Sapphira. "This is a list of resurrections!"

"No wonder it's short. There probably haven't been that many bodily resurrections. How many are listed here? Fifty, maybe?"

"Looks like it." Bonnie touched a symbol closer to the bottom, a small bird.

"Bonnie Conner, otherwise known as Bonnie Silver. Called back to Earth by Ashley Stalworth, dragon healer."

Now staring at the mounted egg, Bonnie swallowed through a lump. What could it mean? Had she come to this place? Had she been a statue, dragged to this room by the dragon and placed inside an egg? But how could that be? She had traveled to Heaven.

She had seen Jesus and rested in his embrace. Could it all have been a dream?

She touched the entry again. "I wonder how we can find the right page that will tell what happened to me."

The parchment bent. As Bonnie withdrew her hand, the pages flipped and stopped at a point near the back of the book. She touched one of the symbols, a humanlike figure, and, as before, the characters rose from the page and painted a scene, the quaint village in the sixth circle of Hades, complete with the street, the pitcher pump, and the building where Bonnie and Shiloh tried to escape through an electrified doorway.

In the image, Bonnie, less than a twentieth her normal size, pushed her wing into the doorway, blocking the light. Shiloh leaped through and disappeared. The charge slung Bonnie away, and she tumbled across a road, her limbs and wings flopping wildly. She came to rest in a cloud of dust, gasping for breath.

148

A man appeared out of nowhere, a tall man walking slowly toward her. An aura of light surrounded him from head to toe, much brighter around his face, blurring his features.

The miniature Bonnie called out, "Jesus, help me!"

The man drew closer and sang out, "Contentment holds eternal keys to days of peace that never pass."

As her breathing eased, Bonnie whispered, "Contentment," and closed her eyes.

The man leaned over, scooped her spirit effortlessly into his arms, leaving her dead body behind. He kissed her forehead. "Come, my child, my beloved lamb, and see what awaits you in your final resting place."

As the man held her aloft, the village faded away. Seconds later, a new scene took shape, a dazzling city with streets of gold, gem-coated ivory buildings, and a lush tree heavy with enormous fruit. People strolled along the streets, singing and talking, each one with a brilliant smile.

The man covered Bonnie's mouth with his own, a kiss of sorts, but much more than a kiss, the passing of breath from one soul to another. As he pulled his head back, she gasped and inhaled. As gentle as a first-time father with a newborn, he set her down feet-first. She looked all around, her eyes wide. The man pointed at various people, whispering to her, as if telling her each person's name.

Finally, she turned and gazed at him, her eyes sparkling. "Jesus?"

"Yes, little lamb," he said, extending his arms.

She leaped into his embrace and disappeared for a moment within the light. When he released her, she bounced on her toes. "Am I in Heaven?"

His voice, fine and resonant, seemed peaceful, unhurried. "You are at Heaven's boundary so that I may give you this glimpse of what awaits you. Remember what you have seen, for you will need this vision to encourage another child of mine in the near future."

"So I'm not staying?" Her head drooped a fraction.

Smiling, he set his finger under her chin. "After one of my angels leads you on a brief tour, I will take you to the Valley of Souls where you will await your resurrection to Earth. When you rise, you will not remember that valley at all, for it is a land between the worlds where all events are lost, save for what is recorded in Abaddon's log book."

As if blown by the majestic voice, the book's projected image faded away.

"Abaddon?" Sapphira asked. "That name sounds familiar."

Bonnie rolled her eyes upward as she tried to recall the Scriptures. "In Revelation, Abaddon is the angel of the abyss. In the Old Testament, the name was used side by side with Death and Sheol."

"Do you think he's the dragon?"

"Maybe." Bonnie touched her chin, repeating the words from the vision. A land between the worlds, a place to await a resurrection. So she really *was* here!

149

After finding Makaidos's page again, she kept her finger there and flipped back to the index. "Let's see what the other column is all about." She touched one of the symbols near the center of the list.

"Unborn hybrid," the voice said. "Daughter of Tamara, the former dragon. Killed in the womb."

Bonnie touched the name again. The book flipped back to the appropriate page, but this time, instead of characters, English words spelled out the logged entry.

> This is an unusual case. The female child came to me as a hybrid, part dragon and part human, as if an incomplete metamorphosis had taken place. Although she was weak and malformed, the spirit in her pulsed with a radiance I have rarely seen. Because of her dual natures, I decided not to give her a rubellite ring as I had given the human child who became Angel, that is, the unborn offspring of Rebekah, the former dragon. Instead, I assigned two companions to her, one of dragon essence and one of human essence, and they seemed at odds with one another immediately. I granted one the right to name the child, and it decided immediately, much earlier than the usual one-year standard. Why it chose "Listener," I do not yet know. I then sent the child to Second Eden.

150

"What about my father?" Bonnie turned back to the index. "If he's in this place, maybe Abaddon wrote about him."

Sapphira set a hand on Bonnie's arm. "I thought I saw something, a flash of light down the hall."

Bonnie looked that way. "I saw it earlier. I'll hurry."

She touched several entries in the first column in rapid succession, listening to each name the book announced, but none seemed familiar. Then, beginning at the bottom of the second column, she touched those entries until it said, "Matthew Conner. Killed by Devin the dragon slayer."

When she touched the entry a second time, the book flipped back a few leaves of parchment. Again, the page contained only words.

> After I received Matthew Conner and used my rhetoric to turn him into stone, he escaped, and I have not been able to locate him. Because the land of Second Eden cries out for his medical expertise, he was scheduled to go there at this time of danger. I will continue to search for him, for the days in that land continue to darken. Without him, many could die.

Sapphira jerked Bonnie's arm and hissed, "Someone's coming."

Bonnie flipped the book to Makaidos's page and ran with Sapphira back to the column. As they hid behind it, Bonnie tried to settle her breathing, but to little avail. Knowing now that the dragon was probably the dreaded Abaddon, a powerful angel, her heart thumped wildly.

As before, lantern light drew close and filled the hallway, ushering in the draconic shadow. The new light played on the walls, but something was different, a tiny competing shadow.

Bonnie looked back at the table and gulped. The candle! It was still lit!

She grabbed Sapphira's knee and pointed. With a wave of her hand, Sapphira whispered, "Extinguish." The candle's flame withered and disappeared.

The dragon shuffled into the room and set the lantern on the table along with a large hourglass. His scaly brow arched down. Picking up the candle, he stared at a thin string of smoke rising from the wick.

His blue eyebeams flicked on again. "Intruder," he said with a calm voice, "if you insist on snooping and stealth, then you are

151

proving your lack of love for truth. Those of high character live in the light, unashamed of being seen no matter where they go. I entreat you, in the name of integrity and incorruptibility, make the choice to show yourself, and your punishment will not be pitiless. If you ply a treacherous trade in this domain, you will surely fail, and the injury will come upon your own head. So I will not seek for you. The choice is yours."

CHAPTER

ABADDON'S LAIR

B onnie measured the dragon's words. Of course she wasn't being treacherous, but she didn't want to suffer punishment, severe or not. Yet, if he was Abaddon, he was really an angel, but was Abaddon a good angel or a fallen angel? She couldn't remember if the Bible made that clear.

She looked at Sapphira, who was now staring straight at her. Sapphira raised her hand, as if conveying a stop sign. Silently they agreed to take their chances and wait where they were.

The dragon flicked off his beams and let out a long, "Hmmm."

Turning back to the table, he flipped over the hourglass. Sand trickled through the pinched glass and collected in the lower half, each grain sparkling as if electrically charged.

"The time of resurrection approaches," the dragon said. "When the last grain falls, the ceremony in Second Eden will commence, and those on the table who are called from that realm will rise to resume life there. But what brings life to them will bring strife to others. If you are in this chamber when the table is energized by power from on high, and you are unprepared, you will die." Breathing a spark-filled stream, the dragon turned and walked toward the hall.

When the lantern light died away, Sapphira rose and lit up one of her fingers. "Should we try to open the portal here? That would be the quickest way out, and maybe we could help the people of Second Eden."

Bonnie scooted to the table and eyed the hourglass. At the rate the sand fell, it looked like they had at least several minutes. "We have to get my father to give himself up to the dragon. Second Eden needs a doctor."

"But we'd have to find both your father and Abaddon before time runs out." Sapphira touched the bottle of liquid the dragon used to put Timothy into an ovulum. "We could try to do it ourselves."

"Should we follow the dragon?" Bonnie asked. "Maybe he would help us if he thought I could talk my father into going."

Lighting a fireball in her hand, Sapphira looked around the room. "I don't see any other way to get out, so following him makes sense."

"Then we'd better take this." Bonnie picked up the hourglass. From top to bottom, it was about the size of her head. "That way we'll know how much time we have."

"Fair enough. He probably left it here for us anyway."

Sapphira led the way through the hall. With their wet shoes squeaking on the stone floor, they had to soften their steps. Even the weakest squish echoed in the cavernous corridor.

A warm breeze blew past. Although permeated by camphor and garlic, it felt good as it swept through their wet clothes. Bonnie touched her sweatshirt, merely damp now. The humidity in this place had to be extremely low for it to dry that quickly.

As Sapphira's fireball washed the hallway in pulsing light, Bonnie scanned the surroundings. Vibrant frescoes decorated each side wall—men and women rising from coffins and hospital beds, babies hatching from plant sacs, and a man walking out of a cave, bound like a mummy in linen wrappings.

At the border of each mural, a painting of an open door ushered in the next fresco. The doors were old and wooden with hinged iron knockers, and a dragon ducked his head to pass through. Each dragon at each door carried a lantern at eye level, the glow extending behind him halfway across the previous mural and also forward to meet the glow from the next dragon's lantern. The series of dragons seemed to be a guide to passersby as they walked through the corridor in this museum of resurrection.

Bonnie looked from side to side, trying to find any of the biblical accounts of resurrection. One might have been Lazarus coming out of his tomb, but without labels it was impossible to tell for certain.

Soon, a new arc of light came into view far ahead. As the flickering aura bobbed up and down with the dragon's now familiar gait, Sapphira blew out her fireball. They slowed their pace further.

155

After a few more seconds, Bonnie spotted the dragon. An old wooden door swung out on its own, and he disappeared through the opening, leaving her and Sapphira in the retreating light of his lantern.

A shiver ran across Bonnie's skin. She felt like a character in one of the murals, or a lost museum patron trying to find the exit. It seemed that Abaddon was leading them along. He had even left the door open. They had to keep following. They didn't have much choice.

Still pressing their shoes down quietly, Bonnie and Sapphira kept pace. After traversing another long hall, this one without frescoes, they stopped at a second door. This one was closed, and the dragon's lantern hung on a hook attached to the ceiling. A long shepherd's hook leaned against the wall next to the doorjamb.

With the warm breeze still flowing, the lantern swung lazily from its perch.

Sapphira grasped a metal handle and pushed the door, then pulled, but it wouldn't budge. "Should we look for another exit?"

"It doesn't make sense," Bonnie said. "I think Abaddon was leading us. He even left a lantern here, so why would he give us a dead end now?"

"A test?" Sapphira asked.

"He did talk about a test to prove wisdom."

Sapphira knitted her brow. "Just what we need. We're in a hurry to save lives, and this dragon wants us to solve a puzzle."

"But to him we're intruders. Why shouldn't we have to pass a test?"

Sapphira blew out a sigh. "Okay. Time's running out. What could the test be?"

"Do you sense a portal?"

Sapphira furrowed her brow for a moment before shaking her head. "It seems normal."

"A secret word, maybe?"

"I have no idea what it would be. I doubt that 'Open sesame' is going to work here."

Bonnie glanced at the hourglass. It looked like about a fourth of the sand had drained to the bottom. "How about a series of knocks? You know, the six, nine, thirteen combination you told me about."

"How would Abaddon know about that?"

"It can't hurt to try, can it?"

"It *can* hurt." Sapphira lowered her voice a notch. "He'll know for sure that we're here."

"I think he already knows."

"Okay. I guess it's worth a try." Sapphira stepped up to the door and tapped six times with her knuckles. After a moment's pause, she tapped nine times, then thirteen.

Nothing happened. It seemed that the door glared at them impatiently.

Sapphira picked up the shepherd's staff. "Should I knock with this?"

Bonnie touched the curved end. What could it be for? There weren't any sheep around, and knocking with a staff wouldn't be any different than knocking with a hand, would it?

As she thought, a slight squeaking sound made her look up. The lantern continued to sway in the breeze.

"I have an idea." She set the hourglass down, took the staff, and reached the curved end toward the lantern. With a deft twist, she looped the end through the handle and lifted the lantern from the hook. As she brought it down, she backed away from Sapphira, allowing her to take it.

"I remember now," Sapphira said, holding up the lantern. "The dragon said something about light being a key."

"A key to every locked door." Bonnie put the staff back in place and picked up the hourglass. "I guess we just walk toward the door."

157

Extending the lantern, Sapphira waved it across the door from left to right. With a low creak, the heavy panel swung toward them. Daylight spilled in, though still muted by the gray overcast.

Bonnie shielded her eyes and stepped out into the valley they had left behind. As her vision adjusted, she scanned the scene— grass under her feet, a river only fifty or so paces away, and several statues standing at various places.

Sapphira joined her. "Now to find your father."

The rusty hinges sounded again. Bonnie spun back, but there was no wooden door, just a rectangular hole in the scenery that led into the hallway. When the panel closed, the gap filled in, leaving no sign of the passage to the resurrection chamber.

She tried to touch the invisible door, but her hand passed right through. "How are we going to find this place again?"

"With this." Sapphira set the lantern on the grass. "If we find the lantern, we find the door."

"That might be a big *if.*"

"We'll make a sign at the riverbank."

The two ran to the river's edge. Sapphira fished a grapefruit-sized oblong stone from the bed and drove it far enough into the soft ground to make it stand on end. "That ought to do it," she said, clapping her hands together.

Bonnie nodded upstream. "Let's go. The sand is almost half gone." Holding the hourglass steady, she took off in a trot. As they ran, she searched for Abaddon, but he was nowhere in sight. Within a minute, they arrived at the waterfall. Bonnie stopped at the edge of the pool.

"Daddy!" she called. "It's Bonnie!"

Sapphira looked into the deep water. "No sign of him down there."

Bonnie scanned the sandy edge for footprints. She found tracks leading in but nothing leading out.

"Look!" Sapphira pointed at a long indentation closer to the waterfall. "Something was dragged away from here."

Bonnie and Sapphira followed a trail of flattened sand and grass that ran parallel to the waterfall's cliff. It led into a sparse forest of skinny pines and a few oaks. Since needles coated the ground, the trail was easy to follow. Finally, they rounded a massive oak and found his body sitting upright against the trunk.

"Daddy?" Bonnie dropped to her knees next to him. His clothes felt damp, and his eyes were closed. "Are you all right?"

"He is alive," a female with a French accent replied, "but he is unconscious."

Bonnie turned toward the sound. A teenager sat on a knee-high boulder only a few feet away. With waist-length blond hair, a long white dress overlaid with a brown tunic, and a sword scabbard attached to a leather belt, she seemed to have stepped out of a medieval storybook. A shield leaning against the boulder completed the portrait.

"Who are you?" Bonnie asked.

The girl slid down. As soon as her feet touched the needle-strewn path, her body burst into flames.

Bonnie gasped and stepped back, but Sapphira held her ground, staring.

The girl walked toward them, her beaming face still clear through the flames. Although her feet blazed, the needles didn't catch fire. "I am a sojourner, like your father, yet I am not a fugitive from the dragon." With her hands folded behind her, she leaned to the side as if trying to look behind Bonnie. "May I ask who you are? I have never seen a winged maiden before."

Trying not to tremble, Bonnie drew a wing around to her front and touched the tip. "I guess you could call me a sojourner, too. I'm from West Virginia in the United States."

"I see. And as you have likely guessed, I am from France." She added a gentle laugh, the same laugh Bonnie heard during their search for the ovulum. "I have been told that my English carries my native land's flavor."

Bonnie looked at the hourglass. Two-thirds of the sand had spilled into the bottom. "We have to get him to the resurrection table. Can you help us?"

She gazed at Bonnie's father. "I have watched this one. He fears Abaddon's enchantment and has hidden for quite some time. But all who will rise from the table must willingly come under the dragon's control."

"What about you?" Sapphira asked. "You're not one of the statues."

"Until it is my turn to rise to new life, I have been assigned to watch over the reluctant ones. I am here to show them what they must become, spirits enflamed by an indwelling passion to serve God with body, soul, and mind. You might say that I am an illustration." She withdrew a sword from her scabbard and rested it on her shoulder. "Your father was attacked by the pool's guardian, a stingray of sorts. I rescued him and purged the water from his lungs, but he now suffers from the stinger's poison."

"Poison?" Bonnie reached into her pocket and withdrew Elam's vial. After jerking the stopper out with her teeth, she pushed the top between her father's lips and tapped the bottom, forcing the last drops into his mouth.

She pushed the vial back into her pocket and drummed her fingers against her thigh, watching for the slightest hint of change as she spoke through clenched teeth. "Come on. Come on."

Her father blinked his eyes. As he looked at her, his brow shot up. "Bonnie?"

"Daddy!" She hugged him briefly, then grabbed his arms, grunting as she pulled him up. "Come on! We have to resurrect you from the dead."

Billy felt a nudge. Was it part of his dream? Maybe.

Then again, maybe not. He turned his head. More sleep. He just needed a little more sleep.

The nudge came again. "I'm sorry to wake you, but we have a lot to talk about."

Forcing his eyes open, Billy looked up from his straw-stuffed pillow. "Elam?"

Elam stood next to his bed, dressed in his new battle uniform, an orange short-sleeved tunic over two shirts—a thick, silver shirt with sleeves almost to his elbows and a red one with sleeves reaching to his wrists. "I talked to Ashley. It sounds like you and Walter had quite a night."

Billy scanned the room. Sir Barlow and Candle stood near the open door, their hands loosely gripping the hilts of their swords. Candle's companion rushed through the boy's dreadlocks, making them sway.

"Yeah, we did," Billy said. "How's he doing?"

Elam touched the front of his tunic where a red dragon marching on his hind legs was superimposed over a circle divided into twelve sections, emblematic of the twelve dragons who were called to become humans in the time of King Arthur. "The chest wound is still pretty bad, but thanks to some heroic surgery by Ashley, Steadfast, and you, it looks like he'll be all right, though he'll be laid up for a while."

Billy rose to a sitting position and focused on Elam's face. Although a smile dressed his lips, his eyes seemed far more serious. "What time is it?"

"Almost second hour. That's why I woke you. You said you were going to test the portal with Acacia, so you need to get started. Also, Candle would like another flying lesson, and we have some other business to discuss before the ceremony tonight."

161

"Other business?"

Elam turned and nodded at Barlow and Candle. "Go ahead and gather the men and horses. I'll be at the training field in a few minutes."

"Valiant and Windor gathered them," Candle said. "Dikaios and Ember are already at the field. I thought you knew—"

"Ahem!" Sir Barlow grasped Candle's arm. "Very good, warrior chief," Barlow said. "We will see you at the training grounds." He turned and hustled Candle out the door.

As they departed, Barlow's powerful voice carried back to the hut, fading as they grew more distant. "Never *remind* a commanding officer of something both of you already know. That was just his way of telling us that he wanted to speak to William in private. It is important to learn ..."

Smiling, Elam reached down, locked wrists with Billy, and hoisted him to his feet. "Emerald told me about her guest, the woman who brought her son, the burn victim."

"Right. Semiramis." Billy stretched his stiff back. He wasn't quite accustomed to sleeping on straw. "Her son was pretty bad off. I didn't know what else to do."

Elam patted Billy on the shoulder. "You did fine. Apparently she tells a convincing story."

"You think it's not true?"

"I'm not saying that, but after encountering her at the bridge, I'm not sure what to believe. She tried to get me to go another way, and that would have been the wrong choice."

Billy picked his cloak off the floor and put one arm through a sleeve. "Being wrong about something doesn't make a person evil."

"Trust me. I know. I've been wrong plenty of times. And her story about being betrayed by Arramos makes sense, too, but there are holes she needs to fill." Elam rested his hand on the hilt of a sword protruding from a scabbard at his hip. "Why does she live in the Bridgelands while her son lives in Second Eden? If she has a son who looks about fifty, why does she look no older than twenty-five? Why hasn't anyone here ever heard of the village he's supposedly from? Yet, Hunter has a companion, so it's hard to dispute that he's a true Second Eden resident."

"And she doesn't seem to pose any danger," Billy added. "Clefspeare didn't detect any."

"Neither did Thigocia or Hartanna. They talked to her this morning."

"How about Ashley? Could she pick up anything?"

Elam shook his head. "But that doesn't really prove much. Back when they first met at the bridge, Ashley didn't detect Semiramis's presence. And since Semiramis is somehow able to block her thoughts, Ashley doesn't trust her. If Semiramis didn't have anything to hide, she wouldn't be putting up a shield."

162

"Makes sense, unless Semiramis doesn't trust Ashley."

Elam tightened his grip on his sword, and his voice lowered. "You weren't at the bridge. If you had seen her that day, you would know that my low regard for Semiramis needs no further proof."

They stared at each other for a moment. Billy firmed his chin and gave Elam a nod of surrender. Obviously this thousands-of-years-old warrior had a lot more experience. "I'd better check on Walter." Billy finished putting on his cloak. "Maybe a good pep talk will cheer him up."

Elam grabbed his arm. "Do it when you get back. Acacia and Listener are already waiting at the dragon launching field. And Listener made breakfast for you, so after you wash up, you can get started."

"I guess you're right." Picking up a basin and Excalibur, Billy headed to an area behind the hut, filled his basin from a pump, and hurried to the men's bathhouse, one of two in the village. Although it was little more than a five-station outhouse with wooden tubs for bathing, it had everything anyone really needed. After a quick face wash, he hustled toward the dragon launching field.

As he ran, it seemed that something pulled him back. So many needs beckoned him. How was Walter feeling? What was Semiramis up to? Did anything change in the garden during the night? With Ruth's next attempt to resurrect Makaidos at hand, would the Vacants try to disrupt it?

Billy heaved a sigh. Others would have to take care of those issues. He had his own job to do.

When he arrived at the field, Acacia and Listener had already buckled two seats on Grackle, the purple dragon, and one on Albatross, the white. Listener, wearing a rabbit-hide tunic with a belt that held her spyglass in place, patted Grackle on his flank. "You and Acacia can take him, and I'll lead the way with Albatross."

Billy held out his arms. "Hugs first!"

163

Listener leaped into his embrace, her twin pigtails flying. As he pulled her close, he relished the delightful warmth, even the tickle of her companion as it nuzzled his cheek. In less than a month this sweet little girl had become like a sister, so loving, so innocent, pure joy in a feminine little package.

"So how's the best dragon pilot in all of Second Eden doing this morning?" he asked as he let her down.

She grinned. "Valiant's the best flyer. Everyone knows that."

"Okay. Second best." Billy reached for Acacia and gave her a hug from the side. "Ready to open a portal?"

"I'm not sure." Acacia laid a hand on her forehead. "I woke up dizzy this morning."

He cocked his head and looked into her vibrant blue eyes. "Any idea why?"

"I had an unusual dream. I saw Mardon shining a strange light in my eyes. It had many colors—red, blue, purple, yellow. Even in the dream, I felt dizzy. Then I felt a sharp pain in my scalp, and I woke up. It seemed that someone ran away from me, but my head was swimming so much, I couldn't tell for certain. The dizziness has lessened, but it never went away."

"Are you sure you should go? If you're feeling weak, we wouldn't want you to catch a cold or something."

"I'll be all right." She tightened a belt that wrapped her tunic, jostling a coiled rope dangling from a clip. "I think I'll be warm enough in this."

"I know what you mean." Billy said, giving his arms a flap. "I'm getting used to the cold here. Just a cloak is enough. I think the fireproofing stuff Ashley put on it makes it warmer."

Listener looked up at the cirrus-scattered sky. "It's the clouds. We never got clouds here before, and now it's warmer. But the season of death starts tonight, so everything could change very soon."

"Speaking of cold," Billy said, "did you pack extra clothes in case we get some visitors through the portal?"

"Yes, sir." Listener nodded toward Grackle. Two garment bags had been tied behind his rear seat.

Billy scanned over the village roofs and locked his gaze on the trees bordering the field leading to the birthing garden. "Where's the rest of our firepower?"

"Thigocia was meeting with Clefspeare and Hartanna," Acacia said. "Something about the lady in red and her son."

"What's your take?" Billy asked. "Can we trust her?"

"When I saw her with her son, her love seemed convincing, but I'm not sure." Acacia folded her arms over her chest and looked skyward. "I think we should keep her far from the birthing garden during the ceremony. I'm suspicious about her showing up the night before."

Billy nodded. She was right. The last time they tried to bring Makaidos back, a deceiver prevented it from happening. Semiramis's arrival seemed too coincidental. "My dad will keep an eye on her," he said, "and I'll watch her with both eyes when we get back."

Listener reached into a shoulder bag on the ground and handed Billy a fist-sized roll. "It's berry bread. I baked it this morning."

"Thank you." He raised the warm roll to his nose and drew in its aroma—rich grain, ripe fruit, and something sweet, maybe honey. "What kind of berries do you use?"

"We call them pucker berries, because they're so tart when you first pick them. If you let them ripen on the vines, the birds get most of them, so we pick them early and wait for them to get sweeter before we eat them. Walter says they look like the raspberries from your world."

Billy bit into the roll. "Mmm, good," he said, muffled by his mouthful.

"There's Thigocia!" Listener pointed toward the village. A beige dragon flew over the treetops, casting a shadow on the village's huts. With a flurry of wings, she settled down next to Billy.

The other two dragons, about a fourth smaller, bowed their heads. Albatross seemed nervous, shuddering his wings and even spilling ice pellets from his nostrils. It hadn't taken the dragons of this world long to assume a subservient position to the dragons from Earth, yet their only negative reaction was a hint of fear rather than resentment.

Listener trotted up to Thigocia and touched a stitched portion of her wing. "How does it feel today?"

"I am perfectly well, thank you." Thigocia curled her neck and set her eyes near the wound in her canopy. "I considered asking the seamstress to remove the stitches, but she is so busy making military uniforms, I had not the heart. I would have pulled them out myself, but my wing bonded with the stitching material, so I need the assistance of skilled hands."

Billy touched one of the stitches. "I can probably do it. Mom made me learn how to sew."

"Perhaps later. I can fly well enough, so I will have no problem completing this mission."

"Sounds good." Billy pointed toward the northern forest. "When we get to the highlands, we'll scan the area for Vacants. If all is clear, Grackle and Albatross will drop us off on the plateau and we'll hike up the volcano while all three dragons patrol. Once we're there, our return plan depends on whether or not Acacia is able to open the portal."

Listener whistled a sharp note. Albatross lowered his head to the ground, making his neck into a staircase. Picking up the shoulder bag, she scrambled up to the seat and strapped in. "I've never been to Mount Elijah through the air. This should be fun."

"I agree," Acacia said as she climbed aboard Grackle in the same fashion. She settled into the rear seat. "We can bypass the skunk lizards."

Billy laughed. A month ago, when he went with Acacia, Listener, and her brother, Candle, to Mount Elijah, Candle led Acacia home and took a shortcut through a swampy area inhabited by four-foot-long lizards that sprayed a foul liquid on intruders. Acacia wasn't quick enough and suffered the consequences.

After strapping into Grackle's front seat, Billy wolfed down the rest of the berry bread as he scanned the darkening skies. Clouds rolled in from the east. Though not yet ominous, they might soon obscure the mountain. Traveling by dragon rather than by airplane, however, would simplify matters. They could buzz across the tops of the trees and follow the footpath until they reached the lava field that signaled the approach to the volcano. Once there, they could land anywhere they chose.

Listener had warned him, however, that although the ice-breathing dragons were adept at landing on areas as small as the top of Mount Elijah, the volcano frightened them, so it was much safer to disembark close to the base.

Listener whistled again and slapped Albatross's flank. Beating his wings, the white dragon lifted into the air. Grackle followed, apparently not needing a command. As soon as they rose above the tree line, the top of Mount Elijah came into view far away, its decapitated profile obvious in spite of thin fog veiling the landscape and the miles between them and the volcano.

As expected, Listener kept Albatross on a low trajectory as she leaned over and peered through the thick tree canopy below. Grackle stayed a few feet higher but still close enough to the trees for his wings to fan the tops as they raced by.

Listener extended her finger downward, apparently pointing out a skinny dirt trail through the underbrush, but the rushing wind kept Billy from shouting his understanding. She had found the path and would stick to it for as long as possible.

Billy looked back. Thigocia trailed them, flying much higher as she skimmed the bottom of the thickening clouds.

After nearly half an hour, the trees thinned out, giving way to gray and black lava fields dotted with scrubby trees. With sparse pinelike needles and twisted trunks, they looked like they rarely benefitted from the eclipse-cycle mists that once watered the land.

As light drizzle dampened their faces, the terrain gradually sloped upward, signaling their approach to the highlands, but with the cloudbank now obscuring the mountaintops, and the trail imperceptible in the lava beds, Listener took Albatross down for a landing. Grackle again followed and came to a stop nearby. Both dragons beat their wings and scattered droplets over everyone. Apparently they had not yet learned how to politely carry riders in this kind of weather.

Billy dismounted, and after helping Acacia down, he searched the sky. "Do you see Thigocia anywhere?"

Listener snatched the spyglass from her belt. Peering into the eyepiece, she swept the tube slowly from one side of the horizon to the other. After a few seconds, she pointed. "Over there. I think she's showing us the way to Mount Elijah."

"Okay," Billy said as he tightened his scabbard belt. "Let's hoof it from here."

Listener stroked Albatross's neck. "If Vacants show up, go ahead and leave without us. We'll all ride Thigocia if we have to."

Albatross spat a spray of ice on the ground and blew a series of whistled notes, low and chaotic.

Listener giggled. "That's a challenge to fight. He's telling me he's not afraid of the Vacants."

"Good for him." Billy nodded at the sky, his hair now dripping. "Better keep track of Thigocia. The rain's getting heavier. We don't want to lose her."

Listener raised the spyglass again. "We won't. I can see her red eyebeams."

"Perfect." Billy set a hand on Listener's shoulder. "Keep watching and lead the way. I'll make sure you don't fall."

With Acacia following, Billy and Listener marched across the lava field—furrowed rock that made for good footing as the rain fashioned crooked rivulets in the gaps. Soon the terrain steepened, and the field narrowed. The surrounding mountains funneled wet wind that bit through their inadequate clothes.

Now shivering, Listener stopped and lowered the spyglass. "I lost her. Maybe she's not blowing fire anymore."

Billy pulled her closer. "Thigocia's around somewhere. She would never—"

A sudden burst of wind made them turn. Thigocia landed behind them and shook out her wings. "The path to the volcano is clear," she said, "but the wind is fierce as you go higher. Once you reach the top, a firestorm might be impossible. Perhaps another day would be better."

Billy looked at Acacia. "What do you think? Are you feeling okay?"

She pushed a strand of wet white hair from her eyes. "I don't think my dizziness will affect my fire. I once created a firestorm in a swamp, so I don't think wind will stop me. As long as we have plenty of time to get back to the village before evening, I think we should try."

169

"Very well," Thigocia said. "I noticed an encampment of Vacants on the far side of the mountain to your left, but they seem hunkered down for the weather. I will keep an eye on them."

"It's good to have you around." Billy shielded his eyes as he surveyed the misty landscape. "How far to the base of the volcano?"

"The upward path becomes clear about a hundred paces in the direction you were heading, so you should have no trouble."

Billy nodded. "I'll recognize it when I see it."

"Would you like a Sahara treatment before you continue?" Thigocia breathed a stream of dry air that bathed his face in warmth.

"It feels great, but we'd be wet again in just a few minutes. No use wasting time."

"As you wish." Thigocia beat her wings and lifted into the air. After flying in a low, tight circle, she ascended toward the clouds. "I will be watching."

CHAPTER

A New Lake

Billy withdrew Excalibur an inch or two from its scabbard, then slid it back. Even without a shield, they would have enough protection—his sword, his fire-breathing, and a dragon's flames from above, not to mention the firestorms Acacia could whip up.

With a wave of his hand, he nodded forward. "Let's climb."

After a minute or so, a steep path came into view, smoother than the surrounding lava field. It switched back and forth across a vertical rock face, obviously cut intentionally to provide an easy way to climb the volcano. Although he and Walter had already climbed it before, the misty gloom made it look like a path through the unknown. They could see only several paces in front of their feet, not exactly a comforting view.

Without a word, the trio ascended the path, Billy leading the way as they pushed against the wet incline, and Acacia trailing, one hand on Listener's back.

When they reached the vantage point where he had first seen the Vacants on the volcano's top, he halted. As fog streamed past his eyes, he searched for the flattened cone above, but it was shrouded in clouds. An odd pinch in his gut sounded a weak alarm. Was it danger? To this point only one of his former dragon traits had returned, his fire-breathing, but a tingling sensation hinted that another trait was trying to live again.

"Is something wrong?" Acacia asked.

"Maybe." The cloud at the peak thinned, allowing a veiled look at the top. Nothing. Just the heap of stones still plugging the volcano's throat. He nodded forward again. "I guess it's safe. We can trust Thigocia to watch over us."

When they reached the top, Billy stood at the edge of the rock pile. Although he would have to carry the larger stones himself, most were small enough for the females to carry and throw down the slope. There was no need to call on Thigocia or the native dragons for help. As she had warned, a bitter wind cut across the peak. This would be a pain-filled job.

172

He detached Excalibur's scabbard from its belt and laid it on the ground. "Okay. Let's get to work."

Acacia set down the rope as well as a hammer, an iron spike, and a small roll of mesh, while Listener added her spyglass to their pile. Then, retying their outer cloaks and keeping their gloves on, the trio began clearing the stones.

While they labored in the cold rain, now mixed with snow, Thigocia appeared below the clouds from time to time, her eye-beams bright. During one of her visits, she reported on the encampment of Vacants. They seemed to be stirring, as if getting ready to break camp, so she would keep an eye on them.

After a few minutes, only a few stones remained jammed in the volcano's throat. Hot air rose through the gaps and transformed into streams of white mist as the cold breeze swept it away. Although the wind had diminished somewhat, and the hard work had warmed their bodies, the air brought a piercing chill.

Billy picked up the scabbard and withdrew Excalibur. "Better stand clear." He pushed the sword's point into one of the gaps between the stones.

While Acacia and Listener backed away a few steps and huddled close in the frigid wind, Billy dislodged the stones. They dropped silently for a moment, then a plume of steam burst forth, a brief but vivid surge of white.

Billy scanned the valley. Did the Vacants notice? Would the steam be a signal that might rouse their curiosity?

Gesturing for the girls to rejoin him, he looked into the hole. "See anything?"

Listener peered down with her spyglass. "Yes. I see the tree I saw last time."

"That's good enough for me," Acacia said. "I'll try to open the portal."

While she created a swirling column of fire within and over the hole, Billy drove the spike into the ground and tied the rope to its exposed head. The wind whipped the cyclone of flames but not enough to blow it away from the volcano's throat.

173

"We're ready," Acacia called. "The portal's open. I can see the tree now."

"Just a second." After stretching the rope between the spike and the firestorm, Billy selected a spot near the hole and wrapped the rope with the roll of mesh—a fibrous, asbestos-like netting—covering a three-foot section. He tossed the remaining coil through the wall of fire and into the volcano's throat. When it tightened, the mesh sizzled in the flames, but it seemed to stay intact.

"You first," Acacia said. "Then Listener. Then me."

"You bet." After refastening Excalibur, Billy pinched the fringe of his cloak. "I hope the stuff Ashley painted on these cloaks works."

"It will," Listener said. "She tested it."

"With normal fire, not Acacia's." Billy raised his hood, grasped the rope, and faced away from the hole and its surrounding fire. Listener did the same at a spot two paces in front of him.

"Let's do it," Billy said.

Ducking low, he backed through the fire and began sliding down the rope, glad for the thick gloves protecting his skin. Just a foot or so above, Listener followed. With her spyglass back in its harness, it dangled only inches from Billy's eyes. Obviously this little girl had spent many hours climbing the vine-covered trees of Second Eden. She kept pace with Billy effortlessly, apparently unafraid of the flames that swirled all around them.

As the heat dried his clothes and warmed his skin, he looked down, trying to find a place to set his feet. The fire illuminated the chamber below, the museum room Acacia had told him about. The cylindrical wall of flames enclosed the Tree of Life. Still on fire but not burning up, it would likely be too hot to stay close to it. They would have to move fast.

As soon as they reached bottom, the rope reeled up and disappeared. Billy and Listener burst through the wall of flames and hustled to the museum room's bookshelves. They grabbed one of the tall ladders, and when they pulled it away from the shelf, a scroll of parchment fell to the floor and rolled through the wall of flames, stopping at the base of the Tree of Life. An edge of parchment near one of the scroll's dowels caught fire.

Carrying the ladder, Billy and Listener punched through the vortex and pushed the top of the ladder toward the portal opening.

"It reaches!" Listener shouted.

"Shhh!" Now sweating, Billy leaned the ladder against the edge of the hole above. "Let me get that scroll before it burns up."

Wrapping his fireproof sleeve around his hand, he reached under the lowest branches and grabbed the unlit end. He batted the flames away and hurried back in time to help Listener support the ladder for Acacia.

When Acacia climbed down with the rope coiled over her shoulder, she looked at the scroll. "Why are you carrying that?"

"It fell from the shelf." Billy ran a finger across the scroll's skin. A thin film of white residue coated his fingertip. "This stuff is strange."

"It glows," Listener said.

Billy peeled back the scroll's edge. "Maybe we'd better take a look at it."

"You should move the ladder first," Acacia said, taking the scroll. "It will fall when the firestorm dies away."

Billy pulled the ladder down and dragged it toward the shelves. "Better get away from the tree," he called back. "Your cloak won't keep you from roasting."

As the portal flames dwindled, Billy walked with Acacia and Listener through the museum's exit, a partially broken doorway. When they emerged into cooler air, he mopped a sleeve across his brow. "That plan worked perfectly."

Acacia's brow dipped down. "If I had thought of the ladder last time, we could have avoided a lot of trouble."

"Don't be so hard on yourself. I thought the rope would work, too." With light from the flaming tree illuminating their surroundings, Billy took the scroll and pulled the parchment out several inches. "Most of it is blank, but there are a few lines written in a strange language."

Acacia looked on. "It's in Hebrew. When Sapphira and I took turns going on scavenger hunts in the world of the living, sometimes we were able to pick up scrolls and books that had been discarded." She pointed at a line near the edge. "This says it's from the book of Jeremiah. It must be a Bible text that a scribe was copying. He likely threw it away because he made an error."

Billy touched the ragged edge with a finger. "It's burned up to this point. Can you make out the rest?"

"I'll do the best I can." Squinting, Acacia read, pausing at times as she translated out loud. "Is there no … ointment in

Gilead? Is there no ... doctor? Why then is not the health of the daughter of my people ... restored?"

"Any idea what it means?" he asked.

"Maybe," Acacia said. "It's already damaged. Why don't you tear off that part, and we'll talk about it later."

"Right. We're wasting time." After stripping off the section of parchment and folding it into his pocket, Billy scanned the area. The huge chamber was exactly the way Acacia had described it— big, empty, and lonely.

Acacia reached up and removed a lantern from the sill of an open window. With a nod, she ignited the wick. "Not much oil in this one, but it should last."

"Right again." Billy took the lantern. "Let's make this quick."

Acacia dropped the rope at the door and pointed into the dim chamber. "The exit tunnel is that way."

After adjusting Excalibur in its belt scabbard, Billy lifted the lantern high and strode ahead. He passed under an arch and entered a tunnel, high enough to navigate without ducking and wide enough for all three to walk together. The light flickered on the side walls, revealing dark clefts and caves that gave no hint as to what lay inside.

All three stayed quiet, more from instinct than from fear. It would be senseless to make a lot of noise when they didn't know who or what might be lurking around the next bend.

After passing through another chamber and two more tunnels, they reached a hole in the floor.

"Strange," Acacia said. "This wasn't here before."

Billy stooped. As he peered into the hole, cool air dried out his eyes. At least fifty feet below, a river flowed from left to right, illuminated by the glow of what looked like hardening magma on either side. "An underground spring?"

Setting a hand against the floor, Acacia knelt next to him. "That's very strange. The springs feed a reservoir, but we never learned where it flows out. We had a magma river down there that ran much farther below, and this new river seems to be running in between volcanic residue."

"Maybe the reservoir sprung a leak," Listener said.

"If so, then the water level might be rising." Acacia rose to her feet. "We'd better hurry."

Billy lifted the lantern again. "So what's that way?" he asked, pointing beyond the hole.

"Our hovels and the springs."

"That sounds like a good place to look." Billy stepped around the hole and continued marching along the corridor. Calling for Sapphira and Bonnie, they checked the hovels and the springs to no avail. Further searching revealed a massive collapse in another tunnel.

"No way we can move that many rocks," Billy said. "What next?"

"The mines level." Acacia started back the way they came. "This way."

When they reached a shaft embedded in the wall, Billy grabbed a dangling rope and looked down. "I can't see anything, but I hear water."

Acacia shivered. "I have a bad feeling about this."

Billy spread an arm around her and pulled her close. "Sapphira knows what she's doing. I'm sure she and Bonnie and Shiloh managed to get out. I mean, they're not here. They wouldn't have gone below and let themselves drown."

Acacia let her shoulders sag. "You're right. But now we have to go back to Second Eden without any dragons."

A new voice broke through from the darkness behind them. "Not exactly."

Billy pushed the lantern toward the sound. "Who's there?"

Two women walked into the light, both so saturated, water streamed down their faces, their clothes stuck to their bodies, and

177

their hair dripped. One of the women extended her hand. "I am Rebekah, also known as Legossi." She nodded toward the other woman. "This is Dallas, formerly Firedda, daughter of Makaidos and Thigocia."

Billy took her hand, noting a ring on her finger with a white mounted gem. "Oh, yeah. We met back in Maryland. Sorry I didn't recognize you."

"Our meeting was brief." Rebekah pulled her soaked shirt away from her skin. "And we didn't look like this."

"I was wondering about that. What happened?"

Before Rebekah could reply, Acacia piped up. "Have you seen Sapphira? Or Bonnie or Shiloh?"

"Not lately," Rebekah said. "Shiloh was kidnapped, but that's—"

"Kidnapped?" Acacia raised a hand to her mouth. "By whom? Where did they take her?"

"As I was about to say," Rebekah continued, "that's a long story. The rest of us were being chased by intruders, so Dallas and I hid in the springs. Sapphira was going to find another hiding place for her and Bonnie. She said something about the magma river overlook. When you came into the springs chamber, we heard you calling, but we didn't want to answer until we were sure who you were. It took a while for us to get out of our hiding place, but ..." She spread out her dripping arms. "Here we are."

Acacia pointed at the elevator shaft. "The river overlook is on the mining level."

"I'm going down," Billy said.

Acacia grabbed the rope. "I'm with you all the way."

He handed the lantern to Rebekah. "Keep an eye on Listener, okay? She can fill you in on what's going on in Second Eden, and you can tell us about Shiloh when we get back."

Rebekah nodded. "Will do."

Acacia climbed down the rope and out of the lantern's glow. Billy followed, glad once again he had kept his gloves on as the rope slid through his hands. Now in darkness, he listened for a signal from below, but only the sound of splashing water filled his ears. Finally, he felt a tug on his pants.

"Swing out here," Acacia said.

Billy obeyed. A flash of light erupted in Acacia's palm, a new fireball, shedding a bluish white glow all around.

"This way." Acacia broke into a trot.

As Billy followed again, he watched Acacia's lithe body glide along effortlessly. With white hair and petite frame, she seemed more like a phantom child than an ages-old oracle. He couldn't help but admire her. With unfailing love and steadfast purpose, she seemed so ... so perfect.

Soon, they turned through an archway to the right and stopped at a lake. They stood on a dark beach, a slab of solid rock. Acacia walked to the water's edge and let the tiny waves lap over her feet.

179

"Does this lake have a name?" Billy asked.

She looked back at him, her brow bent with concern. "It's not supposed to be a lake. This used to be an overlook, and the river of magma flowed way down below."

Billy stooped and touched the water. "It's warm. Real warm."

"Can you tell if it's still rising?" She held her ball of flame higher.

Squinting, he scanned the shoreline. By fractions of an inch the water crept higher. "Nothing to make us run out of here, but it's gradually moving up."

Acacia bent over and squinted. "Do you see something sparkling over there?"

"Yeah." He stepped to the water's edge and picked up a string of beads from the shallows. As he drew the string close to his eyes, they reflected Acacia's fire in an array of rainbow colors.

"A necklace?" she asked.

Billy had to swallow hard before he could speak. "It's Bonnie's."

Acacia touched the necklace. Her voice fell to a whisper. "That doesn't mean they didn't get away, you know."

"I know, but she wouldn't have taken it off and laid it here. It's not broken. Something must've pulled it over her head."

Billy stared at the water. A rushing flood could have easily done the job. If Bonnie had been caught in a sudden rush, it might have taken her away in the flow and stripped the necklace off.

Cupping his hands around his mouth, he shouted, "Bonnie! Can you hear me?"

A distant echo replied. *Hear me. Hear me.*

Acacia joined in. "Sapphira!"

Sapphira. Sapphira.

A wave of cold chilled Billy's skin and penetrated his heart. His legs trembled, and his arms fell limp. Again, he had to swallow through his tightening throat. "Do you think they drowned?"

Acacia sat down. Now an inch of water covered what had recently been a stony beach. She pulled Billy down to join her. "Rest for a minute, and we'll talk."

As he lowered himself to a sitting position, the warm water soaked his pants. It felt soothing, like soaking in a luxurious bath. He pulled his sword belt around to keep Excalibur out of the rising lake.

Acacia blew out her fireball and took his hand. All was dark. Only the sound of running water and the gentle lapping of waves against his body gave a hint that anything existed at all.

Still hot from the flames, her skin radiated warmth into his. "Billy, I have been alive for thousands of years. I have seen toil, torture, and cruelty more times than I could ever count. I was even thrown over this very precipice, and I plunged into a river of magma.

"As I fell, complete despair washed over me. Although I was a slave girl, I still had hopes and dreams. Sapphira and I used to read about the upper lands and daydream about going there someday. We would draw pictures of us dancing together under that strange light the people up there called the sun. 'Can you imagine?' we would ask. 'How could a ball of fire hang in an endless sky?'"

She compressed his hand. Her touch felt comforting, soothing.

"Billy," she continued in a lamenting tone, "we had never seen the sky. To us it was a fantasy that someone invented in a story-book. We wanted to believe it. Oh, Billy, we wanted to believe it so badly we would talk about it for hours on end. But when I was falling toward the magma, I remember thinking that I would never see it. There must be no sky, no sun, no upper lands at all. These mines are all there is, and I'm just a slave girl, forsaken and lost. And nobody cares."

Billy felt a tear trickle down his cheek, but he didn't bother to brush it away. "That …" He cleared his throat, trying to steady his voice. "That must've been awful."

"Worse than awful. But I think you know how it feels. You lost Bonnie once before. You carried her dead body through the seventh circle of Hades. It doesn't get much worse."

"I can't argue with that. That was the lowest I ever felt." Finally wiping the tear, he added, "But it turned out all right."

"That's what I'm trying to say. You have a prophecy that says you'll get married. You have to hang on to that."

"Well, that's how we interpreted it. We're not completely sure. Maybe our union won't happen till we get to Heaven."

"Prophecies are often like that. Sometimes they have spiritual fulfillments." She pulled his hand up to her lips and kissed his knuckles. "I trust that yours will come to pass with a physical kiss."

Warmth again radiated through his body. It was a good warmth, a holy warmth. This girl was as pure as an angel.

Again steadying his voice, he said, "I hope so."

She let go of his hand. "Sapphira and I are also the subjects of prophecy. I believe she is destined to wed Elam, son of Shem."

181

With a sudden burst of energy, she clapped her hands. "Oh, that will be a glorious day! She has longed for that day for centuries!"

"What about you?" Billy asked. "Is there a husband in your future?"

Her voice lowered to a whisper. "My lot has always been to serve others. I cannot hope for the blessings of a journey beyond maidenhood, or the adventure a husband and children would bring. I believe I will not see the end of suffering before I pass on to the next world."

"But you've already suffered so much. Doesn't it make sense that God would allow you to have a little bit of joy before you die?"

"Why should we assume this, Billy? To serve is to live. To suffer is to serve better. Why should I hope for more? If God is pleased with my humble efforts, then I am fulfilled. There is nothing else."

Billy shook his head. "It just doesn't seem right. No one has suffered more than you have."

"Not so, Billy." A tiny fireball, no bigger than a dime, formed in Acacia's hand, illuminating her lovely face. "No one has suffered more than Sapphira. No one, save our Lord Christ. And when she takes Elam's hand in marriage, her journey of loneliness will finally come to an end."

Billy gazed into her sparkling eyes, so rich, so filled with mystery. They were pools too deep to fathom, yet he longed to dive in, to gain the ages-old wisdom this fairylike maid had to offer. "You said you were the subject of prophecy, too."

"Just a hint, really." Her brow lifted. "Shall I sing it for you?"

"Please do."

Her eyelids lowered, hiding the deep pools. As she touched the water with a fingertip, her ivory throat vibrated, and a beautiful voice trilled from her pursed lips, seeming to blend with the sound of running water.

Sapphira bends, but will she break?
Depends on Elam's safe return.
For if he fails to bring the ark,
Her life is chaff and soon will burn.

She set the little fireball between herself and Billy. "What do you think?"

Locking on her gaze, he played the words over in his mind, but the song was so cryptic it didn't make much sense. "I ... uh ... I didn't hear your name mentioned."

"I am the ark," she said, pointing at herself. "That's why God made sure I was named Acacia. The ark of the covenant was made of acacia wood, and just as it carried the word of God, I brought Paili to Second Eden to bring a word from God."

"So what does the song mean?"

"Elam asked Enoch about it, but, as prophets sometimes do, he avoided answering. So Elam thinks he has to bring me back to Earth for some reason. Since he's from Earth, it makes sense that a return would be to Earth, and if he doesn't do it, Sapphira's life will burn like chaff."

183

"Sapphira's life? I thought it meant the ark's life."

"The ark's life?" Acacia lowered her gaze. Her lips moved, as if replaying the words in silence. Finally, she looked at him again. "I see what you mean."

Billy tried to read her expression. She seemed puzzled. She had believed an interpretation of a prophecy that had been guiding her thoughts and motivations, hoping somehow to be used by Elam to save Sapphira's life, but now that interpretation crumbled, leaving her without a foundation.

"Well," he said, trying to build her up again with a livelier voice, "one thing I've learned about prophecies is that sometimes you just have to wait and see what happens. No sense in banging our heads against the wall trying to figure them out."

"I suppose that's true." As a tear traced down Acacia's cheek, her voice trembled. "Will you pray for me?"

He took her hand in both of his. "Of course. What do you want me to pray about?"

"That God will give me the courage to do what I have to do."

He rubbed his thumb across her knuckles. "What do you have to do?"

"I cannot tell you. I think I know the prophecy's meaning. Your question has brought it to light."

"My question? How?"

"Please." Tears dripped to her lap as she squeaked, "Please don't ask me again."

"Okay. I won't." As he looked at her, wave after wave of emotion crashed over him. This great prophetess, packaged in a diminutive body, was breaking his heart. She had asked him to pray, but how could he? Praying with Ashley hadn't been so hard; she was a friend, a fellow Earthling. But Acacia? She was a thousands-of-years-old Oracle, an otherworldly creature that transcended understanding and even mortality, almost like an angel. And how should a regular guy pray for an angel?

184

Finally, he decided. The best prayer would be a short one, straight from the heart.

Caressing her knuckles again, he looked into the darkness above and spoke clearly. "Father, you have watched your faithful servant Acacia for thousands of years. No one needs to remind you of what a brave, noble, and sacrificial person she is. She has served you faithfully in Hades, on Earth, and in Second Eden. Now, after listening to your voice from three different worlds, she believes she knows how she's supposed to fulfill a prophecy, and the thought of it makes her heart quake. Please let her know if she's right or wrong. Help her to clearly see the next step she should take. And I ask that she not become chaff to be burned, because ..." His throat tightened, pitching his voice higher. "Because we would ... *I* would miss her terribly."

After swallowing, he breathed a quiet "Amen."

Acacia leaned forward and kissed him on the cheek. "Thank you, warrior, for lifting your sword for me." Her whisper was weak, yet it carried a hint of relief, as if a burden had been lifted from her shoulders.

"It's an honor." He forced a tone of resolve into his voice. "Let's get back to the others. They'll be worried about us."

"Okay."

Still holding her hand, he rose to his feet and helped her up. "Before the night is over, we should have three new dragons in our army, Legossi, Firedda, and Makaidos."

She took the necklace from Billy and, using her non-fiery hand, pushed it over his head. "And who knows?" she said, touching one of the beads now dangling just below his throat. "Maybe a certain dragon girl will show up, too."

185

12

CHAPTER

SAND IN THE HOURGLASS

Bonnie pushed her shoulder under her father's arm on one side while Sapphira helped from the other. He seemed groggy. Although he stood well enough, his weight sagged their shoulders a bit. Since his eyes wandered, he probably hadn't fully recovered his wits.

Bonnie looked at the girl who had rescued him. Although flames created a fiery aura all around her body, her face shone through, peaceful, joyous. Bonnie nodded toward the hourglass sitting on the ground. "Will you get that for me?"

The girl glanced at it. Now only a fifth of the sand remained in the top half. "I see no reason for carrying a time-keeping device," she said. "If watching it would increase your speed, then your passion for completing your task is based on a wisp, an illusory figment called time, something you can neither capture nor contain. And time is a wicked taskmaster."

Bonnie narrowed her eyes at the girl. Blond, lithe, and beautiful, she seemed far calmer than the situation demanded. "Look," Bonnie said, trying to keep her voice steady, "if we don't get to the resurrection chamber before the sand runs out, it will be too late. Abaddon said so."

"That is easily solved." The girl knelt and pried the top off the hourglass. Then, looking up at Bonnie and Sapphira with a coy grin, scooped a handful of sand and poured it into the top half. "There," she said, pushing the top back in place. "The sand will not run out soon."

Heat surged into Bonnie's ears. What was wrong with this girl? She didn't appear to be a simpleton. But what could they do now? Their way of telling time was ruined.

The girl stood and, flashing a bright smile, showed Bonnie the hourglass. "Do not be dismayed. In this realm, solutions to problems are not what you would expect. My action was a prayer for more time, and if it had not been granted by our Lord, I would not have been able to do it." She set the hourglass in front of Bonnie's feet. "Go in peace, Bonnie Silver. You have proven your faith while inside the candlestone, and you will be tested even more severely in coming days. Yet, you are precious in God's sight, so the sands of your hourglass will not run out before the purposes of God are fulfilled."

Bonnie squinted at her. Not only did this girl rescue her father and apparently buy them more time, she seemed to know everything about her. "Who *are* you?"

The girl curtsied. "You may call me The Maid."

"Thank you … uh … The Maid." Bonnie tried not to frown. Calling her that name was clumsy, to say the least. "I appreciate your help in rescuing my father, but if you knew who I was, why did you ask earlier?"

"Revelation comes to me in strange ways." As she tilted her head slightly upward, her fiery hair swayed at her waist. "If you stay here long enough, you will learn."

Sapphira grunted under the increasing weight of their load. "Do you have a litter or something we can transport him on?"

"Perhaps." The Maid hurried back to the boulder and picked up her shield. She laid it on the ground and waited at a distance while Bonnie and Sapphira lowered Bonnie's father to a sitting position on it. Laying a gentle hand on his head, Bonnie looked into his eyes. "Can you sit here okay, Daddy?"

His head still wavering, he whispered, "Yes, I think so."

The Maid spread out her arms. The flames made a whooshing sound as she moved. "Remember, he must surrender to Abaddon willingly, for only the dragon can prepare him for the journey that lies ahead."

Bonnie nodded. "I understand, but how will we find Abaddon?"

"I do not know." Smiling, she touched the base of the hourglass with her toe. "Remember the lesson of the sand, and let wisdom guide you."

"I see." Bonnie studied the shield. There was no rope to pull it, and no way to tie a rope to the shield even if she had one. She could try to fly while holding him, like she did with Billy and a few others, but her father was taller and more muscular, probably too heavy. There seemed to be only one option. "If we push him, your shield will slide easily on the ground, correct?"

189

"Oh, yes, Bonnie. You really *do* understand, don't you?"

"And once we get back to the river," Bonnie continued, "the shield will float, even under my father's weight."

The Maid clapped her hands. "Excellent! I had not even thought of that."

Smiling, Bonnie locked gazes with The Maid. Sincerity poured forth from her youthful face, along with a blend of complete confidence and deep faith. This was a girl after her own heart, yet The Maid's exuberance wasn't as contagious as her confidence.

Bonnie sighed. "It doesn't work that way in our world, at least not all the time."

"Sadly, no." The Maid drew close and hovered her flaming hand over Bonnie's cheek. Warmth flowed over her skin. "Enjoy it while you are here. There will come a day when every desire of your heart will be granted without even a prayer, for you will be in the Messiah's presence, and his light will fill the temple."

"Does that mean Sapphira and I can leave this place just by wanting to?"

The Maid laughed again. "Oh, that prayer won't be so easy to act out. It is not the same as pouring sand in an hourglass or sliding a shield. If it were, I would have departed long ago. Still, I am content to stay and serve in whatever way I can. Abaddon and I have a working relationship you might call …" She rolled her eyes upward, searching for a word. "Tolerable, I suppose. Since I work for him, I thought he might stop trying to turn me into a statue."

"How did you keep from changing into one?" Sapphira asked.

The Maid's brow wrinkled. "Why would you ask me such a question? Since you have also escaped that fate, surely you know."

"We didn't die to come here," Sapphira said. "I thought that was the reason."

The Maid laughed gaily. "Oh, no. That is not the reason. But if I tried to explain the method, surely my words would endanger you, for the seeking of this knowledge would handicap your efforts."

"But you know the method," Sapphira said, "and you're not a statue."

Bonnie looked down at Sapphira's feet. Mud again caked her legs from her knees downward. She grabbed Sapphira's arm and pulled, forcing her to move. As before, the mud crumbled away.

"We should leave now," Bonnie said. After setting the hourglass in her father's lap, she laid her hands on his back and pushed. At first, he budged only a few inches, but when Sapphira joined in, the shield glided easily through the woods and out to the river.

When they stopped at the river's edge, Bonnie stepped around to the front and looked at her father. His head had stopped wobbling, but his eyes looked glassy. "Are you all right?" she asked.

Blinking at her, he whispered, "Bonnie?"

"Yes, Daddy. It's Bonnie."

"Is your mother home yet? I made lunch. Grilled cheese sandwiches and tomato soup."

Shaking her head, Bonnie dipped a cupped hand into the river and drew out some water. She washed his face with it, though much of the water dribbled down his shirt.

Sapphira carried two handfuls of water and splashed his face. He shook his head hard, slinging drops all around. Then, looking up at Bonnie, he gasped. "The pool! You got out!"

"Welcome back!" She kissed him on the forehead. "Yes, we found a portal that led us to a chamber where dead souls are resurrected from this realm, and we need to get you on the schedule right away."

"The schedule?"

"To get resurrected."

Giving her a confused look, he picked up the hourglass. "What's this?"

"I'll tell you about it in a minute." Bonnie grabbed his wrist and hoisted him to his feet. He staggered for a second but quickly gained his balance.

"So ..." He kept his focus on the sand running through the hourglass. "If I get resurrected, where would I go?"

"To Second Eden," Bonnie said. "They need a doctor there, so the dragon wants to transport you."

"A doctor?" He gave his head a rapid shake. "I haven't practiced in years, since before you were born."

Taking his hand, she gazed into his eyes as she spiced her voice with a lamenting tone. "But they need you there. At least you'll be better than no doctor at all."

191

"I'm not so sure of that. Sometimes a bad doctor is worse than no doctor."

She hooked her arm around her father's and leaned her head against his shoulder. "Did one of your medical decisions hurt someone?"

He lifted his head and gazed at the sky. For a moment it seemed that he wouldn't answer at all. Finally, he looked at her, his eyes glistening. "A little girl died. I thought she had the flu, so I sent her home with the usual liquids and bed rest regimen, but it turned out to be bacterial meningitis. Of course, I went to her funeral, and when I walked to the front to express my condolences, her parents wouldn't even look at me, much less speak." Shoving his hands into his pockets, he let out a sigh. "I quit my practice the next day. I couldn't take it. But I swore that I would dedicate the rest of my life to finding ways to stop suffering and somehow cheat death."

Bonnie looked at the hourglass. There was still plenty of sand at the top. "And that vow led to your experimenting with dragon blood."

He pushed a hand into his pocket and nodded. "I thought we had found the key to a long and pain-free life, but it wasn't until the day of my own death that I saw how much suffering I caused you and your mother. I could never make that up to you."

"Maybe you can." She pulled him forward. "Come on. This will be a chance to redeem yourself."

He followed with halting steps. "What do I have to do?"

"When we find the dragon," Sapphira said, "you have to surrender to him."

He stopped in his tracks. "And become a statue?"

"If need be." Sapphira hooked his other arm, and the two girls forced him to continue. "Maybe he won't have time to turn you into one."

As they followed the river's gently meandering shoreline, he gathered his strength and regained his senses. He provided more details about the girl who died and continued lamenting about how much suffering he had caused.

Bonnie listened patiently. It was probably better to let him vent than to try to talk him out of his sorrows.

When they reached a shallow stream, a tributary for the larger river, he hopped over it in a single bound before reaching out from the other side to help the girls. His chatter grew livelier for a while, but when Bonnie explained The Maid's way of giving them more time, he became silent and stayed that way for the rest of the journey.

Soon, they arrived at the spot where they had set the oblong stone. Turning toward the ridge of highlands, they walked to where the door should have been and searched for the lantern in the ankle-high grass, but it was nowhere in sight.

Bonnie stopped at a point that looked familiar. Although the grass was uniform in consistency and color, this spot seemed a little flatter than the surrounding area. Maybe this is where they had jumped out of the corridor. "I'll bet Abaddon found the lantern," she said. "Maybe he took it back inside."

"Probably." Sapphira brushed her foot along the grass. "It was his lantern, so why not?"

Bonnie set her hands on her hips and looked at the hills in the distance. "There's got to be a way to figure this out. If adding sand to the hourglass bought us more time, this place must allow for the most unusual solutions. We should be able to solve this new puzzle."

"So how does it work?" Sapphira asked. "I'm not very good at coming up with illogical solutions."

"Maybe it's like this. Think of the simplest way to solve the problem, something that doesn't seem like it would work. Then give it a try."

Bonnie's father raised a finger. "You mean like a child's solution?"

"That's exactly what I mean. If you have to get to the resurrection chamber before the sand runs out, add more sand."

"So what do we do if we have to find an invisible door?" Sapphira asked. "That doesn't seem quite as easy."

Bonnie's father set the hourglass on the ground. "My guess is that once we solve it, we'll wonder why it seemed so hard, just like adding sand does now."

"How about if I just open it?" Bonnie reached into the middle of the air, hoping to grasp a knob, but found nothing. "Well, so much for that idea."

"Light from the lantern opened it last time." Sapphira lifted a ball of fire in her palm. "Let's see if my light will work."

"But if we don't even know where the door is, how will your light open it? We had to stand close to the door before it opened last time."

Sapphira waved her ball of flames back and forth. She painted the grass with a wash of yellow light, easy to see under the dismal sky, but no door opened.

Bonnie stepped in front of Sapphira and into the fireball's light. Her shadow appeared on the grass, a winged girl shrouded in black. She whispered, "I think I know how to find the door."

"How?" Sapphira's firelight dimmed. "Should I—"

"No!" Bonnie waved a hand at her. "Keep it going! Stronger, if you can."

New light blazed, arcing over Bonnie and clarifying her shadow. Off to the left and several paces away, another shadow loomed, not as dark, but still recognizable as a rectangle, skewed into a diamond shape by the light's angle.

"We find the door by locating its shadow." Bonnie stepped toward the dark diamond, curling her finger to signal for Sapphira to follow. As she neared, the shadow straightened in the moving light. When it drew a perfect rectangle on the grass, Bonnie raised her hand.

Sapphira halted, stopping the light's progress.

Bonnie set her toes a few inches in front of the shadow's edge and reached out. Her fingers passed through where she thought the door would be, but her hand's shadow disappeared. "It's here. Bring the light."

Holding the hourglass once again, her father walked with Sapphira to the spot. As the light closed in, it drew a yellow circle on and around Bonnie's hand.

Bonnie eased her hand back. A low creak sounded as the door swung away from them.

For a few seconds, the hinges continued squeaking a half-hearted complaint, then, all was silent as the three stared at the doorway that had appeared out of nowhere.

Bonnie stepped inside and nodded toward the ceiling. "The lantern's not there."

Her father and Sapphira joined her in the narrow corridor. Sapphira's flame blazed and painted the ceiling and walls with Bonnie's larger-than-life shadow. Her silhouette looked like the dragon guide who haunted the museum's frescoes.

She glanced back at the hourglass in her father's grip. If they hadn't put more in, the sand would have run out long ago, but even now it seemed dangerously low. Although The Maid had added a good deal more sand, she hadn't filled it beyond the bottom glass's ability to capture every grain. Overfilling it would probably have violated the rules of this place. Still, it would run out soon, and there would be no sand to gather here.

Now walking abreast, they passed through the hall of frescoes. Strangely enough, the dragons in the murals were again walking in the same direction they were, opposite of the way they were facing during their previous visit.

Bonnie shivered. This was all too weird to believe, like the creepiest nightmare of all time coming true.

Soon, they passed by the mural depicting the mummified man walking out of a cave. Sapphira blew out her light and whispered, "We're close to the chamber."

As darkness shrouded them, the trio crept along, Bonnie's father leading the way. A light appeared in the distance, reddish and flickering as it moved from left to right across their field of vision.

When they reached the end of the hall, they crouched and watched the scene in the chamber. Abaddon carried the lantern to the table in his clawed hand. With a red flame burning inside the smoky glass, the glow looked more like thin mist than light, as if fog had settled into the room and created a blood-tinged haze.

As soon as he set it down, his blue eyebeams flicked on. They knifed through the red mist, creating purplish rays that scanned the wall adjacent to the exit corridor. When they moved to the corridor itself, the beams sliced through the darkness above Bonnie's head.

196

She held her breath. Should they just stand up and announce their presence? If her father was going to surrender to him, maybe that would be the best plan. Still, it wouldn't make sense to reveal everyone. If Abaddon meant them harm, it would take only one of them to find out. The others could escape.

She touched her father and whispered, "Stay here and watch closely."

He grabbed her wrist. "I can't let you face that dragon without me."

"Just trust me, please. I've dealt with a lot of dragons."

Pulling away from his grasp, she picked up the hourglass, rose to her full height, and marched forward, letting the blue lasers strike her chest. "I am Bonnie Silver, and I am surrendering myself to you, Abaddon, and to your mercy. The first time I came, I was an unwilling intruder, drawn here by a portal at the bottom of a pool. This time, I have come, not as an intruder, but as a wanderer seeking counsel. As a lover of truth, I am sure you understand my motivation."

Abaddon's eyebeams turned off, and he gave a deep, throaty laugh. "Well, well, the winged wonder has shown herself. Why did a lover of truth forsake asking me for counsel during her first foray here?"

"I was confused, scared, and soaked to the skin. I wasn't sure what to do. I thought you might be angry."

"Ah, I see. You projected your own feelings upon me, judged my character, and deduced my response to your innocent intrusion." His brow lifted. "Are those just actions? Are they in keeping with the truthfulness you cherish? Are you not a hypocrite for casting such shadows upon me?"

Bonnie took a step closer to him. "I hope you will pardon my boldness, but I have been in the company of dragons before, one in particular who did everything he could to get me to doubt my character. I will not be tempted to do that again."

197

Twin plumes of smoke rose from his nostrils. "If you speak of Arramos, indeed, he is a crafty creature." His ears rotated, as if alerted by a sound. "As you must have noticed, I am not he."

"I apologize for any lack of respect." Bonnie dipped her knee as if offering a curtsy. "If I have understood your book correctly, you wish to prepare Matthew Conner for resurrection."

He again raised his scaly brow. "Ah! So you have also intruded upon my personal journal. You who are so confident in your character, how do you rationalize your rashness?"

"You left it open. I assumed it wasn't private."

"Private? If you left a diary open in your bedroom, would you consider it a violation if someone walked in without warning and pried into your prose?"

"I would never write anything that I wouldn't allow others to see. My mother has read every word I've written in my diary."

"Your mother? Not your father?"

Bonnie's cheeks burned. She ached to look back and see her father's expression, but she dared not.

"Your silence speaks truer than trumpets, and since you already know my name, you must have read more of my writings than what you saw on the open page. Indeed, I am addressed as Abaddon. As one who is a serious student of the Bible, you must have heard of me."

Bonnie offered the slightest of nods. "I have."

"Many think of me as an evil being, a crafty creature, especially those who believe in tall tales." He spread out his wings, broad, thick, and muscular. "I am the fifth angel of Revelation. I hold the key to the abyss, and I am the king of the punishers that lie therein. One day I will leave this place and bring God's wrath upon the wicked people of the Earth." His blue eyes flashed. "I am destruction."

Bonnie swallowed. Had any dragon ever looked so strong, so noble? Maybe he really was an angel of some kind, an avenging angel. She cleared her throat and spread out her own wings. "Excuse me for not understanding who you are. Since we've never met, I—"

"Oh, but we have met, my pet. Did you not find the entry in my journal? Did you resist the temptation to mollify your meddlesome nature? If so, then perhaps I have misjudged you."

She fidgeted. She was losing ground to this dragon, and losing it fast. Steeling her resolve, she looked him in the eye. "I found the entry."

"Then you know that you have voyaged through my valley before." Abaddon touched the ovulum on the central mount with the tip of his wing. "I set your soul in this very spot and sent you back to those who love you. From the depths of her heart, the healer Ashley called you from this place and restored you."

"So, is that the key to resurrection? Someone calls you?"

"When the Lord called for Lazarus, and a girl called for Goliath using his human name, and tiny companions in crystalline eggs called for their charges using names of wisdom, they rose in answer to the heavenly empowered calls."

Bonnie tilted her head. "Goliath's human name? I don't understand."

"His abode was in the abyss, a most unpleasant place in this realm, reserved for those of evil intent. When the slayer killed him, he came to me in dragon form, a foul creature, and I cast out the Nephilim nesting within him and sealed their spirits in the abyss. He transformed into a human spirit and was sent to Second Eden, the place of new birth. There he lived for over a hundred years as a man of manners, becoming a fine father and holy husband, and, as is true with most who pass through this valley, he maintained no memory of his visit.

"When he died in that life, he came to me again, still as a human spirit. Michael the archangel told me that Goliath, or Dragon as he had been renamed, must have another opportunity to withstand the workings of the evil Nephilim. He had failed the first time, but perhaps his experiences as a man of nobility had regenerated his resolve.

"This test of character was crucial, and it would likely be his last chance to prove himself. So, he was sealed in the abyss with the evil spirits and without a Second Eden companion to help him. Our plan was to keep him there for only a short time, but when I opened the seal, he had already transformed to his dragon self, as malevolent as ever."

Abaddon finished with a long sigh. "In fact, Goliath conspired with Arramos to deceive his former mate in Second Eden. As a result, she took of that world's forbidden fruit, which led to the further fouling of the land."

Bonnie glanced at the hourglass. Even with the extra sand, it was almost empty. This dragon's long story had wasted a lot of time. Still, he seemed to be in no hurry. "How soon till the next resurrection takes place?"

"I have not kept count of any time elements." He extended his neck, bringing his head so close, his hot breath stung her cheeks. "It seems that *someone* has taken my hourglass."

She lifted it to his eye level. "I assumed I could take it."

"You assume a great deal. I merely said that the chamber would be energized when the sand is spent. I said nothing about anyone taking it."

"It's about to run out now, but there's no room to add any more sand."

"It seems that the simplest solutions elude you." Abaddon took the hourglass, flipped it over, and set it on the table. "Now we have plenty of time."

Bonnie's face again flamed. This crazy world was getting crazier by the minute.

"Now, where was I before I told you about Goliath?" Abaddon's snout pointed at the ceiling for a moment. "Oh, yes, your diary. We both know why you never showed it to your father, do we not?"

200

Again she resisted the urge to look back. Could her father hear everything? Would Abaddon reveal her secrets? Maybe it was better to stay quiet. He probably wouldn't wait very long before continuing.

"Shall I recite for you some of the secrets you shared during your previous visit here?"

Bonnie tried to reply with a formal air, hoping she could convince him. "There is no need for that. If we are both aware of my diary's content, what good would it do to give it voice now?"

"You are a lover of truth, but you seem to have forgotten how powerful words can be. They pierce. They penetrate. They both break and bind. Let us test them once more and see if your incisive lament is the sword of a slayer or the scalpel of a surgeon."

Abaddon shuffled to the opposite side of the table and flipped through the pages of his journal. When he stopped, he touched the surface with his claw.

As before, a three-dimensional image rose from the book, this one depicting a bedroom with pink and purple striped wallpaper. A winged girl lay on the bed, a pen in hand as she wrote in a spiral journal.

Nausea curdled Bonnie's stomach. The scene was all too familiar—her thirteenth birthday, the night the slayers killed her mother. Her father had drawn her blood that day, yet another attempt to further his longevity experiments, though he had promised so many times not to do it again. He had broken his promise only hours earlier and callously filled another tube from her arm.

As the Bonnie in the image picked up the journal and read her entry silently, her voice came through, the tone matching the emotion in her words.

Dear God,

I descended into the shadowlands today. A specter of fear wrapped his cold, cruel fingers around my heart and led me into his chamber of treachery, a sanitary cube of torment that once again enclosed my mind in darkness. Can any instrument of torture deliver cruelty as savage as love betrayed? Does a dungeon's rack stretch a body as sadistically as betrayal stretches trust? Can faith endure a traitor's sinister hand as it turns the wheel, each notch testing conviction until the sword of despair separates peace from its rightful habitat?

He bared my skin. He pierced my flesh. He robbed more than my life's blood; with his brazen face and callous dismissal, he robbed my innocence. He shattered my image of a father's love.

Once upon a time, a tall, strong knight took my little hand and led me to the edge of a cliff. Comforted by his powerful grip, I felt no fear, for this valiant knight would never let me fall. Below lay the jagged rocks, the raging river, and a thousand feet of cold, empty air. As I leaned over the precipice, the joy of beholding danger with unflinching eyes flooded my soul. I have an anchor. I have a sure hold in the land of promise. My father would never let me go.

Yet, he did let me go. Nay, he pushed me over the side. And now I fall, staring up at him as he coldly walks away. The wind chills my heart, and the certainty of eternal torment rushes at me with no savior in sight.

God of wonders, catch me now in your loving hands. Fly down on your stallion and rescue me from this plunge into despair. Let us ride together, buoyed by wings of faith and energized by the love that delivered your only begotten son, for he is the king who catches his falling sparrows. Let us waltz together in this dance of death, for you have called me to suffer with you in willing sacrifice and to burn the image of your crucifixion in my heart. Let us live together in the light of your resurrection, for I cannot survive this walk of faith without the comfort of knowing that you will never let go of my hand.

You are Jehovah-Jireh, my provider in times of trouble. You are Jehovah-Shalom, my peace in the midst of turmoil. And above all, you are Jehovah-Shammah, the God who is always there, a true father who rises to my aid when the specter has taken off his fatherly mask and exposed his treacherous heart.

Ask me for my blood, and I will give it freely. Yea, ask me for my life, for you have already crucified me on Calvary's hill and raised me from the dead, purging the life of sin I left behind. Ask me for my soul, for you have already paid for it with your own precious blood, the holy blood of Jehovah-Yasha, my savior.

And now I see it. I can give you nothing that you have not already given to me. I am purchased, a slave of love. I am your vessel to be used in whatever way you wish. If you make me an urn for ashes, a common earthen jar to bear incinerated bones, leaving me to collect dust in a forgotten tomb, even then, I will be content. For just as you would not leave your son forever in the ground, I know you will raise me up from the land of the dead. You have not ignited

202

this fire in my heart to be wasted in Sheol's pit. Though dead, buried, and forgotten, I will rise again.

No matter what happens, I will never forsake you, for you will never forsake me. You are with me, no matter where I go.

Love,

Bonnie Conner

The projected Bonnie laid the journal down, and the image faded away.

The real Bonnie wept. The words brought back every tortured memory, the pain of every needle that gouged her skin, the scarring of her soul that only savage betrayal can leave behind.

Abaddon looked on quietly, giving no hint of emotion. As Bonnie tried to stifle her sobs, the sound of weeping continued, as if stirred up in an echo behind her. This time, she had to look.

Her father strode out from the shadows, tears streaming. Not bothering to wipe them away, he held up his hands. "I am the traitor," he said, his voice quaking. "I am the one who pushed Bonnie off the cliff."

203

Abaddon nodded slowly. "Does your posture mean that you are giving yourself up to me?"

"I'll do anything to make up for what I've done. I was supposed to be a doctor, and I gave it up because a little girl died on my watch, but instead I became a torturer, a torturer of my own daughter." He covered his face with his hands, unable to control his sobs. "I am such a fool."

Bonnie ran to him and wrapped her arms around his chest. "I love you, Daddy." She rocked back and forth with him and cried. "Will it help if I say, 'I forgive you' again? I'll say it a thousand times!"

"You *were* such a fool," Abaddon said. "My sources tell me that you finished your life as a hero. You forsook your foolishness and embraced the faith your daughter so valiantly lived in front of you, in spite of your betrayals."

"What good is that?" He kept his gaze low, his head bobbing. "I died! I couldn't make up for all the harm I did. I couldn't stay around and be her daddy."

"Since you have acquiesced to my authority over you, I can now prepare you for a potential resurrection. You will not be able to abide with your daughter yet, but you might have the opportunity to, as you say, make up for all the harm you did."

Bonnie drew back from her father. "A potential resurrection? You mean, he might not go?"

"It depends on the decisions the Second Eden dwellers make. If they do not call for a doctor, the fuel that gives this place the power to send him there will not be set aflame."

Bonnie checked the hourglass again. With most of the sand now in the top half, she had plenty of time to figure out her next step. Fortunately, Sapphira had stayed put. She was smart enough to figure out that Abaddon might not be aware of her presence. If he had decided that Bonnie was the only intruder, Sapphira was free to roam without suspicion.

"Okay," her father said, spreading out his arms. "I'm yours, Abaddon. What do you want me to do?"

The dragon's eyes flashed blue. "For months now you have avoided becoming a statue, because you had no idea how important that initiation was in your preparation for resurrection."

"How could I know? You never told me."

"You refused to listen and learn." Abaddon pointed a claw at him. "You ran and hid."

"I was turning into a statue, and when I ran, my feet started catching on fire. Wouldn't you run from whatever was causing that?"

Bonnie looked down at her father's shoes. Thin smoke rose from the toes and heels, and they seemed to glow.

"We were discussing truth," Abaddon continued. "One must never run from such revelations."

"Even if I'm about to burn? I would suffer excruciating pain and then become a pile of ashes."

"Or so you say, yet you have seen a fiery resident of this place. She neither cries in pain nor burns up, and every statue holds another flaming soul who lives on without suffering. So it is your false perception you fear. If we were to strip the solid shells, to outsiders, the inhabitants of this land would appear to be unapproachable apparitions, sources of discomfort, fit only for viewing from afar or perhaps in videos viewed in museums that display such oddities for parents and children to ponder with head-shaking disapproval. Yet, the one who sees from within the fiery body observes others with new eyes. He sees beyond the blinders that most men wear, some willingly and some in ignorance. The inferno's eyes foil façades and unmask the heart, stripping away lies, pretense, and cultural correctness that cause men to live the lie, though they really do not believe the lie at all. Those who fear this flame value acceptance and approval above truth."

Bonnie glanced down again. Now her father's shoes had sprouted flames, and they crawled up his pant legs.

"That would mean that seeking and believing truth is penalized," her father said. "You have to give up freedom to interact with others."

Abaddon gave him a grim nod. "In the fallen world, yes, this is true. Every man and woman who ever plied truth's trade learned this awful fact. Once he or she strips off the outer shell to try to interact with others, the inner fire becomes clear. From Jeremiah to Joan of Arc, one who treasures truth beyond all things becomes a pariah or a paragon, either of which makes him or her hated with passion or admired from afar, and therefore friendless until the day of martyrdom."

Bonnie's father looked down. Now he knew that flames had

205

enshrouded his legs, but he didn't seem to care. "So what's the purpose of doing this here, I mean, in this valley of souls?"

"To train *your* soul. When you resurrect, you will remember your time here for only a short few moments, but your mind will be prepared for the heartache that accompanies the martyr's path, for no one who resurrects from the dead can ever return to a normal life. To others, you will be considered a prophet or a demon. There is no middle ground."

"So be it." As the flames reached his waist, he lifted his arms, grimacing at the heat. "I am ready. Send me wherever you wish me to go."

"It is not I who sends. It is the one who calls. Both you and another will be ready to go, and either one of you will be able to help in the perils the people face, but I do not know which of you they will choose. Yet, I will prepare you, both by the fire that now envelops you and by these words, which you will remember only while your feet are firmly planted in the garden."

As the flames rose to his chin, Bonnie's father tilted his head upward, like a drowning man reaching for air. Agony strained his voice. "Speak, Abaddon. I am ready."

"Heed my words, Matthew Conner. The death of a little girl and the blame you heaped upon yourself have seared your heart, creating scars that enabled you to cruelly punish your wife and another girl. By this fire, I burn those scars and peel away their remains."

The flames covered his face. His fiery head still tilting upward, he screamed loud and long.

"Your heart will be raw, vulnerable, bleeding. If the Second Eden dwellers call you to resurrection, they will ask you to do something that you will not believe you are able to accomplish. Fear will grip your newly wounded heart, causing pain beyond words, and you will be sorely tempted to deny their request. Yet, you must accept immediately. If you delay, you will soon forget my warning, and all will be lost."

His fire-wrapped body now heaving, he nodded. "I will … try."

Abaddon opened the bottle he had used earlier, tipped a drop out onto his hand, and touched the flaming head. As before, a shroud of fog enveloped the fiery body, and when it disappeared, a large egg sat in Abaddon's grasp. "Now you will await word from above."

Inside, Bonnie's father cried out so loud his words penetrated the glass. "Call to me, and I will answer you."

His glass shell radiating orange, he lowered himself to a sitting position. The words repeated again and again, fading each time. His fingers stood out clearly as they pressed against the inside wall.

Abaddon set the egg on one of the table's mounts. "His suffering is great, but it is only temporary."

"Temporary?" Bonnie raised a hand to her mouth and bit her finger. It was terrible! Her father was suffering so much! And there was nothing she could do about it. Nothing.

She looked at the hourglass. About half of the sand had passed through to the bottom. What did that mean? Fifteen minutes? Twenty? However many, with Daddy in so much pain, it would seem like hours. And what of Makaidos? Surely his pain was just as great. When would one of them be able to go to Second Eden?

Abaddon set a wing tip on Bonnie's shoulder. "It is time for you to go. When the call comes, the room will be swept with fire, and only those already in flames will survive."

13

CHAPTER

PIERCING A GEM

With the coil of rope in hand, Billy reached the top of the ladder and emerged back in Second Eden. He pulled the hood over his head and jumped through the wall of fire. Working quickly, he tied the end of the rope to the iron stake, reeled it out, and tossed the other end into the volcano's throat, making sure the mesh still protected the rope.

Listener climbed to the top of the ladder and leaped through the fire, grinning. "I feel like Superman."

"You've been listening to Walter's stories, haven't you?"

"Superman, Batman, and Spiderman." Squinting, she looked up at him. "Are there any women superheroes?"

As Acacia's snowy head appeared, Billy nodded toward her. "You'd better believe it."

Acacia stood and waved her arms inside the fire ring, keeping the cyclone going. When Dallas and Rebekah climbed to the top of the ladder, Acacia looked at Billy. "It's time to close this door."

He checked the knot at the stake. "It's secure. Let's do it."

While Dallas and Rebekah stood inside the fire circle and looked on, Acacia stepped down a few rungs and, hanging on tightly to the rope, kicked the ladder until it slid away. She climbed back up, grunting and slipping. Rebekah reached down, grabbed Acacia's tunic, and hoisted her the rest of the way.

The fiery vortex slowed. As soon as the flames cleared, a plume of gray vapor rose from the volcano. Mount Elijah was once again open.

Billy helped Acacia reel the rope back into a coil. "I saw you write something on a scroll down there," she said. "What was it?"

"Just a note telling what we did and who we took with us." He shrugged. "I don't know if it'll do any good, but maybe someone will find it."

Dallas wrapped her arms around herself. "This place is freezing," she said, her teeth chattering.

Billy stripped off his cloak and tossed it to her. "That should help for now. We'll call Thigocia and get you a Sahara treatment right away. We brought some extra clothes, but we'll have to wait until we find our passenger dragons before we can get them."

Looking up, Billy shouted into the sky. "Thigocia, are you up there?"

Twin lasers cut through the clouds. Seconds later, the tawny dragon dropped into sight. Since five people now stood on the volcano's top, she had to perch on part of the demolished wall that once covered the cone while slowly beating her wings to keep her balance. "I see that we have new arrivals."

"Mother!" Dallas leaped forward and clutched Thigocia's foreleg. "It's so good to see you. We hardly had a minute to speak after our resurrection."

Thigocia sniffed Dallas's hair. "Ah! Firedda! My gentle one!" As she rubbed Dallas's back with her clawed hand, she looked at Rebekah. "And is this my granddaughter, Legossi?"

With a frigid wind whipping her blond locks, Rebekah bowed her head. "It's a joy to see you again, Thigocia, yet I notice you did not call me a gentle one."

Thigocia gave her a toothy smile. "Warriors like you and myself are rarely called gentle, my dear."

"Thigocia," Billy said, "can you give us all a Sahara treatment and take these two to Grackle and get them the clothes we brought? The rest of us will hoof it back."

"Very well. They can mount here, and we will meet you at the rendezvous point, though I will watch over you along the way. The Vacants are on the move, but I cannot tell if they will take a path toward us or to the river."

As Dallas rejoined the others in a huddle, Thigocia took in a deep breath and poured out a jet of hot dry air through her mouth and nostrils. All five humans spread out their arms and basked in the flow. After four repetitions, everyone was dry and toasty.

With freezing drizzle still falling, Billy nodded at Dallas. "Keep the cloak. I'm getting used to this place, and Grackle can heat up his scales for me."

211

Dallas hugged the cloak close to her body. "I am grateful for your chivalry."

Rebekah nodded toward the volcano's throat. "Are you going back to the mines with explosives to blow a hole in the escape tunnel?"

"Probably in the morning," Billy said. "When we resurrect Makaidos at the ceremony, we'll tell him everything that's going on. Maybe he'll have other ideas."

After Rebekah and Dallas mounted and flew away on Thigocia, Billy, Acacia, and Listener retraced their steps down Mount Elijah's switchback trail. With every footfall, an unsettling feeling in his stomach grew stronger, a stewing swill that raised foul odors in his throat and into his nostrils.

When they reached the lava field, Billy grasped Excalibur's hilt at his hip and scanned the ridges on each side, both partially veiled by fog. "I sense danger."

Listener looked into the clouds with her spyglass. "I don't see Thigocia anywhere."

"If I sense it, then she probably does, too." Billy withdrew his sword. "Come on. Let's get to the dragons."

Now jogging with Acacia on one side and Listener on the other, Billy searched through the mist, watching for Vacants as well as for any sign of the Second Eden dragons. Did they fly away, perhaps trying to escape from the enemy? Might they be circling somewhere overhead?

Listener stopped and pointed at the ground. "Here is where we left them."

Billy joined her and studied the rippled rock. "How do you know?"

"White-spotted scat." She nudged a pile with the toe of her boot. "Normally Albatross goes in the woods. He must have been scared."

Billy nodded. "I get the picture."

While Listener again peered through her spyglass, Billy turned in place, scanning the skies again. "We're sitting ducks out here. If we don't see a friendly dragon soon, we should head for the woods ourselves."

"They likely fear you and your sword," Acacia said. "The Vacant who escaped surely told them of your skill."

"Maybe. But I'll bet they're afraid of an Oracle of Fire. They see a powerful warrior at my side."

"I will do what I can." A ball of flames appeared in each of her palms, sizzling in the mix of snow and drizzling rain. "At least we can try to keep them hiding in their holes."

"A dragon just dove out of the clouds!" Listener called.

Billy swung toward her. "Where?"

She pointed at the ridge to the north. "Behind that hill."

A loud growl erupted from that direction. Orange firelight painted the clouds, like flashes of lightning within the mist.

Billy spread out his arms, his sword in one hand. "Get ready. Thigocia's attack might flush them out."

"Should we flee to the woods?" Acacia asked.

"They might already be there by now. We could get ambushed." Billy grasped the hilt with both hands. "I'd rather see what I'm fighting."

Listener put her spyglass back in its holster and withdrew a six-inch dagger from her belt. "Candle taught me how to fight, too."

Suppressing a laugh, Billy gave her a wink. "We'll need all the help we can get."

Listener pointed at a pass in the hillside. "Here they come!"

A line of soldiers poured through the gap, running with swords drawn and spears raised. Fog obscured the landscape. Billy couldn't tell who they were, but his danger sensors sounded a loud alarm.

At least twenty soldiers ran straight toward them. Soon their identity became clear. With small fish-like mouths and big dark eyes, there was no doubt about it.

"Vacants," Billy said. "A bunch of them."

As another dozen Vacants stormed through the pass, Thigocia followed, two riders on her back and her wings beating as she flooded their rear flank with a streaming firestorm. Two Vacants at the back erupted in flames, and a third fell on his face in the lava field. A purple dragon trailed Thigocia, spewing ice on the field, and a white dragon followed, adding another coat of frost.

Acacia stepped out in front of Billy and Listener. She wrapped her arms around herself, then thrust them out to her side and shouted, "Ignite!" White flames shot from her hair and hands, and waves of bright blue sparks coated her body from head to toe. As her fire blazed, her entire body shook, and her face twisted into a pain-streaked grimace.

The leading line of soldiers slowed, their black eyes wide. One charged ahead, screaming a strange word as he raised a curved sword.

Billy jumped in front of Acacia. Excalibur met the monster's sword with a loud clank and broke it in two. He ducked under the Vacant's arm and, with a deft spin, swung his sword into its waist, cutting deeply.

As the Vacant collapsed, Thigocia flew over. "One more pass ought to do it!" she called.

While she made a tight turn, somewhat slowed because of her riders, Billy looked back at the army. More than half were either in flames or blackened and lying on the ground. At least ten retreated toward the hills, but while they slipped on the now frozen ground, the other two dragons coated them with sprays of ice.

Five remaining Vacants charged. Acacia threw flaming balls at two and set their clothes on fire. Billy leaped ahead and cut through the leader's spear at its grip, then with a backswing lopped off his hand. Lowering his shoulder, he rammed into the Vacant and sent him flying backwards.

Thigocia flew over and scorched the fourth with twin jets, but the fifth ducked underneath her fire and dashed by Billy.

With a quick leg thrust, Billy tripped him. The Vacant staggered a few steps before falling to all fours in front of Acacia. Grunting, he raised up, thrust his spear into her leg, and yanked it back out.

Acacia fell backwards. Her flames vanished. Listener dropped to her knees at Acacia's side, while Billy ran toward them.

Still on his knees, the Vacant thrust his spear again, this time through Listener's arm and into her ribcage.

"No!" Billy screamed. Fire spewed from his mouth and splashed over the Vacant's body. Then, he swung Excalibur with all his might and sliced off the Vacant's flaming head.

As Listener toppled backwards, Billy caught her in his arms. "Oh, dear God!" he cried. "Not Listener!"

Her chest heaving, Listener looked up at Billy with glazed eyes. "I ... I'm hurt."

He kissed her forehead. Tears dripped from his cheek to hers as he gasped, "Yes ... but you'll be okay. You'll be ..." He couldn't finish. As blood leaked from her arm, cruelly pinned against her side, he wept.

"Do not remove the spear!" Thigocia shouted as she landed. "Her only hope is to leave it intact until we get her to a surgeon."

Rebekah leaped to the ground and helped Acacia to a sitting position. Dallas followed and dragged the Vacant's burning body away.

Blinking away tears, Acacia reached for Listener's hand and caressed it. "Fear not, precious one," she said, her voice quaking. "We'll get you to Ashley."

"I ..." Listener swallowed. "I'm not afraid. I thought I was going to die by Timothy's hand, and I wasn't afraid then."

Billy looked up at the weeping sky. "God! Please help us! Don't let this little girl die!"

215

Albatross landed next to Thigocia. Ice crystals dripped from his eyes as he looked at Listener, whimpering.

"Albatross," Thigocia said in a commanding voice. "Take Rebekah to the village and find Ashley. We will need something to cut the spear's handle."

"And we will bring a stretcher." Rebekah grabbed Albatross's strap and vaulted to the pilot's chair. "Let's fly!"

Letting out a loud trumpet call, Albatross leaped into the air and flew toward the village.

Thigocia looked up at the purple dragon circling low overhead, apparently watching for more Vacants. "Grackle!" she called. "Follow Albatross. We might need another transport. I will stay here and keep everyone warm."

Grackle beat his wings hard and charged after the white dragon. Soon, both disappeared in the fog.

Thigocia covered Listener with a wing and breathed a warm wind over her shivering body. "Try to calm yourself, little one. The more you shake, the more damage you might do."

Acacia scooted under the wing and pushed her fingers through Listener's hair. "Do you remember what you told me this morning?" Acacia asked. "The story about finding the spyglass?"

Listener nodded.

"And the song you and Candle made up about it?"

She nodded again, this time wincing.

"May I sing it for you?"

As her eyes closed, she offered another weak nod. "I would like that," she whispered.

Acacia looked at Billy, then at Dallas. "When you figure it out, please join in."

After clearing her throat, Acacia gazed into Listener's eyes and sang.

> My prayers go up;
> Your love comes down;
> You make me smile
> On days I frown.
> Our Father above
> Sends us baskets of love,
> The blessings from his heart.

As Acacia repeated the song, Billy joined in, barely able to whisper the words. But when he saw Listener's lips bend into a weak smile, he reached for more strength and gave it all he had. Soon, Dallas and even Thigocia joined them, the pattering of rain acting as a rhythmic beat.

More snow mixed in. A bitter wind blew. Billy shivered. He looked at Excalibur's blade, still wet with the Vacant's dark blood.

216

It wasn't enough—the sword, his skills, his wisdom in planning for battle. Nothing in his power could have kept this sweet little girl from such an awful fate. And nothing he could do would restore her ravaged body. Saving her now would take a miracle.

When the song ended, he looked up at the cascading flakes of white and whispered, "My prayers are going up, Father. Please make this precious one smile again."

Marilyn sat on the tunnel's cold stone floor and leaned against the rocky wall. It wasn't the most comfortable seat in the world, but with her arms and legs aching, it was a lot better than nothing.

Gabriel stooped beside her and set a box searchlight on the ground, pointing it down the long tunnel. The high-powered beam illuminated Yereq and two former dragons as they rested nearby.

"Any other ideas?" Gabriel asked. "Think they found a portal or another way out?"

She shook her head. "No ideas. Let's wait for the diver to come back. If he comes up empty-handed, I'll try to think again. My brain's just too tired right now."

"Well, you already know what I think about his chances."

Marilyn bit her lip. Gabriel was probably right. If they had drowned, their bodies would probably be under several layers of hardened magma by now. And with water rising to within a few feet of the top level, every access would be cut off soon.

"I have some great news, though." He unwound a scroll a few inches and showed her the parchment. The leading edge was charred, but the hand printed text, written in dark pencil, was bold and easy to read. "Check this out."

Marilyn leaned closer and read the carefully printed words.

This is Billy Bannister. Acacia and I took Rebekah and Dallas to Second Eden. We couldn't find anyone else. We'll try to come back tomorrow.

217

Underneath the text, Billy had drawn a sketch of himself and a dragon, both spewing fire.

She took the scroll and hugged it to her chest. Billy was alive! And so were Acacia and two of the former dragons. As tears welled in her eyes, she whispered, "Thank God."

"I heard water running while I was in the museum chamber," Gabriel said. "It's dry in there, at least for now, and a tree's on fire, but it's off by itself so it's not hurting anything. A ladder had been pulled down from the shelves. I guess they used it to climb through the portal."

She clenched her fingers around the scroll. "And we missed them!"

"Yeah, I guess they were here while we were buzzing around in the helicopter."

Marilyn nodded. She was about to ask why Yereq hadn't seen them, but then remembered the huge new hole in the escape tunnel's rubble. Obviously, Yereq had spent most of the time working on the opposite side of the rubble heap. If Billy and Acacia had ventured that way, they wouldn't have seen him from inside the mines.

She read the scroll again. It seemed so wondrous and filled with life, and it communicated so much more than what the simple words said. The drawing meant that Jared was alive, too, or else Billy would have mentioned losing him.

"So," Gabriel said, "assuming the diver doesn't find them, what's the next step?"

"Keep working on Apollo, I guess. We don't have another portal opener."

"Right. That should work great for getting into Second Eden." The muscles in Gabriel's forearms tensed. "But we have three missing in action. What about them?"

Marilyn looked into his fiery eyes. He wasn't ready to give up any of the girls for lost. But how could anyone guess where they were now? Shiloh was in the hands of dragon slayers, who apparently sent their goons back to get the former dragons, and it seemed that Bonnie and Sapphira had simply vanished.

She reached out and took Gabriel's hand. "I don't know what to do. Do you have a suggestion?"

"We have their chopper and some partial names. I'll bet we can find enough clues to get a good start."

"We'll need Larry for that," Marilyn said, "so we should get home and feed him the information."

"Only after we scour the helicopter for data, and maybe by then Mr. Foley will be well enough to travel. But we can't wait around too long. Whoever sent the chopper might come looking for it."

"I'll call Edmund and see what he can do about keeping Carly at my house for a while. If they can make progress on Apollo without us there, staying here for a couple more days should be fine. No matter what happens, if Billy's coming back tomorrow, we have to wait for him."

Gabriel pointed at the floor. "And Yereq will stay longer and keep searching. He can't fit in the airplane anyway."

"And I'll camp out in the museum room. I don't want to miss Billy."

"If it's not flooded."

"Right. That could be a problem." Marilyn touched Gabriel's cheek and changed her tone, hoping to communicate confidence. "We'll find them. You know that, don't you?"

He firmed his lips and nodded. "I know."

"But something else is bothering you."

"Well … nothing important. At least nothing that anyone can do anything about."

"Tell me anyway," she said, pulling on his sleeve. "Just getting it off your chest will help."

He rocked from his crouch to a fully seated position. "I'm working like crazy trying to save everyone and get the world back to normal."

"Yes, I know. You've been wonderful."

"But do you know what will happen if we succeed?"

"I'm not sure what you mean. Some kind of trouble?"

Gabriel set his fingers together and let them spring apart. "Poof! If we separate Earth and Hades, Gabriel loses his physical body and becomes nothing but light energy."

Marilyn covered her mouth. "I forgot about that!"

"I can't say I blame you. This world merging thing is pretty crazy. And the only place I can have a real body will be in Hades. I don't know about you, but that's not even a nice place to visit, and no one would want to live there."

"We'll find an answer. Between Sapphira and Acacia and Enoch, someone has to know how to make you permanently whole."

"Maybe." He stayed quiet for a moment. Then, his voice spiking in anguish, he said, "And what if they do solve it? Will I have to live life as a freak? How could anyone ever love a teenaged senior citizen with dragon wings?"

Marilyn took his hand. Intertwining his fingers with hers, she kissed his thumb. "Oh, Gabriel. I know who brightens your eyes. I know who makes your heart flutter. Everyone does. And she's also a teenaged senior citizen."

Redness colored his cheeks. "I guess I haven't hidden it very well."

"There's no need to hide it. Who would ever say you're too young for romance? Shiloh has to know that you'd make a wonderful husband."

"I'm glad you think so." He pulled a wing tip in front of his eyes and rubbed the leathery canopy. "But would she want to marry a freak?"

"If you insist on using that term, then I'll oblige." She pointed at herself. "I'm a freak, too. I married a former dragon. And of course, my husband's a freak, and so is my son." She began counting on her fingers. "Bonnie's a freak for obvious reasons, as is Sapphira, Acacia, and even Shiloh. Who ever heard of a girl surviving for forty years eating only a poisonous plant? And she didn't age a day!"

Gabriel let a thin smile break through. "Okay. You got me. But there's still the light energy issue to deal with."

Marilyn climbed to her feet and reached down a hand for Gabriel. When they locked wrists, she hauled him up with a strong pull. "You feel solid to me, and if we have to move Heaven and Earth to keep you that way, we'll do it."

221

IS THERE NO BALM
IN GILEAD?

Billy pushed a finger through Listener's hair, no longer braided in her usual pigtails. Someone had brushed it out and splayed it on the soft pillow beneath her head. Lying on an elevated cot, her face pale, her skin soft and smooth, she looked like a sleeping angel. Yet, every few seconds, her lips puckered, and lines dug into her forehead, signs that pain tortured her unconscious brain. This angel was being tormented.

Standing next to Billy, Sir Patrick read the pressure meter. "Eighty over forty, William. The rate of decrease is slow, but it is dangerously steady. Her internal bleeding must be significant."

Billy looked down at Elam as he sat on a nearby cot. "Did you hear that?" Billy asked.

Elam nodded, his face as pale as Listener's. "How much longer does she have?"

223

"At this rate of blood loss?" Patrick looked up at the ceiling for a moment as if calculating. "Perhaps two hours. It is difficult to be certain."

As tears welled in his eyes, Billy moved his hand to Listener's arm, now bandaged and resting under a three-inch wooden stub, the new end of the spear. Earlier, Rebekah sawed it off and Steadfast withdrew the severed end from Listener's arm. Steadfast was able to patch up the wound in the fleshy part of her bicep, but the more dangerous puncture through her ribcage still lay untouched.

Covering Listener's bare chest up to her collarbone, a white sheet was turned up at the side to expose the wound. Listener's companion floated just above her hand as it rested on her stomach. Emanating a pale blue light, the companion blinked at a tube that protruded from her skin, leading to a bag of blood hanging from a hook attached to an upright wooden pole. Valiant, after learning that his blood matched Listener's, had donated as much as Ashley would allow. And since five other villagers also matched, they still had donors eager to help, yet, at the rate Listener was fading, it seemed hopeless.

As blood oozed from her side down to the lower sheet, Billy glared at the sawed butt of the spear. He had been too slow, too confident, too stupid. Why had he allowed her to go with them? Why hadn't he taken her to the forest when the Vacants came into view? Sure, an ambush was possible, but he could have hidden her somewhere and fought those beasts alongside Acacia. Risking a child was stupid. It was criminal.

Raising a clenched fist, he muttered under his breath. "I should have taken that spear and—"

"William?" Patrick grasped Billy's wrist. "Are you punishing yourself?"

Letting out a long breath, Billy slowly loosened his fingers. "I guess so."

"May I suggest that we concentrate on what we must do now rather than what we have done? A very important decision must be made without delay."

Billy shifted his gaze to Listener and kept his voice low. "You mean, surgery?"

"If we fail to make the attempt, she will die."

"But who could do it without killing her even faster?"

"Our best chance is Ashley. Steadfast told me he can brew an elixir that will give her a burst of energy. It won't last long, and it will make her recovery take longer, but she might have enough strength to give surgery a try."

Billy looked at Ashley lying on a cot next to Walter's. She had stripped down to shorts and a T-shirt, and no blanket covered her flushed body. Pearl knelt on the floor and mopped Ashley's bare arms with a sponge. If Ashley hadn't attempted a healing, Listener would have died hours ago. At least they had bought some time.

"But Ashley's never done anything like this before," Billy said. "Not even close."

"I suggest consulting with Elam and Valiant. They must make the decision soon."

"I guess you're right." Billy shuffled over and sat next to Elam on the cot.

Elam buried his face in his hands. "Now what are we going to do? If I wasn't so stupid …" His voice faded away.

Billy laid an arm over Elam's shoulders. "Don't kick yourself." He glanced at Sir Patrick. He was listening, his knowing smile indicating his pleasure at hearing Billy pass along his words of wisdom. "We should concentrate on what we have to do now," Billy continued. "You made the right decision."

"The right decision?" Elam jumped to his feet and spun back toward Billy. He waved a hand toward the other cots in the triage hut. "Ashley's fever is a hundred and five. Acacia's hurt, her flames

225

are spent, and she's supposed to energize the bones in less than an hour."

Billy said nothing. It was probably better to let Elam give himself a swift kick in the pants, in spite of what Sir Patrick had said.

Running a hand through his mussed mop of hair, Elam lowered his voice to a whisper. "She'll probably die anyway, and now we can't call for Makaidos. Everything's messed up."

Billy lowered his voice as well. "Sir Patrick said we have to make a decision. Do we give Ashley an artificial energy boost so she can try surgery, or do we just let Listener die, probably in the next two hours?"

Elam stayed quiet for a moment before answering in a whisper. "I didn't know about the energy boost. We should give it a try."

"But there's another option I haven't told anyone yet." Billy licked his dry lips, unsure of how to explain his idea. It sounded crazy even to him. "When we go to the garden tonight, maybe instead of calling for Makaidos, we should call for a doctor."

"A doctor?" Elam gave Billy a puzzled stare. "What are you talking about?"

"Just play along with me here. Suppose I said there might be a way to use the garden to call for a doctor instead of for Makaidos. What would you do?"

"I guess it won't hurt to speculate." Elam sat next to Billy again. "We're preparing for war, and sometimes innocent little girls die in wars. We need more warriors. You've seen the people here. They're loving and kind, but only a few are real soldiers."

"But if the garden works, we'll have Legossi and Firedda. I have seen Legossi fight with Sir Barlow riding her. If she's at full strength, watch out."

Elam stroked his chin. "With the wall of fire still intact, we'll probably have enough warriors for a while."

226

"Exactly what I was thinking."

Letting out a quiet laugh, Elam shook his head. "Wishing for a doctor isn't going to get us one."

"But maybe calling for one will."

Elam propped an elbow on his knee. "Okay. Give it to me straight. What's your idea?"

"Just something I saw in the mines. It reminded me of a story Walter told me." Billy touched Bonnie's string of beads, still draped around his neck. "Back when all this started, Devin's cronies were trying to find Bonnie in her house, so she hid in her attic. Walter and his dad were in her bedroom looking for her, and they saw a poster of a girl praying, and a Bible verse on it said, 'Trust in the Lord with all thine heart; and lean not unto thine own understanding.' But I don't remember the rest of it."

"In all thy ways acknowledge him," Elam said, "and he shall direct thy paths."

Billy flushed. He should have known that a guy who's been around for thousands of years would know the Bible so well. "Right. Anyway, another poster said, 'Call to me, and I will answer you, and I will tell you great and mighty things, which you do not know.' The words 'Call to me' were underlined in red. So Walter decided just to call Bonnie's name."

227

"And it worked?"

Billy nodded. "Bonnie came down from the attic. She was kind of beat up, but she made it through."

Elam mimicked Billy's nod. "Just like the other verse said, 'Trust in the Lord with all your heart.'"

"Exactly. And Bonnie always trusted. She never doubted." Billy studied Elam's face. Although he had listened attentively, a look of doubt shaded his expression.

"Okay," Elam said. "I think I see where you're going. When Paili switched the words in her song to "the dragon," Goliath came out instead of Makaidos."

"And he was once a human named Dragon," Billy added. "Maybe if we call for a doctor, we'll get one."

"But how do you know a doctor is available? I mean, is someone from every profession lying around under our garden waiting to be called up? I'm not trying to be funny or cruel, but if we called for a plumber, do you think we would get one?"

Billy grinned. "Maybe he could get running water to our bathhouses."

"I know what you mean. But do you get my point?"

"Sure, but that's where what I saw in the mines comes in. When Listener and I were moving a ladder from the museum room shelves, a scroll fell off and rolled to the Tree of Life. It caught on fire, so I grabbed it and snuffed it out. When I unrolled it there wasn't much left besides this sentence." Billy pulled the strip of parchment from his pocket and showed it to Elam. "Do you know Hebrew?"

228

Elam murmured his translation. "Is there no balm in Gilead? Is there no doctor there? Why then is the health of the daughter of my people not restored?"

Billy touched one of the strange characters. "That's pretty much how Acacia translated it."

"It's from Jeremiah," Elam said. "That wasn't even written when the museum was built."

"Acacia said she or Sapphira picked it up during one of their scavenging hunts." He gave the parchment to Elam. "Since it kind of fell in my lap, and since it glowed white, I thought it might be something we should pay attention to."

"It glowed white?"

"Kind of like a phosphorescent powder. I think the scroll picked it up at the Tree of Life. The dirt in the tree's planter is covered with the stuff."

"I see." Elam rolled the parchment into a miniature scroll and then back out again. "So you believe this is some kind of sign from God that we should call for a doctor instead of Makaidos."

"I'm not sure what I believe, but I was thinking—"

A new voice broke in. "Billy doesn't have much experience with calling people back from the dead in resurrection gardens."

Billy turned toward the sound. "Walter?"

Sitting up on the cot and holding a hand against a bandage that wrapped around his bare chest, Walter nodded. "You guys sound like there are only two choices."

"Is there another?" Elam asked.

"I've been around Ashley the logic queen long enough to recognize a false dilemma. Why should you have to choose between Makaidos and a doctor? Why not call both?"

Elam stared at him. "Call both?"

"Sure. That garden changed a girl into a woman, and it's been sprouting dragons right and left. It's already proved it can handle multitasking."

Billy looked at Ashley, still asleep. If she knew Walter was sitting up, she would have a heart attack. He was supposed to stay in bed until morning.

"Okay," Elam said slowly. "We can try both, but if the theory is wrong and the ceremony is good for only one resurrection, which should we call first?"

Setting a hand against his forehead, Walter lay back down in his cot. "Sorry. I'm overloaded now. My brain is choking."

Billy interlaced his fingers into a double fist. "I say the doctor."

"And you?" Elam said, looking up at Sir Patrick.

Patrick eyed the blood pressure meter. "My heart cries out for a doctor for this precious girl, but my head says this might be our last opportunity to call the king of the dragons." With a sigh, he added, "I usually listen to my head, but my heart is holding sway. I think surgery is demanded, so to give this little fighter the best chance, we should ask God for the best surgeon."

"Well stated," Elam said, "but what about Enoch's commands? We didn't call for Makaidos the first time, and our choice ended in a disaster. Are we going to fail again to—"

The door swung open, ushering in a snowy breeze. Acacia and Ruth entered, dressed in heavy cloaks, their shoulders and hoods coated with snow. Acacia limped, but not badly. Apparently her leg wound wasn't severe.

Billy and Elam rose to their feet. "Greetings ladies," Elam said with a bow.

As Ruth closed the door, Walter waved from his cot. "I'd be chivalrous and stand, too, but I might drop a lung on the floor."

Smiling in spite of her pale and haggard face, Acacia brushed snow from her shoulders. "The time has come," she said softly.

"Will Ruth recite the same poem?" Elam asked.

"We see no reason why she shouldn't."

Elam showed Acacia the strip of parchment. "I assume you and Billy talked about this."

She nodded. "If you wish to change the word 'Makaidos' to 'a doctor,' we will do as you ask. We are the couriers of the call, not the composers."

"You know what happened the last time I authorized a change."

Acacia looked at Listener, motionless and quiet on the elevated cot, save for her rapid, shallow breaths. "You are the warrior chief," Acacia said, her eyes sparkling with tears. "We will trust and abide by your decision."

"Warrior chief?" Elam shook his head and sighed. "I'm just a rookie general from another world. This isn't a war decision. This is ethics. This is spiritual. And it's about the life of a girl from a world I barely know. I'm just not qualified."

"So who is?" Billy asked.

"Abraham appointed Valiant to take his place. We'll have to get him up to speed fast. The ceremony is in about half an hour."

"Where is he?" Billy asked.

"Praying at the garden, most likely."

"In the snow?"

Elam nodded. "Ever since he became Second Eden's new prophet, he's spent as much time praying as he has training the troops. Since there's a portal at the garden, he likes to pray there. It gives him a peaceful feeling."

Ruth bowed her head. "I will go to him now and explain the situation."

"Good idea," Elam said. "I'm sure Ember will give you a ride. She is likely staying warm in Emerald's hut."

"I will find her."

As Ruth hurried out the door, Billy nodded toward the garden. "My father's taking his turn patrolling out there. I told Dad about the doctor, so maybe he gave the message to Valiant already."

"Good. He'll have some time to think about it." Elam picked up a cloak from the cot. "Acacia, I don't mean to offend you, but you look spent. I have never seen you like this."

She laid a palm on her cheek. "I have felt ill all day, and the healing exhausted me."

"You should ride, too. Dikaios is in my hut. He'll be happy to carry you."

Acacia lowered her head. "I would like that."

"Sir Patrick," Elam continued, "please give Ashley the elixir that will give her more energy, and the two of you can prepare Listener for surgery. I'm hoping we'll come back with a doctor, but even if we don't, we'll have to try to save her without one. "

"Very well," Patrick said. "We will be ready."

Elam turned to Billy. "You should go. Make sure Valiant knows the whole story. I'll gather the villagers and meet everyone at the garden."

"I saw no villagers on my way over here," Acacia said. "Maybe the weather has kept them inside."

Elam furrowed his brow. "No villagers? Not even the children?"

"Only Cliffside preparing the lanterns for the night. I thought it odd, as well. The snow would be quite a draw for people who have never seen it before, especially the younger ones."

"I'd better get moving," Billy said. As he turned to go, he glanced at Listener again. She was so weak, so close to death. Should he keep trying to persuade them to choose a doctor? Was what happened on Second Eden really his business? Was Elam right about innocent little girls dying during times of war?

He picked up his own cloak and hurried out of the triage hut. He thrust his arms through the sleeves and balled his fists. They had to ask for a doctor! They just had to! Warrior or no warrior, it didn't make sense to watch Listener die without trying to do something, anything, even following a wild hunch, a crazy guess that fell from the sky in the guise of a burning parchment in an ancient scroll.

Jogging through gently falling snow, he approached Cliffside, who was lighting a hanging lantern at the end of the street. "Good evening," Billy said.

Cliffside nodded. "It is evening, to be sure, but it is not a good one."

Billy stopped, puffing white vapor. "You're right. It's a greeting we have in my world. We don't always mean that it's good."

"I have used the greeting many times, Sir Billy, but with that precious girl bleeding to death, and a season of more death upon us, I see no reason to call it good."

Billy dragged his shoe through the snow. Cliffside was right. Listener was a favorite among the villagers because of her willingness to sacrifice herself. With her suffering so much, a heavy gloom seemed to blanket everything. "Well spoken," was all Billy could muster as he resumed a steady jogging pace.

As he entered the forest, he looked down at the path. With snow and rain moistening the ground, mud had formed, revealing recent footprints, dozens of them from child-sized to adult.

Kicking into a higher gear, he rushed out into the field. At the edge of the garden, a sea of lanterns lit the area, highlighting hundreds of people kneeling in the midst of thousands of swirling snowflakes.

Billy slowed his pace. The weight of gloom had lifted, and now a feeling of holiness took over. This place of prayer was a sanctuary that pleaded for silence or quiet singing.

As he neared, he found Valiant kneeling in the middle of a circle of villagers. Quite a number of the younger girls wore pigtails, perhaps in honor of Listener's style. Or perhaps they were from Peace Village, Listener's home, and the girls there often wore their hair that way.

Billy's father sat on one side of the crowd, extending his neck to breathe warm air across as many as he could, while Hartanna and Thigocia sat on the other side doing the same. Ruth knelt next to Valiant, apparently whispering into his ear while Ember, the sorrel mare, stood nearby.

233

Stopping at the outer edge of the circle, Billy crossed his arms over his chest and took in a deep breath. The scene spoke volumes. Valiant the warrior had called his people to battle.

Hoofbeats sounded. With the lantern light making her eyes gleam, Acacia rode Dikaios across the field. When the great horse stopped, Billy took Acacia's hand and helped her dismount. Her skin felt cold, her hand thin and frail. Her woolen tunic and trousers hung loosely on her as if on an emaciated waif. Again, Acacia's call to sacrifice had drained her vitality. How could she once again summon the fires of heaven to ignite the garden of resurrection?

"Are you all right?" Billy asked.

She nodded firmly. "God will provide. He always does."

Billy gave her an affirming smile. Although her fragile voice didn't match the fire in her eyes, there was no doubt about the passion in her heart. She could do this.

As Billy released her hand, allowing her to walk toward the waiting people, Dikaios whispered in his ear. "I fear for her. She is wasting away. Although she has taken from the Tree of Life, she should eat more to gain strength. A morsel of berry bread for each meal will not sustain her."

"When this is over, I'll talk to her. Maybe I can—"

"Look!" Dikaios bobbed his head toward the crowd.

As Acacia walked toward Valiant, the people stood as she passed, every man, woman, and child pressing their hands together and bowing their heads. Acacia herself glowed from head to toe. A bluish white aura dressed her in sparkling brilliance as she seemed to float across the snow-covered grass.

Valiant stood as well. With a sweep of his arm and a low bow, he said, "Welcome, great Oracle. The garden awaits."

15

CHAPTER

An Oracle of Fire

I want to stay," Bonnie said to Abaddon. "I figured out what it means to become ablaze with fire."

"You have, have you?" In the dimness of the resurrection chamber, the dragon's head seemed to hover in midair. "You do not fear pain?"

His hot breath stung her skin, raising a shudder. "I fear it. I never enjoy pain. But if that's what I'm called to do, I'll just endure it. I'm strong enough."

Abaddon's eyes sparkled. "How refreshing, a human who is willing to reveal both weaknesses and strengths. Most of your race would interpret self-deprecation as the only honesty, but such expression is usually nothing more than false humility." He shook his head sadly. "Masks. Nothing more than masks. When in the company of cats and clowns, mice and cowards paint on frowns."

"So do you think I'm wearing a mask?"

"Do *you* think you are?"

"No. I was wondering if you thought I was."

Abaddon looked her in the eye. "You have confidence, but even that can be a disguise. Pride is the most sinister of masks, for it blinds the wearer. The parading peacock does not recognize how ridiculous he looks. He fans his tail, and no one is impressed, save for the foolish fowl himself."

Bonnie spread out her hands. "I have confidence because of who gives me strength. Without God, I'm nobody. But with God, I believe I can do anything."

"Is that so?" His gaze ran up and down her face. "Are you also confident that your motivations are pure?"

She nodded. "I am. I have confidence in the one who has made me pure."

"Then tell me, dragon girl, are you ready to be set aflame in order to go to Second Eden and give yourself up for those who need your help? Or do you really want to go there to see a young man to whom you *think* you are prophetically promised?"

"*Think*?" She half closed one eye. "What are you trying to say?"

"You believe you have trusted in prophecy, yet you have merely trusted in your interpretation. Surely you cannot fail, you say to yourself, because the prophecy guarantees your future betrothed bliss. Shall I quote the verse that has emboldened you to risk your life in the past, the one upon which you rely, thereby making you think of yourself as indestructible?"

Bonnie stared at him. Should she answer, or was this rhetorical? She didn't have to wait long to find out. The dragon spoke the words in a low sing-song voice.

The child of doubt will find his rest
And meet his virgin bride
A dragon shorn will live again
Rejecting Eden's pride

His head shot toward her, stopping just before his snout touched her nose. "There are other children of doubt. There are other virgin brides. Elam and Sapphira fit this prophecy as well as Billy and you do, and when Makaidos rises, the dragon shorn will live again. He was the dragon king who tried to hold his family together in spite of the rebellion of his own children. Surely that qualifies him as one who has rejected Eden's pride, does it not?"

Closing her eyes, Bonnie lowered her head. "I see what you mean."

"Now you know that this prophecy promises you nothing. If you go to Second Eden, you could die, and you would lose the life you have dreamed about for these many months."

Smelling something burning, Bonnie opened her eyes. Her shoes smoldered, and her laces were on fire. The heat stung, but it wasn't too bad yet. "I still want to go. My purposes don't conflict. I mean, I can see Billy and give myself up for people at the same time."

"Your point is valid, but if a situation arises in which you must choose death to save someone, will you do so, knowing that you will certainly lose your future with the young man?"

Bonnie closed her eyes again, this time tightly. She had faced danger so many times, but had she been willing to die for someone else? Did it occur to her during each instance of danger that the prophecy protected her, or did she just act sacrificially without thinking about herself at all?

As if answering her question, a memory rose from the depths of her mind, the image she had recently seen played out above Abaddon's book. In the vision, she pushed a board into an electrified doorway in order to let Shiloh out of the sixth circle of Hades. When it sprang back and flew out of her grip, she replaced it with her wing, blocking the deadly field. Shiloh escaped, and Bonnie was thrown out into the street. A few moments later, she died.

She opened her eyes and looked straight into the dragon's. "I would choose death."

237

"Would you really? Have you enough courage to face the flames? Would you refuse to recant your testimony or recoil at the agony of rejection and repudiation? When the fires of persecution scald your skin, and the daggers of those who were once your friends cut out your heart, will you give praise to the Maker that you were found worthy to travail through these torments?"

With heat now burning her ankles, she grimaced but nodded firmly. "I would never recant or recoil, and I will always give praise to Jehovah Yasha, and my savior, Jesus Christ."

Abaddon's nostrils flared. "We will see about that."

Flames shot up to Bonnie's knees, melting the skin on her legs. Pain ripped through her body. Screaming filled her ears. Was the screaming her own? Darkness trickled across her vision like blood vessels filled with burnt oil. The agony was unbearable. How long would it last?

Bonnie let out a long wail. "Oh, God! Oh, God, help me! It burns!"

She glanced at the ovula on the table mounts. Makaidos and her father stared at her, obviously sharing her pain, but they could do nothing to help.

Seemingly unaffected by her anguish, the dragon continued. "Now for another question." As the sizzle and stench of her burning flesh permeated the room, he turned on his lasers and focused the beams on her eyes. "You say that you now know why you must be set aflame." He paused for a moment as if to let his words add to her suffering. "Why?"

"I ... I ..." She couldn't speak. The flames climbed to her waist and slowly crawled up her back, onto her wings, and up to her chest. Heaving, gasping, panting, she tried to force out an answer, but the words wouldn't come. Were they even in her mind? Did she really not know after all?

"Bonnie Silver!" Abaddon shouted. His call echoed throughout the chamber, repeating again and again. "Why must you be set aflame?"

238

Even as he finished his question, her name continued to echo. *Bonnie Silver ... Bonnie Silver.*

She spat out her words, each one a torture. "My ... my name ... is Silver. All dross ... is purged ... and my body ... is a living ... illustration."

"But you must have some dross remaining. Hidden lies in secret places?" His eyebeams brightened. "Envy? Lust? Or do you seriously want me to believe this notion that the dross is already gone? Is your mask one of pride after all?"

"No!" she screamed. "Not a mask. ... God purged ... my dross ... long ago."

The flames shot out across her arms and up to her neck, forcing her to lift her chin. Gasping, she screamed again, this time a wordless, gut-wrenching cry.

The book on the table flipped open on its own, and a feather-tipped pen flew into Abaddon's clawed hand. An image rose from the pages, taking shape as it expanded. It looked like a three-dimensional Christmas card, dozens of people gathered in a circle in the midst of a heavy snowfall.

239

Abaddon pointed the pen at her. "You, dragon girl, hid your wings in a backpack from the time you were six years old. Were you protecting your mother from a slayer, or were you just afraid of being called a freak? When you had the opportunity to give up your wings, what went through your mind? Were they a gift from God, or were they a curse?" He snorted twin jets of fire from his nostrils. "Oh, I know you display them now, but you have cleverly concealed your earlier decision from all except your mother. Such is the character of hidden dross."

With light fading in and out, Bonnie shook her head hard. She had to stay conscious, no matter the pain. Still, she couldn't answer. Agony clamped her throat shut.

Abaddon transferred the pen to his tail and reached it toward the book. He poised it over the page as if ready to write. "What did you decide? If you kept your wings, was it to parade like the proverbial peacock because of the power they gave you?" He let out a low laugh. "Yes, that would be it. Power. A greedy lust for power is surely your hidden dross."

Summoning all her strength, Bonnie cried out. "My dross … is gone! … Leave me alone!"

"But you have not answered. Did you give up your wings?" As Abaddon scratched something down with the pen, smoke rose from the page. "Perhaps that is it. You considered a gift from God something to be spurned. You lacked contentment with how he created you."

Bonnie pressed her lips together. The torture was awful … worse than awful.

He set his head directly in front of her face and shouted, "Answer me!"

"No!" The fire leaped over her nose and roared across her eyes. Heaving scalding breaths, she coughed out each word. "I … will … not … answer!"

240

Suddenly, the pain vanished. The broiling heat eased to gentle warmth. Bonnie looked at her hands, still on fire. Flames crackled on her arms and legs, yet there was no pain, not even a hint of discomfort. She looked up at the dragon. "What happened?"

With a flick of his tail, Abaddon dropped his pen and smiled. "You have withstood the test, precious child. Your confidence in God's purging power is exceedingly rare, and your steadfastness has proven the purity of your silver." He let out a long sigh. "It is such a shame that others choose chastisement. Those who hide God's purifying handiwork will never learn to stop suffering. They will wear the masks of fear, false humility, and fetters until they discover freedom."

She turned her hands over and back and watched the flames curl with her motions. "So will I stay on fire now?"

"Physically? Yes, for a time. When you are called from the place of resurrection, you will rise without perceptible fire, but those who love you will know that you still burn. They will enjoy its warmth and rally with its unquenchable passion. Those who despise truth, however, will flee from your fire. You will be a flaming sword that cuts deeply to the heart, exposing the lies they tell themselves. They will not understand that you strike with love, for your words will feel like flaming arrows."

Bonnie gazed at her fiery torso. It felt wonderful, like floating in sunshine. Her vision had magnified. Every scale in the dragon's hide seemed divided by deep crevices, and the capillaries in his eyes looked like pulsing rivers of red.

The scene floating over the book also clarified. A small group of people huddled at the center of the circle, apparently talking about something, concern bending their expressions. Their emotions seeped into her mind—turmoil, lack of trust, indecisiveness. And a familiar face turned toward her. Was it Billy? Yes, it was! Maybe this was a picture of Second Eden, and they were getting ready to call someone to resurrection. Soon either her father or Makaidos would be swept into that world, and their suffering would be over.

241

Still, something was wrong. A strange sense of melancholy weighed down her mind—troubled thoughts, sadness, heaviness of heart.

"I ... I feel strange."

"You do?" the dragon asked. "Describe your feelings, please."

She laid a hand against her chest. "Heartache and loneliness, the despair of souls wandering lost."

"Your eloquence is exquisite, and your emotions are inexpedient, to be sure. Now that you have become what you are, this will be your burden forevermore."

"What am I?"

"There is someone else here who could tell you." Abaddon's eyebeams lifted over Bonnie's body and settled over a shadow on a wall behind her. "You may come out, Sapphira. I know where you have hidden yourself."

Bonnie turned that way. With all the pain, she had forgotten about Sapphira.

A white-topped head poked out from the shadow. "I am here."

"Bonnie Silver has questions that you are able to address, but first, I will ask *you* one."

Folding her hands at her waist, Sapphira stepped fully into the light. "I will try to answer."

"Why did you stay hidden while your friend suffered?"

"Because I figured out what you were doing," Sapphira said. "It was not my place to interfere or distract from your purpose. During this initial suffering event, Bonnie had to be alone."

"Your years of experience have produced a great deal of wisdom, Oracle of Fire. Now you may address Bonnie's questions."

"What questions?" Bonnie asked.

"You asked what you are," Sapphira replied, "and you wondered about your feelings of heartache." She raised a hand. Her fingers caught fire and caressed Bonnie's flaming cheek. "To become what you are now, you had to suffer, and you had to suffer alone. You can now see what others cannot, and you feel the pain of those who lack your perception. They toil in misery and heartache. Because of their bondage to the things they see with their physical eyes, they cannot see the light of freedom and the key that will unlock the chains of slavery."

Sapphira's flames crawled down her arm and spread slowly across her body. "And even as you offer them the key, they will flee from you, because your light is too bright, and your fire is too hot. They are so accustomed to slavery, they cannot comprehend the freedom that comes from walking in the fire of God. They fear the pain of purging. They disbelieve the results. They cannot conceive of pure silver, unsullied by even a pinch of dross. You are an illustration, as you put it, a portrait that ignites their fears and raises their retaliating fists, yet instead of fighting back, you reach out again and again, because you feel their pain in your heart, their lostness, their despair."

Now fully engulfed in flames, Sapphira took Bonnie's fiery hand in hers. "You sense the pain because you are now an Oracle of Fire."

Holding his sword in place at his hip, Elam ran across the field toward the birthing garden. Ahead, a gathering of villagers had split into two groups, allowing Acacia and Billy to pass between them as they walked toward Valiant, who had bowed low when Acacia drew near.

When he caught up with Billy, he slowed his pace and walked at his side. "Cliffside is guarding the triage hut," Elam said.

Billy whispered, "Why didn't anyone tell you about the villagers gathering out here? Aren't they keeping you informed?"

"I'm not sure." Elam patted Billy on the back. "Let's talk about it later. The moon's about to rise. When the light strikes the garden, it'll be too late to do this."

As Elam and Billy approached, Valiant bowed, though not quite so low as he had for Acacia.

"Valiant," Elam said, returning a quick bow, "we have only a few minutes before we must begin. Have you considered our dilemma?"

The cold breeze tossed snow from Valiant's black curls, but he seemed warm enough in his thick, fur-lined cloak, though the front was partially open, revealing his battle uniform. "I agree that the matter raises serious questions. Another from your world has provided more information than perhaps even you know." He nodded at Rebekah, who sat with Dallas at the inner part of the circle. "It seems that a surgeon, a former dragon named Kaylee Saunders, wants to come here to aid our cause. If we call for a doctor, perhaps she will be able to pass through the portal."

243

Elam crossed his arms and shivered. "*Perhaps* is a crucial word. I already erred in changing Enoch's words once, and it brought an evil force to this world that waits for an opportunity to attack. Do you think it's wise to alter the prophecy again? Are these events a sign from God, or nothing more than a coincidence?"

"A little girl lies drowning in her own blood, and there is no one here who can save her life." Valiant touched his chest, his thumb lingering on a dragon insignia. "I am a warrior. Whether I fight with weapons of steel driven into the dark hearts of our enemies, or weapons of song lifted to the Father of Lights, I do so for one purpose, to protect the little ones. It is true that casualties of war are inevitable, and losing one or two might not seem much of a sacrifice when compared to gaining a warrior of Timothy's caliber, but if we gain his help at the cost of Listener's life ..."

His voice faltered. Gripping the hilt of a dagger attached to his belt, he swallowed before continuing. "I have been in many battles, and it is always for the little ones that I take my blade into the midst of bloody conflicts with no thought for my own life. Without the Listeners of this world, there would be nothing to fight for. If we do not do all we can to save her from perishing ..." He withdrew his dagger and dropped it to the ground. "I will not fight, for I will then be a traitor to the very cause for which we have shed our blood."

244

Elam looked at the dagger lying on the ground. As it reflected the light of Pegasus, which peeked over the horizon, he could only stare at the blade in silence.

Valiant picked it up and shoved it back into its sheath. "Timothy himself refused to sacrifice that precious girl, even at the cost of his own life. He had no assurances that his sacrifice would bring about the salvation of his daughters, just as we do not know if our call for a surgeon will raise one from this garden. But do you believe that he would fight for traitors, the betrayers we would be if we sacrificed this child now? I say no. And I would join him in his refusal. I say we trust the Father of Lights to honor our faith in him, whether we are foolishly believing in scrolls falling from a museum shelf or a spyglass falling from the sky."

Without a second's hesitation, Elam nodded at Acacia. "Let it be so."

Acacia reached for Ruth's hand and helped her stand up. With the people again rising and bowing, she and Ruth walked hand in hand and stopped at the edge of the garden. As she faced the rows of plants, Ruth lifted her hands and called out, "Let every lantern darken, and I will begin when the last light fades."

As the flickering lights died away, Elam whispered to Billy. "She's repeating the ceremony."

"I guessed that. I was standing at the side last time, so I couldn't hear much." Billy watched Ruth, a woman he had only recently learned much more about. Although she seemed normal, she was once Paili, a plant hybrid much like Acacia, and she blossomed into a lovely woman who eventually became Patrick's wife. And, like Patrick, she was able to turn a red rubellite into a white gem, which meant, she thought, that her hybrid status had passed away for good. Since she wasn't one of the Oracles of Fire, who were able to change a rubellite even in their hybrid state, she was probably right.

245

With the rising moon shining on her white hair, Acacia raised her hands. Two balls of blue fire appeared in her palms, though not as bright and sparkling as they were during the previous ceremony. They had been effervescent and alive. Now they seemed dull by comparison.

Ruth hummed as she and Acacia walked single file along one of the garden rows, stepping carefully to avoid the scattered bones of Makaidos. The blue glow spread out from Acacia's hands and enveloped them both. When it reached their feet, the radiance crawled along the ground, instantly devouring the snow. As it touched the bones, each one burst with a glow of its own, whiter, like luminous frost. Soon, the entire garden, the soil, the plants, and the two women, pulsed with an eerie light.

Acacia waved her arms in a circle, though not as fast as usual. The balls of fire narrowed into spinning cylinders of blue flames. With a grunt, she threw them farther into the garden. They splattered into hundreds of dots of blue light that sat on the soil like glowing marbles.

Unlike last time, the flames crawling along the ground didn't rise up into a dome over the plants. The glowing bones sizzled and popped as before, and the fire ate away their white coats, but the entire scene was dimmer than last month's spectacle, less vibrant.

Her brow furrowing, Acacia turned and left the garden, leaving Ruth alone as she stood in the midst of the sparkling dots of blue. Ruth raised her hands again and sang, her voice resonant as it passed like a wave across the hushed crowd.

246

> When phantoms knock on doors of light
> To open paths to worlds beyond,
> A friend replies, "Insert the key
> To leave the dark and greet the dawn.
>
> "The key is light, the words of truth;
> No lie can break the chains of death.
> A whispered word of love avails
> To bring new life, the spirit's breath."
>
> So now I sing a key for you,
> The phantom waiting at the door;
> We call for you, a doctor who
> Will join us now in holy war.

As she lowered her hands, she kept her gaze on the garden, quiet and still. Like glittering gems, the blue lights continued to twinkle, but nothing else happened, certainly nothing similar to last month's events, no earth-shaking rise of a shadow in the midst of the plants.

A low murmur ran through the onlookers. Elam looked for the reason and found Hunter and Semiramis standing at the garden's edge, Semiramis holding something in her closed hand.

Elam stormed toward her. "What are you doing?"

Still cupping her hand, she turned his way, trembling. "I most humbly beg your pardon, Elam. The people are whispering that the Oracle's fire is lacking power. We all want the doctor to come and rescue Listener, so I offer my services to bring increase to her energy."

Elam looked up at Pegasus. In a few minutes it would rise above the line of trees that shaded the garden. As he looked into Semiramis's eyes, a hundred thoughts blazed through his mind. Acacia lacked energy because he had authorized her attempt to heal Listener, but without that try, Listener would probably be dead already. Had he made the wrong decision? Had God wanted him to let Listener die and call for Makaidos after all? But how could that be? And now with only moments remaining, he had to make another decision that might save or destroy the entire population. Would it hurt just to listen to this woman's idea, the same woman who insisted that he couldn't cross the bridge that provided the key to Heaven's Gate?

247

Glancing at Pegasus again, he gave her a quick nod. "Let's hear it, and make it fast."

She opened her hand, revealing a small rectangular box, tied with twine and sealed with wax. "This morning, while I was out walking in the launching field, the dragon I told you about came to me and offered me this box. At first I refused to take it, knowing him to be a crafty deceiver, but he said that it would help energize the garden during the ceremony, that I need not open it unless the power to resurrect runs dry. If it is opened and the gem is placed in the garden, the energy will increase tenfold."

"The gem?" Elam took the box and looked it over. The wax bore an insignia that looked like a dragon. Apparently Semiramis hadn't opened it, or so she would have him believe.

He untied the twine, broke the seal, and lifted the lid. Inside, a severed finger rested in a bed of bloody cotton, a gold ring with a red gem still in place around it.

Elam's stomach knotted. Heat flashed across his skin. Backpedaling, he nearly fell, but Billy caught him just in time.

"What is it?" Billy asked.

When Elam showed it to him, Billy's mouth dropped open. "That's ... that's evil!"

Rebekah, sitting on a blanket, pulled Billy's sleeve. As they whispered to each other, Elam thrust the box toward Semiramis. "Did the dragon say who owned this finger?"

Semiramis looked inside. Her face turned pale as she backed away, holding a hand against her chest. "My lord! I hope you do not think that I did this thing!"

248

Barely able to keep from gagging, Elam put the lid back in place and shouted, "I repeat! Did the dragon say who owned this finger?"

Her eyes darting back and forth between Elam and the box, Semiramis spoke as one begging for forgiveness. "His words were cryptic, my lord. He said that the energizing gem would be familiar to the dragon boy, the son of Clefspeare."

"Is that all? Nothing more?"

Heaving fast breaths, Semiramis's eyes grew wider. "Now that I perceive his malice, I hesitate to repeat his foul words."

Elam gripped the hilt of his sword. "Tell me! You must!"

She gulped before continuing. "He said that if the dragons and their offspring continued to ally themselves with the residents of Second Eden, this gift would be accompanied by more of the precious puzzle at a later time."

"Precious puzzle!" Elam gritted his teeth. "How dare you bring this serpent's poisonous words here!"

Semiramis trembled. "His words sounded gracious, an act of surrender to our noble cause. I had no idea that the gift was a cruel gesture designed to mock my lord and his valiant army. I see now that the dragon desires to weaken your spines through an instrument of terror." Steeling her body, she clenched her fist. "But I assume you will fight back. This mad dragon cannot be allowed to use fear to make you cower in submission."

"On that, we can agree." Taking the lid off again, Elam turned toward Billy. "Do you recognize the gem?"

His face twisting in pain, Billy nodded. "It looks just like Bonnie's ring."

"That's what I was afraid of." Elam studied the contents again. Something besides cotton lay under the finger. Was it hair? Careful not to touch the finger, he pulled out a two-inch lock of light brown hair. "Do you recognize this?" he asked.

Billy stared at it. As he tightened his jaw, he nodded again but said nothing.

249

Rebekah jumped up. "The finger is probably not Bonnie's."

"What makes you think that?" Billy asked.

"When some people came to kidnap Bonnie, they mistakenly took Shiloh instead. She pretended to be Bonnie."

"But Bonnie was gone when I got there. How do you know they didn't get her, too?"

Lowering her chin, Rebekah shook her head. "I don't."

"And does it really matter?" Elam asked. "Whether the finger was Bonnie's or Shiloh's, will it cause us to alter our course? Will we submit to this wicked beast who taunts us, who believes that we can be shaken by threats? We cannot allow ourselves to be diverted from the path God has set before us."

Hunter stepped up and pointed at his face, still oozing from the dragon's blast. As his companion floated near his chin, flashing red, he spoke with a firm tone. "Do not doubt that Arramos will chop that girl to pieces, and he will do so in a way that will prolong her suffering. First her fingers and toes, then her hands and feet, then her eyes and tongue. She will be nothing but a writhing head and torso with no eyes left by which to weep and no tongue remaining by which to cry out to God for the mercy of death."

"Are you saying that we should appease this devil?" Elam asked. "That we should allow his minions to rule Second Eden by the edge of a sword?"

"I say that when this girl's body parts arrive one piece at a time, the sympathetic hearts of these people will melt. When the wall of fire dies away, they will be unable to fight the onslaught of Nephilim, Vacants, and shadow people that will swarm into the village by night and slaughter them without mercy or pity."

"Hunter!" Semiramis snapped. "Do not speak from faithlessness! Such cowardice is not becoming of a son of mine." She clasped her hands together. "My lord, if I see the dragon again, allow me to spy out his secrets. Since I have stupidly followed his will in the past, it will be easy to feign allegiance to him and learn where he holds the girl captive, whoever she may be."

Elam looked at Valiant. He stood with his arms crossed over his muscular chest. As if summoned by his glance, Valiant stepped closer to Elam and whispered, "If she is a spy for the evil dragon, her pretense is against us, not him. I say that it will do no harm to send her to him, but we should keep our counsel away from her ears."

Elam nodded. "Agreed. But what of energizing the field?"

"Perhaps this so-called gift would help," Valiant said. "If she is a deceiver and the gem fails or causes a disaster, she would not want to stay in our presence. Give her leave to go to the dragon, but only after the gem has proven its value. If it causes us pain, then she will suffer as well. Yet, you know her better than I, so I leave the decision in the warrior chief's capable hands."

Elam glared at the box. This was just too much. He couldn't afford to make another mistake and thereby erode the villagers' trust in him further.

250

He looked at the people, each one staring at him as they waited for something to happen. The moon's light spread across the snow, sparkling as it crawled toward the garden. When it illuminated Semiramis's face, his mind flashed back to the time she stood at the foot of the bridge as he dangled from its ropes.

"Oh, the folly!" she had shouted. "The folly of those who think themselves holier and wiser than the sages who went before them!"

Elam winced as the words echoed in his mind. Was she right? How could he make such important decisions for these people he barely knew? Should he risk everyone's safety for the sake of a dying little girl? Yet, two truths kept echoing in his brain. One—he wasn't ready to trust Semiramis, and two—Valiant's idea was sound.

Finally, he reached into the box and carefully slid the ring off the withered finger. "If this gem energizes the resurrection garden and all is well, then you may go and spy out Arramos's secrets. But you will remain with us for tonight and tomorrow so we can make sure nothing evil befalls us because of this choice. If it becomes clear that this is an instrument designed to bring us harm, then you will suffer the same fate as the owner of this finger."

251

She bowed her head. "You are wise not to trust me, for I have doubted you and tried to dissuade you from crossing the bridge. Arramos sent me here to plant seeds of evil, but when he burned my son's face, I rebelled against him, and I am now in your service. God has provided the power to energize this garden, and I hope you will trust in it though it was delivered by a hand you are not willing to trust. Surely you know that the ring and the finger that wore it are holy." She fell to her knees and pressed her wrists together. "Lock me in chains until my worth is proven. I trust you to make the right decision."

Now shaking, Elam glanced at Ruth, still waiting patiently in the midst of the garden's blue gems. He then checked the moon's encroaching light, only inches from the garden. Clenching his fist around the ring, he nodded at Valiant. "Have your men take her to the triage hut and bind her hand and foot. It's warm there, and Sir Patrick and Cliffside will keep an eye on her."

"Very well." Valiant gestured for a trio of men to follow Elam's instructions. As they led Semiramis away, Elam grabbed Hunter's wrist and pushed the ring into his hand. "You will take the gem out to Ruth. If there is harm in this, you and your mother will suffer the consequences."

Hunter bowed his head. "I trust that your faith in us will soon be restored." He marched into the garden and handed the gem to Ruth. Stooping, she placed it on the ground next to one of the bones.

When Hunter spun back toward the field, he lost his balance and toppled over. As the garden's radiance crawled over his body, he pawed at the soil with one hand and reached out with the other. "Help me!" he called.

Elam ran into the garden, still arguing with himself. Of course this "accident" might be a ruse, but he didn't have any choice. He couldn't let a wounded man flounder in the mud.

As he followed one of the furrows, new sparks erupted around Ruth and spread out, like fire on oily water. Feeling a stinging sensation through his trousers, Elam broke into a trot. When he arrived, he grabbed Hunter's hand and pulled him to his feet. "Are you all right?"

"Yes," Hunter said as he brushed off his clothes. "I think so."

Billy pointed from the edge of the garden. "Elam! Look!"

Elam turned toward Ruth. As the newly energized light dressed the garden in a dawnlike aura, a human-shaped shadow rose from the ground just a few feet beyond her.

"Can you tell what it is?" Elam waded toward her through the rising flood of radiance.

"A man," Ruth said. "At least, I think it's a man."

Elam stood at her side. Rebekah had said that the doctor was one of the former dragons. Shouldn't a woman appear?

252

As the shadow took on a distinct masculine shape, Elam set his hand on the hilt of his sword again and shouted. "Who are you?"

The man, still more ghost than human, laid a hand on his forehead. "I am ..."

Suddenly, he solidified and collapsed. Elam charged ahead and helped him up, taking an arm and hoisting him to his feet. Since the newcomer's legs remained unsteady, Elam had to keep a shoulder under his arm. "What's your name?"

Wearing a long-sleeved dress shirt and khaki pants, the man shivered in the snowy breeze. "Conner. Matthew Conner."

Elam pulled off his cloak and helped the man put it on. "Are you a doctor?"

"Yes. ... Well, I was one." Dr. Conner looked at Elam curiously. "How did you know?"

"We called for a doctor, so we were expecting you. ... Well, not exactly you, but ..."

253

"Oh, yes. I remember now." He firmed his stance and looked around. "Who needs me?"

"A little girl."

Dr. Conner's eyebrows shot upward. "He was right!"

"Who was right?"

As if dizzied by the sparkling lights, Dr. Conner's eyes darted all around before settling. "Never mind. I think I was dreaming."

Elam took him by the arm. "Come on. You'll need to do surgery right away."

"Surgery?" He followed along, though staggering somewhat through the fading radiance.

Ruth trailed them by a few steps. "Shall we try it again and call for Makaidos?"

"The moonlight is already touching the garden," Elam said, "so we'll have to wait for the next eclipse. Just pray that we have enough warriors and that Acacia is healthy by then."

CHAPTER

THE PHYSICIAN

Bonnie and Sapphira approached the hologram that floated
over the book. Keeping her flaming hands away from the
wooden table, Bonnie bent over to get as close as she could. With
her vision so sharp, every detail was clear, and since they were
inside a portal, Sapphira likely could see just as well.

In the image, two females walked into a garden, the shorter
one a white-haired teenager.

"Acacia," Sapphira whispered.

"I guessed that. She looks just like you."

Acacia created a ball of fire in each hand, and the radiance
spilled to the soil and spread out. Something sparkled near her feet,
something white and luminescent. She threw the balls into the garden. The flames crawled along the ground and spread a shimmering radiance. Acacia then walked away, leaving the other female
alone.

"That's Ruth," Sapphira said, pointing. "She was once Paili,
an underborn."

A rushing wind blew through the resurrection chamber. Like a wave catching a sandcastle, the gust picked up the hologram and spread it around the room, repainting it as if everyone in the image had grown to life size.

The air seemed charged with electricity. The garden radiance danced at their flaming feet. Soon fire swirled in the air until it created a cylinder that spun slowly in place.

"The portal is opening," Sapphira said. "But it looks kind of weak."

Bonnie walked close to the image of Billy and looked into his eyes. She felt his emotions streaming into her mind—confusion, distrust, fear. Yet, something wonderful colored every feeling. What was it? Love?

She passed her hand, orange and flickering, across his eyes, then tried to hold his hand. Yes, that was it. Love. That was the truth that kept him from despair.

256

"Keep trusting, Billy," she whispered. Now her own emotions blazed, almost overwhelming her. "I hope to be there soon."

With her hands raised and her head tilted upward, Ruth seemed to be singing. As with most of this vision, they couldn't hear the words, but after a few seconds, a woman's lovely voice broke through, as if spoken from a loudspeaker above.

"We call for you, a doctor who will join us now in holy war."

The ovulum holding Bonnie's father floated upward and hovered about six feet from the floor. Inside, still glowing orange, he pressed his palms against the glass, obviously confused.

When Ruth finished, she stood in the midst of the radiance, as if in a trance, and no further sounds broke through the portal barrier.

The people in the middle of the circle seemed agitated. A young man marched to the edge of the garden and confronted a man and a woman Bonnie hadn't noticed before.

"Elam!" Sapphira said, this time louder than a whisper.

Bonnie pointed a fiery finger. "The one with the strong chin and dark hair?"

"Yes." Sapphira guided her body in front of Elam. Raising her hand, she wiggled her fingers in front of his face. Although she said nothing, her emotions came through loud and clear. She was homesick, homesick for Elam.

Soon, Billy and a few others joined Elam, and they argued with the man and woman while looking at something inside a small box.

"Can you tell what's in there?" Bonnie asked.

Sapphira eased closer. "It's a finger. Is it from a human?"

The woman Elam confronted dropped to her knees. While some men led her away, another man walked into the garden. His face was swollen and marred, as if recently burned.

Sapphira gasped. "It's Mardon!"

"It is? I didn't know he had burns on his face."

"He didn't. But I worked with him closely for a long time. I would recognize him anywhere. Even the way he walks gives him away."

257

The man fell and clawed at the soil. Elam chased after him. The radiance covering the soil suddenly blossomed. The swirling cylinder strengthened and spun faster. The ovulum holding Bonnie's father lifted higher and faded as it neared the ceiling. Seconds later, it was gone.

The fiery cylinder slowed and quickly fizzled out. From the spot where the ovulum once sat, something broke through the ground in the hologram projection. As it rose, it took on a human-like shape and cast a shadow over Ruth. After a few seconds, it became a man and fell limply to the ground.

Bonnie ran to him and instinctively reached down to help. Elam did the same, but only Elam's hands could provide support. As he lifted the new arrival, Bonnie backed away. "It's my Daddy!" she cried. "He made it!"

Suddenly, the wind gusted again. The book blew shut with a thud. The projected scene broke apart, and the pieces scattered into nothingness.

As the breeze died away, Abaddon shuffled to the table and set his pen on top of the book. "This entry has ended."

Bonnie stepped closer to Makaidos's ovulum. "Will they ever call for him?"

"Second Eden has the opportunity with every eclipse, but during this resurrection, I sensed a foul wind blowing in that realm—snow in a world that never knew it before, sweetness in the lips of liars, evil intentions disguised in deceptive words. These were never part of Second Eden before. They portend terrible trouble."

"So what do we do?" Sapphira asked. "When do we leave?"

Abaddon lifted the ovulum from the mount and looked at the miniature dragon within. "Did not Enoch tell you that you would wait for a long time?"

"Yes, but I thought he meant in the mines."

"I am sure he did. Yet, the only word he received was that the two of you would have to wait in a lower level, and that you would need each other. The precise place was merely his interpretation." Abaddon looked at Bonnie. "And you have learned that an interpretation of an obscure oracle is not the same as certainty."

Bonnie let out a sigh. The feelings of heartache and loneliness returned, heavier than ever. "Yes, I remember."

"So now you will wait." Abaddon waved a foreleg toward the exit hallway. "There is a room that holds a treasure trove of wisdom, books similar to my journal that will show you story after story in the same lifelike way. Listen. Learn. Live. If the people of Second Eden call you to their realm, you may well need every precious poem you find in those treasures."

Bonnie looked at her fingers as she pressed them together. Although vague within the flames, she could distinguish their outlines. "What about our bodies? Will we have to eat? Will we age?"

"Your food will be knowledge and wisdom, and these will cause you to age at the same rate as those you love in Second Eden." Abaddon chuckled. "I am not a heartless fiend. I know that you both long to be with your young men. If God so deems that you unite, your apparent ages will be acceptable to all."

Bonnie took Sapphira's hand. As their fingers intertwined, Sapphira's thoughts streamed into Bonnie's mind, though she said nothing. *We can do this, Bonnie. I'll show you how to endure.*

Bonnie smiled. This felt like the way she communicated with others in the candlestone. Concentrating on the connection between them, she sent back a stream of thoughts. *I believe you. Let's use the time to make ourselves ready to fight alongside our men. From one Oracle of Fire to another, they might need some woman power to back them up.*

When Elam and Dr. Conner returned to the field at the garden's edge, they stopped and looked around. With snow still falling lightly, the people studied the new arrival, some with curious smiles and others with skeptical frowns.

Billy stepped forward. "Dr. Conner?"

"Yes?" Dr. Conner looked at Billy, his eyes narrowing. "Billy Bannister?"

Billy clapped him on the shoulder and shouted to the crowd. "It's all right, everyone. I know him. He's Bonnie Silver's father. He's a doctor."

A buzz spread across the field, then cheers. Dr. Conner wrapped Elam's cloak around himself and shivered. "The last thing I remember is being in my laboratory. The mountain had collapsed, and Devin was shooting bolts of electricity at us. I think I was hit."

"You were." Billy waved for Clefspeare to come closer. "Dad, can you and the dragons warm him up?"

"With pleasure." Clefspeare, Hartanna, and Thigocia aimed their jets at Dr. Conner. Within seconds, he loosened his grip on the cloak and blew out a long breath.

"Thank you," he said as he marched in place. "I think every joint is in working order."

Billy looked at Hartanna. The gleam in her eyes spoke volumes. Her husband was now alive, but for some reason, she stayed silent, apparently waiting to see how this new miracle would play out. There was no need to distract him now.

"I'll get him started right away," Billy said, nodding at Elam.

"Good. I want to talk to Valiant for a minute. I'll be there soon."

Billy pulled Dr. Conner's arm. "Come on. It's warm in the triage hut. That's where we need you to do surgery."

As they walked briskly toward the forest boundary, Dr. Conner spoke through his chattering teeth. "I have done only simple surgery, removing warts, excising hemorrhoids, and one appendectomy, that sort of thing."

"Okay." Billy grimaced. What should he say? Should he warn him what to expect? A spear embedded in a girl's side that might have punctured her lung was a lot worse than an inflamed appendix. As they hurried through the forest, guided by the lantern lights in the street ahead, he sighed. "Then this is going to be a challenge."

"What kind of surgery is it?"

"You'll see." Billy opened the door to the triage hut and guided Dr. Conner inside. As they shook snow from their clothes and shoes, Billy looked around the room.

As before, Walter lay on his cot, apparently asleep. Ashley stood next to Sir Patrick, both watching Listener as she lay on the elevated cot. Ashley, still in a T-shirt and shorts and her hair now tied up in a bun, swabbed Listener's side with a wet cotton ball. "I think we'll have to make an incision here," she said, pointing. "And another right here."

Billy whispered to Dr. Conner. "She's too absorbed to notice, as usual."

"She looks familiar." Dr. Conner took a step closer and squinted. "Ashley?"

Ashley looked up. For a moment she just stared, as if caught in a trance. Her lips formed a word, then repeated it, this time adding in a quavering voice. "Doc?"

Dr. Conner echoed his own call. "Ashley!"

She rushed around the cot, slipping for a moment before running into his arms. "Doc!" As they hugged, Ashley chattered at her usual breakneck pace. "I heard about the resurrection garden, and I hoped that maybe you might be the doctor who would come, but I didn't really believe it, because you haven't practiced medicine in years. I mean, Listener needs a thoracic surgeon, and you're not really a—" She pulled away, her cheeks flushed. "I'm sorry. I didn't mean to—"

Dr. Conner set a finger over Ashley's lips. "Never mind that." He looked at Listener as she lay motionless on the cot. "Is this our patient?"

Ashley nodded and pulled him closer to Listener. "A spear penetrated her ribcage here," she said, pointing. "I can't tell how far it went in, but it might have pierced her right lung. I can't tell if the point went into her heart, but her loss of blood would indicate that the damage is significant. We're guessing that the spear itself is plugging the holes and keeping her lung from collapsing and hemorrhaging even worse, so obviously we couldn't pull it out."

Dr. Conner's face turned ashen. As he stared at Listener, his mouth dropped open. "I … I can't possibly do surgery like this. I removed ingrown toenails. I stitched up playground cuts. I mended a few monkeys."

"Don't talk like that!" Ashley grabbed his arm. "Remember back in Missoula what you did for Stacey in the alley? That man had a dagger against her throat, and when you kicked him in the head, he sliced her jugular." She shook him hard. "Don't you remember? You stitched her up with a sewing kit! You saved her life! And when you heard Karen had a compound leg fracture, you grabbed a first-aid kit and ran into a dark tunnel ready to do whatever you could to rescue her."

"But this is … this is different. Far worse."

"I *know* it's worse!" Ashley lifted her hands and splayed her fingers. "Look at these. Together you and I built the most advanced mechanical photosynthetic lab in the world, and now these are healing hands. You cut and I'll cauterize." Shaking him again, she yelled, "We have to save this little girl's life!"

He stared at her, as if in a daze. After a few seconds, he laid a hand on her shoulder and nodded. "Show me the tools we have. I'll do the best I can."

Ashley clenched her fist. "Yes! That's the Doc I remember!"

While Ashley showed Dr. Conner the instruments on a nearby table, Walter rose to a sitting position and waved toward Billy. "Come here a second."

Billy hurried over and sat next to him. "What's up?"

Walter nodded toward a corner of the room, whispering. "Check it out."

Turning, Billy found Semiramis sitting on the floor, bound hand and foot and leaning against a wall. She stared back at him, her face melancholy.

"I heard the deal Elam made. Since a doctor showed up, are you going to let her go?"

"I suppose we'll have to. Why?"

Walter lowered his voice further. "Don't trust her, not for a second. I saw her at the bridge. She's as smooth as silk. She could take your wallet, your shoes, and your belt, and you wouldn't even notice."

"I don't think Elam trusts her, but a deal's a deal. Did they tell you about the finger?"

Walter shivered. "Yeah. That's twisted."

"It's probably Shiloh's." Billy felt the blood drain from his head, making him dizzy. "It has to be."

"Yeah. That makes sense. But just because it's not Bonnie's finger, it doesn't make any difference."

"No." Billy shook his head hard. "No, of course not. I was just saying ..." He let his voice drift away. He wasn't sure what he meant.

"Don't worry about it." Walter patted him on the back. "I get the picture."

"Billy!" Ashley called. "Wash up in case we need more hands." Turning toward Walter, she frowned. "Lie back down. I don't want to stitch you up again."

As Billy rose to his feet, he grabbed a blanket and tossed it in Walter's lap. "Don't get used to the easy life. I'll have you back out in the sparring circle by the end of the week."

"Against you?" Walter waved a hand. "Piece of cake. I expected a real challenge."

Billy kicked the cot's leg. "Not me. Listener. She'll need an easy opponent if she's going to get her confidence back."

"That's cool." Walter's smile slowly diminished. After a few seconds, a grim expression took over, and he lay back on his cot. "Give me a blow-by-blow from the surgery table. I'll be praying for that little warrior."

Abraham's hut had become the operating room. With the exception of Walter, who lay on his cot in obedience to Dr. Ashley's orders, no other patients remained for recovery. Still, the interior was crowded, helping raise the temperature, a benefit on this snowy night. Besides Ashley, Dr. Conner, Sir Patrick, Billy, and Semiramis; Listener's family—Candle, her brother; Mantika, her stepmother; and Windor, her stepbrother—stood in the close confines, huddled near the door as they watched in silence.

And many who hoped to join them waited outside in the frigid weather, praying for Listener on the coldest night the villagers could remember, the beginning of the season of death, as they had called it.

Billy had listened to some of their prayers, so warm, so thoughtful, and so filled with passion. Valiant had reconstructed the circle of people and lanterns in the middle of the street just outside the hut, and every once in a while his deep voice would drift in, reminding everyone inside that heartfelt appeals were constantly rising to the Father of Lights. With tight lines on every face in the triage hut, and more than a few trembling hands, prayers riding upward on brisk winds outside created a comforting thought indeed.

Billy stood next to Ashley, trying to keep his eyes on her and away from Listener's exposed body. Of course, since Listener was still prepubescent, the sight of her bared torso didn't bother him at all. It was the open cavity, the split sternum, the beating heart . . . and blood, lots of it. Too much of it.

Fortunately, the lung machine kept her lung from deflating, though it added a network of homemade tubes going into and out of her body, making her look even more pitiful than she had before. Running on a combination of springs and a solar cell, the machine let out a low hum, not unpleasant, but a constant reminder of the life-and-death tightrope Listener was walking.

Her companion floated lazily back and forth in front of her closed eyes. Much dimmer than usual, it seemed sluggish. Every few seconds, it would flash blue light from its core, but it quickly died away. Candle had explained that the companions often reflected the health or vigor of their charges. A brighter light and more active companion signaled a well-rested person, and a dimmer glow and lethargic companion usually reflected exhaustion.

Billy shifted his gaze to the IV stand. A bag of blood hung there, dripping rapidly into a tube. Three more bags lay on a table near Listener's head, recent donations from villagers. If this kept up, they would run out in a hurry, but they had found six more matches, and the donors were told to be ready at a moment's notice.

Sir Patrick stood next to the table, leaning toward the cot, his body arched over Listener's face. With Ashley's stethoscope draped around his neck and a suction tube in his hand, he extended the tube toward the wound every time Ashley nodded in his direction. It took only a few minutes for him to learn where to whisk blood away and how long to keep the tube in place. The blood pressure gauge lay in his other hand, ready to be pumped and checked, which he did precisely every thirty seconds. From the start of surgery until now, Listener's pressure had stayed low but fairly steady, a miracle really, considering how much blood she was losing.

Near the door, Mantika, Candle, and Windor fidgeted. Candle held the spyglass and Windor fingered the hilt of his sheathed knife. Candle's companion perched on top of his head, its blue light strobing. It was his job to watch the lung machine and wind up the springs if the solar cell ran low. So far, that hadn't been necessary, but Candle kept his ear close to the machine, just in case.

Dangling from ropes, several lanterns hung directly over Listener's cot. They cast several competing rays over her body, some brighter than others, but all steady enough to keep the surgical area bright. With a barricade of empty cots in front of the door, no one would come or go and stir up the air, which would surely disturb the burning wicks.

Ashley, her hair tied back and covered with a tight bandana, stood next to the cot, her elbows up and her fingers inside the cavity. Her eyes darted back and forth, riveted for a second at one spot, then at another. "I got this vessel, Doc. Sealing it off."

Dr. Conner, his sleeves rolled up to his tense biceps, lifted a piece of the spear's shaft out of the hole and showed it to her. "That's the last big piece of wood. I'm going after the point."

"Perfect. Good work."

He pushed his fingers back in. "The point's just barely touching the heart, so we're good there. I'm taking it out."

"There's a splintered piece attached," Ashley said. "Be careful."

265

"I see it. If I pull straight out, the barb will get caught on lung tissue on your left."

"I can't push the tissue back, Doc. My hands are full." She looked at Billy. "I need a finger."

Billy raised one. "Show me what to do."

She gestured with her eyes. "See where the spear point's barb touches the lung?"

Billy licked his lips. "Yeah."

"Push down on the tissue until it's clear."

He eased his finger into the cavity. "This pink stuff?"

"That's it. ... Good. Perfect." Ashley looked up at Dr. Conner. "I think we're clear, Doc. Take it real easy."

"Don't worry." Using both hands, he eased the point toward himself, then lifted it out of the cavity. "Got it."

Billy looked at Ashley. "Can I pull out now?"

"Yes. Slowly."

266

As Billy eased his hand away, Ashley's brow knitted tightly. "I've got bleeding, Doc! Big time!" She looked at Patrick. "Suction! Now!"

Patrick reached the tube toward her, but Dr. Conner grabbed it. "It's the heart. Have to be delicate."

Listener's companion landed on her forehead and dimmed further. Billy looked at Sir Patrick. Their gazes met. As the old former dragon pressed his hands together, Billy nodded. The prayer posture. Doctor or no doctor, Listener's only real hope lay in the hands of a higher power.

"I don't know what's wrong," Ashley said. "My hands aren't sealing the leaks like they were before."

"What's going on?" Walter asked, still lying on his cot.

His throat tightening, Billy could barely talk. "Bleeding," was all he could manage.

"Patrick!" Ashley barked. "Hang another bag!"

While Patrick hurried through the procedure, Billy let his gaze wander over to Semiramis. She stared back at him, still sad, still as innocent looking as a lamb.

"May I speak?" she called in a quiet voice.

Billy nodded. "I guess that won't hurt."

"My words were proven true. The garden energized, and you have a doctor."

"We don't know why that happened," Billy said. "Maybe it was the ring. Maybe not."

"In any case, please allow me to offer my assistance. I am skilled in many arts."

"What kind of assistance?"

"When Steadfast worked on my son, I noticed that the doctor who was once here was a mistress of exotic potions, and I am familiar with her craft."

Billy turned to Ashley. "Did you hear that?"

The sweat-dampened bandana over her brow slid higher as she nodded. "We're already using Angel's clotting factor."

"I assumed so," Semiramis said. "I saw it on the table earlier. There is another potion I thought she might have, but I did not see it."

"What does it do?" Billy asked.

"It will slow Listener's functions, including her heart, until she will be near death, though still safely in the grip of life. While her bleeding is slower, you can repair her body."

Dr. Conner looked up at Ashley. "A chemically induced coma?"

"Sounds like it." Now breathing rapidly, Ashley shot Semiramis a suspicious stare. "What's in it? Tell me quick!"

"Ingredients with which you would not be familiar."

Sir Patrick's voice pierced the tense air. "Blood pressure has dropped. Seventy over thirty-five."

267

"I can't seal it!" Ashley cried. "My touch isn't doing anything!"

Dr. Conner lurched toward the table. "Sutures!"

While they scrambled, Semiramis pushed against the wall and struggled to her feet. "Untie me!" she shouted, extending her bound hands. "I can help you!"

His sword hand covered with blood, Billy set his fingers just above Excalibur's hilt. Should he release her? Would she really help, or would she brew poison?

The sound of metal sliding on metal made Billy twist toward his scabbard. Walter stood next to him, holding Excalibur in both hands. "There really isn't any choice, is there?" Walter stalked toward Semiramis. Although he staggered a bit, his path was straight and true. With a deft swipe, he cut through the rope, and the pieces fell to the floor.

268

While Ashley and Dr. Conner continued working frantically, volleying sharp commands back and forth, Semiramis massaged her wrists and turned to Mantika and her sons. "Dwellers of Second Eden. I will need narla root, sempian bark, and one drop of venom from a cave spider. The other ingredients are already here."

Candle pointed at himself. "I know a burrow where two cave spiders live."

Windor nodded. "I get root and bark."

Tossing aside the pile of cots in front of the door, Candle and Windor dashed outside. As a snow-filled draft rushed through, Mantika quickly shut the door.

The hanging lanterns stirred, troubling the light over Listener and her surgeons. Ashley looked up at the swinging ropes. "Somebody stop those things! I can't see!"

"Sixty-five over thirty-five," Patrick announced.

Billy grabbed Excalibur from Walter. He slid a cot close to the surgery table, stood on it, and reached the sword toward the ceiling. As he touched the ropes one at a time, he looked down at the steadying light. From this perspective, Listener's pale body seemed small and faraway, yet the hole in her chest seemed cavernous as blood flowed over the four frantic hands. Her companion wobbled as if ready to fall.

Semiramis marched to the potions table, slid a wide-mouthed jar to the front, and, one by one, picked up small glass bottles filled with crushed red, green, or brown leaves. "Yes, the other ingredients are here." She looked up at Billy. "This potion must be heated. Where can I find a fire?"

He jumped down from the cot and slid it out of the way. "I've got that covered. Just say the word."

Windor burst in. In one hand he carried two thick wet roots, still covered with dirt. In the other, he clutched a hunk of green bark and a serrated knife. "Covered with snow," he said. "But Windor find."

Mantika immediately closed the door. The lanterns swayed, but only a little. Her dark face taut and her eyes wide, she pointed at the ingredients table. "Roots need skin peeled."

"Yes, yes, I know," Semiramis said. "Bring them here."

As Windor dropped the ingredients on the table, Candle hurried in, his dreadlocks flying. He lifted a gray spider between his thumb and forefinger. Its wiggling legs spread out as wide as his hand. "I got him!"

"Hurry it over here before it bites you!" Semiramis reached for Windor's knife. "I have to draw out the spider's poison."

Windor pulled it away and looked at Billy, his brow arching. "Windor give?"

"Sixty-five over thirty!" Patrick announced.

Ashley called from the surgical cot. "Get that potion! We're losing her!" Her voice seemed strained, weaker. Listener's companion toppled from her forehead and fell to the cot.

Raising Excalibur, Billy nodded. "Go ahead."

Semiramis glared at him. "Your faith in me is so inspiring."

"Just get the potion done. If it works, I'll be the first to apologize."

17

A POTION FROM POISON

Windor extended the knife. Still glowering at Billy, Semiramis snatched it and drove the blade through the spider's head, pinning it to the table. Dark blood oozed from underneath and inched along the wood grain. A blue stream, bright and sparkling, added to the flow, but the two colors stayed unmixed. She freed the knife and, using the tip of the blade, picked up a drop of the blue liquid and let it fall into a jar.

Her hands zipping from the ingredients to a mortar and pestle to a bottle of water, Semiramis seemed to be a woman possessed. As her hair fell in front of her eyes, she just blew it back and kept working. In less than a minute, she presented Billy with a glass jar containing about half an inch of brown liquid at the bottom. "Heat it until it turns green."

Billy pulled a glove from his pocket and put it on. Holding the jar by its top, he blew a stream of fire just under the glass base. For a few seconds, nothing happened. Then tiny bubbles formed on the surface and began popping, releasing a brown gas that rose over the brim and dribbled to the floor.

271

"Give me an update!" Ashley wiped her sleeve across her brow. "I think the invigorating potion is losing steam. I'm not going to last much longer."

"I see green!" Billy shouted. "It won't be long."

Semiramis grabbed the jar. "It's enough!"

"Wait. That jar has to be as hot as—"

"I know!" Stirring the concoction with a tongue depressor, Semiramis rushed to Ashley's side. "Drinking it is too dangerous and slow. You must rub it directly into her heart."

Ashley looked at Dr. Conner, alarm blazing on her face. "Doc?"

"Just do it. She's a goner if we don't try something."

Turning away from Listener, Ashley extended a bloody palm. "Pour some on."

"It will sting like no wasp you have ever felt." Semiramis held Ashley's wrist and tipped the jar just enough to let a trickle of greenish sludge fall.

When it touched her skin, Ashley cringed but made no sound. Coffee-colored fumes rose from her hands, and tears streamed down her cheeks. She gasped for breath. Sweat poured. "I'm … I'm all right. It's not really that hot. It's just having a weird effect on me."

"It's slowing your metabolism," Semiramis said. When a small pool had formed in Ashley's palm, Semiramis pulled the jar upright. "Now, massage it in. Hurry."

Ashley turned back to Listener, let the potion drip onto the exposed heart, and massaged it in with her other hand. After a few seconds, she looked up at Dr. Conner. "It's slowing down."

"I see that. So is the bleeding."

"That's enough." Semiramis pulled Ashley's hand back. "Too much will kill her."

Ashley staggered backwards, but Patrick caught her before she fell. "I'm so dizzy."

Walter jumped up. "Ashley!"

272

"She is not in danger," Semiramis said, "but she must rest."

Ashley stared at her, her eyes wide and glazed. "Your mind is unguarded. I sense … I sense … murder." Her head lolled to one side, and her eyes closed.

"Take her, Walter," Patrick said. "I must return to my suction duties."

As Walter eased Ashley to the floor, Billy pressed Excalibur's tip close to Semiramis's throat. "What did you do to her?"

Her eyes riveted on the blade, she swallowed. "I assure you, gracious knight. This is a natural result of the potion in concert with her exhausted condition. The invigorating elixir is wearing off, and she absorbed some of my potion. She has merely passed into a swoon."

He set the point against her skin and growled. "She said she sensed murder."

"Please forgive my indiscretion and the weakness of a mother's protective instincts. I sorely wish to kill Arramos to avenge what he did to my son. Surely this is what Ashley detected."

"Her heart is down to ten beats per minute," Dr. Conner said, "but the bleeding's almost stopped. I can sew up the worst hole now."

"As you can see," Semiramis continued, "my potion is working. I have no intent to hurt anyone in this village, especially an innocent little girl."

Billy pulled the sword away and nodded at Candle. "You and Windor tie her up again. I'll go out and speak to Valiant and Elam."

"I willingly submit to your authority." Semiramis pressed her wrists together. "I am trustworthy. You will see."

As Candle led her to the corner, Billy shoved Excalibur back in place. "How's she doing, Doc?"

"Whatever that potion was, it has done much more than simply slow Listener's bodily functions. If I may venture a guess, that potion absorbed some of Ashley's healing characteristics, her photoreceptors, and her heart is pumping them throughout her body. It's as if the wounds are sealing themselves."

"Her diastolic pressure has stabilized," Patrick said. "With the slow heart rate, her systolic is difficult to measure, but I believe it, too, has stabilized."

Walter piped up from the floor where he cradled Ashley. "Her palm's bleeding. I'll bet her blood mixed in with that potion."

"Is she all right?" Billy asked.

"I think so. She's breathing okay. Knocked out cold, though."

Candle tapped on Billy's shoulder. "We tied up Semiramis. Windor showed me a new knot. She'll never get loose."

"Thank you." Billy unhooked his scabbard and gave it to Candle. "Keep an eye on her. I'm going out to talk to Elam."

As he reached for the door, Semiramis called from the corner. "Son of Clefspeare!"

He turned toward her. "Yes?"

274

With her eyes reflecting the lantern light and her voice calm and soothing, she seemed more like a storybook muse than a woman. "I have saved the little girl's life. If she and Ashley arise from their slumbers, I will await the apology you promised."

Billy looked at her for a long moment. Turmoil swam through his mind. There were just too many conflicting signs, too many hard decisions to make. Figuring out if this strange woman was truthful seemed impossible. First she seemed in league with the Nephilim, and now she breathed murderous threats against Arramos right after working so hard to save the life of someone who couldn't help her in the slightest.

He looked back at Listener. Her companion again perched on her forehead, but it was still dim.

Finally, Billy nodded. "We'll see very soon, won't we?" He opened the door, stepped outside, and shut it behind him. After taking two steps to the edge of the wooden walkway, he stopped and scanned the area.

Illuminated by lanterns at each side of the street, Valiant stood at the center of a throng of seated villagers, his hands uplifted as he paced back and forth in the midst of falling snow. Wearing a fur cap that covered his ears but not the dark curly hair that protruded from underneath, and a thick forest green cloak that fell to his knees and fanned out as he walked, he looked like a warlord exhorting the troops. Yet, his words said otherwise. Though his voice resonated in a rich baritone that demanded attention, and his companion's light flashed in cadence with his rhythm, each syllable carried the flavor of entreaty rather than the bark of command.

"Father of Lights, now that each man, woman, and child has lifted up cries for a miracle, songs begging for deliverance, and lamentations for this precious girl, this selfless little lamb, I add my final appeal."

He paused for a moment and swung back to pace the other way. As murmurs of "Hear him" mixed in with the whistling breeze, he continued. "Listener is a precious flower. Though she sprouted from our garden soil weak and fragile, mute and masked in scaly skin, we loved her. For no child in this world is ever considered of lesser value than any other. We have heard from our visitors that people in the world she came from cast away unwanted children, even butchering them more savagely than they would a murderer or a dog. So you sent her to us, and we have cared for her, this daisy, this rose of suffering, and she carried within her frail shell a heart of fire, proven by her willingness to suffer and die for the deliverance of others."

Again he paused and turned. Billy wanted to shout out, "Listener's recovering!" but the news was premature. It was still touch and go, and besides, interrupting a prayer like this seemed irreverent.

He spotted Elam across the street walking his way around the perimeter of the circle. With snow capping his black hood and a slight bend in his slow gait, he looked like a gray-haired old man trying to cross a slippery street.

275

Valiant glanced at Billy. Heaving a sigh that blew out in a stream of bright white, he continued. "Perhaps even now the struggle in that hut is over. Perhaps you have touched her with your healing power or provided the skills necessary to heal our little flower. Or perhaps you have decided to take her to your heavenly home and leave us bereft of the beauty and joy she has brought to our world. Whatever your decision, we will never forsake the love that you have called us to give to you and to our neighbors. For it is love that courses through our souls as blood courses through our veins, and by that love we will survive and carry on your work in this land." He clasped his hands together and shouted, "Father of Lights, hear our prayer!"

Young and old, the crowd echoed his call. "Father of Lights, hear our prayer!" Companions flashed all around, like twinkling blue lights in a Christmas display.

Valiant turned and walked slowly toward Billy, weaving past the villagers who were now rising. Elam arrived at the sidewalk first and, hugging his dampened cloak close to his body, whispered, "Any word?"

Billy clutched Elam's arm and moved him under the protection of the roof's overhang. "Let's wait for Valiant." Rising to tiptoes, he scanned the heads in the crowd for Rebekah's blond locks. "Are Rebekah and Dallas here?"

Elam shook his head. "We decided to let them transform while there was still some energy in the bones of Makaidos. They are now Legossi and Firedda, and they are at the garden with the other dragons."

"Excellent. Where is Acacia?"

"At her hut. Asleep, probably."

"All for the best." Billy imagined the dragons huddling in the snowy garden. How would they stay warm? Could the villagers build shelters for them?

Valiant jumped up to the walk. "How is our little flower?"

"Still alive," Billy said, "but barely. Semiramis concocted a potion that—"

"Semiramis!" Elam's voice spiked. "You let her loose? You let her brew a potion?"

"Calm down. It looks like it worked. Listener was about to die, and Semiramis said she could help. What was I supposed to do?"

Valiant clapped Billy on the shoulder. "A wise decision. Choosing a potential danger over certain death was your only option."

Elam gave a nod of surrender. "Okay. If she's decided to help us, I guess we can accept it, but I won't believe it's not for her own benefit until proven otherwise."

"Same here," Billy said. "Apparently handling the potion knocked Ashley out, or at least aggravated her exhaustion, so that's more than suspicious. And another strange thing. Just before Ashley conked out, she got an impression from Semiramis's mind, something about murder. Semiramis claimed that she wanted to kill Arramos because of what he did to Hunter, but I'm not sure I'm buying that story yet."

277

"A reasonable concern," Valiant said. "For we now also suspect Hunter is not genuine. He no longer has a companion, and no Second Edener can be separated from his companion without immediate sickness and eventual death."

"And he shows no signs?" Elam asked.

"He seemed healthy for a while, but after one of our little boys mentioned that he should be ill, Hunter began complaining of nausea and dizziness."

Billy rolled his eyes. "How convenient."

"Indeed. We would not let him go into the medical hut to see his mother. He is now at Cliffside's hut with Cliffside guarding him."

"What about the companion?" Billy asked. "Any sign of it?"

Valiant shook his head. "We searched the garden, but with snow and darkness covering the field, any further attempts by humans seemed impossible. The dragons, however, will begin melting the snow and searching the grass with their laser eyes. If the companion is out there, they should be able to find it."

"Companion or no companion," Elam said, "we can't take any chances. Given Hunter's charade and Ashley's report about Semiramis's murderous intent, I say we send them away."

"Banishment to the northern lands?" Valiant asked. "During the season of death?"

Elam rolled his fingers into a fist. "If we're going to stay strong, we have to make sure all corrupting agents are gone."

"I'm not sure of that," Billy said. "If she's really an enemy, I'd rather have her close where I can keep an eye on her."

Valiant smiled. "A keen observation. Yet, if your enemy desires to be close to you, then you can be sure that her intent is to watch and wait for the moment when your back is turned."

Elam gazed at the door to the triage hut. He seemed pensive, worried. "We will discuss it in the morning. By then we'll know if Listener and Ashley are going to recover."

278

"And if Hunter is a true resident of Second Eden," Valiant added. "If he is, he will be dead by dawn."

The door opened behind Billy, and Walter shuffled out with a blanket draped over his shoulders. "Brrr! It's colder than Morgan's heart out here."

"How's Listener?" Billy asked.

"That's why I came out. The bleeding stayed under control, and her pressure went up. Just a little, but it's positive. Not only that, her companion's buzzing around again, happy as a lark."

Valiant spun toward the street and clapped his hands. The villagers, some milling around and others dispersing toward their homes, stopped in their tracks. "Praise the Father of Lights!" he shouted. "Our little flower is recovering!"

Some of the villagers jumped in place, repeating, "Praise the Father of Lights!" while others joined hands and danced, sliding on the snow-covered street and laughing gaily while their companions flashed and zoomed in tight orbits around their heads.

Billy laughed with them. Seeing such an outburst of happiness after so much tension felt fantastic.

Walter nudged Billy's side. "And Doc says Ashley's okay, too. Her vitals are stable, and she's sleeping like a baby."

Billy clasped Walter's shoulder. "That's cool, Walter. That's really cool."

"Not to put a damper on the celebration ..." He flicked his head toward the triage hut. "What're we going to do with spooky Semiramis and her suddenly companionless son?"

"You heard about that?"

"Yeah. You guys are loud."

Billy pushed a hand into his pocket. "First I'm going to have to apologize to her."

"And then banish her?" Walter smirked. "Not exactly a believable apology."

"That part's not my decision." Billy reached for the door. "Come on. I might as well get it over with."

Once inside, Billy scanned the room. Walter walked straight to Ashley's cot, while Mantika sidled up to Billy and took his hand. "Listener lives," she said, smiling at him.

Billy patted her hand. As he looked at her dark, gleeful face, tears welled in his eyes. "I heard, Mantika. It's a miracle."

"Miracle. Yes. It is miracle." Mantika compressed Billy's hand. "Praise the Father of Lights." She pulled away, joined Candle and Windor near Listener's side, and kissed both boys on the cheek.

Billy took a few steps closer to the surgery cot and peeked at Listener. Still unconscious and pale, she seemed barely alive, but with her chest now sewn back together with thick dark sutures and her skin free of blood, at least she didn't look like the victim of a bomb attack.

Dr. Conner sat on a nearby cot, his elbows resting on his knees as he looked up at Billy. "Pressure's eighty over forty. Her heart's strong. Her lung inflated. If infection doesn't set in, I think she'll make it."

"Way to go, Doc." Billy tightened his trembling fingers into a fist. "You were amazing."

Dr. Conner nodded toward the opposite corner. "If not for our prisoner, we would be telling a different story."

Billy looked at Semiramis as she sat with her back to the corner. Once again she had taken on the aspect of a mythical siren, her eyes wide, her gaze entrancing, her lips quivering in a mournful pose. With her bound wrists resting on her knees and her hands clasped, she looked more like a supplicant begging for mercy than an imprisoned witch.

With a shrug of resignation, he walked toward her, trying to avert his gaze, but something about her deep pleading eyes kept him entranced. He pushed his hands into his pockets again and stopped in front of her, shifting back and forth. "I ... uh ... I guess I owe you an apology."

"You owe me nothing, son of nobility. If you wish, however, to offer a gift of gracious words, then I am ready to receive it."

Billy cleared his throat. "I'm sorry for what I said. Your potion made all the difference in the world."

"My potion, as you call it, is nothing more than a mixture of natural elements." She lifted her eyebrows. "Do you understand my meaning?"

"I think so. You're trying to tell me that you're not a witch or a sorceress. You didn't conjure the stuff up through some magical power."

"Yes, Billy. It is your trust I crave, not your willingness to praise a jar of green liquid. I am merely a mother who lost her way. I trusted a vile dragon and obeyed his command to guard a dangerous bridge. I had no idea that he wished to use the chasm to bring these people to destruction. Now that I have rebelled against him, I am a woman without a country, without a home, for I have deduced that the people of this village will send my son and me away."

"Probably. Hunter lost his companion, and since he doesn't seem to be suffering, they think you lied about him being a Second Edener, especially since he started putting on an act. Elam and Valiant said they would decide your case in the morning."

"Ah, how I pity these villagers! Their lack of knowledge begets such naïveté. Hunter comes from a village in the northern lands, a place these people have never visited because of their tradition that these two villages hold God's only chosen people. They assume that all true Second Edeners are like themselves. If there is the slightest difference, prejudice is born, and they assume the peculiar man or woman is one of the altered tribes. And now Hunter is trying to be something he is not. He is frightened and wishes to preserve his life and mine. You see, his companion will return to him. Have no fear of that. While he waits for it, imprisoned by a people who mistrust him, Hunter is doing what he can to survive."

281

"So what do you want me to do? Try to convince them?"

"No, Billy. It has become clear that we cannot live in harmony here, at least not until the people learn to tolerate those who are different." She lifted her wrists. "Cut my bonds. Allow us to go in peace. If we wait until morning, the pass through the mountains might well be blocked with snow."

He shook his head. "I don't have the authority to do that. I'm just a soldier. Elam and Valiant make all the decisions."

"Then make an appeal for my release now. If your apology is sincere, if your words of trust are more than mere sounds from your lips, then do whatever you must to let us leave this place with our lives and a scrap of dignity intact."

"I guess I can do that." He dragged his toe across the floor. The tension felt thick, heavy. The struggle between loyalty to Elam and trying to get justice for this woman was too intense for words.

Curling a finger, she whispered, "Come closer. There is something else that must remain a secret between us, at least for now."

Billy closed the gap and stooped. "I'm not promising to keep anything secret."

"Very well. But choose wisely whom you will trust and when you reveal it." She scooted so close, her breath warmed his ear. "The finger in the box haunts you, does it not?"

He nodded. "Yeah. It shook me up."

"Although I am not a sorceress, I am familiar with the arts of the evil dragon who devised that cruel plan. He knew you would need an energizing device, so he provided it, also knowing that your use of it would create an advantage for him."

"What advantage?"

"The garden will now generate a plant that will look unlike the others. It will be ugly in comparison, and some might be tempted to uproot it as a weed. But they must not. The life of that plant will be tied to the life of the girl who wore the ring. If it dies, she will die."

Billy tried to draw back an inch, but the woman's tractive draw seemed stronger than ever. "How will the plant help Arramos?"

"By causing the people to do someone harm. As you have heard, when the people of Second Eden do any sort of evil, it allows greater evil to enter the world, as happened with Angel's lie and the coming of the Nephilim. With the new dragons you have in your army, Arramos knows that he has to fortify his own army. He cannot do this without help from someone willing to do evil."

"But if they don't know it's wrong to uproot the plant, it won't be evil to do it. I mean, not a real evil. Just an innocent mistake."

Her whisper lowered even further. "You are correct, and that is why our enemy's plan is so diabolical. Since I know the secret tie between the plant and Bonnie, I am bound by goodness to warn you, and since your love for her obligates you to protect her, you are bound by goodness to warn the others, and since they are bound by goodness to heed your warning to protect Bonnie and prevent a new assault of evil, they will allow the plant to grow unhindered."

"Will the plant spawn anything? I mean, will it carry a life inside like the others?"

"That I do not know. I can only guess that it will spawn a life, something that will be in league with Arramos, perhaps even worse than the evil that would come as a result of uprooting the plant."

"Then we'll watch it night and day," Billy said, touching the hilt of his sword, "and if it delivers, we'll destroy the fruit, whatever it is."

"Destroy it?" Semiramis grasped his hand. "Billy, you cannot kill something that has not proven itself evil. As I told you, I do not know anything about what might be spawned. That is part of the dragon's plan that extends beyond my knowledge. As the bridge's guardian, I had the opportunity to learn about some of his ways, because he would often pass to and fro in that land. But it is clear to me now that he always kept his darkest counsel to himself. All I know with certainty is that the plant's life will be tied to Bonnie's."

283

"You keep saying Bonnie. How do you know the finger didn't belong to ... to someone else?" Billy was tempted to mention Shiloh, but giving Semiramis more information than she needed probably wasn't a good idea.

"There is no need to hide your thoughts. I heard your theory about Shiloh. It holds merit, but neither of us has any way of knowing. Since Bonnie is missing, I think it is wise to assume that our enemies have her in their grasp."

"What about Arramos's threat? Will he send more body parts?"

"I am not sure." Semiramis gazed at one of her long, narrow fingers. "Perhaps he will send more fingers and maybe some toes until the plant is well established. Once he is sure that it will be protected, he would be a fool to slice her further. At that point, we would hold the plant hostage in the same way he is holding her hostage. We each will be demanding a ransom of protection."

As he tried to untangle the web of possibilities, the message Semiramis delivered repeated in his mind. *"If the dragons and their offspring continued to ally themselves with the residents of Second Eden, this gift would be accompanied by more of the precious puzzle at a later time."*

"He's got us in a bind. If we don't want any more body parts delivered here, the dragons have to vow not to fight with us, and he's free to keep slicing her up until the plant sprouts."

Looking away, Semiramis nodded. "Yes, it is ingenious, I must admit. Yet there is a way to stop him."

"What's that?"

"To rescue Bonnie ... or Shiloh, whoever he is holding hostage."

"How? Do you know where he might be keeping her?"

"I do. That is one of my purposes for leaving. I must try to get to his lair and attempt a rescue."

Billy grasped Excalibur. "Let me come with you. I think Arramos is the dragon I faced in the abyss below the seventh circle."

"Then who will protect the plant? Is there anyone here besides you who will believe my words? Will Elam believe me?"

As he stared at Semiramis's gleaming eyes, Elam's words rushed back into Billy's mind. *"I won't believe it's not for her own benefit until proven otherwise."*

"You know that he wouldn't," Semiramis continued. "And Valiant would heed his counsel. It would be up to you to protect the plant, and if you are not there ..."

Billy pointed at himself. "But how do *I* know you're telling the truth about the tie between Bonnie and the plant? Maybe I would be an idiot to believe something like that without proof."

"If Arramos is using the binding tie that I believe he would use, then a simple test would prove the connection." She looked toward the hut's door. "You preserved the finger, did you not?"

"Elam put it on ice. The ring's gone, but, yeah, we still have the finger."

"When you see the first tender leaves of a new plant sprout, which should be very soon, check for orange and black tips. Those are the colors of Arramos, which will be the sign that you have the correct plant. Retrieve the finger and let a drop of blood touch a leaf. If the leaf withers, it is because of the connection between it and the prisoner of Arramos. The spillage of blood is reflected in the plant, just as harm to the plant would be reflected in Bonnie. Then quickly pinch off the withering portion so that death does not spread to the rest of the plant."

285

Billy imagined a voodoo doll with Bonnie's face on it. If not for Semiramis's serious expression and tone, he would have dismissed her story as ridiculous superstition. It just didn't make sense.

"I sense disbelief in you," she continued, "so you would be wise to wait for this proof before you commit to anything. Still, while you await the first leaves, you run the risk of receiving another body part from Arramos. The only other options would be either to get the dragons to vow to refrain from battle or else to rescue Bonnie quickly. My hope, however, is that the plant will show itself immediately; then the risk will be low."

Billy imagined once again the severed finger lying in blood-stained cotton. His thoughts then wandered to a dark room where Bonnie sat crying in a corner, her hand covered with a bandage, red where her finger used to be. The thought churned his stomach. And even if the hostage was Shiloh instead of Bonnie, the image stayed the same. It was tragic.

Billy shook his head. "You're right. No one else would be willing to do all that. I'll stay here."

"Then appeal for my release. When I find Bonnie, and you have had time to prove to the others that the connection is real, I will send for you. Then together we will rescue her before she loses another finger ... or worse."

RETURN TO PERDITION

M arilyn let her head droop until it tapped against the desk. A pencil fell from its perch atop her ear and rolled. Looking at it from the corner of her eye, she watched it fall to the computer room carpet. No matter. She was too tired to use it anyway.

With only a lamp and Larry's panel monitor illuminating her work area, the surrounding dimness eased her eyelids downward. Tomorrow. She would do more research tomorrow. Gabriel was already following up on the best leads—the helicopter registration, the pilot's license, and a flight log. Apparently the soldiers didn't cover their tracks very well, likely not thinking their chopper would be commandeered by their prey. Still, that didn't mean they were sloppy enough to leave a link between the pilot and whoever held Shiloh, so making that connection might be impossible, but it was worth a try.

A feminine voice reached her ear. "Mrs. Bannister?"

She lifted her head. Carly stood at the doorway to the hall, wearing the flannel pajamas she had borrowed from Shelly. "Yes, Carly?"

"Still no word from Bonnie?"

287

"No, dear." She touched the telephone on the desk. "Yereq called an hour ago. The water finally stopped rising, but the museum chamber and all the tunnels are flooded, so no one could be there."

"And the other divers?"

"Neither one found anything. I think Bonnie and Sapphira must have escaped through a portal. That's Sapphira's way."

"I hope so." With her hands behind her back, and her head low, she walked in, half sliding in a pair of oversized slippers. "I'm sorry we didn't get Apollo working."

Marilyn waved her hand. "Don't worry about it. It's not your fault. It took Ashley longer than you and Adam have had to work on it."

"Ashley worked from scratch. We had all the schematics and software."

"Don't beat yourself up. Ashley's a super genius." She tapped a finger on Larry's main keyboard. "He's a genius, too, but he doesn't have hands and eyes to help you with."

"Marilyn," Larry said. "May I be so bold as to offer my insight without being asked?"

"Certainly."

"Some of our failures are due to lack of supply of the newest generation parts. The panic that has arisen because of strange creatures lurking in the streets and long-dead people surprising the populace has put quite a pinch on commerce."

"Especially the appearance of long-dead dictators, mass murderers, and gangsters."

"Precisely. I suggest using these phenomena to our advantage."

"How would we do that?"

"You need a human genius. My guess is that there are a few geniuses residing in Hades who are unable to fit back into society, perhaps due to fear or a desire to be alone. Find one of them and request his or her help. I think he or she will be happy to be of use in a concrete way."

"But one of our goals is to separate Earth and Hades," Marilyn said. "The genius will be helping us condemn himself."

"Questions of ethics are beyond the scope of my programming, but my commonsense engine suggests that you tell the genius everything so that your conscience will be clear. He or she will likely dismiss your concerns because of eagerness to work on the project."

"So how do we find one?"

"I am already searching news stories for appearances of the dead. I will filter them using a list of physicists who would have enough brainpower to help us."

Marilyn looked at Carly and winked. "They would have to be physicists who didn't go to Heaven. Good luck with that."

"Their eternal destination is not in my database. I will check all on the list."

"Okay, Mr. Data Sleuth. You and Carly come up with the best option. I'll help her contact our condemned physicist in the morning."

289

Shiloh sat on the familiar bench in front of the abandoned dry goods store. Sniffing back tears, she rubbed her index finger along the marks she had etched into the backrest, one for each of the forty years she had spent in the sixth circle of Hades. Her release had been the most wonderful day imaginable, and when she leaped into her father's arms and felt his warm embrace, she knew, she just knew without a doubt, that all the suffering, all the fear, all the anguish had finally ended.

She stared at the stub on her hand, bandaged and still damp with blood. She was wrong. The suffering had begun all over again, worse than ever, and she was back in the clutches of her never-ending nightmare. And who could rescue her this time?

When Morgan kidnapped her, at least her father knew where she had gone, but now no one knew. With Daddy, Billy, Walter, Acacia, and so many others in Second Eden, who on Earth would guess that she had been taken to this God-forsaken place? Sapphira and Bonnie? Maybe. But they were being chased, too. How could they come out of hiding to rescue her? And even if they did try, could they get into this part of Hades at all? Even with Hades and Earth combining, would they figure out the path?

A loud rumble sounded from her abdomen. She pressed the heel of her hand against her stomach. Four days without food. The first three weren't so bad. Pressure made the pain go away. But not this time. Now she would have to face the part of the nightmare she had avoided since coming here. The watering trough near the stables had kept her from getting thirsty, but the only source of food lay in the direction she hadn't yet dared go.

She got up and shuffled to the street. With her hands folded behind her, she strolled toward the central circle, kicking any pebble that happened to be in her path. There were no wandering spirits, no Frankie, no Bat Masterson, no humanlike entities to alter the stark deadness that settled around her. With her hand throbbing and the threats of more disfigurement looming, what could be worse? Could anyone survive the misery of being slowly butchered in a strange world?

Yet this wasn't really a strange world. She knew exactly what to expect—the same routine she suffered through for forty years.

When she reached the town's circle, she found the pitcher pump, exactly where it had always been, anchored in the raised garden area with the spout extending over the dirt at the side of the street. Shading the pump from the morning sun, a twenty-foot-tall statue stood in its usual spot, Captain Autarkeia riding a rearing horse.

Shiloh pumped the handle. Water poured out and made a swirling puddle in the mud. Yes, it was all the same. Soon, the plant would grow, she would eat its fruit and get violently sick, and once she felt better, she would wander around until nightfall until she made a bed among the broken crates in an alley.

She sat on the raised curb and waited. Nights were the worst. Sleeping inside the abandoned buildings always produced the most horrible nightmares, and strange noises seemed to stalk the streets. Maybe it was always the wind rattling broken window shutters and rusty chains, but the sounds were enough to keep her in hiding behind the alley crates. Besides, they provided shelter from the wind's chill.

Soon, the plant sprouted, and its green stalk grew at its usual fast rate. When the five-leafed bulb appeared, she plucked it, peeled away the stubborn leathery leaves, and tossed them to the side. With a sigh, she stared at the fibrous white fruit. Just looking at it brought stabs of pain to her stomach. But it had been four days since her last meal, and it hadn't killed her the previous ten thousand times she had eaten it, so it didn't make sense to fret about it now.

291

Just as she opened her mouth, someone called from the other side of the circle. "Greetings!"

Shiloh turned toward the voice. A woman dressed in red from head to toe walked out from behind the statue.

"Who are you?" Shiloh asked, remembering to continue faking an American accent.

Smiling, the woman lowered her hood and sat next to her on the curb. "I was going to ask you the same question."

Shiloh half closed one eye. "I asked you first."

She laughed and touched herself on the chest. "I am Semiramis. I have come to find a way to rescue you from this place."

Shiloh leaped to her feet. "You have? Who sent you?"

"Why, your friends in Second Eden, of course. Billy hasn't so soon forgotten you."

"Billy?" Shiloh's face flushed hot. Obviously Semiramis thought she was Bonnie. Had she already blown her cover? And if Semiramis was a friend, would it be okay to let her know the truth? Probably not yet. Better to feel her out and get more information.

Shiloh sat down again and calmed her voice. "Yes, of course. I know Billy would send for me if he were able, but how did he find out I was kidnapped?"

"Your captors sent us your finger, a hideously cruel act designed to instill fear in our hearts. Not only did the finger have your rubellite ring still on it, the box included a lock of your hair, and Billy recognized your blond highlights. Also, two former dragons, Rebekah and Dallas, have come to Second Eden, and they told us that Shiloh had been taken and Bonnie went missing later. We wondered if the finger might have been Shiloh's, but since the kidnappers did not deliver it until after Bonnie's disappearance, we decided that they had waited until they had her, the real former dragon girl, in their clutches."

Semiramis pulled a wad of gauze from her pocket along with a small bottle. "Here is material for a clean bandage and an infection-fighting potion. When I heard about your finger, I assumed you would need these. There is an adhesive strip in there as well."

"Thank you." Shiloh peeled off her old bandage, red and sticky from the still oozing blood.

"Here," Semiramis said. "I will dispose of that for you."

Shiloh gave her the old bandage and took the gauze and bottle. As she applied the potion, she said, "Where did they take Shiloh?"

"I do not know. I suspect that, once they discovered that she was not who they thought she was, they simply did away with her. There would be no need to hold her captive."

Shiloh drooped her head. "I see."

"It is tragic, I know, but we must put that aside and concentrate on how to get you out of here. As you likely have discovered, the path to freedom is not easy to find."

292

"I know." Shiloh finished constructing the new bandage and looked up at Semiramis. "On the way here, they blindfolded me, so I couldn't tell how I got here. I felt a lot of wind, like I was flying on something with wings, but I don't know for sure. And now whichever way I go, I run into a transparent shield. I can see a land covered with snow beyond it, but I can't get through. What's even stranger is that it doesn't snow here like it does out there. It's like I'm in a big bubble of some kind."

"Yes, and that is just the first obstacle. Even if you were able to get beyond the shield, you would find a long journey through snow and ice that you are ill prepared to take."

"Then how did you get here?" Shiloh asked.

"If I told you, you would likely not believe me. You see, I was once in league with Arramos, the mastermind of this sinister plot to destroy Second Eden and overthrow Heaven itself, so I have abilities you would not understand. I am able to travel here with relative ease."

"But where is here? I mean, where physically? If you came from Second Eden, and Hades and Earth merged, how did you get here?"

"An excellent question. When Earth and Hades joined, the seven circles had to reside somewhere physically, so most took up space in their earthly counterparts, and some moved elsewhere. The physical attributes of one land gave way to another, so that both reside together, though one set of attributes necessarily became invisible to the eyes of the inhabitants.

"For example, Morgan's former home in the third circle is now at the Glastonbury Tor, and the grass fields of the second circle are in the plains of the United States while the bordering forest land where the Caitiff once lived is now in the eastern U.S."

Semiramis spread out her hands. "This village was unique. It already had a close tie with Dragons' Rest, which you know much about. When Dragons' Rest was destroyed, God granted Arramos's

293

request to move this village to the northern lands of Second Eden, and since I dwell in Second Eden, I was able to come to you."

"How?" Shiloh asked. "Do you just walk through the shield? Is it passable going one way and not the other?"

"It is passable only to those who are dead." She lowered her gaze. "This is the truth that I dared not tell you earlier, but now I think you need to know. You see, I, in fact, am dead."

Shiloh drew her head back. "You're dead?"

"Ah, yes," Semiramis said, looking at Shiloh again. "It is true. I died to Earth's realm millennia ago. Being dead is a great disadvantage most of the time, but it allows me to come and go from this village as I please. And the presence of the sixth circle created a gateway for me to come from the Bridgelands where I once worked for Arramos as the guardian for Zeno's Chasm.

"When Arramos learned that I had lost faith in him, he decided to put me away for a while, until I, as he put it, came to my senses. I was far too valuable to destroy. So he snatched me up in his claws, flew down here, and deposited me in this very spot. That is why you felt the sensation of flying. You likely rode on his back to get here." She looked up into the clear blue sky. "It is impossible to get back up without help from another flying creature, perhaps a helpful dragon."

"So how did you know to find me here?"

"A guess, really. I had to come to this region, anyway, so it made sense to look here. You see, I had to leave the village where Billy is, because, although I saved the life of one of their children, they did not trust me. I felt, however, that Billy trusted me, at least a little, so now that I have found you, I will send for him. It took me more than a day to get here, and with the mounting snow, it will likely take more than that to get word to him, then another day for him to come. Perhaps he can fly on a dragon and get here more quickly. We will have to see."

Shiloh stood again and, sliding her hands into her jeans pockets, walked a few paces away. "That would be great, but …" Heaving a sigh, she looked at the doorway to the Feed Store, the place where Bonnie had given her life to save her own. She had been so sacrificial, so willing to do what was right no matter the cost to herself.

Raising her hand, she looked at her bloody bandage. Sure, being Bonnie was costing her body parts, but if word got out that she was Shiloh, the kidnappers would likely kill her. But did that matter? Shouldn't she be willing to risk death, just like Bonnie did? Yet, if she revealed who she really was to this woman, could she be trusted? The whole point of her masquerade was to protect Bonnie, and any hint that Bonnie was still free would put her in danger. Still, it wouldn't be right to ask Billy to put his life on the line to rescue her without letting him know who she was. Yes, he would do it no matter what, but giving him the opportunity to make the decision based on truth would be the honorable thing to do.

295

Semiramis rose from the curb and touched Shiloh's arm. "What is it, Bonnie? Speak your dilemma, and I will try to solve it."

She spun back to Semiramis. "Don't tell Billy I'm here."

"What? Why not? Don't you want to escape?"

"Of course. It's just that …" Shiloh looked away

"You are not willing to draw Billy here on pretense."

"That's right. I wouldn't want to—" Shiloh swung back toward Semiramis. "What did you say?"

Semiramis laughed gently. "Do not fret or fear, Shiloh. It was not difficult for me to discern who you are."

Shiloh reverted to her British accent. "How did you figure it out?"

"When I mentioned that Billy might be coming, you were seized by a dilemma. If you were really Bonnie, there would be no hesitation."

Shiloh crossed her arms and scowled. "I'm such an idiot."

"It is an unfortunate truth that those who hold to high morals have a very hard time deceiving others. Withholding truth creates dilemmas that do not occur to the unscrupulous, and even if they did, they would not be bothered by violating codes of honor."

Shiloh looked at Semiramis again and spoke in a pleading tone. "So what are you going to do?"

"Send for Billy, of course. Since he is honorable, he will not view you as any less valuable than Bonnie."

Shiloh tightened her chin and nodded. "Okay. Thank you."

"Come with me," Semiramis said, taking her hand. "I want to show you something."

Flinching at Semiramis's touch, Shiloh went along, pondering the strange woman. Maybe this is what dead people felt like, cold and tingly. It stood to reason that she would be different, even in speech and mannerisms, but why was she so willing to help? What was in it for her?

Semiramis led her past the final building in town and into a field of bare ground, decorated only by prickly pears and acorn-sized stones. Of course, Shiloh had walked through this field many times in search of a way out, so she knew the invisible shield lay only twenty or so paces away. Yet, even if she didn't know, the boundary was obvious enough, an abrupt line that separated the dry, desertlike landscape from a sea of snow.

From her vantage point at the top of a high hill, she could see tens of thousands of acres of valley lands. Only the tops of evergreen trees and a few boulders protruded, creating splotches of green and gray that dotted the white expanse.

"As you can see," Semiramis said as she gestured toward the scene with her hand, "the snow has already mounted beyond what can be easily traversed, and it is still falling. I will do what I can to fetch Billy, but if the snow persists, I might have to wait a few days.

Keep watching through this wall, and when the thaw comes, know that your deliverance is at hand."

Shiloh nodded. "I will watch. I was here for forty years. I can handle a few extra days."

Semiramis kissed her on the cheek, a frigid kiss that made Shiloh shiver. "Whatever you do," Semiramis said, "do not trust Arramos. He is treacherous."

"Don't worry. I won't."

Semiramis raised a finger. "And one more thing. I will need a token of some kind that will prove that I found you. Elam and Ashley do not trust me. In order to mount a rescue, Billy might need their support, and—"

"You don't have to explain. I understand." Shiloh pulled her sweatshirt over her head, then the long-sleeved shirt underneath, leaving only a thin undershirt. After putting the sweatshirt back on, she handed the shirt to Semiramis, letting her hand linger over the imprint, a sketch of a majestic lion.

Semiramis lifted the shirt and read the lettering. "What does, 'He's not a tame lion' mean?"

"It's hard to explain. Just give the shirt to Billy. He'll know it belongs to me and what it means. And if anything happens to me or Bonnie, and he discovers that you're part of the reason, you'll find out what it means, too." She tried to bend her brow just enough to show a fighting spirit. "You'll find out the hard way."

A nervous smile quivered on Semiramis's face as she folded the shirt. "Well, we won't have to worry about that, will we?"

Shiloh smoothed out her sweatshirt and drilled her stare at Semiramis. "I hope not."

"Well, then, I will be going now." Semiramis stepped through the shield and out into the waist-high snow. A man walked out from behind a boulder and tromped toward her on snowshoes. With severe burns marring his face and a limp in his gait, he seemed to be in pain, but when he reached Semiramis and gave her a pair of snowshoes, a strange smile appeared. They spoke for a moment, both laughing afterward, but Shiloh couldn't hear their words or their laughter.

She pressed a palm against the shield. Apparently soundproof, it felt like glass, but her hand left no mark. Backing away, she sighed. Even if Billy showed up, how could he rescue her? Thinking about a knight in shining armor charging in on a noble white steed sounded like the most wonderful sight in the world, but if he could only stand outside and knock, what good would it do? She had already tried to break the barrier with a hundred different objects—stones as big as her head, an old sledgehammer, and even a rusty drill. Nothing worked.

Closing her eyes, she turned away and took a deep breath. She could do this. She could endure another few days, even a week or two. At least someone knew where she was and how to get to her. After forty years of dreadful misery without hope of rescue, these days would pass quickly, wouldn't they?

She lifted the plant's fruit to her mouth, bit off a large hunk, and marched toward the town's circle. As she chewed, the familiar sweet taste coated her tongue, and the gentle scent of honey filtered into her nostrils. The flavor was even better than she remembered, probably because she was so hungry and hadn't tasted it in such a long time.

When she reached the circle, she squinted at the statue. The descending sun was just touching Captain Autarkeia's head, and as it continued its downward journey, his shadow fell over her eyes.

Pain stabbed her insides, like ten spears being driven into her belly. Clutching her stomach, she dropped to her knees and then to her side, now lying fully within the lengthening shadow. As the agony increased, she looked up at the man's face. He seemed so kind, so caring, as if he would reach down from his mount, scoop her up, and ride off to safety, far away from this hellhole. Yet, he

298

just sat there and looked. He wasn't Timothy Autarkeia or the great Makaidos. He was nothing more than a hunk of carved stone.

"Augh!" More stabs. More ripping pain. She panted, wheezed, groaned. As the roaring spasms climaxed, she cried out, "Jesus, help me!"

Within seconds, the spasms eased. Still breathing heavily, she closed her eyes and let her hands fall away from her stomach. It was almost over … almost over.

As she lay on the cold ground, she let her mind wander to images of apple pies and ice cream sundaes. Maybe this place was all a dream. Maybe she had eaten too many goodies and her stomach ached from the overindulgence. Soon she would wake up from this nightmare and find herself in bed snuggling one of her stuffed animals, probably Winnie, her longtime favorite. Oh, when would that alarm clock go off? When would her father come in with a cheery greeting? "It's time to get up, Shiloh!"

299

She blinked her eyes open. No bed, no alarm clock, no Winnie, just the town's central garden with the dead eyes of the high-riding man still staring at her.

She climbed to her feet, brushed the dirt from her clothes, and strode to her alley hideaway. She pulled crates to the side and arranged the straw and horse blanket she had found at the stables the day before. Then, after pulling the crates again to hide her from any peering eyes, she nestled into her bedding.

It would be all right. Billy would come. And a dragon, too. And maybe even the noble steed. No matter how long it took, she would wait patiently. If God could help her endure this place for forty years, surely he could do the same for a few days. Just a few more days.

As evening fell, darkness arrived with it. It felt heavy, oppressive, and lonely … very lonely. Shiloh pulled her knees close to her chest and wept.

CHAPTER

THE PROTECTED WEED

B illy knelt next to the tiny plant. With only two circular leaves, each the size of a quarter, and a thin green stalk supporting them, the plant seemed fragile. The leaves weren't even green. They were black on one side and orange on the other, more like a fungus than a harvestable plant.

He looked up at the field. Elam struggled toward the garden, his head down as if in deep thought as he pushed through the waist-deep snow. His dark cloak fanned in the cold breeze and floated above the drifts.

When Billy reached the garden, he picked up his pace, now walking on mud between two rows. Although the dragons had done a great job keeping the snow from freezing the plants, the huge green leaves still seemed cold as they trembled in the breeze, as if the babies inside were shivering.

After sidestepping a bone and hopping over another, apparently honoring the man who once owned them, Elam arrived, shivering as he set his hands on his hips. "So this is it?" he asked. "It's not even in the right place. It's in between the rows."

Billy touched one of the sickly leaves. "I'm not sure if it's the right one. That's why I called you out here to witness the test."

Elam stooped beside him. "Have you heard from Semiramis yet?"

"Not a word. With all the snow, we might not hear for a while." Billy pulled a small glass vial from his pocket and removed its cork stopper. He stared at the red liquid inside and gave it a swirl. "I have to hurry, or it'll clot."

Snow flurries began to dance around their faces. "No argument from me. The clouds look pretty ominous."

"I noticed. That's why we canceled Mount Elijah again. Dad did a flyover. The flat part on top has a mound of snow and ice. He tried to melt it, but with no place to land, he couldn't do much, and the path up the side is impassable." Billy tilted the vial and let a drop of blood fall on the tip of one of the leaves. Instantly, it curled and rotted. As if burning, the rot spread toward the stalk.

302

Billy pinched off the tip and dropped it to the soil. The leaf, now only three-quarters its original size, no longer shriveled.

He put the stopper back in the vial. "Exactly the way she said it would happen."

Elam picked up a clump of dirt and crushed it. "Witchcraft!"

"Witchcraft?" Billy straightened to his full height, adrenaline pumping his muscles into tight knots. Of course, Elam had good reason to doubt Semiramis, but how far would he take his lack of trust? "So do you think she's a witch?"

"Whether she's a witch or not, it doesn't really matter. The connection might be real, even if her black magic caused it. So now we have to protect something that Arramos put here." Elam shook his head. "It's like giving a burglar a gun and the keys to your house."

"What choice do we have? We can't uproot it."

"Of course not. I'm just venting." Elam gestured with his head. "Let me show you something."

Billy followed him to the rear part of the garden. They reached a circular area that contained no growth except for a single plant near the middle, smaller than the one they had just tested. This one, however, was green and lively.

Elam crouched and touched one of the twin leaves. Like the others in the garden, the leaves resembled praying hands, though these weren't yet touching each other.

"Cliffside told me that when the leaves come together, the baby usually shows up in between within the next week, though sometimes it takes a month. He enjoys shining a light through the leaves to see its early development stages, and he has a journal filled with drawings that show the typical growth pattern of the plants and the expected shape and size of the baby inside.

Billy nodded. "That's very cool. He must really love babies."

"He does. He wants one of his own, but he has never married, so he can't be part of the parent lottery."

"Any candidates?" Billy gave Elam a wink. "I mean, is he looking?"

303

"I heard just today that he and Emerald are betrothed. You should have seen Cliffside. He was like a young buck, picking snowball fights with the other unmarried males, and he even went door to door and left candy boxes for the kids."

"Nothing like requited love to perk a man's spirits."

"Trust me," Elam said. "I know what you mean."

"Sapphira?"

Elam's smile provided the answer.

"I heard the story from Acacia," Billy said. "Why didn't you ever tell me?"

"It hurts too much. I have loved that girl for thousands of years. Ever since she risked her life to feed me stew on her fingers, I knew there would never be another one for me. When I worked in the shipyards in Glasgow, lots of girls tried to charm me. A few even proposed marriage. Some were very attractive, both in appearance and in depth of spirit, but I couldn't entertain any notions like that. They were nice, but they just weren't Sapphira."

"Does she feel the same way about you?"

"Well, I saw her briefly a few weeks ago. I was standing near Heaven's Gate, and she was on Earth. I guess that's about as far away as you can be from someone and still see her. She wiggled her fingers at me, so I have hope."

Billy cocked his head. "Wiggled her fingers?"

"That's our love sign." His voice pitched a notch higher. "It reminds us of when she fed me."

Billy grasped Elam's wrist. "Then there's no doubt about it. She's as tied to you as you are to her."

"How about you?" Elam asked. "Do you miss Bonnie?"

"Well ... sure. I mean, it's not like I've loved her for thousands of years or anything, so I can't compare with what you're going through, but ..."

"Come on. I spilled my guts. It's your turn. No one's listening but me and the birthing plants."

Billy looked into Elam's eyes—piercing, wise, gentle. He would guard any secret. "I love Bonnie. She's the most amazing girl I've ever met. It's like she's so perfect, it's unbelievable. I mean, if you described her to someone—her kindness, her faith, her self-sacrifice—most people either wouldn't believe it was true or they would hate her for being so good. Do you know what I mean?"

"Jealousy, I think. The spitefulness of inferiority that tries to defame their betters in order to drag them down to their pitiful level."

"Something like that, but Bonnie would love them anyway, no matter what they thought of her." Billy rubbed his finger gently across the top of the plant. "She's a gem, a lump of coal that God made into a perfect diamond."

Elam stroked the side of the plant as if caressing a girl's hand. "It's amazing what suffering can turn someone into. Some become bitter and hateful, and others reach out with love."

"Right. So, yeah. I miss Bonnie. I miss her a lot."

"Anyway," Elam continued, "there's something special about this plant, too. This is the place where Abigail landed. A plant sprang up here much faster than the others, and Roxil came out of it. When I looked at the remains of the plant, I found a seed-like thing, kind of egg-shaped in the roots. I decided to plant it to see if it would grow."

"And this is the result?"

Elam nodded. "It grows slower than anything Cliffside has ever seen, maybe a fourth of the normal rate."

"Any idea what it means?"

"Not really. I've had dreams that a dragon came out of this one, like Roxil did. But it was probably because of the swamp peppers on my sandwich. Fire breath, you know."

Billy laughed. "Trust me. I know."

"Yes, you would." Elam rose to his full height and scanned the skies. The snow had thickened across the darkening canopy. "If we get another storm like the last three nights, the dragons will have to clear the garden again. They've been working much too hard. They haven't even had a chance to build good regeneracy domes."

"I know what you mean," Billy said. "I asked Legossi and Firedda to get some rest. I'm hoping they'll take Acacia and me back to Mount Elijah tomorrow. By air is the only way now, but if we don't get more sunshine, no Earth dragon will be able to take us. Valiant said he would help us get there on Grackle and Albatross, if we can find them."

Elam tilted his head upward and let the tiny flakes collect on his forehead. "No one's seen them. Candle even tried to use Listener's spyglass from the top of the ridge, but no luck."

"How is she?" Billy asked. "I haven't seen her since this morning."

"Still on the heart machine, but Dr. Conner thinks she'll be off it in a few days."

"Speaking of Dr. Conner, did he and Hartanna reunite? I remember when my mother and father got back together after he became a dragon again. It was pretty clumsy for a woman and a dragon to show affection."

"They spoke," Elam said. "They were friendly, but, like you said, there's a barrier they really can't cross. And since he was part of the reason she died ... yes, *clumsy* is a good word. But I think they'll warm up to each other."

"Look." Billy nodded toward the field. "Here comes the dynamic duo."

Walter and Ashley plowed through the snow side by side. Soon, their chatter reached Billy's ears.

"If you had worn boots," Ashley said, "your socks wouldn't be wet. Didn't your mother ever teach you how to dress for the snow?"

"Of course she did, but my boots are in my closet back home. If you know how to get Federal Express to deliver something across dimensional barriers, I'll use your new radio to give them a call. I'm sure they'll rush my boots here by overnight delivery."

Billy grinned. "Will they ever stop?"

Elam shook his head. "They enjoy it. Look how they're smiling."

"I'll give you a Federal Express package!" Ashley scooped up a handful of snow and threw it at Walter, smacking him in the chest.

Walter covered his heart with his gloved hands. "Oh, no! You opened the wound! I can feel blood in my lungs."

"Really?" A look of concern flashed across Ashley's face. "Let me see."

When Walter leaned close, Ashley pulled his collar, grabbed another handful of snow, and stuffed it down the front of his shirt. "That ought to seal the wound!" Laughing, she ran toward the garden. Walter followed, but at a much slower pace. As he shook out his shirt, his grin stretched from ear to ear.

Billy held up his hand. "Stop! Wait!"

Ashley halted. "What?"

Quick-marching through the mud between the rows, he pointed at the weedlike plant just a few feet in front of Ashley. "Don't step on that."

She edged closer and stooped. "What is it?"

When Billy arrived, followed by Elam and Walter, Billy retold the story. Of course, Walter and Ashley asked so many questions, it took longer to tell it this time than the first. By the time he finished with Semiramis's claim that Bonnie or Shiloh was imprisoned in the northern lands, the snow had thickened in the air, and a thin coat of white dressed the soil.

Walter grasped Billy's arm. "Let's hit the northward trail right away. Ever since I saw those fountains from the top of Mount Elijah, I wanted to see what was out there."

"If Semiramis is telling the truth about where Bonnie or Shiloh is," Ashley said.

"What's the consensus?" Billy asked. "Is Semiramis on our side or Arramos's?"

Elam raised his hand. "Arramos's. I don't buy her story."

"I agree," Ashley said, lifting her hand. "The murder I sensed in her heart didn't feel like righteous indignation to me."

Billy lifted his eyebrows at Walter. "And you?"

"I think Semiramis is working for Semiramis. She's playing both sides. You can't argue with real burns. They were recent, and her care for Hunter wasn't fake. She doesn't like Arramos, but she's no friend of ours, either." He gripped Billy's arm again. "But it doesn't matter. If she comes back and says she found Bonnie or Shiloh in the northern lands, and you want to head that way, then I'm at your side, no matter what."

Ashley poked Walter's stomach. "Not until you're completely healed. You can't even swing a sword yet."

"Is that so?" Walter rotated his shoulder. "With all the tender loving care I'm getting, I think—"

"Uh-oh," Elam said, pointing toward the field. "Speak of the devil."

Billy and the others turned. A tall slender woman trudged through the snow. Dressed in a thick hooded cloak, red from head to toe, she broke through the final drift and walked into the garden. As she approached, she lowered her hood, revealing her familiar auburn locks.

"Semiramis," Billy whispered. "Her timing is—"

"Suspicious," Ashley interrupted. "I still didn't sense her presence."

When Semiramis came within ten feet, she dipped low, her head bowed, apparently unconcerned that snow and mud seeped into her cloak as her knee pressed down. "I have come, just as I said I would."

Billy set a hand under her elbow and helped her rise. "Did you find her?"

As she straightened, she trained her eyes on Billy. "I have." She reached under her cloak and withdrew a folded shirt. "Shiloh said you would recognize this."

"Shiloh?"

"Yes. For a while, she concealed her identity, trying to protect Bonnie, I am sure, but I discerned the truth soon enough."

Billy took it by the collar and let it fall open. "It says, 'He's not a tame lion.'"

"Aslan," Walter said. "The Narnia shirt Bonnie gave her."

Billy nodded. "I remember."

Elam crossed his arms over his chest. "So why didn't you bring her with you?"

"It is a complex situation, Elam. She is once again in the sixth circle of Hades, but it has been moved to the northlands of Second Eden. It is now behind a shield that is impenetrable to the living."

"To the living?" Walter pointed at her. "Then are you ..."

"Dead?" Semiramis gave him a sad nod. "Yes, Walter. I died millennia ago. Arramos received permission to use me in the

Bridgelands for his purposes, and now, before I am cast into the Lake of Fire, I want to make amends for my many misdeeds. Perhaps by the grace of Elohim, I will be allowed to wander in the lands of the dead and delay my suffering."

"Then how are we supposed to get her out?" Billy asked.

"You must break the shield. I know of no way to do this deed, but perhaps between your brilliant scientist and the many dragons at your disposal, you will be able to penetrate it."

Ashley furrowed her brow but said nothing. Billy looked at Ashley's narrowed eyes. It was easy to read her mind this time. She didn't trust Semiramis, not in the slightest. This dead woman who seemed impenetrable to Ashley's powerful mind was hiding something, something sinister, something deadly.

"We'll discuss it," Elam said, nodding toward the field. "Alone."

"I understand." As Semiramis bowed her head again, her eyes suddenly widened. "The plant!" She stooped and touched the torn leaf, then looked up at Billy. "You tested it."

"Yeah. It worked, just like you said."

"Then can there be any doubt about my allegiance?" She straightened and looked around, her gaze pausing at each person. "I have told you everything, Arramos's plans regarding this plant, how it is tied to his prisoner, and the location of his prison. I have kept nothing from you."

"Like I said ..." Elam's tone grew stern. "We will discuss it alone."

For a moment, Semiramis just stared at him. Then, her lips trembling, she bowed her head again. "Very well." She raised her hood, turned, and walked toward the field. "I will wait for word at the center of the village."

Billy and the others watched her in silence. She retraced her steps through the furrow, and when she reached the forest bordering the village, Elam spoke up.

"She plays this game well."

"Maybe." Billy let the shirt flap in the snowy breeze. "But we can't ignore this."

"So what's the verdict?" Walter asked. "Round up the dragons and assault the northern lands?"

Elam shook his head. "That's exactly what she wants us to do. If we send our dragons up there, we're vulnerable. There's no way I can allow that, not with the Vacants lurking."

Billy wadded up the shirt and held it close to his chest. If Bonnie were imprisoned, he would stop at nothing to rescue her. It wasn't right to do anything less for Shiloh. "Then I'll take my father, and the two of us will check it out. With Legossi and Firedda here, you should have plenty of firepower."

"Fair enough." Elam gazed toward the north through the snowy air. "If Clefspeare can't break through, no one can."

Walter pointed at himself with his thumb. "And I'm going with Billy."

310

"Over my dead body," Ashley said. "You won't be ready for dragon riding for at least a month."

"But if Billy gets in trouble—"

"Don't worry about me, Walter. My dad will—"

"Wait just a minute!" Elam waved for everyone to settle down. "Let's plan this calmly. If we can agree on a course of action, and Valiant adds his vote, we can move ahead as a team. It's important to be unified. That way, no one can say, 'I told you so.' We're in this together."

Billy nodded. The warrior chief was right, and he was showing his talent as a leader.

"You," Elam said, pointing at Billy, "will try to find Shiloh. Get directions from Semiramis, and we'll hold her in custody until you get back with a report." He shifted his finger to Walter while looking at Ashley. "Is he well enough to oversee construction of shelters for the dragons so they can build regeneracy domes?"

Pressing her lips together, Ashley nodded. "I don't see why not. As long as he uses his brain and not his brawn, I'm fine with that."

Again Elam moved his finger, this time pointing at himself. "I'll alert Cliffside and the dragons regarding the new plant. We'll rotate armed guards to make sure it stays safe, and we'll capture anything that comes out of it."

"What about me?" Ashley set her hands on her hips. "With Dr. Conner here, I'll be freed up to help. Everything's in deep freeze mode, so we're not likely to get attacked anytime soon."

"Three projects," Elam said, holding up a trio of fingers. "Keep working on the radio. We need to get in touch with Earth to get the other dragons here. And the second is to come up with a way to get back to Mount Elijah. That's our only portal. Number three is to figure out how to survive in the cold. We'll need greenhouses, more solar power cells, and a way to tap geothermal energy."

"Sounds doable." Ashley raised two fingers of her own. "And a couple more projects. I want to build a microscope for medical use. I learned a lot about glass grinding when I had to reconstruct my regeneration light at the visitor center back in Maryland. I'm also going to research my fireproof coating for the cloaks and make it stronger. If we can get someone into enemy territory, we can spy on what they're doing and maybe figure out how to use the tunnel portal in the Shadow Lands."

Walter let out a whistle. "You go, girl!"

Ashley drew her head back. "*I'm* not going to be a spy. I'm just cooking up the protectant." She sidled up to him and rubbed his upper arm. "We need a strong, brave, chivalrous knight who would surely be healed by the time the cloak is ready."

Walter scratched his head. "Can't imagine who that would be."

She gave him a hefty shove. "Oh, just knock it off!"

He faked a backwards stumble, then quickly regained his balance. "Well," he said, holding out his arm for Ashley. "Shall we go back to the village and rustle up something hot to drink?"

"Sounds good." Ashley hooked her arm around his and looked at Elam and Billy. "You two coming?"

Billy waved a hand. "In a minute."

As Walter and Ashley exited the garden and high-stepped through the snow, Billy laid an arm over Elam's shoulders and spoke in a low tone. "Whoever goes to Mount Elijah or the Shadow Lands in search of a portal will need Acacia to open it."

"Sure." Elam matched Billy's tone, his face expressing mild curiosity. "Then we would need two protected cloaks."

"That's not my point. I'm worried about her. She seems to be getting weaker. Her fire-making power isn't what it used to be. And her mind-set is ... well ..."

"Just say it, Billy. No use holding back."

"She's kind of down. Not really depressed. Just sort of ... I don't know how to describe it."

"Wishing it were all over?" Elam offered.

"Yeah. Maybe that's it."

Elam patted Billy on the back, and the two walked slowly out of the garden. "I know the feeling. She and Sapphira and I are thousands of years old, and living in a corrupt world gets kind of old after a while. Sometimes I just want to quit fighting and go to Heaven."

When they reached the snow, they shifted to walking single file, Billy in front. "I think I understand," Billy said. "I can't relate, of course, but it makes sense."

Elam heaved a sigh. "Acacia just wants to go home. With her firepower decreasing, she probably feels kind of useless."

"Then maybe a new mission to the Shadow Lands will recharge her spirit. I get stoked just thinking about opening the tunnel portal. I'm going to ask Ashley to get three cloaks, so I can go, too."

Elam laughed. "We'll see about that."

Billy stopped and turned around. "Let me take Acacia to find Shiloh. Maybe her fire would do something to the shield that my father's wouldn't. If not, just keeping her busy might help."

"Sure," Elam said, shrugging. "I don't see why not."

"Super! I'll get Semiramis to give us good directions."

"And while you're flying around, could you check on the guards at the wall of fire? With all the snow, we haven't been able to see if they need more supplies, and I'd like a report on how the wall is faring, especially at the river entry and exit."

"You bet. We'll pack some extra food and supplies for them and leave first thing in the morning."

With a hint of dawn lighting the horizon, Semiramis stood at the entrance to the alley in the sixth circle's rundown village. It had taken all night to make the journey, but time was of the essence. Now that Billy knew where to go, he would likely arrive soon, so she had to prepare the bait.

313

Since Mardon was free, escaping from Elam's guards had been easy enough. A little sleeping powder worked wonders. Of course, it would be impossible to convince Elam that her escape was for a noble cause. She would have to stay away from him and Billy, at least for now, and Mardon would never be able to go back to the village, since "Hunter's" companion didn't return. For now, she would stay scarce until the next step in her plan was complete.

She searched the sky. Arramos would be there soon, flying down from the Bridgelands and demanding a report. So many times she had been tempted to laugh, point at the barrier to Second Eden, and say, "If you are so powerful, then get your own report. Of course, you would have to die to penetrate the shield, so be my guest."

Yet, Satan dwelling in a dragon's skin would not be pleased with her lack of outward obeisance. Since all her plans danced on such a thin thread, now was not a good time to show him her true feelings.

With light now filtering into the alley, a haphazard collection of crates became clear, including Shiloh's legs protruding from the pile. She had slept fitfully for the past half hour, but the powder Semiramis had sprinkled in the air would keep her asleep long enough.

Soon, Arramos flew down and alighted next to her. With a shudder of wings, he settled and growled his question. "Shall I assume our plans are on course?"

She crossed her arms over her chest. "Have I ever failed you?"

"You answer a question with a question. This is the pattern of a deceiver."

"As well you should know."

Arramos let out a throaty laugh. "This I cannot deny. Nor can you. Your deception prowess far exceeds Morgan's. She was clever, but she was too straightforward. Her inability to avoid direct confrontation proved to be her downfall." He set his eyes near hers. "That is why I must always watch you closely."

For a moment, she froze, but she couldn't let this foul dragon intimidate her. She drilled her stare directly into his and spoke with a confident air. "To answer your question, our plans are coming along better than I ever thought possible."

"How so?"

"Mardon's reprogramming is working, and Acacia is weakening. If she dies, we will be able to safely collect her blood and perhaps her ova. Also, I kept Shiloh's bandage, and Mardon analyzed her blood. Her exposure to the plant she eats created a high amount of antitoxins, making her immune to Morgan's poison. We believe the blood Billy poured on the plant will surely transmit a similar yet even more substantial invulnerability to the fruit."

"Of course," he growled. "I planned this long ago."

314

THE PROTECTED WEED

Semiramis forced herself to keep her face calm, but deceiving a deceiver wouldn't be easy. "As I suspected. You would not be fooled by Shiloh's pathetic disguise."

"She was the one I wanted in the first place. What do I care about capturing the winged girl? That is Devin's obsession, not mine. As long as she comes to Second Eden with your rope intact, her purpose will be complete, and our greatest enemy will see to that."

"So, you were already acquainted with Shiloh?"

"Of course. I saw Shiloh's invincibility, so I wanted to harvest it. I knew she would act as Bonnie's substitute. She has fooled Morgan with that act before." His scarlet beams flashed into her eyes. "I recognize liars quickly."

"And since I am a liar, it would be foolish to try to hide lies from you."

His growl sharpened. "Do not patronize me. I know you hate me because of what I did to your son, but your loyalty, if you still have any, will be rewarded. We must remain on the alert. During the time we wait for Bonnie Silver to arrive, the boys you have deceived will grow into men. They will not be so easily blinded by your wiles."

"I know. Elam is older and wiser than Billy. He sees through me already, but he suffers from a wound that hinders him. When he forced Angel to tell the lie she had concocted, the results were disastrous, and since the lack of trust among the villagers grows, he will not be quick to pass judgment on me."

"Excellent. All is well. My only concern is the ropes that bind the realms together. When the final piece of our interdimensional puzzle is set in place, the Bridgelands will crumble, and our ropes will be exposed. Anyone who comes upon them will be able to cut them."

"Not without a staurolite blade," Semiramis said.

"The winged boy Gabriel had one. Do you know what became of it?"

She shook her head. "That is a concern, but if we kill them all, even that worry will be eliminated."

"When the army I am assembling is able to enter Second Eden, killing them all will be an easy task."

Arramos lifted into the air and flew straight up. Soon, he disappeared from view.

Semiramis tiptoed into the alley and moved the crates that protected Shiloh's body. Giving her arm a gentle shake, she called out, "Shiloh. I have news for you."

After stretching her arms, Shiloh blinked. "Oh. You're back." She pushed up to her feet, wincing as she laid a hand on her head. "I have a terrible headache."

Semiramis steadied her. "I apologize. You are suffering from a side effect of a sleeping powder I gave you. You seemed so fitful, I wanted you to sleep more deeply, but now that dawn has come, I was sure you would want to hear my news. I told Billy that you're here. He will be coming for you as soon as possible."

She smiled through her grimace. "That's really cool! Thank you!"

"There is another reason I made sure you were asleep." Semiramis looked up again. Arramos was now long gone. "Arramos, the foulest creature in all the cosmos, visited here, and if he thought you were awake, he might have done you harm. He does not want anyone to know his plans. The only reason he keeps you alive is to make sure Billy protects a certain plant, but that would take too long to explain right now. When Billy comes to rescue you, I am sure he will tell you all about it."

Shiloh nodded. "Thank you again. I'll be watching for him."

"Excellent." Semiramis stepped back and pulled her hood up over her head. "For now, it is important that Arramos never know that I am working against his plans. I am a double agent, of sorts, and I hope to destroy him for what he did to my son."

Enoch stepped out of the anteroom, the small library that welcomed anyone who entered Heaven's Gate. Now walking in the great altar chamber, he listened to the buzz—prayers whispered and shouted from the lips of thousands of petitioners. With high and low voices rising and falling, it sounded like a choir warming up for a performance.

He strode along the side aisle and looked down the rows of praying stations. With each person kneeling on pillows, their hands folded on chest-high, wooden shelves, surely it would be easy to spot the two females. Both were shorter than most, and the distinctive red hair of one of them would be obvious even under a prayer shawl.

As he searched, he took in the sweet aroma. Of course, he had smelled it thousands of times. The prayers of the saints always carried this rich fragrance, but for some reason it seemed especially vibrant today, as if something unusually important stirred the hearts of the white-robed prayer warriors.

He stopped at row forty-one and scanned the heads and faces. The two he was looking for sometimes used this row because of its proximity to the painting of Stephen's stoning at the far end.

Standing on tiptoes, he spied the redhead and her dark-haired counterpart. Each wore sheer lacy veils that draped their heads and fell past their ears.

Sidestepping between the two rows, he hurried toward them. Of course, calling their names was allowed, but there was no use distracting people from their fervent prayers.

As he passed, he eyed each hologram in front of the prayer stations. One scene, floating in front of a male teenager, showed an elderly lady lying in a hospital bed. The boy prayed out loud,

317

asking for healing for this missionary, the lady who had led him to faith only days before he was killed for converting from Islam.

The next scene showed a man, bound and gagged. A hooded man stood next to him with a machine gun barrel pushed against his prisoner's head. A lady knelt at the altar, praying for her son, her only son, a victim of terrorism.

Enoch hurried on. Listening to this lovely chorus of prayers could captivate him for hours, but there was too much work to do, and he would have many more years to bask in this rich flood of love.

When he arrived at the end of the row, he stooped between the two females and whispered. "Karen. Naamah. I must ask you to come with me."

Karen raised a finger. "Can you wait one second?"

"Yes. Yes, of course."

Naamah glanced up and smiled. "And I will be only a moment, as well."

Enoch looked at their holograms. In front of Karen, Ashley sat at a table with a collection of beakers containing liquids of various colors. Holding an eyedropper, she let a few drops of blue syrup fall into one of the beakers.

"Father," Karen whispered. "Please help Ashley find the best formula for protecting the cloaks." Breathing a sigh, she added, "And let her know that I love her."

In the hologram, Ashley looked up, as if listening. She gave the ceiling of her work area a curious glance before smiling and going back to work.

In front of Naamah, Elam and Walter stood next to a different table. With a lantern at one side, Walter pointed at something that looked like plans for constructing a building. The words at the top of the oversized page read, "Dragon Shelter."

318

Naamah sang her prayer, her voice lilting sweetly.

Grant them wisdom to increase;
Grant them vision to find peace;
Help them build a dragon's lair;
Gracious Father, hear my prayer.

When the song ended, Karen and Naamah stood and followed
Enoch to the closer aisle. He marched toward the first row, turned
in front of it, and passed a giant altar—a high table covered with a
white cloth. As he walked swiftly by, the cloth's purple tassels
swayed, so low, they nearly swept the floor.

Upon reaching the anteroom door, Enoch raised his voice
above the choir's din. "You may take off your coverings now."

"Yes, sir." Karen pulled off her veil and helped Naamah remove
a pin that held hers in place.

Enoch lifted the latch and led them inside. As he closed the
door, the song died away.

319

"It is time to plan," he said, gesturing toward an old table and
the benches that sat on either side.

Karen and Naamah sat on one side, while Enoch sat on the
other. "I've been wondering when you'd pull the trigger," Karen
said. "It's been in the prayer wind for quite a while."

Smiling, Naamah gave Karen a nudge with her elbow. "I think
you have been putting most of it in the wind yourself."

"Well, that's true, but Prof was talking about it before he left.
I didn't plant the idea in his mind."

Enoch lifted his brow. "Did Charles say when he would
return?"

"Not to me." Karen shrugged. "When he got the news, he was
like a man on a mission. He almost danced down the aisle."

Enoch laughed. "Well, it's no wonder."

Karen laid her palms on the table. "So, what are we supposed to do? Call the Seraphim and ask them to go to war? They could beat Flint's army in a heartbeat."

"No one in this realm will be allowed to participate directly in the battle, though I have heard that a temporary visit may be allowed later. In any case, God delights in using weaker vessels, so . . ." He forked two fingers at them. "So your request to be in charge of planning has been granted."

Naamah enfolded her hand in Karen's. "We are weak in body, Father Enoch, but we are strong in spirit."

"Yes," he said, laughing again, "I know that quite well. You are the two copper coins, the widow's mites that toppled Mardon's tower. No one will ever doubt your courage."

"This is going to be fun." Karen rubbed her hands together. "I have some cool ideas."

"Excellent, and since Charles is also so interested, you may want to include him in your strategy."

Naamah's lips spread into a lovely smile. "We have already consulted him about the portal situation. We think—"

The latch clicked. As the door opened, the choir of prayers again filled the library. A head poked in, the face wrinkled, the hair wild and white. "Enoch, you sent for me?"

"Professor Hamilton!" Karen jumped up and hugged him around his robed waist. "You look like yourself again!"

He smoothed back his hair and sat down next to Enoch. "Yes, the youthfulness I gained when I entered the heavenly realm was splendid, but, in light of the coming events, I thought it best to revert to this appearance."

Naamah smiled. "You are dashing in either form."

Professor Hamilton bowed his head. "I thank you, fair lady. The beauty of Heaven's grace rests upon you, as well."

"So ..." Karen set her finger on the table and began an invisible sketch. "I think we should—"

"Dear Karen," Enoch said. "The technology here is not so lacking that we must imagine what you are scribbling there."

"Oh, yes." Professor Hamilton withdrew a pen from a pocket in his robe. "It seems that restoring my old body has also brought back my feeble brain, so I almost forgot about your request for this sky marker."

"Perfect." Karen took the pen and drew in the air. As the tip swept up and down and left and right, a full-color, three-dimensional image took shape, a battle scene with dragons, giants, humans, an airplane, and a white horse. "This is what I was imagining during the last prayer cycle." She pointed at a dragon. "The battle is inevitable, and since Goliath knows how to protect the army from Excalibur's beam, we will have to counteract that protection."

"The beam has not yet been restored," Enoch said. "What good will that do?"

Karen pointed at Charles. "That's where Prof comes in."

"Yes, I have already consulted with the angel who controls the portals. The tunnel portal in the Valley of Shadows has been redirected to the former mobility room, which, of course, is at the bottom of a pit in Montana. Now we must rely on the wisdom and intelligence of Marilyn and company as they learn how to use it."

"I have a prayer song," Naamah said, "for the reconstruction of Apollo and for guiding the rubellite from Earth to Second Eden. It will take a miracle to get it into Billy's hands."

Enoch nodded. "Indeed it will. I have not even imagined how it could happen."

"Our plans depend on it." Karen pointed at her drawing. "Anyway, since we control the weather, here's what we have to do. When Goliath's army brings out their secret weapon, you can bet that the weapon will be looking for the most dramatic way to make his appearance. My guess is that he will wait for the lesser minions to thin our ranks and then ride in on a horse at the rear

321

of the attack forces. When that happens, we will begin our weather changes."

"I see," Charles said. "The ice cap over Mount Elijah will cause the pressure to build until it explodes in an enormous eruption. The chemical composition of the cloud mass should be perfect."

"And the reason for the long season of death in the first place," Karen added. "But the difficult part will be controlling the weather with enough precision to do the job while keeping it from hurting the plants in the birthing garden."

"Quite right," Charles said. "It would be toxic, indeed."

Enoch patted Charles on the back. "Have you selected appropriate attire, my friend?"

"A cloak that matches the one you plan on wearing. The colors will be dazzling."

"I wish our Father would let us go," Karen said. "The clothes Naamah and I are making for the celebrants are going to be amazing, too."

322

The professor set a hand on her shining red hair. "Keep asking, my dear. The glorious one has not yet denied your request. He has merely said to wait. We must see how events unfold. Nothing involving the will of mankind is set in stone."

"Speaking of that," Enoch said, "Bonnie and Sapphira come to mind. Have you decided how you will guide the new Oracle of Fire?"

Naamah borrowed Karen's pen and drew a sketch of two flaming bodies. "I have also composed a song for Bonnie. She will have to be aware of the Spirit's voice and listen carefully, but I think she has the wisdom to understand where her protection originates."

Enoch rose from the table. "I think the three of you have this well under control. I must go back to my viewing room to see if God has granted me access to the Valley of Souls. Since my contact with Bonnie and Sapphira has been cut off, and since I am not allowed to journey to Second Eden, I have very little else to do."

"Your screen still doesn't work?" Karen asked.

Enoch shook his head. "It has happened before. When God decides to allow his warriors to battle on their own, I must be content to stay out of the action. If they really need my help, God will again open my communication window."

He left the library and closed the door behind him. Again walking along the aisle, he searched for an empty prayer station and found one next to the teenaged male he had seen earlier. His hologram had switched to a primitive playground where one little girl pushed another riding on a tire swing.

As Enoch knelt on the soft pillow, the young man looked at him. "You're still among the disadvantaged, aren't you?"

Enoch smiled. Heaven's euphemism for those who had never left the shackles of physical life would seem odd to the "disadvantaged" ones on Earth, the living souls who had no idea what real life was all about. "For whom are you praying?" Enoch asked.

323

The young man pointed at the girls. "My sisters, that they won't fear death when the missionary tells them about the Messiah."

Enoch watched the two dark-skinned girls playing on the swing while a middle-aged woman stooped and laughed with them. As he gazed over the sea of prayer holograms, his words came back to him. *Since I am not allowed to journey to Second Eden, I have very little else to do.*

Shaking his head, he waved his hand across his empty hologram area. "Young man, being in my disadvantaged state, I am unable to create a prayer image. Would you please bring up your parents? I would like to pray for them."

A broad grin spread across his face. "Absolutely!"

As the image took shape in front of him, Enoch folded his hands on the altar. There was plenty to do, and for now he would be content to wait for God's next assignment.

CHAPTER

BREAKING THE BARRIER

R iding atop Clefspeare's back, Billy pointed to his right. "Is
that the lake?"

Acacia, hanging onto his waist from behind, shouted, "Probably. It looks like a flat icy area."

"We shall see," Clefspeare said as he banked that way. They
had been flying north with a tailwind, which had made for speedy
travel and tolerable breezes, but with the shift into a crosswind,
bitter cold returned with a vengeance.

Billy felt Acacia's shivering body, but she offered no com-
plaints. When he had asked her to go, she jumped at the chance,
and the sparkle in her brilliant blue eyes returned. Still, her silence
through most of the journey and her shaking arms proved that her
exhaustion lingered. He would have to keep a close eye on her.

Patrick had also wanted to come on the journey. After all,
Shiloh was his beloved daughter. But Clefspeare told him that a
third rider would make the burden too great, and bringing another

dragon into unexplored territory was unwise. What Clefspeare did not say, but later confirmed to Billy, was his concern for Patrick's age and the bitter cold they expected to encounter. Disappointed, but eager to help, Patrick opted to pack the supplies for the boundary guards and draw an excellent map based on directions Semiramis supplied the night before.

Of course, her escape had set everyone on edge. Elam wondered about a possible ambush and questioned the wisdom of continuing with the search plan, but, in the end, it seemed best to go ahead. Clefspeare would see to their safety.

When they flew over the snow-covered expanse, Billy pulled a scrap of parchment from under his cloak and looked at Patrick's map. The lake, the final landmark before Shiloh's prison, was roughly elliptical with at least five wiggling streams that protruded to the north like gnarled fingers. These, too, were frozen. The season of death, the worst Valiant could remember, had taken its toll here as well.

Billy glanced back and forth between the map and the landscape below. The widest stream bent away on the northeast side. That would lead them to the valley, their final destination. Since they were now heading east, they would have to adjust.

"Head left about forty-five degrees," Billy called. "Follow that river with the cluster of evergreens on each side."

Clefspeare's eyebeams flashed on. After making a slow turn, skimming the bottom of the low cloudbank, he followed the river upstream, but it soon disappeared under a deep blanket of snow. Keeping the same heading, they traveled over a ridge and then a valley on the other side. A few trees and large boulders managed to find daylight above the snow's surface, marring the smooth blanket of white.

"What is that?" Acacia asked.

Billy looked back. She pointed toward something glimmering to the east. With barely any sunshine leaking through the clouds, whatever it was had to be huge to capture the light and reflect it. "It looks like a curtain of glass."

"I sense a portal," Acacia said. "If it's behind that glass, it must be enormous for me to feel it from so far away."

"It is less than a mile," Clefspeare said as he turned toward it. "Get ready. We will be landing in a moment."

With a great beating of his wings, Clefspeare settled to the ground between a high snowdrift and a dragon-sized boulder, about ten paces or so from the glass. Billy jumped down and helped Acacia dismount Clefspeare's neck.

All three hurried to the glass, Billy arriving first. With the surface curving slowly away in each direction, it seemed to be a huge cylinder. It would probably take at least fifteen minutes to walk around it.

Snow had piled in drifts against the glass except at one three-foot-wide section where it seemed that someone had recently cleared it away, allowing Billy to walk right up to the partition and peer through. On the other side, the landscape looked more like a desert than a snow scene. A few scrubby trees dotted the area here and there, and some old buildings stood in the distance. The closest one seemed very familiar. This place definitely looked like the old town in the sixth circle of Hades.

Standing in knee-deep snow, he pressed a finger against the glass, but it left no mark. "This is really weird, Dad. What do you make of it?"

Clefspeare set his snout close to the window and blew twin flames, narrow and orange, and kept them there for several seconds. When he pulled away, Billy touched the spots. "Cold. Cold as ice."

Acacia pushed her body against Billy's side and shivered harder than ever. "I will try my fire, but first we should see if we can call Shiloh. If our voices won't penetrate the glass, maybe she can hear us knocking."

Billy rapped on the window with his knuckles and shouted, "Shiloh! It's Billy! Can you hear me?"

He pressed his ear against the glass. "I don't hear anything, but the wind's in my ears, so that doesn't mean much."

Clefspeare swung his tail and whipped the partition. A loud *thwap* rocked Billy's eardrums. Although the glass shimmered slightly, it showed no sign of cracking.

"It is clear," Clefspeare said, "that Semiramis's story has proven true to this point. Perhaps we should also assume that Shiloh is, indeed, trapped in there, which would give me reason to make a more strenuous attempt."

"A full-speed body slam?" Billy asked.

He focused his eyebeams on the glass. "With white-hot blasts of fire aimed at the collision point immediately before I strike."

Billy touched the scarlet target. "I can help with that. I'll blast it with my fire while you're on your way."

"Look!" Acacia laid a palm on the window and pressed her nose next to it. "I see someone."

A girl peeked around one of the buildings. She seemed hesitant, frightened, and too far away to be recognized.

"It's Shiloh," Acacia said. "My vision is so sharp, I can see her wounded hand."

Billy rapped on the glass again and waved. "Shiloh! It's me, Billy!"

Shiloh crept around the corner, easing one foot in front of the other. Suddenly, she burst into a sprint. With her blond-streaked hair flying behind her and a beautiful smile decorating her lovely face, she looked exactly like Bonnie.

Swallowing down a lump, Billy shouted again. "Can you hear me?"

Shiloh stopped a few feet away from the glass and mouthed something, but he couldn't read her lips. She pointed at her ear as if to indicate that their voices weren't coming through.

Acacia narrowed her eyes. "I think she said, 'Do you know Mars code.'"

"Probably Morse code," Billy said. "She wants us to tap out our words."

"I learned it long ago." Clefspeare touched the partition with a wing tip. "If a tap vibrates the glass enough to transmit sound, then why do our voices not penetrate?"

"It's a barrier between dimensions," Billy said, "probably not real glass at all. Maybe she'll watch our taps and figure them out, or, then again, maybe it responds somehow to physical touch."

"If that's the case ..." Acacia stripped off her rabbit-fur cloak and handed it to Billy. Then, spreading out her arms, she flattened her body against the partition. Her white hair streaming in the breeze along with her long woolen skirt, she called, "Ignite!"

Starting at her bare hands, two-inch-high firelets crawled along the sleeves of her leather tunic. Although the flames looked hot enough, they didn't burn her clothes or even raise a puff of smoke. Soon, her body blazed.

329

Laying her cheek against the glass, she called out, "Shiloh! Can you hear me now?"

Shiloh stepped closer. A smile trembled on her lips. "Yes! Yes, I can!" Her voice seemed far away, like a call from a distant canyon.

Billy stood directly behind Acacia. The warmth from her body thawed his frozen cheeks. "Shiloh, do you know of any spots in this wall that look weak? Clefspeare and I want to try to break through."

Shiloh shook her head. "I walked every foot of this thing and hit it with a big hammer until it wore me out. It's tougher than steel."

"Then we might as well try here," Billy said. "Stand back."

As Shiloh stepped away, Acacia did the same. At the spot where she had pressed her body, the glass seemed darker, as if smoke-stained.

Billy touched it. The surface felt warm, but not hot. "Let's concentrate here, Dad. Acacia might have made the dimensional barrier thinner."

"Then perhaps she should try a portal opening cyclone," Clefspeare said. "We have enough firepower."

Billy looked at Acacia. "Could you?"

Acacia spread out her arms. "It feels like the portal wraps around the entire town she's in. To open it, I would probably have to make a vortex at least as big, but with your father's help, perhaps we could do it."

Billy read her sincere expression. She seemed so weak, yet she wanted to help. But should she? Did it make sense to drain her energy if they didn't have to? Yet, allowing her to use her gifts might be the emotional boost she needed. "Dad," Billy said, "let's try brute force first. If it doesn't work, we'll give Acacia a shot at it."

330

"Very well." Clefspeare launched into the air and flew in a wide circle, gaining altitude with every second. When he turned back toward the window, Billy pushed Acacia behind him and, taking a deep breath, blew a narrow stream of fire at the target. The flames bounced to each side and spilled to the ground, melting the surrounding snow.

He slid to the side to give Clefspeare room to attack. As he took another breath, a volley of flames rocketed out of the sky and blasted the same spot. Billy added his jet again. With steam rising and water streaming at their feet, he glanced at Shiloh. Bouncing on her toes, she folded her hands at her chest, the bloody bandage obvious over her stub of a finger.

Seconds later, Clefspeare stormed through the fire and, his wings now folded, slammed the side of his body into the partition. With a thunderous *smack,* he bounced to the side and slid through the snow. The wall trembled for a moment but quickly settled down.

Billy ran to where his father lay. With his tail turned one way, his neck turned the other, and his head lying motionless near a spine on his back, he looked dead. "Dad! Are you all right?"

A puff of smoke rose from each nostril. "I think so. I feel no broken bones, but I will likely have a very large bruise."

Billy touched Clefspeare's side. Some of the reddish scales had already turned purple. "Can you get up?"

"I will try. Perhaps you should speak to Shiloh while I gather myself together."

Billy ran back to the wall. Acacia was already standing in front of the impact point, touching the glass with a fiery hand as she spoke. "Shiloh, I am going to try to envelop as much of this area as I can. If it looks like the wall is deteriorating, try to walk through it."

Shiloh nodded and backed away again.

Her facial features sagging, Acacia lifted her hands high and called out, "Flames! Come to my fingers!"

Instantly, two enormous fireballs, twice the size of beach balls, erupted in her palms. Closing her eyes for a moment, she took a deep breath and began waving her arms in tight circles. The fireballs expanded and stretched out horizontally until they merged into a sphere the size of three elephants. Acacia appeared to be a diminutive Atlas carrying the world in her little hands.

With her face tense and her lips pursed, she continued to swirl her arms, letting out high-pitched grunts every few seconds.

As the ball continued to grow, Clefspeare shuffled close to Billy. "I am concerned for her," Clefspeare said. "She is likely too weak to undertake such an enormous task."

"Yeah. Me, too. It hurts just to watch her."

Acacia slid her feet through the mud and again pressed her body on the window. Like a bursting bubble, the fireball broke apart. Flames spread across the glass, crawling in every direction. Acacia rubbed her palms on the surface in wide circles. As

331

if propelled by her motions, the flames continued to spread up and around the cylinder.

"It is time to add more fire," Acacia called. "And fan it with your wings!"

Clefspeare raised up on his haunches. "Son, climb aboard and come with me. We will both add fire from the air."

Billy ran up his father's tail section and along his back, dodging the longer spines. As soon as he seated himself at the base of the neck, he shouted, "Let's do it!"

Beating his wings, Clefspeare rose into the air. The wing on the bruised side seemed to falter, making him tilt for a moment, but he soon righted himself and began an orbit around the transparent cylinder.

"You aim low," Clefspeare shouted, "and I will aim high."

Angling his neck toward the sky, he sprayed a flood of orange from his mouth and both nostrils. Billy joined in, bending over to strike the glass several feet lower. As soon as the flames met the partition, they spread out in the same way Acacia's did, and gusts from Clefspeare's wings added to the momentum.

It took a few minutes for Clefspeare to complete one orbit. When they passed Acacia, she was still leaning against the glass and still moving her hands in circles, though she seemed slower, and her eyes were now tightly shut.

Billy continued shooting fire into the storm. With each splash, the flames made a whooshing sound as they joined in with the rest of the fire. Breathing in cold air, then blowing out hot, he pressed on, though each barrage grew weaker.

Clefspeare's fire remained strong, but his flight angle tilted again. The bruise on his side was definitely taking its toll.

The glass shook. As if boring holes through the partition, fire spilled to the inside and dribbled downward. A slight dizziness swam through Billy's head, likely a touch of hyperventilation, but he couldn't stop now. Something was happening. Maybe it was working.

As they approached Acacia again, the entire wall dissolved, and the fire dropped to the ground like a burning curtain. Her flames ceased, and she stumbled through and fell into Shiloh's arms. Shiloh sat down and, cradling Acacia, called, "She's okay! Just exhausted, I think."

Clefspeare and Billy shut off their jets. As they glided toward the snow, Billy shouted, "Yes! She did it!" But before his final word passed through his lips, the village began to fade.

"Dad! Get on the ground! Quick!"

As soon as Clefspeare landed, Billy jumped down. Sliding in the snow, he dashed toward Shiloh and Acacia, but the scene vanished before he could get there. They were gone.

He stumbled forward and plowed into a drift. As he rolled, snow pushed into his mouth, cooling the sensitive skin inside. When he came to a stop, he looked up at the cloud-blanketed sky and rested for a moment. His heart thumped. His head pounded. Every part of his body ached.

333

"Son!" Clefspeare called. "Are you all right?"

"I think so." Slowly rising to a sitting position, he looked at his father. Now his heart pounded even harder. Tears came to his eyes, and the chilly wind pushed them back toward his temples. They had failed. Not only did they not rescue Shiloh, they lost Acacia, an Oracle of Fire, no less, probably a great asset in the battle if Abraham's protective wall should ever fail. She had the best chance of opening the portal at Mount Elijah. Now what would they do? Could a dragon open it? With no good place to land, it wasn't likely. And poor Shiloh. Within seconds of being rescued, her hopes were dashed.

He rose to his feet and batted the snow from his pants. Or maybe they weren't dashed after all. Could she have transported to a safe place, away from those who wanted to slice her into pieces? Maybe Shiloh's captors had no idea where she ended up.

Sighing deeply, he pushed through the drift until he worked his way back to the muddy section. He leaned against his father's side and draped an arm over his neck. "Now what're we going to do?"

Clefspeare picked up Acacia's cloak with his teeth and laid it over Billy's shoulders. "We will go back to the village. What choice do we have?"

"We could try to open it again. You know, create another circle of fire."

"We can, and we will, but not in my weakened state. I will return later with Hartanna, and we will see what we can do."

Nodding, Billy looked up into his father's eyes. "Any speculation?"

"If you mean their destination … no. When the firestorm toppled the Tower of Babel, the bottom third transported from Earth to Hades, so it seems that these portal jumps are unpredictable, at least for us who have no knowledge of the cross-dimensional paths."

Billy touched Clefspeare's bruise. "How does it feel? Going back will be mostly against a headwind."

Clefspeare bent his neck until his head hovered in front of the purple blotch. "I would not want to do battle for a while, but I am confident I can make it to Founder's Village."

"If we go another route, maybe it won't be so bad."

"I assume you mean that you still want to check on the wall of fire and deliver the supplies."

"Right. Do you think you could make it that far? I can go with Hartanna later."

"I see value in going now. The warrior chief will be glad to get a report, and the men could be hungry." Clefspeare shuffled to the large boulder. "But first, I want to create a landmark to ensure that we are able to find this place in the future." He heaved in a breath.

Then, with a narrow, laserlike stream of fire, he chiseled into the boulder's surface. As he guided the stream, smoke shot out, veiling his mark, but after several seconds, he finished, and the breeze cleared the smoke, revealing a letter X about the size of a human head.

"X marks the spot?" Billy asked.

"Indeed. It is a simple but well-known symbol."

Billy laughed, "Mom used to put an X on maps when we played Treasure Island together. She would even put one on the ground at the place where she buried ..." He let his voice dwindle away.

They stayed silent for a moment until Clefspeare breathed a sigh. "I know, Son. I miss her, too."

After resting for a few minutes, Billy remounted Clefspeare and the two rode southeast to the north side of the Valley of Shadows. A wall of flames stood before them, rising from the ground on the northern border of the valley, through the clouds and out of sight.

As they passed around to the northeastern side, Billy looked back at the river. Before the start of the season of death, one of Valiant's warriors tried to cross into the valley by diving into the cold water, a test to ensure that no one could come through from the other direction. Under the surface, the water boiled at that point, but most of the flow passed through, proving that this was a vulnerable spot. The same was true where the river exited the walled-in zone. So Valiant stationed armed guards at each point. Even if the enemy breached the wall, they wouldn't be able to get more than one soldier through at a time, making them easy prey for the guards.

Billy spotted two men wearing thick coats and huddling under a makeshift shelter, more of a lean-to than a hut. With a spear in hand, one faced the river while the other appeared to be sleeping under a pile of blankets.

After delivering a fresh supply of food and clothing to the guards, Clefspeare and Billy took off again and rounded the valley's eastern boundary. Billy looked down at the rugged terrain. Snow dressed the trees in skirts of white, though the depth whittled down with every inch closer to the wall, until only mud and scorched trees lined the area nearest the flames.

Several minutes later, Clefspeare flew around a bend and reached the south side just beyond Adam's Marsh. When the river came into sight, Billy patted his father's neck. "I see the guards."

His wing obviously faltering again, Clefspeare angled down and landed in a deep drift near the eastern side of the river. As he slowed, he toppled over, spilling Billy, and then slid into the water.

"Dad!" Billy jumped up and splashed into the chilly flow. His father's wings splayed over the surface, and his head had disappeared underneath. Chunks of ice bounced against Billy's thighs as he waded deeper, pumping his arms and churning his legs. Finally, in waist-deep water, he plunged in, hooked his arms around his father's neck, and hoisted his head above the surface.

Shivering, Billy listened. Was he breathing? The river's rush made it impossible to tell. But his father was definitely unconscious. How could he possibly drag him out?

Loud splashes sounded behind him, then a voice. "Hold on, Billy! Help is on the way!"

He twisted around. Two men waded in, a tall and hefty man in front carrying a rope. Billy heaved in a shaking breath and let it out through chattering teeth. "Thanks ... uh ... Sorry, I don't remember your name."

"Name's Stout." He threw the rope over Clefspeare's back, dove under the water, and resurfaced with the end in hand. After shaking away droplets from his hair, he tied the rope in place. "Just keep his head above water, and Frank and I will haul him out."

336

Billy looked at the other helper, a short, skinny man with a thick beard. "Frank" seemed like an odd choice for these folk who were usually given names based on their personalities.

The two men charged back and forth with the rope, looping and tying until they had fashioned a makeshift harness. Then, with each man pulling on an end, they began hauling Clefspeare to the river's western shore.

Still holding his father's head, Billy trudged along with them. For a few seconds, they moved into deeper water that rose to his neck, but soon they angled up and slid Clefspeare up to the snow.

Frank shook his body and shivered. "We'd better get a fire going here. The dragon is likely dead already, but until we're sure, we should do what we can."

"Just b-bring wood." Billy's teeth chattered so hard, he could barely spit out his words. "I c-can light it."

While the two men hustled to their camp, Billy knelt and set his ear close to his father's nostrils. A wheezing breath warmed his skin. It sounded awful, but it was still music to his ears.

After a few minutes, Stout and Frank had set piles of split logs around Clefspeare's body. Billy moved from pile to pile. The intense cold had chilled his belly, making his fire weak, but as he ran around, reigniting each log as it burned low, he managed to get them all blazing nicely.

With warmth now spreading all around, melting the snow underneath and around his father's body, Billy sat down and rested. His father's breathing had grown deeper and even, but he showed no signs of waking up.

Stout and Frank stood on the other side of one of the fires, Stout now holding a spear. "What brings you to this guard station?" he asked.

Billy pulled his wet clothes away from his skin. "We were checking the wall's security. I wanted to get a report to Elam."

Frank slapped Stout's arm with the back of his hand. "The warrior chief lacks trust in us."

"Lacks trust?" Billy untied the second box of supplies from Clefspeare's back and shoved it into Frank's chest. "Elam sent this for you."

Frank staggered back but regained his balance. "What is it?"

"Food, socks, clean underwear, compliments of your distrusting warrior chief, though they probably aren't dry now."

Stout took the box from Frank and set it on the ground. "I apologize for my partner's frivolous words. We are grateful for Elam's concern. Please let him know that all is well, and there have been no breaches."

"I also apologize," Frank said. "I fear that listening too often to the concerns of other villagers has skewed my thinking."

Billy squinted at him. "Concerns? Other villagers? What are you talking about?"

Stout nudged Frank with an elbow, but Frank didn't seem to notice as he rattled on. "Some believe that Elam is unqualified. First, he is a foreigner and does not understand our ways. Second, he seemed to force Angel to lie. Why would he do that? Third, he commanded the singing girl to change the words to her song, and that brought the giants and the evil dragon into our world. Quite a number of our people died as a result. Now our great prophet is gone, we have strange weather that paralyzes us, and a constant threat looms beyond this fiery wall. And it seems that each one of these problems can be attributed to—"

"Hush!" Stout batted Frank with his huge hand. "You have said far too much."

Frank stepped back, his eyes wide. "Oh, I do not believe this blather myself. Heaven forbid! I merely said that it skewed my thinking, and this noble knight asked me to explain."

Billy scowled at Frank. "Has anyone suggested to these doubters that Angel's lie, and not Elam's decisions, led to all these problems?"

Frank parted his lips to speak, but Stout clamped a hand over his mouth. "I have spoken to several, Billy. Most are merely frightened. Doubts do exist, to be sure, so we should be wary. If doubt is allowed to fester, idle talk can cause it to spread, and seditious talk can set it on fire. Fortunately, Flint has been the only seditious influence in our villages, and he is now on the other side of this wall, so we need concern ourselves only with idleness. Discipline and purposeful hard work will surely be of great benefit to everyone and will silence the mouths of the busybodies."

As soon as Stout lowered his hand, Frank added, "Including the dragons. People think they are not working hard enough."

Stout gave him another punch. "Remember what you said when you are eating the food this dragon nearly died to deliver to you."

Billy looked back at Clefspeare. His breathing was steady and strong. The firelight had to be helping his photoreceptors recharge, but was the bruise a sign of internal bleeding? Would his photoreceptors promote healing fast enough? Maybe a healer could get the process moving faster.

"If you don't mind," Billy said, "could one of you go back to the village and ask Thigocia to come out here? And one of the other dragons, like Hartanna, Legossi, or Firedda."

Frank pointed at himself. "I will go. Stout is stronger than I, but I am swifter. In these conditions, Stout might take until next week to arrive."

"He speaks the truth, as usual," Stout said, laughing as he delivered another punch to Frank's arm, "but he could learn a bit of diplomacy."

"Thank you." Billy reached back and touched Excalibur's hilt, but his arm felt stiff, and a hard shiver shook his body. "I can take Frank's place here till he gets back."

"You will need dry covering." Stout hurried to a tent, returned with a thick blanket, and draped it over Billy's shoulders. "Now you will be much more comfortable."

While waiting for the guard to return, Stout provided Billy with a long and eloquent account of the history of the two villages, at least what he could remember. Since he was only one hundred twenty years old, his recollections didn't reach as far back as some of the elders. Still, he recalled tales that Abraham had told, as well as some of Valiant's adventures. With Abraham gone, Valiant was now the oldest citizen in either village, but no one knew exactly how old he was, and he would never tell. Some said six hundred years, some said well over a thousand, but his physical vigor and mental acuity had not faded in the slightest.

During the stories, Clefspeare shifted his body from time to time and let out a low groan. The bruise spread farther across his scales, red giving way to purple from just above his right foreleg all the way back to the base of his tail. It looked bad, very bad.

After a few hours, a booming call sounded from above, a dragon's trumpet, then another. Billy looked up. Two dragons slashed through the lower layer of clouds and angled toward them. As they drew closer, their identities became clear, Thigocia and Legossi, both with wings folded in and diving fast.

The next few minutes seemed like a blur. With barely a word, Thigocia snuffed out the surrounding fires and covered Clefspeare with her body and wings while Legossi coated her with flames. Under the barrage, Thigocia's scales slowly turned from beige to reddish orange. Again and again Legossi applied new coats until Thigocia called out, "Enough!"

She lay motionless, save for the normal rise and fall of respiration. As her glow diminished, Clefspeare began to stir. Thigocia rose and stepped out of the way, giving him room.

"He will soon rise," she said.

Billy knelt at his father's side. The bruise had diminished to the size of a grapefruit, and even the color of his healthy scales seemed bolder and brighter than ever.

Soon, he blinked and lifted his head. His blazing red eyes shifted to each onlooker in turn. With a low rumble, he murmured, "It seems that I have taken a spill."

Billy patted him on the neck. "You just went for a swim in the river, that's all. You seemed kind of cold, so I called in a heating specialist."

Clefspeare draped a wing over Billy's back. "A healing?"

His throat tightening, Billy nodded. "It looked pretty bad for a while."

Clefspeare climbed to his haunches and spread out his wings. "I am still quite sore, but I think I will be able to fly back to the village."

"No riders for you," Thigocia said. "I will carry Billy."

Legossi shuffled close to Stout. "And I will remain with this guard until the other returns. Frank is not fond of riding dragons, so he chose to walk back."

"I welcome your presence," Stout said, bowing low. "As an amateur historian, I would like to learn more about dragonkind from your world."

After a minute or two of stretching and testing his wings, Clefspeare lifted into the sky and flew in a wide circle, apparently without difficulty. Billy climbed up Thigocia's tail and settled at the base of her neck. Seconds later, she joined Clefspeare, and the two dragons headed back to the village, slowly but steadily.

As they ascended to just under the cloudbank, Billy watched his father's flight, his eyebeams aimed straight ahead. He seemed to be in deep thought. Was he thinking about his vulnerability? His relative weakness in this place of cold and so little sunlight? How long could these dragons maintain their power?

Billy's thoughts turned to his conversation with the two guards. Apparently, Elam had vulnerabilities of his own. Stout's words came back to mind. *If doubt is allowed to fester, idle talk can cause it to spread, and seditious talk can set it on fire.*

Sure, Flint was gone, but could there be another source of sedition? Semiramis definitely talked a good talk, but it seemed that everything she was involved in turned into a disaster. Because of her, a new plant was growing that was a spawn of Arramos, and they couldn't do anything to stop it. Her discovery of Shiloh's prison led to Acacia's disappearance. And even her help with healing Listener could be explained as a stealthy way of gaining trust rather than a truly caring gesture.

Billy lowered his head to get out of the stiff breeze. The coming weeks, months, and maybe even years would seem so long, especially without Bonnie around to talk to.

Bonnie stood near the waterfall in the Valley of Souls and looked into the pool. Her rippled reflection, a human-shaped statue of flames stared back at her. It was all so strange, good in a way, yet awful in another. It was like the passions in her heart burned on the outside of her body—love, faith, zeal—but was it always the best idea to show these feelings to everyone so plainly?

Two other flaming people joined her, one on each side. To Bonnie's right, The Maid's French-flavored voice sang out. "Do not fear." She dipped her toe in the water. Although the girl's skin and the outline of her foot clarified, the fire kept burning. "Nothing is able to extinguish your flame, unless you allow it."

Standing on Bonnie's left, Sapphira looked at the waterfall. "Can we try to go back through the portal?" She let her fire die away. "I can try it by myself and see what happens."

"Oh, please do not," The Maid said. "Abaddon has already warned me that this portal is closed at the other side by thick layers of rock. You would drown if you made the attempt. And if you wish to perish by water, the pool would be more efficient. It would be easier to retrieve your body."

"Thanks," Sapphira said, "but that's not exactly comforting."

342

The Maid withdrew a dagger and set it on the ground next to Bonnie. "Abaddon said you must take this."

Sapphira stared at it. "It's the staurolite dagger! How did you get it?"

"It washed down from your world, and Abaddon found it. I can only assume someone threw it into the portal."

"I did that," Sapphira said. "It's evil. It tried to get me to kill myself."

"I see." The Maid picked it up again and looked at it. "Perhaps its evil nature has been purged. Since Abaddon insisted that Bonnie keep it, the dagger must be safe. He is quite adept at exorcising an evil spirit."

Bonnie took it from The Maid. "I don't have a sheath for it."

"That is easily remedied. I think we will be here long enough to make one."

Sapphira pulled the ovulum from the pouch and stared at the clear glass.

"Still no Enoch?" Bonnie asked.

Sapphira pushed it back in place. "I think we're on our own."

"The heavenly viewer will work here," The Maid said. "There is likely a problem on the other side."

"That's not good news," Bonnie said. "If Enoch's in trouble, then everyone else is, too."

The Maid laughed. "There is no need to fear. An Oracle of Fire surely understands this."

Bonnie stared at her hands again. Somehow she could see the outline of her fingers a little better. It was almost like being in the candlestone. When she first dove into the stone, she was just a mass of energy, but over time her details grew clear.

She looked at The Maid. She, too, seemed to be clearer. Her eyes were sharp and piercing, and her hair flowed behind her, clearly blond, even within her fiery shell.

343

Yet, The Maid had been there for years, so the reason for her clarity had to be a sharpening in Bonnie's vision. Would they soon be able to see each other plainly? Could The Maid already see every detail in Bonnie's face and form?

Bonnie sat down and dipped her feet in the water. Although it felt neither warm nor cool, it was refreshing. "How much warning will we have if we're about to be called?"

The Maid stooped beside her. "Abaddon receives word of possible callings at least an hour in advance, by Earth's reckoning, but with the will of man as part of the equation, it is rarely certain. He sometimes prepares, and the call does not occur. Only when the call is a fulfillment of prophecy is he ever certain."

After a pause, The Maid added, "But since you are an Oracle of Fire, I am sure you suspected this."

"Why do you keep saying I should know these things?" Bonnie asked. "I've been an Oracle of Fire for what? Three days?"

"Do you mean to say that you did not know these things?" The Maid cocked her head, a curious expression behind her flaming aura. "Do you not know that God would give you time to respond to a resurrection call? That there is no need to fear the future? If not, then how can you be an oracle?"

"Okay, I did know those things." Bonnie shook her head sadly. "Now I'm not sure why I thought I might not have known. I feel kind of foolish."

"It is because you have lived so long among people who love their slavery. Although the key to the lock has been provided, they refuse to employ it, even those who verbally profess the same faith. They hold on to the chains, because a faithless life seems easier to them than the sacrificial suffering that you and every other oracle is called to live. They even drag these chains and moan about their weight, yet they still refuse to let them go, even though they are told time and again that every lock has been rendered powerless by the Lord Christ. Such is the madness of this generation of mankind."

"And living among them," Bonnie said, "I guess I caught the mind-set and got used to the language."

"Even though you threw away the chains long ago." The Maid's fiery hand touched Bonnie's. "Speak the truth. Live the truth. Be the truth. Never let the faithless ones change any of those three principles. Remember that you are an Oracle of Fire, as is every faithful follower of our Lord. For all true disciples possess the pure silver, purged of all dross, and the fire of God's love burns within, an everlasting flame that others, even those who give lip service to the truth, will never comprehend until you are able to pass along that fire from heart to heart.

"As an Oracle, you will look through portals to their hearts, you will feel the heavy sadness of their lonely and dark estates, and you will possess crystal-clear vision that will allow you to see what will bring them deliverance from their sorrows. In trying to bring this deliverance, you will say and do things that will make them shake their heads in pity. 'That poor girl,' they will say. 'Her passion has addled her brain.' Your confidence, they will call arrogance. Your faith, they will call wishful thinking. Your purity, they will call self-righteousness. Your firm standing, they will call pride. Yet you will know, because of that fire within, that they are the ones dwelling in darkness, and you must touch your lighted wick to their darkened lamps.

"While you are here, I will remind you of these things daily. Not only that, I will train you in the art of the sword, both the physical art and the spiritual."

Bonnie felt warmer all over. The Maid's touch seemed so real, so energizing. And her words made the inner flame burst into an inferno.

"Have no fear," The Maid continued. "For as long as you stay here, you will neither hunger nor thirst, and you will always walk in the light. Since Jehovah has called you to this place, you must believe that all is well."

Bonnie let every syllable sink in. They felt peaceful and good as they filtered through, like hot soup poured into a cold belly. After a few silent moments, she nodded. "I am an Oracle of Fire, so I know without a doubt that God will not forsake me in this place. I will rise again."

BOOK 2
FROM THE ASHES

CHAPTER

TONGUES OF FIRE

B illy crouched behind a bushy tree, Walter on one side, Ashley on the other, and Elam guarding their backs with a drawn sword. As twilight faded into darkness, they huddled without a sound. It was finally time to make the boldest move yet. It had taken months of preparation, and tonight, with neither Pegasus nor Phoenix rising to reveal their presence, they would launch their plan.

After being dropped off by Clefspeare, Hartanna, and Thigocia, they had hiked a mile to get to this point. Although the enemy stayed behind a wall of fire, it was impossible to know if they could see anything beyond the flames. If they could perceive the shadow of a dragon, they would likely be on the alert for any activity near the wall, and that might ruin everything.

For now, the dragons had to stay back and meet them later at the southern rendezvous point, the river's exit from the flaming wall. Even there, they would need dragons for passenger transport only if their plans didn't work out. Candle was supposed to fly

Merlin to the rendezvous and park it nearby for Billy's use when they arrived, and Ashley brought a transmitter for calling either the airplane or the base radio station in case they needed help.

So, with their powerful winged friends absent, it was time for Billy and company to be quiet and wait for the cover of darkness. That would be their greatest ally.

He peeked between the velvety green leaves. This "ghost lily tree," as the locals called it, reminded him of the rhododendrons he once hid behind in West Virginia while trying to stay out of the dragon slayer's sight. Ahead, just ten paces separated them from the towering wall of flames near the northern boundary of the Valley of Shadows. To their right, Twin Falls River, maybe fifty paces away, flowed under the fire and rushed toward the valley for about a quarter mile before plunging from a height of several hundred feet into the land of the shadow people.

350

Now that the sound of thundering water crashed into his ears, he couldn't help but shiver. Although he had grown accustomed to the never-ending frigid weather and frequent snowfalls, the thought of taking that plunge into the domain of shadowy fiends brought an icy chill.

He reached to his back scabbard and fingered Excalibur's hilt. It was still there. Why wouldn't it be? Checking it every few minutes served no reasonable purpose. Yet, somehow touching it settled the goose bumps.

Ashley whispered, "They know we're here."

"They?" Billy asked, also whispering. "The shadow people?"

"No. Abraham and Angel."

Billy looked at the wall of flames. Of course, it was more than flames. Ever since Abraham had marched around enemy territory four years ago, his and Angel's life energies had fueled this barrier, a living wall with two embedded souls. "Are they communicating with you?" he asked.

"In a way. I don't sense words, only impressions. They are weaker than when I first sensed them. Their energy will soon be spent."

Elam joined them in the low bushes. "Do they approve of our mission?"

"I'm not sure." The fire billowed upward in Ashley's wide eyes. "I don't sense *dis*approval. It's more like a contented sigh. They are at peace and happy to see us."

"Will they help us?"

"They will do what they can, but I'm not sure how. I get the feeling that they aren't able to make a hole in the wall without falling apart completely."

"At least we'll have fired-up cheerleaders," Walter said. "Can't hurt."

Elam straightened, picked up a shoulder bag, and motioned for the others to join him. Raising his hood over his bushy hair, he said, "I think it's dark enough. Let's go."

After raising their own hoods, Billy and Walter each hoisted a hefty pack while Ashley picked up two smaller ones, more like leather briefcases than the canvas haversacks the others toted. All four carried swords, either in a belt or in a back scabbard, though none had brought along shields. They already had as much as they could handle.

With Elam leading the way, they marched over packed snow that marked a deer trail they had scouted out earlier, perfect for a silent approach. Under the cover of trees, some just dry woody skeletons from the perpetual winter and others still green and vibrant, they followed the river's call.

Soon, they broke through the forest edge, and, hunched over and jogging, they hurried to a point near the intersection of the flaming wall and the river. A guard on the other side of the river stood next to a weak torch sticking up from the beach sand. He stared but said nothing. He knew the plan. No words. No gestures

351

that might signal a guard on the valley side that something unusual was taking place.

Billy quietly set down his pack. Walter, Elam, and Ashley did the same with their loads. When Elam's bag clinked, everyone froze. The metal-on-metal sound had plagued their trial runs, but it couldn't be helped. Even though the snowboards were part of a backup plan in case the raft failed, they decided to bring them. No matter how confident they were in Plan A, it didn't make sense to forsake Plan B, even with the risk of the telltale sounds. They had hoped the river's noise would mask them. Now the theory would meet the test.

They stared through the flames. No shadows moved. Yet, since plumes of vapor shot up at the river's entry point, it seemed impossible to know if any guards on the other side had noticed their presence.

Elam waved his hand, the signal to continue. Billy untied his bag, withdrew a large raft, and unfolded it on the beach. Inflating it would be the first step. Ashley had installed a tiny motorized fan that would draw in surrounding air. Since they couldn't risk a loud sucking noise, she opted for a quieter, slower fan energized by a battery she had fashioned from local metals.

Billy flipped the switch and listened to the low whir as it inflated. It would take quite a while, but at least it was quiet.

Walter tied a rope to a hook on the left side of the raft's front, one of the guidelines for the parachute. There would be three other ropes, one on the opposite side of the front and two in the back. During their tests, mastering a directed fall had taken longer than any other step, but after so many successful trials, everyone seemed confident. Still, the swirling winds in the valley's sheltered bowl could be far less predictable than at their test range. This wouldn't be easy.

Elam laid four snowboards and eight ski poles in the raft, careful to keep the poles' sharp tips away from the sides. The metal points had been wrapped with a blanket just to be safe. One hole would end their mission before it began.

Ashley attached the transmitter to the back of the raft. As she adjusted the eight-inch antenna with one hand, she looked at a signal meter in her other hand, the flames from the wall giving her enough light to see. She flashed an okay sign. The transmitter was working.

When Walter tied the last guideline in place, the foursome unfolded an oblong parachute, laid it over the raft, and attached it to the lines. It had taken weeks to design the canopy's shape to allow for precise guidance, and their low-level trial jumps had cost the test pilots a few bumps and bruises, but with each new design, they were able to launch from higher elevations until all four had mastered the skill from the necessary height.

Elam raised three fingers—three minutes until the raft would be full. After thousands of years of life, his internal clock had become flawless. With Walter and Elam at the front and Billy and Ashley at the rear, they carried the raft to the river and set it in the water.

353

All four waded into the icy flow. While the men held the raft in place against the swift current, Ashley threw back a rear corner of the parachute and stowed their packs. The men's bags were nearly empty now, while Ashley's still carried the gadgets they would need later. She then crawled under the parachute and stationed herself at the raft's right rear corner.

Elam entered next, followed by Walter. With the raft now barely buoyant under the added weight, Billy shoved it toward the center of the river, pushed an anchor into the sandy bed, and jumped in. In the darkness, he had to squirm as he slid under the parachute as quietly as possible. For a moment, Excalibur caught the canopy, but Ashley pried it free and guided him the rest of the way in.

When he finally settled in his corner, he pulled the parachute over his head and waited in silence with the others. With the wall's firelight radiating through the protective covering, he could see each taut face. Elam had planned this pause, a time for everyone to slow down and collect themselves.

He held up a pair of fingers—two minutes. Again, this precision-minded warrior chief would run this mission like clockwork. Yet, the next sequence of events would require guesswork. Five seconds till they hit the fire, a minute and a half to the waterfall, and thirty seconds till they floated safely to the river again. They hoped.

Safety through the flames, however, was certain. The parachute's retardant chemicals worked. The first few tests using volunteers who braved the wall with chemically coated cloaks had been painful failures, but Ashley's newer formulas proved extremely effective. The tests had also drawn Flint's troops to their attempted penetration points on the south side of Adam's Marsh. With Valiant and Candle making another attempt an hour ago, they hoped even the shadow people might have migrated from the valley to help guard that region.

With the current pushing heavily and chunks of ice bumping the rear, the raft rocked back and forth. Elam paid no attention. His head bowed and his eyes closed, he seemed to be praying.

Billy nodded. Elam had never failed to begin every trial run with prayer. He wasn't about to take the real plunge without it.

Reaching over, Billy took Ashley's hand. She gripped it tightly and tapped Walter's. Soon, all four joined hands.

Taking in a deep breath, Billy prayed silently—for their dangerous mission; for his mother, whom he hadn't seen in four years; for Bonnie, wherever she was, that God would watch over her and bring them together someday; and even for Flint, that somehow he would realize how his actions had brought them to the brink of all-out war, that he would have a change of heart, and when the wall of fire faded, that he would come out with an olive branch instead of a spear.

Soon, Elam pulled his hands back and pointed at Billy. That was the signal. It was time to fly.

Billy untied the anchor. The raft shot forward. Elam splayed his hands and counted down the seconds.

Four fingers. The light inside the raft grew brighter.

Three. The raft jerked and kicked.

Two. The temperature shot up.

One. A sizzle erupted—water striking fire.

Elam closed his fist. Ashley squeezed Billy's hand. A whoosh sounded. Crackles, pops, and sizzles beat against their ears as steam warmed the floor of the raft and lifted them into the air. The wall was thick here, an impossible scenario to duplicate in tests. They would just have to ride it out.

Sweat dampened Billy's armpits and trickled down his back. Soon he would be soaked, and facing the frigid wind during their upcoming plunge would be torture. Yet, they had trained for that as well by spending several weeks sleeping outdoors with minimal clothing and covering.

355

Finally, they dropped back to the river with a splash. Their raft bounced twice before settling into a gentle rocking motion. Staring through the parachute's material, Billy listened. Had anyone out there heard the commotion? During their planning, no one had talked about the steam's elevating surge. But now it was too late to worry about it. They would just have to ride it out.

As they rushed away from the wall, the light faded. The sizzles died away. Coolness filtered in. For the next minute or so, they would wait in silence. It would do no good to peek out and watch for the upcoming drop. It was just too dark. And this section was uncharted. No one knew the exact distance between the boundary and the waterfall. Only a brief sense of flying and a sudden drop would signal their arrival.

During their tests in complete darkness, Billy had tried to use his danger sensing gift to guess when the fall would come. But it seemed that darkness and constant danger somehow blunted his ability to sense a coming peak. Knowing exactly when the moment would arrive seemed impossible.

Billy slipped out of Ashley's grasp and reached for the left rear guideline. She, Walter, and Elam held their lines, as well. They had practiced this in the dark before. They could do it again, four parasailing pilots flying an overloaded raft into a valley of death. No problem.

Every bump felt like "the" bump. Every sudden jerk made them flinch. Finally, it seemed that the river fell away. Then, they dropped.

Elam and Walter threw their lines out first. The parachute flew upward, billowed out, and grabbed the air. Billy and Ashley cast out theirs. The entire canopy beat above them, sounding like a dragon trying to hover in place.

356

As their descent slowed, falling water splashed in from behind. Gusts of wind blew the spray all around. Without a visible target, they had to use dead reckoning, listening to the roar of water and constantly adjusting to stay at the center of it while gliding away from the waterfall itself.

At this point, they had decided that necessary commands could be given. The background noise would have to drown them out.

"Left five degrees," Elam grunted. "There. Keep it there."

"Tilting right," Ashley called. "Billy. A few inches slack. … Perfect."

Soon, they slid back into the river with a barely perceptible splash. Billy gave Ashley a silent high five, almost missing her hand in the darkness.

As the chute began to droop behind them, Billy and Ashley reeled it in and folded it into a wad at the center of the raft. With the masking noise dying away, it was time for silence again.

Darkness enveloped them like a heavy blanket. Billy searched for Ashley's eyes. Nothing. Total darkness.

Her hand touched his. He slid his fingers under her palm and rubbed her knuckles with his thumb. The touch felt good. Reassurance. Comfort. In spite of the darkness, they were all in this together.

Billy kept his ears trained on the water's flow. It had died down to a consistent, low-level rush. Now he had to listen for another rise in volume, their only signal that the next waterfall, the exit from the Valley of Shadows, was fast approaching.

He pulled Excalibur from his back scabbard, taking care not to make it glow. Because of his four years of training and physical maturing, he had become one of the best, if not *the* best swordsman in their army. So, taking into account Billy's expertise with Excalibur, Elam appointed him the mission's strong-arm man. Everyone else would work while he stood guard.

After a few minutes, the water's percussion began to increase. Elam tapped Billy's knee. Billy tapped Ashley's. He tried to watch Ashley pass the signal to Walter and Walter back to Elam, completing the cycle, but it was too dark. Of course, there was no doubt. They passed it along, and now everyone knew the first water-ride phase was coming to an end.

Seconds later, the front side of the raft lifted. Elam had slid into the river, as planned. The raft turned to the left, lifted again, and, with a sliding noise at its floor, came to a stop.

Billy lifted his leg over the side and felt for solid ground— beach sand. Although the valley had likely received as much snow as any other place, the rise and fall of the river probably scoured any snow from its beach.

When he had steadied himself, he helped Ashley step out. As they had practiced many times in the darkness, Walter handed the packs to Elam and Ashley while Billy walked a few steps away from the river, listening.

357

No unusual noises. In order to prepare his ears, the younger villagers had tried to imitate the sounds the shadow people made. Candle had sent a chunk of ice sliding across a table, but he admitted that the shadow people were quieter. In reality, the dark creatures crawled along the ground with more of a hush. Windor poured oil on the table and tried again. That was closer, they decided, but still too loud.

Finally, Valiant offered a hint that all agreed was the best. "Hear them?" he had said. "Yes, you can hear them, but once you do, that will be too late. By the time the first breath reaches your ears, they will have you in their clutches. You *feel* them first. The hair on the back of your neck rises, and a tingle on your skin tells you that a dark hand is stretching out to drag you into their swarm of devouring black oil."

Billy shook off a shiver. It was time to concentrate. He reached out with his danger-sensing "radar" and tried to feel for the signals. After a few seconds, he shook his head. Nothing. And no sound, either. Even the expected noises of his fellow spies didn't rise over the river's din. Maybe the shadow people had no clue that intruders were present, and the months of training had paid off. But maybe their silence wouldn't be enough. Valiant had said that those creatures could smell a human a mile away.

Billy sniffed the air. Wood smoke. Something burned somewhere close by. Maybe that would mask their presence, too.

As he let his thumb rub across a gemstone embedded in Excalibur's hilt, a memory rose in his mind, the event that birthed the plans for this mission in the first place. Stout had found this rubellite on a tiny raft floating through the southern wall boundary. It had been tied down by wire, and a resin-coated note had been attached, obviously prepared by someone who wanted to keep it safe through the fire.

In an almost illegible scrawl, the note read, "Found in valley cave. Roxil."

A note on the other side, written in beautifully familiar penmanship, said, "Billy, if by some miracle you get this, here is an update. We have finally rebuilt Apollo. We found a portal near the mines that, according to Larry, emits signals that are not of our world. I attached his note to the missing stone from Excalibur's hilt. If it goes through the portal, we will begin working on strengthening Apollo to the point where we can make a hole big enough for Gabriel to go through. Then, if he is successful in finding Second Eden, we will send the other dragons. We are praying for you. Please tell your father that I love him."

Billy imagined Roxil tying the gem and note to the little raft. If only he could have replied! But now, months later, his mother had no idea that they had received it. He couldn't tell her that they had worked every waking minute since that time to get safely to the cave. And did anything happen in the meantime? Did she manage to open a bigger hole? Did Gabriel try to come through? If so, he would have been trapped. With no way out of enemy territory, he would have been taken prisoner … or worse.

Yet, most of the note's news had brightened their outlook. Mom was working hard to get the dragons into Second Eden, and putting the rubellite in its proper place had given Excalibur more power than ever before.

A hand touched his shoulder. Billy jumped but quickly settled down when Walter whispered, "We're ready."

Billy raised his arms and allowed Walter to tie a rope around his waist. The others would hang on to the lead rope and tag along with Elam at the back, guiding the raft along the shallows, as planned. He had to let it drag a bit on the sand to keep it from taking off in the current, but the noise wasn't discernible above the water's constant rush.

Billy drew a map in the darkness in front of him. Candle and Listener had created a nearly life-sized copy of the cave's surroundings, including a man-made stream with precise bends; rocks that protruded from each side of the river, signaling the exit waterfall; and the most important landmark, a head-high boulder embedded in the beach sand. Once they reached it, they would be even with the cave. They would then turn left, walk through the forest about fifty paces, and search for the opening in the mountain face.

Unfortunately, the boulder sat an unknown distance away from the river's edge, so they had to fan out, Billy on the left, then Walter and Ashley, and Elam on the right. Depending on the river's current level, it could be anywhere from one to ten paces from the edge.

Billy crept along, keeping his left hand out in front as he tried to feel for anything solid. At the same time, he kept his danger radar going. Using every sense but sight had been hard to learn, but the training was paying off again.

Finally, he touched a rock. With a quick tug on the rope, he brought everyone to a halt. He groped higher until his hand moved over the top. Yes, it was just about head high.

After giving Elam a moment to pull the raft fully on shore, he led the way toward the forest. With every step, he lowered his boot carefully. The terrain underneath would provide important clues that might reveal his location. The beach sand ended abruptly, giving way to soft turf of some kind. After tugging the rope again, he stooped and felt the ground. A thin layer of snow covered long, stiff leaves that crumbled as he pinched them.

Billy brought a sample to his nose and sniffed. Musky. Candle had said that the callow ferns couldn't have survived the weather. They always died back during the season of death, and with this season lasting four years, they would all be dead. He also warned that walking on them would raise a crackling racket as well as a musky odor that would alert the shadow people to their presence. Their only hope would be a deep enough layer of snow to mask both.

The river, however, had kept this section relatively free of a protective snow layer. Deeper snow, and safer ground, likely lay farther away, but how far?

Billy gave the rope two more tugs, letting everyone know that it was time for Ashley's magic. As soon as he returned Excalibur to his scabbard, he felt her hand touch his. She put Walter's MP3 player in one hand and a spray bottle in the other. Only days ago, she had captured the river's distinctive rush using the airplane's radio transmitter, which she had modified into a digital recorder. Now, they hoped, replaying the recording at this point would wash away the crackling noise.

After turning on the player and setting it on the snow, Billy began spraying the bottle's contents on the ground as he walked gingerly forward. The liquid emitted a strangely sweet fragrance that quickly vanished. Since the same species of ferns once grew near the village, Ashley had been able to formulate a counter odor that would, as Walter loved to put it, "mask the musk." Fortunately, no one had to reinvent an Earth spray bottle. They had found a bottle of window cleaner in the airplane.

361

When he reached deeper snow, Billy stopped spraying and passed the bottle back through the line. He withdrew Excalibur again and marched on. The snow under his feet made almost no sound at all, but he still had to be careful. With trees ahead, protruding roots could trip him up, and their mission would be over.

Keeping the sword in front, he waved the blade back and forth in a wide arc. Soon, it brushed against something. A low branch? Probably.

He signaled with another yank on the rope. They had arrived at the forest. Since Candle had reported that most of the trees were not evergreens, they likely had no leaves and had allowed the snow to fall through. The march could continue in silence.

A slight tingle crawled along Billy's skin. It wasn't much, but it was very real, definitely danger. The shadow people were in the forest, but where? Since they couldn't live in sunlight, wouldn't they take refuge in the evergreens where the boughs would give them shelter?

Billy drew in a long breath through his nose. The smell of pine was pretty strong. If it got any stronger, they would have to find a new path. After another minute or so of dodging roots, evergreen scents, and danger signals, the blade touched something solid that felt like stone.

Pulling the rope, he gathered the other three into a huddle. "We veered right," he whispered. Then, setting his hand on the cliff, he turned left and followed the mountain's stony face, his fingers feeling the crags for any hint of a recess.

The scent of pine grew stronger. The danger alarm heightened, but now was no time to find another route. He had to go on. Should he allow just a bit of glow? He could slice a few attacking shadow people with Excalibur's newly restored beam, but could he handle the storm of darkness that thousands of those creatures would bring? It wasn't worth the risk, at least not yet.

After a few seconds, the cliff fell away from his guide hand. He leaned and reached farther. Still nothing. This had to be the cave. Now it was time to plunge into the depths of another mysterious darkness.

CHAPTER

2

THE PORTAL HOME

With three tugs, Billy signaled the others. It was time for the next step. While he stood with Excalibur at the cave's entrance, Elam would start the new march inside. He had been in this cave before, and since the shadow people feared it, or at least everyone hoped they still feared it, they would not be likely to venture into its depths.

As Ashley passed by, she touched his hand again, prompting him to smile. What a comfort she had been during the four-plus years he had been separated from Bonnie. Now that he was twenty and his tough training had molded him into a man, he longed to fulfill the prophecy and marry Bonnie. Surely she would be ready, too. She was always far more mature than anyone else her age.

He turned and followed the pull of the rope. He could sense Ashley in front of him, and she likely sensed him as well. She always did before. Over the years his emotions had let her know that he needed a woman's support. Of course others had wanted to help. Several fathers of village girls had inquired about his availability, which explained the friendliness of some of the twentysomething females and the giggles rising from teenaged girls as he walked by. But there was no way he could offer them hope. He and Bonnie would eventually get together. Even if it took a hundred years, he would wait for her.

For the time being, Ashley had been able to tell when he needed a boost. A kind gaze, a caring smile, a soft touch—she gave each one at the right time, never hinting that her gestures suggested anything beyond a sister's love. She was salve for a Bonnie-sized wound.

After nearly a minute, the rope's steady pull slackened. Elam had stopped. Billy turned and set his feet, taking his stance as rear guard while Walter unfastened everyone from the line and let it drop to the ground.

With the rush of water now a distant whisper, every footstep and every popping joint sounded like thunderclaps. Ashley ventured a whisper of her own. "I'm going to let you know what I'm doing step by step. Right now I'm examining the cave's back wall with a photometer. It's definitely showing readings that are consistent with what I have seen at other portal locations. The key is in finding the strongest signal." A few quiet seconds passed before her whisper continued. "Ah! I think I have it."

After a rustling sound crackled in the motionless air, her volume rose a notch. "I'm setting my flash unit on the ground at the focal point, and I'm about to turn it on. There's no way to stop the noise." A click sounded, and a low hum reverberated in the cave. "Billy, I'll let you know when it's ready. The last time I tested it, the light-bending ions took twenty-three seconds to charge. We'll assume the same now. Elam will give us a five-second warning, and we'll all stand back."

As Billy faced the cave entrance, the tingle returned. Its level of intensity grew quickly, and his danger alarm spiked. Something was coming, something deadly.

He turned on Excalibur's glow to maximum and searched the nearby floor. Nothing.

"Billy," Ashley said, "it's not time yet."

"I know, but we have company." He turned on the beam. It shot into the cave's ceiling and bored into the rock. The brilliant light cast a wave of energy out onto the cave floor. A skittering mass of black halted about ten paces away, then began a slow retreat.

"Looks like a bunch," Walter said. "I counted six sets of beady eyes in the front line."

"Five seconds," Elam called as he and Walter and Ashley backed toward the side walls. "You'll have to risk turning the beam this way," Elam said. "It's do or die now."

"Great choice of words." Billy flexed his biceps and swiveled toward Elam. "Ready!"

Elam chopped down with his hand. "Now!"

Billy copied his motion, slicing downward with the beam. As it cut a vertical line from top to bottom on the back wall, sparks exploded as if he had cleaved a high-voltage cable. He angled his head away from the arcing fireballs and finished his sweep. The beam struck Ashley's ion box, a baseball-sized black cube with mirrors on the top and sides. As sparks continued to fly, he kept the beam in place. Yellow bolts shot from the top of the box and cut jagged lines all across the back wall.

"Is this supposed to be happening?" he called.

Ashley stared wide-eyed at the fireworks display. "No! The ion box was supposed to open a portal, but I think that wall was already a gateway of some kind, like a portal that just needed a burst of energy."

"Keep it up!" Elam shouted. "At this point it's better to go forward than back."

Billy firmed his grip. The tingling sensation mounted. His danger alarm blared. "Something's behind me!"

"Uh-oh." Walter leaped and hacked with his sword. "Just keep energizing that gateway. I've got your back."

Sparks flew everywhere. Light poured from Ashley's box, creating a rectangular aura on the rear wall that looked like a glowing door.

Ashley raised a hand. "That's enough!"

Billy swung the beam up and turned. Walter was hopping and hacking his sword against the floor so fast, it looked like he was dancing a violent jitterbug.

"Get back!" Billy called. "I'll fry the vermin."

Walter jumped out of the way. Billy chopped down with the beam and waved it back and forth across the stony ground.

Sizzles and squeals echoed, and purple smoke filled the cave with a burnt carrion stench. The shadows melted away, leaving a scattered collection of flat white bones.

Billy spun around. Ashley and Elam stared at the aura, which now looked like a golden painting on the back wall, a door as wide as the cave itself, stretching from floor to ceiling and as bright as Excalibur's beam.

"Our portal?" Billy asked, shielding his eyes.

"I think so." Ashley pushed her fingers against the wall. Her hand disappeared up to her wrist.

Walter joined her. "Feel anything?"

"Just air." Ashley retrieved her hand and flexed her fingers. "I think it's safe to go through."

"Will the shadow people follow?" Walter asked.

"Not likely." Billy put Excalibur away. "They risked a lot by coming this far, but going through a door of pure light?" He shook his head. "I don't think so."

Elam gave them a firm nod. "No time like the present." Leading with a hand, he walked into the glow and disappeared. Ashley followed, then Walter. After a final look at the steaming pile of bones on the floor, Billy joined them.

He broke through into a bath of cool air, though not nearly as cold as what they had left behind in Second Eden. A quick scan revealed a high wall encircling him, its perfectly vertical face interrupted only by a pile of rocks at one point of the base. A tent big enough for two campers had been set up in front of the pile, and a campfire smoldered a few feet from the tent's entrance flap. Nearby, a huge man slept on the ground, obviously Yereq.

Ashley grabbed Billy's shirt. "This is the old mobility room where Walter and I found Sapphira." Her voice pitched into a squeal. "We're in Montana! We're home!"

Walter slapped Billy on the back. "You did it!"

Billy let his mouth drop open. The portal opening hovered in place, a brilliant rectangle sitting an inch above the ground right over a large *X* that someone had painted in black. On one side, the portal was bright and shining, an obvious doorway, but from the other side it seemed that nothing was there at all. The window to the other world was completely flat, invisible from any angle beyond ninety degrees in either direction.

367

Everything made sense. His mother had found the portal at this spot and had marked it to make sure she could find it again. She was probably the one camping out, maybe waiting for some kind of response after sending the rubellite, and Yereq, her guardian, slept close by.

Smiling, Billy rubbed his hands together. A reply to her note had arrived. Pressing a finger against his lips, he crept toward the tent. Judging from the sun's angle, it was getting close to midday. Why would she be sleeping so late? Maybe they had been up most of the night.

As he approached, the tent flap pushed to the side. His mother came out, stooping to fit through the opening. With her head down, she didn't notice Billy. Carrying a cooking pot, she shuffled to the campfire, picked up a small log from a nearby stack, and threw it onto the embers.

Billy walked to within reach and looked at her from the back. Her hair was shorter, grayer, and her posture just a bit more stooped. Was it from the heavy burden of losing her husband and son and trying to retrieve them from an invisible world for more than four years, or had those years physically aged her body that much?

She crouched and stirred the ashes with a stick, deathly quiet. Billy's memories drifted back to another morning when his mother prepared breakfast, the morning he kissed her cheek and left a burn, giving her proof that he was different, that he was genetically a dragon child. She was humming that morning, her sign of peace and contentment, but now, not a sound.

Billy spoke softly, yet clearly. "Mom. I'm back."

She stopped stirring but neither spoke nor turned. Yereq woke and sat up with a start, his eyes wide as he stared at Billy.

Trembling, his mother straightened. The stick shook in her hand. Then slowly, ever so slowly, she turned. For a moment, she just stared. Her eyes darted, first side to side, then up and down, as if drinking in every detail. A teardrop fell from one eye. She laughed, then sucked the breath back in, her lips quaking.

Finally, she raised a hand and caressed Billy's cheek. A smile breaking through, she spoke with a hoarse, tremulous voice. "Who is this handsome young man who looks so much like my son? You are taller, your face is thinner, your body more muscular, and …" Her voice cracking, she shouted, "Oh, Billy!" She threw her arms around his neck and wept. "You're here! Oh, thank God you're here!"

Pulling her into a tight embrace, Billy patted her on the back. "Yes, Mom, and you're the reason."

She pushed herself away and looked into his eyes. "I am?"

He gripped her shoulder. "We found the rubellite."

She gasped, and her eyes grew wide. "You did?"

"Yep. I don't know where you got it, but it was made for Excalibur's hilt." He flicked his head toward his back scabbard. "Now it lights up like nobody's business."

She stared at him for a moment, blinking. Her head tilted, and her voice dropped to a whisper. "That was six months ago."

"Well, it's complicated. You see—"

She looked past him and locked her gaze on the others. "Then you didn't come with Gabriel?"

"Gabriel? No. Why would we?"

Her voice spiked. "Because we sent him through the portal to find out what was over there!"

Ashley, Walter, and Elam joined their huddle. "How long ago?" Walter asked.

Her eyes darted back and forth between Walter and Billy. "Late last night, maybe eight hours ago." She nodded at her tent. "That's why we camped out here. We finally got Apollo to open a large enough portal, so we did it as soon as we could, even though it was at night. I hoped to follow when he reported that it was safe."

369

"It's far from safe," Walter said. "There are these shadow people that—"

Ashley nudged his ribs. "We'll find him. Since he can fly, he's probably fine. He just won't be able to get past Abraham's wall."

"He won't be fine if Goliath sees him. Gabriel's probably not as fast as—"

"Walter!" Ashley nudged him again and looked back at Billy's mother. "Don't worry, Mrs. Bannister. We'll find him."

Billy's mother touched his cheek, tears again falling. "How is your father?"

"He's doing great. He has a shelter and a regeneracy dome, and ever since the dragons started taking turns resting by Abraham's wall of fire, they've all stayed strong. But I guess you didn't hear about the transformation, did you?"

"I heard he's a dragon again and that you have your fire-breathing back. When Acacia came through the portal, she told everyone in the mines, and Gabriel told us."

He slid his hand into hers. "Then you also know we need reinforcements. We think an army of giants and shadowy beasts are going to attack some peaceful villagers soon, so we need more dragons."

"Yes, the former dragons are lodging close by. Yereq can have them here in less than an hour."

Billy looked at Elam. "How much time do we have?"

"First light of dawn is about two hours," Elam said. "We still have to parasail down to the marshlands and then float out the southern wall, but I think we can make it." He glanced at the glowing portal. It was still bright and showed no signs of weakening. "We can wait an hour."

Billy laid a hand on Elam's back. "I almost forgot. Mom, this is Elam, son of Shem, grandson of Noah."

She nodded and offered a weak smile. "I'm glad to finally meet you."

"Likewise," he said, bowing. "I appreciate the politeness, but we should hurry. The longer we wait, the more danger for Gabriel."

"Yereq!" Marilyn called.

Yereq walked up and replied in a deep, echoing voice. "Yes, Marilyn."

"It's time to summon Kaylee, Tamara, and the others. We're going to Second Eden."

Elam raised a finger. "We can take only one at a time. Our raft is too small for more."

She gave him a quizzical stare. "Raft?"

"We have to navigate a river," Billy said, "but we'll explain the whole thing while we wait. We talked it over and decided it would be best to start with Dorian. Then we'll come back for the others, one each night until Pegasus rises too early in the evening."

"Pegasus is our moon," Walter added. "We need at least four hours of total darkness to do this safely."

"I think Dorian will be happy to be first. Kaylee is burning up the Internet and the phone lines searching for her son and Dallas's daughter. Elise is helping, so they'll want to keep working on that."

Yereq pulled a cell phone from his trousers pocket. "I will climb into cellular range and summon Dorian." Tromping with heavy footsteps, he headed for the wall where a rope ladder dangled from above.

Billy's mother let her head droop. "When will I be able to come with you?"

"Well," Billy said, glancing at Elam, "we talked about that. You see, we have to get five dragons into Second Eden. By the time we get the fifth one in, Pegasus will—"

"We'll get you over there," Elam said. "By that time, maybe we'll be faster and can do it in a shorter window."

371

Billy looked into his mother's eyes. She desperately wanted to come to Second Eden and see her husband. "Elam's right, Mom. We'll make it happen."

With her gaze still on the ground, his mother sighed. "Only five more days. I can live with that."

After a few seconds of silence, Billy took in a deep breath. It was time to ask the question he had been avoiding ever since he arrived. "Uh … Mom? Have you heard from Bonnie?"

She compressed his hand, a new tear sparkling in her eye. "Not a word in more than four years. Some of the Caitiff chased her and Sapphira in the mines, but every tunnel is flooded now, so there was no way we could keep searching. Even when the waters were rising, we sent in cave divers, but we didn't find any sign of either of them."

Billy tensed his jaw. He couldn't say a word.

A gentle hand rubbed his back—Ashley. She, too, stayed silent, but her touch said it all. "Don't give up hope," she was saying. "We're here for you."

As usual, Ashley's healing hand did wonders. His muscles loosening, Billy touched the string of beads around his neck. "Acacia and I found this on the ledge while the floodwaters were rising. Since it wasn't broken, I was thinking she left it there on purpose, like a sign that she's okay."

"There is another clue," his mother said. "When I arrived at the overlook in the mines, I thought I saw Bonnie flying Sapphira off the ledge, but it was dark, and it happened so quickly, I wasn't sure. But Yereq found one of the Caitiff, and it confirmed what I thought I saw. Bonnie and Sapphira were definitely there, and they did jump."

372

Elam pointed at himself. "I've been through a portal in that river. The magma was cool back then, and it got too hot later. But now that it's water—"

"They could go through it," Billy finished. "And that means we can go, too."

"I'm game," Walter said. "Compared to what we just did, diving through an unknown portal at the bottom of a flooded chasm should be a piece of cake."

"You can't." Billy's mother flattened her hands and set one on top of the other. "According to our diver, the magma hardened in layers. You have lava rock, then water, then lava rock, and so on. We don't know how many layers there are or how thick each one is."

Billy ground his teeth together. All the clues led to the same lousy conclusion. Even if Bonnie escaped through a portal, she was stuck somewhere without a way to call for help. Obviously, in four years, she would have contacted her friends if she had been able.

"And we haven't heard from Shiloh," his mother added. "Not a word since she was kidnapped."

"And Acacia's missing, too," Billy said.

After several seconds of awkward silence, he motioned for everyone to sit around the fire. While they waited for Yereq to return with Dorian, he related the story of how he, his father, and Acacia found Shiloh in the protected ghost town and failed to rescue her, and worse yet, how Acacia fell into the prison herself and disappeared with Shiloh.

As the minutes ticked away, all five exchanged stories, including how Billy's mother, Adam, and Carly had reconstructed Apollo. It had taken over three years to get a working model, and it would have taken longer if not for the help of a dead physicist who made them promise to keep his identity secret because of his shame. Obviously, being a resident of Hades meant that all his brainpower had been for naught. He had lost his soul. Still, he was willing to help. Why? He never said, and no one thought it proper to ask.

Shelly was now married and living in Morgantown. Since she was pregnant with her first child, she had to excuse herself from the adventures and make her home ready for the new arrival. Walter's parents were in Castlewood watching Monique and Rebecca. His father retired from his law practice and was running Ashley's computer company, Stalworth Enterprises, with help from a local computer wizard named Fred. For a while, people asked where Ashley and Walter had gone, so Walter's father kept brushing them off with a story about them traveling somewhere with Billy and Jared on a secret mission. Eventually people stopped asking.

373

Stacey was attending the local community college now, so she was relatively independent. Carly moved into the Bannister home on a fostering basis and later began attending the same college part-time while still working on the Apollo project. Adam and his father started an electronics supply business, which helped in finding parts for Apollo.

"Speaking of Apollo . . ." Ashley excused herself and returned a moment later with the hourglasslike portal device.

As the storytelling continued, she looked it over, practically taking it apart and reassembling it with her practiced fingers.

Billy's mother touched Walter's hand. "Your father walks with a cane now. He took a bullet in his spine and was in physical therapy for months. He's doing great, considering the circumstances."

A tremor ran across Walter's face. He looked at Ashley. She took his hand and interlocked their thumbs.

Walter fished a small, rolled-up parchment from an inner pocket. "Mrs. B, can you give him and Mom something for me?"

"Yes, of course. I can mail it to them." She took the scroll and looked at it. "It's sealed with wax."

"It's personal." A distinct jitter rattled his voice. "I want them to be the first people on Earth to read it. Then they can tell you what it's all about."

"Okay." She laid the scroll on her lap. "But that makes my brain go wild with speculation."

374

Billy suppressed a grin. Since Walter was being so secretive, it wouldn't be right to give anything away. The message explained to his father that he had asked Ashley to marry him, and he hoped that somehow his family could come to Second Eden for their wedding. Of course, they were waiting for the expected war to be over first, so maybe it would be safe when the time came.

After a few more minutes of storytelling, Yereq climbed down the rope ladder, followed by Dorian. Billy and company greeted her and explained the transformation procedure. They had figured out long ago that each former dragon had to wear a rubellite ring while in the garden. Yet, Patrick was still unable to transform into Valcor, even after borrowing one of the rings Elam still had in his possession.

"I do not have one," Dorian said, showing them both hands.

"I have two." Elam pulled a ring from his pocket. "This one used to be Ashley's. She's wearing her mother's now."

Dorian slid it over her finger. It was a little loose, but manageable.

After they had gathered at the portal, Billy kissed his mother on the cheek, careful to hold back his scorching breath. "I read your note, and I told Dad that you love him. Is there anything else you want me to tell him?"

She nodded, her eyes sparkling. "Tell him scales or skin mean nothing; my love will never fail." She returned his kiss and, raising a fist to cover her mouth, said no more.

Ashley read her photometer. "The doorway deteriorated a little bit. At this rate, it will be gone in about three and a half hours. Yereq should guard it to make sure nothing comes out from the other side. You won't like what resides over there."

"Flat shadow critters." Walter twisted his shoe on the ground. "Yereq can probably stomp them like cockroaches."

Drawing his sword, Billy led the way through the portal. When he stepped back into the cave, it was darker and colder than before, but no shadow people slithered about, likely frightened by the portal's glow and the sight of their fellows' bones.

When the others joined him, Walter again fastened everyone together with the rope, Billy in front, then Ashley, Walter, Dorian, and Elam. Billy strode ahead, quickly at first, but when the portal's light faded, he slowed, listening for movement and tuning his danger radar. Since the shadow people had been alerted to their presence, they might have amassed at the cave's entrance. An ambush seemed likely.

Soon, the exit arch came into sight, barely visible now that the portal was well behind them. The tingling sensation crawled along Billy's body, and his alarm sounded. They were close, very close.

He halted. Ashley bumped into him, but only lightly. She tugged on his shirt and breathed a ghost of a whisper in his ear. "I sense a presence."

Billy pointed at himself, trying to signal, "So do I."

From her belt clip, she pulled a flashlight, modified for use with her homemade batteries. "It's real close." She shone the light at the base of the wall. A dark form turned its ribbonlike body away from the light and shivered as it emitted a series of high-pitched clicks.

"That's strange," Billy whispered. "It stayed here alone."

Ashley stooped. "It's scared, but it wants to communicate." She flicked off the light. "What do you want to say?"

The portal at the back of the cave painted a dim glow on Ashley's profile. As more clicks sounded, she nodded several times. "This one seems quite intelligent," she explained. "I sense mostly feelings. That noise it's making doesn't mean anything to me, but I'm getting a few words from its mind."

Billy glanced back and forth between the shadow person and the cave exit. His danger alarm heightened. Could this one be a decoy, told to get their attention while the others massed for an attack?

Ashley looked up at Elam. "I think he knows you. He said something about being sorry for not building the fire."

"The fire," Elam repeated in a whisper. "Where could that have been?"

She half closed one eye. "Does 'skotos' mean anything to you?"

"It's a forest in the Bridgelands." Elam crouched beside Ashley. "Does he have a name?"

Ashley turned back to the shadow. "What is your name?"

A short burst of clicks rose from its dark face.

Ashley shook her head. "He's saying it with his language, but I can't pull it from his mind."

"Zane?" Elam asked. "Is your name Zane?"

376

C H A P T E R

THE FACELESS PROTECTORS

The clicking noise pulsed rapidly, sounding like an excited cricket.

"Slow your thoughts," Ashley said. "Your mind knows English. Just concentrate on each word and say it inside as forcefully as you can."

After a few seconds, she began nodding again. "Okay. I see. That's good to know." She rose to her feet with a sigh. "Apparently he was banished here when he lost his courage during the battle against the giants, and now he wants to make up for his faithlessness by giving us a warning. There are a few dozen of his people immediately outside the cave entrance, but the rest of them, thousands maybe, have gathered on the main path between here and the river. So if we want to survive, we'll have to go another way."

Elam slid his hand under Zane's paper-thin head. "Thank you for the help. Is there anything I can do for you?"

The tiny eyes turned toward Ashley. Once again nodding, she spoke while shifting her gaze between Zane and Elam. "He says he had his chance in life, and he chose the ways of the hypocrite, so it's too late for him. When the others learn of his treachery, they will tear him apart and end this phase of his suffering, which will be all for the better. Just go in peace and remember that he finally did something right."

Elam kept his hand in place, apparently struggling in his mind.

"We can't take him," Ashley said. "Among us, he would suffer all the more."

Drawing his hand away, Elam rose to his feet and whispered, "So be it."

"If they're gathering at the path we took to get here," Billy said, "we can use all the light we want to go around them. We won't run into them."

"Until we get to the river," Ashley said. "They'll see us there."

Billy untied the rope. "Just stay close." He took in a quick breath, lit up Excalibur's beam, and ran. Swiping the laser back and forth across the floor, he flew through the opening. Sizzles again erupted, and the now familiar stench of roasted shadow people permeated the air.

He stopped just outside the arch and mowed the ground with a blast of flames from his mouth. The firelight revealed at least thirty shadowy forms, some writhing in pain, others fleeing along the ground.

Billy waved his arm. "This way!" With his sword lighting the path, he headed straight into the forest, dodging low-hanging branches and leaping over roots. When he broke into the clear and found the beach, he sprinted along the boundary between sand and snow, running parallel to the river. On his left, a sea of black shadows boiled with activity. The escape raft floated on top of hundreds of black fingers.

When his four companions joined him, Ashley now leading with her flashlight, Billy waded into the blackness. "Stay here and get ready to grab the rope." He blasted a wave of fire on the ground and slashed the beam back and forth. Dark body parts flew in all directions.

"You're not going without Elam and me!" Walter called.

When Billy reached the raft, he grabbed the rope and tossed it past Walter and Elam as they cut and hacked at the ground. Ashley caught it, and she and Dorian dragged the raft toward the river. "We got it!" Ashley called.

A hand reached out and grabbed Elam's ankle. He sliced its arm with his sword, but five more hands latched onto his legs. As if running in glue, he lifted his feet in slow motion, constantly swinging his sword behind him.

Billy sprinted up to him from behind and yelled, "Jump!" He swept the beam along the ground. Elam leaped over it just in time. The dark arms snapped like rubber bands, and the sea of bodies underneath melted into a steaming oil slick.

"Run!" Billy and Walter jumped over the black mass, and Elam joined them in stride. Following Ashley's waving flashlight beam, they ran in leaps. When they arrived at the raft, it had been pushed out to the river's edge, and Ashley and Dorian were already inside. Dorian sat in the center with the empty bags in her lap.

"Get in!" Ashley shouted. "The parachute's almost ready."

While Walter climbed in, Billy doused and sheathed the sword. Now in total darkness, he slid into his corner and checked his guideline. It was good and tight. "Did you get your noisemaker?"

"Check," Ashley said. "And my musk masker."

"Launching!" Elam called as he shoved the raft fully into the river. He leaped aboard and settled in place. The current sent them hurtling forward.

379

"What may I do to help?" Dorian asked.

"We're the flight attendants," Walter said. "Just relax and enjoy the flight."

Elam snapped his fingers. "Silence!"

A hush fell across the raft. Elam seemed tense, in turmoil. Seeing Zane and leaving him behind had shaken him badly, and now it would be only seconds before they would launch over another waterfall where a new danger lay, Adam's Marsh, the home of Flint, Goliath, and the Nephilim.

Billy slid two metal tubes from one of the bags and fastened them end to end. He then put on a pair of fireproof gloves. There would be no time later.

Suddenly, the river fell away again. As before, Elam and Walter caught the air with the front of the parachute, and Billy and Ashley let out their guidelines to allow the canopy to fill. This fall would have been shorter, but their plan was to stay airborne and use the persistent breezes to fly as far away from the pool as possible in case enemy soldiers guarded the valley exit.

A queasy feeling churned in Billy's stomach. Was it fear? Not likely. He had made it this far without getting sick from fear. It was a deeper sickness, a nausea that seemed familiar somehow, but this was no time to figure it out. It was time to put their plan into action.

After filling his lungs, he lifted the connected tubing, hoisted one end near the apex of the billowing parachute, and pressed the other against his lips. Mixing in the gasses from his belly, he blew with all his might. The flames shot out the opposite end of the tube and struck the middle of the parachute, giving it an upward boost. The tube shielded the fire stream from any onlookers. Of course, a few orange tongues were visible at the exit point, but someone would have to be looking directly at it to notice.

Heaving in breaths and shooting more fire, Billy helped the raft stay aloft. Ashley had slid in behind him to control both rear guidelines. Since they had practiced this procedure many times, she had no problem steering the back of the raft.

When he began to feel dizzy, he pulled the tube down, broke it apart, and put it away. It was time to come in for a landing. Where? With nothing but darkness all around, they could only guess. Since this part of the river meandered, the best they could do would be to follow a straight line and listen for the rush of water as they descended.

He grabbed his guideline again. Looking below didn't help. The darkness was complete, and the wall of fire was too far away to provide any light at all.

After sailing at least a thousand feet, they settled on a patch of sand. The river splashed along on their left about ten paces away.

Billy jumped out and lifted his corner. The raft was light. Good. Walter had already guided Dorian to his corner and helped her disembark, just as planned. They carried the raft to the river, and all five slid silently back into place.

381

After securing the wadded parachute next to Dorian, Billy picked up the two tubes, still warm to the touch, and reached one forward. Someone took it, probably Walter. He was supposed to use it to push off from the right front corner and Billy from the left rear in case the current rammed them into a beach.

Billy kept the far end of his pole in the water. Of course, he wouldn't be able to see any bends coming, so he had to navigate by feeling the river's depth.

As they rode the current in silence, Billy kept his stare fixed on the right-hand side. Adam's Marsh lay there, and if anyone would challenge them, the attack would come from that direction.

A pair of torches came into view, maybe a stone's throw away. Billy ducked low. As the raft passed the lights, he peeked up. One of the Nephilim stood next to a bitternut tree, his torches planted in the sand. As he ate one of the fruit, a torch fizzled out. He plucked it up and extended the top toward a dark mass. "Light it," he growled.

A blast of fire shot out and coated the torch, illuminating it with a vibrant flame. A dragon sat on the beach, a small dragon, too small to be Goliath or Roxil, and it couldn't be a Second Eden dragon. They breathed ice.

The dragon's eyebeams fell on Billy's cloak. He desperately wanted to brush them away, but that would just make him more obvious. Whoever this dragon was, it had spotted them, but it made no motion or sound, and the Naphil didn't seem to notice.

When they reached a bend to the left, Walter pushed off the beach, and they passed out of the dragon's sight. Billy let out a long sigh. Ashley took his hand and gave it a gentle squeeze. She knew. Something strange was going on. That dragon could easily have sounded an alarm, but for some reason, it chose silence.

After pushing off the edge a few more times, Billy rested. The river had straightened, and the southern part of Abraham's wall came into view. It was time to get ready for another plunge through fire.

Of course, the dragons had tried several times to blast through, but it repelled their blows, as if their bodies and the wall were similar magnetic poles. Was it their scales? Their photoreceptors? No one knew. But the effect was likely for the better. If Clefspeare and Hartanna couldn't get in, then Goliath couldn't get out.

Billy stared at the flames, searching for a shadow, any hint of Flint's guards. So far, nothing. If all went according to plan, Valiant and Candle were now raising a ruckus a hundred paces to the west, close enough to lure any guards away.

Elam tapped Billy's knee. Billy sent the signal along. They spread out the parachute again, and everyone ducked underneath. As before, the light grew brighter. Their raft was now exposed. The most dangerous part of the journey had arrived. If any guards were on duty and paying attention, this voyage was doomed.

Someone shouted. Another answered. Something whizzed above. Was it an arrow? A dull *thunk* struck the parachute, then another.

"Time to fire back," Ashley said. She pulled a thin cylinder from her bag, yanked out a strand of twine from one end, and tossed the cylinder out from under the parachute. Within two seconds, it exploded. While more arrows rained down, whizzing by or piercing their covering, she threw out three more. With each explosion, the number of attacking arrows lessened.

The temperature spiked again. With a loud whoosh, blinding light flew over the raft from front to back. The arrows ceased. Tongues of fire shot through the chute's holes and licked at their bodies. Finally, steam lifted the raft. The front tipped down, and the rear slung the passengers headlong into the river.

Billy tumbled through icy water. After a breath-stealing surge, he thrust his head above the surface and searched the turbulent river for the others. Ah! Ashley was treading water within reach, her wide eyes reflecting the nearby flaming wall. He grabbed her around the waist with one arm and began to swim for shore with the other, but something pulled his collar and jerked him up. Swinging toward Ashley, he locked his arms and legs around her. She relaxed and allowed herself to be dragged along.

Within seconds, he felt his body sliding on the beach. As strong arms helped him stand, he hoisted Ashley to her feet.

"Are you well?" came a deep, strong voice.

Billy looked at his helper. "Valiant! Thank you!"

"Yes," Ashley said as she wrung out the fringes of her cloak. "We didn't expect you to be here."

Valiant draped a blanket over Ashley's head and back. "I will explain soon. I must help Candle tend to the others." He ran downstream, firelight dancing on the back of his cloak.

"He's dry," Billy said, shivering.

Ashley drew the blanket together. "I noticed. Then who dragged us from the river?"

A hot breeze swept across their bodies. Billy spread out his arms and let his wet clothes flap in the luxuriant draft. "I think we have our answer."

383

Hartanna blew the stream of hot dry air while Clefspeare sat at her side. "Yellinia is hurt," Clefspeare said. "Thigocia and Candle are tending to her."

Billy translated his father's words. Yellinia was Dorian. One of the arrows must have hit her, but she hadn't made a sound. "How bad is it?" Billy asked.

"It does not appear to be a deep wound." Clefspeare inhaled and took a turn blowing a warm wind.

Ashley pushed her fingers into her hair and shook out the water. "I'll check on her in a minute."

"I think your smoke bombs did the trick," Billy said. "They couldn't shoot what they couldn't see."

"I was afraid one of those arrows would puncture the raft." Ashley let a smile break through. "When you think about it, every part of the plan worked pretty well."

Walter and Elam joined them in the warmth, both shivering and wet. "Valiant thinks Flint got wind of our mission," Elam said. "He and Candle tried their diversion, but no matter how much noise they made, only one Naphil stood guard at that part of the wall. When Valiant heard the ruckus over here, he and Candle ran to try to help, but there wasn't anything anyone could do."

Billy stripped off his cloak and let the heat radiate through his inner tunic. "But if they had a spy, wouldn't they have stopped us a lot earlier?"

"I would have thought so," Elam said.

"Did you see that dragon at the side of the river?" Walter asked. "Could he have flown ahead and warned them?"

Turning to give his back a chance to dry, Billy nodded. "I saw him, and I'm sure he saw us. If he betrayed us, why did he wait?"

"And who could he be?" Elam asked. "He was too small to be Goliath or Roxil but he was almost as big as Grackle."

"A youngling?" Hartanna asked. "Has Roxil given birth?"

Clefspeare let the breeze die away. "There has been ample time to have two younglings by now, though only one could be old enough to fit the description."

"I'd better check on Dorian now." Ashley pushed her hair back and fastened a rubber band around it. "She might not be able to make the hike, so we'd better bring Merlin closer."

"On my way." Billy ran downstream with Ashley and stopped for a moment to check on Dorian before continuing into the prairie. As he hustled through the snow-covered grass, light from the wall dimmed. At least the dangerous part was over. Lions no longer hunted these fields, having migrated farther south. All he had to do was taxi Merlin across the snow, pick up a few human passengers, and fly back to the village.

Although cold air dried his throat, he pressed on. At one time, running a mile would have winded him, but now, even tromping with heavy boots through snow, it seemed like nothing. A warm rush flooded his body. His mother had noticed the change—taller, more muscular, she had said. He had become a warrior, and her affirmation felt good.

385

After jumping into Merlin and starting the engine, he eased it into a low-speed taxi and settled back in the pilot's seat. What would they do now? Of course they could patch the parachute, but with Flint's troops knowing how they had breached the border, would it be possible to try again the very next night? If not, how could he get word to his mother that they would be delayed? She would be expecting them. And what about Gabriel? Without the ability to penetrate the wall, how could they search for him?

The silhouettes of his comrades moved about across the backdrop of the towering wall of flames. Somehow the view seemed appropriate, faceless shadows hustling about under the watch of an immeasurable light. Without desire for recognition or acclaim, these small, nondescript forms served the light's will. Would they live through the trials? Die in the effort? Those questions seemed unimportant. The only end that mattered was whether or not the purposes of the light would be fulfilled—to protect the innocent ones and hold back the fiends who would drag them away to slaughter.

Billy locked the scene in his mind. He would draw this portrait someday, maybe in charcoal with a splash of color for the background. Yellow and orange pigments from sempian bark would do nicely. He would call it, "The Faceless Protectors."

As he drew closer, one of the dragons spread its wings. With no other features visible, the shadow brought Bonnie to mind … again.

Four years and no word. Where could she be? Had Arramos's goons captured her? Maybe she was with Shiloh and Acacia in yet another world. And what about Sapphira? Could all four be together?

Billy stopped the plane and flopped back against the headrest. His mind raced with jumbled thoughts. Bonnie's face, so young and lovely. What did she look like now? The marriage prophecy, odd words that many agreed pointed to their eventual union. But did they really? The words seemed less certain than ever.

Gabriel came to mind. Someone had to rescue him. Sure, he was one of the faceless shadows, and he knew the dangers of his mission, but that didn't matter. No warrior should be left behind.

Pulling his hood up, Billy hustled to the back of the plane, hopped down the airstair, and marched toward Walter. "Are you ready?"

Walter raised his own hood. "Time to find Gabriel?"

Billy glanced at Valiant and Ashley helping Dorian into the airplane. Dorian was on her feet. That was good news. "Right. I think everything's under control here."

"Yes!" Walter said. "Another wild water slide!"

Billy shook his head. "By the time we get there, they'll have posted plenty of guards."

"Then what do you have in mind?"

Billy thrust out his fist. "Punch straight through the wall at an unguarded point."

"With just our cloaks to protect us?" Walter tapped himself on the head. "Did that tumble in the river rattle your brain?"

"Look, we already tested the cloaks partway into the wall, and the raft proved that we could go the rest of the way. We just need to get enough momentum."

"A dragon could throw us, maybe with its tail," Walter said. "Then we could—"

"Cool your jets, boys." Ashley walked up, inspecting a broken arrow. "Your plan won't work."

"Why not?" Walter asked.

Ashley pushed the arrow between her fingers. "A dragon might be able to propel you through the wall, but how are you going to get back?"

"I was just about to say that Roxil could shoot us back through," Walter said. "We're hoping she's still on our side, right?"

"If you can find her. If you can dodge Goliath and the Nephilim. You can't rely on help from allies who don't even know you're coming."

"But we have two allies who know we're coming," Billy said.

Walter and Ashley both stared at him. "Who?" they said at the same time.

"Abraham and Angel. I think we won't need a dragon at all. Just running with a full head of steam ought to do it. I'm counting on our allies to thin out the wall for us."

"Well … maybe." Ashley crossed her arms, her brow bent low. "You're missing one ally in your plans."

"I'm starting to sound like an owl now," Walter said. "Who?"

She elbowed his ribs. "Me, silly! How else are you going to find Gabriel in the dark? I should be able to detect his presence."

"Fair enough," Billy said. "But we'd better get back to the village first. We should reapply the flame retardant to our cloaks and get a fourth one for Gabriel."

"A big one," Walter said. "We have to cover his wings."

"Good point. We can't cut holes in the back, or the fire would get through."

Walter rubbed his stomach. "And I'm starved. Blasting through walls of fire really burns the calories."

"Food sounds good. And a quick nap. We'll go back in the middle of the day. Flint won't be expecting us to come back so soon and in broad daylight, and we won't be bothered so much by the shadow people."

"From the north," Walter said. "Climbing up from the south would be impossible. Besides, we didn't get to use the snowboards."

Ashley rolled her eyes. "The boards were Plan B, in case the raft didn't make it through."

"Plan A, Plan B, what do I care? I practiced too hard. Let's boogie on those boards!"

CHAPTER

SEEING THE INVISIBLE

Billy lay awake on his straw bed. With thoughts of trying to rescue Gabriel dominating his mind, getting to sleep would probably take a while. Their next mission could be the most dangerous yet, but they had no choice, and Gabriel might be out there dodging shadow people and Flint's troops, so they had to go as soon as possible. He had to make this nap a short and efficient one.

Although dawn was breaking outside, only a bare candle near his pillow illuminated his surroundings. The hut's window had been sealed tightly for the cold weather, so total darkness had become a way of life. But it was better that way. It would help him employ his usual plan for falling asleep.

He blew out the candle and settled in. Darkness gave him a canopy for painting pictures in the air, a way to begin his dreams. He would mentally draw Bonnie's face, and, since closing his eyes made no difference in the darkness, she would stay in his mind's eye as he drifted off to sleep.

Soon, his portrait expanded. Bonnie, now fully drawn from head to toe, knelt at her bedside. This was definitely one of his favorite scenes. Years ago, back when her father had come to West Virginia to take her home to Montana, Billy had found her praying in this position, her hands folded on her bedspread. Back then, her wings were hidden in her backpack, but now, in his imagination, they spread out behind her in all their glory. With her blond-streaked hair draped over her back, and her sparkling eyes lifted up toward Heaven, she looked like an angel.

Billy walked into the bedroom scene and listened to her lovely voice as she prayed out loud, her cadence lacking rhythm as the words missed their obvious metric beat.

> Call to me, and I will answer you;
> Say my name, and my light will shine.
> Draw me out, and I will rise again;
> Take my hand, and I will be thine.

390

Billy let the words echo in his mind. These were different, not her usual prayer, and her lack of rhythm felt odd, like a drum striking at the wrong time. Normally she asked for help to escape whatever prison she was in, and she often prayed for him, for his safety, courage, and enduring faith. This was the first time his mind ever invented the scene with her praying a poem. And the opening line was familiar, the words on her poster, the phrase that helped him understand that he had to call for a doctor instead of Makaidos.

Makaidos. Billy let that name bounce around in his thoughts. Twice they had changed the poem and called for someone else, and now that the season of death had arrived and stayed, and with Acacia's energizing light no longer available, a third opportunity never arose. The eclipses had ceased, and with clouds and snow often obscuring the sky, they rarely saw Pegasus or Phoenix anyway. The moons would sometimes peek through breaks in the clouds, and their light would bathe the covering blanket in a silvery glow. Even with those glimpses, the villagers agreed that until the season of death finally ended, the cycles would never return to normal. And no cycles, no Makaidos.

Bonnie sang her prayer again, this time with more emotion. Every word seemed drenched with sorrow, yet buoyed by hope as they rose toward the sky as an offering to God. And Bonnie glowed. Oh, yes, she glowed, far brighter than Pegasus, and with a shimmering radiance that outshone a regeneracy dome, even with all the glittering gems the dragons had gathered over the years.

He reached for her, but, as usual, a barrier stood between them, invisible, yet impenetrable. He would have to wait still longer. Someday it would be broken. Eventually it would dissolve. ... Wouldn't it?

Bonnie turned and stared at him. Billy gasped. She saw him! This was new. They had never made eye contact before.

She opened her mouth, and a harsh call burst forth.

"Billy!"

Something shook his shoulder.

"Billy. It's me, Walter. It's time to blast through the fire."

Yawning, Billy blinked his eyes open. "Already?"

Walter stood over him with a lantern in hand. "You said three hours, and you got an extra five minutes."

Billy looked at the bed on the other side of the hut. Elam had still not slept. "Where's our warrior chief?"

"Interviewing Yellinia. He never gives up on our missing-in-action troops, so he's trying to get every clue he can about Sapphira and Bonnie." Walter threw a cloak over Billy's legs. "It's got a fresh coat of fire-be-gone. You're all set. I told Ashley we'd meet her at her hut."

Billy climbed to his feet, put on the cloak, and strapped on his scabbard. "When does Elam want to try the transformation?"

"It's done. That's why I called her Yellinia instead of Dorian. They decided it was better to go ahead and transform her so Thigocia could heal the arrow wound."

391

"Great! Now we have six dragons."

Walter nodded toward Billy's scabbard. "I put Excalibur back, but you might want to move it to your belt for this mission."

"Right." As Billy made the adjustment, Walter pushed open the door and allowed Billy to go through first. Still working on the belt, he blinked at the morning light. Snow was falling again, but not heavily. "If the beam worked on the garden soil, I guess the bones of Makaidos are still functioning."

"They sizzled up a storm. Excalibur worked great."

Billy and Walter jogged toward Ashley's hut. "Any effect on the two plants?" Billy asked.

"Zero. They're both still bulging. The ugly one looks about ready to pop."

When they reached the hut, Ashley was standing outside the door, her arms crossed tightly as she bounced on her toes. "Which dragons are we flying?"

"Grackle and Albatross," Walter said. "They're good and rested."

Ashley shivered hard. "Perfect. Heated scales."

Walter picked up a duffle bag near Ashley's feet. "Does this one have the snowboards?" he asked.

She nodded, tight-lipped and still shivering. "And more flame retardant and a few smoke bombs, just in case."

"Are you okay? It's not any colder than usual."

"Just tired, I think." She bundled her cloak tighter against her body. "That makes me colder."

"What did you get? One hour of sleep?"

"Maybe two." She nodded toward the door. "My other bag's inside, the one with a cloak for Gabriel, and my ion box."

"I'll get them." Walter disappeared inside.

Ashley smiled at Billy but said nothing. A ring glittered on her finger, a new one Walter had given her when he proposed marriage.

Billy grinned. Even after three months, it was still hard getting used to thinking of his old buddy as an engaged man. For most of the four years they had lived in Second Eden, Ashley had said many times that he wasn't old enough, that their ages were too far apart, but when he single-handedly mowed down four Vacants who had trapped her in one of the greenhouses, she changed her mind.

Sure, he was still only twenty, but living in the rigors of this world had definitely made a man out of him. He had helped Ashley design the farming greenhouses and suggested a great way to funnel geothermal energy to a heating coil system throughout the greenhouse network. Although digging through the frozen ground was bitter, backbreaking work, he never complained or took a day off. And his ability to organize and teach the villagers the intricacies of the technology was amazing. He had translated the scientific jargon into the common language so that everyone understood well enough to work without constant supervision.

And the results spoke for themselves. Without Walter's labors, by now everyone might have starved, but their food supply had proven to be more than adequate. So one day while he was showing Ashley his new idea for keeping snow from overloading a roof, he took her to the top of one of the greenhouses where he had built a snowman kneeling in front of a snowwoman.

393

As Billy and Ashley continued waiting for Walter, Billy imagined the roof scene, having heard every detail from Walter a dozen times.

"What's going on here?" Ashley said as she pushed off the top ladder rung and stepped onto the roof.

"The snow dude is asking the snow dudette a question." Walter touched the kneeling snowman's head. "But he's younger and a whole lot dumber, so it took him a long time to get enough courage. That's why he took her up on the roof, to do it privately. Down on the ground there's always someone asking a question or needing help."

"I see." Ashley crossed her arms and looked back and forth between Walter and the snow sculptures. "What question did he ask?"

Walter got down on his knee, mimicking the snowman. "I'm not a hundred percent sure. That's the reason I brought you up here. I was wondering if you could read his mind and figure it out for me."

"Is that so?" Ashley stood in front of him and copied the snow-woman's stance. "Judging from their facial expressions, my guess is that he's asking her to have a cup of hot cocoa with him."

"I doubt it. They'd both melt."

"Good point." Ashley stroked her chin with a gloved hand. "I guess I'll have to do a little mind reading."

As new snow began to fall, Walter pushed his finger into the snow dude's ear. "You'd better hurry. I'll bore a hole into his head so his thoughts will leak out."

After several seconds, Ashley shook her head and gave a mock sigh. "I just can't imagine what he's thinking. His brain must be so cold, it totally choked."

394

Walter took off his glove and then Ashley's. Taking her bare hand, he looked into her eyes. "For years I felt like a snowman in your sight—stiff, stoic, and stupid."

"Alliteration?" Ashley said. "Very clever."

"Shhh. I worked on this a long time."

"Oh, sorry." Taking on a doe-eyed expression, she gazed at him lovingly. "Please go on."

"Anyway, I felt like a snowman. I knew I was too young for you and too immature, but as I worked year after year, I grew up a lot faster than I would have at home, and I melted away my shallow shell until I became limber, lithe, and loquacious."

"Loquacious?"

"Right. Elam gave me that word, but he wouldn't tell me what it means. Anyway, ..." He pressed a button under his coat. A sizzling sound rose from the snowman, and the snow covering his outstretched hand melted, revealing a metallic coil holding a ring. Walter took the ring and extended it to Ashley. "I have no doubt that I am now ready to be a husband to an angelic anthrozil." Swallowing, he paused for a moment to steady his voice. "Since your father isn't available, I asked your mother for her blessing, and she gave it without hesitation, so now I ask you. If you believe me to be worthy of taking your hand in marriage, I vow that I will never let it go. We will be side by side in everything we do, together in every adventure, just like we said when we clasped hands after you sang 'Amazing Grace' for your grandfather. I now ask for your grace." He cleared his throat and spoke the final words with power and clarity. "Ashley Stalworth, will you marry me?"

As Billy let the image melt away, Ashley smiled at him. "I hope you don't mind," Ashley said, "but your thoughts were so vivid, I listened in."

"Was that the way it happened?"

"Word for word, except you didn't finish. My answer was, 'O worthy warrior, you need no grace from me, for your request fills my heart with joy. I am the one receiving the blessing, for a noble knight has asked for my hand, the same knight who willingly laid down his life for me time and again. He melted my heart of ice so that I could hear the heralds of Heaven proclaim the amazing grace of God. I gladly accept, and it is most appropriate that you brought me here, for I want to shout from the rooftops that Walter Foley has asked for my hand in marriage."

395

"I know. You shouted so loud I thought the war had started."

As they laughed together, Walter exited Ashley's hut, her bag in hand. "Sorry," he said. "Emerald's father stopped me. He wanted to give me some pointers on being a good Adam."

Billy patted him on the back. "No problem for a noble knight."

The three hurried to the dragon launching field. Listener had already strapped on the seats and waited next to Albatross.

"I explained your mission to them," Listener said. "They know what to do. They promised not to get scared if Vacants show up."

Even from where he stood, Billy could feel heat from the passenger dragons. They would definitely provide a comfortable ride, but since they had disappeared after the battle with the Vacants, Elam wasn't comfortable with using them for important missions. When they finally came back after several weeks, they seemed contrite, so they were allowed to return to service in non-battle situations.

Albatross lowered his head, allowing Billy to climb his neck. Walter and Ashley mounted Grackle, Walter taking the front seat while Ashley tied her bags to the back.

Listener let out a shrill whistle and slapped Albatross on his flank. As the two dragons beat their wings, she yelled, "I'll be waiting at the radio station. We'll be praying for you!"

"Thank you!" Billy shouted. As they rose, he gazed down at the little girl. Well, not so little anymore. Although not much taller than when he first met her, she had definitely blossomed into a young lady, filled with love and laughter and no hint of the terrible wound she had suffered at the hands of the spear-wielding Vacant.

As expected, the dragons' heated scales helped immensely, making the flight through the snowy skies bearable. It would be a long journey. Flying north, they planned to stay well west of Adam's Marsh and the Valley of Shadows before circling east to the northern border of the valley, again wishing to avoid being sighted from within Abraham's wall. That would put the enemy on alert, and Goliath would see to it that every guard around the perimeter kept close watch, especially at the river entry.

With Twin Falls River in sight, they landed in a woodlands clearing about a mile from the valley's northwest border. Several years ago a landslide had flattened a section of the protective mountain range, so a thick blanket of snow would make that slope into the valley passable for someone on a snowboard.

After dismounting, Billy watched the dragons fly away in the same direction they had come. Since they had no idea when this mission would be accomplished, they planned to use Ashley's transmitter to call Listener at the village's radio station, and she would send the dragons back for them.

Walter joined Billy at his side. "Checking out the weather?" Walter asked.

"Just watching the dragons and thinking about the return plan."

"You do that. I'm still trying to figure out the meteorology here." Walter nodded toward the protective barrier, easily visible as its flames rocketed skyward. At the point the cloudbank collided with the wall, the fire seemed to absorb the vapor. "How do the clouds get inside? Shouldn't the heat evaporate them?"

Billy shrugged. "Beats me. It was dark when we went in there, so I couldn't see the sky, but the snow wasn't as deep in there as it is out here. Maybe the clouds redevelop inside."

When they had strapped into their snowboards, Billy and Walter each carrying a bag on his back, Ashley raised her hood and tied it closed. "Do you remember wearing those cloaks that protected us during portal jumps in the Circles of Seven?"

397

"Yep," Walter said. "The ones with the microchips."

"Same principle. When we get to the fire, keep your head low, and try to cover up as much as you can."

Billy raised his own hood and checked his gloves. Every article of clothing smelled of the freshly applied flame retardant. The odor wasn't strong enough to detect beyond a few inches, so the shadow people probably wouldn't notice, at least that's what he hoped.

With a little jump, they started down an easy slope that would lead them to the wall. As they dodged trees, some toppled from decay and heavy snow, Billy traced the course in his mind. The slope's angle would increase, allowing them to pick up speed for their plunge through the wall. Then, if they survived and stayed on their feet, they would use their momentum to slide as far up the valley's protective ridge as they could. From that point, they would hike to the lowest summit, the point where many of the rocky peaks had broken off and contributed to the landslide.

Whizzing past stumps and boulders, Billy led the way. Of course, Walter would want to stay at the rear where he could keep an eye on his fiancée. That worked out fine. Billy would cut through the powder and make an easier trail for both of them, and Ashley could save her energy for probing the forest in search of Gabriel's thoughts. And since Walter had been busy with Dorian's transformation, he couldn't have gotten much sleep. There was no use taxing his body further.

As they closed in on the flames, the snow thinned. According to Valiant's scouts, there was a slight rise within several feet of the wall that spanned a thirty-foot-wide section. The slope protected the side facing away from the fire, so it should be snow-covered, but the strip of land between it and the wall would be bare. They would have to slide up the rise at full speed, curl their bodies, and fly through the wall.

Billy scanned the forest. The rise had to be close by. If he didn't find it in the next few seconds, they wouldn't have a decent launch pad, and they would have to turn back and try again.

Ah! There it was, a short, sharp incline. Perfect. But would Abraham and Angel see him? Would they thin out the wall for his entry? Would he land in snow on the other side or crash onto bare ground?

He crouched low. They would all find out soon enough.

Giving his body an upward jerk, he launched over the rise and flew through the air. As the flames zoomed toward him, searing heat chafed his face. He ducked low. Unable to watch the collision, he tightened his muscles and prayed for balance.

The sound came first, the now familiar whoosh of flames, then heat, scorching heat that sent a shock wave straight to his bones. He bit his lip. *No screaming. Just ... get ... through it!*

The whoosh faded. Coolness freshened his skin. He opened his eyes just as his board pounded down on snow-coated grass. Bending his knees, he absorbed the impact and continued hurtling down the slope.

With clear sailing ahead, Billy looked back. Ashley burst through the flames, then Walter a split second behind her. With twin *swishes*, they landed and followed his trail.

Ashley's hair had blown loose, and one section was on fire. Since the burning ends flew behind her, she likely didn't even know it. Needing to stay quiet, he couldn't yell, and Walter couldn't catch up, even if he was able to see the problem.

Leaning over, Billy scooped up a handful of snow and threw it at her. He missed the flaming hair but caught her attention. She bent her brow and mouthed, "What's wrong?"

He jerked down his hood, pointed at his own hair, and formed the word, "Fire!" with an exaggerated alarm in his eyes.

An annoyed huff blew from her lips. She batted the flames away with her gloved hands, as if her hair catching fire was an everyday occurrence.

The terrain, a grass field speckled with tall pines and dead deciduous trees, flattened out and then rose in elevation. Soon, they came to a stop and unfastened their boards. The rocky ridge lay ahead, a short hike, and not too strenuous. The slope was fairly steep, but with only a little snow covering the ground, the rocky projections would make for an easy climb.

As they pushed silently against the incline, Billy looked up. The air rushing through the fiery wall at cloud level quickly transformed into white vapor and formed billowing clouds that joined into a thick dark blanket drifting away from the fire.

When they reached the top of the ridge, Billy peered into the bowl-shaped valley. Several hundred feet below, the river carved the floor into two halves and spilled out through a narrow divide

399

at the southern end. On either side, trees filled the landscape. The evergreens seemed healthier here, perhaps a result of less snow and proximity to the surrounding wall's warmth. Even the deciduous trees seemed alive. Although none carried any leaves, only a very few had fallen prey to rot and the domino tumbling that had plagued the higher elevations outside the wall.

Walter and Ashley joined him, one on each side. Ashley let her hair flow in the stiff breeze, only a few ends showing signs of the earlier scorching. "I don't sense anything," she whispered. "At least nothing as intelligent as Gabriel. Just a mass of senseless beasts, hungry, craving, violent. Zane was different. These feel more like a pack of wild dogs than anything."

With the wind blowing the treetops, the shadows on the valley's snow-covered floor shifted back and forth, creating a hypnotizing dance of black on white. It wasn't hard to imagine those flat beasts lurking within the splotches of black.

Billy sat on the top of the ridge, set his feet on the valley side, and strapped into his snowboard again. Of course, these boards weren't as fancy as those on Earth. With leather straps, unvarnished boot braces, and no steel on the edge, they looked rough and primitive, but a special wax for the base made them tough and fast. When they first discovered it, Walter joked about bottling the wax and selling it to the snowboarders on Earth, but as the months and years passed, his jokes about what he would do at home diminished. He had settled into life here as if he would never return home.

As soon as all three were ready, Billy touched Ashley's back and whispered, "Your turn to lead."

She nodded and pushed off. Walter followed, and Billy trailed. On the valley slope, the new alignment made the most sense. Ashley would probe for Gabriel's presence and steer toward him, while Billy would watch for shadow people. Even if Ashley slid right over them, they likely wouldn't be able to react in time to hurt her, so Billy and Walter would be the ones to quell any uprising.

All three zoomed down the steep wall. Pointed rocks jutted out here and there, but they were easy enough to see in the treeless span. Ashley rode her board expertly, digging in for sharp turns and dipping and rising while riding over bumps and ridges. With her cloak flapping around a sword at her belt and her hair flowing back, she looked like a snowboarding elf straight out of a Tolkien story.

As the slope began to level out, she straightened and looked left toward the river, her stare fixed on something, though nothing seemed apparent in that direction other than the water tumbling from the top of the valley wall.

Digging in again, she turned that way. Now that they were near the floor, trees dotted the area, and shadows waved back and forth on the snow. Ashley glided past a tree and across the first shadow without harm and stopped in front of a tall pine. With her eyes wide and her mouth open, she slowly swiveled her head, like an antennae searching for a signal.

401

In a spray of snow, Walter and Billy slid to a stop next to her, listening. The waterfall roared in the distance, more of a background hum than a dominating thunder. Wind buzzed through the trees. A hawk let out a shrill call and flew from the highest branch of a pine to a perch at the top of a nearby deadwood tree.

Finally, without breathing a word, she took off again, this time slowly as she wound past trees and rocks on her way to the river. Billy kept glancing at the ground. Still no sign of life. Maybe the shadow people congregated in the denser woods during the day.

When they arrived at the beach, Ashley unfastened her straps, kicked out of her board, and marched across the sand. Billy and Walter did the same. Unable to figure out what Ashley was doing, they gave each other a shrug and hurried to catch up.

As soon as they reached the edge of the swiftly flowing water, Ashley allowed her voice to rise above a whisper. "I sensed something in the direction of the waterfall, but there were too many trees that way, so I thought we'd come down here and walk back upstream."

"Good thinking," Billy said, glad to uncork his throat.

Walter hustled back, retrieved the snowboards, and quietly set them next to the river. Ashley began a slow march, her head turning from side to side. Every ten paces or so, she stopped and listened, then continued, but since each step brought them closer to the waterfall, all other sounds surrendered to the tumult ahead.

When they drew close enough to feel the spray, she halted and turned in a full circle twice, her brow bent in confusion.

"What's up?" Walter asked.

She pointed at the ground. "I sense a powerful presence, right here, right now."

Billy searched the area. No shadows. Just sand and small patches of snow. He looked at Ashley and Walter in turn and gave each a nod. They were definitely on the same wavelength. Gabriel was here in his light energy form. Leaving Hades had caused him to lose his physical body.

Ashley withdrew her ion box from her cloak's inner pocket and opened a lid on top. "Gabriel, if you're here, would you please enter this box? I'm not sure how small you can squeeze yourself, but this indicates the presence of light energy, and it will allow us to carry you out of here."

Holding the box in her palm at chest level, she waited. After a few seconds, a glow emanated from the mirrors on each side.

Walter pumped a fist. "We got him!"

Smiling broadly, Ashley spoke into the opening. "Hello, dear brother. The circumstances could be better, but I'm glad to be with you again. I'm going to close you in. It's the only way to keep you safe when we jump through the wall of fire."

She began pushing the lid down but stopped. Her brow furrowed deeply. "What? I don't understand."

Billy looked at Walter. Obviously she was talking to Gabriel. Her ability to pick up words had been increasing all the time.

Ashley glanced back and forth between Walter and Billy. "If you stay in Second Eden, you'll just be light energy." Between every response, she paused, listening while the box's glow pulsed, as if energized by Gabriel's words. "Theory? What theory? ... So how would you find the way? There was no trace of Shiloh. ... I see. Did you hear that Acacia went with her? ... But how would Flint know? He's stuck behind the wall. ... Oh. So we're not the only ones using the river that way. ... Who?"

Her eyes grew wide as she riveted her gaze on Billy. "Gabriel's been listening in on Flint's conversations with Goliath. Apparently someone is getting messages through the wall, but they haven't said who's doing it. Flint and Goliath talked about what happened to Shiloh and Acacia, so Gabriel wants us to get him out from behind the wall so he can find them."

"But how?" Billy felt a twinge in his belly. Was it danger? He gave the sky and ground a quick scan but saw nothing. "There's no portal out there for him to go through."

403

"Not that we know of, but in his energy form he can sense a portal, and maybe he'll be able to go through it."

Billy nodded. That would be worth a try. He might even be able to locate a way to find Bonnie and Sapphira. "Sounds good. So let's pay my mom a visit and let her know what's going on, and then we'll—"

"Incoming!" Walter grabbed his sword and pointed it toward the sky. "Two dragons!"

5

CHAPTER

RETURN TO EARTH

Billy pulled Excalibur from its scabbard and looked up. The dragons, both bearing red scales, flew over the mountain boundary. The larger of the two was clearly Goliath, and the smaller one had to be the dragon they saw at the side of the river. "Think they've seen us?" Billy asked.

Ashley snapped the box's lid closed. "I sense anger in their minds, but nothing violent."

"Stay still or run for cover?" Walter asked.

She nodded toward a tree that stood about thirty paces away. "Slowly. Very slowly."

As they crept along the river's beach, Billy kept his stare trained on the dragons. The smaller one had its eyebeams turned on and was sweeping them across the valley floor.

The moment Billy set foot on the snow-covered turf, the beams brushed over his body. A loud screech rode the wind. Goliath's roar followed, and the two dragons dove toward them.

"Get under the tree!" Billy lit up Excalibur's beam and sliced the air, barely missing the smaller dragon. The dragons broke from their dive and separated. Goliath sped to the right, and the smaller one wheeled around one of the tallest trees to Billy's left.

Walter ran with Ashley to the tree before returning in a sprint to Billy's side. "Back to back!" Walter said. "Just like Sir Barlow taught us."

They pressed their backs together. Billy swiped the beam at the smaller dragon but missed again. "He's quick!"

"Turn it off and wait till he gets closer. He'll shoot fire, and then you can nail him. But if you miss, watch out for his tail."

Billy let the beam die away but kept the blade glowing bright. The dragon zoomed down, its mouth wide and its teeth bared. "He's coming! Cloaks up!"

Walter ducked low. "Goliath's coming, too!"

Both men let their cloaks cover their exposed skin. Torrents of fire lit up Billy's darkened vision, and heat blistered his face. The moment it passed, he leaped up and shot the beam from Excalibur's blade. The smaller dragon zoomed toward him, only two seconds away. He reared back and swung, but something smacked his head and knocked him to the ground, dousing Excalibur.

As he sprawled, still clutching the hilt, he covered himself again. Was it a tail? Goliath's tail?

A sudden pull jerked him to his feet and set him upright. A beige dragon sat next to him, spewing fire into the air. When the flames died away, she growled, "I will protect you from my mate, but I cannot allow you to use that weapon to kill my son."

"Roxil?" Billy rubbed his head. "I'm just trying to save my own skin."

Walter jumped to his feet and stood next to Billy. "You okay?"

"Yeah. Better check on Ashley."

Walter ran to the tree where Ashley stood, her sword drawn. She seemed fine.

Goliath landed on the other side of the river, and the smaller dragon joined him. "Roxil!" Goliath called. "You are not allowed to fight with the humans. Your vow is to stay at my side."

Roxil shot her eyebeams toward Goliath. "At *your* side? I stopped him from slaying our son. Even now he has the power in his sword to slay you, but he stays his hand because of my presence at *his* side. Do you really want me to leave him and allow him to disintegrate you?"

Goliath growled but added no words.

"Then be off," she continued, "and I will lead them out of this place."

"Only to return with that sword," the smaller dragon said.

Goliath's ears rotated toward him. "An excellent point, Karrick. If your mother were really on my side, she would kill that cockroach now and be done with it."

Billy pushed Excalibur's tip against Roxil's underbelly and shouted, "If she tried to kill me, she would be dead before you could blink. Just do as she says, and I'll let all of you live." He whispered out of the side of his mouth. "No offense, Roxil."

A growl masked her response. "None taken, but he will not be persuaded."

"Feel free to kill her," Goliath said. "I have my son, so I have no need of her any longer."

Billy caught a glimpse of Walter and Ashley skulking his way. He whispered again to Roxil. "What now?"

This time she didn't try to cover her words. "I am under a vow that I cannot break. I cannot fight with you. The only reason I was able to fend them off was because of my duty to protect my son. I knew you would slay Karrick if I did not interrupt the battle."

"So are we at an impasse?"

"Not for long. If you delay, he will attack the other humans. If you defend them, I will stop you from hurting my son, and your friends will be doomed. He knows this, but he is likely waiting to see if you will kill me. Since he is faithless, he does not trust me, so he wants me out of the way."

"But if you stop me from defending Walter and Ashley, I would have to kill you."

"Precisely." Roxil's eyes followed Walter and Ashley as they approached, but she seemed not to be concerned. "And after killing me, you would turn your sword on Goliath and Karrick, but they might have killed your friends already, and you would have to fight two dragons alone."

Billy made eye contact with Walter. Walter took Ashley's hand, whispered something to her, then nodded at Billy.

With a burst of strength, Billy jumped to Walter and Ashley, and the trio stood back-to-back-to-back in a triangle, all with swords at the ready. Billy turned on Excalibur's beam and slashed at Goliath, but he jumped out of the way and took to the air. Flicking his wrist, Billy swiped the beam over Karrick's head before he could follow. When the younger dragon ducked low, Billy stopped the buzzing laser within inches of its neck.

He shouted at the top of his lungs. "Don't move, or I'll disintegrate him!"

Roxil roared. "If you do, you will die! Goliath will kill you, but only if I do not kill you first!"

Eyeing Goliath as he circled overhead, Billy shot back with a growl. "We're willing to do battle to see if either one of you can kill us. Don't underestimate our abilities."

Karrick trembled. He looked up at his father with terrified eyes. Goliath landed on Karrick's side of the river but far enough away to keep Billy from shifting the beam to him. With a spiteful snort, he said, "Even with that weapon, you cannot defeat Roxil and me when we fight together. If you kill our son, her rage will be beyond anything you can imagine."

Walter mimicked Goliath's snort. "Then we'll provide a lesson in anger management at the point of a sword!"

"Walter!" Ashley hissed. "Cut the trash talk."

"I'm trying to get them mad. They won't think straight."

Roxil aimed her beams directly into Billy's eyes. "Are we at another impasse?"

"Not necessarily." Billy averted his gaze. Her eyebeams weren't blinding, but they had a dizzying effect. "Just let us go, and we'll all stay alive."

Roxil spat a ball of flames on the sand. "Fool! Even if we agreed to allow you to leave in peace, Goliath would break the vow and attack you when you are most vulnerable. He is a liar."

Goliath snorted again, louder this time. "You are a witness, Karrick. Your mother, the faithful dragoness, is displaying her undying loyalty!"

"Karrick already knows of your lying ways all too well." Roxil pawed deeply into the sand. "You cannot deny it."

"But *I'm* not a liar," Billy said. "Will you trust me to keep a deal?"

409

Roxil dipped her head. "You are the offspring of Clefspeare, and therefore the son of my son. I will gladly assume that he has passed on to you his undisputed integrity."

"I will hear your offer first," Goliath said. "With death hanging over my innocent son's head, it is difficult for me to believe that your integrity is as high as Roxil assumes."

Billy glanced at Roxil. "Is Karrick able to carry a passenger?"

"He is able," she replied with a suspicious stare, "but he has had only a little practice with one of Flint's men."

"Good enough." Keeping the beam in place, Billy pulled away from his companions' backs. "Roxil, fly Walter over there."

Walter sheathed his sword. "I'm not sure what you're up to yet, but I'm game."

"Karrick's a youngling," Billy said. "He should still have a vulnerable spot where his neck meets his back. Have him fly you to the cave and keep the point of your sword on that spot."

Walter cocked his head. "I didn't know you've been studying dragon anatomy."

"I guess you skipped that class." Billy suppressed a grin. Listening to his father's dragon stories for the last four years had paid off. "Just keep your hostage at the cave entrance. I'm sure you can persuade him to help you fight off any shadow people. Ashley and I will meet you there."

"And what do you offer in exchange for my trust?" Roxil asked.

"Simple. We won't kill your son. This way, we don't have to worry about Goliath breaking any promises."

"Then how will you leave this place? You cannot safely navigate the river in daylight, and Karrick is unable to carry more than one human."

"Once we get to the tunnel, we'll take our chances from there."

Roxil lowered her head to the sand. "Very well. In the name of my son, Clefspeare, I will trust you."

Walter scrambled up the neck stairway and settled on her back. "I'm ready."

"You are playing the fool!" Goliath shouted. "Your loyalty is with me, yet you are making deals with the vermin."

"I have conflicting vows," Roxil said as she raised her head again, "and I will honor my obligation to Karrick first."

While Billy held the beam steady over Karrick's head, Roxil flew with Walter over the river. Ashley drew close to Billy's side, trembling, but she stayed silent.

"He'll be all right," Billy said. "He's a true warrior."

"I know." Her voice shook. "Billy, I love him so much."

He nodded but stayed quiet. He couldn't add anything to such a profound statement.

As soon as Walter dismounted Roxil and climbed aboard Karrick, he set the point of his sword against the dragon's neck. "Ready!" he called.

"Okay. Get going!" Billy turned off the beam but kept the sword raised. "Roxil, if you will carry Ashley and me to the cave, we can finish this quickly. Otherwise, we have to cross the river at Lilith's Shallows and walk all the way."

"I will carry you." Roxil turned to Karrick. "Just do as he says, and all will be well."

"Fool of a dragoness!" Goliath shouted, still keeping his distance. "Your loyalty to these sewer rats will be the death of you!"

Roxil paid no attention. She and Karrick launched into the air at the same time. While Karrick headed south, she flew over the river and landed at Billy's side. "Let us fly immediately," she said as she made a neck stairway. "Goliath is no fool. He will devise a counter plan."

"I agree." Billy put his sword away and hustled with Ashley onto Roxil's back. As soon as he got a good grip on the spine in front of him and Ashley wrapped her arms around his torso, he yelled, "Let's go!"

411

Roxil took off and made a beeline toward the cave. In the distance, Karrick was already descending toward the river near the exit waterfall. Walter would get there less than a minute ahead of them.

"We have but a moment," Roxil said. "I must tell you something very important."

Shivering in the gusting wind, Billy gritted his teeth again. "Go for it!"

She turned her head back toward them as she spoke in rapid-fire fashion. "Someone smuggled in soil from the resurrection garden along with one of the bones of Makaidos, and Flint now has a resurrection garden. Since Goliath was once in a place called the Valley of Souls, and calling him out of there allowed him to rise in the garden, he deduced that we could resurrect others who reside in that realm simply by energizing the bone and calling for the resident to come forth. Goliath learned that I was carrying an unborn youngling when I died, though I did not know it myself, and it seems that he discovered this youngling's existence in the Valley of Souls. He likely also learned what kind of fire was necessary to energize the bone, and he reproduced it with his own breath."

As Roxil began her descent toward the river, Billy looked past Ashley's flying hair. Yes, Goliath was following, but quite a ways back.

"So," Roxil continued, "Goliath, being his father, assigned him a name and called him to this world, but he needed me to care for him, because he was ill equipped to handle an infant dragon."

Billy nodded. "I was wondering where he came from. I thought maybe you and Goliath—"

"No!" Roxil turned her head to the front. "My vow was to stay at his side. Nothing more."

When they landed on the river's beach, Billy and Ashley slid down Roxil's side and sprinted toward the cave, both drawing their swords as they ran.

"I will stay here and fend off Goliath," Roxil said. "Restore my son to me, and all will be well."

Now tromping over a thin layer of snow, Billy looked back. "You have my word."

The ferns crunched underneath their weight, raising a musky odor. "See any shadow people?" Ashley asked as she ran two steps behind him.

"I sense danger, but it's not real close. My guess is that they're holed up in the cave in the daytime. It's the darkest place around."

"Perfect. Dragons ready to scorch us outside the cave, and a horde of shadow people ready to strangle us inside."

When they reached the cave entrance, Walter stood just outside the dark arch, his sword planted against Karrick's underbelly. "We had a good talk," Walter said. "You might say that he gets the point."

Karrick snorted the same way his father had. "I fear to die only because it would break my poor mother's heart. If not for that, I would do battle with you cowardly worms."

"And he has his father's charm," Ashley said.

Billy lit up Excalibur's beam and stepped inside the cave. "You do well to honor your mother. Go to her now, and I advise you to heed her counsel and not your father's."

Karrick spat a stream of sparks. "And I advise *you* to drink your own poison." With that, he shuffled away a few steps, then used his wings to help him scoot to the edge of the forest.

Waving Walter and Ashley inside, Billy marched ahead. "Let's see if we can get to Earth."

"Reinforcements?" Walter asked.

Billy looked back. "Are you a mind reader now?"

"Nope. Just guessing that you had a reason for walking into a cave full of spooks with no way out but into a dragon's mouth."

"Speaking of spooks." Ashley pointed into the darkness. "I sense something ahead."

Billy swept the sword's beam across the floor. Sizzles echoed through the cave, along with mournful cries. "They're here, all right."

"They're in pain," Ashley said. "Aren't we invading their territory?"

Billy took several steps into the cave and motioned for the others to follow. "Elam told me they're like vermin. Abraham said so himself. This is more like exterminating rats than anything."

Ashley sighed. "If you say so. I know it didn't bother me last time, but things seem different in the light of day, especially after talking to Zane."

Billy looked at her sad eyes. Again, her thoughts were clear. Goliath had called the three of them vermin, and he was ready to kill them, and now they were doing the same to these creatures, whatever they were. They had Abraham's word, but was that enough?

As the cries of the dying shadow people faded, Billy touched Ashley's cloak. "Better let Gabriel out."

413

She pulled the box from her pocket. "Why now?"

"We're going to make a run for it."

"Run for it?" Walter asked. "Through that mass of snakes?"

Billy nodded. "No use killing more than we have to."

"Gabriel," Ashley said as she opened the ion box's lid. "Have you been listening?"

The glow inside the box pulsed.

"Good. Hop out. After we open the portal, we'll see you on the other side."

A surge of danger flooded Billy's senses. As he turned to the entrance a dark form shaded the opening.

Walter swallowed. "Running for it works for me."

A blast of fire shot into the cave. Walter ducked his head and fanned out his cloak just in time to cover Billy and Ashley.

"Run!" Walter shouted.

As another flood of fire rushed in, the three sprinted farther into the cave, Billy leading the way with Excalibur's glow. Sticky hands grabbed at their feet and ankles. It felt like running through tar, but their momentum allowed them to snap away from the dark predators.

Soon, the end of the tunnel came into sight. Billy turned on the beam and slashed it vertically across the back wall. As before, sparks flew, and a rectangular aura took shape.

"It's open!" Ashley called.

Billy waved a hand. "Everyone go!"

While Billy kept the shadow people at bay, Ashley leaped into the glowing doorway, followed by Walter. As he turned off the beam and jumped, a dark hand grabbed his ankle, but his thrust carried him through the portal. He broke into daylight and landed on his side, the black limb still attached and stretching into the cave. With a quick jerk, he pulled away, and the arm sprang back and disappeared.

Squinting, Billy looked around. Ashley propped herself on hands and knees. Walter, a new abrasion on his forehead, helped her rise to her feet, then reached for Billy.

As he rode Walter's pull, Billy looked at the portal. A radiant human shape passed through and instantly solidified into Gabriel. He stretched his wings and lifted his legs up and down. "That box was a tight fit even for me."

Ashley ran into his arms. "It's so good to see you!"

Pressing his palms on her cheeks, he kissed her on the forehead. "Thought you got rid of your brother for good?"

Grinning, she swatted him on the backside. "Behave yourself!"

Billy called toward the tent, still staked out in front of the mine entrance. "Mom! Are you there?"

"Are we going to bring home another dragon?" Walter asked.

Shaking his head, Billy called again as he circled around the portal and headed for the tent. "Mom, it's Billy!"

A woman crawled out of the tent and looked at them, blinking. "I am Tamara," she said meekly.

"Oh, sorry. One of the dragons, right?"

"Yes." She tilted her head. "Do you seek Mrs. Bannister?"

"Yeah. She's my mother."

Tamara pointed at the pile of rubble that blocked the entrance to the mines. "In there with Yereq. The flood is …" She rolled her eyes upward, searching for a word. Finally, she looked at Billy again. "Receding."

"Thanks." Billy ran to an opening in the rubble. Just as he took a breath to yell, his mother walked out, her shoulders slumped, her face dirty, and her hair wet.

"Mom!" Billy hugged her close. His mother's arms slid around him, weak at first, but they tightened to a firm embrace.

She pulled back and looked at him. "I thought you'd come later. Is it night in Second Eden already?"

415

He shook his head. "Change of plans. Listen. We're going to need all the firepower we can get, and we can't wait to take one dragon at a time. Are there any other dragons available?"

She glanced at Tamara. The former dragon picked up a stick from the fire, then jerked her hand away and licked her finger, apparently nursing a burn.

Billy's mother whispered. "Tamara is available, but Kaylee told me she's not exactly the brightest bulb in the chandelier. When Devin killed her, she was carrying a message from Patrick that allowed Devin to find the courier and track down other dragons. She was supposed to destroy the message immediately after reading it. The former dragons would never have learned about the mistake if not for Devin's bragging about it to Patrick. But since Morgan wouldn't let Devin kill Patrick, the dragons were able to change the way they communicated."

Billy drew a picture in his mind of the slayer grinning as he read the message, but he quickly shook the image away. "If Tamara can breathe fire and wants to fight for our side, then I don't care about her IQ."

"Oh, she's loyal to a fault, and she's as loving as the day is long."

"Then sign her up." He looked back at the campfire. Walter, Ashley, and Gabriel had gathered around to warm themselves and were chatting with Tamara. "Anyone else?"

"No. You said you could take only one at a time, so I told the others they could follow up a lead Kaylee found about the missing younglings."

"Fair enough." Billy looked into the tunnel. "Is Yereq around? We could use him."

"He'll be out soon. He loves Sapphira so much, he'll never give up looking for her."

Billy dragged his boot across the stony ground. "I know exactly how he feels."

416

"You mean Bonnie?"

"Yeah ... Bonnie."

She embraced him again and laid her head on his chest. "I know how you feel, too."

As he patted her on the back, he looked at the portal. "I can get you to Second Eden, but I don't know if I can restore Jared Bannister for you."

For a moment, she said nothing. Her body trembled slightly, but after a few seconds, the tremors died away. "When do we go?"

"We'll have to wait for Second Eden's nightfall. A couple of dragons out there are waiting to fry us."

She took his hand and pulled him toward the campfire. "Then let's sit and make our plans."

417

6

THE EMPTY VALLEY

Bonnie thrust her sword. Sapphira blocked. When the two blades crashed together, they pushed against each other, grunting. Metal slid on metal until the two hilts met. With their hands blazing a pulse of flames, the two girls locked stares. Now that Bonnie had been an Oracle of Fire for more than four years, she could see through the fire easily, as if the flame coating were no more than an aura of light.

Flashing a grin, Sapphira looked up at Bonnie, her blue eyes sparkling in the midst of her fiery aura. "Giving up?"

"Never!"

Bonnie dug in and pushed with her legs, but Sapphira didn't budge an inch. Bonnie glanced at the smaller girl's bulging shoulder muscles. So much strength in such a small package!

After several seconds of stalemate, Sapphira glanced away and gasped. "Oh! Will you look at that?"

Bonnie tilted her head upward. "Look at what?"

"The sky!" Sapphira planted a foot in Bonnie's stomach and shoved her backwards.

Bonnie fell on her bottom with a thud and nearly completed a somersault before flattening herself on her back. "Such a fiend!" she shouted, a laugh shaking her voice. "Thou hast deceived me, rogue!"

Sapphira marched forward, set her foot on Bonnie's stomach again, and spoke in mock lament. "Oh, woe is me! I am smitten with anguish over my dastardly plot to fell this fair maiden! I deserve nothing but scorn for my vileness."

Bonnie grabbed her ankle and pushed her away. As Sapphira stumbled, Bonnie jumped up and shoved her again, knocking her flat. Then, with a mighty heave, Bonnie plunged the sword between Sapphira's fiery chest and arm and into the turf behind her.

Splaying her limbs, Sapphira cried out, "Thou hast delivered thy revenge in full measure, O virtuous maiden. If perchance I see you in the hereafter, I will be your eternal servant!" Her head lolled to the side, her tongue protruding. For a moment, she didn't move. Then a giggle erupted and grew into a full belly laugh.

420

Bonnie yanked out her sword. A dozen corny replies came to mind, but when she tried to speak, she just sputtered and laughed. This show was definitely over.

A third laugh joined theirs, then a clapping of hands. The Maid, her aura as bright as the sun, sang out with delight. "A wonderful performance, my friends! Your swordplay was excellent and your footwork exquisite. You are now the finest of sword maidens."

Sapphira climbed to her feet and saluted with her sword. "And the best of actors, don't you think?"

The Maid smiled. "Of all the sword-bearing actors I have seen in this realm, you two are the best."

Bonnie gave her an exaggerated bow. "You do us an ambiguous honor, fair Maid."

After another round of laughter, Bonnie slid her sword into a scabbard at her hip. "Can you tell us now?" She stared into The

Maid's eyes. Her fiery orbs turned solemn, pensive. She had told them earlier that she had received a message from Abaddon, but she wasn't free to release it until the final swordplay examination was complete. They had studied every stance, every move, even every verbal joust from "En garde" to their dramatic Old English wordplays. They were ready for the next step.

The Maid nodded. "The time has come, my dear friends."

Sapphira hooked her arm around Bonnie's and leaned against her. "To go to Second Eden?"

"Perhaps. Abaddon has learned that your friends now have enough information, and their wisdom will likely guide them to attempt a call. At the very least, you should prepare for the journey."

Bonnie looked down at Sapphira's ovulum, still in its pouch. "So we'll shrink down into eggs, too?"

"Not you," The Maid said, "for the two of you entered here alive."

Bonnie shook her head. "I guess I don't understand all the rules. Will we arrive fully grown? I assumed my father did, because they needed a doctor, but I heard that most of them show up there as babies."

"The rules, as you put it, are fairly simple. One who has died goes to Second Eden in the form in which he or she arrived here. Most were killed as unborn babies, so they go to Second Eden in uterine plants that complete the gestations. Your father was too big for a plant, so he simply appeared in his adult form, like a flower sprouting from the soil. There are, however, a few exceptions. Roxil came here as Abigail, a human who died in a terrible plunge from the Bridgelands to Second Eden."

She raised a pair of fingers and continued. "Since that was her second demise, she passed into a state in which her body had to be regenerated by other means than the usual straightforward resurrection. Abaddon decided to use a birthing plant. He thought

421

it would take a full nine months in the plant, but her rebirth was nearly instantaneous."

"Do you know why?" Bonnie asked.

"I have a theory." The Maid touched her sternum. "A crystalline egg dangled from her necklace. I know not what it was, but it had the aura of life within, so I assume that it provided the energy to regenerate her body."

Sapphira looked up at Bonnie. "That's the egg I told you about, the one that formed from the diamonds I collected when Timothy's tears fell from the sky."

"What about Timothy?" Bonnie asked. "He died three times. Does he need an egg's energy, too?"

"Abaddon and I have discussed this, and he thinks Timothy, or Makaidos, as we came to know him, will need that and more. His sacrifice was singular in that he gave up his right to have his soul resurrected. Even now as his body grows in a birthing plant, it will not come to fruition without three steps." The Maid raised a finger. "The first step is the call. The plant will wither and die without his name being verbally called by those who need his aid." She lifted another finger. "The second step is the crystal, for the body inside will not quicken without the necessary energy from his previous life. And the third step," she said, raising another finger, "is a sacrifice, the willing death of an innocent lamb, and the blood of the lamb must be applied to the plant to restore the soul of the one being reborn."

Sapphira gave her a quizzical look. "A sacrifice? Who?"

"Ah! But that is not for you to know. Since the lamb will make the decision without coercion either to sacrifice or withdraw, no one will be told ahead of time; neither you, nor I, nor Abaddon, nor even the lamb." Like a glowing tong touching a flaming coal, The Maid caressed Sapphira's cheek. "Who knows? Perhaps even you will be the one to offer your body to the wolves of Second Eden."

422

Bonnie watched as Sapphira stared at The Maid, their faces glowing and fresh, yet so serious. Was Sapphira thinking about becoming the sacrifice? Had her thousands of years of life and suffering been a preparation for an ultimate sacrificial act? She had to be in turmoil. She wanted to be united with Elam, but if that was really what God wanted, why weren't they together already? Why was it taking so long?

Filled with a blend of joy and heartache, The Maid's eyes communicated empathy. Somehow she understood the impact of her words, what it meant to be offered to the wolves. At the center of each pupil, a flame erupted. Shaped like a teardrop, the fire consumed something in its midst, a girl … a weeping girl.

Blinking away the image, Bonnie cleared her throat. "But there's something strange about all this. The Second Edeners couldn't have known about the three things necessary for Makaidos to be reborn. If they had called him too soon, he would have—"

"Come back as a corpse," The Maid said. "And that would have been tragic, truly tragic."

423

Sapphira shook her head as if throwing off a trance. "So … I guess it's really fortunate that it worked out the way it did."

"Fortunate?" The Maid laughed again, her eyes merry. "You may call it that, but nothing in this matter has been left to chance. You heard Abaddon tell the story. Were you surprised that Elam allowed Angel to tell the lie? And did it seem odd to you that he commanded Paili to alter the poem?"

"I was surprised," Sapphira said. "It didn't sound like something Elam would do at all."

"Elam prayed for wisdom. He received it. When God gave those words to Paili through Enoch, the delivery of the crystal and the sacrifice were planned, but certain events transpired that necessitated a change."

"Planned?" Sapphira repeated. "I know Ashley had a crystal, but who was supposed to be sacrificed?"

"Once again you ask the identity of a potential lamb, but consider for yourself the damage that could be done if you were to learn who the sacrifice was supposed to be, and then he or she chose not to walk the path of blood and fire."

Sapphira lowered her head. "I see what you mean."

"So Elam ordered the change," Bonnie said, "because not everything was ready for Makaidos to rise."

"Yes." The Maid's flames heightened. "Is it not an exciting thought to ponder? Even Elam was unaware of the reason, yet God moved his heart to do what appeared to be a mistake in many eyes."

"Especially since it gave rise to Goliath," Bonnie added. "That still looks like a mistake."

"Indeed it would to eyes that see through a glass darkly. Perhaps if you are called to that world, you will witness how the results of that decision unfold. Even the return of Goliath has a reason behind it." The Maid laid a hand over her heart. "Every call to life is an echo of a longing in the heart of the caller. It is like a thunder within, a drum that beats without a rhythm, yet it searches for the power to set the thrumming into a new heartbeat for the resurrected loved one. It combines words of love with the music of sacrifice and the rhythm of a disciplined purpose. All of these create passion, a heart set on fire, and without that fire, no one can be reborn."

Bonnie let the lovely words soak in. They seemed true, yet mysterious. Maybe they would become clear later when she needed them. "But will we remember what we learned here?" She lifted her sword. "It would be a shame to forget all the fighting techniques and the stories you and Abaddon have told us."

"Since you are alive, there is no need for you to revert to the form with which you entered this land. You will go to Second Eden four years older and four years wiser, remembering all that happened here. In fact, you will not even need the ovulum. Its usefulness has now passed away."

Bonnie looked down at her body. Although ripples of fire coated her clothes and skin, there was no doubt about the changes—subtle, yes, but she had definitely matured from a girl to a woman.

"Shall we go to the resurrection table?" The Maid asked as she extended a hand to each of them.

Sapphira removed the ovulum from its pouch and set it on the ground. "I'm ready," she said, taking her hand.

Bonnie slid her hand into The Maid's. When they touched, it seemed that a holy warmth radiated from her fingers and pulsed throughout her body. "How long will we be there?" Bonnie asked.

"Until they call you." The Maid walked with them along the edge of the river. "There is nothing more to tell."

As they walked, the image of the hourglass entered Bonnie's mind. The dragon's scaly hand would grip it and turn it over, beginning the process of waiting for the Second Eden dwellers to make the call. When the last grain of sand fell to the lower glass, their transport would take place, but how many times would Abaddon have to turn the hourglass over?

425

Bonnie checked the staurolite dagger in a sheath at her belt. It didn't really make any difference. No matter how long they had to wait, she and Sapphira would be ready.

Billy stood with his back against the cave's dead end wall. It had taken hours to gather everything they needed, and transporting them to Second Eden had been a nightmare. Since the portal opening contracted every hour or so, he had to reopen it four times. Twice he stepped back into the cave to reopen it with Excalibur, and twice he opened it from the Earth side using the new Apollo.

He looked around at his companions. Each one held a light of some kind to help ward off the shadow people. Yereq, who had to hunch way over to avoid the cave's ceiling, carried two sets of scuba diving gear, two tanks under his arm and the other pieces in a backpack he lifted by a strap on his shoulder. Billy's mother and Gabriel had used the equipment several times in the flooded mine tunnels, but not lately. Only Yereq had not given up the search. Since he was able to hold his breath for almost ten minutes, he dove without gear.

Billy's mother, decked out in a scuba dry suit, had packed her clothes and her pistol in a duffle. She carried a two-person inflatable raft, though they hoped to squeeze three inside for the dangerous journey. Since Elam had told of his own survival after plunging down the exit waterfall even during flood stage, it seemed reasonable that three in a raft could make it, especially with three others swimming in the river to help them right the boat if it capsized.

Ashley held up the ion box and spoke into it. "Gabriel, are you ready?"

The box pulsed with light.

"Everyone else?" Ashley asked.

Lifting his legs up and down, Billy looked at his mother. "I could use another lesson, and this diving suit doesn't quite fit, but I'm ready."

She set her hand over her nose. "Just don't forget to hold your mask and regulator in place. When we splash down after the falls, the impact might jerk them off."

He gave her a thumbs-up. "Gotcha."

Walter stepped out in front, Excalibur in his grip. The beam shot out into the darkness. "My guess is that with all of us here, the shadow people might not bother us, but let's go double time anyway."

Kicking into a fast jog, he led the way. Yereq followed, still hunched over as he pounded his huge boots, apparently trying to ward away any shadowy lurkers.

Billy ran a few steps behind the giant. The combination of Yereq's thudding feet and his own squeaking suit sounded strange, like bats succumbing to hammer blows. He waved a scuba flashlight back and forth along the cave floor. No sign of shadow people. Where could they have gone? Since it was now dark outside, maybe they were congregating between the cave and the river again. Not knowing where they were seemed worse than facing them. The advantage of surprise was on their side.

When they reached the cave entrance, Walter paused and searched the area, using the beam to illuminate the ground and nearby trees. Again, no shadow people.

He resumed jogging, slower now. Yereq straightened his body and followed, obviously taking care to silence his thunderous gait.

Billy suppressed a laugh. Such a huge man running on tiptoes seemed comical, but this was dead serious. He had to keep a straight face.

When all six arrived at the river, Billy dug the scuba gear out of Yereq's pack, while his mother turned on the raft's inflation motor. Although the rush of the river was loud enough to drown out the motor and any whisper, no one spoke a word.

Once Billy and his mother had strapped on their gear, including an air tank and buoyancy compensator, they waded into the river with Yereq. Billy clenched his teeth together, forcing them not to chatter. Even with a scuba dry suit, the chill seemed to plunge knives into his bones. He clipped the waterproof flashlight onto his belt and let his body shiver. At least that was a quiet way to suffer.

While Ashley, Walter, and Tamara climbed into the raft, Billy searched the sky and the surrounding sand. Still nothing. No shadow people or dragons. Something was up. Something big.

Yereq swam into the flow and dove under. With a final kick, he disappeared. He would be the first to brave the plunge to the next level and wait in the pool to support the raft when it fell.

Walter pulled Tamara's hood up for her. Since she was wearing Billy's cloak, the hood and sleeves seemed to swallow her body.

427

It would cover her well when it was time to blast through the wall of flames.

Billy looked over the surrounding mountains, but Abraham's wall was not in sight. The clouds must have been very thick tonight to mask its usual glow.

Walter doused Excalibur, leaving the area in total darkness. Billy pulled his mask down and inserted the regulator. It was time to go for it.

Placing their hands on a rope attached to the back of the raft, he and his mother guided it to the center of the river and let the current take over. As they picked up speed, he listened to the waterfall's heightening rumble. Within seconds the icy river would send them hurtling through the air and then straight down.

Suddenly, the water fell away. Holding his mask and regulator in place with one hand and the rope in the other, Billy twisted and dropped feetfirst. When he plunged in, he pulled on the rope to haul himself back to the surface. A light flashed on from the bouncing raft, and Ashley's face appeared at the back. She shone the beam in his eyes.

428

"Are you all right?" she whisper shouted.

Billy pulled out his regulator. Spray from the pounding water flew all around and tossed droplets on the flashlight's lens. "I think so."

Ashley shifted the beam to Billy's right, illuminating his mother. "You okay, Mrs. B?"

"Fine. And Yereq?"

"He's good. He's getting ready to guide the front end."

The light flicked off. As the current pushed the raft forward and out of the deep pool, Billy reinserted the regulator and dove under water. He grabbed his flashlight, turned it on, and pointed the beam up at the raft's bottom, allowing him to follow its course. Immediately to his right, his mother set her beam on the riverbed.

Although it was made up of sand and pebbles, they had to watch for sharp projections that might rise up ahead.

The flashlights' glow provided a view of Yereq's feet as he kicked. Since the river was only about four feet deep here, his powerful legs churned up sand at the bottom, clouding their view.

Soon, the channel deepened, and the bottom cleared again. Instead of sand, slabs of rock appeared, black with sparkling crystals embedded within that made the bed look like a star-filled nightscape. A hole appeared ahead, so deep, the bottom of the river seemed to fall away into nothingness. The hole's surrounding walls were covered with the same crystalline stars.

Billy studied one of the crystals. It didn't merely reflect the flashlight; it seemed to radiate a light of its own.

As they drifted over the hole, the bitter cold jabbed deeper into his body. Queasiness turned his stomach. He shivered hard, so hard his beam shook on the bottom of the raft.

429

His mother aimed her light at herself and raised her eyebrows as if to ask how he was doing. Billy laid a hand on his stomach and shook his head. Whatever the problem was, it seemed to be getting worse, a lot worse.

She dove and shone the light on one of the crystals. Billy followed her progress with his own light. After a second or two, she hurried back and caught up. Reaching out of the water, she jerked on the rope and surfaced, pulling Billy with her.

Keeping her light under water as they floated with the raft, she whispered, "I think they're candlestones!"

Billy pressed a fist into his gut. "No wonder I'm so sick. There must be a hundred of them down there."

Ashley whispered from the raft. "What's up?"

"Candlestones," Billy said. "Lots of them."

"Did you feel sick when we came through before?"

"We flew over this part, but I remember getting sick while we were in the air. It's worse now, a lot worse."

"Let's hope they're only in one spot," his mother said.

Billy pulled his fist away from his stomach. "Could be. It's easing up already. But since Goliath's been here four years, he probably felt them, too, so you can bet Flint knows about them."

"Something else has me worried," Ashley said. "I haven't seen the wall's glow since we came back."

"I was thinking it was cloud cover." Billy looked up at the sky. "It's pretty clear now."

"It's all adding up. No shadow people in the valley and no one guarding the river. They're probably massing their troops somewhere. Abraham's wall must be dwindling."

Billy let out a long breath. The pain was almost gone. "I guess we'll find out soon."

"Right." Ashley set her transmitter on the raft. "Hold this for me. I'm calling Listener. They need to know right now."

Kicking with his fins to stay upright, Billy held the small box and antenna in place, while his mother kept her light trained on his hands.

Ashley tapped her jaw and began speaking in a hushed tone. "Listener, can you hear me?"

As he held it, the antenna turned slowly. Their tests had worked several times before. Ashley's tooth transmitter sent her voice to the box, which boosted the signal, but since the antenna needed to point in the right direction, she had to find the correct angle as she spoke.

"Listener," she said again, this time a bit louder. "Are you there?"

A static-filled voice sounded from the box. "I'm here, Ashley. I can barely hear you."

"I know. The river noise is terrible. Is Candle with you?"

"He's right outside the door."

"Have him call Valiant and Elam immediately. This is an emergency."

"I'll be right back."

Ashley looked at Billy, a worried frown on her face. Behind her, barely visible in the flashlight's glow, Walter and Tamara looked on. Both stayed silent.

Listener's voice returned, clearer now. "Ashley, Candle is on his way."

"Good. Now here's what I want you to do. Run to Clefspeare and tell him that the wall of fire is either weak or gone. Flint's army is getting ready to attack, and they might have candlestones."

"That's awful. Billy told me about those."

Ashley kept her voice steady and calm. "We also need a ride back to the village, enough dragons for six passengers."

"But if Flint attacks," Listener said, "won't Elam want to keep the dragons here to help?"

"Good point, but it'll take us too long to walk."

"I can send Candle in the airplane."

Ashley looked at Billy. "What do you think? Can he fly in the dark?"

"He can do it. If we light up a landing strip, he'll be fine."

Ashley set her finger on her jaw again and looked toward the village. "Listener, that should work. Have him come to where the river meets the wall on the south side. It might not be there anymore, so he'll have to look for our signal. When we hear the engine, we'll shoot Excalibur's beam into the air."

"I'll tell him."

"If the tank's almost empty, there's a new barrel of fuel in greenhouse number four."

"Got it. I'm on my way."

Ashley breathed a sigh. "Four years of preparation are coming to an end. I hope we're ready."

"We didn't count on candlestones," Billy said.

Tamara tapped Ashley on the shoulder. "Walter says he sees the wall. It is weak and not as high."

"Okay," Ashley said to Billy. "We'll cover up. Maybe now it won't be so bad for the three divers when they go through the barrier."

Billy glanced ahead. The fiery wall did seem weaker, and there was no sign of a guard anywhere. But even with the prospect of an easier-than-expected exit, the thought of imminent war brought a new wave of shivers. Soon, good men would likely die. Soon, the once innocent and naïve villagers would learn if their hardened muscles and honed skills were ready for a real battle, a battle for blood.

When they drew within a few seconds of the wall, Billy and his mother submerged. The water grew warm, then hot. After spiking to a scalding peak, it suddenly cooled again.

Billy surged above the water, and he and his mother, working in concert with Yereq in the front, pulled the raft to shore. He took his mother's hand and led her to the dwindling flames, a wall that now rose to about thirty feet in height. Basking in the heat, they stripped off their dry suits and straightened out their wrinkled clothes. Yereq joined them, and the three dried out their hair and shook out the river's chill.

Ashley drew near, walking at Walter's side. "I can hear Abraham and Angel again."

"What are they saying?" Billy asked.

She edged closer to the wall, so close it seemed that the flames might reach out and scorch her skin. As she stared straight at the fire, she took on a strange tone, like a song, except all in one note, and breathed, not spoken, a breeze with blended voices. "It is time for us to go. We have protected you these many months, and our energy is spent. We will now fly to the Father of Lights, but we leave you three gifts. One is a final burst of energy that will release Second Eden from the shackles of the season of death, and your dragons will find new strength in the warmth of this world's first

432

true summer. The other two gifts you will find as wisdom guides you."

She stepped back and again took Walter's hand. Then, smiling, she let out a long sigh. "They're so happy, happy to be together and happy that they're going to Paradise."

Suddenly, the wall of fire brightened. Like a rising curtain, it shot into the air, an irregular ring of flames that once drew a boundary around enemy territory. When it reached the remaining clouds, the fire absorbed every trace of vapor. The sky cleared. Stars twinkled. And far away, Pegasus peeked over the horizon, offering a scant glow over the dark area.

A loud shout sounded from somewhere in Adam's Marsh. A dragon's roar followed, then silence. Only the river's splashes reached their ears.

Billy pulled Walter and Ashley close. "Flint's troops. They're getting ready to march."

"How much time do you think we have?" Walter asked. "The shadow people are pretty slow, but we need time to set the trap."

Billy watched the clouds over the village dwindle and disappear. "How long will that take?"

433

"Setting the nodes will take maybe fifteen minutes. But we still have to spread the net with the airplane before we place the nodes. The fuel lines are already in place."

"If I'm flying Merlin," Billy said, "and you're spreading the net on the ground, who'll use Excalibur to energize the bones and get Tamara transformed into a dragon?"

Billy's mother joined their huddle. "Just tell me what to do. I can fly Merlin for whatever that prep run is."

"Mom, that's perfect. Candle can show you what to do. The maneuvers are too precise for him to do the flying, but the two of you together can pull it off."

"I'll help Walter," Ashley said. "That'll speed up his part. Cliffside can run the magneto."

Billy pointed at himself. "Then I'll get Tamara to the birthing garden, but everything depends on Candle getting here soon."

"There's one thing I missed," Walter said. "When you told us what Abraham and Angel were saying, you mentioned three gifts. What were the other two?"

Ashley flicked on her flashlight and aimed it at the ground. "I got the impression that it would be—" She dropped to her knees. "Here they are."

Billy looked over Ashley's shoulder. In her palm she held a ring and a small white object that looked like a bone.

Rising to her feet, she slid them into her pocket. "Maybe Valiant can give us an idea of what these—"

A new voice erupted from the radio. "Ashley? This is Elam."

Ashley touched her jaw. "Elam, did you get the word?"

"Yes. We're all hustling to get prepared. Is there anything else we need to know?"

"The wall's completely gone now. We heard a lot of commotion, so they're probably getting ready to march."

"Seen any shadow people?"

Ashley stared into Adam's Marsh. "The valley's empty. We can assume they'll be coming in full force, but it'll probably be a slow march. They might send a dragon as a scout, so you'll have to stay alert."

"We'll be ready. We're keeping the village lights at normal levels for now. Better to make them think we don't know they're coming."

"Unless Merlin gives us away," Billy said. "But we've done nighttime reconnaissance before. If they hear a motor, they might not think anything unusual is happening."

Ashley lifted a finger. "One more thing. You probably noticed the clear skies. Before the wall vanished, Abraham and Angel spoke to me. They said the first true summer will be coming to Second Eden."

"We noticed," Elam said. "It's a lot warmer. We'll discuss how to use that to our advantage."

"I have some ideas cooking. I'll let you know when we get there."

Elam's voice faded as if he had stepped away from the microphone. "It shouldn't be long. Candle has already taken off."

"Okay. See you soon." Ashley withdrew the ion box from her cloak. "I'd better let Gabriel out."

Walter stretched, popping his back. "Yeah, I get a backache just thinking about being stuffed in there."

She opened the lid and spoke into the opening. "Gabriel, do you remember the directions?"

The glow within the box dimmed. Ashley's gaze shifted upward as if watching something rise, apparently following the source of Gabriel's voice.

"Good." Ashley pointed upstream. "That's due north, so try to keep your bearings. When you find the lake, you shouldn't have a problem locating the boulder with the *X*. If the portal's still there and you can't get through it, come back and let me know. We can send some dragons to try to open it again."

435

As Ashley put the box away, she looked at the river. After a few seconds, she turned toward Billy. Breathing out her words in a sigh, she said, "He's gone."

Billy searched for any sign of Gabriel's light, but, of course, nothing appeared. "I guess there's no other way he can help us in that condition, but my father and Hartanna tried to open that portal at least three times. What makes Gabriel think he'll be able to get through?"

Ashley smiled. "Do you need a lesson in the power of love?"

"What do you mean?"

"Love believes all things. This is a love journey, you know."

"You sensed that?"

A trembling smile bent Ashley's lips. "Very deeply."

"Acacia or Shiloh?"

"Oh, it's Shiloh. Definitely Shiloh. When he said her name, I could feel his love."

Billy nodded. It made sense. Gabriel had watched over Shiloh for a long time, so developing an attachment was normal. And since they were both much older than they looked, their differences in age didn't really matter much.

He waved for Yereq and Tamara to join them. "Yereq, I have a dangerous assignment for you."

Even in a whisper, the great giant's voice seemed to shake the air. "Speak it. I will do whatever I must."

"Flint has no idea you're here. Since you look so much like the other Nephilim, and since it's still dark, you can try to infiltrate their troops. See what you can do to sabotage their plans, but don't give yourself away. The longer you can work behind the lines, the better for us."

"It will be an honor." Yereq rubbed his chin thoughtfully. "I will attempt to subdue one of my kinsmen and take his clothing."

Ashley pulled a white hair band from around her head and gave it to Yereq. "Use this as an arm band so we'll know which one you are. In the heat of battle, I doubt Flint's troops will notice."

"Very well." He took the band and pushed it into his pocket. "Yet, if you see me in the heat of battle, I am likely to be noticeable as the Naphil who is killing Goliath with his bare hands."

Billy handed Yereq his diving flashlight and grasped the giant's wrist. "We'll see you at the victory feast."

Yereq gave Billy a sad sort of nod and walked into Adam's Marsh, following the direction of the earlier shout.

Heaving a sigh, Billy laid a hand on Tamara's shoulder. "When we arrive at the village, I will rush you to the birthing garden to get you transformed into a dragon. Are you ready and willing?"

Her eyes sparkled in the moon's strengthening beams. "I am both, and I am also excited."

"Great. The other dragons will teach you everything you need to know."

Ashley took off her rubellite ring and slid it onto Tamara's finger. "You'll need this."

"Thank you." Tamara lifted her hand and looked at the gem. "Some of the other dragons had one. I did not."

After a few minutes, Merlin's familiar drone reached them, steadily increasing. Billy ran out to a flat area, lit up Excalibur, and pointed the beam at the ground. It drew a long line through the snow, creating Candle's runway.

As soon as the plane rumbled to a stop, Billy hustled everyone on board. His mother jumped into the pilot's seat, while he settled into the copilot's. "Think you can take off in the dark?" he asked.

"Just watch me, flyboy." With a wink, she throttled up and rolled Merlin down the bumpy runway. A few seconds later, they were airborne.

437

Billy nodded at the windshield. "See those pinpoints of light way out there?"

"Yes. What are they?"

"The village's lanterns. The birthing garden is on the north side; that's to the right. There's room to land, but you'll have to make a quick drop and stop. Then you and Candle will take off again."

She pushed the airplane toward top speed. "Let's get it done."

7

CHAPTER

THE HYBRID'S SEED

Billy climbed the stairs to the village's rampart, an eight-foot-high mound Valiant and Sir Barlow had constructed a year earlier to provide a good view to the northeast where Adam's Marsh lay. He crossed the rough beams that made up the rampart's eight-by-eight-foot deck and stood next to Windor behind a waist-high parapet. The teenaged boy had stayed at his lookout post for hours, his keen eyes surveying the field in the light of the moon.

After four years of bitter cold, the temperate air felt stifling, though it was likely no more than sixty degrees Fahrenheit. Billy aimed Listener's spyglass toward Adam's Marsh. Since Enoch's gift had not provided prophetic glimpses in years, Listener had stopped using it so frequently, but it still provided a great view of the surrounding area.

With Pegasus casting its radiance over the fields and forests, Walter and Ashley were easy to find. Riding Firedda northwest and southeast along the village's northeastern border, they were spreading out a thin-filament net across a field.

439

In preparation for the construction of the rampart, the villagers had cleared the dead and dying trees just outside the village. They hoped to be able to see the enemy coming, and now they had room for the huge net. Coated with iron filings, it would serve as a heating coil for the unsuspecting shadow people who were likely to make up the first wave of invaders. Then, when the second wave arrived, the villagers could spring trap number two, the fuel lines that lay underneath the net.

Firedda landed gracefully. Walter and Ashley jumped off and dashed around for a few seconds, pulling the net and staking it down. After camouflaging it under the melting snow the best they could, they climbed back on Firedda to fly to the next spot.

Billy looked at Pegasus, still low in the sky. At this rate, Walter and Ashley would be done pretty soon. Ashley's idea was brilliant, as usual, but would it work? No one knew exactly what the shadow people were made of, so all this preparation might be worthless. At the very least, it should light up the enemy, allowing the villagers to better attack their shadowy bodies.

He shifted the spyglass to the south and spotted Merlin. His mother and Candle had made the initial drop of the net and were now flying toward the dragon launching field. Soon he would be able to reunite his mother and father, but not right away. Clefspeare would be gathering the dragon air force and their pilots together for battle, and his mother volunteered to work with the women of the village. They and the children were preparing for their part in the battle, setting up the hospital, which once flew high above but now sat just outside the village's western border.

Nodding at the progress in the field, he lowered the spyglass and looked at Windor. "Report to Elam and Valiant and tell them the net's in place. I see no signs of enemy troops yet."

"I will tell them." Windor hustled down the rampart's five wooden steps and nearly ran into Elam.

Elam grabbed the teenager's shoulders and kept him from falling. "I heard the message. You will find Valiant with the dragons at the launching field."

When Windor disappeared in the darkness, Elam joined Billy at the parapet, carrying a lantern and wearing the village's battle uniform. The lantern's flame seemed to be mimicked by the sunburst design on Elam's tunic, a symbol of the fire God had given both man and beast, a demonstration of power and light from above.

Billy pointed with the spyglass. "The shadow people are probably on the front lines."

"Hoping to strangle us in our sleep, I assume."

"That's what I would guess."

"The dragons sense them," Elam said, "but they say that danger is closing in from the north at a faster rate, and it's a different kind of danger."

"The Vacants?"

441

Elam nodded. "We already caught a scout. The conspiracy between them and Flint's army has now reached its climax."

"Who's watching the birthing garden?"

"Sorentine."

"Sorentine?" Billy shook his head. "That won't work. My mother said she's …" He paused, searching for a kind word. "Well, she's not exactly a genius."

"Don't worry," Elam said, laughing. "Patrick's with her. With his brains and her brawn, they're a perfect combination."

Billy breathed a sigh. "You scared me for a minute."

"Give her a chance. Courage and love are more important than brains." Elam set his hands on the parapet. "So now we wait."

"Yeah. I guess so." Billy eyed Elam. Those words stung. Again it seemed that the ages-old warrior chief oozed more wisdom than Billy could learn in a lifetime. And he was right. He needed to give Sorentine a break. She was doing the best she could.

"Are we missing any steps?" Elam asked. "Can you think of anything else you heard or saw behind enemy lines that might help?"

Billy began counting on his fingers. "You already know what Yereq's doing. You know about the candlestones and Karrick."

"Right. Since we don't know who has candlestones, we decided to split up the dragons. Most of them will assist on the northern side again the Vacants, while Clefspeare and Legossi patrol the northeastern front. They should be enough to fight Goliath and Karrick. When we figure out if Flint has candlestones and how he'll use them, we'll decide how to shift our dragon army. In the meantime, it's best to hold Thigocia back until we have a handle on the situation. We don't want our dragon healer injured."

Billy touched a third finger. "There's one more thing. I didn't tell you how Karrick was born. Somehow Flint got some soil from the resurrection garden and one of the bones, and Goliath used them to call Karrick from a place called the Valley of Souls. When Devin and Palin killed Roxil, her unborn youngling went to that valley, and all they had to do was call him out to resurrect him."

"But when could they have done that? We haven't had another eclipse cycle."

"They must have done it at the same time we resurrected Dr. Conner," Billy said. "I guess they already had their garden by then. I described Karrick to my father, and he says four years old is about right."

"But who provided the soil and bone?"

Billy tightened his grip on the spyglass. "I already know what you think."

"Look," Elam said, grasping Billy's arm, "I'm not blaming you for putting any trust in Semiramis. If she stole soil and a bone, she must have done it before that night. You're in the clear."

Billy nodded. It was true. Semiramis had convinced him to find Shiloh after they called for Dr. Conner, so Flint must have already had his garden set up. Then why would Arramos need to plant something in the village's garden if they already had one of their own? Was Semiramis able to transport the bone and soil under the wall at the river but unable to transport the plant's seed? Or did she have some other reason for making sure their plant grew in the original birthing garden? "All that aside," Billy said, "there's another issue. With the season of death over, we're bound to have another eclipse cycle, so we can call Makaidos and probably anyone else in the Valley of Souls."

"Anyone else?" Elam raised his eyebrows. "Do you know who's down there?"

Billy looked away for a moment. Explaining this part wouldn't be easy. "It's like this. I've been having dreams where I see Bonnie praying. Sometimes she's alone, and sometimes she's with Sapphira, but she keeps praying the same thing over and over." He paused for a moment. A lump was forming in his throat, and he had to get rid of it. Just before a life-or-death battle was no time to get so emotional. "She always says, 'Call to me, and I will answer you.'"

"You've mentioned that before. That's on Bonnie's poster."

"But there's more. In the dream she mentions rising again if I'll say her name."

Elam nodded and stretched out his reply. "Oh, I see."

"I know, I know. You think I'm probably conjuring up some kind of hopeful daydream, but this one's not like that. You'd have to experience it to understand."

"Trust me. I've had dreams about Sapphira like that, especially one where we're dancing near a fountain, sort of like the fountain in our village, only it's in a ballroomlike setting." He tilted his head upward and inhaled deeply. "It's so real I can almost feel the spray."

"So you get what I mean. Maybe our dreams are prophetic."

"Hard to say for sure," Elam said, shrugging. "But if Bonnie and Sapphira went to the Valley of Souls, it would explain why no one's seen them."

443

"Then is it worth a try?"

"Maybe, but we don't know when the next eclipse is supposed to be."

"True." Billy looked at Pegasus. It seemed bright, similar to the brightness it had shone after the first eclipse, but since they hadn't seen its fullness in years, it was hard to remember for certain. "Valiant would've kept up with the calendar, but if tonight's the night, we can't wait to ask him."

The moon's glow reflected in Elam's eyes. "If it is, the moon's already getting close to the crucial angle."

"Do you think I have time?" Billy touched Excalibur's hilt. "I have all I need to energize the soil."

Elam looked toward Adam's Marsh. "Probably plenty of time before Flint's troops arrive, but it's such a long shot. According to the prophecy, it's possible only two nights out of the month."

"Wouldn't it make sense for Abraham and Angel to time their departure for the very day we needed to use the garden? We can't miss this opportunity."

"But if Abraham planned it that way, he would want us to resurrect his son. We can't miss another chance to call back Makaidos, especially when your idea is based on a dream."

Billy tensed his jaw. Elam's logic was right on target. How could a message in a dream overcome basic common sense? Dreams were just wishful thinking more often than anything, but sometimes they meant something more, and his vision of Bonnie was so deeply rooted, this dream had to be one of those times.

Years ago, he had read Bonnie's prayer in her journal, and a vision of her appeared in his mind, her wings spread in full flight. She begged him to take Excalibur from her hands. Not long before that vision, Professor Hamilton had said of Excalibur, "It was bestowed to you as a gift from above. It was meant for you to wield in battle." But he had refused the professor's wisdom, and rejecting divine revelation when it defied his ill-informed logic had led to a huge mess.

Elam shook Billy's shoulder. "Hey, we can't wait forever. If you want to give the garden a try, you'd better go now."

Tightening his muscles, Billy set his feet. "Elam, your reasons for calling Makaidos are right on the mark, but I think something's going on, something we don't understand. I'll go to the garden, and I'll do what you told me, but I'm asking for a little slack."

Elam set his stare on Billy and held it for several seconds. Finally, he exhaled and nodded. "I expect you to call Makaidos, but if wisdom guides you otherwise, you may do as you see fit."

"Thank you." Billy hustled down the stairs. "Don't start the war without me."

"If we get attacked," Elam called. "I'll send up a flare. But don't forget. The Vacants could show up from the north at any minute."

"Got it!" As Billy jogged along the path to the village, he imagined the resurrection procedure. Would he have to get Ruth to recite the poem? Apparently Flint performed a rebirth without her, but could Goliath have provided the words? He was at his own resurrection, but not really physically present until after the poem's recitation. Maybe they forced Roxil to sing it, but exactly when she showed up during the ceremony wasn't clear at all, and how could she have memorized it in one hearing?

When he arrived at the central circle, he stopped and pulled off his cloak. The air was getting warmer by the minute.

A sweet voice reached his ear. "Billy?"

"Listener?" Turning, he found her standing by a street lantern. She was dressed in the village's uniform, much like Elam's but without the marching dragon, signifying that she would not be in the battle. A troubled frown wrinkled her face. "What's wrong?" Billy asked.

"I was napping, and I had a strange dream. An elderly man asked me to do something. He was kind and gentle, so I hope it comes true someday, but I didn't understand his request. It was so puzzling."

Billy ached to take the time to hear more, but he couldn't delay much longer. "Dreams are like that sometimes. Maybe it'll become clear later."

"Where is your uniform?" she asked.

Billy clutched his tunic. "I haven't had time to put it on, and now I have to go to the garden."

"I can bring it to the garden for you."

"That would be great. Would you also ask Ruth to come? I need her to recite the resurrection poem."

"Really?" In the light of a dozen street lanterns, Listener's eyes sparkled. "Are you going to call Makaidos?"

"Yeah." Billy cleared his throat. No sense in letting her in on the other option. "Anyway, that's the plan."

Listener ran toward Billy's hut. "I'll meet you there!"

He watched her young legs, so light, so strong. No conflicts did battle in her mind, while his own conflicts made his legs feel like slabs of concrete.

Pushing his feet forward, he trudged toward the birthing garden. No use hurrying. He couldn't do anything until Ruth got there.

As he walked into the bordering forest, his view darkened. He had forgotten to carry a light, but it didn't matter; he knew the path well. With blackness ahead of him, his dream of Bonnie took over his senses, and the first line of her song repeated, *Call to me, and I will answer you.* Her delivery was quiet, as if she called from another world, yet it was forceful, a plea that reached from heart to heart.

Billy clenched a fist. It had to be real. It just had to be. But how could a dreamer convince anyone of a feeling? Elam had made his wishes clear, so Billy had to make those his priority, but how could he ignore the inner turmoil? He had said, "Don't start the war without me," but it felt like the war had already begun, at least in his mind, and this decision might be the first salvo for either side, and maybe a decisive one.

When he reached the field and the path to the garden, he forced his legs into a jog and focused on a single lantern light in the distance. His shoes squished. The surrounding snow was obviously melting, and the ground felt like a blend of dead grass and mud.

"Patrick!" he called as he drew close. "It's Billy." He slowed to a stop, sliding a bit in the mud. Patrick stood at the garden's edge while Sorentine sat on her haunches behind him.

Patrick's bushy white eyebrows arched up. "I'm glad to see you, William. What brings you out here?"

"We need to try a resurrection."

Patrick looked up at the moon. "I was just thinking about that. The shadow angles are precisely what they were when we began Dr. Conner's ceremony. I suspect that, if not for the season of death, we would have had a normal eclipse last night or perhaps the night before."

Billy cocked his head. "Really? You remember details like that?"

"Oh, yes. Charles Hamilton and I were both avid astronomy buffs, so I take careful note of celestial events."

As Billy looked up at the stars, a memory flowed into his mind, the early morning when he and the professor were in England waiting for Bonnie to arrive with Clefspeare and Hartanna. Prof pointed out Ursa Major and Polaris, as well as another star Billy had never heard of. The wise old professor definitely knew the celestial sky.

"Listener is bringing Ruth." Billy touched Excalibur's hilt. "I suppose I can go ahead and energize the bones."

447

"Ruth might not be able to come. She has taken ill, and I believe Dr. Conner is examining her as we speak."

Billy looked toward the village. Listener strode quickly down the path, alone, sloshing through the mud. When she arrived, she slipped and nearly fell, but Billy caught her in time.

Breathless, she handed Billy his uniform. "Ruth is too sick to come. Dr. Conner says it was probably something she ate, and it will pass soon, but she is so nauseated, she can hardly move."

Billy stripped off his tunic, leaving him bare-chested. He had learned long ago that the people of Second Eden had few modesty standards, so Listener wouldn't give his appearance a second thought. "So what can we do?" he asked as he pushed his arms through a long-sleeved red shirt. "If this is the second night, we won't have another chance until next month."

"True," Patrick said, "but must my wife be the one to sing the words?"

"Well, no." Billy put on the second layer, a short-sleeved silver shirt made of a woven cloth as tough as chain mail. "At least I don't think so."

"Then we have a solution." Patrick patted his torso, speaking slowly as if distracted by his search for something buried in his clothing. "Ruth has practiced it many times since her previous recital. I helped her by writing it down and following along while she practiced, and when the season of death ended, she asked me to find the transcription, so I located it …" He pulled a wrinkled piece of parchment from inside his coat. "Ah! Here it is."

Billy looked at the palm-sized scrap. Patrick's handwriting was sloppy but readable.

"The only problem that remains is the tune," Patrick said. "Do you know it?"

"No. Didn't Ruth practice it?"

"Only the words. Adding the tune slowed us down."

"Maybe the tune doesn't matter," Billy offered. "The words have the power, right?"

448

"I wouldn't be so certain, William. Music has great power. One tune can make a man rise up with his muscles flexed, while another can sap his energy."

"May I see the song?" Listener asked, reaching for the parchment.

"Certainly." Patrick handed it to her. "Have you heard it?"

Listener shook her head, her eyes trained on the words. "I wasn't at the garden either time, but I heard Ruth humming a tune many times, and I told her it sounded like one I have had running through my head for as long as I can remember. I wanted to see if the words fit."

"And?" Billy prompted.

Looking up from the parchment, she nodded. "I think so, but I should practice first to make sure."

Rapid-fire thoughts raced through Billy's mind. They couldn't drag Ruth out there on a wild hunch that it might be the appropriate resurrection night, and if Listener, the little girl who was known for her listening and memory prowess, was sure, then maybe her tune was the right one. Besides, they had to hurry. The battle might start at any minute. "Okay. Listener will sing the words, and I'll light up the bones."

"Is there any way I might be of service?" Sorentine asked.

Billy looked into her hopeful eyes. How could he find a way for a not-so-bright dragon to do something useful? "Uh ... how about if you help Listener practice? Every singer needs someone as a sounding board."

Sorentine's brow drooped, and her long neck swung her head away. "Very well."

Billy's heart sank. He had hurt her feelings. She might not be brilliant, but she knew a veiled dismissal when she heard one. Yet, what could he do about it now?

He took Patrick's arm and guided him a few feet into the garden. "I have a dilemma," he said in a low tone. "I've been having these dreams that Bonnie wants me to call her. I think this is where

449

I'm supposed to do it, but Elam thinks it would be wrong to bypass resurrecting Makaidos for the third time just because I've been dreaming about Bonnie."

Patrick stroked his chin for a moment before answering. "Do you have any corroborating evidence?"

"You mean, something more than just the dream?" He shook his head. "Not really. Just that the phrase Bonnie sings in the dream is the same one that led me to suggest calling Dr. Conner from the garden."

"Ah, yes, and that worked out quite well. We needed a doctor far more urgently than we needed Makaidos that night."

"True, but we sure could use Makaidos now."

"Indeed." Patrick looked down at one of the garden's pregnant plants and used his shoe to push soil over an exposed root. "It seems that, absent corroborating evidence, you should heed Elam—"

"Billy," Sorentine called. "I must tell you something."

He looked back at the village. No flare yet. "Sure. What is it?"

"Listener's song. I know the tune."

"You know it?" Billy walked back to the edge of the garden where Listener was staring up at the dragon with wide eyes. "How could that be?"

"It is a lullaby we dragons sing to our smallest younglings. Before the transformation, I sang it to my unborn little one. She moved so much inside me, I thought she must have heard my voice."

"She?" Billy asked. "How did you know?"

"When the time gets close, we dragons sense the gender. Yet, I know not what happened to my little one when I was transformed. Her movement slowed greatly, so I sang nearly all day, hoping to wake her up, perhaps to regenerate her as I was regenerated. But I never learned why she was so quiet. The slayer killed me before she was born."

As Billy looked at her serious face, a tingle ran across his skin. Something strange was happening. The mysterious dragon and the even more mysterious girl couldn't possibly know the same tune. "How ..." Billy swallowed. "How does your song go?"

"It is not exactly the same as other dragons sing. I ..." She looked up as if searching for a word. "I invented the last part, because my youngling was yet unborn, so it is not as good as the rest."

"It'll be fine," Billy said. "Please sing it."

"Very well." Sorentine moved her head directly in front of Listener, and, looking into her eyes, sang in a low, yet feminine voice.

> When younglings play so hard all day,
> They need to rest in mother's care.
> Regain the light your play has spent;
> My bed of gems I now will share.

> So leave your eyes as open doors
> To gather truth, to gather light,
> For truth and light will call as one,
> "Rebuke the false and scatter night."

> And now I call to you in song;
> Regenerate within my womb.
> Above all gems you are to me,
> I call you from your hidden room.

451

Tears flowed down Listener's cheeks. Sniffing, she petted Sorentine's neck. "That's the exact tune, and some of the meanings are the same, too."

"Yes," Patrick said. "The theme of calling to rebirth is similar in both."

Billy let the lyrics sink in. *I call to you ... Above all gems ... Your hidden room ...* There was so much there! Each word seemed to reach into his heart and play its note from within. Furrowing his brow tightly, he turned to Patrick. "Which gem is the most valuable?"

Sir Patrick tilted his head. "A surprising query, William, but the answer would depend on a number of factors, such as color and clarity and how it is cut."

"Forget about cut." Billy stared hard at the ground. "What if it had perfect color and perfect clarity?"

"I suppose it would be a ruby. A flawless ruby usually fetches a higher price than a diamond of equal size and quality."

"A ruby?" Billy looked up at him. "Not a sapphire?"

"William, a sapphire is the same gem. They are both corundum. A red deposit is a ruby, and any other color is a sapphire. They have the same basic chemical composition, a type of aluminum oxide."

While Billy pondered the words, Patrick added, "It seems to me that we have discovered the reason for Listener's knowledge of the song."

"We have?" Billy looked up at him again.

"Indeed. My guess is that a certain unborn dragon was not completely transformed when her mother underwent her transformation. After the youngling died as the result of her mother's death, she resurrected here, much later, to be sure, but we haven't learned much about the timing of these events, so that should be no surprise. Since Listener was born with two companions, one of which gave her dragonlike scales, there seems to be only one explanation. Listener and the youngling are one and the same. The song is the binding tie that proves the connection. After hearing it in her mother's womb, Listener, who never forgets what she hears, remembers it to this day."

Listener covered her mouth with her hand. As more tears flowed, she reached up and touched Sorentine's cheek. "Mother?" she said meekly.

A large teardrop fell from the dragon's eye. "My little one?"

Listener rose to her tiptoes and wrapped her arms around the dragon's neck. "Mother!"

Sorentine wept. "Oh, my darling! At last we meet!"

As they nuzzled cheek to cheek, Listener spoke through her sobs. "Acacia said she thought my mother probably killed me before I was born. She wasn't really sure, and I always hoped she was wrong, and now I know you never stopped loving me. Never!"

Billy bit his lip. If he kept watching these two, he would start crying with them. Poor Listener had lost two mothers, first Sorentine and then Angel. Yes, Mantika was a fine surrogate mother, but this was different, a bond that lasted for centuries, tied together by a song that a tiny youngling never forgot.

Billy pulled Patrick away again. "You mentioned that we needed corroborating evidence." He nodded at Listener and the dragon. "Does it get any clearer?"

"If I am following your thinking, William, you are connecting the lyrics to our situation. Since Sapphira is linked to a sapphire, you are suggesting that we call her instead of Makaidos."

"Exactly. I was hoping I could call Bonnie, but I guess we'll have to wait for another time."

"I see." Patrick began stroking his chin again. "This is most extraordinary. I have to agree with your assessment."

Billy spread out his hands. "Elam is the warrior chief. He told me to follow wisdom, but is this enough proof to go against his wishes?"

"If he heard the evidence, he would likely acquiesce, but we have already lost so much time. Searching for him now with an army pressing in on us would cause too much of a delay, especially with Pegasus nearly at the crucial point in the sky."

"Then what do we do?"

Patrick raised a hand. "I will vouch for you. Since he long ago submitted to my authority as my servant, Markus, and has not

453

rescinded that duty, he will trust my judgment. I hereby call upon you to change the name in the song from Makaidos to Sapphira."

A flare arced across the sky, brightening the field. "The signal!" Billy withdrew Excalibur, lit up the beam, and took Listener's hand. "We have to hurry."

They ran into the garden, passed by the plump weed they had been protecting for Shiloh's sake, dodged the dozen or so other plants, and stopped in front of the one Elam had grown from a seed.

Billy touched the soil with the beam, careful to avoid the plants. The light crawled across the garden like flame on a dry prairie. The bones began to glow, as if burning within and emanating a chemical fire that oozed radiance. Soon, the garden came alive with sparkling white embers, the bones of Makaidos again providing energy to the soils of rebirth.

After putting Excalibur away, Billy laid a hand on Listener's head. "Sing it now, daughter of Sorentine. Sing it with all your heart."

Blinking away tears, Listener began the song, not bothering to look at the parchment.

> When phantoms knock on doors of light
> To open paths to worlds beyond,
> A friend replies, "Insert the key
> To leave the dark and greet the dawn.
>
> "The key is light, the words of truth;
> No lie can break the chains of death.
> A whispered word of love avails
> To bring new life, the spirit's breath."
>
> So now I sing a key for you,
> The phantom waiting at the door;
> We call for you, Sapphira who
> Will join us now in holy war.

As she rolled up the parchment and held it in her fist, the garden's glow ran up her legs and painted an aura around her body. She was the new Paili, another prophetic songstress in a petite shell.

Billy steeled his shaking legs. What would happen now? She had called for Sapphira, but leaving Bonnie out felt like a stab in the heart. Could they call for two at once? No one had said they couldn't. Bonnie's name didn't really fit the poem's meter, but did that matter? Resurrection couldn't hinge on singing perfectly placed syllables, could it?

Shaking his head, Billy glared at the shimmering soil. So many questions! And too few answers.

The ground shook. Just a few paces ahead, a bump formed between two rows. For a moment, it grew, like an expanding mole-hill. When it reached a foot tall, the soil began spilling away, revealing a head of hair, dirty, yet obviously white. Then, a face appeared, and two blue eyes blinked away the dirt.

455

CHAPTER

THE REUNION

S apphira!" Billy rushed forward, and taking her hand, helped her step out of the erupting garden.

Brushing dirt from her clothes, Sapphira looked around. "Where's Bonnie?"

"Bonnie? I thought she might have been with you."

Sapphira's eyes widened. "Didn't you call her?"

"Not yet. I wasn't sure how—"

She wrapped her arms around him and laid her head on his chest. "Billy," she cried out, "I feel your thundering heart. It is a drum that beats a call, a call for Bonnie. Can't you hear it? Can't you feel it?"

Billy lifted his arms and looked down at her soiled white hair. What a strange reaction! His heart racing, he stumbled through his words. "I ... I do feel something. I just don't know what to do about it. We thought you were the one we were supposed to call."

"I was the one." Sapphira released him and picked up one of the glowing bones. "Rebirth has its genesis in love. Makaidos demonstrated that love by dying for the sake of his daughters, and he left behind the power to bring others to life. Yes, the prophetic song is one way to call specific people back from the Valley of Souls." She swept her arm across the garden. "But look around you. It is love that calls these little ones to spring forth from the valley of dead souls. Just sing your own song of love and call Bonnie from the valley."

A shout sounded from the village. "Billy! The Vacants are attacking!"

Billy spotted Walter swinging a lantern at the edge of the village's bordering forest. "I'll be there in a minute."

"A minute!" Walter's voice spiked. "We need Excalibur now! Goliath was seen flying this way!"

Billy gritted his teeth. War would have to wait. He spun toward Sorentine. "Are you willing to go with Walter?"

"Willing?" Sparks flew from her snout. "I will fight with the best of the dragons!" She dipped her head to the ground next to Listener. "Mount, my precious one. I will take you to safety, and then I must go to battle."

Listener scrambled up her neck and settled on her back. New tears gleaming in her eyes, she nodded at Billy but said nothing. The potent mixture of emotional filling and catharsis had drained her of sound.

Sapphira took Billy's hand. "You must call her now before it's too late. I will pray for the words to leap from your heart."

"Okay." His heart still racing, he closed his eyes. Again, the song from his dream entered his mind, yet this time spoken in his own voice.

458

Call to me, and I will answer you;
Say my name, and my light will shine.
Draw me out, and I will rise again;
Take my hand, and I will be thine.

As he added the tune, he let his new thoughts fill in the words, and he sang them out.

Hear my call, and I will raise you up;
Heed my words, and look at my eyes.

He stretched out his arm, his hand open.

See my love, and know my words are true;
Bonnie Silver, I bid you rise.

The moment the last note died away, the ground shook again. Billy searched the soil for another rising bump, but the shadows cast by Pegasus overwhelmed Patrick's lantern. He reached for Excalibur, but just as his fingers touched the hilt, something slammed into his body and knocked him flat.

459

Billy looked up from the ground, his head throbbing. "What was that?"

Spreading out her arms, Sapphira shielded him with a ring of fire. "Stay back, foul dragon!"

A deep growl sounded, but it was too dark to see the source. "I am not here to trifle with boys and girls. Stand aside so that I may collect my prize."

Strong arms lifted Billy to his feet. "Get up, brave knight." The voice was soft and gentle, but not Sapphira's. "Don't let this lizard defeat you with mere words."

Billy tried to focus on his helper. "Bonnie?"

As a pair of wings spread out behind her, her beautiful smile shone in the moonlight. "I heard your call, and now I'm looking into your eyes. I see a man, not a boy, a man who can stand up to this scaly bag of hot air."

Her words pulsed through his body, hardening his muscles. He embraced her and whispered into her ear. "I'm glad to see you, but I have to take care of business right now."

She kissed him on the cheek. "Go get him, tiger!"

Flexing his biceps, he turned toward the intruder. Now able to see the dragon in the shadows, he called out, "Goliath! Leave it to a coward like you to wait for the dragon guard to fly away."

"I will wait no longer for my prize." Flames shot from Goliath's mouth and slammed into Sapphira. Her body bent backwards, and her hair and clothes streamed as if flapping in a strong gust of wind. The fire arced around her, missing Billy and Bonnie, but it splashed into three plants behind them.

"No!" Billy lunged for one and batted the flames away with his hand. "You coward!" While Patrick ran to tend to the other burning plants, Billy rose to his feet, withdrew Excalibur, and took three heavy steps toward Goliath. Sapphira stood at his side, the balls of fire in her hands swelling.

"What is this prize you want?" Billy growled as he summoned the beam.

460

"Merely a weed. I am sure you have seen it." Goliath reached down and wrapped his clawed hand around the supporting stem of one of the plants. "It is very different from this one, which I will incinerate if you do not put away that sword. I wager that I can kill its fruit before you can strike."

Billy scowled at him. He didn't have much choice. Goliath had already proven that he would kill these unborn babies without a thought.

He doused the beam. "Okay. What next?"

"That's a good boy." Goliath released the plant and stretched his neck to see around Billy. "There is my prize. Stand aside, and I will take it and be on my way."

Billy glanced at the weed without moving his head. Of course, he didn't care a whit about the plant itself, but if Goliath took it, what would happen to Shiloh? If Arramos created the life connection between them, did Goliath's appearance mean that its fruit was ripe and could be harvested safely?

"I can't let you uproot the plant," Billy said. "I don't want you touching it."

"I understand what you fear. Open its leaves, and bring the fruit to me, but if you do harm to it, I will destroy every plant in this garden."

Bonnie touched Billy's shoulder. "I'll do it. You and Sapphira can keep an eye on him."

Billy nodded toward the plant. "It's the ugly weed with a big pouch on top."

Glancing back at Goliath, Bonnie hurried toward the edge of the garden and knelt. "This one?"

Patrick set his lantern down next to her. "Yes. We have been watching it for four years."

While Billy and Sapphira eased closer to get a better look, Bonnie peeled back one of the leaves. A sac with a gauzelike, semi-transparent shell tipped into her hands. As she rose to her feet, she held it out for everyone to see.

Billy eyed the strange object, an egg the size of a large cantaloupe. The ovular sac began to glow. Inside, a man pressed his palms against the lining.

"It's too fuzzy to see his face," Bonnie said. "But it looks like he's trying to get out."

Goliath let out a low growl. "Bring it to me."

She looked at Billy. "Should I?"

He tightened his hands into fists. "I guess we don't have much choice."

Beating her wings, she floated over the other plants. With every second, the egg grew larger and brighter. By the time she set it down next to Goliath, it had already doubled in size.

The dragon scooped it up, and as he rose into the air, he grabbed the back of Bonnie's shirt with his clawed foot.

Bonnie screamed. As her outer shirt rode up to her armpits, she beat her wings and kicked wildly.

"Insurance," Goliath said with a low rumble.

461

Billy thrust Excalibur back into its sheath and sprinted along a row, chasing them. Goliath rose higher. Bonnie's feet dangled only six feet above the ground, but Billy couldn't catch up enough to reach her. And with the dragon's tail swinging back and forth, he had to duck to keep from getting swatted to the mud.

Finally, with a leap and a desperate stretch, he grabbed her shoe with one hand. As his fingers began slipping, he swung up with his other arm and latched onto her ankle.

A rip sounded. He looked up. Was that her shirt tearing? Another rip reached his ears. Suddenly, they dropped. Billy landed into a snowdrift, breaking his fall. Less than a second later, Bonnie landed softly next to him, her wings fanning the air.

Scattering the slush around him, Billy scrambled to his feet. "Sorry, but I have to leave you. There's a war to fight."

She glared up at the escaping dragon. "Get me a sword. I'm going with you."

"A sword?" He laid an arm on her shoulder. When his fingers touched bare skin, he pulled back. "I'm not sure you understand. This is life or death fighting and—"

"Just trust me, Billy." Bonnie pulled her torn shirt higher on her shoulder. "Sapphira and I have been training with an expert for four years."

He took in a deep breath. "Okay. I trust you. Ask Patrick to take you to the outfitters and meet me at the rampart."

"The rampart?"

He nodded at Sapphira and Patrick, who were now hustling toward them from the garden. "Patrick will show you."

As Billy turned to run, Bonnie took his hand and pulled him back. "Thank you for calling me."

Drawing closer, he took her hand into both of his. "I'm sorry. I called Sapphira first. There was this song—"

"Don't explain. We watched everything from the Valley of Souls. You did exactly what you had to do, and you *did* call me. I heard every word."

Her loving tone sent tremors through his body. "I hope Elam understands. I went against his wishes."

She looked at their clasped hands and smiled. "You did?"

"I was supposed to call Makaidos."

Her eyes snapped back to him. "And if you had called him, he would have died."

"Died?" He squinted at her. "How? Why?"

"Just trust me." She pulled his hands close and pressed them against her cheek. "Now get going. I'm looking forward to fighting alongside you."

Billy ran toward the village with her face and shining eyes still in his mind. In spite of the warming temperature, a chill ran from his toes to his head. *Bonnie's alive! And she's here in Second Eden!*

With renewed strength, he sprinted down a village street, now crowded with people as they made ready for their defense. Women and children rushed toward the western side carrying towels and basins. Ashley and Dr. Conner marched together, Ashley holding a basket of medical supplies with both arms and Dr. Conner lugging a cot under each arm.

When Billy reached the path to the northeast, he ran past the border of the village and bolted up the rampart's steps, nearly colliding with Walter and Elam. "Sorry I'm late," Billy said, breathless.

Elam looked through the spyglass toward the northeast but said nothing. Blood on his uniform and a deep scratch across his chin proved that he had just come from the battle.

Walter whispered, "Did you resurrect Makaidos?"

"No. It's a long story, but—"

"Save it. We're here because the Vacants on the northern front seem to be trying to draw us away, so Elam wanted to check out the path to Adam's Marsh."

"A diversion?"

"That's what we're guessing. Maybe you should take Excalibur to the northern front and show those Vacants a little diversion of your own. Valiant's troops and the dragons are handling it, but if you could sweep through the Vacants with that roasting beam, the battle would be over in a heartbeat."

Still looking through the spyglass, Elam raised his hand. "No. Wait."

Walter leaned on the parapet and peered into the dim landscape. "What do you see?"

Elam kept the spyglass trained, moving it slowly for several seconds before answering. "A dragon is flying away from us, and he seems to be heading for a dark mass in the distance." He handed the tube to Walter and pointed at a draconic silhouette sinking toward the ground beyond their trap area. "Do you recognize it?"

Walter guided the spyglass. "It's hard to tell, but I think it's red, so it's got to be—"

"Goliath," Billy said. "I just had a scrap with him out in the garden."

Elam narrowed his eyes. "Goliath was in the garden? What happened?"

"He wanted the fruit of the weed."

Elam pounded his fist on the parapet. "I knew it! They were growing something they wanted to use in the war."

"Whew!" Walter patted Billy on the back. "Good thing you were there. I guess you sent him off with his tail on fire, right?"

"Well, not exactly. You see—"

"Elam!"

The new voice was loud and joyful. All three turned. Rapid footsteps clopped up the stairs, and Candle burst into the moonlight's glow. "The Vacants retreated," he said, breathing heavily. "The battle on the northern front is over."

Walter interlocked wrists with Candle. "Great work! We have them on the run."

"I don't think so," Billy said.

Elam looked at him. "Why not?"

"It's the timing." Billy walked to the parapet and looked out at the field. "Ask yourself. If it was a diversion, why didn't Flint's troops attack from the northeast? They didn't even send the shadow people. With the dragons distracted, the conditions were ideal. My guess is that they lured the dragons to the north, so Goliath thought it would be safe to get the plant's fruit. They didn't know we have Sorentine now."

"So what happened out there?" Walter asked. "You're dancing around the bottom line."

"Well, it's a long story." Billy tapped his knuckles on the parapet's stone top. "You see, we never called for Makaidos."

"You decided it wasn't the proper night?" Elam asked.

Billy shook his head. "No. It's the night after eclipse. You see, there's this song Sorentine used to sing—"

"Hello, Elam. Hello, Walter."

Every head turned toward the voice. Bonnie climbed the stairs, slowly and with deliberate footfalls. Dressed in the village's orange and red uniform, a sword at her hip, and her hair tied back, she halted at the top and took a soldier's stance. "What are my orders?"

Billy tried to smile, but she looked so radiant he could barely keep his jaw from dropping open. "Elam," he said, working hard not to squeak, "I'd like for you to meet Bonnie Silver."

"It's a pleasure, my lady." Elam offered a formal bow. "I'm glad to finally meet you."

Bonnie bowed in return. "The pleasure is mine, son of Shem, grandson of Noah. It is truly an honor to serve under your command." She then leaned close to Billy and whispered, "Have you told him about you-know-who yet?"

Billy shook his head. Bonnie's impish grin indicated that she wanted to have some fun with Elam. He wasn't about to spoil it.

"You've learned a lot about me." Elam brushed his hand across the dragon on his tunic. "You're dressed as a warrior. Do you intend to fight?"

With a lightning-fast move, she withdrew her sword and set the tip near Elam's chin. Flashing a wide grin, she said, "Only in your service, my liege."

465

Elam touched the end with his finger. "I get your point."

She slid the sword back to its scabbard. "Since my point is well taken, may I ask the warrior chief if the current crisis is under control?"

"It seems to be. For the moment, at least."

"Then come with me." She reached for Elam's hand. "An old woman has begged me to request an audience with you on her behalf."

Elam allowed her to lead him down the stairs. "An old woman? A lot of the women here are well over a hundred, but no one looks that old."

Nudging Walter, Billy whispered. "Come on. This is going to be very cool."

As they followed, Candle trailing the group, Walter laid his arm around Billy's shoulders. "You're as cool as a snowball. You haven't seen Bonnie in four years, but you're acting like she's one of the guys."

"Hey, Mr. Engaged Man, I have no idea what to do. Should I just go ahead and ask her to marry me?"

Walter pointed at him. "Perfect. But don't build a snowman. It's not cold enough, and, besides, you should be original."

"Thanks for the advice. But just thinking about asking her to marry me makes my knees knock together."

"Good. It ought to." Walter gave him a light punch on the arm but said nothing more.

Still holding Elam's hand, Bonnie led him southwest down the street leading toward the village's central circle. To the left, a fountain gushed sparkling water several feet into the air. Normally they kept the pressure low at night by blocking the feeding stream, and in the daytime the children would romp in its spray. But ever since the stream froze, they had to chop the ice to get any flow at all. Apparently the rising temperatures had thawed the blockage, and no one had bothered to dam it up.

Bonnie pulled Elam onto the dead grass and closer to the fountain. "This is the place," she said.

When she released his hand, he fidgeted and pressed his fingers together, more like a little boy than a centuries-old warrior. "So . . ." He cleared his throat to arrest his high pitch. "Where is this old woman?"

Smiling, Bonnie just stepped away and pointed at the fountain.

Veiled by the spray, Sapphira stood with her hands folded over the hilt of a sword, the tip resting on the ground. Dressed in the village's orange and red, her hair as white as hailstones, and her face aglow in a fiery corona, she looked like a radiant angel.

She stepped through the mist and stopped three paces from Elam, her hair and cheeks sprinkled with tiny droplets that glittered in the moonlight. A tear dripping from one eye, she lifted a hand and wiggled her fingers.

Elam's jaw dropped. His arms trembled. He took one step toward her, but his other foot seemed anchored to the ground. He, too, wiggled his fingers, his voice barely more than a whisper. "Sapphira."

467

She walked another step and stopped again. Her eyes followed a moth as it flitted across the space between them. "It's good to see you again," she said with an air of nonchalance. "It's been a very long time."

"A long time," he repeated. He seemed distant, as if lost in a dream.

Billy winked at Bonnie. She covered a wide grin with her hand.

"So, I was wondering ..." A coy smile spread across Sapphira's face as she stepped within reach. "I asked for this audience, because I was wondering if there's a place in your army for a five-thousand-year-old woman."

Elam mouthed the words, "five thousand," but no sound came out. His chest heaved through rapid breaths. Finally, he leaped toward her, gathered her into his arms, and twirled. Her sword clattered to the grass, and her petite legs, covered by the uniform's green trousers, swung out as she and Elam laughed and cried.

Stopping the wild ride, he laid a hand behind her silvery hair and pressed her cheek close to his chest. "Oh, my dearest Sapphira, how I have longed for this day!" As he caressed her hair with his cheek, sobs shook his entire body.

Sapphira wept with him. As her own body trembled, she stroked his arm. "Elam, before we go out to battle, I have something to tell you."

He pushed her gently away and lowered himself to one knee. "Please tell me, and then I have a question to ask you."

"Elam," she said softly as she caressed his cheek. "Elam, I lo—"

"Warrior chief!" Valiant ran toward them from the direction of the rampart. "The enemy is advancing from the northeast. We must activate the trap immediately."

468

Elam raised his hand. "No! I have waited for this moment for thousands of years, and I will not delay it again. I'm not moving until my Sapphira has said what she must say."

Walter gave the spyglass to Billy. "Take your time, Elam. Candle and I will make sure the trap's ready to go."

Valiant bowed his head, a grave expression on his face. "I will see you on the battlefield." Then with a twinkle in his eye, he added, "Or perhaps floating above the battlefield."

When Walter, Candle, and Valiant departed, their footsteps faded in the distance. Only the gentle sound of spraying water filled the nighttime air.

Elam, still resting on one knee, looked into Sapphira's eyes. "Now, what did you want to tell me?"

Still trembling, she twirled a lock of his hair around her finger. "Thousands of years ago I threw morsels of food on the floor for a little mouse I named Qatan. The food disappeared, so I knew he had to be around somewhere. Little did I know that a lost and lonely boy was pushing his hand through that mouse hole and gathering the tidbits just to keep from starving. When I learned about that boy, I fed him stew from my own hand, and he licked my fingers clean."

She lifted a hand and wiggled her fingers again. Elam did the same. Then, they joined their hands together and intertwined their fingers. "Now the boy has become a man, a general, a warrior chief, and he has a war to wage, a battle to win, so I will curtail my speech and say only one more thing."

As she took a deep breath, she met his gaze. A single tear coursed down her cheek and dangled from her chin. "Elam ..." Her lips quivered as she steadied her voice. "Elam, I love you."

Elam caught the tear on his finger and touched a tear on his own face, blending them into one. He suspended the droplet from his finger and spoke in a near whisper. "Sapphira, I love you more than my words could ever say, yet I will attempt to put my thoughts into a simple pledge. As our tears are bound together as one, so our lives will become one, impossible to differentiate and impossible to separate." He pulled their clasped hands close to his lips. "What I'm saying is ... will you marry me?"

469

Sapphira's tears flowed. As tiny firelets ran across her snowy hair, she nodded. "Yes, Elam. Yes, I will marry you."

He reached into his pocket and pulled out a ring. "This belonged to Makaidos. It's the only one I have, so I hope it will serve this purpose."

She extended her finger and let him slide it on. As he straightened, she lifted her hand and gazed at the rubellite, now as white as a pearl. "I will wear the ring of my great friend, the king of dragons, with gladness."

He pulled her close, and the two wept together again.

Billy felt Bonnie's hand slide into his. As he gripped it, he shifted his gaze absently toward the rampart. What did her touch mean? Did she want him to propose, too? Yes, they were old enough now, and the prophecy was still intact, but was it the right time?

He turned toward her. She was already looking at him, her eyes probing. He studied her expression, searching for a clue. After clearing his throat, he whispered, "We have some things to talk about, too."

"I know." She gave him a tender smile. "We have a war to win. Let's talk when everything settles down."

"That sounds good to me."

Elam touched Billy's shoulder. "Shall we go?"

Billy checked Excalibur's position at his hip. "I'm ready."

"I'm ready, too," Bonnie said, drawing her sword again.

"As am I." Sapphira picked up her sword from the ground, slid it into a hip scabbard, and tossed back her fiery hair with a shake of her head. "I'm going with my warrior chief."

The foursome marched toward the northeast field. Billy walked between Bonnie and Sapphira, turning his head from side to side to speak to both. "We'll have to maintain silence in a few seconds, so I'd better tell you a few things. Walter, Sir Barlow, and Valiant will be out in a field waiting for the shadow people to crawl out over some netting we spread on the ground. Our trio will be stationed at intervals. Valiant will be the farthest out, Walter next, and Barlow the closest to the village. When the shadow people attack each of our warriors, we'll know how far along the net they've come. You see, these creatures are flat like shadows, and they creep along the ground, but they can reach up and drag you down. When they swarm, they can smother you in a hurry."

"So, basically," Bonnie said, "our warriors are acting as bait."

"Exactly. But they'll be bait that fights back."

"Now that's courage," Sapphira said. "Just waiting for the enemy to jump on you."

Billy nodded. "It's courage, but it's also strategy. We want to make sure we trap as many in the net as we can. If we can get some to mass at each point, we'll probably get most of them when we heat up the net."

"Will it hurt our warriors?" Bonnie asked.

"A few burns, maybe, but not enough to leave scars. We tested it on some volunteers, and Ashley declared it safe."

"Ashley?" Bonnie's eyes lit up. "Where is she?"

"At the hospital with your father, getting ready for casualties." Bonnie grabbed his arm. "So my father *is* here!"

"I should've told you earlier, but, yeah, he's here. I'll tell you more later. It's time to be quiet."

Smiling broadly, Bonnie gave Billy's arm a hearty shake. Billy smiled back at her. As they left the village lights, her face grew dim, but the glow in her eyes remained. Billy bathed in that glow. Seeing her happy was like being in heaven.

When they reached a grassy field on the northeast side of the village, Billy crouched in the darkness and pulled Bonnie down with him. He glanced at Sapphira. She and Elam had stooped as well.

471

As Billy's eyes adjusted to the moonlit area, more bodies took shape. Dozens of crouching villagers lined up to his left and right, swords and shields ready. Dikaios and Ember stood behind a bushy evergreen. Ember was saddled, but Dikaios had chosen against taking one. His long mane made it easy for a rider to hang on. Although Ember's sorrel coat helped her blend in with the shadows, Dikaios's white body made him stand out, forcing him to stay in his hiding place, at least for now.

Sir Barlow stood at his position on the net about twenty paces in front of the rest of the villagers. Barely visible another twenty paces beyond him, Walter walked slowly from side to side. If not for his movement, he would have been invisible in the darkness.

Billy tried to see past Walter. Pegasus provided enough light to reveal dim outlines, but any one of several phantom shadows could have been Valiant. Standing completely still was his way—a tower of strength, immovable.

Valiant's companion stayed dark. Either the villagers knew to keep their crystals hidden in their hair, or the companions knew not to flash in these dangerous situations. Either way, no blinking lights would betray their presence.

As Billy waited, only his own heartbeat and Bonnie's gentle breathing interrupted the deathly silence. Somewhere out there, a crawling horde of vicious life stealers drew close. Unable to resist the scent of a village victim, they would reach out and attack Valiant, maybe before he could detect their approach.

Still, the miserable wretches would likely squeal, first for joy when they found a victim, and again in agony when Valiant sliced their skinny black arms and legs from their bodies. That would signal the beginning of the battle.

Walter stopped pacing. Now he, too, blended into the darkness. Bonnie held her breath. Even Billy's heart seemed to stop beating. In the growing warmth, the silence felt heavy, oppressive.

A squeal sounded, high-pitched and feverish. Another echoed, and then a third. In the distance, a tall shadow swung an object. More squeals erupted, some fearful and truncated. Valiant, the greatest swordsman among the villagers, was now at work. In just a few seconds, Walter would try to bait them with—

"Hey, you low-life vermin!" Walter shouted. "Come over here and pick on someone closer to your own stunted size!"

Billy whispered to Bonnie. "They should be distracted enough now. It's time to inch closer, but I'm the only one who's supposed to draw his sword. It would be too noisy for everyone to do it."

He rose to his feet and slowly withdrew Excalibur, careful to soften the sound. As he and every villager in their line crept toward the net, Walter shouted again, swinging his sword. "Eat steel!"

Now within a few feet of the net, Billy could see the battle clearly. Valiant fought the dark beasts as he staggered toward the village. With so many shadow people hanging on, it looked like he wore a cape of living blackness.

472

Sir Barlow called out, "Walter, are you injured?"

Walter trudged toward him. He dragged a host of shadows hanging on to his legs. They bit and clawed as he chopped at them with his sword. "I'm fine. I think I picked up a few hitchhikers. I wish—"

He dropped to his knees. Shadow people swarmed over his body. Their squeals sounded like mice possessed by ecstatic demons. Barlow rushed toward him, but the energized monsters overwhelmed them both in a tsunami of darkness.

473

9

THE SMALLEST ENEMY

Valiant struggled toward Walter and Barlow, but with the weight of hundreds of shadow people dragging him back, he would never make it in time to help.

"Get ready," Billy said. He summoned Excalibur's beam and let it soar into the sky. When Cliffside saw the signal, he was supposed to turn on the magneto and fry those fiends. It was time to spring the trap.

The beam's glow lit up the faces around him, including those of Candle and Windor. Wearing anxious expressions, they waited while the battle ahead of them raged on without the expected sounds and smells of cooking shadows. All three warriors faltered under wave after wave of shadow people.

Elam jumped on Dikaios and drew his sword. "I'm going in!"

As Dikaios galloped toward the melee, Sapphira charged after him, her body ablaze. Several other villagers ran to join them, one riding Ember.

Bonnie looked at Billy. "Are we going?"

"Come with me!" Dimming Excalibur to a glow, Billy sprinted toward a corner of the net where the primary node was anchored. Kneeling, he searched through the grass with one hand while reaching Excalibur toward Bonnie. "Hold the sword."

The sword brightened in her grip. Billy glanced at it while continuing his search. "Here it is." He fished the net from the slush-covered grass and held it up. "Now touch the blade to this."

She obeyed. When the metal edge made contact with the net, sparks flew up. Billy dropped it and shook his hand. "Ouch!"

"What's supposed to happen?" Bonnie asked.

"I'm trying to heat up the grid." Now sweating, he nodded at the sword. "Do you know how to summon the beam?"

"I think so. I've done it before." Bonnie closed her eyes. As she concentrated, the blade brightened further. Suddenly, the laser shot out from the tip and burrowed into the ground, raising more sparks and a foul odor. The filament turned orange, then crimson, and the color spread out along the netting, disappearing under the snow and reappearing again as it moved across clear ground.

Holding his breath, Billy watched the battle scene. Thousands of shadow creatures mobbed the villagers. It seemed that someone had dumped a legion of tar-covered demons over their army. The humans fought back—hacking, wrestling, and prying strangling fingers away from throats. They staggered about, desperately trying to keep their balance. Falling into the sea of demons would be a fatal mistake. Companions flashed like strobes, then winked out one by one.

Atop his warrior horse, Elam bent over and sliced at the attackers, while Dikaios stomped with his powerful legs, but Ember and her rider were nowhere in sight. A bright column floated from place to place, Sapphira, her body a flaming fountain. Wherever she went, the blackness fizzled, but she was so small, and their army was so massive. She was like a matchstick in a dark canyon.

When the heat reached the battleground, the batlike squeals changed from joy to terror. Sizzles and pops flew about everywhere, and steam shot up from bubbling black pools.

Billy shouted, "Everyone drop down and roll."

Most heeded Billy's call and pressed the dark attackers against the pulsing red matrix. More squeals erupted. Plumes of steam shot into the air. Two villagers continued staggering, and with their heads covered with black hoods of clawing vermin, they probably never heard Billy's shout.

"Keep the beam going." Billy leaped up and ran toward the battle. When he reached a standing villager, Billy pushed him to the ground. Then, after tiptoeing around several rolling masses of black, he grabbed the second warrior and did the same.

Walking from body to body, he tore away shadow people and stomped them against the heated net. With each uncovering, a village soldier heaved a breath of air and then jumped up to help in the rescue effort. Three of the villagers had to search the blackness and pry their companions from rigid black fingers, but every flashing little egg finally broke free.

As the pungent air grew thick with the stench of boiling shadow people, Billy worked even faster. The lack of oxygen would soon take its toll on their strength. They had to finish up and get out.

Near one corner, Ember walked backwards, dragging a villager by the collar. Now dismounted, Elam ripped a shadow person from Ember's legs while Dikaios stomped another one hanging on to the villager.

Billy tore away another squirming black shroud, revealing Walter. Grasping his friend's wrist, Billy heaved him to his feet.

"Thanks, buddy." Grimacing, Walter peeled a severed hand that had been plastered on his cheek. "I have a good name for these critters. Skunk tape. Sticky and smelly."

"Can't argue with that." Billy nodded toward the village. "Let's get everyone back. I want to sweep the whole net clean with Excalibur."

477

"I see Elam. I'll ask him to give the order." Walter ran into a rising column of steam and out of sight.

Billy hustled back to Bonnie and reached for Excalibur. "Great job. Time to clean up the mess."

Bonnie turned off the beam and set the hilt in his hand. Her face downturned, she spoke in a sad tone. "I guess if I'm going to fight alongside you, I'd better get used to killing the enemy."

He gazed at her sorrow-filled stance. She was right. A warrior had to be ready to use deadly force against an evil army, and when their numbers overwhelmed those of the innocent, everyone had to take up arms.

After giving her an encouraging clasp on her shoulder, he turned away and summoned the beam again, training it on the net at a forty-five degree angle. When he drew near the bubbling mess, he crouched and swept the beam across the matrix. Wherever the radiance touched, the black pools disappeared in a dazzling explosion of purple sparks.

Some of the closer eruptions sent arcing embers over his body that stung if they happened to land on exposed skin. As he breathed in the fumes, his lungs tried to repel the noxious gas. He coughed and spat, but the residue left a film on his tongue and the back of his throat.

Underneath the vanishing blackness, the net appeared, now fading from red to orange. As the beam moved from one part of the ground to another, it seemed to paint the dark canvas with orange paint until no smudge of black remained. Fortunately, the network of tubing beneath the net would likely be unaffected. Ashley had constructed the second-stage trap out of various plastic and rubber pieces she had found on the airplane, including a box of drinking straws and dozens of feet of wire insulation.

When the final spot disappeared, Billy straightened and let Excalibur fade. A breeze cooled his damp face and brushed away

478

the remaining fog of shadow remnants. His legs shaky, he jogged back to where he and the other villagers had waited for the attack. With Pegasus now high in the sky, the villagers were easy to see, at least twenty standing at the edge of the field, touching each other as they examined their wounds.

Walter greeted him with a hearty pat on the back. "That's what I call cleaning up!"

"I guess so," Billy said as he slid Excalibur back into its scabbard, "but I feel like I need to scrub with lye soap."

"Tell me about it." Walter touched a raw spot on his forehead. "But not lye. Most of us already look like we had a losing battle with a flame thrower."

Elam and Sapphira stepped out of a shadow. "What happened to the plan?" Elam asked.

"No idea." Billy looked toward the southeast where the magneto station lay. "Maybe there's a break in the circuit between here and the magneto."

479

"Or something's up with Cliffside." Walter drew his sword and began jogging southward. "I'll check on him."

Billy looked out over the field toward Adam's Marsh. In the distance, a single torch drifted away, small and fading, like a lit match dwindling as it burned down to the nub.

"A scout running back to tell the news," Elam said. "Soon Flint will know that his first wave failed."

"Does that mean he won't attack with the rest of his troops tonight?" Billy asked.

Elam tilted his head upward as if trying to get a better view. A crisscross pattern of thin lines marred his cheek. "That's my guess. We'll station fresh guards, but if our theories are right, the Nephilim will do much better in the daytime, and the warmer season will help them a lot."

"It'll help our dragons, too," Billy said.

"And theirs as well."

Sapphira touched Elam's arm. "I'm concerned about Walter going to the magneto by himself. We should give him support."

"You're right. There might be trouble." Drawing his sword with a sagging arm, Elam waved for everyone to head back to the village. "Sapphira and I will ride the horses to the magneto. The rest of you report to the hospital for some healing salve."

Billy weaved through the crowd. He found Bonnie kneeling next to Valiant and Candle. Both sat leaning against a fallen log, their legs straight out with their trousers rolled up past their knees. Sir Barlow sat on the end of the log. As he pulled black goo from his mustache, he frowned. "Back on Earth, the Caitiffs' sticky blood dissolved after we skewered them. I doubt that we will have the same benefit with these creatures."

As the clops of the two horses passed by, Bonnie touched Candle's leg near a long burn. "Will you be able to walk?" she asked.

Sweat glistened on his handsome dark face. "I think so. I just need to rest. I'm not used to the warmth."

Billy reached for Valiant's hand. "Need a lift?"

"I gladly accept." Valiant wrapped his hand around Billy's wrist and pulled himself up. When he gained his balance, he rubbed a finger across a mark on his chin that looked more like a bite than a burn. "I am grateful for your quick thinking, Billy. Those creatures were more ferocious than I realized."

Looking into Valiant's noble face, Billy kept their wrists locked. Watching his courage had sent a charge of bravery through his own muscles. "Good job, my friend," Billy said. "You're a true hero."

After Valiant and Barlow began a stiff-legged march toward the village, Billy and Bonnie supported Candle from each side and helped him limp. They took their time, chatting with him as they shuffled through the damp grass. There was no hurry. He wasn't badly hurt, and listening to him recount his battles with the shadow people gave Billy another boost. This teenaged warrior had a heart the size of a mountain.

As soon as they set foot on the street leading to the center, Pearl and Mantika ran toward them with a stretcher. They set it down and helped Candle lower himself to it.

"Such a warrior," Pearl said as she mopped his brow with a soft cloth. "You were brave and strong for us. Now we will serve you with our healing skills."

Mantika brushed her hand through his mud-caked dreadlocks but said nothing. Even after four years in the village, she still maintained her habit of speaking only when necessary. Yet, her eyes spoke volumes. She loved her adopted son, and her pride in his courage poured forth.

As they rushed Candle toward the hospital, Billy looked around. Several pairs of women hauled other wounded warriors in the same direction. Obviously, Ashley had stationed a battery of stretchers and orderlies at the edge of the village, ready to tend to the wounded.

Billy shuffled to the village's central circle and plopped down on a bench. He leaned forward and rested his arms on his knees. It was dimmer here than on the streets that fed the circle, and it felt good to rest in the shadows, out of the limelight, far from the bustle.

Sitting down next to him, Bonnie touched his arm. "How did you know Excalibur would do that?"

Billy looked at her through the shadows. When his eyes adjusted, he tried to read her expression. She seemed tired, yet charged up by the excitement. "Something that happened a few years back. I'm not sure if I told you about it or not. When I was staying at that old mansion in England, one of the New Table goons attacked me. He was wearing a black cloak that was covered with metallic mesh. When I hit him with Excalibur's beam, it didn't hurt him at all. The mesh just heated up, and it protected him from being disintegrated. Prof looked at the cloak later and said it was coated with iron oxide, a fancy term for rust. I thought if Excalibur did that then, it might do it again."

481

"Good thinking."

They paused, looking at each other in silence. Billy pondered her new expression, meditative, uncertain. For many other people, this would be an awkward moment, but a break in conversation never bothered Bonnie. She often searched for the best words, always willing to risk discomfort in her quest for eloquence, and those who had a chance to listen to her were rewarded for their patience.

As he waited, a woman ran toward them from the direction of the hospital and passed by without glancing their way. Stripped to jeans and a T-shirt, she hurried down the road toward the birthing garden, her slender and muscular form now recognizable.

"Was that Ashley?" Bonnie asked.

"Yep. She was in a big hurry. I guess we'll find out why soon enough."

"I'm sure we will." Bonnie touched the string of beads around Billy's neck. "Did you make that? It looks exactly like mine."

"I found it in the mines. Acacia and I went there looking for you, but the magma chasm had filled with water, so we had to give up." He lifted the necklace and then let it fall back to his skin. "We were worried that you and Sapphira had drowned, but I've been wearing it ever since, because . . ." He looked down for a moment before regaining eye contact. "Well, because I believe in the prophecy."

Bonnie took his hand into hers. "Before we go to the hospital to see my father, I have something to tell you."

Billy studied her expression again. She looked so serious, so grave. Swallowing, he nodded. "Okay. I think I'm ready."

She averted her gaze, apparently focusing on a woman helping one of the wounded soldiers walk past. "I spent over four years in the Valley of Souls training to help Second Eden on the battlefield. And I did a lot of thinking." She looked back at him. "About us."

The lump in Billy's throat grew, this time more painful. "Go on."

"Someone pointed out to me that the prophecy wasn't exactly clear. It might not mean that you and I are supposed to get married."

The lump's pain increased. A tear welled. He fought against the emotions, but they were winning, breaking through to the surface. And although a million words raced through his mind, he swallowed them down. It was better to let her finish speaking her mind.

As she continued, she kneaded his hand with her thumb, and her voice rose to a plaintive pitch. "There are other children of doubt, Billy. There are other virgin brides. Maybe it wasn't talking about you and me. You know, Elam and Sapphira fit the poem perfectly. And Makaidos might be the dragon shorn that lives again."

She paused. Now her eyes searched for a response. It was time for him to say something. But what? His emotions were twisting into a knot. After years of believing he was destined to marry the most wonderful girl in the world, she seemed to be pulling back. She was drifting away. He was losing her.

483

He breathed a silent prayer. How could he put his feelings into words? Just be quiet? Just ask a question and hope for a clue?

Clearing his throat and hoping to keep his voice steady, he said, "So does that mean you don't want to marry me?" He cringed. Was that too bold?

Her face displayed half amusement and half anguish. "No, no. That's not it at all. I just want to know that I don't *have* to marry you. I want us both to be sure that we *want* to. If you love me, I want you to pursue my heart with your courage, your kindness, and your godly manner. And I want to freely give my heart to you in love, not by compulsion because of a prophecy that seems to chain us together without a choice."

As she continued, tears streamed down both cheeks. "Ever since someone labeled me as the prophetic virgin bride, I was okay with it, because you're such a great guy, but it felt like an arranged marriage. We didn't have any choice. Then, when I heard that the prophecy might not be for us, I felt free. I didn't have to marry you if I didn't want to."

She caressed his cheek, her voice shaking. "But that's a good thing, Billy. If we really do get married, neither one of us will ever wonder about being bound by someone else's words, a predestined edict that denies our free will and forces us to obey its irresistible decree. Instead we can come together by a choice to love that is free and resistible, because if we aren't able to choose to walk away from each other, then our coming together wouldn't be because of love at all, would it?"

As she drew back her hand, a torrent of conflicting emotions flooded his mind. She was so right. Being bound like that wouldn't be love. Freedom to choose a life partner was the basis of love in the first place. Being dragged by fiat into a relationship would be nothing more than bondage. Still, not knowing for sure that he would forever be with this amazing girl nearly tore him apart. Finally, he squeezed out a reply. "I … I think you're right. But it's scary. It was kind of …" He paused. The words had to be just right. "It was comfortable, I guess, knowing that you would be in my future. I didn't have to guess what was going to happen."

Her fists clenched in her lap. "But I don't *want* you to be comfortable. I want you to win my heart. I want you to fight for me, sweat for me, bleed for me. I want you to know that you had to pay a valuable price for me, and that I am a treasure in your mind, not a trophy that was handed to you because of a divine proclamation."

Billy looked into her fiery eyes. She had been bold, confident, and true. Again she was right, and he couldn't say a word.

She laid her palms on her chest, covering the sunburst on her uniform. Then, slowly, ever so slowly, she extended her arms, her palms up. "Here is my heart, Billy. It's yours if you want it. But

484

you have to buy it. And since it's the most valuable possession I have, it will be very expensive."

He glanced between her palms and her pleading eyes. "How much will it cost me?"

With a quivering smile, she wept through her words. "Everything. It will cost you your life, your devotion, your commitment to love me for the rest of your life till death do us part." Sniffing back a sob, she added, "But don't answer now. I don't want words. Show me. Show me that you'll pay the price for my heart, and I'll show you that it's worth every drop of sweat and blood you spend."

Billy cupped his hand over her palms, making a covering for her "heart." Firming his jaw, he pushed every ounce of energy he had into his voice, giving it strength, yet a sense of calmness, like a lighthouse in the midst of a storm. "Watch me, Bonnie. We have battles ahead. We have enemies to conquer. And we have women and children to protect from some of the greatest evils imaginable. But I will not neglect this mission. I will show you how much you mean to me, how precious your heart is to mine. And when you see how much I'm willing to pay, then you can decide if it's enough to buy what is priceless."

A new voice broke in. "Billy!"

Her face now striped by tears, Bonnie turned. "That sounded like Ashley."

Billy stood up and looked around. "Ashley! Over here!"

Ashley ran toward them on the southeast road, breathless. "Oh, thank God I found you."

When she arrived, Billy grasped her forearms. Her face was red and glistening with sweat. "What is it?"

"It's Walter." She held a hand against her chest and swallowed. "He was captured by Flint's army. Elam and Sapphira tried to help, but they had a Naphil and a dragon. They barely escaped and came back here for reinforcements."

485

"An ambush?"

Still trying to catch her breath, Ashley nodded. "They killed Cliffside. That's why our net trap didn't work. Then they waited for someone to check on him."

"That's terrible!" Bonnie said. "The cowards!"

Ashley gasped. "Bonnie!"

Bonnie pulled her into an embrace. "I'm so glad to see you again."

Ashley began sobbing. "Me too, Bonnie ... but it's so terrible. ... Did Billy tell you?"

Bonnie pulled away. "Tell me what?"

"Walter." Her weeping nearly overwhelmed her words. "Walter is my fiancé now."

"Your fiancé!" Bonnie pulled her close again. "Oh, Ashley, we'll find him. We'll get him back."

While they held their embrace, Billy pelted Ashley with questions. "Which dragon was it? Did Elam and Sapphira see which way they went? Did either of them get hurt?"

"They're fine." Ashley pushed back from Bonnie, sniffing. "While Elam battled the Naphil, Sapphira rode Ember, trying to follow the dragon when he flew away with Walter, but she couldn't keep up. I don't know which dragon it was. Maybe you should ask Elam. He's with your father and my mother. They're planning a rescue."

Billy grabbed Excalibur's hilt. Redness blinded his vision. He imagined Walter and Elam battling those creeps while he, Billy, relaxed in the village. The thought made his blood boil. "Are they at the garden field or the launching field?"

"The birthing garden. I guess Sapphira and Elam cut straight through from the hospital, so you didn't see them."

"Let's go!" Billy jumped into a quick jog, drawing his sword as he hurried. Of course, holding it now wouldn't do any good. It just felt better to have something to strangle.

Bonnie caught up, half walking, half flying at his side. "Would they take Walter back to their … camp, I guess? I don't know where they came from."

"It's a marsh area, and yes, they would probably go there. They know the territory better than we do, and after four years, they might have all sorts of traps set up."

When they arrived at the field, they slowed to a walk. Most of the snow had melted, leaving wet grass, thin and sparse, in the midst of a quagmire. Although Billy's shoes slid at times, slowing him further, Bonnie hovered over the mud and kept him from falling.

Ahead, Elam, Valiant, and Sir Barlow huddled with Dikaios, Ember, and a group of dragons. Billy recognized Clefspeare, Thigocia, and Legossi. Two others blended into the darkness behind them. Sapphira stood a few paces to the side, her arms spread and her body ablaze to add more light to the moon's glow.

As Billy drew nearer, the conversation reached his ears.

"They have us in a bind," Elam said. "If we attempt a rescue, they will have the advantage. The marsh is dangerous enough in the daytime; more so at night. So we can't just march in, and any sign of a dragon or airplane will alert them to our presence."

487

Valiant gave him a solemn nod. "It seems as if they knew our plans. How else would they know to attack the magneto station?"

"An informer," Billy said as he drew into their huddle. "I think we can assume Semiramis has been lurking."

Elam looked at him. Billy offered a nod of surrender. The warrior chief had the right to say, "I told you so," but he didn't. He was too noble for pettiness.

"I am torn," Valiant said. "My heart burns to rescue Walter, but my brain is shouting that this is exactly what Flint wants. He knows that battles fought in his territory will give him an advantage, and he wishes to deplete our forces. We would bring back a single warrior at the cost of twenty. Flint will gladly make that trade."

Sir Barlow drew his sword and traced a line along the ground. "True, my good fellow, but there is a line we cannot cross. At what cost do we forsake a rescue and allow Walter to suffer alone? Our morals? Our dignity? Our character? We are willing to die to do what is right, and retreating from our purpose now is the very line we should not step past."

"Remember what happened to Shiloh," Billy said. "They won't hesitate to torture Walter."

Ashley joined them. With her arms wrapped around herself in spite of the warmth, she listened quietly, her unkempt hair draped over one eye.

A deep growl rumbled in Clefspeare's throat. "You are correct, son, but he is not a kidnapped hostage. He is a prisoner of war. At the risk of sounding callous, he knew this possibility existed. He is not a boy playing at war with a sharpened stick, and he is prepared to face whatever befalls him."

Billy tightened his grip on his sword, and a growl spiced his own voice. "I agree with Sir Barlow. We pledged to spill our blood for each other. What kind of soldiers are we?"

"Wise soldiers," Ashley said. "Reasonable soldiers."

Everyone looked at her. In spite of the tear tracks, her face seemed peaceful, serene. "Walter and I already talked about this. He's ready to die if he has to, and he wouldn't want anyone else dying to save him. If you try to rescue him, and you lose soldiers in the process, you'll put more people at risk, including women and children. Walter would rather die than let that happen."

Bonnie pushed Ashley's hair out of her eyes. "Would you object to a precision rescue attempt?"

A new tear followed a well-marked track. "A precision attempt?"

"One person, or maybe two. They couldn't walk in safely, but they could fly in."

"Goliath would sense one of us from far away," Clefspeare said. "He would meet us in the air before we had any chance to locate Walter, much less rescue him. I could match him in a head-to-head battle, but the element of surprise would be lost."

Bonnie gave her wings a quick snap. "I could fly in. He might not recognize me as a danger to him."

"Alone?" Billy shook his head hard. "No way."

"Why not?" She touched her sword. "I can fight, and I can fly away if I get outmatched."

Billy looked at her narrowed eyes. How could he protect her without offending her? "But you don't know the marsh, where Flint might keep a prisoner, or—"

"Or where the muskrats roam," Dikaios said.

Billy pointed at him. "Exactly. Elam says they have these huge rodents that are more like bears than our muskrats, and they nearly had him for dinner."

"It's true," Elam said. "I faced several. If I hadn't been lifted out by a dragon, they would have killed me."

"So," Billy continued, "at least you would need an escort."

Elam pointed at him. "But you don't know the marsh either. It's been closed off ever since you've been here."

"He doesn't," Dikaios said, "but I know it quite well. I have already participated in two escapes from there."

Elam stroked the horse's neck. "Are you saying you would be her escort?"

"I would be honored. And her flying ability would allow her to escape if capture or injury seems imminent. And remember, we have two allies somewhere in the marsh, Yereq and Roxil. Perhaps we will be aided in our rescue from within."

Billy chafed. He couldn't let Bonnie ride into the marsh without an armed escort, and he couldn't risk insulting her by suggesting that she wasn't capable of handling the rescue. And if he just let her go, she might think he didn't care about her safety. There was no easy answer. He had to buy time. "Give me a minute to think."

Everyone looked at him. They couldn't wait long. Walter was in trouble, so every second of delay might make rescue even more difficult. But how could he sort out the pros and cons under such pressure? Haste was always a poor general, but delay, based upon fear of doing the wrong thing, was even worse.

He looked at his father's fiery eyes. He seemed to think that rescue was foolhardy; better to risk losing one life than many. Mom would likely agree with Barlow; better to show how much we value a single life and trust that a rescue attempt would work. Seeing her in his mind's eye, now packing a pistol more often than not, he almost grinned. Even with her tender heart, she had become a warrior.

As he concentrated on the image, he focused on his mother's holster. Of course! She still had it, and she had mentioned keeping it with her to protect the hospital in case of attack.

Billy pushed a hand into his pocket and looked at Elam. "We have a weapon Flint won't expect—my mother's gun. She brought one clip, and it has only eight rounds. It's not much good for a war, but it would be perfect for a precision rescue effort, and after fending off the Caitiff back on Earth, I probably know how to use it better than anyone else here."

"You're probably right." Elam shifted his gaze upward, as if trying to remember something. "I had a revolver back when I worked in the shipyard, but I rarely used it."

Billy turned and gave Bonnie a courtly bow. "Fair lady, I do not mean in any way to minimize your capabilities, but, taking notice of your fair gender, I consider it my duty as a knight to offer my services as a pistol-packing flaming torch and as a bodyguard of your person."

Smiling, she bowed her head. "I accept your noble offer."

"I will let Marilyn know of our need for her weapon," Dikaios said. With a quick turn, he bolted toward the village.

Billy looked at Clefspeare. At the sound of "Marilyn," his brow rose for a moment but quickly settled. Their reunion had been delayed by preparations, a battle, and tending to the wounded. Would she now come to the garden field to see her husband? Or was the thought of him as a dragon again too much for her to bear? Maybe the delay had been intentional.

Sapphira let her energy dim to a white aura. With the moon casting its light over her body, she seemed to be a small moon herself. "If our rescue party is captured or killed, our only clue will be that they didn't return."

"If Flint expects a second rescue after a failed attempt," Barlow said, "he might assume that we have depleted our guard at the village. It would be a prime opportunity for an attack."

"Then we'll double our security here." Elam looked at the village. "If we have enough guards remaining."

Ashley raised her hand. "I can implant my tooth transmitter in one of them and stay in touch the entire time. We have plenty of helpers in the hospital and only minor burn cases, so I can go to the radio station and stay in contact with our rescue party."

491

"As long as you have a dragon guard," Elam said. "You'll need a danger detector. We don't want to lose you, too."

Ashley raised her eyebrows at Thigocia. "Mother?"

"Of course I will go with you," Thigocia said. "Anything to help my future son-in-law."

After a few minutes of discussion, including how they could bolster the guard, Dikaios returned with Marilyn's holster clenched in his teeth. He laid it in Billy's hand. "Marilyn sends her love, and she wishes to convey her appeals for a safe journey. She cannot come right now. Apparently several people have become ill, and she is helping Dr. Conner with …" He shook his mane and blew through his flapping lips. "I suppose the best words would be, 'cleaning up messy expulsions.'"

"This is very strange," Valiant said. "We have had no such sickness here before. I have heard of it among the marsh people, but these expulsions are new to us."

Billy turned to Ashley. "Biological warfare?"

As she nodded slowly, her voice turned somber. "Delivered by the shadow people. Maybe Flint implanted something in them."

"Could that be what was growing in the garden?" Elam asked. "Did that weed carry an infection?"

Bonnie shook her head. "A man was inside, not a virulent bug."

"A carrier," Ashley offered. "Maybe they raised up a man to bring the bug into the world."

"So ..." Billy raised a hand to his chin. "Maybe the shadow people weren't sent to slaughter us. They were sent to *be* slaughtered so they could deliver the infection and be disposed of."

"Semiramis again?" Elam asked.

"Who else?" Billy smacked his palm. "With her spying on us, they're always a step ahead. They knew about the magneto and the net trap, and now they'll probably be content to wait for the infection to take hold. They'll strike when we're at our weakest."

Ashley took on her rapid-fire voice of command. "Valiant, ask Dr. Conner if he saved any of the shadow people remains. We need to culture it. I already showed him how to use my microscope, so if the infecting agent is big enough, he might be able to spot it. We need to isolate the bug and see what we can do to counteract it. If it's fast-spreading, we can't delay for a second. We have to isolate everyone who came into direct contact with the shadow people, including those who took care of the wounded. Put them all in the hospital, and don't let anyone enter or leave without permission, including yourself. I'll be there soon to organize the quarantine and the effort to find a cure."

Without a word, Valiant ran toward the village. As he faded into the darkness, Thigocia touched Ashley with a wing. "What will you do about monitoring the rescue effort at the radio station?"

Ashley stared at her. She seemed lost, perplexed. "I ... I have to do both. I can't let them try the rescue without someone monitoring their progress."

"You have to help Dr. Conner," Elam said. "I'll man the station. Besides, you took care of the wounded. You're subject to quarantine."

"But so are you," Ashley countered. "We all are."

Billy pointed at himself. "Bonnie and I are leaving the village, so we won't infect anyone."

"And I'll be outside the village at the station," Elam said. "You need to be with Dr. Conner."

Looking at the ground, Ashley furrowed her brow. "It could be that the Second Edeners are the only susceptible ones, anyway. Since they haven't been exposed to diseases, they don't have as many immunities."

"Perfect," Billy said. "Then you can probably take care of them safely."

493

"And I have a portable receiver," she added. "I'll see if I can pick up your broadcasts while I work in the hospital. It'll help me keep my sanity ... what little I have left."

CHAPTER 10

BEHIND ENEMY LINES

B illy rode low on Dikaios. With Pegasus almost directly above them and Phoenix rising, ducking into the shade of the over-arching trees felt like a good idea. Although the silence gave no hint of any enemy observers, his danger sense told him otherwise. Something lurked close by, something unusual. It didn't feel like an evil presence; more like a natural danger, the foreboding of a storm. Could it be an animal? Maybe Vacants? Their bestial ways seemed more like instinct than premeditated acts of evil.

Bonnie leaned forward on Ember, her arms loosely wrapped around the mare's neck. With her wings folded in tightly, they appeared to be a backpack, though an occasional flutter at the tips ruined the impression.

The two horses stepped quietly through the last strip of forest between the village and the marsh. The trees here were healthier than in most forests in Second Eden. With evergreens dominating the population, only a few rotting logs lay across the ground.

The two moons made the landscape look like a jungle on a stormy evening. It was more like dusk than the middle of the night, barely dark enough to veil the horses' hoofprints in the mud. Fortunately, Billy's cloak covered most of Dikaios's shimmering white coat, and, as before, Ember's coloring blended in with the shadows and the mud below.

Dikaios stopped at the forest's edge and whispered. "The marsh begins in about two hundred human paces. There is only grass between here and there, so we will risk exposure until we reach the bulrushes. Now is the time to send our scout."

"Got it." Billy tapped his jaw. The transmitter vibrated with a barely perceptible hum, accentuating the pain from having the device jammed between his teeth. Ashley had told him he would get used to it, but that hadn't happened yet. Bonnie had offered to wear it, which made more sense. After all, she would be flying reconnaissance alone. But her molars were too close together, forcing them to go with Billy.

"Elam," Billy whispered. "Two hundred paces to the marsh. I'll leave this on for a while."

Elam's voice buzzed. "I'll be listening."

Billy checked the holster fastened to his belt on his right. With Excalibur on his left, he felt balanced, ready to draw a weapon from either side. A bulge in one pocket reminded him of the ring Ashley had given him, the same ring she had found with the bone where Abraham's wall had been. Valiant said the ring once belonged to Flint, a gift from Abraham as a symbol of love.

Even after his rebellion, Flint had kept it for a while, though no one in the village knew why. Valiant noticed it on Abraham's finger after he had turned into a marching column of fire, so it seemed that Flint must have returned the symbol. Everyone agreed that Billy could take it with him, just in case he had an opportunity to use it as a gift of love again. Although Bonnie heard the story about Flint and the ring, she didn't know that Ashley had given it to Billy. That would be his secret, at least for now.

Bonnie slid off her sword belt and draped it over Ember's neck. Then, without a word, she spread out her wings and took to the air.

Ahead, her shadow slid across the grass, black and undulating with the strokes of her wings. Billy tried to find her in the sky but gave up. Watching her shadow was easier.

The dark form glided to the right, circled back, and passed across a cluster of short trees among the bulrushes to the left. After about a minute of back and forth surveying, the shadow began a slow return to the forest. When it disappeared in the trees, Billy looked up. With her wings beating rapidly, Bonnie floated down and landed gently on Ember.

Breathing hard, she swallowed before giving her report. "I saw the central village, but I didn't see anyone there except for two giants." She forked her fingers and pointed at the marsh. "There's an encampment on each side, like lookout stations, with a dragon at each. One is about forty toises to the left of a straight-ahead entry point, and the other is about half that far to the right. I spotted a few tents at each one, but no people."

"Toises?"

"Sorry. My sword trainer always used it. After four years it kind of sticks in your mind. One station is about eighty meters to the left, and the other is forty to the right."

Billy paused and listened. Although the danger signals stayed constant, no sound reached his ears. "Did anyone see you out there?"

"I think one of the giants saw my shadow, but when he looked up, I don't think he could find me. He didn't sound any alarm, so maybe he thought I was a big bird."

"I guess the dragons didn't sense any danger."

"Because I'm not a danger," Bonnie said. "That's why I left my sword belt on Ember."

"I thought it might have been too heavy."

She wrapped the belt around her waist. "Part of my training was to fly with it. I'm a lot stronger than I was that day I dropped Excalibur while flying."

"I'm sure you are. I could tell."

497

As she rebuckled her belt, a curious grin crossed her face. "You could? Have I changed that much?"

"Well … yeah." Warmth oozed into his cheeks. Bonnie's form had definitely changed, and her womanly blossom was impossible not to notice, but he had to keep his mind on the question at hand. "I could see the muscles in your forearms. Those are the first to get toned when you do sword training."

Her smile now radiant in the moonlight, she patted her belt. "I'm ready."

"Wait." Billy set a hand on his sword's hilt. The foreboding sensation suddenly spiked.

"Danger?" Bonnie asked.

"I don't get it. It's strong, like it's real close, but I don't see—"

Something fell on his head. Pressed under a heavy weight, he fell to the muddy ground. He grabbed at anything within reach but could find only air.

498

"Billy!"

Bonnie's voice! He clutched his attacker's slippery arm, threw the weight off, and leaped to his feet. A Vacant rolled through the mud. Dikaios reared up and stomped it with his hooves.

"Over here!" Bonnie shouted, her voice muffled.

Just beyond Ember, another Vacant held Bonnie around her waist. With one long-fingered hand over her mouth, he dragged her deeper into the forest.

Billy charged toward them. The Vacant stopped, pressed a dagger against her throat, and shouted in a weasely voice. "Come no closer!"

Billy halted within five feet of them. Setting his feet, he scowled. "What do you want with her?"

His little ovular mouth opened and closed from the sides as he continued in his squeaking, raspy voice. "She is the one our master wants. He has put a ransom on her head that will provide us food and clothing for life."

"Us?" Billy looked back at the dead Vacant near Dikaios's legs. "I think you're outnumbered."

"You are mistaken." He let out an odd croaking sound. From the low-lying shrubs, several more Vacants appeared, each one looking like clones of the first. All carried long spears and shields.

"We know how powerful you are," the Vacant continued, "so we make you this offer. If you leave with your horses now, we will let you live."

Billy wrapped his hand around Excalibur's hilt. If they wanted Bonnie alive, this beast wouldn't be quick to do her any harm. He could afford to be bold. "You can't be serious."

The Vacant's low-set eyes blinked. "You wish not to live?"

"I will die before you take her anywhere." Setting his jaw, Billy withdrew Excalibur. "How many of you wish to stay alive?"

Bonnie bit the Vacant's finger and stomped on his foot. With a lightning-fast spin, she whipped out her sword and cut off her kidnapper's head. In a mad rush, the other Vacants swarmed over her. For a moment, her sword glinted in the moonlight as limbs and spear points flew right and left, but she quickly fell under the mass of bodies.

499

Billy leaped into the fray, blowing fire. He blasted a Vacant's chest, but the cloak deflected the stream. Using his sword, he whacked off an arm, then plunged the blade through a torso. The Vacant twisted, jerking Excalibur from his hand. Another pulled him into the sea of struggling bodies and threw him down next to Bonnie. The tip of a spear pushed against his chest and pierced his skin. Within seconds, blood soaked into his tunic.

A second Vacant set his foot on Bonnie's chest. Grimacing, she bucked under his crushing weight, but when he pressed down harder, she settled down, her chest heaving shallow breaths.

"Surrender," the first Vacant ordered. He pushed the spear another fraction of an inch into Billy's chest. "Or die."

Billy steeled his muscles. He couldn't let them see an expression of pain. The sting of the cold metal pulsed across his body like an electric shock, but as he remembered Naamah's staurolite blade plunging through his heart, the pain seemed to ease. Nothing would ever be worse than that.

He looked around at his captors. Their numbers had swelled to thirty or more, and they all stared down at him with their big black eyes. These Vacants were dressed strangely. They wore dark cloaks that exposed only their hideous faces. The others Billy had faced wore thick, fur-lined tunics and long woolen trousers. Apparently someone had supplied them with cloaks that would repel his fire.

One of them held Excalibur and stared at it curiously. He wouldn't know how to use its power, but he could still do a lot of damage with its indestructible blade.

500

Billy glanced at Bonnie. With her brow knit into three tight lines, she looked ready to kill. It was time to show confidence, maybe make them wonder if he had a trick up his sleeve. "Surrender?" He laughed. "If you let Bonnie go unharmed, then I'll let *you* surrender. We'll treat you like prisoners of war. Otherwise, I will have to kill you all."

Dikaios trotted close. "I advise you to listen to this young warrior. You have said that he is powerful, but now you have angered him by threatening the girl he loves."

"He cannot fight without arms." A third Vacant stomped on Billy's right wrist and thrust a spear into the meaty part of his left forearm.

"Arrgh!" Billy bit his lip. He couldn't cry out again. He had to stay focused. But the spear's blade pressed against his bone, piercing and grinding. It felt like a superheated drill.

When the Vacant pulled out his spear, Billy grunted but managed not to cringe. The release in pressure helped, but the wound continued to shoot bullets of pain up and down his arm.

At his waist, he felt Bonnie's fingers fishing for the gun. Lifting his bleeding arm to point at the Vacant, he kept his glare riveted. He had to keep him distracted. "I repeat. Release us, and I will let you live."

A squeaky laugh spilled from the Vacant's puckered mouth. "I am tempted to let you up to see how well you fight in this condition, but we must return with our prize to the one who hired us."

Billy felt his holster grow lighter. A shot rang out. The Vacant pinning Billy's chest flew backwards. Another shot. The one over Bonnie toppled.

Before Bonnie could shoot again, the Vacant standing on Billy's wrist jerked the gun away. Swinging his legs up and back, Billy caught the Vacant's neck between his ankles and slung him into the air. He leaped to his feet, hoisted Bonnie to hers, and snatched Excalibur while Bonnie scooped up her own sword. Then, standing back to back, Billy and Bonnie stared at the surrounding enemy.

501

Trying to ignore the pain in his arm and chest, Billy spoke in a commanding tone. "This is my final offer. Leave now or die."

"You are still greatly outnumbered," a Vacant holding two spears said. "You cannot defeat us all."

Excalibur's beam shot into the inky sky. "If you knew what this sword could do, you would think otherwise."

The Vacant tied a sash at his cloak's waist. "Our master is acquainted with your weapon's light, and he assures us that it will do us no harm."

Billy tried to focus on the Vacant's cloak, but it was too dark to discern any details. Did a rusty mesh cover the material? Probably. The uselessness of his fire was his first clue, but there was only one way to find out for sure.

He swept the beam across the Vacant's body. Light splashed, and sparks drizzled on the cloak, but the Vacant stood erect, undisturbed. A matrix of orange and red lines radiated on his cloak, the same effect Excalibur had on the cloaks of the New Table knights.

The Vacant's fishlike mouth spread into a vertical smile. "Will you now surrender the girl? We want her alive, but we will gladly kill you."

Billy let the beam die away and whispered to Bonnie. "Are you ready?"

"Just say the word, warrior." Bonnie's wings flexed against his back. "I'm ready."

Billy looked at Dikaios. The horse nodded and said, "At your command."

Letting his wounded arm hang limply, he tightened his grip on the hilt and shouted, "Now!" He lunged. Swinging Excalibur, he lopped off the Vacant's spear arm. Then, with a quick spin, he cut through another's head at the ear and a third at the base of his skull.

502

Bonnie thrust her sword into a Vacant's belly, jerked it out, and leaped into the air, her wings lifting her over a hurled spear. Slashing while flying, she toppled four Vacants before settling on Dikaios's back.

Billy ducked under two spears, sliced through the ankles of three Vacants, and plunged through their ranks until he popped out on the other side.

As he raised his sword to attack again, Bonnie extended hers and shouted, "Charge!"

Dikaios bolted into the confused throng and stomped on Vacants, rearing up and crashing down on their bodies. Leaning over from her perch, Bonnie hacked with a two-fisted grip, her wings keeping her balanced as her mount rose and fell. Ember trotted all around the battle circle and gave any exposed Vacant a vicious kick with her back hooves.

Billy dove into the fray again. With powerful, one-armed sweeps, he killed one Vacant after another. A spear point grazed his head. A shaft banged against his ribs. A fist thumped his chest. But he kept swinging with Excalibur's razor-sharp edge again and again.

Vacants pulled and clawed at Bonnie's legs, but she continued flailing away at their groping arms. Finally, a Vacant grabbed her wing, slung her to the ground, and set one foot on her sword arm and the other on her throat.

Billy pulled Excalibur from a dead Vacant's chest and glared at Bonnie's captor. "Let her go!"

Two surviving Vacants scrambled away into the woods. Ember chased them to a line of shrubs before turning and walking slowly back.

The remaining Vacant pressed harder on Bonnie's throat. Gagging, she kicked and thrashed for a moment, but with her wings splayed on the ground, she couldn't get any leverage.

The Vacant growled like a cat. "Drop your weapon."

Billy let Excalibur fall to the ground. "Just let her breathe."

"Very well." The Vacant lifted his foot from her throat, picked up a broken spear, and set the splintered end over her eye. "Now get on your horse and leave."

503

Bonnie, her eyes closed under the broken spear, cried out. "I'll be all right, Billy. He wants to take me alive."

"I do want her alive," the Vacant said, "but losing an eye will not kill her."

Billy raised his arm. Blood soaked his sleeve from elbow to wrist, and streams ran down to his fingers. He smeared blood across his chest, but his tunic was already soaked from the first spear wound. "Look at me," he growled. "Do I look like I'm ready to just walk away? She is the most precious treasure in the world, and the only way you'll take her is by draining the last drop of blood from my body." Gritting his teeth, Billy set his feet firmly. "Now what do you think my answer will be?"

Another hideous vertical smile broke through. "Yet you dropped your weapon at my command."

Billy kept his stare on the Vacant. Ember had positioned herself behind the monster, her rear hooves set, but he couldn't let his eyes focus on her. "I dropped my weapon," Billy said, "so I could kill you with my bare hands."

Ember hammered the Vacant's back with both hooves. It flew into Billy's arms, knocking him flat. Hooking his arm around the Vacant's neck, Billy made ready to break it, but the body felt limp, like that of a rag doll.

He rolled the body to the side and, rising as fast as his aching bones would allow, he hurried to Bonnie and helped her up. "Are you okay?"

She caressed her throat. "I think so. A few scratches, but I'm okay."

"That one looks nasty." He touched her cheek just above a deep scratch. "Deep and bleeding."

She dabbed her finger in the oozing blood. "It doesn't hurt. I doubt it'll even leave a scar."

"If it does, it will remind me of the bravest girl I've ever known."

"Brave?" She cradled his bleeding arm. "I'm nothing compared to you."

He shook his head. "We both did everything we could. It's—"

Dikaios snorted. "How long will this mutual admiration meeting last?"

Laughing, Billy picked up the gun and slid it into its holster. "At least long enough to thank Ember." He patted the sorrel's neck. "Great job!"

Dikaios bowed his head. "Indeed. A most exquisite strike. I am very impressed."

Ember nuzzled Dikaios's cheek and swished her tail.

"Speaking of mutual admiration," Bonnie said with a wink.

Dikaios shook his mane. "Oh. Yes. Well, shall we continue with our rescue efforts?"

504

"Definitely. And we'd better hurry. If Flint sent those Vacants, the two that got away will report what happened." Billy put Excalibur away and helped Bonnie find her sword among the dead bodies. Then, using his good arm and getting a boost from her, he climbed aboard Dikaios.

Bonnie flew up to Ember's back, and the foursome returned to the edge of the forest. "There is a channel between the two encampments," Dikaios said. "The depth of the water has probably increased because of snowmelt, so they might not be paying much attention to that path. It would be difficult for intruders to negotiate it without making a lot of noise."

"After all the noise we just made," Bonnie said, "their guards might be on the alert."

Billy nodded. "They had to hear the gunshots."

"I suspect," Dikaios said, "that Flint and company were well aware of the ambush. They likely believe that you and Bonnie are in the hands of their allies. Perhaps now is the safest time to proceed."

505

"Let's go for it." Billy scrunched down. "But we'll keep a low profile. No use taking chances."

As Dikaios loped along, Ember kept pace close to his side. Since the ground had moistened to soft mud, no telltale clops would travel to the outposts' ears, though a slight squishing sound occasionally reached Billy's.

His wounds aching, he laid his head on Dikaios's neck and looked at Bonnie. She looked back at him, smiling. Apparently the battle didn't faze her. Compared to running from an insane slayer, being trapped in a candlestone, dying in Hades, and battling demons, this was just another death-defying night.

After a few minutes, the horses reached a line of reeds and walked into the marsh single file. Finding water almost immediately, Dikaios slowed his pace. To keep from splashing, he pushed his legs forward instead of raising them. Ember did the same.

Soon, the channel water rose to Billy's knees and stayed at that level.

As they crept along, Billy whispered as quietly as he could. "Elam, we're in the marsh. So far, so good."

Elam's whispered voice tickled Billy's jaw. "After all I heard, I was wondering. But I'll stay quiet. Just give me an update when you can."

Dikaios eased to a stop. As he sniffed the air, he looked around, his ears bending back. "Muskrats," he whispered. "We will have to leave the channel and go directly to Flint's village to the left."

Bonnie leaned so close her leg pressed against Billy's. "It should be safe. I think we passed the encampment."

Dikaios turned and climbed up the incline with his powerful legs. Ember copied his movements, but she slid back, forcing her to spring ahead. With a series of loud splashes, she reached level, shallow-water terrain.

When Dikaios joined her, Ember lowered her head, obviously ashamed. He rubbed his nose against her neck and said, "Do not fret. No one is angry. But we must leave this area immediately."

As they moved on, a whistle sounded from somewhere to the left. Another answered.

The horses stopped. Billy held his breath. Bonnie reached over and grabbed his hand. With the usual breezes deathly still, the marsh fell into complete silence.

About thirty feet away, the tops of the reeds shook, and a deep voice called out. "Muskrats?"

"I see none," another replied, "but I smell them."

"Very strange. I thought we killed the last one." He let out a hearty laugh. "Muskrat hams have a strong flavor, but they taste better than boots."

Billy cringed. They were Nephilim. That distinctive throaty laugh gave them away. He set a hand on his gun but kept it in its holster. Shooting in the dark wasn't a great idea, especially without knowing exactly who or what was out there.

Soon, a face appeared above the reeds. Billy, Bonnie, and the two horses lowered their heads.

"Maybe one traveled here after the wall disappeared," the first Naphil said.

Another head protruded from the marsh's foliage. "Maybe. If you can spear it, I will keep it a secret between us."

"Flint would have our scalps if he found out."

"You have been at your outpost too long. The rules have changed. With the wall of fire gone, we have no energy source, and Flint's people have freedom to hunt beyond the boundary now. Flint will not begrudge us a muskrat that we kill ourselves."

"The survivors are too weak to hunt. The sickness has left none with arms strong enough to throw a spear or legs swift enough to run down a prey."

"The dragons will hunt in their place."

"Roxil, perhaps, but Goliath will guard the prisoner. Flint will not risk losing that little dog."

Another Naphil laugh boomed. "He has quite a bark, does he not?"

"More than a bark. Chazaq is not pleased with the wound the mongrel delivered. From what I hear, this was not their first skirmish. Chazaq is looking forward to when Flint decides it is time to dispose of … What was the dog's name?"

"Walter. It will not be long. It seems that the warrior chief has chosen to forsake our prisoner. If Goliath detects no approaching dragon by dawn, we will not have to worry about sharing our muskrat with him. Walter will make a fine meal."

Billy eased his grip on the gun. These guards didn't know any intruders were present. Yet, their conversation seemed odd—forced, contrived, as if they were trying to communicate in code.

507

Laughing, the two Nephilim parted, each one sloshing through the shallow water. Dikaios took the opportunity to mask the sound of his own movements and plodded ahead. After a few minutes, they reached a clearing. Ahead lay the village, a collection of rundown huts built on a raised area of mud. Some of the homes had partial roofs with perforated thatching and others had no roof at all. A few tilted to the side, the supporting logs either crumbled or missing, the apparent victims of rot or theft. Nearly every home had damage of some kind, though one brick-and-mortar house closer to the water seemed strong and sturdy.

Dikaios nodded at the brick house. "Flint's," he whispered as he continued. When they climbed up the rise, Billy looked from house to house. No movement. No sound. During the past four years, he had imagined Flint's people training for war behind the fiery wall, making ready to attack and kill innocent people, but apparently disease and lack of food had devastated them. No wonder they hadn't attacked. They couldn't. With only a few Nephilim and two enemy dragons, they wouldn't stand a chance. Now the strategy of sending the shadow people alone made sense. They hoped to bring the same devastation to the villagers and win the war through attrition.

Then why capture Walter? They were better off staying in hiding and waiting for the disease to take hold. They must have known that Elam wouldn't attack first, especially after winning the initial battle. Why would they risk bringing the wrath of a host of dragons down on them? They would lose in a rout.

When they came within a stone's throw of Flint's house, the horses stopped. "Ember and I will wait here," Dikaios whispered. "Any closer and our scent will be detected by dragons or humans."

Billy and Bonnie slid to the ground and tiptoed through the mud until they reached the front door. Billy pressed his back against the wall on one side of the door, while Bonnie stooped at the other.

All was quiet. Of course Elam would want a progress report at this point, but the danger was too great. Risking even a whisper now was out of the question.

He edged in front of the door and laid his ear against the panel. Again, not a sound. He looked at Bonnie, pointed at his ear, and shook his head, trying to signal his findings.

As he moved his hand to the door's lift latch, he let his eyes dart around. Both horses stood still, mostly veiled by shadows. A muffled laugh sounded from the marsh, a Naphil likely returning to his post. Sweat streamed down Billy's cheek, and dried blood made his tunic stick to his skin, raising the agonizing sting once again. There really wasn't much choice. He had to go in, ready to fight.

Just as he touched the latch, a hiss came from the side of the house. He jerked his head around. A hooded figure skulked toward him. "Billy," a woman whispered. "Do not go in."

He slid out the gun, pointed it, and spoke with a low, commanding tone. "Stop in your tracks."

The woman halted and let her hood fall back. "It is I, Semiramis."

11

CHAPTER

LOVE NEVER FAILS

I am your ally," Semiramis said, "not your enemy."

"I doubt that." Billy kept the gun trained on her. "Why did you escape?"

She scowled. "That was four years ago. Are you still holding that against me?"

"If you had waited, we would have let you go. All we wanted was to confirm your story about where Shiloh was being held, and you were right, so—"

"Of course I was right," she said, her voice sharpening. "Why should I acquiesce to imprisonment when I had committed no crime? I helped you once again, did I not?"

"Okay, okay." He lowered the gun but kept it drawn. "What do you want?"

"To deliver your friend, Walter. He is unconscious, so I had to drag him to the corner, but when I saw you, I left him there." She backed slowly away. "Come. You will see."

Billy motioned for Bonnie to follow. When they arrived at the corner of the house, Semiramis stooped next to a body lying face-up in the mud. With the moon shining directly on him, his identity was clear.

"Walter," Billy whispered.

Bonnie gripped Billy's shoulder. "Is he all right?"

"He's been drugged," Semiramis said. "His hands and feet are still bound, but he is fine otherwise. I was in a hurry to get away, so I have not yet cut him free." She withdrew a knife from under her cloak.

Billy extended the gun, watching her every move. With a quiet snick, she cut through the ropes binding Walter's ankles and wrists. "You are familiar with my apothecary skills, Billy. I slipped a powerful sleeping potion into the drinking water, powerful enough to subdue two Nephilim guards, so there is no need for whispers. Unfortunately, it seems that Walter also drank the water, but I think he will recover. He is breathing well."

512

"We'll see about that." Billy nodded at Bonnie. "Cover me."

As Bonnie drew her sword, Billy put the gun away. Then, lifting Walter over his shoulder, he carried him to Dikaios and Ember. His wounded arm throbbed, and the cut on his chest stung, but he had to push through the pain.

"Lay him over me in riding position," Dikaios said. "Ember will keep him from falling over until you return."

With help from Ember, Billy pushed Walter onto Dikaios and balanced his body. Now semi-conscious, Walter instinctively gripped Dikaios's mane and stayed in place, while Ember stood at his side, watchful.

When he ran back to the house, he pulled out his gun again and nodded at Bonnie. "I'll keep an eye on her now."

Semiramis's brow bent angrily. "I have helped you time after time, Billy. I saved Listener's life, I guided you to Shiloh, I have been spying on Flint, and now I have rescued Walter. What else must I do to prove myself?"

Billy looked at Bonnie again. The confused expression on her face probably mirrored his own. There had to be a way to prove if she was a friend or an enemy. Maybe a prodding for information? "If you've been spying on Flint, maybe you know how he learned about our plans to defend against tonight's attack."

"I do know. Arramos has entered Second Eden." She laid a hand on his arm. "Billy, Arramos is the devil himself. He is crafty and powerful, and if someone is giving away your secrets, you can be certain that Arramos was involved."

"Why would Flint kidnap Walter? I figured out his army is sick, so why would he invite an attack?"

"You are correct. Disease has ravaged this village, and even Flint is deathly ill. He was desperate, so he was willing to listen to Goliath's counsel. I was close at hand only an hour ago, and I overheard the conversation. Goliath and Flint do not believe the warrior chief would attack and risk dropping his village guard. As long as he was unaware of the epidemic here, Elam would always choose to keep his forces in a defensive posture."

513

She raised a narrow finger. "Remember, the devil is cunning, and he surmised that the two of you would come, because you need someone to fly without alerting Goliath, and you would never let her go alone. With Excalibur and your fire-breathing, you make a formidable army on your own, so the two of you together would be a sufficient rescue party. Once they captured you, it would prove to Elam that rescue attempts were futile and costly, and he would send no more warriors."

"Why would they want us?"

"Not both of you. They want Bonnie. Arramos has longed to have her as a prisoner for years, and he will do anything to capture her."

Billy watched her eyes, sincere and piercing. Did she know about the Vacants' kidnapping attempt? Had she noticed their wounds? Should he probe her to find out if the ambush was planned by Arramos through Goliath and Flint? No. It was probably better to keep the attack to themselves. "So why do they want Bonnie?"

"May I show you something?" Semiramis asked, flashing her knife.

Billy pulled out the gun again. "Just move slowly and let me see your hands at all times."

"You are making me angry." Semiramis pushed the knife into his free hand and spread out her arms. "If you do not trust me, then slay me now. I cannot help you if you are constantly fearful of betrayal at my hands. While it is true that I am already dead, that blade will send me to my eternal punishment."

Billy glared at the knife, a stony blade at the end of a rough wooden hilt. Of course he couldn't take her offer, and she knew it. This act could be a dramatic bluff. Still, if she was bluffing, she was the best actress he had ever seen. What else could he do? He had to play along for now.

He gave her the knife. "Go ahead."

Shifting her gaze, Semiramis touched Bonnie's waist. "Have you ever felt anything odd here, as if something was attached to your body?"

She nodded. "All the time. It started back when my mother and I were running from a slayer. We never figured out what it was, so I just got used to it."

Semiramis glanced at Billy. "It is an invisible line that connects your body to Earth. Flint wants to make sure you stay here, so you can act as an anchor in this world. With the attachment, he will be able to call upon the unredeemed dead in Hades and raise up a new army that you and your dragons will never be able to withstand."

"If the rope's invisible," Bonnie said, "how do you know about it?"

Semiramis lowered her head, her tone weaker. "I was the one who sent Mardon to put it on you."

"Mardon?" Billy repeated. "Elam mentioned him. He's Nimrod's son."

"The same." She looked up at him again. "I used Mardon to do the bidding of Arramos before I rebelled and escaped."

Bonnie brushed her hand across her waist. "I can sense a pull, so why can't I feel it out in front of me?"

"It is so thin now, it passes by your hand like the thinnest of spiders' webs." She showed her the knife. "Only this can cut it. It is a staurolite blade. There are only a few in existence."

As if grabbing a string, she wrapped her hand around the air in front of Bonnie and made a vertical slice. "There," she said, holding up her fist. "I have the rope, and you are now free."

"What will you do with it?" Bonnie asked.

515

"I must go on a long journey to destroy it. If it stays here, the anchor will be set, and the armies of Hell will gather at the command of Arramos. Yet, I have foiled their plans, and you are free to go and tell Elam that Flint's army is broken and must be routed by a swift and forceful attack."

Billy looked at her face, trying to cut through any feigned sincerity. If this was all a bluff, it was the most cunning bluff he could imagine. If Elam attacked in full force, his own village would be undefended. Then, if Flint's army was actually still intact, they could devastate the villagers left behind. Maybe that was why this place was so deserted. They were lying in wait somewhere, ready to spring their trap. If only there was some way to find out for sure.

Billy reached for the door's latch. "Bonnie, keep an eye on her."

Letting out a huff, Semiramis crossed her arms over her chest, one hand still gripping her knife and the other holding fast to the invisible rope. "You seek truth in strange and deadly places, but if you must see for yourself in order to trust someone who has done only good to you, then step cautiously, for if you arouse those behind this dwelling, your lives, the very lives that I just saved, will be forfeit."

Billy nodded at the horses. "Bonnie, maybe it would be better if you get ready to escape with Walter, just in case."

She walked slowly backwards. "What about Semiramis? Who'll watch her while you're in there?"

Semiramis huffed again but said nothing.

"As long as you're safe," Billy said, "I'm not worried about her."

After waiting for Bonnie to get to the horses, he lifted the latch and peeked inside. It was dark and quiet.

"You will find Flint near the back door," Semiramis said. "After his conversation with Goliath, he returned to the house, and the drug made him collapse on the floor."

"How do you know all of this?"

"Your suspicions never end, do they?"

"Just tell me."

"When Goliath flew away, the drug began taking hold of Flint and his two Nephilim guards, so I was free to walk boldly in their presence. They had no power to subdue me, and since I am leaving to destroy this rope, they will never see me again."

"What about Hunter? Where is he?"

"He is waiting for me in the northlands. We will start our journey by returning him to his home."

Billy wanted to hurry, but another question dogged him. With Semiramis spilling so much information, now was a good time to ask. "Goliath took the weed from the garden. What was in it? Someone who carried the disease?"

"No. The disease began weeks before the wall collapsed. The weed held a warrior, a man of strength and stature. As far as I know, he did not succumb to the illness, but I do not know where he is now."

"Then he might be back soon."

"Indeed. In fact, he was riding Goliath when he flew away. Perhaps they went in search of food. If so, their return could be at hand."

"I'll be ready." Billy withdrew his sword and let its glow shine brightly as he entered the house. Tiptoeing, he waved the blade from one side to the other. The front room was spacious but empty, with holes in the walls that exposed decaying lattice work. Dikaios had mentioned seeing the inside of Flint's house and described it as relatively rich in décor, but it was certainly far from rich now. Without furniture or wall decorations, and with piles of nondescript debris lying here and there, it seemed no more than an abandoned shack.

As he pushed deeper into the house, the sounds of creaking footsteps followed. He looked back. With her hood again covering her head, Semiramis walked a few steps behind.

"Curious?" Billy asked.

"A better word would be, 'Cautious.' If Goliath returns, perhaps I can be of service, in spite of your never-ending suspicions."

517

"Have it your way." Leading with Excalibur, Billy picked up his pace until he reached the back wall where he found a blond-haired man lying faceup on the floor next to a wooden table and a single chair. A cup sat atop the table along with a pile of dried fruit, apparently partially eaten.

He leaned through an open back door and looked around. As expected, two Nephilim lay stretched out in the mud, one with an empty cup still in his hand. He walked closer and examined their sleeves. Neither wore Ashley's band around his arm.

Billy curled his fingers tightly around the hilt. It would be so easy to kill them and take out two powerful enemies without risking anyone else's blood. But, of course, he couldn't. The professor's wisdom had been emblazoned on his heart. *A knight opposes his enemy face to face. A stab in the back is the way of the coward. If you must fight, attack your enemy head-on. That is the way of valor.*

Killing a sleeping giant would be the coward's way, the way he killed Palin. And he would never return to the life he had left behind.

He pulled back into the house and knelt next to the man's body. At the end of a necklace, a glass egg, much like a villager's companion, lay on his chest, dark and lifeless.

Billy looked up at Semiramis. "Is this Flint?"

When she nodded, her hood fell back again, revealing her long tresses, shimmering in Excalibur's light. "He is drugged to be sure, but he was quite ill before my potion took effect. He will likely remain unconscious for a long time."

Billy used his tongue to feel for the tooth transmitter. It still buzzed. "Elam, I'm inside Flint's house. We rescued Walter. He's out of it, but I think he'll be fine."

Elam's tiny voice tingled in his jaw. "That's great, but how did you get into Flint's house? What's going on?"

"It looks like they have no army. The disease killed most of Flint's people."

"What about Flint himself, and the dragons?"

He turned away from Semiramis and whispered. "Flint's here, and he's out cold, but the dragons aren't around. Semiramis is here, and she explained—"

"Not her again. Did you wonder why she showed up?"

"Yeah. Kind of convenient, wasn't it?"

"Exactly. She was probably assigned to wait for you and tell you the story they want you to hear."

"Yeah, I thought of that, but we have an ace in the hole."

"What's that?"

Billy turned back toward Semiramis. She was looking out the open back door. Was she listening? Probably. She had already admitted to being an expert eavesdropper. "We have Flint."

"You mean you'll take him prisoner?" Elam asked.

"As a prisoner of mercy. Can you send three dragons? We'll need extra cloaks that can be made into litters a dragon can carry underneath. Be sure to send my father. If Goliath shows up, he might be the only one who can handle him."

"How many sick people are you talking about?"

"I don't know. I haven't searched their village."

"Perhaps six or seven," Semiramis said. "But I also have not searched everywhere."

Billy glared at her. "So you *were* listening."

"You did not say it was forbidden. I cannot hear Elam, but I can deduce what he is saying."

"I'm not surprised." After putting Excalibur away, Billy pulled Flint up and carried him over his shoulder. He marched quickly toward the front, hoping to keep Semiramis and her radar ears far enough behind. Although it was now dark, his memory of the empty room guided him toward the moonlight peeking through the open front door. "Elam, I'll send the horses back with Walter, and we'll wait for the dragons to arrive. And make sure Sorentine is in the group. This is a perfect job for her."

519

As Billy hurried out the front door and closed in on the horses, Elam replied. "What will the horses do if trouble shows up?"

"That shouldn't be a problem." Billy laid Flint next to Bonnie and, rising again, smiled at her. "I'll send a winged transport with them, someone in whom I have complete confidence."

"Okay," Elam said. "I think we have enough dragons. We can spare three. I have to leave the radio station to call them, so you might see the dragons before you hear from me again."

"Great. Thanks."

Semiramis called from the doorway. "I will be leaving you now, Billy. It grieves me that you never learned to trust me, but perhaps in later years when you remember these days, you will find it in your heart of love to look upon me with greater mercy." She raised her hood once more and walked slowly toward the marsh. With every step, her slender form faded into the darkness.

"She mentioned a staurolite blade," Bonnie said. "I have one of those." She touched a sheath at her hip. "According to Sapphira, it once belonged to Morgan, but my trainer in the Valley of Shadows thought I should keep it."

Billy eyed the narrow wooden hilt. "Maybe it will come in handy, but if Semiramis uses one, I wouldn't be too sure it's a good idea."

"You still don't trust her?" Bonnie asked. "I don't feel that pull anymore. She must have been telling the truth about that."

Billy moved to her side and watched Semiramis's shadow meld with the darkness. "I'm not sure what she's planning to do with that rope, but I thought it would be better for her to have it than to keep it tied to you. And I just wanted to get her out of here. It's better if she doesn't know what we're doing. If Arramos is so good at predicting our actions, we have to do the unexpected."

"Is that why you're taking Flint?"

"Right. Drugged or sick, their general is in our hands. If Semiramis is in a conspiracy with Goliath and Arramos, then she's too evil to expect us to show mercy."

She hooked her arm around his and laid her head against his shoulder. After sighing deeply, she whispered, "Love never fails."

Billy took in a long breath. Her touch felt good, a touch of approval, a blessing, maybe even a hint of an opening door. When she had said that he needed to win her heart, he imagined a dramatic rescue by which he suffered horrible wounds and shed a gallon of blood to prove himself worthy of her most precious gift. Yes, he had delivered that sacrifice, and gladly, but now this moment felt even more important.

Standing in the glow of a brilliant moon, it seemed that Pegasus illuminated more than a devastated village and a muddy marsh. It revealed the truth about an enemy. Flint needed healing.

Billy looked down at Flint's pallid face. Yes, if necessary, he would have gone to war against this pitiful man, but the opportunity to offer him medicine instead of the tip of a sword seemed like medicine to Billy's own soul. More than four years of preparing for battle, toning his muscles and sharpening his skills, had made him a formidable soldier in the eyes of his enemies, ready to go to war to protect the innocent. Four years spent away from the opulence of life on Earth and, instead, worshiping with the villagers in their simplicity of life and faith, had honed his heart into one that longed for peace.

"Bonnie?" he whispered.

"Mmm?" She kept her gaze locked on the marsh.

"We're alone now."

"How can you say that? Dikaios and Ember are here."

"I meant we're the only awake humans."

She laughed gently. "Okay. I guess that's close enough."

He slid his hand into hers and faced the two horses. "Before you take Walter back, will you be our witnesses?"

521

Both horses nodded. "What will we be witnessing?" Dikaios asked.

"A question from my heart to hers." Still holding Bonnie's hand, Billy lowered himself to one knee and looked into her eyes. Pegasus sparkled in her irises. A warm breeze tossed her blond-streaked hair, making it flow behind her like a banner of tawny linen embroidered with gold. Oh, if only he could borrow some of this beautiful woman's eloquence, something that would pour out his heart in a sonnet of love, words that would bare his soul and allow her to see the man of God he had become. Silently he begged for those words, if only for these next few moments.

After clearing his throat, he spoke loudly and clearly, unafraid. "Bonnie Silver, together we have plunged into the heart of territories unknown, and, with love as our sword, we have captured the captain of those who threatened to harm the innocent. He was a rebel who shook his fist at the one who showed him love and mercy in spite of the rebel's clenched fist. Two thousand years ago, the Lord of the universe entered a world of rebels and washed the feet of those who denied him in both word and deed. Because of your witness, the life you have lived in your words and in your deeds, I was able to clearly see this God who became a man. Because of the purity you displayed, I witnessed a reflection of the sinless life he lived. Because of the light you shone every moment you were in my presence, his light was able to break through my stubborn shell."

He swallowed, trying to loosen his tightening throat as he kept his gaze on her lovely face. Tears streamed down her cheeks. She squeezed his hand but said nothing as he continued.

"The day I opened your journal and read your prayer was the day I saw that light in all its glory, and I never wanted to depart from its blaze. I thought being with you would be the only way to walk in the sunshine. Yet, strangely enough, while I spent more than four years without you, I learned something very important. The light of Jesus shone wherever I went, and spending that time away from you strengthened me in ways I never imagined. I learned how to find the light that God planted within me. I learned how to seek his power without looking to you for instructions." Swallowing again, he raised his eyebrows. "Do you understand?"

Her chin quivering, she nodded.

"So, Bonnie Silver, now that I have spent those years without you, and I have learned what those days were designed to teach me, I never want to live another day without you. I want to spend the rest of my life with you." He withdrew Excalibur and summoned a strong glow. "So here, in the heart of darkness, I shine my light without fear. Instead of looking to you as my source of illumination, I look to God alone, and I will lead you through the darkest of places, arm-in-arm and heart-to-heart, as together we storm the gates of the enemy and rescue those he has taken captive."

Now trembling, he rubbed her knuckles with his thumb. "What I'm trying to say, Bonnie, is this." With his own tears flowing, he returned Excalibur to its scabbard, pulled out the ring, and lifted it between his thumb and finger. "Will you marry me?"

Her eyes sparkled. The moon bathed her milky cheeks in a soft glow, highlighting the trickling tears. She took in a deep breath, and spoke, her voice as smooth and lovely as her spirit. "Yes, Billy Bannister. I will marry you."

Taking in a deep breath, he pushed the ring onto her finger. Since it was far too big, it slid easily over her knuckles. She rolled her fingers to keep it in place, smiling as she gazed at the red stone.

He rose to his feet, his legs shaking. Just as he opened his mouth to speak, a clapping sound made him turn.

Walter leaned against Dikaios, clapping his hands. "Bravo! That was simply fabulous!"

Bonnie laughed. "How long have you been listening?"

"Let me think ..." Walter shrugged. "Ever since you said you were all alone, I think. But it's kind of fuzzy. The water here really packs a wallop. Good thing I only took a sip."

Billy pulled Bonnie close, leaned his head against hers, and extended his hand to Walter. "Come here."

Staggering slightly, Walter joined them in a tight huddle. Billy kissed Bonnie's head, then Walter's, and wept. "I'm with my best friends in all the world. I couldn't be happier."

After a minute or so, Billy pulled back and looked at his friends in turn. "We have a lot to do, so ..." He sniffed and wiped his eyes with his sleeve. "So let's start with checking on Flint."

Walter's brow shot up. "Maybe we'd better draw our swords."

Billy lowered his voice and slowly withdrew Excalibur. "Did you hear something?"

"Yep. After listening to those Nephilim, I'd recognize them anywhere, even the sloshing of their big, ugly feet." As if working in tandem, Walter and Bonnie pulled their weapons. A shimmer

523

of light ran along the metallic blades, and the two warriors set their feet.

A huge figure crashed through the wall of reeds and rushed toward them.

Billy lit up Excalibur's beam. "Stop!"

The Naphil halted and raised his hand to block the brilliant light, revealing Ashley's band on his arm. "Billy? Is that you?"

"Yereq!" He let the beam fade. "Where have you been?"

The giant crossed his massive arms. "For the last half hour I have been keeping the other Naphil guard away from you. You have been making a great deal of noise."

"Where is he now?"

"I subdued him. He will not be a threat any longer."

Walter slapped Yereq's back. "Thanks. We owe you one."

"Perhaps more than one. The two Nephilim who were asleep behind the house woke up, so I had to put them to sleep again. And when you rode here with the horses, I kept the other guard from finding you. Did you not hear me?"

"We heard," Billy said, "but I didn't know who you were."

"I spoke as a witless monkey, loud and obvious. I hoped you would recognize that I was trying to send you information. We heard gunshots, and I convinced the other Naphil that it was likely just a series of thunderclaps. Fortunately, that giant did not possess more than a squirrel's brain."

"We were wondering about that. Thanks for covering for us."

"Well, I see that you learned what has been afoot here. Goliath never intended to use Flint or his people as part of his army, but he speaks about another army that he hopes to gain by capturing Bonnie, something about anchoring her in Second Eden."

"Let's save that thought for a minute. Did you figure out who was in the plant?"

"I never saw him, but I heard his name. Sir Devin. Your mother told me many stories about him, so if he is here, we have another great concern."

Billy breathed the name quietly. "Sir Devin ..." Years ago that name would have given him a shiver. Now it seemed little more than a bad memory, and the miracle of his resurrection seemed commonplace, just another villain back from the dead. "How did he get into the plant?"

"A traitor in the village had a companion that was actually a seed of sorts. It contained Devin's life energy, and the traitor planted it in the garden."

"A fake companion?" A thousand thoughts raced through Billy's mind—Hunter falling in the garden, his lost companion, Semiramis protecting the plant, finding Shiloh only to lose Acacia, and now ...

Billy kicked at the mud. "Semiramis has the rope!"

"Yes," Bonnie said. "What do you mean?"

"This is exactly what she wanted. We followed her plan from start to finish. They didn't want Bonnie; they just wanted the rope. And only Semiramis knew how to cut it and what to do with it. She'll anchor Second Eden to Earth and Hades herself."

525

"So their army's on its way?" Walter asked.

"Probably." Billy searched the dark edges of the marsh. Every shifting shadow seemed to hide a crouching warrior. Although the potential danger was real, nothing prodded his alarm, just a bit of background uneasiness. "We need to get out of here."

Bonnie marched toward the nearest hut. "Then we'd better search the homes and find the survivors out. Our dragons might be here at any minute."

Looking at Walter and Yereq, Billy let his shoulders slump. "You're right. Let's do it."

"I'm still kind of woozy," Walter said, "so I'll stay with Flint and the horses and watch for our dragons." He pulled Billy's gun from its holster. "But I might need this."

Billy and Yereq caught up with Bonnie, and after searching through at least twenty houses, they found three women and two men between thirty and fifty years old. All five were either unconscious or too sick to walk, so Yereq carried them to Walter. By the time they brought the fifth patient, three dragons had arrived: Clefspeare, Thigocia, and Sorentine.

After Billy and Bonnie wrapped the five in cloaks, Thigocia and Sorentine snatched up two bundles each and took to the sky.

As Billy laid Flint on a cloak, his body jerked. His eyes blinked open, and he stared at Billy. "Who are you?"

"Relax. I'm a friend. I heard you're sick, so I'm taking you to a hospital."

"What hospital? The only hospital I know of is …" A frown bent his face. "Abraham's village?"

He tried to get up, but Billy pushed him back to the cloak. "Don't worry. We're taking you there to help you."

Venom laced his voice. "I cannot accept help from Abraham. He kept us trapped in a circular prison of flames. We had so little food, we were always weak. We had no way to fight disease."

"You're not accepting help from Abraham," Billy said. "He's gone forever, so you won't have to swallow your pride. Just take it easy and let us get you and your people to the hospital."

Closing his eyes, Flint gave a nod of resignation. "I am too sick to fight. Do with me what you will."

12

FINDING SHILOH

Floating several inches above the lake, Gabriel pushed forward. Of course, using his mental power to travel in his light energy state was never physically tiring, but it put a drain on his brain. Yet, that didn't matter. Finding Shiloh and Acacia couldn't wait for him to sit and rest. And now that he had found the lake, this was no time to slow down. The portal was probably only moments away.

After crossing a snow-covered valley, he found a large boulder that matched the description Billy had provided. He let his hand float above a letter *X* on one side. No doubt about it. This had to be the place.

He drifted around the area. The sixth circle village was pretty large, so its location shouldn't be hard to find. The problem wouldn't be sniffing out a portal if it was still here; it would be breaking through. It might take all his energy, but he had to find Shiloh and Acacia. Nothing was more important.

Something moved near the boulder, a human crouching at the base. Gabriel eased closer. The man, shorter than average, seemed to be manipulating something with his hands, as if tying a knot with an invisible line.

When the man straightened, his oval face came into view. Badly scarred from burns, he wore glasses over his narrow eyes, and his scant white hair blew back in the cool breeze, uncovering a nearly bald head. He pulled against his invisible rope, as if testing the knot he had fastened at the base of the boulder.

Gabriel studied his countenance. He seemed to be too serious, too focused to be a madman. Yet, what sane man would be playing an imaginary game of tug-of-war with a boulder?

The man withdrew a bottle from his pocket, pulled out a stopper, and poured a shining yellow liquid onto his "rope." A splash of sparks sizzled in the air and shot out from the boulder like a lit fuse, following a line until it disappeared far away.

Suddenly, Gabriel's body dropped. He looked down. His shoes made indentations in the snow, and his energy field gave way to physical legs and torso. Quietly, he patted his chest and stretched out his wings. It was true! He had regained his body!

The man gasped and jumped back. "What are you doing here?"

Gabriel raised his hands. "Hey. Don't be scared. I know I have wings, but—"

"I am not frightened of you. We have met before."

"We have?" Gabriel narrowed his eyes. "Now that you mention it, you do look familiar. Did we meet before your burn accident?"

The man snorted. "Accident. That's a laugher. The only accident is that you're here, so now I have to decide what to do about this unfortunate meeting." He withdrew a dagger. "I doubt that I could catch you, so it would be better for both of us if you would leave as quickly as possible."

Gabriel gave his wings a quick flap and scooted away. As the man's voice and manner registered in his mind, everything grew clear. This was Mardon, the mad scientist who tried to lasso Heaven and join it with Earth, and the dagger looked like the staurolite blade from Dragons' Rest, though the hilt was slightly different. "Where'd you get the knife?"

"Don't play me for a fool with your small talk. I wasn't born yesterday." Mardon looked upward, apparently in thought. "Upon reconsideration, it might be advantageous for us to work together. As you can imagine, I am not happy with what happened to my face, and I want to exact revenge upon the beast who did this to me."

"Beast? What beast?"

"The devil himself. He masquerades as Arramos, one of the dragons of old. If I could get back to the Bridgelands, perhaps I could find him and use this dagger to end his charade. My sources tell me that only a staurolite blade is able to cut through his scales, and such a cut will force that devil from his body so that he won't be able to deceive or maim anyone else."

"Well," Gabriel said, "I'm all for taking a shot at him, but I have to find some friends who were trapped in the sixth circle of Hades. Do you know anything about that?"

529

"I know more about your friends than you do."

Gabriel resisted the temptation to roll his eyes. Mardon's dramatic pause was annoying, but he had to play along. "Well, then, please tell me where they are now and how to find them."

"I will tell you, if you will agree to help me foil Arramos's plans."

"Yeah. Sure. As long as it doesn't conflict with what I need to do."

"We will not be at cross-purposes." Mardon nodded toward the boulder. "I have anchored a line that attaches Earth and Hades to this realm. I did it here because, when I transported from the Bridgelands, this is the point where I appeared in Second Eden. I thought it best to try to return by this route. Shiloh, too, was here, so it stands to reason that she might have gone there as well.

Therefore, your journey is tied to mine. My sources tell me that you are also seeking Acacia. Although I have not seen her, the story of her disappearance would indicate that she is likely with Shiloh. Finding her would serve my purposes well."

"Why is that?"

For a moment, he paused, nervous, uncertain. "I gave her life in my laboratory thousands of years ago. So, of course, I want to see her again."

Gabriel studied Mardon's uneasy manner. He had balked. Was he lying? Either way, it didn't really matter. He had to complete his mission. "Right," Gabriel said. "I heard about how you did that with Acacia, and Sapphira, too."

Closing his eyes, Mardon took in a deep breath and let it out slowly. "Yes, Sapphira. I wish to see her more than any other. She was a wonderful assistant to me, intelligent, thoughtful, kind, even when my father brutally misused her." He shook his head as if tossing off a wayward thought. "In any case, if we work together, perhaps we can signal the Bridgelands that we are here and request safe conduct to that realm."

"Signal the Bridgelands?"

"Yes, my mother knows the gatekeeper there, and he monitors attempts to enter. If we can make an attempt to open the portal, whether successful or not, perhaps he will come and see who is, shall we say, knocking at his door."

"Fair enough." Gabriel looked around for a loose piece of wood. "What do we do? Spin a flame like Sapphira does?"

"Exactly. I was able to do it when transporting from Shinar to Hades, but that was a wide-open portal. I'll wager that this one won't be so easy. Otherwise, the people of this land would have gone there long ago. So, I am hoping you will fly around with a flame. Perhaps that will attract the gatekeeper's attention."

Gabriel shrugged. "Sure. I don't have any other way of getting there."

"Very well. I brought flint stones and parchment, so I will start a fire, while you search for a suitable firebrand. There are fallen trees within a mile, so with your wings, I assume you can locate a branch and return quickly."

"I'll see what I can do." Gabriel lifted into the air and scanned the valley. As Mardon had said, several trees had succumbed to the long winter, leaving rotting logs with spindly branches reaching upward like a man drowning in frigid water. He zoomed down to one, snapped off a branch, and again rose into the air.

As he flew, memories of battling Mardon's giants flowed back into his mind. This madman had been the cause of so much trouble over the centuries, including very nearly destroying the entire world. Would it be right to help him? Was there really any choice?

Gabriel eased into a descent. The air carried a nasty chill, but the prospect of working with this snake in the grass made him shiver even harder. He had to keep a close eye on Mardon's every move, a very close eye.

531

Acacia searched for an appropriate branch, something easy enough to break from a limb, yet thick enough to hold an enduring flame. Although nothing seemed suitable so far, the search had been relaxing. The woods here were always a delight— shade from the never-setting sun, a breeze tossing the treetops into a melodic swish, and blossoming vines to flavor the air with hints of honeysuckle and jasmine.

Ever since their transport to this realm and the subsequent vanishing of the sixth circle's village, life had been sweet and easy. With Shiloh for company, as well as a variety of animals, both familiar and exotic, including unicorns, every day brought new sources of pleasure and mental stimulation. But with her strength still ebbing daily, any strenuous exercise taxed her body. Even breathing seemed to erode her from within.

Although she didn't need food to survive, she occasionally took small meals to see if something would revive her energy. They brought some strength at first but later burned like fire in her bones. Shiloh was always worried and daily cajoled her into a few more mouthfuls of this fruit or that herb, warning her that she had grown so thin, her Second Eden garments now hung like rags on a skeleton.

Not only that, thoughts about worried loved ones haunted them both. Shiloh spoke about them more often, especially Gabriel.

Acacia crouched next to a bush that bore a yellow flower the size of her hand. She took in the lovely fragrance—sweet, mellow, and buttery. This was one of the edible flowers, but the thought of eating it made her feel queasy.

She looked back at Shiloh as she worked on her latest effort to contact Gabriel. She had abandoned any pretense about her love for him, choosing to believe that he would be the one to find her and sweep her off her feet. Years ago he had watched over her and proven his devotion. Even after all this time, he wouldn't have forgotten his commitment to keep her safe.

And now new hope had arisen. They finally learned where they were. Although Acacia had long suspected this to be the case, a strange old man had confirmed today that they were in the Bridgelands. She had been here before when she, Joseph, and Ruth came through, but they had been in such a hurry, and Ruth's condition had so dominated her thoughts, she didn't pay much attention to the details of this world.

During their journey, Joseph, while carrying Ruth, led Acacia across a bridge over an apparently bottomless chasm. Yet, the bridge Acacia more recently found here was very different, so she wondered if it was the same one. Most of the planks connecting the supporting ropes were either gone or broken, and the ropes themselves were so frayed, in some sections only a few strands held them

532

together. With every gust, the span swung wildly, making the broken steps clack and creak. If this was the same bridge, there seemed to be no way to get to the other side where Heaven's Gate awaited.

The old man said just moments ago that they need not make an attempt to cross the bridge. Why? In his strange and mysterious way, he hinted at bringing someone from another realm, but he just cackled merrily when she or Shiloh tried to press him for details.

As a heftier breeze swept past, Acacia looked up. A limb hung low with a protruding branch that seemed perfect. She reached up and snapped it off. It was time to give their new plan a try.

After exiting the woods, she held up the arm-length tree branch and called out, "Ignite!" A flame erupted at the end and burned steadily. Lowering it to eye level, she showed it to the withered old man seated on a stone. "Will that be sufficient, Glewlwyd?"

Glewlwyd eyed the flame and spoke in a squeaky voice that sounded more like a rusty hinge than a man. "Perhaps. Perhaps. We shall see. When the circle of stones is complete, we can test it."

533

Shiloh pointed at the stone Glewlwyd sat upon. "May I use that one? I can't find any others close by, and I need one more."

Smiling, the old man pushed on a cane and rose to his feet. "I will be most satisfied when this is finished. The body I received has aged slowly while in the Bridgelands, but not slowly enough to keep these old bones from complaining."

Shiloh picked up the stone in both arms and, with knees bent, carried it to a flat, grassy area nearby. She had already set out eleven similarly sized stones in even intervals, one short of creating a circle with a diameter roughly matching hers and Acacia's combined heights. After letting the stone roll out of her arms and onto the grass, she shoved it into place. "There. That should do it."

Acacia walked to the center of the circle. "So how will we know when someone passes through this spot in Second Eden?"

"That is where you need my help." Glewlwyd shuffled across the perimeter boundary. The moment he passed the stones, his body morphed into a transparent, liquidlike substance. Only his slow movements allowed them to detect his presence at all.

When he stopped at the center, he seemed to disappear, but his voice was clearer than before. "I am the gatekeeper of the Bridgelands, and I am able to discern if anyone is trying to pass through an entry portal. Since this is the spot that you appeared, a portal remains, and that is why I asked you to build this new gateway. Someone, indeed, is at the gate, and the stones will create a dome of safety for the traveler." For a moment, he paused. His liquid head shifted slowly from side to side, as if he smelled something odd. "This is a strange portal. I cannot discern what is different about it, but it feels … dead."

"'Dead' might be a good word," Shiloh said as she joined them in the circle. "When I was in that old ghost town in Hades, Semiramis told me only dead people could travel through the barrier."

"Hades is an unusual place, but when it merged with Earth, all the rules of travel changed. The dead were able to pass into the lands of the living, but the living ones were still shackled by their corporeal existence."

Acacia raised a finger. "But I'm not dead. Clefspeare, Billy, and I were able to open it, and I fell through the barrier."

Glewlwyd's barely visible head nodded. "A most perplexing mystery. Perhaps there is something about your existence that even you do not yet know. In any case, I am the gatekeeper here, so I have the power to open any portal in the land, and now I will peer into Second Eden to see who is about." He took the branch from Acacia and waved it over his head. It seemed that a flaming, crooked stick floated in midair. "Take heart. I will return as soon as I am able."

The old man, or what was left of him, disappeared, along with the branch.

Shiloh let out a breath and sat on the grass. "Well, since he's gone, at least we know the portal still works."

"True enough." Acacia sat next to Shiloh and took her wounded hand in both of hers. "Have you been keeping track of time?"

Shiloh gave her a shrug. "Not really. Since my watch quit working and since we have constant daylight, it seems impossible. I kept track for a while by watching my body changes, you know, counting my cycles, but even those got out of whack. Maybe it's the food here. I don't know."

"I've been watching." Acacia looked up at the sky. "Even though this world's sun never goes down, it still makes a circuit in the sky. If that equals a day, then we've been here between four and five years."

"Sounds right. It didn't make much difference in Hades, but now I'm finally aging, so the passing of time feels more important than before."

Acacia caressed Shiloh's cheek. "You still look very young, no more than twenty years old, and you're as lovely as ever."

Shiloh looked down and plucked a blade of grass. "When Gabriel shows up, I hope he thinks so. In reality, I'm practically a senior citizen."

"And he's even older." Acacia gave her a gentle push and laughed. "Come now, Shiloh, don't fret. He loved you before; he will love you now."

Still looking down, Shiloh let a smile break through. "I hope you're right."

"I am. Trust me. He will sweep you off your feet and fly you to the wedding altar. After all you've been through, I'm certain God will reward you with the desires of your heart."

"After all *I've* been through," Shiloh said, pointing at herself. "What about *you*? You've been around for thousands of years, suffering loneliness and pain for a lot of that time, and you've never had anyone, no husband to lift you up when you're down, to offer you a shoulder to cry on, or to ..." She looked away. "Or to give you babies."

"Oh, Shiloh, is that what's troubling you?" Acacia turned Shiloh's face toward her. "Don't worry about your womb. I'm sure it's as youthful as your face, and Gabriel will prove to be a marvelous father. You have nothing to fear."

"There you go again," Shiloh said. "You're always concerned about me, never about yourself."

"That's because I'm not sad about these things. Although I have often longed for strong, embracing arms, I have them in my Lord Jesus. Day after day I needed a shoulder to cry on, and he gave me one that never tires of hearing my lamentations. And now that I have seen him, I know that his presence was real every moment."

"You've seen him?"

Acacia looked up at the sky. "Only once, but it was so strange. One day while I was praying at Heaven's Altar, a group of martyrs rose up and cried out, 'How long, O Lord, holy and true, will you refrain from judgment and avenging our blood on them that dwell on the earth?' During that moment, I could look up into Heaven itself and see the Lord, and he instructed an angel to give each martyr a white robe." She shifted her gaze back to Shiloh. "You see, I'm not a martyr, so I wore a blue cloak while I was there, but when new martyrs come to the prayer room, they are given white robes. Anyway, that's when I heard his voice. He said, 'Rest, my beloved, for a little while longer until your brethren who will be killed as you were fulfill their purpose.'"

"Wow! That must have been amazing!"

"Oh, Shiloh, I can't even begin to describe it. But here's my point. Ever since the day Sapphira restored me after my fall into the chasm, I learned to turn my focus outward, never inward, and I find complete fulfillment in serving others. I have no need of a husband or children. All I want to do is make my savior, my only husband, happy with me, so that when I finally get to meet him, to touch him, he will smile and welcome me into a physical embrace and ensure that I never need a shoulder to cry on again."

Looking up into the sky, Shiloh breathed in the fragrant air. "Just think. It's going to be even better than this place." Then, half closing one eye at Acacia, she added, "Do you think they'll have unicorns in Heaven?"

Acacia shrugged. "I don't see why not. Maybe they'll even let you take Cornelius with you."

"Speaking of Cornelius," Shiloh said as she rose to her feet, "have you seen him lately?"

Acacia pointed. "He was grazing in a meadow just beyond the stream we crossed. He seemed to like the clover there."

"Let's bring him over here. Maybe Glewlwyd will be back by then."

Shiloh ran through the calf-high grass. Acacia followed, though more slowly. Her legs hurt too much, and today they felt worse than ever. Her body seemed empty, like a sail without wind. Her flames had been adequate for starting campfires, and she could still fashion a small fireball, but the days of creating blazing infernos seemed to be over.

Was age finally creeping up on her after all these centuries? Did her years in Heaven's Altar leave her pining away for the sweet fellowship of the martyred saints and another glimpse of the Holy One, the blessed Messiah Jesus?

Urging her legs into a quicker walk, she searched for Shiloh. There she was, petting Cornelius, the leader of the unicorns, at least the leader of the herd that grazed on this side of the chasm. After Cornelius and Shiloh met, he left his herd to stay with her, apparently realizing that she needed a strong, tactile companion, someone who could physically return the love she poured out.

537

Acacia stopped and waited while Shiloh led the unicorn back. Acacia crossed her arms over her chest and smiled. The way Shiloh treated Cornelius proved that Gabriel would someday have a sweet, gentle wife, a real treasure. All would be well.

A tear dripped from Acacia's eye, and she quickly swiped it away. Yes. All would be well.

A Double Plunge

Holding the flaming branch, Gabriel landed next to Mardon, out of breath. "I don't think … it's working. I did … about thirty orbits."

"Yes, I know." Mardon glared at the dwindling flame. "Thirty-two, to be precise."

A squeaky voice broke in. "I counted exactly thirty."

Gabriel turned toward the voice but saw nothing, only the snow-covered ground he had flown over so many times. "Who's there?"

A vague outline took shape and slowly filled in. After several seconds, a stooped old man stood barefoot on the snow carrying a flaming branch similar to Gabriel's. His brow suddenly scrunched tightly, and he looked down at his feet as he lifted them in turn. "If you don't mind, please state your business quickly. Since you are not trying to enter from Hades, I will bypass the usual required examination protocol."

Mardon stepped forward. "Glewlwyd, I request—"

"So you know my name, do you?" He pointed his branch. "Let me know yours before you make your requests."

"Very well." Mardon cleared his throat. "I am Mardon, son of Semiramis."

Glewlwyd's eyebrow shot up, but he said nothing.

"I seek passage to the Bridgelands," Mardon continued, "in order to provide a great service for all the realms. I intend to find the devil who assumes the body and the great name of Arramos so that I may slay him. He must no longer bring shame to dragons."

"A noble task. Impossible, but noble." Glewlwyd turned to Gabriel. "And who might you be, winged boy?"

"I am Gabriel, son of Makaidos and Thigocia. I am searching for two friends, and they were last seen here before they disappeared through a portal. We suspect that they might be in the Bridgelands."

"I assume you mean Shiloh and Acacia."

Gabriel nearly leaped out of his shoes. "Yes. Are they there?"

"Indeed, they are." Glewlwyd waved his branch. "Come nearer, and we will go immediately. I have not stood in the snow since the days of Arthur. I did not like it then, and I do not like it now."

Gabriel and Mardon stepped close, one on each side of the strange old man. Then, with a quick, snappy motion, Glewlwyd waved his firebrand. Instantly the snow scene disappeared, replaced by a field of green grass and lush forests as well as a surrounding circle of stones.

Inhaling deeply, Gabriel took in the warm, fragrant air, allowing it to chase away every shiver. "So," he said as he turned to survey the new scene, "where should we start looking for—"

"Gabriel!"

He spun toward the sound. Shiloh and Acacia were riding toward him on a unicorn, but it suddenly stalled, as if frightened. A slight tremble ran across the ground, gentle but noticeable.

Shiloh slid down and ran, her arms outstretched. Gabriel gathered her into an embrace and pressed his cheek against hers. "Shiloh! Praise the Maker! I finally found you!"

While they hugged, Acacia dismounted and stood nearby, smiling as she looked on.

Gabriel studied her petite frame—thin, fragile, almost cadaverous. Although pale and gaunt, her face was still lovely, yet it carried a morbid sort of beauty, like a comely child dying of cancer.

As another tremor, stronger this time, rolled through the meadow, Gabriel extended his arm. "Acacia, it's good to see you as well."

Acacia glanced at Glewlwyd. He had dropped to his knees and set his palm against the ground, his head tilted upward as if listening. She joined in an embrace with Gabriel and Shiloh for a moment before pushing away, her eyes narrowing. "Your traveling companion looks familiar."

Gabriel looked over his shoulder at Mardon. The mad scientist was staring at Acacia, seemingly mesmerized, or perhaps appalled at her appearance.

Acacia stepped closer to him, her face drooping into a piteous frown. "Hunter, I see you never found your companion. I hope—" She paused and stared. "You look different here ... more distinct, more focused."

Mardon held out his hand. "I was worried that you would recognize me in Second Eden, but apparently there are no secrets here in the Bridgelands, so I will no longer disguise my voice. My usual voice is hampered by burn damage, but you will likely recognize it."

Gasping, she raised her fingers to her lips. "Mardon!"

"Yes, my child." Mardon stepped closer and gazed into her eyes. "You are wasting away."

Acacia inched back and pulled her tunic higher on her bony shoulders. Her voice lowered to a whisper. "I have been ill."

541

A tear slipped down Mardon's ravaged cheek. "I created your genetic blend. Perhaps I can do something to help you if you will let me examine you thoroughly."

"Uh ... thank you, but that won't be necessary." She shot Gabriel a look that seemed to communicate, "Why are the two of you together?" but she said no more.

Gabriel stepped between them. "Mardon and I sort of ran into each other while I was looking for you." He gave his wings a quick shake. "For some reason, I got my body back in Second Eden. Mardon says that Second Eden has now combined with Earth and Hades, so that would explain the change."

"And your explanation," Glewlwyd said, rising to his feet, "tells me all I need to know."

Gabriel slid his foot across the grass. "Is that what all the shaking is about?"

"Indeed, and it will increase to catastrophic proportions. In fact, the portal by which you entered here has already dissolved." Glewlwyd waved his arm. "Come. The Bridgelands will crumble. We must go to the bridge. It is our only hope of escape."

"The bridge?" Acacia said. "It's in ruins."

Glewlwyd's voice grew animated. "Do not judge by appearances, for salvation often comes in broken vessels."

"How far is it?" Gabriel asked.

"If we hurry on foot, perhaps fifteen minutes by your measurements. If, however, the ladies ride the unicorn and you fly, the three of you will get there more quickly. Mardon and I will get there when we can. We are both already dead souls, so the worst that can happen to us is a quicker entry into our ultimate destination."

"The worst is right," Mardon said. "I hope to convince Elohim that I be allowed into Heaven. My current destiny is one that I would like to avoid."

Gabriel flapped his wings and drifted behind Acacia. "I'll carry her, and Mardon can ride with Shiloh. But what do we do when we get there?"

Glewlwyd raised a pair of fingers. "You have two choices. You may cross the bridge and go from there to Heaven's Gate where you may petition for entry into the altar, or you may go into the chasm, which would lead you to Second Eden. The problem is that if you are unable to slow your descent, you will be crushed when you arrive."

"I might be able to carry two," Gabriel said, "but not all three."

"Then the ladies should go, and Mardon will cross the bridge with me. That way—"

"No!" Mardon shouted. "I must return to Second Eden! I must complete my mission!"

"What mission?" Gabriel asked. "To convince Elohim that—"

"Never mind." Mardon thrust a finger toward Acacia. "I know what's wrong with her, and I can heal her. But if you refuse to let me come, I cannot help, and she will surely die."

"But you're probably as heavy as both girls combined. I can't carry everyone."

"Gabriel," Acacia said. "Have no fear for my health. I have lived for thousands of years, and I am glad to go to my Lord. Our embrace has been delayed far too long. Take him and leave me to Glewlwyd's care."

Firming his jaw, Gabriel wagged his head. "I will not trade you for this mad scientist! I'd rather leave him here and have you die in my arms!"

"Then leave me," Shiloh said. "I'm not afraid to die."

A strong tremor raced across the ground, nearly knocking them from their feet. Gabriel grasped Acacia's arm and helped her stay balanced. "We can't keep arguing. I'm carrying Acacia and Shiloh, and that's the end of it."

543

"Then more will perish," Mardon said, shaking his fist. "Sapphira has identical genetics, so she will suffer the same fate Acacia does unless you take me to her."

His words hit Gabriel like a hammer. How could he let both Oracles waste away like this? These twin beacons couldn't be allowed to fade. No! It just couldn't happen!

"Gabriel," Shiloh said softly as she eased up to him. "Take Mardon and Acacia. After you jump into the chasm, I will wait two minutes and follow. When you land safely, fly back up and catch me."

"But what if I can't—"

"You will catch me." She laid her head against his chest. "I trust you with all my heart."

Gabriel drew in his lower lip. How could he let her take such a risk? Impossible! Yet, there seemed to be no choice. He had to trade one impossible situation for another.

Laying a hand on the back of her head, he whispered, "I'll do it. Your faith in me is beyond anything I have ever seen."

After getting directions from Glewlwyd, Gabriel flew Acacia to the chasm and waited near the edge for Mardon and Shiloh to arrive. In the distance, the muscular unicorn galloped across the expanse of green, a magnificent sight.

Another tremor shook the ground. Again Gabriel held Acacia in place. As he grasped her shoulders, the reality of her emaciated state crushed his heart. She was so thin, so frail. How much life could be left in this broken jar of clay?

As if sensing his dismay, Acacia turned and, staring at him with her still brilliant blue eyes, spoke with firm resolve. "Fear not, Gabriel. Although I am now but dust in the wind, I still have one gift remaining that I might yet use to great purpose in Second Eden."

"What gift? And how will you use it?"

"The gift will remain my secret. How I will use it, I do not yet know, but I assume when the opportunity presents itself, I will recognize it."

An even stronger quake rocked the earth. Acacia's legs gave way, but Gabriel caught her and lifted her into his arms. He beat his wings and hovered in place, now immune to the unstable ground.

A loud groan sounded from across the chasm, a low, creaking grumble of rocks grinding against rocks.

Acacia whispered in his ear. "There is a portal here. It's making me sicker than ever. But my eyesight is sharp, and it appears that the other side of this chasm is coming this way."

"The chasm is closing?"

"Not quickly, but steadily." She seemed ready to say something else, but she just leaned her head against him and sighed.

When Shiloh and Mardon arrived, they dismounted and stood with their feet spread apart. Shiloh petted the unicorn and pointed in the direction they had come. "Cornelius, wait here for Glewlwyd. He'll figure out how to get you to safety. And thank you for allowing Mardon to ride."

As the unicorn's head bobbed, Gabriel studied the splendid creature. The legends revealed that they couldn't be ridden by anyone but a virtuous maiden. Apparently Cornelius was willing to make an exception for Mardon.

Gabriel elevated to about three feet off the ground. "Mardon, you'll have to hang on to my legs, but you'd better hang on tight, because we'll be dropping like a rock. I won't put on the brakes until I see the ground."

Mardon wrapped his arms around Gabriel's legs. "I am ready."

As he rose higher and lifted Mardon, he looked at Shiloh. She blew him a kiss, but, straining against Mardon's weight, he could return only a grimacing smile.

545

Flapping his wings mightily, he drifted over the chasm. Mardon trembled and squeezed so tightly, Gabriel's legs ached. The chasm groaned again, and now the narrowing of the gap was easy to see. The bridge drooped farther, and rocks tumbled in from either side. Shiloh crouched to keep her balance. The quake was really rocking this world now.

Gabriel took in a deep breath. It was time to go for it. He lunged horizontally, then folded in his wings. Instantly, they plunged. Mardon's weight eased, though his death grip continued. Acacia buried her face in Gabriel's shirt, but she showed no other signs of fear.

As the wall on each side raced by, rushing air whistled in Gabriel's ears. He tried to breathe, but the wind snatched away most of any mouthful he could grab.

Soon, their surroundings grew dark, too dark to see the walls, much less any sign of ground below. Would he be able to see it in time? Even if he could, would he be able to grab the hurricane-like wind and put the brakes on three hurtling bullets?

After a minute or so, the darkness faded, and they floated for a moment in a clear blue sky before descending once again. Although they dropped quickly, that brief pause seemed to start the process over again, so the plunge wasn't as fast as it had been earlier.

Acacia whispered, "I see the ground, but it's still far away."

"Yep. I'd better start slowing down now." He let his wings out a few inches at a time and tried to catch a slowly increasing amount of air. The wind beat against the webbing, and everything heated up, from his toes to his face to the tips of his wings.

The ground drew closer. He stretched his wings farther. The blast of air lessened, and Mardon's weight seemed to increase until he felt three times as heavy as before. Acacia sagged in Gabriel's arms. Fingernails dug into his legs. Pain flooded every limb.

Gabriel gritted his teeth. He had to make it. There just wasn't any choice. Letting out a loud groan, he spread his wings fully. The raging wind ripped against his canopy. Agony shot from his wings to his spine. Below, Mardon screamed and dug his nails farther in.

Finally, just a few hundred feet above the ground, they slowed. His wings aching, Gabriel swung the trio into a controlled, spiral fall until they landed in a muddy field. Mardon dragged on the ground for a few seconds until he let go and slid in the mud. Then, settling his own feet, Gabriel lowered Acacia gently to the ground.

"I'll be right back," he said, stretching out his wings again. "Wait for me here."

He shot up into the sky. As he rose higher and higher, he searched the blue ceiling, desperately trying to spot the tiniest speck, the slightest hint of a plunging human body. Of course, the greater the elevation, the better chance he had of slowing her down enough to prevent injury, but since she would be plummeting at an enormous rate, and he would be ascending, timing their meeting would take incredible precision. Fortunately, the physics of Earth didn't match the rules here, and the brief pause would likely work in their favor. Otherwise, he would have no chance of catching Shiloh. She would be dropping much too quickly.

547

Once he reached about five thousand feet in the air, he caught a glimpse of a speck much farther above. It had to be Shiloh.

He hovered for a moment, trying to gauge her rate of descent. Stretching out his wings, he used them as a parachute and descended slowly. As Shiloh approached, he drew them in a little at a time until he dropped in a feet-first plunge. She had spread her arms and legs, slowing her descent just enough to match his.

When she came within a hundred feet, her face clarified, wide-eyed and flushed. He reached up for her. She reached back, her fingers groping.

Slowly, the gap decreased. Gabriel glanced down. The muddy field rushed toward them. Acacia was already easy to see, her white hair a beacon of danger.

Gabriel let out his wings another inch. Shiloh dropped into his arms. Stretching out fully, he slammed on the brakes. Again, agony shot up and down his spine. The base of his wings strained against his back, feeling as though they might rip away.

Finally, his feet slammed into the mud. The soft turf absorbed some of the momentum, but as he rolled, he couldn't keep Shiloh from getting a face full of sloppy soil.

When they came to a stop, he helped her up. Her face, chest, and arms were covered with mud.

"I'm so sorry." He tried to wipe her cheeks with his sleeve but managed only to smear more dirt.

Shiloh laughed. In fact, she laughed so hard she couldn't speak. She wrapped her arms around Gabriel's waist and buried her face in his muddy shirt.

He laughed with her, feeling light and carefree, but only for a moment. As wonderful as it felt to land safely, they had to figure out what they should do next.

He set his hand on the back of her head and looked at Acacia and Mardon. "So, where are we?"

Acacia stooped next to a strange plant. With two big leaves pressed against each other and a lump in between, it seemed to be praying. "This is the birthing garden where once-dead people are given new bodies for life in Second Eden."

"I guess that means we made it. Is anyone hurt?"

"I'm fine." Acacia straightened. "How about you?"

After breaking his embrace with Shiloh, Gabriel pulled up a pant leg, revealing a long, deep gash. "It looks worse than it feels."

"If anyone cares," Mardon said as he tucked something away under his tunic, "I am unharmed."

Gabriel eyed Mardon. It was better not to trust even his slightest movements. "What are you hiding?"

"I am hiding nothing." Mardon withdrew the object, a long strand of white hair. "I persuaded Acacia to give it to me so that I may confirm my theory about her illness."

548

"You can tell what's wrong from her hair?"

"And from the skin cells still attached. I believe her genetic structure has been altered. This will be sufficient."

Gabriel offered an approving nod. What could it hurt? Maybe he could help Acacia and Sapphira. He looked around at the surrounding field and bordering walls and forest. "So if we can find a place to clean up, maybe—"

"Oh, my!" Acacia jumped up and away from the plant.

Behind the two praying leaves, a bright rectangular light flashed, like sunlight shining through a window. As the rectangle grew, its edges drawing away from the center, its brilliance dimmed, and a transparent circle took shape at the focal point, growing at the same rate the entire box expanded.

After a few seconds, it looked like an enormous sheet of glass, easy to see through, like a window into another world. On the other side, a stooped old man and a unicorn appeared, standing in a room that looked like an old library.

549

Shiloh clapped her hands. "Glewlwyd and Cornelius! They're safe!"

Glewlwyd bowed. He moved his lips to speak, but no sound came through. As he straightened, his stoop disappeared, his face smoothed out, and his hair filled in, turning from white to brown.

Gabriel bowed in return. He reached a hand toward the window, but a sharp tingle made him draw it back. "I guess we can't go that way."

"Is that Heaven's Gate?" Mardon asked.

Touching her chin, Acacia studied it. "When I last saw it, it was blue, but I recognize that room. It's the antechamber that leads to the altar. Since the Bridgelands are likely gone now, maybe it's the same gate."

Gabriel stared at the barrier. The chamber faded away, as did the man and unicorn, leaving a transparent glass-like sheet. Glare from the sunshine provided the only hint that it was there at all.

Now the back of the garden came into view, as if the gateway to another world had become a window.

"We should go to the village," Acacia said as she pointed toward a forest on the other side of a field. "It's just beyond those trees. We can get cleaned up and find someone to look at the scratches on your legs."

Gabriel looked at his filthy body. Acacia was right about cleaning up, but it was more important to get Mardon's research going than to get a doctor to look at a few scratches. With only a strand of hair and some skin cells providing clues, Mardon might need help in figuring out what was wrong with Acacia. Could Ashley provide what he needed? Maybe. Certainly by now she would have advanced the technology in this world.

"Okay. Let's go." Walking between Shiloh and Acacia, he took their hands and headed toward the trees. Mardon followed quietly. As Gabriel glanced back at the dirty, scarred mad scientist, a tingle ran up his spine. Maybe trusting him was a mistake, but there seemed to be no choice. Acacia was dying, and saving her was all that mattered.

THE CALM BEFORE THE STORM

Billy lay on a hospital bed, a proper bed with sheets and a blanket, far better than the cots in the old triage hut. A leather bandage wrapped around his ribcage several times, covering his otherwise bare chest. After pushing the blanket down to his toes and stripping to thin, pajama-like trousers, he had done all he could to stay cool. For some reason, the room had grown much too warm.

Underneath his arm bandage, sweat stung his wound. That was by far the deeper of the two cuts, but the spear didn't rip any tendons, so it would heal fine.

Ashley bustled in, carrying a thin stack of parchments and a feather pen. After scratching a few marks on the top page, she smiled. "Are you ready to check out?"

"You bet." Billy sat up. "Only five hours in a hospital. That has to be a new record."

"The record is the temperature outside. My homemade thermometer says thirty-two degrees Celsius."

He half closed an eye. "So that's about ninety Fahrenheit?"

"Very good. It's eighty-nine point six, but my meter isn't exactly precise, so give or take a couple of degrees."

He let out a whistle. "The locals must be roasting."

"They are, especially the sick ones." She poked his shoulder with her finger. "That's why I want you out. You got a few hours' sleep. That should be enough for a warrior like you."

He gave her a thankful smile. "What's the rush?"

"We're taking the hospital back into the air. It should be cooler up there, and if the new army shows up, everyone will be safer."

A knock sounded at the door, and a sweet voice sang out, "I have something for you." Bonnie walked in with a bundle of clothes, his village battle uniform. As her wings waved at him, she patted the top of her pile. "All clean and ready for my warrior."

Billy reached for her hand. Her own uniform looked sharp, obviously freshly laundered, though a rip in her right sleeve revealed that she hadn't had time to mend it. The scratch on her cheek was already healing nicely. Although it probably wouldn't leave a scar, it made her look like the sword maiden she was.

He caressed her knuckles, causing her to grimace. "Oh. Sorry." He looked at her hand. A deep gash ran across her knuckles from her index finger to her pinky.

She pulled her hand back and examined her wound. "It's not bad. Just superficial. But I didn't want a bandage. I need to keep my fingers free."

"I don't blame you. A sword maiden needs her hands to be unbound."

Smiling, she showed him her other hand. "And I hope you don't mind. I moved the engagement ring for now. It irritates the wound."

"I don't mind at all."

She touched the bandage on his arm. "How's your wound?"

Billy nodded at Ashley. "Better ask the doctor."

"It's pretty deep, but he'll be fine." Ashley took the clothes from Bonnie and tossed them on Billy's legs. "Get up, tiger. Bonnie and I'll meet you outside."

Giving him a wave and a smile, Bonnie spun on her toes and hurried to the door with a bounce in her step. When the door closed, Billy got up and put on his long-sleeved undershirt. Wearing all three layers would be warm, but necessary. The second layer, the metallic shirt, would chafe his skin without protection, and the tighter over-tunic held everything in place.

When he pulled up the uniform's green pants and tucked in the shirt, a loud knock sounded. He buckled his belt and called, "Come in."

The door swung open, and Bonnie ran through. Alarm filled her eyes. "They're coming!"

"Goliath's army?" Billy threw the mail shirt over his head and pulled it down.

553

She nodded briskly. "Your father was on patrol and saw them leaving the marsh."

"Did he describe them?"

"They look like something out of a history book; Romans from Caesar's time, Egyptians from the days of Moses, Chinese from an ancient dynasty, and they have full armor, horses, and chariots."

Billy stuffed his head through his tunic and thrust the hem down his torso. As he looked into her wide eyes, he spoke in a calm tone. "How many?"

"Two hundred, maybe. But that might be just the first wave. They're not marching very fast, but they could be here in about forty-five minutes."

"Let's move!" Billy grabbed his sword belt, Excalibur still attached, and swung it around his waist. As he buckled it on, they hurried through the hospital's long hallway. "Were they wearing cloaks like the Vacants had?"

"No," she said as she jogged at his side, "but your father said they seemed to be coated with something reddish, like powder."

"Rust." He burst through the double exit doors, held one for a moment while Bonnie hurried through, then ran across the dragon landing platform. Taking Bonnie's hand, he leaped to the ground three feet below, bypassing a makeshift stairway.

"Hey! Wait up!" Walter jumped down and joined them. "Ashley sprung me from the hospital. I'm ready to roll."

"Did you hear about the army?" Billy asked.

Walter shrugged. "What's a few hundred historically misplaced soldiers? They won't even speak the same language. They have to be as confused as a herd of cows landing on Mars."

"Charging bulls, maybe, but good point. We'll see." Together, all three dashed into the village. When they reached the central circle, Valiant, Elam, and Sapphira stood next to the bell, each wearing full battle gear as well as somber faces. With the bell still and silent, they obviously hadn't sounded an alarm.

"Where's everyone else?" Billy asked.

Flexing his forearm, Elam strangled the hilt of the sword protruding from its hip scabbard. "Sick or helping with the sick. It looks like Ashley was right. Only the Second Edeners are getting it. They don't seem to be immune like we are."

"We're guessing it's a bug from Earth," Sapphira said.

Elam took Sapphira's hand. "We speculated that it came with the rubellite Billy's mother sent. The timing would be about right."

"A bug actually on the gem?" Billy shook his head. "That doesn't make sense. It would have to survive exposure and then a trip through a fiery wall."

"Or maybe," Elam said, "a certain witch introduced the virus through one of her witch's brews."

Billy shifted his weight from one foot to the other. Elam was probably right again. Semiramis had been following a plan from day one, and this disease was likely just part of the scheme. The huge army they were building proved that she didn't need Flint or his people. They were pawns, and their sickness provided a way to spread the virus, both through the shadow people and through the survivors in Flint's village. Ruth's illness had been short-lived and her symptoms were quite different, so that seemed unrelated. This was definitely biological warfare.

"No matter who brought it," Elam continued, "it's here, and we have to deal with it. Since most of our villagers have it, the remaining healthy women and children are taking care of the sick. Valiant is one of the few Second Eden warriors left standing."

"Candle will join us soon," Sapphira said. "He's flying the plane to get an update on troop count and movements, and Yereq and Sir Barlow are at the field by the birthing garden waiting for him to return."

Billy imagined a thundering horde stampeding toward the little village—iron chariots, charging horses, and savages with blood-thirsty hearts. "That's just not enough," he said. "How can we possibly defeat so many?"

555

Lifting a hand, Valiant looked up at the clear sunny sky. "Only by faith. Without help from above we are doomed. Listener is organizing a prayer vigil in the hospital. When Candle returns, we will gather and send our prayers into the sky as an appeal to the Father of Lights."

"So we have …" Walter lifted his fingers in rapid succession. "Me, Elam, Billy, Bonnie, Valiant, Candle, Yereq, Sir Barlow, and Sapphira. That's nine of us and the dragons." He let out a whistle. "I don't know about you, but if we're facing hundreds of crazed warriors trained to kill, I'd like at least ten."

"You got it!" Ashley strode toward them wearing an oversized battle uniform and clutching the hilt of a sword at her belt. Stopping at Walter's side, she squared her shoulders. "I'm not as skilled as any of you, but I've sparred enough with Walter."

Walter grinned. "I won't argue with that!"

She nudged him playfully with an elbow. "Don't get me started."

"What about the patients?" Bonnie asked.

"They have Doc, Patrick, Ruth, Steadfast, Marilyn, and Listener taking care of them," Ashley said, "and one very interesting addition. It turns out that Hunter is really Mardon, the crazy scientist who tried to bring Heaven and Earth together. It's a long story, but Gabriel met him while trying to find Shiloh and Acacia. Gabriel's body has been restored, and he brought all three back here."

Sapphira nearly leaped off her feet. "Acacia's here?"

Ashley nodded toward the hospital. "She's here, but she's not well. She has some sort of degenerative disease." She touched Sapphira's arm tenderly. "I don't think she'll last much longer. Doc's working with Mardon to figure out what's going on. If anyone can solve the puzzle, I think they will."

"We can't trust Mardon," Elam said. "He's been posing as Hunter and working with Semiramis for years. You can bet that he'll use his research against us. He just wants to get into Heaven by force."

Ashley laughed under her breath. "Believe me, Patrick and Marilyn already accused him of every crime in the book. He claims that he has always loved the two Oracles, and he won't betray them. There are plenty of people in the hospital to watch his every move."

Sapphira looked up at Elam, tears brimming. "Isn't there any way we can let him try? If he can save Acacia, then maybe we can stop him from doing anything else."

Tightening his jaw, Elam gazed at Sapphira for several seconds. It seemed that a battle was raging in his mind, a struggle between judgment and mercy. Finally, he nodded. "Only if Acacia stays away from him."

"Don't worry about that," Ashley said. "Gabriel won't let him touch her. Mardon has a strand of Acacia's hair to work with, and that's all he'll get. But it should be enough. He and Doc will use my lab equipment in the hospital, and they'll be floating high above the village while Gabriel, Shiloh, and Acacia stay here."

"So, where is Acacia now?" Sapphira asked.

"Getting cleaned up. Shiloh's helping her in the ladies' washroom, while Marilyn's patching up Gabriel. He got some nasty-looking scratches on his legs."

"Did my mother ever get to talk to my father?" Billy asked.

Bonnie touched his arm. "While we were rescuing Walter."

"I was there," Elam said. "It was pretty good. I think you could call their interaction 'subdued joy,' but they talked more about you than each other."

Biting his lip, Billy nodded. He could picture the scene. Mom hadn't seen Dad in almost five years, and now he was a dragon again. They probably just looked at each other while they talked, both aching to embrace. But the scales-on-skin contact would have been like acid, a reminder that they were still worlds apart. Mom's love was still as strong as ever, but the blend of joy and pain had to be tearing her heart in two.

557

"Anyway," Ashley continued, "back to the original topic. We weren't able to isolate the bug, but I mixed up an elixir that might help. There's really not much more I can do. Doc knows more about cell structures and medicines than I do." She curled her arm around Walter's. "And I want to be with my fiancé. Someone has to watch his back."

"I'm glad to have you with me," Walter said, "but I'm afraid I might be watching out for you more than fighting the bad guys."

She raised a finger near his eyes. "If you do, I'll kick you in the backside. And if you're going to die, I'm coming with you. You're not going to Heaven without me."

Walter raised his hands. "I wouldn't dream of it."

"Besides," Ashley said, "I have to make sure our fuel trap works."

"Are we sticking with Candle flying the plane?" Billy asked. "If their troops are protected with rust, Excalibur won't do much good, so maybe I should fly it."

Elam touched the hilt of his sword. "We still need Excalibur in the battle. Maybe some of the enemy won't be as protected as others. Windor's sick, but he still wants to be the bombardier for Candle, so we'll go with the original plan."

"Good thing they didn't bring Nazis with machine guns and tanks," Walter said. "I'm not sure who's in Hades, but you've got to figure some of them were."

"So, where are the dragons?" Billy asked.

Elam nodded toward the northeast. "They're lining up along the village border. Since most of our dragon riders are sick, we'll have to fill in. Dikaios is with the dragons, and he's supposed to meet us with a new report soon."

"Sounds good," Billy said. "We'll just have to do the best we can."

558

"Let's get moving." Elam gripped Billy's elbow and led him down the street. "There's something I have to show you, something strange in the garden."

As the others followed, Billy tried to read Elam's face. "Have you taken care of the plants?"

"All but the one I planted. Before he got sick, Windor dug them up and hauled a lot of the soil to the new garden in the hospital." Elam broke into a jog. "You'll have to see what I mean."

Billy kept pace. Behind him, the sounds of running footsteps echoed in the empty village. When they reached the field, now completely free of snow and basking in warm sunshine, they slowed to negotiate the mixture of mud and grass. Yereq and Sir Barlow stood at the far end of the field, looking up at the sky. The low buzz of a propeller sounded from somewhere, signaling Candle's approach. With the snow gone and the mud drying, his landing wouldn't be as difficult as usual.

Ahead, something shimmered in the garden, a rectangular shape so large, it seemed to have no borders on either side or at the top.

Elam quick-marched along a furrow while Billy followed in the one next to it. With the plants gone, no one had to worry about tripping and hurting one of the babies.

Coming to a sudden stop a few paces away from the shining rectangle, Elam stretched out his hand and waved it over the light. "It's like a force field. It tingles when I get close, so I wasn't sure if I should touch it. It reminds me of the wall I saw at the Bridgelands, but it was blue there, and you couldn't see through it. This one's transparent."

Billy shielded his eyes. "It's like sunlight on water, almost blinding."

"And look at this." Elam pointed with the toe of his shoe. The only remaining birthing plant stood just inches in front of the base of the wall. The leaves, although green on the surface, emanated a reddish glow from within.

559

"Too close for comfort?" Billy asked.

"Right. Windor moved the others before this wall showed up. I told him to leave this one here, because I thought there might still be a chance of resurrecting Makaidos. I hope it's okay where it is."

When the others caught up, Sapphira stepped close to the force field. "It's a portal. I can sense it."

"Your eyesight?" Elam asked.

"My sight and the feeling of sorrow." She knelt next to the plant. "I can see inside this fragile shell. Our dear friend Makaidos is within, but unlike other unborns at this stage, he cannot survive without two essential catalysts that will give him life. We can provide one of those now." She looked up at Ashley. "Do you have the crystal egg I formed out of your father's tears?"

"Always." Ashley pulled a thin necklace and lifted a glassy egg from behind her tunic.

Sapphira extended her hand. "May I have it? This is the first catalyst."

"Of course." Ashley reached behind her neck, unfastened a clasp, and laid the necklace in Sapphira's palm. "Anything for my father."

"I hope I'm doing this correctly. Our teacher in the Valley of Souls had no egg to demonstrate with." Sapphira closed her fist around the crystal. For a few seconds, a flaming halo encircled her hand. When she spread out her fingers, the egg glowed with a blinding white light. Using a finger, she dug a shallow hole directly under the roots and pushed the egg in. As soon as she covered it over with soil, a stream of light crawled up the stem, as if an iridescent dye flowed vertically through its channels. When the stream flowed into the pair of leaves, they vibrated with a rhythmic beat.

Soon, the light faded, and the plant returned to normal. Sapphira petted the leaves softly. "I see a heart beating. Perhaps it was there before, but it's clear and strong now."

"What's the second catalyst?" Elam asked.

She rose to her feet, her expression sad and forlorn. "A sacrifice. Someone will have to give his or her life for Makaidos to be reborn. My teacher said that I must apply the blood of our willing victim to the plant's leaves."

"Who will it be? Has it already been planned?"

"Our teacher wouldn't tell us," Sapphira said. "It's hard to explain, but, in the Valley of Souls, the concept of planning is very strange."

A ripple of light ran across the wall, and a voice sounded as if echoing the tremors of energy. "The lamb has been preparing for this sacrifice for many years, though he or she does not yet know it."

Directly behind the plant, a vertical line of dazzling light split the wall. A leg protruded, then an arm. Finally, a man appeared.

He stepped around the plant and stood with his arms crossed over his Second Eden-style leather tunic and breeches. His white hair and thin white beard dressed him with many years, but his sparkling eyes told of youthful vigor.

"Father Enoch!" Sapphira hugged him around the waist. "It's wonderful to see you again!"

He laid a palm on the back of her head. "And you, dear child."

"It's good to see you again," Elam said, shaking Enoch's hand. "I assume you're aware of the coming army."

"Indeed. And you are ill prepared. They outnumber you at least a hundred to one."

"A hundred to one!" Elam looked at each member of his company. Billy read Elam's dismay. It felt like a stab in the gut. All of their planning now seemed like spitting into a hurricane.

"They are still gathering their forces," Enoch continued. "Many have been summoned from a great distance, and Arramos, whom I will now call by his real name, Satan, has timed their arrival for this date and hour."

561

"Why do they need so many to conquer two little villages like ours?" Elam asked.

"Oh, they haven't assembled this army to conquer you." Enoch spread out his arms and called out. "Gather around, everyone, and I will explain. We can take the time, for I must give you a solemn charge."

Yereq, Sir Barlow, and Candle, who had been standing at the edge of the garden, walked toward them. Billy, Bonnie, Walter, Ashley, Elam, Sapphira, and Valiant formed a semicircle in front of Enoch, leaving room for the three others to join in.

Enoch touched the wall, raising a bright light around the outline of his hand. "The army has come to attack Heaven itself. The alliance with Flint was merely a vehicle, a stepping-stone of sorts. Satan often uses willing fools in his quest to bring down Heaven's throne. He makes them feel important for a time, then casts them down when they are no longer needed. Now the evil one finally has the means to attack Heaven's Gate with the legions of warrior slaves he has collected throughout history."

"So is this the same Heaven's Gate I saw in the Bridgelands?" Elam asked.

"It is. The Bridgelands were nothing more than a buffer that separated the realms of Earth, Hades, and Second Eden. When the realms joined, the buffer collapsed and brought all three to Heaven's doorstep. The single world now is a blend of three realities. Because of the temperature, my guess is that where we are standing is a temperate or subtropical zone on Earth, and the residents there have been forced from their usual abode and must find a suitable habitat. Fortunately for us, we blended into Earth's environment in a zone that was inhabited by very few humans."

"Do we have other Earth dwellers here now?" Elam asked.

"And Hades dwellers. Except for this barrier to Heaven, all portals have been destroyed. There is no limit to travel between the realms."

Billy looked at the wall at the east side of the birthing garden, the only barricade separating them from the advancing army. "Are you going to send warriors from Heaven that'll mow down the forces of Hades?"

Enoch pulled Billy's sword from its scabbard and lifted it high. Even in the bright sunshine, its glow created a brilliant aura. "We have thousands of angels, and they could wipe out this horde in short order, but that will not be God's way. Since Satan is bringing an army of his followers and not his demonic host, Jehovah wishes to counter with his own servants and not with his angelic advantage." He slid the sword back into the scabbard, extinguishing its glow. "Those who live by faith are always more powerful than those who live by sword and sinew."

Billy again imagined the attacking army, hundreds and hundreds of warriors armed to the teeth. "I guess it makes sense, but I don't see what's wrong with having a few angels on our side."

"Angels on your side?" Enoch chuckled. "I suppose you could say that. Although they are neither Cherubim nor Seraphim, the two faithful witnesses who felled the giants' tower to Heaven are working behind the scenes to help you in whatever way they can." He added a wink. "In fact, I think you know them, an especially spunky redhead and a petite songstress. Although they cannot come out here for the battle, they are at this very moment behind that wall planning their strategy."

Billy looked at Ashley standing near the end of their semicircle. Her broad smile said it all. She knew who the redhead was, her sister Karen. And Elam's melancholy expression revealed his recognition of the songstress, Naamah.

"So what do we do?" Elam asked.

"Defend this gate. Repel the attackers. Take courage, knowing that you have been prepared for such a time as this, and even if some of you die in battle, you will not be forsaken. You will simply pass through this barrier and take your place with the saints who cheer you on from that side of eternity." Enoch raised a finger. "And there is one more issue. It is crucial that you bring Flint to the battlefield. Jehovah wants him to see what his decisions have wrought."

563

Elam nodded at Sir Barlow. "Will you see to that?"

"With pleasure." Barlow lumbered toward the village.

"Now," Enoch said as he stepped back toward the wall, "I must leave you in order to advise our two angels." He paused and looked at the plant, a sad expression sagging his features. "Until the lamb comes to complete the sacrifice, you will likely suffer great losses. Pray that she comes soon."

With that, he turned and disappeared through the split in the wall. Then, as if closed by a zipper, the line sealed from bottom to top.

Billy glanced at Bonnie, then at everyone else. Had they picked up the clue? Enoch said, "She." Who could be the female who would act as a sacrifice that would bring Makaidos back to life?

Bonnie whispered into his ear. "It's better not to guess. Let the one who is called do what she must do."

A low hum sounded from the village. Above the trees, the hospital rose slowly into the sky. With the sun shining on its metallic shell, the glint blinded them for a moment, but when it turned and continued to ascend, the luster faded. Soon, it shrank to the size of a mechanical pencil.

Elam locked wrists with Valiant. "Are you ready, my friend?"

"I will be, after we pray." Valiant's muscular forearm rippled as he firmed his grip with Elam. "With the enemy closing in, a moment in prayer will feel like another layer of armor."

From the forest near the village, two figures appeared, Barlow with his arm around Flint. As the two drew closer, Elam faced Heaven's Gate and lowered himself to his knees. The others joined him in another semicircle. Forming a chain of hands, Elam on one end and Valiant on the other, they waited for Barlow to arrive.

Billy looked at Bonnie. Kneeling with her at Heaven's Gate felt like the fulfillment of the greatest dream of all time. Someday, when their engagement time reached its climax, they would kneel at an altar of marriage, but could it ever match this heavenly altar?

When Barlow and Flint arrived, Candle released Walter's hand at the middle of the line. Barlow knelt, took Candle's hand, and looked up at Flint, who stood shakily. "There is always room for one more," Barlow said.

Crossing his arms, Flint offered a timid shake of his head and stepped back a few paces. "I am ill, and I don't want to infect Candle or Valiant."

"Very well." Barlow grasped Walter's hand and closed the line.

At the end of the row on Billy's left, Valiant lifted a hand and called out in a loud, vibrant voice. "Father of Lights, creator of all, hear our plea. We kneel at the doorstep of Paradise and ask you to grant us more strength than we have in our muscles, more courage than we feel in our hearts, and more endurance than our feeble arms and legs now possess. We are humbled by your confidence in us, that you would deem us worthy to suffer, bleed, and die for the sake of defending your glory. Although you could sweep this rabble away with a breath, you have blessed us with this great honor. Let us be your breath. Let us be your might. Let us be your hand of wrath upon your enemy."

Valiant took a deep breath and continued in a softer, gentler tone. "And let us be your hand of mercy as we extend your grace to Flint, an offer of forgiveness if he would only turn from his rebellious ways and allow himself to be embraced by your love."

Billy sneaked a look at Flint. He kept his stare locked on the eastern wall, shaking in spite of the warmth.

Lowering his hand, Valiant ended with a quiet, "Let this prayer be answered according to your wisdom, by which we all strive to live."

Bonnie whispered, "Amen." Several others echoed with quiet amens of their own.

Pulling on each other's hands, they rose as one. Valiant walked over to Elam and grasped his upper arm. "Warrior Chief, the command is yours."

Elam looked around at his little army, his muscles flexing and his eyes flashing. "Candle, are the bombs ready?"

The teenager's dark face lit up with a brilliant smile. "They are on the airplane. Windor is aboard. He was too sick to come out."

"Get in the air. One or more of the dragon riders will guide your bombing runs." Now animated in his delivery, Elam thrust a finger toward Ashley. "Is the fuel apparatus ready?"

She nodded. "We'll burn the whole village before we'll let them into the garden."

"Excellent." Elam grabbed Barlow's hand with both of his. "My good friend and noble knight, are you ready to go to battle on a dragon?"

Barlow's smile lifted his mustache. "By all means! May I ride on my old friend Legossi?"

Deepening his voice to mimic the knight, Elam said, "By all means!" Adding a laugh, he pointed toward the village. "You go ahead of us and tell the dragons that we'll be there soon. They're probably getting anxious by now."

While Barlow hurried away, Elam paced back and forth in front of the others. "When the enemy comes within reach, Billy will try Excalibur's beam. When he has done all he can with it, he will ride Clefspeare into battle. Walter will ride on Firedda, Ashley on Thigocia, Bonnie on Hartanna, Valiant on Yellinia, and I will take Sorentine. Remember to watch for weakness in the dragons. That would indicate that the enemy has candlestones, and we will have to call off our dragon cavalry. And remember this. If your dragon falls to that evil gem, and you survive the fall, but the dragon is incapacitated, you must leave the dragon and hurry back here to help with guarding Heaven's Gate. There is nothing more important. Our dragon friends will understand."

Billy gauged everyone's expression. Bonnie, in particular, grimaced at the thought of leaving her mother behind, but they all seemed to understand that this strategy was necessary.

"Sapphira will stay on the ground," Elam continued, "and ride Dikaios to light the fires when the enemy gets close enough to our trap. Yereq will stand here at the wall as the final guard. Any enemy who gets past our defenses will have to face him."

He stopped pacing and, with a serious bend in his brow, faced his troops. "Any questions?"

566

"I have one." Bonnie pointed at the forest near the village. "What are we going to do with her?"

Like a timid deer, Listener peeked out from behind a tree. Dressed in the village's battle uniform, she walked slowly toward them, her head low and the spyglass in her grip. With sleeves and pant legs overlapping her hands and boots, she looked like a soldier who had shrunk while wearing her clothes.

Bonnie whispered, but her voice was loud enough for everyone to hear. "I know what she's doing."

"The lamb?" Elam asked.

Bonnie nodded. "At least she thinks she is. She overheard me talking to Sapphira about the need of a sacrifice to resurrect Makaidos. Since she feels like she should have died in his place, she wants to be the one."

As Listener approached, the image of her nearly lifeless body on the surgery cot came back to Billy's mind. During those torturous hours, everyone had worked so hard to keep this precious girl alive. Makaidos had given his own life in her place, choosing flames and forfeiture of his soul to let her live.

567

Billy shook his head. No way. There was no way he would let her die now.

"Bonnie," he said, keeping his own voice low, "can you fly her up to the hospital?"

"I can try, but—"

"No time," Elam said. "We have to go to war. And, besides, the choice of the lamb isn't our business."

Billy gritted his teeth. Like Valiant had said earlier, they were going to battle for little girls like this. How could they let her die now?

Dikaios galloped out of the forest. When he caught up with Listener, he stopped, helped her climb to his back, and carried her to the garden.

"Their army is now complete," Dikaios said when he arrived. "Clefspeare estimates at least nine hundred armed men, perhaps a thousand, along with two hundred horses and fifty chariots. He expects them to arrive within fifteen minutes."

Elam looked into the horse's eyes. "My good friend, when we met in the Bridgelands, did you know that we would be facing such an army together?"

"No, Elam. I was called to serve my master, and that is all I need to know. If I must sacrifice limb or life, I do so gladly, for there is no greater joy than to die in my master's hands."

"Well stated." Elam looked down and dragged his shoe across the drying mud. He seemed ready to speak again, but he just sighed and whispered, "Well stated."

"I have come to help Timothy resurrect," Listener said from atop Dikaios. She sucked in a breath and squared her shoulders. "I can fight almost as well as Candle. I promise not to die on purpose."

Billy turned away. Watching that girl's determined, yet piteous expression would make him laugh or cry, or maybe both at the same time.

"Let her come with me," Sapphira said to Elam. "She can help me set the fires. We certainly can't leave her alone in the village."

"I guess that will have to do." His face melancholy, Elam looked at Billy. "I'm going now. You have a couple of minutes if you need more time with your friends."

Billy nodded. "Yeah. Thanks."

Elam stood face to face with Sapphira. She looked up at him, her eyes moist. He looked back at her. They neither moved nor spoke.

Billy slid his hand into Bonnie's. He could feel the heartache. Elam and Sapphira had waited thousands of years to come together, often in the abyss of loneliness. Now they had to separate once more, and who could tell if one or both of them might die in battle?

Elam lifted his hand and wiggled his fingers. A tear emerged from Sapphira's eye. A spasm shook her body, and as she wiggled her own fingers, she broke into sobs, but she didn't say a word.

Turning abruptly, Elam signaled for Valiant. They each took one of Flint's arms and marched him out of the garden.

Bonnie embraced Sapphira and kissed the top of her head, then, with Ashley's help, boosted her onto Dikaios's back with Listener. Without a word, Dikaios turned and trotted away.

Walter clapped Billy on the shoulder. "You ready?"

"I think so." Billy gripped Excalibur's hilt and looked around. Yereq stood in front of the plant, his feet set firmly and his arms locked over his chest. The great giant was now the only one in the garden besides Billy, Walter, Bonnie, and Ashley.

"We'd better go." Billy reached for Bonnie's hand. "How about you? Are you ready?"

Her eyes a blend of sadness and determination, she nodded. "I am."

Walter pulled Billy and Ashley closer, and Bonnie joined them in a tight circle. "Listen, guys," Walter said with a shot of confidence in his voice. "This is just like old times, the four of us fighting the bad guys. We've battled the forces of Hades before; we can do it again." He put his hand in the middle of their huddle, palm down. "If you don't believe we're going to win this thing, then don't join your hand with mine. But if you think that the God who took us to Hades and back is going to help us kick these guys' butts, then let's see it."

Ashley laid her hand on top of his. "I believe it with all my heart!"

Bonnie's hand came next. "Whether I live or die, I am the Lord's, and he will win the battle."

Billy looked at each set of joyous eyes. What faith! What sincerity! They exuded the overflowing confidence they had been learning through all their incredible adventures. And now, when called to face almost certain death, they showed no hint of hesitation. How could any army, no matter how great, conquer a God who could instill such supernatural courage in his soldiers, no matter how few?

Billy laid his hand on top. He then set his other hand underneath and pressed the layers closer. Reaching for the same confident tone, he let his gaze pass across each face. "Nothing will ever separate us, neither life, nor death, nor the armies of Hell. If I don't see you again on this side of the heavenly wall, I will see you on the other."

THE INVASION

Billy stood next to Clefspeare. Both stared into the northeast-ern field, the same field where they had battled the shadow people.

In the daylight, everything seemed so different—bright, cheery, almost peaceful. Yes, *almost*. Billy's danger alarm was already burning in his stomach. A rise in the landscape prevented them from seeing beyond a half mile or so, but a low rumble from somewhere in the distance agreed with the alarm. Something big was on its way.

Hartanna's recent surveillance report had said that a marauding army was now marching faster and would crest the rise in less than three minutes. Chariots rolled in the front line along with dozens of bowmen and spearmen. The war they had awaited these four years was now upon them.

Billy lifted Excalibur and let it glow. Hartanna had confirmed the rust coating on most of the troops, but not all had been pro-tected. Maybe he could take out enough soldiers to slow them down, or at least spread a little panic.

Hiding in the forest at the left side of the field, Dikaios waited with Sapphira on his back. Nearby, Listener rode Ember, her pigtails swinging in the warm breeze as she carried an unlit torch in each hand. Dikaios pawed the ground with a hoof. The warrior horse was ready for action.

On the right side of the field, Ashley and Thigocia also hid among the trees. Ashley held a hose that led up into a tall evergreen where it split into several feeder tubes attached to bags of airplane fuel. In the other direction, the hose split again into a web of tubes that spread out over the field. Ashley had drilled tiny holes throughout the tubing network and laid it in the grass several weeks before she and Walter covered the field with the filament net. Now, with the net removed, the tubes would be ready for the attack.

With her hand on a valve, she waited for the right time to open it. Gravity would force the fuel into the tubes and spray both the ground and the invaders. Then she and Thigocia would take to the sky while Sapphira set everything ablaze. Her timing would have to be perfect.

Above, Merlin flew back and forth over the expanse between the fire trap and the rise. Candle and Windor were ready. The bombs would soon be falling.

To each side of Clefspeare, dragons had lined up in a row, leaving a gap of about ten paces between them. Bonnie sat atop Hartanna to their left, and Elam rode Sorentine to his right. To Elam's right, Walter sat high on Firedda's neck, his muscles flexed. He was ready to go to war. Beyond him, Sir Barlow rode Legossi. She had brought her head back toward him, and he was whispering something in her ear. Dragon and warrior grinned, both apparently in good humor.

To Billy's left, beyond Hartanna, Valiant rode Yellinia. Both were stoic, perhaps even sad. As many times as Valiant had gone to war, it seemed strange that he appeared to despise it so much.

Such was the character of nobility—a hatred for violence, yet a willingness to perform it to protect the innocent from its jaws.

Billy tried to settle his heart. As soon as Excalibur disintegrated as many enemy troops as possible, the ground on which they all stood would erupt with dragons flying into battle.

Behind the line of dragons, Flint sat against a tree. Still very sick, his arms hung loosely at his sides. Obviously, he couldn't do anyone harm, and Elam and Valiant wanted him to witness the trouble his alliance with Goliath had caused. If the attacking army managed to break through, Flint would be at their mercy, though no one thought they would show him any.

In a cloud of dust, a chariot appeared at the top of the rise and halted. Two horses reared up and stomped the newly dried mud. Four other chariots joined the first, and the lead driver steered his horses to the side, allowing him to view the land ahead.

Billy clenched Excalibur. Just a few were in sight. It would be best to wait as long as possible. Besides, he had never tested the beam's power from this far away. Still, with the restored rubellite in the hilt, it would probably work.

573

The lead driver shouted. His horses wheeled the chariot around and charged. The other four pursued in a wild gallop. Like a rush of ants, men clad in dark armor swarmed over the rise and flooded the landscape, some on foot and some on horseback. Brown dust flew all around, masking their churning legs. At least three invaders stood taller than the others, the surviving Nephilim, and the oddly shaped heads of a few Vacants were obvious in the midst of the throng.

Elam drew his sword. "Billy, you may attack when ready."

As battle cries pounded his ears like a sonic hammer, Billy lit up Excalibur's beam and pointed it straight up. The horde's front line would be in the fuel trap in less than two minutes. It was time to thin them out.

A flutter of wings made him look back. Gabriel flew horizontally along the ground and settled between Billy and Elam. Dressed in the village's battle uniform, he withdrew a sword from a scabbard at his hip. "I'm reporting for duty."

"Excellent," Elam said. "We can always use another warrior."

"Warrior?" Gabriel waved his sword. "I have zero training, but I might be able to take someone out from the air."

"Where are Shiloh and Acacia?" Billy asked.

Gabriel pointed toward the village with his thumb. "Behind me. I told them to stay put, but I'm not sure they will. Acacia thinks she can muster up a little more fire, but—"

"No more time to talk." Billy angled the beam toward the rushing mass and swept it from right to left across the field. As soon as the beam made contact with a soldier, sparks flew. One man disappeared, but four surrounding him continued running, though the one following had to leap over the tumbling armor.

As if jumping from place to place, the sparks erupted in a ragged pattern. A horse vanished, sending its rider flying. Three men running side by side disintegrated, but the next five merely glowed red.

Finally, the last line charged over the rise. A lone man rode a horse at the top of the crest. Tall and dressed in black from head to toe, he stopped and watched the scene, apparently content to let the advance troops do the dirty work before he came to add to the carnage. His entire body seemed to sparkle in the sunlight, as if he had been painted with reflective powder instead of rust.

Two red dragons flew over his head, one half the size of the other. As they zoomed toward the village, a third dragon with tawny scales trailed them.

Billy swept the beam back across the invaders. More disappeared, but far fewer. Gaps dotted the black sea. The disintegrating laser made it seem as if a rain of arrows had fallen among them, taking out about a fourth of the troops—not nearly enough.

"I think that's all I can do." Billy ran up Clefspeare's tail and sat at the base of his neck. "Let's go!"

In a massive flurry of wings, six dragons lifted into the air. As Clefspeare rose in a tight circle, Billy tapped his jaw and shouted into the transmitter. "Candle! Make a bombing run!"

Elam called from Sorentine's back. "Tell him to take out the lead chariots!"

"Got it!" Billy kept his grip on his sword and clutched his father's spine. "Bomb the front row, Candle. Send the charioteers on a ride they'll never forget!"

Clefspeare leveled out at an elevation high enough to avoid the expected onslaught of arrows. As soon as they sailed over the attackers, arrows zinged into the air, but most fell back to earth before reaching their altitude. A few made it that high and finished their ascension in lazy arcs. One pinged harmlessly off Clefspeare's scales and another drifted past Billy's ear, too slowly to do any harm.

575

He looked back at their takeoff point. Acacia and Shiloh now stood there, Gabriel in front of them with his wings spread and his sword in front of him. In the rush, Elam hadn't told Gabriel what to do, so he would have to fend for himself and hope Ashley's firetrap warded off the invaders.

Clefspeare drew his head close to Billy. "Candle is making his run. Are you ready?"

Bending low, Billy nodded. "Let's smoke 'em!"

Clefspeare angled downward. To his right, five other dragons did the same. The plan was to follow Candle, fan out, and blast fire at anything the bombs didn't stop. So far, the dragons seemed strong, and no one on the ground flashed any glittering gems. Maybe they didn't have candlestones after all. Still, the lone man on the ridge held up a fist as he patiently watched. Was he Sir Devin? He was too far away to tell for sure. Could he be holding their ultimate weapon? If so, what was he waiting for?

As they dove, the airplane came into view. A bomb dropped, a leather bag loaded with fuel and explosive powder that would ignite on impact. Before the first one landed, five other bags flew out the airplane's door.

With the warm wind stinging his eyes as he and Clefspeare zoomed downward, Billy squinted. The bombs exploded one by one, the first one blasting a chariot to bits and sending a cloud of fire and smoke skyward. The cloud obstructed their view, but the loud bangs and thick plumes told the story.

Danger alarmed from every direction. Death lurked in too many places to count. Dodging the smoke, Clefspeare took aim at the invaders to the rear of the bombing run. Just as he drew in a breath, a red dragon blasted out of the cloud and slammed into Clefspeare's flank.

Clefspeare rocked to the side. Billy jerked with him but held on. As the attacking dragon bounced away and righted himself in the sky, Clefspeare beat his wings to keep his balance. "Goliath!" he roared. "Only a coward like you would attack from a cloud!"

Goliath wheeled around and zoomed toward him again, shouting, "It is not cowardly to attack when I am so outnumbered in the sky."

Fire gushed from Goliath's mouth. Clefspeare folded in his wings and dropped. Billy hung on. The stream of flames flew just above his head, and Goliath's claws snatched at his hair, barely missing. As they fell, Billy's stomach pressed up toward his throat. When Clefspeare spread his wings again and caught the air, Billy's organs surged into reverse and dove straight down into his pelvis.

Now that they flew close to ground level, the details of the battle came into view. The bombs had blown craters in the ground, and iron wheels and broken pieces of several chariots lay strewn about. The surviving invaders in the front lines were now scrambling around the holes, while five dragons swooped, one after the other, flooding the field with fire.

Clefspeare added his own barrage. Men became torches—flags of flames as their horses galloped away with them, terrified. Still, at least a third of the attackers broke through the wall of craters, fire, and smoke and charged toward the village, now within seconds of reaching the final barrier, Ashley's trap.

Above, Goliath gave chase, his laser eyes aimed at Billy. Obviously he knew Clefspeare's greatest vulnerability was his son.

"Dad!" Billy shouted. "Take me to where we launched! I have to protect Shiloh and Acacia! You'll fight Goliath better on your own!"

Without a word of objection, Clefspeare veered away and beat his wings madly. Like a shot out of a rifle, they zoomed toward the village.

Billy looked back. Goliath followed but at a slower rate. Behind him, Karrick blew a stream of flames at Legossi, but she shook them off and slapped him across the face with her tail, sending him tumbling downward with a shriek.

From atop her back, Sir Barlow shouted, "Well struck!"

Goliath banked and flew toward the point where Karrick fell. Smoke engulfed both dragons, blocking the view.

As they rocketed past the lead runner and horses in the invading horde, Clefspeare swooped low and flew so close to the trapping field, the tips of his wings touched the ground at the bottom of their down sweeps, even brushing the tubes that lay in the dead grass.

He tore past Ashley to the left and Sapphira to the right as they continued waiting in the bordering woods. At the launching site, Gabriel sprang out of the way. Rearing up, Clefspeare beat his wings furiously and landed on the run, fanning Shiloh and Acacia as he passed by.

Before he came to a stop, Billy leaped to the dried mud. "I'm down! Take off!"

Clefspeare banked, his feet clawing the ground and his wings swerving his massive body. Then, in another flurry, he vaulted again into the sky.

577

The stampeding army swarmed over the booby-trapped field, chariots rumbling, horse hooves thundering, men shouting. Billy dashed in front of Shiloh, Acacia, and Gabriel and raised his sword. "Get down! Now!" Billy gave Flint a quick glance. He sat motionless against the tree, his eyes wide, but he showed no other signs of alarm.

In the woods, Ashley twisted the valve, then mounted Thigocia. As they scrambled from the forest, thin fountains spurted across the field. A few soldiers slipped and fell under the tromping feet and hooves, but the rest charged on.

Dikaios leaped into action, carrying Sapphira in a mad gallop. Ember and Listener followed close behind. At the near end of the field, Sapphira tossed a ball of fire to the ground. Listener slung a flaming torch.

Like a blast from a dragon, the flames shot across the muddy grass, creating a fiery wall. As Dikaios ran along the field's left boundary, Sapphira threw ball after ball, igniting the fuel that coated the ground and the sea of soldiers. Listener tossed her second torch, then ducked low and rode Ember at a gallop.

Chariots, men, and horses burst into flames. Cries of anguish filled the air. The inferno spread throughout the forest-bounded field and roasted every creature caught in the trap.

Standing close enough to feel the searing heat, Billy kept Excalibur raised. The three Nephilim broke through the fiery wall. Two were completely ablaze while the third batted at his flaming legs, apparently in too much pain to fight. Another two men, normal in size and wearing Roman-style armor, jumped out from the forest, their clothes merely smoking. They charged, but there was only one clear path to the village, straight through Billy and Excalibur.

As they sprinted toward him, one threw a spear. With a quick swing, Billy slapped it out of the air and ran to meet them. Just as he heaved in a breath, ready to send a volley of fire, a ball of flames surged past him and splashed in one attacker's face, knocking him back. As he writhed on the ground in a blaze, the other swung a sword. Billy parried and dropped to a crouch. When the man's momentum carried him over Billy's body, Billy shoved upward with his shoulder and sent the man tumbling.

The attacker climbed back to his feet, dazed. Gabriel strode in front of him and spread his wings. Wide-eyed, the man drew back his sword, but Gabriel drove his own sword through the man's belly. He collapsed in a heap.

Exhaling heavily, Billy scanned the area. The other four attackers, including the three Nephilim, lay on the ground, burning, and no one else had broken through the fire trap. He hurried to Shiloh, Acacia, and Gabriel. "Thanks for the help."

Her face pale and gaunt, Acacia gave him a nod. "It was the least I could do."

Gabriel nodded. "Same here. That guy was so scared of my wings, I think he was having a heart attack."

579

"We have to get you guys out of here," Billy said. "That was our last trap. There are so many of them, more are bound to break through."

"And the fire's spreading into the forest," Shiloh said. "What are you going to do about Flint?"

Billy looked at the pitiful man, still leaning against the tree. "Nothing. Elam's orders. I wish I could take him, but I can't disobey."

Gabriel wrapped his arms around Shiloh from behind. "I can carry one. Just tell me where to go."

A gust blew back Acacia's snowy hair. Thigocia landed with a thump, breathing heavily. Atop her back, Ashley shouted, "Our dragons are faltering! Someone must have a candlestone!"

Billy pointed toward the fire. "I saw someone dressed in black behind the lines, probably Sir Devin. It looked like he was waiting for something."

"Likely to see if I was anywhere in sight," Thigocia said. "I am immune to the candlestone, and if I had seen him, I would have cooked him on the spot."

"Then let me ride with you." Billy stepped toward Thigocia. "I'll show you which one he is."

Ashley shook her head. "You're not immune, but I am. I know what the creep looks like."

"We have to hurry," Thigocia said. "I stopped here to let you know that Goliath is trying to lead a wave of invaders to the birthing garden by a different route. Clefspeare is opposing him, and they are doing battle, but they are getting closer to the garden by the second. If Elam and Valiant are still alive, I will warn them. Otherwise, as queen of the dragons, I will order our survivors to break off this attack and hurry to the garden. We must protect Heaven's Gate."

Billy nodded. "Have you seen Bonnie?"

A streak of pain crossed Ashley's face. "We saw Hartanna from a distance. She was still flying, but she had no rider. That's all we know."

As Thigocia beat her wings to take off, Ashley kept her gaze on Billy. She mouthed the words, "I'm sorry," and then rose into the air.

His legs now trembling, Billy turned to the others. "We have to get to the garden and warn Yereq."

"You bet." Gabriel flapped his wings, but Billy pulled him back.

"I think you'd better take Acacia," Billy said. "She probably can't run as fast as Shiloh."

Gabriel shifted his arms from Shiloh to Acacia. Looking at Shiloh, he whispered, "I'll see you soon." Then, taking a deep breath, he flapped his wings again and took off.

Billy slid Excalibur away and grasped Shiloh's hand. "Come on!"

580

As they ran toward the village, Billy glanced at her every few seconds. Her lovely profile and blond-streaked hair shot pain through his heart. If only Bonnie could be running at his side. Would it be all right just to imagine her presence for a moment? Would it ease the pain of not knowing where she was and cast away the images of her lying dead on the battlefield while those demons from Hell did whatever they wished to her body?

As she began to pant under the strain of their sprint, Shiloh pulled her hand away, a hand with a missing finger. The stump shattered his daydream. Her lack of wings ripped his heart. This wasn't Bonnie. She was still in danger … somewhere.

After running into the village at the northeast side, they skirted the tree-lined border to the north and rushed into the garden's field. Gabriel had already arrived and stood with Acacia in front of Yereq.

Billy and Shiloh joined them. While Billy caught his breath, he scanned the sky. As expected, two red dragons battled overhead, maybe a quarter mile away. If Goliath was leading part of the army this way, the invaders would be here in moments.

Breathless, Gabriel nodded at the plant between Yereq's massive legs and Heaven's Gate. "Ashley filled me in on a lot of your story, but what's the deal with the wall and the plant?"

"We think Makaidos is in the plant," Billy said, "and we figured out that a girl is supposed to give her life to resurrect him. Listener thinks she's the one, but I know Makaidos would not want to live if Listener has to die."

"Is Listener supposed to come here?" Acacia asked.

"If they follow the plan, they should be here any minute. We're all supposed to fall back and protect Heaven's Gate."

Acacia set her hand close to the shimmering wall. "Perhaps we will be entering it very soon."

"Now that's strange," Shiloh said, pointing at the sky. "Storm clouds in one spot and nowhere else."

"They're over the battlefield." Billy took several steps toward the village. The cloud spread out from the northeast and stopped maybe two hundred yards away. A purplish tint between the cloud and ground indicated heavy rain.

Suddenly, the ground shook. A massive explosion sounded from the north. In the distance, a dense cloud of black soot and ash poured into the sky.

"Mount Elijah!" Billy shouted. "It blew its top!"

A fast stream of air in the upper atmosphere jetted the debris into the storm and mixed the ash with the boiling cloud. The purple tint turned darker, almost black. A bolt of lightning forked into three jagged green lines as it crashed to the ground. Rolling thunder followed, deep and menacing.

Billy stared at the ominous cloud. The weather in Second Eden had been strange for years, but this was the strangest yet. With all the supernatural events going on, it had to mean something, but what?

16

CHAPTER

THE SLAYER RETURNS

With a sudden jerk, Hartanna tilted to the side. Bonnie fell from her back and plunged. Just before smashing into the ground, she unfurled her wings, grabbed the rising air, and landed with a heavy, feet-first thump.

A man wearing a head scarf charged. Ducking under his swinging sword, she stepped to the side and gashed his thigh with her own blade. As the man toppled, another swordsman ran toward her. With help from her wings, she leaped over his thrust and kicked him square in the nose. When he crumbled, she dropped on his shoulders and pierced him through his chest.

Swinging her head from side to side, she looked around. The invaders had all passed her except a single man atop a black horse. Apparently she had fallen at the back of the ranks and only this straggler remained. She looked up. Hartanna flew erratically, jerking back and forth as if disoriented or blind.

"Mama!" she called. "What's wrong?"

Flying in a ragged circle, Hartanna descended, finally landing in a rough slide. Bonnie ran toward her mother, but the horse bolted and cut her off.

Bonnie looked up at the man, a muscular specimen draped in black chain mail. He seemed to sparkle from head to toe, as if coated by glittering dust.

He removed his cowl, revealing his face and hair. "So we meet again, demon witch." He extended a hand. Dangling from a thin chain at the ends of his fingers, a gem swung back and forth. "Does this look familiar?"

Pain stabbed her stomach, a hot poker jabbing again and again. She steeled her body. She couldn't double over. Not now. Giving Devin any sign of weakness could be fatal.

She quickly scanned the battlefield. Four dragons had fallen to the ground and were now staggering and beating their wings in their attempts to escape the candlestone's energy drain. She had to come up with a plan to save them, something he didn't expect.

"It does look a bit familiar," she said. Battling the tremors in her arm, she raised her sword and pointed at him. "Would you like to come down off your high horse and let me have a closer look?"

Devin laughed. "You always had a lot of spunk. I admire that."

"Don't patronize me. If you really admire me, then put that stone away and prove it. Fight me sword to sword, unless you're too scared to fight a woman."

"And revive the dragons?" Devin shook his head in a scolding manner. "Bonnie, come now, you know I am not a fool. Your bravado is comely, to be sure, but I do not wish to become dragon fodder."

"You won't. I can arrange it." Bonnie turned toward her mother. She was now fully stretched out on the ground, but her eyes were open, two sad orbs glowing dimly. "Mama, if Devin puts the candlestone away, do you promise to take the other dragons and leave us?"

"Bonnie," she called with a hoarse voice, "we cannot sacrifice you to save ourselves."

"If you don't, all is lost, Second Eden, the garden, Heaven's Gate. If I don't defeat Devin and the candlestone, all the dragons will die, and we will be overwhelmed by their army."

"But Bonnie, he is an expert swordsman, and you are—"

"Do not underestimate me!" Summoning all her energy, she shouted, "You must let me do this! Promise it now!"

Blowing out a weak stream of smoke, Hartanna eased her head to the ground. "Very well. I give my word. If we revive, I will take all the dragons to the birthing garden and leave you here with the slayer."

"There you have it," Bonnie said, looking back at Devin. "If you want your demon witch, then let the dragons go, and come and get me."

"On one condition." Devin slid off the horse and drew his sword. "I had hoped to kill all four of these dragons. What is the head of one demon witch in exchange for four others? I admit that your lovely head would be an excellent trophy, but it cannot replace four dragon heads."

Bonnie squinted at him. "What are you trying to say?"

He raised a gloved finger. "Before I battle you, I will allow three dragons to escape, but I must kill one of the others first. Let us say that this is a demonstration of my intent and resolve."

She gulped. As the candlestone glittered in her eye, pain roared through her body, numbing her senses. With tears welling, she lowered her arm and forced out a weak, "Which dragon?"

"Well, obviously not your pitiful mother. She is the one who has to enforce her promise. One fact I have learned about the dragons who pretend to be good, they keep their word, hoping to veil the evil intentions of their hearts." Leaving his horse behind, Devin marched about thirty paces to one of the other dragons. Her tawny scales revealed her gender, but since she lay motionless on her side, Bonnie couldn't figure out who she was, especially with her vision blurred by the candlestone's influence. And this dragon's rider, by Elam's orders, had fled to the garden to shore up the defense there.

"Wait!" Bonnie cried. With the candlestone farther away, the pain eased a fraction, allowing her to think more clearly, but the awful idea that one of these brave dragonesses might soon feel the demon's blade made her body tremble. Could she do this? The cost was so terrible! "If ... if I agree, will you keep the candlestone put away until we finish our battle?"

Devin flashed an evil smile. "I will." Setting the point of his sword against the dragon's underside, he thrust the blade deep into her belly.

"No!" Bonnie screamed. "I didn't say *I* agreed, I was just asking—"

"Too late." His eyes now wide in a maniacal stare, he twisted the blade and jumped back as he pulled it out, dodging the gushing fluids.

"You fiend!" Bonnie shouted, shaking her fist. "You could've waited a few more seconds for me to decide!"

"The candlestone obviously has had a greater effect on your mind than you are letting on. If you had agreed, I would have killed her. If you had not agreed, I would have killed all four. Waiting a few more seconds would not have altered this dragon's fate." He shifted to the dragon's head and set the blade against her neck. Again smiling, he lifted his sword.

Bonnie turned her head. She couldn't bear to watch. But what could she do? In her condition, she couldn't fight. She had to stay strong to save the other three.

A dull thwack sounded in her ears. Pain knifed through her stomach and soul. One of the valiant dragons had just given her life, and all Bonnie could do was stand there.

Suddenly the pain in her belly eased further. The slayer's shuffling footsteps grew close. Turning toward him, she raised her sword again and backed away.

Devin showed her his empty palm. "As you can see, the candlestone is now hidden. It is on a neck chain behind my mail."

She set her feet in ready position. "When my mother leaves with the other dragons, we can begin. Not before."

Whispering a "tsk, tsk, tsk," he shook his head. "You are such a fool. I didn't have to make this deal at all, and I could alter it at any time."

Bonnie glanced at her mother. Quietly, the weak dragon rose and used her wings to help the others get up. Their heads swayed, and their legs trembled, but the absence of the candlestone seemed to be helping.

"You and your kind are of the devil," Devin continued, "and I will exterminate every scaly beast by any means necessary, including deception."

587

Bonnie kept her sword out in front. "Even if it means proving yourself such a coward that you couldn't even fight a girl?"

"Ah, yes!" Devin said, laughing as he drew closer. "The clichéd challenge, the appeal to my pride as a gentleman and a knight." He spat in her face. "That's what I think of your theatrics."

Keeping her eyes on him, Bonnie wiped her sleeve across her cheek, again refusing to grimace. "If you're not enamored with my acting ability, then what *do* you want?"

Devin looked at the three surviving dragons. One by one they lifted up into the sky. Hartanna called as she flew away. "I will see you again, my love."

A new tear welled in Bonnie's eye. She blinked, letting it fall to her cheek. But where would they meet? Here, or in Heaven?

"What I want," Devin said, turning back to her, "is something that I have tried to get for many years."

"Now you're the one who's being theatric. Just tell me."

In the sunlight, his eyes glinted—evil, hungry, bloodthirsty. "I want the mongrel. I want Billy Bannister. And I want his father, the great Clefspeare. Now that I have you, it will be much easier to lure them into my clutches."

A surge of anger swept through Bonnie's body. Her muscles flexed—the arms, legs, and abdomen she had trained four years to harden into steel. Now feeling much stronger, Bonnie stepped back. "You don't have me yet, and I'll never let you take Billy."

"We'll see about that." Devin raised his sword. Like a raging bull, he charged. Bonnie jumped to the side, but Devin tripped her, sending her into a backward somersault. At the end of her spill, she leaped to her feet and shot into the air, barely avoiding his sword as it swiped just underneath.

She landed behind him and lunged, aiming her sword at his back. He spun and blocked her blade with his. As the two locked, his eyes narrowed. "You are much too strong for a girl of your stature. The blood of demons flows through your veins, but I will puncture the witch with enough holes to drain every drop."

Bonnie narrowed her eyes to match his. "If your theatrics continue, you will soon have to take a bow. Don't think for a minute that your diatribe can scare me. I have been in every realm—Earth, Heaven, Hades, the Valley of Souls, and now Second Eden—and God has been with me every step of the way. It would take more than the venomous spewing of a viper to make me tremble."

"It is not God who slinks like a serpent at your side, it is—" Devin glanced upward. A slight bend in his brow piqued Bonnie's curiosity. She gave the locked blades a shove, jumped back, and looked up. A cloud formed low in the sky, boiling, swelling, darkening. Within a few seconds, it grew to a raging black cumulonimbus that began spreading toward the village.

A tremendous explosion rocked the ground. In the northern sky, a geyser of black shot into the air and flowed southward into the brewing storm. The two clouds mixed into a purple and ebony swirl.

Bonnie stared at the roaring eruption. Ashley had mentioned a volcano called Mount Elijah, but she had said nothing about how active it might be.

As penny-sized raindrops began to pelt her head, Bonnie set her feet again. Should she attack? Wait for his next move? She tried to gauge his level of aggression, but he just stared toward the village, his scowl deepening. Was it a ploy to get her to strike? She mentally shook her head. Even though he was the foulest creature ever to walk the face of Earth or Second Eden, she couldn't attack while he wasn't looking. Billy had taught her that lesson a long time ago.

Something stung her hand, a minor sting, like a mosquito pricking her exposed skin. Was it the rain? She pulled her sleeves down over her wrists. It was really nothing. Maybe the volcanic ash had created an acidic rain.

Devin looked at her again. "You could have run me through just now. Why didn't you?"

"Because I'm not a cowardly snake. I won't stab a man while he's looking away." She pointed her sword at him and shouted, "En garde!"

Devin lowered his sword. "I am looking at you now. Feel free to strike. This is your only chance. If you fail, I will take out the candlestone and imprison you with it."

Bonnie studied his expression. Was this a trick? Did he think she wouldn't do it because she was a girl and too squeamish to run him through? Well, if he did, he thought wrong. Setting her feet, she lunged and thrust the point directly at his chest. When the blade struck his mail, it made a loud pinging sound and deflected away.

She swung it back with all her might and hacked at his bare neck, but the blade bounced again and quivered in her grip. His sparkling aura flashed momentarily before settling back to normal.

589

"This is getting tiresome." Devin reached behind his mail shirt, withdrew the candlestone, and let it sway at the end of the chain around his neck. "I'm in a hurry, and you're too skilled to defeat quickly."

The stabbing pain returned, worse than ever. She staggered, dizzy. Turning, she tried to run, but a sharp pain tore across her scalp. Her neck bent, and her head snapped back. She lost her balance, but as she toppled backwards, something stopped her fall. She twisted to find out why. Devin was dragging her by the hair.

As the rain increased, her heels made ruts in the moistening mud. Reaching back, she hacked weakly with her sword, but he just swiped it away with his own, and her blade thudded to the ground at her side.

His nauseating snicker rose above the intermittent splashes. "I might risk losing your pretty head as a trophy, but having you as bait for the grand prize is worth it. First, I capture the mongrel, then I will use him to lure the most powerful dragon of all." He laughed loud and long. "I can already picture the heads on my mantle, side by side by side. I will let you keep your scalp so your lovely hair will flow all around."

She jerked her body downward, freeing her hair from his grasp, but when her head hit the ground, new pain ripped across her skull. She gasped for breath. Her heart raced, feeling like it did the moments before she died in the Circles of Seven.

"Get up, witch!" Devin grabbed her belt and hoisted her up to his horse's saddle. The feeling of his hands on her waist and backside as he pushed her into place made her want to vomit, but she couldn't. Inside, she felt a void, an aching emptiness. She could barely move at all.

Mounting behind her, he spread out her wings and pushed close as he settled into the saddle. With the candlestone now resting on her back, the agony spiked, and with his body pressing close to hers, the nausea churned to a sickening swill.

Rain poured. The wind howled. Green lightning flashed from cloud to ground with a crackling pop. As water streamed from her hair to her folded hands, all seemed lost. She was a maid being dragged to the stake. Soon the fire would be set, and all her hopes would go up in smoke.

As they trotted past the slain dragon, its head lying a few feet from its body, Devin let out a snort. "I will collect that little trophy later."

Lightning flashed again. Rain fell in sheets. The wind whistled in her ears, and it seemed to form a tune, a familiar tune. What was it? Could it be? Yes, it was the same tune she had always used for her favorite psalm.

Words filled in, but not the usual psalm. A gentle feminine voice sang new words in a vibrant contralto that poured in like the driving rain.

591

Within the gem your light had ebbed,
Entrapped in crystal prison lair.
You cried for help from God on high;
You sang in faith that he was there.

The candlestone, a pseudo-gem,
The bogus beauty now exposed;
By lies, deceit, the hidden heart,
A wolf in wool, the killer's clothes.

For prophets false are like the gem;
They dress in collar, frock, and silk,
Pretending beauty, while within,
They soil their garments, prove their ilk.

The prophets false are but a breeze;
The chains they carry, but a string.
They shackle those who don their garb,
But never children of the King.

The crystal fools the sightless ones;
They give their light away for free,
And even prince and princess have
Become ensnared unknowingly.

But when you sing the faithful song,
The gem will lose its blinding grip.
Defeated foes cannot endure
When faith invokes the master's whip.

After the tune faded, the voice continued, now merely speaking. "Brick upon brick, your song will build your faith until you become an impenetrable fortress. You have already conquered this crystalline enemy. Sing the words again, for the master of that deceiving gem cannot have so soon forgotten the child of God who has already repelled him within those walls. He is a defeated enemy, but you must claim this truth by faith, for only then will the invisible chains be broken forever. Let no shackles bind this valiant daughter of the lamb. Let no darkness overcome the light within an Oracle of Fire."

592

Nodding with the horse's gait, Bonnie hummed the tune. Then, ignoring the bullets of pain shooting through her heart, she began to sing.

Whither shall I go from thy spirit? Or whither shall I flee
    from thy presence?
If I ascend up into heaven, thou art there: If I make my
    bed in hell, behold, thou art there.

"Stop the singing!" Devin slapped the side of her head. "Or I'll start carving you now."

Bonnie's ear rang, but she barely felt the slap. "I'm going to sing. You'll have to kill me to stop me."

He grabbed her hair and twisted her head halfway around. For a moment, he stared at her with hate-filled eyes, but soon, his expression slackened, and he shoved her cheek. "Go ahead and sing! What do I care?"

Taking a spasm-filled breath, Bonnie began again, picking up where she left off.

> If I take the wings of the morning, and dwell in the utter-
> most parts of the sea;
> Even there shall thy hand lead me, and thy right hand shall
> hold me.
> If I say, Surely the darkness shall cover me; even the night
> shall be light about me.
> Yea, the darkness hideth not from thee; but the night
> shineth as the day:
> The darkness and the light are both alike to thee.

593

When she finished, she let out a sigh. The pains eased. Her heart slowed to a steady rhythm. Energy roared back into her muscles. Though the candlestone still lay on her back, it no longer had any effect.

So what now? Devin had a sword, and she didn't. Her only hope was to take him by surprise.

As the horse cantered, Bonnie looked up. About a hundred yards away, the sky was clear, though rain continued pouring from overhead. Above, two red dragons battled at the boundary between storm and calm, while the remaining army, perhaps four hundred, gathered nearby, all soaking wet and standing in mud.

Bonnie watched the up and down movements of the horse's head. Her timing had to be perfect.

She reached out, set her palms high on the horse's neck, and pushed with all her might, thrusting herself upward. She slapped

Devin's cheeks with her wings, kicked him in the chest with both feet, and propelled her body up and away.

As Devin hurled obscenities, Bonnie flew with all her might toward the garden. The downpour beat against her wings, but at least the weather would keep the invaders from looking up and spotting her. She didn't want to have to dodge their arrows now. That would be nearly impossible.

CHAPTER

THE SACRIFICE

Billy stared at the strange contrast in the sky, clear over the garden field but stormy just beyond the eastern wall. The battling dragons drew ever closer. With the invaders following Goliath's lead, they couldn't be more than two minutes away. Soon they would be scaling the walls or pouring in through the narrow path from the village.

The sound of hooves made him turn toward the path. Dikaios and Ember galloped into the field, Sapphira and Listener riding. Walter ran behind them. Holding his scabbard to keep it from bouncing, he favored a leg, but it didn't seem to slow his pace.

When they stopped, Sapphira leaped off and ran to Acacia, shouting, "Oh, my dear sister!" But when they drew close, Sapphira halted and stared at her. She took Acacia's fingertips and lifted her arms. Acacia's tunic rode up, exposing her emaciated frame. "Oh, Acacia!" Sapphira wrapped her up in a tight embrace. "I'm so glad you're here! I'll nurse you back to health. I promise."

"I'm sure you'll try," Acacia said, "but there seems to be no explanation for my decay. Perhaps the fruit I ate from the Tree of Life has finally lost its power."

"How could that be? I am still hale and hearty." Sapphira looked at Billy. "She can't die unless someone kills her with violence, and that can't happen unless she's betrayed by someone who loves her. Even if someone spills a drop of her blood, her attacker will die."

"Elam told me those stories," Billy said. "Let's hope they're true here in Second Eden."

Breathing heavily, Walter clasped Billy's arm. "My dragon fell near the back of the invading line. I killed seven of their goons while trying to defend her, but then the other dragons faltered, and Valiant and Elam were grounded. After we cleared out the enemy stragglers, Elam ordered me to come back here."

596

Another man ran onto the field, shorter and slower than Walter. Sapphira recognized him immediately. "It's Mardon! I thought he was supposed to be in the hospital."

As Mardon drew close, Billy stepped out in front of the others. "What are you doing here?"

Wringing his hands, Mardon bowed his head to Billy and then to the two Oracles. "I have come to confess everything. I sneaked out of the hospital before it departed, because I never had any intention of working with your doctor. There is no cure for Acacia's disease. I altered her genetics in order to study her indestructibility. Even in this state, she will not die, but she will waste away and live on as a walking cadaver." He withdrew a white hair from a pocket. "You see, it's important to study the genes before and after the alteration in order to decode the secret to her power. I plucked a hair from her long ago when I exposed her to the decaying light, so I have the older set of genes and—"

"We don't want a science lesson," Billy growled. "Just get to the bottom line."

"Very well." Mardon put the hair away and again wrung his hands. "My mother, Semiramis, conspired with Arramos to bring this army to Heaven's Gate. I was supposed to use the genetic encoding to make ourselves and our troops indestructible, but I have already learned that without a blood sample, that will be impossible. Her blood likely contains the final clue that will solve the puzzle, but when I considered the possibility of coercing some fool into taking blood from her, I finally woke up to my folly. I was actually willing to kill an innocent lamb to further my own desires!"

He clenched his fingers into a tight knot. "I have been such a fool! I have been following the commands of a dragon who ruined my face and a mother who cares only for her own advance. Now I wish to appeal for mercy and join forces with you. Perhaps with time, I can learn how to reverse Acacia's degeneration."

Billy looked at the two Oracles. Sapphira gave Mardon a skeptical stare, while Acacia gazed at him with forgiving eyes.

Gabriel crossed his arms and shook his head, while Shiloh just glared at Mardon, her stub of a finger obvious as she let her hand dangle at her side.

"What should I do?" Billy whispered to Walter.

"No time to decide." Walter pointed toward the sky. From over the tree line, Thigocia flew in with Ashley, followed immediately by Legossi, Firedda, Hartanna, and Sorentine, each of those four without a rider. All but Thigocia flew haphazardly and flopped to the ground when they landed.

Billy scanned the weakened dragons. Yellinia was missing. Since Valiant was no longer riding her, she must have fallen out in the battlefield and was unable to return.

"They have been weakened by a candlestone," Thigocia said as she settled gracefully. "There is no fight remaining in them, and the storm left them disoriented. The rain carries an unusual odor that has made them dizzy."

597

Legossi lifted her head. "As long as I have strength to breathe, I will fight."

"And that won't be long," Ashley shouted from atop Thigocia, "unless you rest at least a few minutes."

Billy and Walter ran to Thigocia and helped Ashley down. "We've been routed," Ashley said. "Elam, Valiant, and Barlow are on their way, and Roxil is creating walls of fire between them and the invaders."

"Roxil?" Walter pumped his fist. "Yes! She's fighting for our side now!"

"Not exactly. She's creating an escape for our people, but she won't destroy any invaders. I guess she thinks that's part of her vow." Ashley pointed at Mardon. "What's he doing here?"

Billy took in a breath. "It's like this. Mardon was—"

A ball of fire erupted in the village. A beige dragon flew almost straight up from the blaze as if launched by the explosion. She bent into a sharp turn and flew toward Clefspeare and Goliath.

598

"Roxil's heading for the big fight," Walter said. "I don't know if that's good or bad."

Elam and Valiant hustled into the field with Flint in between them. Flint's feet barely touched the ground as his two supporters ran. Sir Barlow followed, backing toward the garden and fighting sword to sword with an armor-clad invader.

New flames shot from the treetops. With much of the forest dead and tinderbox dry, the fire roared from one tree to the next.

Elam and Valiant joined Billy and the others at the edge of the garden. They set Flint in a sitting position in a grassy area. Looking sicker than ever, Flint let his head droop close to his crossed legs.

"We couldn't hold them off," Elam said to Billy, panting. "I think the invaders will be here any minute." He glared at Mardon for a brief moment but said nothing.

"I'll help Barlow." Walter drew his sword, but Elam grabbed his arm.

"He's fine. Stay here. We have only a minute to execute our final plan."

"Final plan?" Acacia asked. "What might that be?"

"We have to resurrect Makaidos before it's too late. We learned that a female has to sacrifice herself and offer her blood to energize his rebirth from the plant."

"And I'm the one," Listener said as she slid down from Ember. "He died in my place, so now it's my turn to die for him."

Ashley pointed toward the sky. "Look! Roxil's trying to break up the fight!"

Above, Roxil flew between the two combatants like a battering ram. Both sets of claws from the male dragons scraped against her sides. As she faltered in the air, Clefspeare made a quick turn as if to check on her, but when he exposed his underbelly, Goliath attacked, his teeth and every claw extended. When they collided, blood sprayed from Clefspeare's belly, red and sparkling.

Thigocia launched into the air. "I will help Clefspeare."

599

As she zoomed upward, Billy wanted to scream at Goliath, but his throat clamped shut. Enraged, he clenched a fist and shifted his stare to another part of the sky. Something appeared from the storm cloud, a human with wings.

Swallowing hard, he managed to whisper, "Bonnie?"

"We don't have time to watch the battle," Elam said. "We have to decide now. Who will be the sacrifice?"

Acacia raised her hand. "I am already weak, and my body is deteriorating."

"No!" Mardon stalked into their huddle and grabbed Acacia's forearm. "You cannot be the sacrifice or someone else will die. Why destroy two lives?"

"Why do you care?" Acacia asked. "I was just a science experiment to you."

Mardon glanced between her and Sapphira. Beads of sweat popped up on his balding head. "You two were the only ones I really cared about. You were wonderfully created by a miracle that went beyond mere genetic logic. It was clear that I had to protect you. By defending you in the face of Morgan's threats, I saved your lives countless times."

Acacia gazed into his eyes and breathed a low, "I see."

A man at the burning tree line screamed. Barlow yanked his sword from the invader's stomach and hurried to the garden. "The fire is keeping them from entering through the forest," Barlow said, "so they are building a ramp to scale the walls. We have a little more time, but not much."

In a spray of wind and water, Bonnie flew down and settled next to Billy. Breathless and dripping wet, she rattled off her story. "I fought Devin … He has a candlestone … and he's invincible. One of my blows should have cut his head off, but the blade just bounced away."

"Bonnie!" Hartanna called as she shuffled on her wobbly legs. "Stand still while I dry you off. At least I have the energy to do that."

While she blew a jet of hot air across Bonnie's body, a black horse and a black-garbed rider burst through the wall of flames at the forest entry. A sparkling aura surrounded his body, making him appear ghostly.

"Speak of the devil," Walter whispered. "Just replace the *l* with an *n*."

Devin eased the horse into a high-stepping trot and approached the gathering. "I see my trophy has flown to a safer haven. It's not wise to send little girls out to battle alone."

Billy jerked out Excalibur and summoned the beam. "Stay back, or I'll fry you and your horse together."

"Oh, don't take out your anger on my horse. He never did you any harm." Devin dismounted and drew his sword. "I, on the other hand, have done you much harm, and I intend to do a great deal more."

"He's so cocky," Bonnie said, "he was spewing dramatic lines nonstop while we fought. I think he knows that Excalibur won't hurt him."

"There's only one way to find out."

Billy swiped the beam across Devin's body. Sparks erupted, but the slayer stayed upright. A grin spread across his face as he set his feet and raised his sword. "I have come for you, Billy Bannister. You have been a thorn in my side for far too long."

"He will taste my steel," Sir Barlow growled. The muscular knight charged and hacked at Devin's midsection with his sword, but it rebounded. Barlow lost his balance and dropped to his knees. With a swift turn and thrust, Devin drove his sword into Barlow's midsection and jerked it back out.

"Sir Barlow!" Bonnie cried. "Oh, dear God! Help him!"

His eyes wide, Barlow clutched his belly and toppled over. Blood spilled between his fingers. Walter and Ashley ran to him and, gripping him under his arms, dragged him back toward the garden.

Ashley peeled away Barlow's fingers, pulled his shirt up, and laid her hand on the wound.

Barlow opened his eyes and winced. "How bad is it, my lady?"

Pressing her lips together, Ashley shook her head. "It's bleeding quite a bit. I can't tell."

His smile revealed a set of crooked teeth. "I am sure your touch will seal it fast. I have confidence in you."

"Sapphira!" Ashley called. "We need to try a healing."

Elam stepped forward. "Billy. Walter. Valiant. Gabriel. Yereq. Let's see if the six of us—"

"No!" Billy waved everyone back. "He's mine!"

"Billy," Bonnie said, staying at his side. "You can't beat him. He's invincible."

He pushed her gently away. "I'll keep him occupied long enough to stop him from killing anyone else, at least for a while. The others can stay alive for the more important battle."

Billy charged and swung his sword. Devin's blade met his with a loud clank. Grunting, Billy pushed away and set his feet to run again, but a deep female voice erupted from the direction of the burning forest.

"Desist!"

A woman emerged from the flames. Dressed in a long red cloak, she marched toward them, lowering her hood as she drew near.

"Semiramis," Ashley said. "No wonder I didn't sense her approach." She covered Barlow's abdomen with her body and looked up at Sapphira. "It shouldn't take too much. Let's try to make it quick."

Semiramis grabbed Devin's arm, scowling. "Didn't I tell you not to seek revenge until the battle was over?"

Billy glanced at Elam. Their gazes met. Again, the son of Shem had every reason to say, "I told you so," but he just averted his eyes. After all her pretense, Semiramis was finally coming out in the open, proving that every good deed she had done had been an illusion.

Devin jerked away. "I have plenty of protection. I can dispatch this mongrel and everyone else in this pitiful company."

Semiramis pointed a finger at his nose. "You will do as I tell you and nothing more."

"You sound just like Morgan." Devin spat on the ground. "And you know where she is now."

"And you refused to listen to her precise instructions. Shall I recount your losses?" Semiramis raised two fingers. "You were imprisoned in a candlestone, not once, but twice."

Growling, Devin aimed his sword at the garden boundary. "Then where are my allies? Let us proceed with the battle and collect our trophies."

"The ramps are in place, and the troops are awaiting my command to storm this refuge." She looked up. "As you can see, the remaining dragons are returning."

Above, Clefspeare and Thigocia descended, Clefspeare dripping blood. When they landed, Clefspeare's head flopped to the ground, and Thigocia immediately covered him with her wings. "Hartanna," she called. "Between you and Legossi, you should have enough firepower to coat me with healing flames."

"I'll put a stop to this," Devin said as he reached for a thin chain around his neck. "I want that devil's head."

Ashley leaped up from Barlow, rushed toward Devin, and grabbed the chain. Devin spun on his heels and swung his sword, but Ashley threw herself backwards, avoiding the blade and breaking the chain. Now holding the candlestone, she slid away on her backside, her cheeks as red as embers.

"Why, you little …"

Devin took a step toward her, but Semiramis pulled him back. "Stand down until I am finished with my business here!"

Flashing a fake smile, Devin bowed. "Then be my guest, your royal highness."

Ashley covered the candlestone with both hands and hurried back to Sir Barlow and Sapphira. "This will help us heal him." She let a drop of her own blood fall from her scraped hands to the gem.

As the flames from the forest crawled out to the field and began devouring the scant brown grass, Semiramis turned toward Billy and company. "With whom shall I speak? I need someone who will make wise and just decisions."

Elam stepped forward. "Say what you've come to say, and then leave."

Her eyebrows lifted. "Ah! My old friend, Elam. You made it safely across the chasm, proving your arrogance; you came to Second Eden, proving your desire for fame; and you forced a grieving widow to lie and face humiliation, proving your misogyny, which you also willingly heaped upon me when I came as a mother in search of help for her son." She let out a contemptuous laugh. "And now what are you? You are the warrior chief of a ragtag gang of weak dragons and sick humans. Will you rally this pitiful menagerie to battle a trained army? While it's true that you have thinned our ranks, we still number over four hundred strong. How long do you think you will last? Five minutes? Three?"

"Like I said …" Elam's brow dipped low. "Say what you've come to say, and leave out the venom."

"Very well." She pointed at Mardon. "Bring the Oracle of Fire forward. I want to speak to her."

Elam looked back at Acacia. "Just to talk. Nothing more."

"Just to talk?" Semiramis repeated. "We shall see."

Holding Acacia's hand tenderly, Mardon guided her to the front of their company. Acacia glanced at Sapphira, who was still on her knees next to Barlow.

The line of fire drew closer, but since the flames were only inches tall, they seemed to pose no danger. Anyone could easily step over them.

Thigocia lay on top of Clefspeare, her scales reddened by the flames of other dragons. Motionless and quiet, she waited for the healing to take effect.

Semiramis's eyes narrowed. "Which one are you, Sapphira or Acacia?"

Elam gave everyone a firm shake of his head. Obviously he didn't want anyone to answer.

Billy glared at Mardon. If this creep really wanted to help Acacia, now was the time to prove it. Obviously Semiramis asked this question for a reason, so giving away Acacia's identity wouldn't be a good idea.

Acacia pulled free from Mardon and dipped into a curtsy. "If you please, my lady, kindly tell me why you wish to know my name."

Her eyes narrowing further, Semiramis glanced between Acacia and Sapphira. "It is my understanding that one of you is ill. I selected you because you appear malnourished, and I wish to make an exchange. Once we learn the secrets behind your DNA structure, we will gladly restore your health. Yet, if I choose the wrong Oracle, everything we worked for will be lost."

"Begging your pardon," Acacia said, "but I do not wish to aid whatever ends you have worked so hard to achieve, so I will maintain my silence regarding my identity."

Sapphira shuffled over to Mardon's other side, adding a pronounced limp to her gait. "We will never help you. We are Oracles of Fire, and we were created to serve God alone."

"Fools! I need no help from you." Semiramis glared at Mardon. "Which one is Acacia?"

Mardon took Acacia's hand and caressed it, then did the same to Sapphira. Keeping his head low, he said, "Even if I told you which one is Acacia, you would not be able to use her genetic changes for your purposes without my expertise."

"Mardon! We are moments from our final triumph. Your father dreamed about this day, the day we would rise up to Heaven, assault its very gates, and demand an audience with the Almighty. You know as well as I do that we cannot complete the assault unless we equip our army with angelic invincibility. Are you now going to forsake that dream, that passion born in his heart millennia ago? Are you going to throw away your place at the throne of the universe because of a foolish infatuation with a pair of pretty pets? Have you gone mad?"

Mardon looked up at her. "They are not pets. Each one sprouted from embryonic cells I put together with my own two hands. If I turned Acacia over to you now, it would be as if God himself turned his back on his own daughter."

Semiramis reached out her hand. "You are my son, and my loyalty is to you. If we can extract this knowledge from Acacia, not only can we become like gods ourselves, your own face will be healed, and we can exact revenge upon the monster who maimed

605

you." Her voice transformed to a tone of entreaty. "Don't you see, my son? If we get Arramos to kill Acacia, he will die because of the Oracle's curse, and then we will be free to harvest her ova for our purposes. You will be whole, and revenge will be yours, delivered in a package of bloody red and snowy white prepared by your own hands."

Mardon touched the scars on his face. His ears flushed red. As new beads of perspiration gathered on his forehead, he grasped Acacia's arm and strode toward Semiramis. "This one is Acacia." Acacia stumbled along with him, apparently too weak to resist.

"No!" Billy lunged toward Mardon and swung Excalibur, aiming for his neck. Devin thrust his own sword in between and blocked the stroke.

As they pushed against each other's blades, glaring eye to eye, Walter charged and stabbed at Devin's side, but his sword merely bent and sprang back. Walter lost his balance, stumbled several steps backwards, and fell to his seat. Billy leaped away from Devin and ran with Bonnie to Walter's side.

Still holding Acacia's hand, Mardon passed Devin and joined Semiramis.

Yereq bellowed from Heaven's Gate, his sword drawn. "Say the word, Warrior Chief, and I will kill all three of these villains."

"And I will join him," Valiant said. "They cannot stand against us."

Gabriel flew over and landed next to Valiant. "Count me in."

Elam held up his hand. "You might hurt Acacia."

Billy and Bonnie helped Walter up. "Let's go after Mardon and Semiramis together," Bonnie whispered. "They won't hurt Acacia on purpose, and if we're quick enough, one of us can snatch her away."

"I'll push Devin to the side," Billy whispered back. "You and Walter can take care of the rest."

When all three rose, Devin rushed toward them. He kicked Billy in the groin, knocked Excalibur away, and set the tip of his own sword against Billy's throat. "I see no one has trained you for a dirty, underhanded attack."

In spite of the pain, Billy refused to double over. He wanted to swallow, but the blade was already cutting into his skin. He growled without moving his throat. "We fight like knights here."

"As if I care." Pulling back the blade slightly, Devin turned toward Elam. "Now you will leave Mardon and Acacia with Semiramis, or I will skewer this mongrel where he stands. If you acquiesce, Semiramis will signal our troops, and at least he will have a fighting chance to survive."

Billy glared at Devin. "My friends will likely want to save my life, but it's not their choice. Whether your troops come or not, you will take Acacia over my dead body."

Devin laughed. "Your demon witch girlfriend complains about my theatrics, yet you drool that pathetic cliché."

"Take it or leave it, you cowardly sycophant. You were under the thumb of a sorceress for centuries, and you still cower behind the skirts of one now. If you weren't covered by her dark magic, you would be tucking your tail and running like a terrified puppy."

607

"Her dark magic?" Devin laughed again. "How little you know!"

Semiramis took a step closer to Billy and crooned. "Do you want to know how Devin was able to gain his invincible shell?"

Billy finally swallowed, brushing his throat against the sharp blade. "Why should I care?"

"Because it was by your hand. Fool that you were, you added Shiloh's blood to the plant, exactly as I requested, and her blood, which carried an extraordinary immunity, added the precise element we needed to provide our seedling a cloak of invulnerability. And all this time, you thought we wanted Bonnie, when we really needed Shiloh. You were such a fool."

"Am I?" Billy knitted his brow. He had to figure out a way to rile Devin, somehow get him to rebel against Semiramis, or at least get him angry enough to make a mistake. "Devin is the real fool. He's still just your toady, nothing more than a fat lapdog that you pet with your bloody fingers. What bone did you toss to get him to lick your filthy boots?"

"You have your Oracle," Devin growled at Semiramis. "Signal our people, and let me kill this rodent."

Semiramis let out a shrill whistle and waved her hand. "Very well. Feel free to take his head. You have earned that reward."

"With pleasure. First a stab through his heart." As Devin pulled back the hilt, Acacia jerked away from Mardon and leaped in front of Billy. Devin thrust his sword. The blade punctured her chest, ran through her body, and slid out her back, pricking Billy's skin.

Devin yanked it out. "Stupid girl."

Acacia slumped. Blood poured from her wound. Billy slid his arms around her chest and lowered her gently to the ground and himself to his knees. Heat blazing in his cheeks, he shouted, "You ... you ..." He couldn't think of a word vile enough to describe the slayer. As he stared at the foul beast, the aura surrounding his skin and black chain mail fizzled and disappeared.

"Sister!" Sapphira screamed as she ran to Acacia.

"No!" Bonnie raised her sword and charged.

As Devin stared at her, a cocky smile bent his lips. "The demon witch comes again—"

"Shut up!" With a mighty swing, Bonnie swept her sword at his neck. The blade struck bare flesh and sliced cleanly through. Devin's head toppled over and dropped to the ground, his eyes wide as it rolled. The mail-clad body crumbled in a heap of black.

Pointing her sword at his eyes, Bonnie added, "Forever."

"We can still use Acacia!" Semiramis shouted. "Get her body!"

Bonnie aimed her sword at Mardon, her arms and voice shaking. "Make one move, and you're dead!"

Mardon backed away a step, then turned and ran toward the village, leaping over the low fire. Semiramis raised her hood and followed. She seemed in no hurry, likely realizing that no one would attack an unarmed, retreating woman.

Flint rose to his feet and hobbled toward Devin's body. He picked up the slayer's fallen sword and propped it against his shoulder as he faced Elam. "Allow me to fight for you."

"You're too sick," Elam said. "You can't possibly survive."

His eyes glistening, he managed to straighten his body admirably. "After all I have seen here, I must demonstrate my repentance. Whether I live or die is of no consequence."

Elam nodded. "Let it be so." He stooped close to Sapphira and touched the white rubellite ring on her finger. "During the four years of waiting here, I think I figured out a prophecy. You'll probably have to use that gem to resurrect Makaidos, but I'll get you another." As he rose, he pointed at Ember. "Take Listener to the far side of the field."

Walter boosted Listener onto Ember's back. As she settled in place, she said, "Sapphira, please tell Acacia that I'm sorry. I'm sorry that I was too slow to take her place as the sacrifice."

609

Her face twisting in grief, Sapphira nodded. "I ... I will tell her."

Gabriel wrapped his arms around Shiloh. "I'll take her to safety with Listener, but I'll be back to join the battle."

As he lifted into the air, Ember followed his path toward the field's western boundary.

Walter shouted, "Get ready! Here they come!"

At the eastern wall, invaders climbed over the top and, one by one, then two by two, dropped to the ground, their weapons drawn for battle.

Thigocia lifted her body off Clefspeare and tugged on his wing with a clawed hand. "Are you able to rise?"

With a lurch, Clefspeare rose to his haunches. For a moment, his neck wavered, but he quickly steadied it and roared. "Follow me!" He vaulted into the air, beating his wings with all his might.

Thigocia followed. Hartanna and Legossi struggled to their feet and flew after them, but much more slowly. Firedda and Sorentine stayed on the ground. They seemed to be trying to get up, but their wings flailed helplessly.

Elam waved his arm toward the eastern boundary. "Defend the garden!"

"Let's do it!" Walter said as he leaped after him. Valiant broke into a full sprint and kept pace at Walter's side.

Yereq shouted from Heaven's Gate. "Take courage, my friends. If any of the snakes slip through your fingers, I will be here to relieve them of their heads."

Dikaios ran to Barlow and lowered his body. "Come, valiant warrior. If you are strong enough to ride, let us go to battle like the knights of old."

"By all means!" Barlow climbed to his feet and crawled over the horse's back.

Dikaios shot up to his full height and jumped into a gallop, Barlow shouting a battle cry as he waved his sword.

Clefspeare stormed toward the garden's boundary. Fire shot from his mouth and nostrils and blasted the invaders as they trickled over the top. Like a dragonfly, Thigocia flew from place to place, seemingly pausing in midair to cook the invaders who had already dropped onto the field.

Merlin the airplane buzzed overhead. A fuel bomb dropped on the opposite side of the wall and raised a fiery explosion. The stream of invaders slowed, but only for a moment.

As Merlin flew away, Billy watched the action, dazed as he held Acacia's body. Was that the last of Windor's bombs? Would Candle land somewhere and try to make more? He ached to join his fellow warriors, but holding the sacrificial Oracle seemed far more important. He had to guard her body until Sapphira did what she had to do.

Sapphira pulled Acacia into her arms, weeping. "Oh, my dear sister! Oh, my sweet, wonderful sister!"

Ashley laid her hand over the wound, but it did no good. Blood continued to pour from Acacia's twitching body.

His heart pounding, Billy looked at his blood-covered hands. Acacia's blood. The sacrificial lamb's blood. She had completed her purpose, her millennia-long journey. For this death she had been born, and for this saving sacrifice she had been waiting all her life.

His hands trembling, Billy rolled his fingers into fists. He couldn't fight. He couldn't even speak. His arms felt like rubber, and his legs were numb.

Groping fingers ran along his arm and found his fist. He loosened his fingers and let the weak hand slip into his.

"Billy?" Acacia whispered.

He leaned close to her as she lay cradled in Sapphira's arms. He had to swallow before he could answer. "Yes. ... Yes, I'm here."

Her lips, now light blue, trembled as she spoke. "I gave my life to save yours."

"Yes." He folded her hand into both of his and forced his body to stop shaking. "Thank you."

Her voice weakened. "It was the greatest thing I have ever done."

He pressed his lips together. As tears dripped, the lump in his throat swelled. He couldn't answer.

"I never had a man in my life," she continued as she raised a hand to his cheek. "But after our talk in the mines, I knew that if I were ever to choose, I would want someone like you at my side."

Her eyelids closed. After a final heave, her chest became still. Acacia, the great Oracle of Fire, had died.

Billy raised her hand to his lips and kissed her knuckles. His tears flowing freely, he whispered, "Good-bye, Acacia. Thank you for saving my life. I will be forever grateful." Then, his voice

611

strengthening as new energy flowed through his body, he added, "I will fight in your name."

"Can we try a healing?" Ashley asked.

Her face stained with tears, Sapphira shook her head. "This is what she wanted. I have to use her blood now to resurrect Makaidos."

"I'll go with you," Bonnie said. "You apply the blood, and I'll guard your back."

As Sapphira lowered Acacia to the ground and rose to her feet, Bonnie touched Billy's arm. "The rain washed the rust off. You need to get to work."

"Right." He scanned the ground and spotted Excalibur a few feet away. Rising on his wobbly legs, he stumbled toward it and snatched it off the ground. He summoned the beam and looked at the battle near the eastern wall.

Goliath had flown in, and as he and Clefspeare fought once again, more invaders and their horses spilled over the top, like rats crawling out of a flooded sewer. Five armor-clad horsemen kept Thigocia at bay with thick spears while fending off her flames with shields. The weaker dragons continued spewing fire at the arriving troops, but they were unable to keep up with the flow.

The battleground resembled a sea—waves of slashing swords, roars of battling men and dragons, and a tidal surge that pushed the entire group toward the middle of the burning field.

He let the beam die away. With everyone fighting in close quarters, using Excalibur would be dangerous. He would have to save it until he met the invaders face to face.

Ashley strode to his side, her sword drawn. "Mind if I join you? I have to keep my fiancé in one piece."

"By all means."

She set a hand on his shoulder and lifted her sword. "For Acacia?"

Tightening his jaw, he nodded. "For Acacia."

18

CHAPTER

WHEN DEATH
BRINGS LIFE

Cradling Acacia's body in her arms, Bonnie pulled the dead
Oracle's blood-soaked tunic up just past her ribcage and held
it there. Blood oozed from under the material, and when it reached
the end of her ribs, it dripped down to her scant waist.

Sapphira cupped her hands and collected it drop by drop. Her
arms trembled, but she kept them in place. She had to angle her
head away to keep her tears from spilling in.

As the blood filled Sapphira's hands, Bonnie wept. This portrait of one sister gathering the blood of another was too much to
bear. They had loved each other for thousands of years. They
longed to be together, but calamity after calamity had kept them
apart. And now, when they finally met again, they were torn asun-
der only moments later.

"Do you think I have enough?" Sapphira asked.

Bonnie took a deep breath and tried to compose herself. "I
don't know, but since her heart's not beating, I don't think you'll

613

get much more." She lowered the tunic and mopped Acacia's waist with the hem. The red liquid against her pale skin painted a stark contrast. Although both colors signified death, maybe one would soon bring life.

With the sounds of a raging battle behind her, Bonnie slid both arms fully under Acacia's body and rose to her feet. The little Oracle was so thin, she seemed no heavier than a bag of bones. Heaving a sigh, she nodded at Sapphira. "We'd better hurry."

Sapphira padded toward Heaven's Gate, glancing back and forth between the plant and her cupped hands. When they arrived, she knelt in front of the plant, while Bonnie set Acacia next to the transparent energy field. Although the wall cast a sharp tingle across her skin, it seemed appropriate to lay Acacia as close to Heaven as possible.

Bonnie sat next to Sapphira, one leg curled under, one knee raised, and the point of her sword planted in the dirt so she could thrust herself to her feet if danger arrived. Yereq took three sideways steps to give them room and watched, his sword clutched in both hands. He, too, would be standing guard. They would be safe, at least for a while.

The bones of Makaidos lay strewn about, so dry and stripped white, even a dog wouldn't bother with them. Lifting her head, Bonnie looked at Heaven's Gate. It shimmered in the vibrant sunlight. Somewhere just beyond that barrier, the God of all creation awaited their fellowship in the glory of eternal light, a place she had visited briefly, but with war raging in the sky and on the ground behind her, the splendor of Paradise seemed so foreign … distant. How could perfect peace abide so close to demonic discord?

Sapphira laid her palms on the leaves and began massaging them in an up and down motion. As blood dripped to the ground, the leaves changed from green to red. The white gem in her ring, stained now with blood, began to glow with a swirling radiance of red and white. She pulled the ring off and forced it under the roots. The radiance pushed up through the stalk's channels, as if red and white phosphorescent paint flowed upward through its veins.

After a few seconds, she straightened her torso, though she stayed on her knees. Then, lifting her hands, she shouted, "Ignite!"

A ball of radiant white appeared in each palm. She swirled her arms, making the balls grow. They burst open, and the radiance spilled to the ground. As the light crawled along the soil, bubbling and sizzling, the bones absorbed the energy and began to glow, turning whiter than ever. The brilliance followed the red and white channels up the plant's stalk and burrowed into the middle of the praying leaves, lighting up the entire womb.

The blood on Sapphira's hands burned away. Like a sponge soaking in water, the plant drew in the blood from the praying leaves. Thin lines of scarlet pierced the membrane, as if creating capillaries from the outside to the life inside. Soon, the redness disappeared, leaving only vibrant green. As wave after wave of energy flowed from the soil, the bones dwindled to thin sticks and finally vanished.

615

When the last sparkle of radiance winked out, Sapphira shouted, "Makaidos, we call you to resurrection. The sacrifice has been made, and the blood of the innocent has purchased your new life." Weeping once again, she cried, "Come to Second Eden and help us rid this land of the corruption that has spoiled the new beginning that Abraham tried to maintain for so long."

As if erupting from the deepest recesses of her soul, words spilled from Bonnie's lips, unbidden words, passionate words that seemed set on fire from the Paradise that lay beyond the gate.

Makaidos, dragon, strong of heart,
Bereft of daughter, son, and mate,
Arise and take thy crown and throne,
Become again the potentate.

Deceivers fly to wrest thy place,
To steal thy seed, thy brood, thy fold;
Forbid the theft, this love betrayed,
And seize the souls from demons' hold.

Bonnie snatched in a breath. For a moment, she had lost her sense of reality. She had to concentrate. As the shouts, roars, and clanking of metal on metal grew louder, she glanced between the raging battle and the plant.

Reaching for the leaves, Sapphira looked at Bonnie. "I suppose I should just peel them back."

Bonnie nodded. "I think it's now or never."

Sapphira pinched the tops and pulled the leaves away from the center. An egg-shaped, transparent ball sat on top of the stem. No bigger than a small pumpkin, it glowed orange. Inside, a miniature dragon tried to spread its wings, but the glass boundary squeezed in the tips. The dragon reared up on its haunches and clawed to get out.

Sliding her hands under the ball, Sapphira lifted it to eye level. She gazed at it, her brilliant blue eyes shining and reflecting its glow.

Hoofbeats sounded. Bonnie glanced toward the battle, barely able to take her eyes off the plant's offspring. Dikaios thundered toward them, riderless and shouting, "Watch out for Goliath!"

Bonnie looked up. A red dragon swooped, his claws extended and fire blazing. Yereq leaped ahead and blocked Goliath's dive, slashing the air with his sword. Bonnie dove on top of Sapphira and spread out her wings. Heat coated them, and something sharp dug in, but it didn't rip her wing.

A loud whinny clashed with a dragon's roar. Bonnie jumped to her feet. Dikaios had reared up and was battling the dragon, hooves against claws and teeth, and Yereq jumped into the fray with powerful sword thrusts, but the nimble dragon dodged every jab.

616

As Goliath drew in a breath to scorch his opponents, Sapphira rolled over and threw a ball of flames into his eyes. Goliath beat his wings and flew backwards, then headed high into the air, apparently making ready for another diving attack.

Dikaios trotted up to Bonnie. "Ride with me to the battle. Yereq and the Oracle will protect the dragon king. Your beloved needs you."

"Billy? Is he all right?"

"He is alive, but there is no time to explain. Just come."

With a flap of her wings, Bonnie jumped onto Dikaios's back and looked at the egg. Now on the ground, it had swollen to four times its original size and was growing at an astounding rate. The outer shell cracked and flaked away. The dragon's snout poked through, then his wings. Surpassing Dikaios in size, he shook away the shell fragments, then, extending his neck, let out a trumpeting call.

Dikaios turned toward the battlefield and took off in a gallop. Bonnie looked back. Above, Goliath dove toward Sapphira. She raised her hands and created a dome of light around herself and the growing dragon while Yereq stood in front of her, his sword raised.

617

Goliath blasted a stream of fire that splashed against Yereq's chest. With a swipe of his tail, he smacked Yereq to the ground, snuffing the flames. Then, reaching out with his claws, he broke through the light, snatched Sapphira's arm, and jerked her off the ground. As he rose into the air, Sapphira screamed, but her voice thinned out in the distance.

The newly birthed dragon, now almost normal size, shot after them. Bonnie jumped to her feet on Dikaios's back and zoomed upward. "Makaidos!" she called. "Attack Goliath! I'll catch Sapphira!"

Now at least a hundred feet in the air and closing in, Makaidos roared. "Release the girl, Goliath, and prepare to feel my wrath."

Goliath flew in a slow orbit another fifty feet higher. "Long ago, you vowed not to fight alongside the human race. What has become of your cherished integrity?"

"I am not fighting alongside them. I am here to reestablish my kingdom, and you are the usurper. Now release the girl, and let us see who is the rightful king of the dragons."

"As you wish." Goliath opened his claws. Sapphira plummeted, but she didn't scream. Her arms and legs flopped helplessly. She seemed unconscious, or worse.

Bonnie flew underneath, caught Sapphira, and pressed her ear close to her mouth. "Thank God," Bonnie whispered. "She's breathing." As she eased her to the ground near the open plant, she looked at the Oracle's face. A dark bruise marked her forehead, but that was there before. Apparently all the jerking around had knocked her out. Someone had to stay to protect her.

Bonnie looked at the battlefield. In the sky, Makaidos fought with Goliath, colliding, snapping, biting, then circling around for another violent collision. A smaller red dragon joined in and helped Goliath. Thigocia dove down from above and snatched him out of the sky with her claws and threw him downward.

On the ground, the invaders had made a ring around the village defenders, but Bonnie couldn't see through to the center. Flames shot here and there, indicating that some dragons were within, apparently holding the attackers at bay. With only Billy and a few other warriors remaining, how long could they hold out against such an onslaught?

Still, the invaders seemed far fewer than before. Had Billy thinned them out with Excalibur? Where was its beam now? If he was hurt, as Dikaios had implied, he wouldn't be able to fight. Yet, she could take his place. If she could locate the sword, she would be able to fly into the circle, summon its beam, and disintegrate men and evil dragons.

Merlin flew over the field again. Another fuel bomb dropped and exploded among the invaders, but it was smaller, obviously

618

something Candle and Windor had pieced together in a hurry. Still, it punched a significant hole in the attacking troops. As the plane flew away, perhaps to try to reload again, Windor stuck his head out the open cargo door and shook his fists, a blend of triumph and worry in his expression.

Something touched Bonnie's shoulder. Twisting her neck, she looked at it—a man's hand, large and gentle.

"Go to him, Bonnie," a soft voice said. "I will watch Sapphira."

Tilting her head upward, she gazed into Enoch's eyes. "You'll protect her? How?"

He set a duffle bag down next to the plant. "Yereq is recovering, so you need not worry."

Bonnie looked at the giant as he struggled to his feet. His uniform was soiled and scorched, but as he straightened and lifted his sword, he seemed strong and alert.

Behind Enoch, the gate had split slightly, allowing a brilliant light to radiate from within. "Go now. The glory of Heaven is an effective deterrent. No one will dare approach while Yereq and I guard the Oracle."

She grabbed his hand, kissed it, then leaped into the air. Flying as fast as she could, she lifted over the invaders' siege circle and landed at the center, dodging a ball of flames launched by Clefspeare. The great red dragon stood next to two fallen men lying under a lean-to of battle shields, ferociously guarding them with a barrage of fire against any invader who dared to draw near.

Hartanna and the other females spewed their own flames, weaker but effective. The invaders held up shields to protect themselves, but they had to stay back.

Elam, Valiant, Barlow, Gabriel, and Flint jumped and jabbed at the closest enemies, each with shields up to ward off arrows and spears. Flint seemed invigorated by the battle, though his movements lacked the crispness and vigor the others displayed.

619

Ashley knelt near Billy and Walter, making sure the shields over their bodies stayed in place while holding another shield over her own head.

"Where is Excalibur?" Bonnie shouted.

"Over here!" Ashley waved her arm. "Get under cover!"

As Bonnie ran, an arrow whizzed by her head. An invader charged toward her. Valiant slung a dagger and pierced the attacker's neck, instantly felling him. Five more attackers charged. Valiant raised a shield and, like a battering ran, drove into them, pushing all five far into the crowd. In a mad flurry of swords and spears, Valiant disappeared.

"Valiant!" Bonnie cried.

Flint ran after Valiant, swinging his sword to cut an opening. As if swallowed by the attackers, he, too, vanished.

Ashley yanked Bonnie down to a crouch. "Stay low! We can't help them now!"

620

"Are Billy and Walter all right?" Bonnie asked.

Ashley shifted the shield, partially covering both herself and Bonnie. "Billy got knocked unconscious, but I don't think it's serious. He's been mumbling your name. Walter's alive, but not for long. I need Sapphira to help me do a healing."

Bonnie shook her head. "She's out cold, but she's safe."

Ashley pulled Excalibur from Billy's grip and passed it to Bonnie. "Go get 'em, tigress."

Billy raised his head and called out with a groggy, "Bonnie?"

"Hush." Ashley pushed his head back down. "You're in no shape to help."

"I'll do you proud, Billy." As Bonnie rose to her feet, Dikaios burst into the circle and joined them. "Karrick has fallen, but when Roxil flew to protect him, Goliath knocked her down. The coward is up to his old tricks and now stands with a claw on Roxil's underbelly threatening to kill her if Makaidos and Thigocia approach. They are at a stalemate."

"We can't do anything about that now." Picking up a shield from the ground, Bonnie used her wings to mount Dikaios. "Let's make like a clock, if you know what I mean."

Dikaios bobbed his head. "I do. Proceed when ready."

"You're a sitting duck up there," Ashley said.

"But I'll get a better angle on the enemy." Holding the shield in one hand and Excalibur in the other, she summoned the beam. The brilliant light shot into the air. For a moment, the surrounding invaders became stone silent. Their wide eyes told Bonnie that they had seen what the beam could do, and now that they were within range and no longer mixed in with the village troops, she could wipe them out in a hurry.

While Dikaios turned in a circle, she swept the beam over the heads of her allies and into the crowd of invaders. The dragons ducked as the beam passed by. Clefspeare blew fire at any invader who lowered his shield to load an arrow or throw a spear.

In explosions of sparks, the enemy troops vanished—fifty, seventy, one hundred. Some retreated while some managed to shoot arrows. A few pinged against her shield, but one hit Dikaios's front leg. He grunted but continued his rotation.

621

Bonnie kept the sword in place. Fifty more vanished. Another twenty. As invaders ran for their lives, the remaining ones shot their arrows wildly. Clefspeare and Hartanna flew into the air and chased the retreating men, blasting their unguarded backs, while Elam, Gabriel, and Barlow pursued the stragglers. Now it seemed that only thirty or so remained.

An arrow whizzed in and knifed into Bonnie's sword arm. She drew her arm back and dropped Excalibur. As the sword fell, the beam died away. Flapping her wings, she jumped off Dikaios and lunged for the hilt, the arrow protruding from her forearm, but a hand scooped Excalibur up before she could reach it.

One of the attackers, a tall muscular man in ancient Egyptian garb, swung Excalibur at Bonnie's neck, but just before the blade could strike, a shield blocked it with a loud clank. The shield bearer lowered his shoulder and bulldozed the attacker, knocking him flat on his back and sending Excalibur thudding to the ground. As Bonnie's defender snatched it up, a dragon flew by and smothered the attacker in flames.

The defender turned and smiled. "That was a close one."

"Billy!" Bonnie gave him a one-armed embrace. "Thank you!"

He whispered into her ear. "You did me proud. Now let's finish the job."

She flew up to Dikaios's back and, using her good arm, helped Billy mount in front of her. With Excalibur's beam once again surging, Billy shouted, "Let's round them up!"

Dikaios leaped ahead. As he passed one fleeing invader after another, Billy raked the beam across them. When a man vanished, his armor kept running for a moment before crashing to the ground. Soon, he had cleared the field of enemy troops.

After dousing the beam, he jumped off Dikaios and ran to Ashley while Bonnie followed, flying a foot or so off the ground. Ashley had tipped the shields over, exposing Walter's pallid face to the sun.

Billy knelt next to him and touched a deep gash across his forehead, placed there by an enemy sword. "How is he?"

She shook her head. "Not good, and Bonnie says Sapphira's not available." She looked at him, her eyes wet with tears. "Can we try a healing with Excalibur?"

"In a heartbeat." He stepped a few paces back. "Everyone stand clear!"

Clefspeare rose into the air. "I must see what I can do about my father's new threats," he said. "I suggest you join us after you restore your friend."

Ashley covered Walter's body and slid her arms underneath. "I'm ready."

Billy reignited the beam, but just as he angled it toward the ground to send its energy through the soil, someone shouted, "No!"

622

With a quick jerk, Billy raised the sword again. He turned toward the voice. In front of Heaven's Gate an elderly man waved an arm. "With the gem intact," the man called, "Excalibur is too powerful in this realm. It will likely heal him, but it will bring great harm to the healer, perhaps even death."

"I'll risk it," Ashley shouted. "Walter's dying."

Billy squinted at the old man. "Is that Enoch?"

Bonnie nodded. "We'd better listen to him."

"Bring him to me!" Enoch said, gesturing for them to come. "I will tell you what to do."

Billy let the beam die away and ran to Walter. "Come on. Let's get him on Dikaios."

Bonnie, Ashley, and Billy hoisted Walter in place, and Ashley mounted with him, holding his limp body in a sitting position. She gave Dikaios a gentle kick. "Let's move!"

As Dikaios galloped toward Heaven's Gate, Billy reached for Bonnie's hand and nodded at a gathering of dragons. "Elam and the others are already there. Come on."

"You go. I have to check something."

He pointed at the arrow protruding from her upper arm. "How bad is it?"

"Just break it off for me, but leave a few inches."

Taking a deep breath, he grasped the shaft. "Here goes."

She closed her eyes and clenched her teeth. The arrow snapped. Pain stormed from her arm, through her spine, and down to her toes, but it quickly eased to a dull throb. As tears welled, she nodded. "I'm okay. Thanks."

While Billy ran toward the garden's western wall, Bonnie scanned the ground and eyed each nearby body. She spotted one of the village's distinctive orange and red uniforms dressing a body that lay underneath a tall thin man sprawled facedown with his limbs splayed.

With a beat of her wings, she half ran and half flew toward the pair. She fell to her knees, rolled the top man over, and slid his blood-spattered body to the ground. His blond hair, dirty and matted, brushed back from his face. He blinked, revealing blue eyes, glassy and dilated. A companion attached to a thin chain floated out from under his shirt and hovered next to his ear. It flashed a dim blue light. As if in response to its light, Flint smiled weakly.

"Flint," Bonnie whispered. "Can you hear me?"

Grimacing, he choked out gurgling words. "Valiant. You must help Valiant."

Bonnie shifted to the other man and, with a heave, turned him over. Valiant's dark curls waved in the warm breeze, but the rest of his body stayed motionless. He was breathing, but with multiple wounds in his chest and his belly oozing blood, he wouldn't be breathing for long.

"I have to get you both to Ashley." Bonnie slid her hands under Flint's back.

"No." Flint clutched her sleeve, pulling the arrow and sending a new shock wave of pain through her body. She tried not to let it show, but a grunt pushed through.

"Take Valiant," Flint said, his voice slightly stronger. "You cannot take us both, so allow me this one sacrifice to make amends for my many sins against Abraham ... my beloved father."

Bonnie looked at her engagement ring. Sunlight made the red gem light up with brilliant sparkles. She pulled the ring off and slid it onto Flint's finger. "Abraham gave this to you long ago, and he kept it with him, even as he burned. For some reason, he left it behind. I think he wanted someone to give it back to you."

Flint drew his hand close to his face. He smiled again, then closed his eyes and let his head droop to the side. As his chest drew in a final breath, the companion settled there, and its light faded away.

Tears once again flowing, Bonnie shifted back to Valiant and slid her hands under his armpits. Using her legs and wings, she dragged him to Heaven's Gate where Ashley sat next to Walter's body. Yereq stood guard in front of the two Oracles, while Enoch knelt over Walter.

Panting, she nodded at Valiant. "No time to talk. Please take care of him." Without another word, she flew to the western end of the field and joined Billy.

Goliath stood over Roxil, a clawed foot resting on her underbelly. Clefspeare and Makaidos stalked around him, apparently searching for a way to catch him off guard, but Goliath's head rotated with them, and when his neck twisted beyond its limits, he snapped it back around and began following them again.

"You must stand down, son," Makaidos said. "Even if you kill Roxil, you can never escape. Between Clefspeare and me, you stand no chance."

"Give me my son back," Goliath growled. "Allow me to fly away with him, and I will release my mate. I will never return to haunt your pathetic tribe again."

Billy whispered to Bonnie, "This has been going on ever since I got here. The words have changed, but the standoff remains the same."

Bonnie searched for Karrick. She spotted a splash of red scales surrounded by Thigocia, Hartanna, Legossi, and Firedda. She then scanned the field again. Two dragons were missing, Yellinia and Sorentine. Bonnie had guessed that Yellinia was Devin's victim out on the battlefield, but what had happened to Sorentine?

Listener had dismounted Ember and was now standing near the ring of dragons, though she appeared to be back far enough to avoid danger. Gabriel and Shiloh stood behind her, while Elam and Barlow, both with swords drawn, watched from the opposite side of the circle.

"Karrick is under our protection," Makaidos said. "He has seen your traitorous ways, your brutal betrayal of his mother, and has requested asylum among us. We will not give him over to you."

"This is new," Billy whispered to Bonnie. "Just keep your eyes and ears open and be ready for anything."

A low growl erupted from Goliath's throat. "You know our law. He is not of age, so he cannot consent to join with you. As his father, I decide his fate."

"I know the law, and the king can overrule a father's rights if a son applies for asylum." Makaidos extended his neck, bringing his head close to Goliath's. "And I am the king."

Goliath spat a wad of fire on the ground. "The king of pride. The king of arrogance. You lord your authority over all your subjects, just as you did over Roxil and me. Your insane loyalty to corrupt humans incited us and other dragons to seek to protect our own kind."

Makaidos snorted. "And you say this with the claws of death ready to rip open your own mate."

"I am willing to sacrifice one for the good of many others. You did that yourself."

"You speak as a fool! I sacrificed *myself*, not someone else." Makaidos stretched out his wing and gently pulled Listener into his webbing. "This is the precious girl who asked to die for the sake of my daughters, but I could not allow her to pay the price of blood for dragon children she did not even know." He touched the other wing tip to his chest. "Roxil and Ashley were bone of my bone and flesh of my flesh. If they were to find deliverance in the ultimate Messiah, I had to be the one to give up my own blood to show them the way."

"It is true," Roxil said as she lifted her head from the ground. "I agreed with you during our days of foolishness, but when I saw our father burn in flames, his joy increasing with every painful moment as he gave his life for my sake, I knew that our rebellion was folly. Our father's every act, whether we agreed with it or not, was fueled by love, and when I saw that love, I knew that his love for humankind was pure and righteous. He loved humans, corrupt and stupid as they were, just as he loved you and me, though we never ceased in our rebellion. It took his suffering and death for me to finally see past my hatred, but now I understand what love really is."

Goliath blew out a stream of sparks. "He was grandstanding. He knew he would come back to life and lord his self-righteousness over us once again. But he cannot fool me. I am wise to his trickery. I can see—"

"My son!" Thigocia pleaded. "The Nephilim spirits are speaking these lies to you. Can you not see their schemes? No matter how great your father's deeds of sacrifice, the spirits burn them into scornful ashes. He can do nothing good in your sight. Your controlling spirits will not allow it."

Goliath's eyes flashed. "There are no spirits! No one has control of me. I am autonomous."

Listener broke away from Makaidos, ran to Goliath, and petted his scales as she looked into his eyes. "Daddy?" she cried out. "Is that you?"

Everyone stared, mesmerized. The little girl was now out of reach, beyond rescue.

"Daddy?" Goliath drew his head back. "This child is proving her madness once again. She who sought to die for her betters now wonders if one is her own father."

"But Daddy ..." Listener laid a palm on each side of his head as she continued staring. "I see you in there. I have not forgotten when you told Candle and me stories in front of the fire. We used to snuggle, and you would look at me with those same red and flashing eyes as you told of the dragons of old who would breathe fire instead of ice and help the humans battle against enormous angels called Watchers who had enslaved the world."

Goliath's words stumbled out like those of a stuttering drunkard. "Many know these ... these stories. It ... it wasn't I who told them to you."

627

"But you did. I will never forget the one about a great red dragon who spoke these vows to his new mate, the same vows you spoke to my mother, Angel."

Listener folded her hands, and, looking up, she spoke in a singsong chant. "Sweet are the days of those in love, yet too short for the breadth of love's endurance. When death comes to end our story, the words of love I write will find another page, for—"

"For our book of affection can have no end," Goliath finished. His eyes now seemed glazed over, a duller shade of red.

She set her hands on his face again. As dragon and girl stared at each other, Listener added, "Those were the words of my father's vow to my mother. He said he would love her even after death."

A thin line of smoke rose from Goliath's nostrils. Almost incoherently, he mumbled, "Even after death."

She pulled his head closer, so close he could have killed her with a single puff. "Do you still love her?"

628

Goliath's eyes rotated toward Roxil, then back to Listener. He seemed lucid now, though his tone was much gentler than Goliath's normal tenor. "Your mother was your father's mate, not mine. He died. She died. Why raise the issue?"

"Are you the great red dragon my father told me about, the one who spoke the vows?"

Goliath drew back again. "How did you learn these words of mine? I composed them, but I never spoke them to my mate. I chose a different vow."

Roxil spoke up, still underneath Goliath's foot. "Your vow was similar, but not exactly the same. You said, 'When death comes to end our story, the words I write will find another page.' You said nothing about love or affection."

A scowl bent Goliath's brow. He snatched Listener's clothes with his wing's claw and set her down next to Makaidos. "This is trickery," Goliath said. "You are filling my mind with confusion."

Thigocia pleaded again. "My son, Listener is reminding you of your true nature. When you were here as a human, you were kind and noble and good. When you are in your dragon form, the spirits of the Nephilim control you and tell you lies. Listen to Listener, for she has listened to you and learned of your integrity. Fight against the demons who have controlled you for all these centuries. If you truly want to think for yourself, then you must win this battle."

Goliath looked at Thigocia. Again his eyes turned dull as he whispered, "Mother, I ... I cannot fight them. ... Help me."

"Father!" Ashley ran into the gathering, her eyes wide and streaming tears as she reached her arms around Makaidos's neck. "Walter is dying. Enoch says that only another sacrifice will allow the birthing garden to restore him."

629

ANOTHER SACRIFICE

Makaidos nuzzled Ashley's cheek. "But there are no remaining bones. How will the garden be energized?"

Ashley dug a bone from her pocket, the finger bone she had found at Abraham's wall of fire. "There is this one. Maybe it will be enough."

Makaidos lifted his foreleg and looked at a gap in his clawed hand. One appendage was missing.

He let out a long sigh. "It will be enough."

"Makaidos?" Thigocia spread a wing toward him. "What do you intend to do?"

"I intend to save another life." He turned toward Heaven's Gate. "If my son-in-law dies, a valiant warrior will perish, and my daughter will be heartbroken. I cannot allow it."

"You have already given so much," Thigocia said. "You have died thrice. Will you be able to cheat death again?"

As he shuffled toward the garden, he shook his head. "No, my love. There will be no more bones, for the ones that fill my frame now have no resurrection power."

She dipped her head. "Very well, my darling. I shall not try to persuade you to turn against the love in your heart."

"It seems that our reunion is short-lived." He stopped and looked at her. "But when we meet on the other side of that gate, we will never be apart again."

"Let it be so." As Makaidos continued his march, Ashley at his side, Thigocia turned back to Goliath. "Is it grandstanding you perceive now, my son? Do you see a charlatan, or a loving father?"

Goliath wagged his head back and forth as if trying to cast off a spider's web. "I ... I cannot see. I cannot hear."

"Concentrate!" Thigocia set her wings on each side of his head. "Look at me and focus on my eyes."

Goliath's eyes flashed back to their more vibrant color, but his manner stayed calm. "I am focusing."

Now speaking softly and slowly, Thigocia continued. "Release your mate."

Goliath lifted his foot. Roxil rolled out from underneath and rose to her haunches.

"Good, my son. Now listen to my words. Your father loves you. He has always loved you. Just as you love your own son and do not want to lose him, so your father never wanted to lose you. You know the pain you suffered in your heart when Karrick chose to leave you. Oh, my son, it was ten times worse for your father, for instead of his wise teachings, you chose to listen to the foul song of demons. His firstborn, the crown prince of the dragons, decided to follow the Prince of Darkness, and how great the darkness has become. Because of your rebellion, his life has been but one death after another, each one a result of a series of events you set in motion. Yet, he has borne these sorrows and suffered these deaths willingly, for ever since you left his loving embrace, he died in his spirit every time he awoke from slumber to find that you were still a rebel."

Sparks drizzled from Goliath's nostrils. "How will he die now? Who will kill him?"

Sudden pain shook Bonnie from a trance. Billy had brushed against her arm and the still-protruding arrow. Since he was also mesmerized by the dragons' conversation, he hadn't even noticed the pain he had inflicted.

Bonnie studied Makaidos's shuffling gait as he closed in on the garden. Goliath's question was valid. Who would kill him? Every enemy had been vanquished.

She looked at Excalibur, the hilt still clenched in Billy's grip. Would he have to do it? Could he bring himself to take the life of a king in order to save Walter?

"Come," Thigocia said. "We shall see what the king of the dragons has in mind."

Still encircling Karrick as he walked, the female dragons half shuffled and half flew to the garden. Goliath and Roxil trailed them, while Bonnie and the other humans followed, Elam in the lead and Gabriel bringing up the rear.

633

Bonnie sidled up to Billy and whispered. "Are you thinking what I'm thinking?"

"I think so, but I can't see how anyone here could kill him."

From his other side, Sir Barlow spoke up. "Nor I, William. It is a terrible task indeed. Perhaps it will fall to the duty of the warrior chief."

Elam shook his head. "After all we've been through, I would rather die myself."

"Billy, you'll probably be called upon to energize the bone," Bonnie said. "I think Sapphira's still unconscious."

Billy nodded. "I can do that, but let's see what Enoch says."

When they had all crossed the garden and drew near to Heaven's Gate, Billy weaved through the crowd, stepped ahead of Makaidos and Ashley, and dropped to one knee in front of

Enoch. "I have brought Excalibur." He laid it on his palms and lifted it up. "A few years ago, Professor Hamilton traveled from Oxford to a little town in West Virginia. His faith in me led to the salvation of all dragonkind, and without his guiding hand, I would never have had the spirit or the courage to give my life for a race that spawned a few traitors who tried to kill me. So now I cannot dishonor the professor by lifting my hand to destroy the great king of the race for which we both sacrificed so much."

"Well spoken." Enoch grasped the hilt and lifted Excalibur. Then, touching Billy on each shoulder, he said, "By the power vested in me by the Majesty on High, I dub you a Knight of Heaven, for although a few precious souls might be willing to die for a friend, anyone who gives his life for those who hate him surely possesses the spirit of the ultimate Messiah."

Billy looked up at Enoch. "I will do my best to wear that title with honor and integrity."

634

Enoch gestured for him to rise. Lifting Excalibur high, Enoch spoke with a commanding voice that seemed to echo throughout Second Eden. "When Billy energizes this final remnant from the bones of Makaidos, the birthing garden will have the power to regenerate all who stand on its soil, including Gabriel, who lost his physical body in the earthly realm. As before, when the dragons passed in front of the Great Key, all who have dragon traits will be able to choose their form, a state they will keep for the rest of their natural lives, but this time, they must bear witness to that choice before we begin. Each of you will speak the words that God's spirit will reveal to your hearts."

He pointed the sword at Billy. "Take the hand of your fiancée, for the two of you will speak first. Have no fear that the wounded are in travail, for God will watch over them until we are finished." He looked at Bonnie's arm. "We will tend to that arrow very soon."

Bonnie joined hands with Billy. As he looked into her eyes, Billy said, "I choose to stay as I am, the way God made me. I will breathe fire and sense danger for all my days."

She pulled their clenched hands close to her chest. "And I choose the same. I will be content to be hounded by the media and to be called a freak." Breaking into a big smile, she added, "I will be a freak for God."

Gabriel raised a hand. "I'm with you. Being a winged wonder is very cool. I never really wanted to be anything else."

"And now you, Ashley," Enoch said as he shifted the sword toward her.

Ashley knelt beside Walter's body. As blood drained from the gash on his head, he heaved shallow breaths.

Enoch leaned down and touched her shoulder. "Fear not, my child. God will sustain him."

A hint of a smile broke through. "I agree with my brother and with Billy and Bonnie. I would like to stay as I am."

635

"Very well." Enoch moved the sword's point from dragon to dragon.

"I will no longer be Irene Silver," Hartanna said. "I will be Irene Conner, for my husband has returned, and he has restored his good name. I am proud to wear it again."

Clefspeare bowed low. "I will again be a husband to my dear Marilyn and a father to my noble and courageous son. I hope soon to take a daughter-in-law under my proverbial, if not literal, wing. I choose to be human."

Legossi lifted her head high. "I was born a dragon, and I will stay a dragon. If humans continue to despise my form, then so be it. I will show them the spirit of true integrity as I guard their backsides whether they like it or not."

"I am sorry, my old friend," Firedda said. "I was never very skilled at being a human, but I wish to return to Earth as a human to continue searching for my youngling."

Enoch shifted the sword and pointed it toward the sky. Everyone turned and looked. Another female dragon flew toward them, carrying two wriggling bodies. When she landed in the garden, she kept a foot planted on each one.

Bonnie grinned. It was Sorentine! And she carried Semiramis and Mardon in her claws!

"I apologize for my absence," Sorentine said. "When I saw these two escaping, I thought it better to make sure they caused no further trouble."

"And what of Yellinia?" Thigocia asked. "Have you seen her?"

Sorentine's head dipped low. "The slayer beheaded her. I assume the others did not tell you because of their grief."

A tear dripped from Thigocia's eye. "She was a valiant warrior." She turned toward Enoch. "Can Yellinia be brought back from the dead when the garden is energized?"

"Sadly, no," Enoch said. "This energy will not restore life or severed body parts."

Everyone stayed silent for a moment. Listener hugged Elam and wept. As he patted her gently on the back, he nodded at Sorentine. "Well done, good dragon. You are among the wisest and noblest of your race."

"You honor me too well," she replied, lowering her head further.

Semiramis, her red cloak now smeared with dirt, grunted from underneath Sorentine's foot. "If you will stop all this chatter for just a moment, I would like to plead my case."

Elam drew his sword and pointed it at Semiramis. "You have borne witness against yourself. We will hear no more from your lying lips."

Mardon stayed still as he stared at Elam. "Perhaps they will hear me. The three realms are still joined, and I know how to sever the rope that binds them. If you will grant me mercy, I will show you how."

"I will address that issue later," Enoch said. "For now, we must continue. Sorentine, what is the desire of your heart? Do you wish to remain a dragon or will you return to your human form?"

"I have learned that my precious little one is alive here in Second Eden, so I would like to become human and be her mother for as long as I can." She bowed her head again. "If that pleases you, honorable prophet."

"It pleases me," Enoch said, smiling. "Now, I need a volunteer who is not going to transform. Kindly take these two miscreants to the village, find a place that isn't in flames, and guard them there until you receive further instructions."

Legossi shuffled over to Sorentine. "With pleasure." She grasped Semiramis and Mardon and lifted them into the sky. Mardon shouted, but only the words, "Sever the rope," survived the buffeting wind.

Enoch moved the sword to Roxil. "And you, dear dragoness?"

Roxil looked at Makaidos and Thigocia in turn. "I have long disparaged the human race, so it is important that I make up for my errors. If I become human again, I would show that I love mankind by becoming one of them, but it was as a dragon that I spat on their shadows, so I will stay a dragon and become what I should have been all along, a servant in scales to the human race."

When the sword pointed at Thigocia, she looked up at Enoch. "What of my other offspring, Carboni, Alithia, and Martinesse?"

"They are humans on Earth, and in that place and state they will remain. Many adventures await them there. They have already located other dragon offspring, but that is not for us to consider at this time."

"And Valcor?"

Enoch smiled. "Patrick's desire to remain human and stay with Ruth prevented him from becoming a dragon here in Second Eden. That decision will not change."

"Very well." Thigocia looped her tail with Makaidos's and spoke with a trembling voice. "When my mate completes his sacrifice, he is going to be with you in glory, so I will stay a dragon and honor his memory within a suit of scales. Since my remaining days will be spent in sadness, let them be days that give tribute to the great Makaidos, king of the dragons."

Makaidos laid a wing over her back. He nuzzled her cheek but said nothing.

"And you, Makaidos," Enoch said, shifting the sword again, "what form do you wish to take? For even in death your body would be left behind."

Makaidos fixed his gaze on Thigocia. "Although my love for humans is well known, my love for my mate and my offspring exceeds all loves, save for the love I have for the Maker. Let me die as a dragon, and let the legacy of my service to both species be preserved forever."

638

Finally, Enoch pointed the blade at Goliath. "What do you wish to be? The dragon named Goliath, or the human who was called Dragon?"

Goliath looked at Makaidos, then at Listener. Although his eyes seemed filled with confusion, he spoke with clarity. "I will not tell you."

Riveting his gaze on Goliath, Enoch raised his voice. "You must!"

Goliath growled through his words. "I ... will ... not!"

Enoch bent his brow. "Then we will have to proceed without you."

"But how do we proceed?" Billy asked. "Who here would kill Makaidos?"

Enoch nodded at Ashley. "Do you still have the dragons' bane?"

She lifted a chain from around her neck and pulled the candlestone from under her uniform. The moment the crystalline facets appeared, Billy flinched. Every dragon showed signs of pain, some grimacing and others drawing back a step.

The chain dangling under her hand, Ashley wrapped the gem in her fingers, concealing it.

"You will give it to the sacrificial dragon," Enoch said, "for he is called to suffer great torment. Every ounce of energy he has gained in this life will be delivered bit by bit to the ones for whom he is dying. This will demonstrate once and for all the great love that he has for humans, and since love covers a multitude of sins, every evil act by dragonkind that has ever been incited against the human race will hereby be nullified in the memories of mankind. Tales of this sacrificial act will be told to generation after generation, and the story will remind them that the evils of the past have been washed away."

Keeping her grip on the chain, Ashley released the gem and let it dangle underneath. Now sobbing, she rose to her feet and held it out for Makaidos.

Bonnie looked at Billy. He was biting his lip. The pain had to be terrible, but he could bear it. If the pain in his heart was the same as the horrible ache in hers, it was much worse than anything the candlestone had ever delivered.

As Makaidos reached out with a foreleg, Goliath beat his wings and shot forward. He snatched the candlestone in both clawed hands and held it close to his chest. "I could not choose a form," he said, his eyes flashing wildly. "For I have chosen death." He settled to his belly, holding the candlestone underneath. "Let the Maker decide what he will."

Thigocia lunged toward him, but Enoch waved her back. "Stand aside!" he shouted. "The Maker's purposes will be fulfilled through this dragon, and every word I spoke will come to pass, for the evils perpetrated through dragonkind had their source in him."

Goliath lay still. His eyes pulsed. Smoke poured from his nostrils. Although his tail and wings twitched, he gave no other signs of suffering.

639

Makaidos dropped to his belly next to Goliath and draped a wing over him. "My son, I love you." Spasms shook his body. "I love you more than I could ever say."

Thigocia did the same from the other side. Sobs punctuated her words. "Oh, my dear son! My dear, dear son. My love for you has never diminished, and my memory of you will never die."

Clefspeare and Roxil guided Karrick in front of Goliath's eyes. "Father," Clefspeare said. "For many years my thoughts of you have been dark, but now they will be filled with light, for I have never witnessed a nobler act."

Tears falling to the ground, Roxil stretched out her neck and nuzzled Goliath's cheek. "Now I will look forward to eternity. Our love will truly survive death, and when I see you in Heaven, we will forever celebrate what you have done."

Karrick nuzzled Goliath from the other side. "Good-bye, Father. I have known you for only a few years, and now I will live the rest of my years as you have lived your final minutes, in sacrificial love for those around me."

Enoch gave Excalibur back to Billy. "It is time to energize the garden's soil, so please move Walter, Valiant, and Sapphira close to Goliath."

Gabriel and Sir Barlow lifted Valiant, while Bonnie and Elam carried Sapphira. As they laid the two limp bodies side-by-side, Sapphira's feet almost touching the dragon's snout, Yereq carried Walter and placed him next to Sapphira.

Enoch pointed at Makaidos's plant. "Set the bone on the ground near the roots."

Ashley laid the tiny white fragment next to the thick stem. "Like this?"

As he nodded, Enoch reached for Bonnie. Cradling her arm, he looked into her eyes. "Prepare yourself, sword maiden. This will hurt terribly, but you will soon be healed."

Gritting her teeth, Bonnie watched Enoch as he pushed the arrow the rest of the way through her arm and pulled it out the other end. Pain jolted her body once again. For a moment, she felt dizzy, and nausea churned in her stomach, but both sensations quickly eased.

Enoch threw the bloody arrow to the ground. "Now we must hurry. We don't want Bonnie or anyone else to lose too much blood before the healing takes place." He turned to Billy. "Summon the beam and cover the bone with Excalibur's energy."

Billy aimed the beam at the spot. The laser coated the bone with light and dug into the soil.

The finger of Makaidos glowed so brightly, Bonnie pulled a wing in front to shield her eyes. The energy spread across the ground and flowed into every human and dragon.

"Now," Enoch said, "the healer must cover the wounded."

Ashley lay on top of Sapphira and spread her arms over the other two. The light crawled up over all four, coating them with a pulsing glow. Beams of light shot out from Ashley's eyes, and, as she guided the beams from body to body, she wept. Her tears sizzled as they fell to Sapphira's chest.

Bonnie held Billy's hand. Her arm had already stopped bleeding, and the entry point seemed to be closing. "The light stings, doesn't it?" she asked.

"Yeah, but it's a good sting."

Goliath groaned but quickly stifled it. Makaidos and Thigocia patted him on the back and whispered into his ears, but their voices were too quiet to be heard.

A violent spasm jerked Goliath's body. A stream of black fog flew out of his nostrils and, like a frantic phantom, darted back and forth, stopping at each human and dragon as if seeking refuge.

Enoch pointed at the stream. "Billy! Strike the foul spirits of the Nephilim! They have tormented both dragons and men for far too long."

With a flick of his wrist, Billy zapped the fog with Excalibur's beam. The beam's energy enveloped the blackness with a halo of sparkling radiance. It evaporated the entire stream in an instant.

Enoch gave Billy an approving nod. "You may now let Excalibur darken."

He obeyed and lowered the sword.

"While the power of light does its work," Enoch said, "one of you must summon the hospital and bring it down to rest. Then, bring everyone to Heaven's Gate. Let them bathe in the radiance, and all will be healed."

Elam raised his hand. "I can run the magneto. I'll set them down in the field." He jumped onto Dikaios, and they rushed toward the forest path to the village. The fire had dwindled, allowing them to pass.

"The transformations will now begin," Enoch said with a bow. "When all is completed, I will come back. I have something very special prepared, and I ask that everyone return here ready for a celebration." Smiling, he added. "Including a good washing."

With that, Enoch turned, passed through a brief rift in the gate, and disappeared.

Hartanna lifted her wings. "I feel something."

"As do I," Clefspeare said.

Firedda and Sorentine stretched out their necks. "I feel smaller," Firedda said. "My neck is shrinking."

Clefspeare's scales smoothed out, and his tail and snout began to shrivel. Hartanna's spines flattened. Blond hair began to sprout at the top of her head.

Bonnie picked up the bag Enoch had left near the plant. "I'll bet I know what this is." She pulled out a beautiful sky blue dress. As she held it up off the ground, Billy reached in and withdrew a man's suit, black with pinstripes.

"Uh …" Billy said as he looked in the bag, "there are two more dresses in here, underwear, too. Men's and women's."

642

Giving Billy a wink, Bonnie placed the bag in front of the dragons and turned toward Heaven's Gate. "Let us know when you're done," she called.

Bonnie gazed at the transparent gate. Although she could see through to the rear of the garden, it seemed that faint shadows passed across the plane, like human phantoms of light scurrying from one place to another. It seemed that much more was going on behind the scenes than met the eye. The precise timing of so many events proved that loving helpers lay behind that shimmering barrier.

"We're ready!"

Billy and Bonnie turned. Jared Bannister, dressed in a perfectly fitting suit, bowed. Holding her ankle-length dress up to keep it from touching the dirt, Irene Conner curtsied. Dallas and Tamara copied her motions but with a bit less grace.

Bonnie ran to her mother and wrapped her up in her arms. "Oh, Mama, I'm so glad you chose to be human!"

643

Billy walked up to his father and extended his hand. "Dad, I—"

Jared pulled Billy into a tight hug. "Son, I watched you in battle. You and Walter both sacrificed yourselves for Ashley and Listener. I'm so proud of you, I might just explode."

As he returned the embrace, Billy laughed. "Don't explode. You'll mess up your new suit."

He pushed Billy back and brushed off the dirt Billy's uniform left behind. "Kind of overdressed for this place, aren't we?"

"You heard what Enoch said. He's planning something special."

Bonnie looked down at her uniform, caked with dirt and blood from her collar to her pant cuffs. "We'd better get cleaned up."

As the radiance continued sparkling on the ground, Goliath also shrank. Within seconds, he had turned into a man, now motionless. Makaidos and Thigocia kept their wings over his naked body from his shoulders to his ankles. Roxil lay down and stretched her neck over her mother.

Listener knelt near the man's head. "Oh, Daddy! It really *was* you!" She ran her fingers through his thick locks and tried to look into his eyes. "Daddy, it's Listener, your daughter."

Tears welling again, Bonnie pulled in her lip. This was too sad for words. The poor little girl had lost her father once again.

Tamara joined Listener and rubbed her back. "My precious little one. I will take care of you now. I cannot replace Angel or your father, but I promise to love you with all my heart."

While they embraced and wept together, Tamara's dark tresses fell over Listener's pigtails. The two colors were perfectly matched. Mother and daughter had finally reunited after over a thousand years.

Ashley lifted herself off Sapphira and helped all three patients rise to their feet. With her hair tossed about, her cheeks scarlet, and her shoulders slumped, she seemed ready to collapse, but when Walter smiled at her, her own smile lit up her tired face.

Rubbing his head, Walter looked around. "Wow! What did I miss?"

"When we hit the washroom," Billy said. "I'll tell you all about it."

Valiant bowed toward Ashley. "Thank you, healer. I am forever in your debt."

Sapphira ran to Acacia's body and fell to her knees. "Oh, my dear sister! I was hoping it was just a nightmare!" She laid her head on Acacia's chest and wept.

As her cries rose into the air, another sound drifted down from the sky, a low hum. Like a slender blimp, the long, tubular hospital descended toward the field. Merlin eased in for a landing as well. Candle threw down the back airstair and helped Windor hobble toward the garden.

Bonnie touched Billy's arm. "I'll stay with Sapphira. Why don't you and the others help the hospital patients come for their healing in the garden. Then we'll all get cleaned up."

"Good idea. I can hardly wait to see Dad and Mom get together."

While Billy, Walter, Ashley, Shiloh, Barlow, and Gabriel headed to the field, Bonnie stooped and touched Sapphira's shoulder. "I will never, ever forget your sister's sacrifice," Bonnie said. "She saved my fiancé, she stripped Devin's invincibility, and she rescued Earth and Second Eden. I have seen many wonderful sacrifices, but never one as beautiful, noble, and loving as hers."

Sapphira looked up at her. Tears poured from her shining blue eyes. "Thank you," she said, barely above a whisper. "That means a lot to me."

Bonnie rose and turned toward the field. Pearl and Marilyn had just carried a patient on a stretcher through the hospital doors and onto the landing platform. Ashley took Marilyn's place at the stretcher and pointed at Jared.

645

Marilyn pressed a hand against her chest, let out a squeal, and very nearly flew into Jared's arms. Billy and Walter laughed, but Ashley got them back to work in a hurry as she barked out her usual rapid-fire orders.

Carrying a stretcher, Patrick and Ruth emerged, with Steadfast walking alongside and holding an IV bag. Whoever that patient was, he or she must have been very sick.

When Bonnie's father came out, carrying a dark-skinned little girl in his arms, Ashley caught his gaze and nodded toward Heaven's Gate. As Sir Barlow took the girl, his resonant voice carried across the garden. "Your wife is waiting for you."

His mouth agape, Bonnie's father ran to Irene, then stopped and stared at her for a moment. After an exchange of inaudible whispers, they embraced warmly. Soon, they pulled apart and, holding hands, walked back to the hospital.

As stretcher after stretcher headed toward the garden, Bonnie leaned over and caressed Sapphira's hair. "I'd better check on our water supply and see if we have any clean clothes. The fire might have burned everything."

"Wait!"

Bonnie followed the sound of the voice. Enoch stepped out of a new rift in Heaven's Gate, carrying a pile of clothing draped over both arms. "I apologize for this last-minute detail, but some good friends of yours have been rushing this project to completion. Karen and Naamah were particularly fussy about your dress." He nodded at the pile. "They guessed correctly that you would keep your wings, but they had to pull out some fastening devices they had put in the back, just in case."

Bonnie touched the dress on top, a gorgeous white satin gown with a silk train. "It's ..." She lowered her voice to a whisper. "It's a wedding gown."

Keeping his voice low, Enoch winked. "I had to wait for Billy to leave. Tradition says that a groom should not view the bride's gown until the appropriate time."

Bonnie kissed Enoch's cheek. "Thank you so much!"

"And there is a fine suit here for Billy and proper attire for everyone. I'm sure you will find that they all fit perfectly. We have access to very accurate information inside Heaven's Gate."

Smiling, Bonnie ran her hand along the hefty load of clothing. "I see two more wedding gowns here. Who else—"

"They are all labeled, my dear." Enoch began walking toward the edge of the garden. "You are all much too dirty, so I will carry these to the village. I will meet you at Abraham's old hut when you're ready."

A surge of joy blended with a fountain of sadness, and both rushed through Bonnie's mind and heart. As she surveyed the garden and adjoining field, scenes of life and death flooded her senses. Her mother and Billy's father were again human—happy, healthy, and content. Billy and Walter hauled sick villagers to the garden to be cured in a bath of life-giving energy. Dikaios and Elam galloped back into the field, and Elam joined in with the helping hands. Listener's father and Acacia lay dead, both a true blend of joy and sadness, and both precious portraits of the tragedy and victory of heroic sacrifice.

Tears flowing yet again, Bonnie heaved a sigh and marched toward the edge of the garden. With every step through the radiant soil, the sadness melted away, giving rise to fuller and fuller joy. Every tragedy, every moment of suffering, had led to life and peace, just as the suffering and death of her Lord Jesus had brought the same to every man, woman, and child on Earth who called upon his name.

She gave herself a firm nod. In this truth she could rest, knowing that the God of the universe had guided her and Billy every step of the way. And now, a final journey lay before her, a new adventure with her beloved, the young man who had proven his worth time and time again.

As Billy and Walter passed by with a patient on a stretcher, Bonnie smiled. Billy smiled back. Turning to the village again, she wrapped her arms around herself, holding the memory of that smile close. Yes, that wonderful man had proven his undying love, and their union would now come about by an act of the will, not a prophetic destiny. He was hers, and she was his, by choice. Could she scream that truth from the rooftops? Her heart felt like it was about to burst.

She unbuckled her sword belt, let it fall to the ground, and walked onto the field. The first step on the final path couldn't come soon enough.

Dikaios and Ember trotted up to her, Listener riding on Ember's back. "Would you like a ride?" Dikaios asked.

Bonnie grinned. "I think I could float back to the village, even without my wings."

"I can see the joy in your eyes." Dikaios bowed his head. "After the celebration, I will enter into Heaven to forever be with my master, so please do me this honor."

Bonnie flapped her wings, rose into the air, and settled on Dikaios's back. "The honor is all mine, great horse." She looked at Enoch as he walked across the field. Even from the garden, she could see the wedding gown on top of his pile of clothes.

Smiling, she stroked Dikaios's neck and cried out, "Let's fly!"

20

CHAPTER

TILL DEATH DO US PART

Lush grass, ankle-high and as green as emeralds, now covered the birthing garden and its adjoining field. Only one flaw interrupted the verdant carpet, a rectangular mound of dirt, a grave for Dragon, formerly Goliath. Since he had expelled the Nephilim in the garden, everyone agreed that his body should be laid to rest here, though all knew that his spirit was now rejoicing somewhere beyond Heaven's Gate.

Bonnie stood at the edge of the field and contemplated the recent events.

Just an hour ago, Enoch guided Bonnie back to Heaven's Gate. A golden rope had appeared, parallel to the shimmering gate and extending out of sight to the right and left. He instructed her to cut it with her staurolite dagger, which he had found buried in her dirty uniform. When she did, the rope snapped and disappeared. The ground shook. Although the sky stayed clear, the air cooled, though not enough to bring a chill.

Enoch explained that cutting the rope separated the three realms, but he wouldn't say what happened to Semiramis and Mardon, only that they would receive exactly what they deserved.

At that moment, thick green grass began to shoot up in the garden's soil around Bonnie's feet, replacing the burnt grass. Enoch went on to tell of several new birthing gardens that would be created so that Second Eden could be populated more rapidly as the inhabitants explored beyond the old boundaries and established new settlements.

Earlier, Thigocia and Legossi burned Yellinia outside the village, along with the bodies of the invaders. Billy and Walter buried Devin in an unmarked grave far from any footpath or water source. When they returned, they seemed stoic, lacking any joy at finally disposing of one of the darkest beings in all of human history.

"Let's just forget about him," Billy had said. "He's not worth the energy to speak his name." And he and Walter refused to tell anyone where they had buried him.

Following the village's custom for fallen warriors, Elam and Valiant burned Flint's body and buried his bones. Instead of the burial grounds outside the village, they created a small plot behind Abraham's former hut. Valiant sang a beautiful song of lament that carried a theme of hope. No one knew the condition of Flint's soul when he died, but the revival of his companion, his apparent change of heart, and his heroic sacrifice spoke volumes.

The two village chiefs also burned Cliffside's body. Taking Emerald along, they interred Cliffside's bones in the traditional burial grounds. Valiant's song prophesied the coming of another Second Edener, a child who would learn the same rock-solid dedication to service and unshakable love of the smallest ones, the unborn lives in the garden. Emerald wept for quite some time, and Valiant stayed with her, both on their knees as they prayed for comfort.

Enoch himself had taken Acacia's body through Heaven's Gate, saying something about preparing a "Welcome Home" celebration for an Oracle of Fire. As the prophecy indicated, since Elam never returned to Earth with Acacia to search for Sapphira, Acacia's life became chaff, a sacrifice of love on behalf of others.

Just before Enoch took her body, Elam asked about the prophecy.

"I don't understand. When was I supposed to take Acacia to Earth?"

"When Billy took Acacia and Listener, you could have gone instead of Billy. If you had kept the prophetic words in mind, you might have realized that."

Elam pointed at himself. "So is Acacia's death my fault?"

"Of course not. Devin killed Acacia. You merely made a mistake. You had set your mind on training the troops. You did not intentionally disobey."

"But what if I had paid attention? Would Acacia still be alive?"

"Yes, my son." Enoch set a hand on Elam's shoulder. "But Sapphira would have perished instead."

"Sapphira? But how could—"

"Shhh …" Enoch stooped and picked up Acacia's body. "I can tell you no more of things that might have happened. Rest assured that God is not angry about your choices. You came to a fork in your journey, and you chose the path that you thought would be most likely to please him. It is a heart of obedience that God cherishes, and yours burns with passion like few others."

He turned toward the gate, and as he passed through a shining rift, Acacia's body burst into flames. Then, they both disappeared.

651

Bonnie sighed. One tragedy in exchange for another.

She shook her head and tried to cast off the sorrow. Only tears of joy would be allowed for the rest of the day. After all, a great celebration was about to commence.

Before she had cut the rope, in anticipation of the celebration, the youngest villagers had washed naked in the fountain. Enjoying the newfound warmth of their land, they scrubbed themselves and each other in perfect innocence. Their parents joined in, not caring that their wet, filthy clothes weighed them down. They made sure their toddlers exited the fountain clean from head to toe. Wearing broad smiles, it seemed that everyone was washing away the past—the conflicts, the deaths, and the sadness of days gone by.

Bonnie and the other Earth inhabitants had chosen to bathe in the private washrooms. Those buildings and half of the others survived the fire, but to the villagers, the losses seemed no more than broken jars. The huts were merely things, temporal and replaceable. They would share their dwellings and the labor of rebuilding what they had lost. Such was the loving character of these precious people.

Now, less than half a day after the climactic battle, Bonnie stood on the field that led to the birthing garden. A line of six bridesmaids and matrons assembled in front of her, temporarily shielding her from the groom who waited for her in front of Heaven's Gate.

They walked ahead in time with the slow music of a trio of pipers playing near the edge of the garden. It seemed appropriate to stretch out the occasion. Her wedding gown felt so heavenly, why not let these moments last for hours? The satin, dazzling white and as soft as silk, brushed against her body from her bare feet to her neck. With Ashley at her left and Sapphira at her right, each also wearing a beautiful white gown, the sensation was like walking among angels in the clouds.

Karen and Naamah knew the hearts of the brides and designed the gowns accordingly. Although they bore many similarities— modest necklines, fully covered shoulders, long sleeves, and ankle-length skirts—the gowns displayed the individuality of each bride.

The lace that covered the bottom third of Ashley's skirt lacked symmetry, but a closer inspection revealed a complex design within the delicate fabric, a tiny mural of scenes from her adventures—a miniature Apollo, a representation of Larry the supercomputer, and a portrait of her departed grandfather.

Sapphira's lace bore images of flames sprouting from plants, scrolls from the museum, couples dancing with fountains of water spraying over their heads, and a blossom from the tree of life. As she pushed each foot forward, the sun seemed to make the flames come alive, the tongues sparkling with her every movement.

Bonnie looked down at her own dress. Of course, Karen and Naamah had cut holes in the back for her wings, but they had added something far more important. Although the satin was already brilliantly white, when the sun struck the bodice and skirt at the right angle, something still brighter gleamed—text stitched in silver thread, her song from Psalm 139. As she read the opening words, though it was upside down in her perspective, tears filled her eyes.

653

> Whither shall I go from thy spirit? Or whither shall I flee
> from thy presence?
> If I ascend up into heaven, thou art there: If I make my
> bed in hell, behold, thou art there.

Yes, whether living on Earth, visiting Heaven, trapped in Hell, or in the midst of battle in Second Eden, God had always been with her no matter what.

As they neared the garden, Bonnie peeked through the line of escorts. Billy stood in front of Heaven's Gate, facing her and wearing a stunning white tuxedo, a jet-black sword belt, and a freshly polished scabbard with Excalibur sheathed within.

She smiled. With his hair brushed back, his handsome face clean and shaven, and his broad shoulders squared, he looked fine indeed. Oh, yes, very fine indeed.

To Billy's right and Bonnie's left, Walter stood ramrod straight, alternately folding and unfolding his arms. Also wearing a white tux, he kept his eyes focused on the ground, shifting his weight constantly, apparently too nervous to behold the lovely treasure he would soon receive.

Elam stood at Billy's left, his hands folded at his waist. Also dressed in white, he moved from side to side, obviously trying to catch a glimpse of Sapphira behind the bridal party wall.

The villagers sat in the grass, as did the dragons and humans from Earth, all facing Heaven's Gate, yet looking back at the approaching procession, every eye wide with anticipation.

Billy's parents sat in the front row next to Bonnie's, all four so close to Billy, he could have reached them with two steps and an out-stretched arm. Makaidos and Thigocia sat on their haunches close to Walter, with Roxil behind them, all three wearing draconic smiles.

Bonnie also spotted Patrick and Ruth seated near Elam. Patrick still felt very close to Elam, though he was much younger. Watching over Elam, or Markus as he was called at the time, had made him feel like a father long before Shiloh was born.

When the bridal party arrived at the front edge of the garden, the escorts stopped. The pipers' song faded, and, except for the cool breeze creating a gentle rustling of nearby trees, silence ensued.

Bonnie let her gaze drift from left to right along her line of escorts—Mantika, Tamara, Dallas, Shiloh, Listener, and a village girl about Listener's age. The two Second Eden maidens began to sing, trilling words in an unfamiliar language. They had explained earlier that Abraham had written the song centuries ago at a time when they did not yet speak English, and it became their tradi-tional wedding song. Of course, he later translated it, but to this day they still sang the first verse in the original language, and that was the cue for Bonnie, Ashley, and Sapphira to lower their bridal veils over their faces.

After the beautiful yet mysterious words ended, the three matrons on the left shifted into single file, and the girls on the right did the same, as if opening a gate to the brides they had veiled with their bodies.

Bonnie and her companions stepped through the gap. The villagers and Earth visitors rose to their feet, gazing in silence. Even the breeze fell to a hush.

All three grooms stared. Walter's mouth dropped open. Tears streamed down Elam's cheeks. Billy's jaw quivered, and his fingers worked Excalibur's hilt. With his gaze locked on Bonnie's, he smiled.

Goose bumps covered Bonnie's arms. That smile ... that wonderful smile—content, satisfied, filled with joy that a great journey was over and a new one, perhaps even more exciting, was about to begin. And now, they would travel the new road together as husband and wife.

655

She returned his smile, hoping to reflect the same excitement, the same joy, a joy so overflowing she could barely keep from bouncing on her toes.

Listener stepped out from her line of maidens and stood directly in front of Bonnie. Now the processional would begin, Listener leading the way, singing the English version of this realm's wedding song, altered slightly for the triple union of brides and grooms.

As she and the maidens proceeded, followed by the three matrons, Bonnie paused for a moment, took in a deep breath, and led the brides, stepping in time with the song's gentle rhythm.

> The brides are ready, sound the call,
> With spotless virtue, virgins all;
> Let pipers pipe and angels sing,
> Let shouts resound and anthems ring.

Extend your hands, O grooms of light,
And be their noble, worthy knights;
With arms of holy strength embrace
Your brides with honor, love, and grace.

When the song ended, Bonnie took her place in front of Billy, facing him and Heaven's Gate, though they didn't yet touch, as was the Second Eden custom. Ashley stood in front of Walter, and Sapphira faced Elam.

Immediately to Bonnie's right, Listener knelt and gazed at Billy with a broad smile. As Shiloh, the gap in her fingers still obvious, took a seat with Gabriel, and the village maiden sat with her parents, the crowd buzzed, some displaying questioning glances.

Tilting her head, Bonnie gave Billy a quizzical look. Why did Shiloh and the other girl do that? They were supposed to copy Listener's pose, one kneeling in front of Walter and the other in front of Elam, virgin females to attend each of the couples, a Second Eden tradition.

Billy seemed to understand her silent question, but his expression said he didn't have an answer. Obviously Shiloh and the other girl knew something the marrying couples didn't. A surprise, maybe?

A bright vertical line appeared in Heaven's Gate. As expected, Enoch stepped out. Instead of his usual tunic and breeches, he wore a multicolored cloak tied at the waist by a purple sash. With his white hair brushed neatly back, he appeared regal and holy, certainly looking like a man qualified by Heaven itself to perform the wedding ceremonies.

As Enoch lifted his hands, the crowd quieted. Speaking with a deep, resonant voice, he said, "I assume you are wondering why the young ladies have broken tradition and not taken their places as attendants." He flashed a coy smile. "I made this agreement with them earlier, so they are following my instructions. Through special arrangement by the Majesty on High, we have two replacements, one whose purity is unquestioned and another whose virtue has been restored."

He stepped away from the rift in the gate and looked at it expectantly. A young woman's head came through the opening, her hair red and shining. As if frightened by what she might find, she set her foot down timidly on the garden's soft turf and looked around, her eyes wide. When her body fully appeared, a shining aura surrounded her sky blue gown, making her look like a radiant angel.

Bonnie bit her lip. She wanted to squeal, "Karen!" but it wouldn't be right. This was a moment reserved for Karen and Ashley.

Lifting a hand to her mouth, Ashley let out a gasp. As Karen's gaze locked on her, Ashley's knees buckled. Walter grasped her arm and held her up, his smile trembling. "It's okay," he said. "It's just Karen. She's—"

657

Walter swallowed his words. Karen, every step touching the ground as if set there by a princess, glided toward him. She knelt at her position and looked up at him with sparkling eyes. With a voice like a strummed harp, she said, "She's what, Walter?"

"She's ..." As he looked at Ashley, his jaw firmed. "She's amazing!"

Another woman, raven-haired and petite, stepped through the rift in Heaven's Gate, wearing a gown every bit as blue and shining as Karen's. Even more timid, she glanced around as if wondering if she would be unwelcome. When her gaze fixed on Elam, she bowed her head.

"Who is that?" Bonnie whispered to Billy.

"I remember Elam's description. She has to be Naamah."

Bonnie mouthed her name. Naamah. Sapphira had told stories about her evil mistress, Morgan's seductive minion. After all she had done, how had she gone to Heaven? What would Sapphira think about this wicked woman kneeling in the place of a virtuous attendant? What did Elam think?

Keeping her head low, Naamah took short, quick steps to her spot in front of Elam and knelt. Sapphira looked at him, her expression asking the questions Bonnie had already raised in her mind.

Suddenly, Heaven's Gate flashed. The transparent wall grew opaque, and a grassy meadow took shape. A woman with dark hair knelt in the field, her body so low she seemed curled in a trembling ball. As she shook, a song emerged, a lament that drifted across the wedding party like a gentle wind.

O who will wash the stains I bear
The harlot's mark of sin I wear?
Exposed and shorn of all I prized,
And now I beg for mercy's eyes.

O Jesus, look upon my strife
And spare this foolish harlot's life.
I bow, surrender, pour my tears;
Forgive my sins and draw me near.

The scene shifted abruptly. Elam stood at the crest of a rise looking out over the expanse. Naamah, wearing an oversized cloak, stared at her hand, standing, waiting, hoping. Elam extended his own hand, grass-stained and bloodied.

She ran to him and dropped to her knees. Grabbing his hand, she kissed his palm, her tears flowing. "You won't regret this, Elam," she said. "I promise, you won't regret your mercy."

He pulled her to her feet and spoke softly. "To be wanted and not lusted for. To be loved and not pitied. To be asked and not commanded." He pushed his hand through her tangled hair, then slipped it into hers, touching their palms together. "Is that right?"

As Naamah's cheeks flushed, she smiled. "And to be believed, even after all my lies."

The scene faded away, and the gate reverted to transparency. Sapphira leaned over and took Naamah's hands. Letting out a little gasp, Naamah looked up at Sapphira and allowed her to raise her to her feet.

Bonnie bit her lip again, trying not to cry. The sight was such a contrast! Although both women stood no taller than five feet, they seemed like giants, one with snowy white hair, pure and undefiled, the other with the shadow of Morgan hanging over her, a raven dressing her locks with memories of darkness, torture, and abuse. Did Naamah's mocking songs still ring in Sapphira's ears? Did the whip and briar nettles still sting like angry hornets up and down her back? Could Sapphira forget all the years of humiliation she suffered at the hands of this servant to a sorceress?

Sapphira lowered herself to her knees and looked up at Naamah. "Will you forgive me?" Sapphira asked.

Naamah's chest heaved. Tears streamed. She swallowed and choked out her words. "Me? Forgive you? I … I don't understand. I need you to forgive me."

Sapphira kissed Naamah's fingers. "I hated you for centuries. I cursed your name both in whispers and shouts. I wanted you to die." Her voice pitched higher. "But then I watched Bonnie Silver. Even though her father treated her with contempt over and over again, she never cursed his name. She never stopped loving him, even after he betrayed her mother and caused her death as well as Bonnie's suffering in foster homes. And when he asked for forgiveness, she gave it, showing the kind of love I needed to learn."

Bonnie looked at her father and gave him an "I love you" sign with her fingers. He returned the sign, his eyes glistening. Her mother took his hand and clenched it tightly, nodding at Bonnie with trembling lips.

"So," Sapphira continued, "that's why I ask you to forgive me. Because of Bonnie, I learned about the same Jesus you sang about, and that's when my hatred for you just melted away. But I have ached for your forgiveness ever since, and now that you're here …" She kissed Naamah's hand again and looked up at her. "Will you please forgive me?"

"Oh, yes! Yes!" Naamah pulled Sapphira to her feet and wrapped her arms around the white-haired bride. "And please do not withhold *your* forgiveness. My wickedness toward you was not in response to anything evil you did. It sprouted from the depths of my black soul."

"And now your soul is clean," Sapphira said. "As white as snow."

They kissed each other's cheeks, smearing the tear tracks. Naamah withdrew a handkerchief from her dress and dabbed Sapphira's face. "Enoch said I would probably need this," Naamah said. "He was right."

Enoch clapped his hands. "Now if everyone will take your places …"

Her smile as broad as an ocean, Naamah knelt at Sapphira's right, glancing back and forth between her and Elam.

Bonnie's father stood at her left. Makaidos shuffled forward and sat next to Ashley. The fathers of two brides were now ready to give away their daughters.

Bonnie looked at Sapphira. She had no father, no one to give her away. They had already wept together, knowing she would need a surrogate, but the one she chose certainly stood head and shoulders above any father. Yereq, dressed in a tailored Earth-style suit, walked up and took his place at her side. Being a brother, of sorts, spawned from the same genetic code and the same soil as her own origin, surely he had the right to offer her to the groom.

Smiling, she reached up and held his hand, barely able to wrap her fingers around three of his.

Heaven's Gate shimmered. Now, instead of a window to the other side of the garden, it became a window to another world.

Dozens of people lined up on the other side, watching the ceremony.

Bonnie let her gaze linger on each face. She spotted Acacia,
Dorian, Brogan, Joseph of Arimathea, and many other souls who
had passed away during her many adventures, a band of heavenly
witnesses who would be watching over all of them for years to
come. She tried to find Professor Hamilton, but with people lined
up at least five deep, he was probably hidden from sight.

"Now," Enoch said, "in order to make sure each union receives
its proper recognition, we will perform the ceremonies one at a
time."

Bonnie grinned. Enoch didn't mention the fact that the best-
man situation made it impossible to perform all three at once, but
that would become obvious very soon.

Enoch walked to Walter's side. "You seemed surprised to see
Karen," Enoch said.

"Shocked would be a better word. I didn't know you could just
pop out of Heaven and into Second Eden like that."

661

"Well, be prepared for another shock. Now that some of the
portals have been restored, I sent a certain pair of couriers to collect other special guests from the cave in the Valley of Shadows."
Enoch lifted a hand to his ear. "And if those are hoofbeats, they
are right on time."

Everyone turned toward the village. Dikaios and Ember trotted across the field, Dikaios carrying Walter's parents, Carl and
Catherine Foley, and Ember carrying Shelly, Walter's sister. All
three were dressed in sharp riding outfits. When they arrived, the
three Foleys took places in the front row, Carl using a cane to walk.
Catherine blew Walter a kiss as she sat down.

Walter grinned and gave them a thumbs-up. "About time you
got here!"

When the laughter subsided and Billy took his place at Walter's side as his best man, Enoch looked over Ashley's shoulder at

the sea of onlookers. "Who gives this maiden to be wed to this warrior?"

Makaidos nodded at Thigocia, then at Enoch as he laid a wing over Ashley. "Her mother and I do."

Enoch bowed. "So be it."

Ashley pressed her veiled cheek against Makaidos's. "Thank you …" She paused, her voice spiking. "Daddy."

She threw her arms around his scaly neck and pulled him close, but only for a moment. When he took his place with Thigocia, Enoch folded his hands at his waist. "Since only one of you has dragon blood, we will proceed with the traditional vows of humans in your culture."

After reciting the vows, saying "I do," and exchanging rings Enoch provided, exquisite gold rings from Heaven's forge, Walter and Ashley knelt in front of Enoch.

He laid a hand on each head. "Seeing that you have made this commitment to one another in the sight of God and these witnesses, by the authority vested in me as a prophet of the Most High God, I now pronounce you husband and wife, or as the Second Eden residents say, 'Adam and Eve.'"

He gestured for them to rise and nodded at Walter. "You may now kiss your bride."

Walter lifted Ashley's veil with both hands. Karen smoothed the veil out behind Ashley's hair, another Second Eden custom. He paused, staring at her lovely face as if hypnotized. Finally, Ashley laid a hand behind his head, pulled him close, and kissed him, a tender lip caress that lingered for several seconds.

Laughing, Enoch turned the couple around and announced to the crowd. "Ladies and gentlemen, dragons and dragonesses, I present to you, Mr. and Mrs. Walter Foley."

"All right, Walter!" Billy shouted, clapping his hands. "You're a married man!"

Walter pointed at him. "You're coming up, buddy!"

"Indeed." Enoch waved for Ashley and Walter to sit with their parents. As he walked toward Elam and Sapphira, he passed Bonnie, whispering as he breezed by. "You are radiant, my dear."

Warmth rushing into her cheeks, Bonnie smiled. Having that wise old prophet performing their ceremony would be wonderful. He was so gentle and kind.

With Patrick as best man, Enoch performed a similar ceremony for Elam and Sapphira. When he asked them to repeat the vows, they spoke in Hebrew. Looking into each other's eyes, Elam pressed his left hand against Sapphira's right. Their fingers didn't wiggle. That expression of longing for togetherness had ended. Now they had come together, their union as husband and wife only seconds away.

After Enoch repeated his pronouncement, declaring them a wedded couple, he turned them toward the audience and said, "These two have waited thousands of years for this blessed day. When the final ceremony is complete, we will have a celebratory feast to end all others."

Everyone rose to their feet and cheered, most clapping while a few children leaped into the air.

"Now," Enoch continued, turning to Elam, "you may kiss your bride."

Elam pushed Sapphira's veil up and paused for a moment while Naamah smoothed it out. Then, without another second's hesitation, he kissed Sapphira, keeping his hand pressed against hers.

Standing on tiptoes, she wrapped her arms around him. A faint glow coated her body, and a ripple of flames ran from her head to her toes.

Elam pulled back and gazed at her. Sapphira's eyes sparkled with a more radiant blue than ever. They both smiled, the two most beautiful smiles Bonnie had ever seen—pure joy, simply pure joy.

From under his robe, Enoch withdrew a journal and gave it to Elam. "A friend of Sapphira's and Bonnie's asked that I restore this

663

to its owner. She said to tell you that 'The Maid' will pray for you both for as long as you live."

Elam and Sapphira caressed the journal's worn cover, their faces beaming. After they sat with Patrick and Ruth, Enoch turned toward Billy and Bonnie. Bonnie stiffened. Now it was their turn. Would Enoch have any surprises for them? Visitors from Earth? Other special guests?

As soon as Walter took his place as Billy's best man, Enoch stood in front of them, his arms crossed and his expression somber. "I am afraid, my two wonderful anthrozils, that I will be unable to perform your ceremony."

Billy drew his head back. "What? Why?"

"The Majesty on High has forbidden it, and someone has been chosen to take my place."

Enoch stepped aside and joined Elam and Sapphira in the audience. The wall to Heaven split vertically again, and a tall, lanky man strode out. Dressed in a multicolored robe similar to Enoch's, an aura shimmered around his body. He bowed, mussing his silvery white hair. "Greetings, my friends."

Bonnie could barely breathe. Now it was her turn to shout out the name of their surprise visitor, but she couldn't get her tongue to move.

Billy spoke his name for her. "Professor Hamilton?"

The professor smiled and dipped again. "William, Miss Silver, I am delighted to see you."

Bonnie ached to embrace him, but would it be proper? He was a heavenly being, not the familiar teacher of years gone by.

As a tear slipped down the professor's cheek, he stretched out his arms. "Come, my three friends. I cannot hold back my affection any longer."

Billy, Bonnie, and Walter eased into his embrace. Bonnie laid her head against the professor's shoulder, but in the warmth and joy of his presence, no tears emerged, only the bliss of feeling those wonderful arms again and hearing his lovely voice.

After releasing them, Walter backed away, and the professor gestured for Billy and Bonnie to turn. When they looked out upon the audience, still standing in response to the previous wedding, he spoke with power. "These are the witnesses to your coming union, and since you both have dragon blood, we will create a covenant veil."

The professor nodded at Walter. "If you would be so kind, Mr. Foley, please split them into two groups with an equal number of dragons and humans on each side."

"You got it!"

While Walter waved for everyone to get together, and Ashley helped him count and separate them into two groups, the professor reached for Listener's hand. "Are you ready to lead them through, my dear?"

Listener nodded. "Should I just do what you said in my dream?"

"Exactly."

Smiling, she reached up and lifted Bonnie's veil. "To pass through the covenant," Listener said, "all other veils must be removed, for your soul is laid bare through your unfiltered eyes."

When everyone assembled, Bonnie's parents on the left, Billy's on the right, and a host of others evenly divided on either side, Professor Hamilton again lifted his voice. "When I say the vows, I want everyone to repeat them by speaking through the gap in between the groups."

The people and dragons on each side faced each other. When the rustling stopped, the professor spoke again, now with a more powerful voice than ever. "I, Billy Bannister, do take thee, Bonnie Silver, to be my wedded wife."

With a joyous outburst of voices—men, women, children, and dragons—the words rocked across the garden in both directions. The gap in between the groups sparkled and began to glow, creating an arching aura. It looked like a shimmering membrane, thin and brilliant, nearly as tall as Yereq and wide enough for two people to pass through.

The professor finished Billy's vows as well as Bonnie's, waiting between each phrase for the witnesses to repeat them. With every utterance, the aura grew brighter, stronger. When the final words sounded forth, the arch pulsed with white energy.

He nodded at Listener. "Now, dear child, you may lead them through."

She stepped in front of Billy and Bonnie. "Each of you lay a hand on my shoulder," she said quietly.

As soon as they complied, Listener marched slowly forward, in step with the cadence of the professor's voice.

"The covenant veil is established, and the bride and groom will be able to pass through only if the words of the vows are true in their hearts. They, too, will speak them as they walk, fulfilling the human tradition."

Bonnie let the words pour from her lips. "I, Bonnie Silver, take thee, Billy Bannister, to be my wedded husband."

666

Billy echoed with his vows. "I, Billy Bannister, take thee, Bonnie Silver, to be my wedded wife."

As they spoke the final phrases, they reached the energy field. Not even slowing down, Listener led them into its light. Taking Billy's hand, Bonnie looked at him as they finished their vows together with "Till death do us part." They passed through—easily, as if gliding through a silk curtain. The radiance tickled Bonnie's skin, forcing her to smile.

When they emerged on the other side, Bonnie blinked. Billy stood at her side, gazing at her as they held hands.

The veil dissipated. A fountain sprang up in its place. Shooting seven streams high into the air, it sprayed a fine mist over everyone within a few paces. While most of the crowd moved away from the water, Sapphira and Elam held hands and stayed under the mist, allowing the tiny droplets to dress their hair and clothes in sparkling raiment.

The professor waved for everyone to gather around in a circle. "William. Bonnie. I have desired to do this for a long time." Setting his hands on their shoulders, he turned them toward each other. "By the authority vested in me as an emissary of Heaven, I now pronounce you husband and wife."

He paused. Bonnie looked at him, noting the gleam in his eye as he winked. When would he say those final, wonderful words?

Smiling, the professor took a deep breath and spoke with clarity and passion. "William, I will now dispense with formalities and call you by the name your bride cherishes." He paused again, his smile broadening. "Billy Bannister, you may now kiss your bride."

Billy set his hands on Bonnie's cheeks. Tears welling, making his hazel eyes sparkle, he drew close. Then, Billy and Bonnie kissed, a slow, satisfying kiss—soft, tender lips touching for the first time.

A shiver ran down Bonnie's spine. All the dangers, pain, deaths, and sorrows melted away. All the waiting, prayers, and lonely vigils had been worth it. She was now the virgin bride, spotless, unspoiled, and pure for her warrior husband, a noble knight, equally unblemished and holy.

667

When their lips parted, Professor Hamilton turned the newly married couple toward their parents. As Walter, Ashley, Elam, and Sapphira looked on, the professor called out, "I now present to you, Mr. and Mrs. Billy Bannister!"

EPILOGUE

Carrying Bonnie's lunch in a paper sack, as well as a stack of about fifteen envelopes, Billy hurried along the hospital corridor. He had left Bonnie in her room too long, having told her he would return in less than an hour. But Walter had stopped by his house with an important message, and Larry kept interrupting their conversation with updated communications from Second Eden. Establishing an open, cross-dimensional channel had worked out great most of the time, but Listener had a habit of reporting every event in Second Eden, no matter how trivial.

Ever since Earth, Hades, and Second Eden separated more than a year ago, everything should have returned to the peaceful paradise that realm had longed for. But Elam and Sapphira, established as king and queen of Second Eden by Enoch's orders, made sure life there stayed hopping with technology updates and deeper explorations of their cleansed world through expeditions led by Yereq, Legossi, Mantika, and Windor.

When Legossi learned that Angel was her resurrected daughter, she felt more at home in Second Eden. She spent many

669

evenings hearing Listener's stories about Angel's love and wisdom.

Valiant relished being relieved of his duties and often took Candle on long journeys, both for physical training and spiritual instruction. Having recently become Emerald's Adam, Valiant felt like he was in training himself. Fatherhood awaited. He and Emerald had won the lottery for an upcoming birth, and both were as happy as they could be.

The companions of those who had died in Second Eden became communication portals between Heaven and Second Eden. The widow or widower, along with any children, could speak to their loved one in Heaven, fulfilling Abraham's word that keeping the companions would someday bring his people joy.

Sharing authority in Second Eden, Makaidos and Thigocia ruled as king and queen of the dragons, with Roxil and Karrick as their ambassadors to Earth. Since every slayer had been vanquished, they hoped to acclimate both worlds to the idea of dragons in their midst, but that would take a while.

On the Earth side, the castle museum run by Sir Barlow and his knights flourished. They no longer hid their identities as knights from the time of King Arthur, thereby attracting more visitors than they could handle. Barlow, in particular, enjoyed the exposure. Every day he would tell a long tale to a gathering of hundreds of children, a tale of knights, dragons, and slayers.

Walter's new message was hilarious, as usual. After he and Ashley resumed her computer business, she built another supercomputer in their home—Lois, a new generation, faster and with a greater learning capacity than Larry. According to Walter, Larry found out about Lois by reading Ashley's e-mail to Billy, and now Larry was "requesting" an upgrade by sending Lois thousands of messages per minute with the same words, "Give me parity, or give me death."

As he reached for Bonnie's hospital room door, Billy laughed to himself. Walter was as funny as ever, and he and Ashley were as happy as any two love birds around. Although as different as night and day, their conflicting ways somehow seemed to mesh, and they never spoke a cross word to one another, though they still playfully fought with snow, water, and anything else that would cause no damage.

Billy pushed open the door and strode in. "Sorry I'm late."

As soon as Bonnie saw him, her face lit up. "Don't worry. I was fine. I just finished feeding the babies." Reclining in a partially raised bed, Bonnie used her wings to push higher, trying not to disturb the infants, one nestled in each arm. Her multicolored necklace draped a blue hospital gown that matched her pretty eyes. "Charles went right back to sleep, but Karen's a little fussy. I couldn't get her to burp."

"I'll give it a try." Billy held out the sack. "I brought your favorite sandwich."

She waved with a wing. "Thank you! You're my knight in shining armor!"

He set the bag on her stomach along with the stack of envelopes. "Christmas cards," he said. "Lots of great news."

While Bonnie opened the first card, Billy set Karen against his shoulder and patted her on the back. The image of tiny wings appeared in his mind. Of course, she was much too young for any wings to sprout, but it was possible, someday. Maybe she would take after her mother.

Now that society had accepted Bonnie Bannister, the strange dragon girl, as well as Gabriel and Shiloh Drake, two more recently married oddities from the dragon line, and now that Earth was negotiating with Roxil for the reentry of friendly dragons into the world, Karen would never have to worry about hiding wings in a backpack.

"This *is* good news," Bonnie said. "The orphanage is well-supplied, and Patrick and Ruth are both healthy and happy."

As Billy continued patting Karen's back, Bonnie showed him a photo from the next card. "Shiloh looks just like me when I was pregnant."

"Stands to reason," Billy said. "Did you read the sales' leads?"

She nodded. "Gabriel thinks he has a buyer for two of them. Do you know which ones?"

"He called me a few minutes ago. He sold 'The Faceless Protectors' and 'The Wedding Ball.' He's really proving to be a great agent."

"And you're a great artist."

Billy smiled at her loving expression. No matter how many times she built him up with her encouraging words, her compliments always felt good. Yet, the wedding painting, in particular, really was a work he could be proud of. Drawing Elam and Sapphira dancing under the spray of a fountain, with a wedding party of dragons and humans surrounding them, had been a labor of love, and it turned out beautifully. The price Gabriel was able to get would pay the bills for quite a while.

672

Karen burped, and heat from her spittle scalded Billy's shoulder. Holding her at arms' length, he gazed into her eyes. "Did you and your brother pull a switcheroo on us?"

She just stared at him, her purplish eyes wide. Billy set her back at Bonnie's side and reached for his son.

"What are you doing?" she asked. "He's asleep."

Billy pulled away. "I just wanted to check for—"

"Wings?" Smiling, she winked. "I already checked. Nothing yet."

He set a hand on the bedrail and gazed at their two newborns. "So now that Alithia and Dallas found their offspring, how many does that make, humans born to dragons or former dragons, I mean?"

"Eleven?" Bonnie guessed.

Billy raised a finger for each name he rattled off. "Ashley, Gabriel, Shiloh, Listener, Thomas, Mariel, Karen, and Charles. That's eight. If Angel were still alive, that would have made nine, but I'm counting only living anthrozils."

Bonnie pointed at him. "And you and I make ten."

"Right," he said, laughing under his breath. "I almost forgot."

"And Ruth's and Patrick's son makes eleven."

"But he doesn't count, does he? They're both fully human."

Bonnie wrinkled her nose. "True. I didn't think about that."

Resting his hand on the rail again, he blew a sad sigh. "I wish Prof could have lived to see our little ones."

Bonnie caressed Karen's feather-soft blond hair. "I'm sure he's seen them. Enoch would make sure of that."

"I guess so. With his portal viewer, he can—"

A knock sounded at the door. "Maintenance."

"Sure," Billy said. "Come on in."

An elderly man dressed in clean blue coveralls walked in, pushing a cart that carried lightbulbs, paper towels, and bathroom tissue. Brushing back his white hair, he nodded at a flickering light in the ceiling. "I heard that you might want a bit more illumination in here."

Bonnie's face lit up. "Enoch!"

He pressed a finger to his lips. "I suppose my disguise lacks authenticity."

"No," Billy said, laughing. "It's great. We just have, I guess you might call it, a heavenly advantage."

"Did you come to see our little ones?" Bonnie asked.

Enoch waved a hand. "Oh, I've seen them, and so have many in Heaven. When you announced their names, more than one tear coursed down your professor's cheek, and Karen's aura shone like the sun." He patted Billy on the back. "Your kindness to their memory is very much appreciated."

Billy grasped Enoch's arm warmly. "So, to what do we owe the blessing of your visit?"

Enoch gazed at the infants. "Just to deliver a prophecy. Be sure that your offspring forge friendships with the others, especially Listener, Thomas, and Mariel. It is clear that their paths, should they choose the way of faith and righteousness, will lead them toward many adventures."

673

"Dangerous adventures?" Bonnie asked.

"Oh, yes. Of course." A wry smile spread across his face. "I assume you wouldn't want it any other way."

Billy slid his hand into Bonnie's. "After all we've been through together, and after all God taught us …" He shook his head. "No. We wouldn't have it any other way."

PRONUNCIATION GUIDE

NAME	DICTIONARY PRONUNCIATION	PHONETIC PRONUNCIATION
Acacia	Ä - kā′ - sē - ä	Ah - kay′ - see - ah
Arramos	Âr′ - rä - mŏs	Air′ - rah - moss
Canaan	Kā′ - nən	Kay′ - nann
Clefspeare	Klĕf ′ - spēr	Kleff′ - spear
Dikaios	Dĭ - kī′ - ŏs	Di - kie′ - oss
Elam	Ē′ - ləm	EE′ - lem
Emzara	Ĕm - zär′ - ä	Em - zah′ - rah
Enoch	Ē′ - nŏk	EE′ - nock
Firedda	Fī - rĕd′ - dä	Fie - red′ - dah
Glewlwyd	Glūl′ - wĭd	Gluel′ - wid
Greevelow	Grē′ - vĕ - lō	Gree′ - ve - low
Hartanna	Här - tăn′ - ä	Har - tan′ - ah
Japheth	Jā′ - fĕth	Jay′ - feth
Legossi	Lĕ - gōs′ - sē	Le - gose′ - see
Makaidos	Mä - kī′ - dŭs	Mah - kie′ - dus
Mantika	Măn - tē′ - kä	Man - teek′ - ah

NAME	DICTIONARY PRONUNCIATION	PHONETIC PRONUNCIATION
Monique	Mō - nēk´	Mow - neek´
Naamah	Nä´ - mä	Nah´ - mah
Paili	Pā´ - lē	Pay´ - lee
Palin	Păl´ - ĭn	Pal´ - in
Qadar	Kā´ - där	Kay´ - dar
Qatan	Kä - tän´	Kah - tahn´
Raphah	Rä´ - fä	Rah´ - fah
Roxil	Rŏk´ - sĭl	Rock´ - sill
Sapphira Adi	Săf - fī´ - rä Ä´ - dē	Saff - fie´ - rah Ah´ - dee
Semiramis	Sĕ - mîr´ - ä - mĭs	Seh - mier´ - ah - miss
Shachar	Shä´ - kär	Shah´ - kahr
Sorentine	Sōr´ - ĕn - tēn	Sore´ - en - teen
Thigocia	Thĭ - gō´ - sē – ä	Thi - goe´ - see - ah
Valcor	Văl´ - kōr	Val´ - kore
Yellinia	Yĕl - lĭ´ - nē - ä	Yell - li´ - nee - ah
Yereq	Yĕr´ - ĕk	Yerr´ - eck